SANTA CRUZ, THE ISLAND OF LIMUW

A Novel By: Dale Kornreich

Give Room! Give Room! Give Room! Give Room!
Do Not Get Discouraged! Do Not Get Discouraged!
Do Not Get Discouraged!
Help Me To Reach The Place! Help Me To Reach The Place!
Help Me To Reach The Place!
Hurrah! Hurrah! Hurrah! Hurrah!
(Chumash Indian prayer at the launch of a new Tomol canoe)

Santa Cruz
The Island of Limuw

By Dale M. Kornreich
www.dalekornreichbooks.com

Published by Dale M. Kornreich, 6165 Fairview Place, Agoura Hills, CA 91301
Website: dalekornreichbooks.com
E-mail: contact@dalekornreichbooks.com
Telephone: (818) 706-0913

ISBN-10: 0996508201
ISBN-13: 9780996508209 (Paperback)
ISBN 978-0-9965082-1-6 (E-Book)

Chumash Indian prayer at the launch of a new Tomol canoe: "Tomol—Chumash Watercraft as Described in the Ethnographic Notes of John P. Harrington," used with permission, courtesy of the Malki Museum.

All scripture quotations are taken from the New King James Version®. Copyright © 1982 by Thomas Nelson. Used by permission. All rights reserved.

Printed in the United States of America

Cover design by Josh Mathis (be.net/joshmathis)

ACKNOWLEDGMENTS

The author wishes to acknowledge the invaluable assistance of the following people: My wife Carole, for her continual faith and encouragement. My children—Nicole, Nathan, and Jaclyn—if you see yourselves in any of my characters, thank you. Author, L.A. Marzulli, my mentor. Novelist, James Scott Bell, for his guidance and suggestions. Michelle Tormey, my exceptional editor, who was also my cheerleader. Gail Kearns and Wendy, my proofreaders at *To Press and Beyond*. Jaclyn Kornreich, my manager extraordinaire. Sherri Del Pozo of Karamad Siberian Huskies, an expert on this exceptional breed. And Dee Pressl, my 10th grade English teacher—who planted a writing seed that has finally blossomed.

PROLOGUE—YEAR 1542
NORTHERN TERRITORIES

JUAN RODRIGUEZ CABRILLO, conquistador, soldier, and captain of the 200-ton Spanish galleon, *San Salvador*, guided his one hundred foot fully rigged flagship on a western course as it headed back toward a cluster of islands located off the Southern California coast. Cabrillo's intended destination was one island in particular, Capitana, where days earlier he had left several of his men to gather provisions—especially fresh meat—in order to replenish the ship's pantry. The *San Salvador's* smaller sister ship, *La Victoria*, at 100 tons was directly behind him. Both vessels had spent the last several days surveying a pristine bay situated along the California coastline. The Captain, captivated by its unique beauty and white-sand beaches, named it Santa Monica, after St. Monica, the mother of St. Augustine.

Juan Rodriguez Cabrillo was proud of his flagship, the *San Salvador*. The four-masted galleon with a square-rigged foremast, lanteen-rigged main mast, and two mizzen-masts with triangular canvas sails supported by swept booms, represented the pinnacle of ship building in the New World.

Cabrillo had personally supervised the building of both the *San Salvador* and *La Victoria* in Iztapa, Mexico. The project began in 1536 and took four years to complete. The ships were then moved to Navidad, Mexico. His journey of exploration from Navidad, up the Pacific North coast, began on June 27, 1542. Rumors of fabulous treasures, including precious stones, gold, silver, as well as the possibility of finding a shorter passageway to the West Indies and the Spice Islands, spurred the funding of the campaign. Unfortunately for the sponsors of the expedition, nothing of any monetary value had yet to be unearthed. However, large tracts of land, bays, harbors, rivers, and islands were being discovered and claimed for both God and Spain, including the San Lucas group of off-shore islands that Cabrillo was now sailing towards. As captain of the exploratory trip, and as part of his agreed upon compensation, Cabrillo was allowed to keep one-tenth of everything he discovered as his own *encomiendas,* or estate. The island of Capitana had so intrigued and charmed Cabrillo that he decided to claim it as part of his *encomiendas.*

Now, as his ship navigated its way back from the California mainland to the island of Capitana, a light breeze moved his galleon at a leisurely three knots. The color of the ocean was a rich indigo, and the sky was painted in soft royal blue, with a few nimbus clouds.

Once they arrived back at the island of Capitana, Cabrillo intended to resupply their two ships with food and water prior to continuing their exploratory journey north. Five sailors had previously been left behind on the island to gather the necessary supplies. The Chumash Chief had agreed to replenish their ships. The island itself was sizable and supported over one thousand Indians. In addition to securing the necessary supplies, Cabrillo looked forward to spending some precious time with his Indian mistress, Luisa, who just happened to be the Chief's daughter.

Cabrillo was a practical man who tackled the challenges of life in a realistic manner. His years of soldiering in Mexico had left him scarred, but his scars were not disfiguring and actually contributed to his mystique. His visage was comprised of piercing dark brown eyes, reddish-brown bushy eyebrows, short thin nose, long wavy red hair, and a sanguine complexion easily burned by the sun. At age forty-four, he was still robust and young at heart though his face was etched with lines of wisdom gained from his many years as a leader of soldiers, and as captain on a Spanish galleon.

His Spanish wife, Beatriz Sanchez de Ortega Cabrillo, lived in his hometown of Navidad with their two sons. As was customary in the age of exploration, having a mistress on a long voyage was the norm and not the exception. The only complication on this campaign was the fact that Cabrillo's mistress, Luisa, was now four months pregnant.

Cabrillo's second in command was Bartolome Ferrer, a stocky Spaniard who thus far had survived their long journey at sea without losing a single pound. Cabrillo suspected that his Chief Pilot had his own private cache of food hidden somewhere in the inner sanctuary of the ship. Ferrer stood just two inches above five feet and was as round as he was tall.

As they neared the island of Capitana, Ferrer spotted a small wooden boat. "Captain, there's a small vessel approaching our ship."

Cabrillo removed his hands from the ship's wooden steering wheel and cupped them to his forehead, blocking the sun in order to obtain a better view of what Ferrer was referring to. "It appears to be a Tomol canoe. I think there's just one person in it."

"Why is someone approaching our ship?" Ferrer asked.

"Probably our welcoming committee."

"That person is definitely in a hurry," said Ferrer. He could tell this by the way the individual was paddling the canoe. The strokes were fast and hard.

Cabrillo picked up the ship's eyeglass to obtain a closer-up view. Raising it to his left eye, what he observed surprised him.

"It's Luisa!"

"Luisa," said Ferrer, "are you sure?"

"Yes, and she appears to be angry."

In the five months that Cabrillo had known Luisa, she had always been lighthearted and full of warmth. She had learned Spanish at an astonishing rate, teaching her father as well. At age eighteen she was a gifted person beyond her years. Though petite, Luisa had strong, muscular arms and legs. Her opulent, jet-black hair flowed in natural wavy curves to just below her shoulders, and her rich olive-colored complexion was enhanced by constant exposure to the sun.

As he peered at Luisa through the eyeglass he could see that from the waist up she was wearing an oblong-shaped fur cape made out of island fox. From the waist down she was wearing a soft buckskin skirt whose outer fringes were adorned with strings of beads, seashells, and color fabric. Around her neck hung a necklace sparkling with several strands of olivella sea shells, interlaced with polished brown cowries. The number of strands worn by Luisa signified her importance and her connection to the Chumash Chief. Even in her agitated state she appeared graceful, and Cabrillo's heart stirred at her beauty.

He could not imagine why, in her pregnant condition, she was racing out to meet their ship.

"Ferrer, have the men lower the sails and bring the ship about."

"Aye Captain."

As the sails were lowered, the momentum of the galleon brought it closer to Luisa's canoe; however, turning the ship sideways slowed it to a near stop. Cabrillo then ordered the starboard anchor released, which dragged along the seafloor until it snagged on some rocks. With the ship at a standstill, Cabrillo hurried over to the leeward side of the vessel to watch as a rope ladder was dropped over the side. After securing her canoe to some lines attached to the ladder, Luisa carefully angled her way up the swaying ladder and into the waiting arms of Cabrillo.

Cabrillo held her tightly against his chest for a full minute. He was acutely aware that his entire crew was watching and waiting, wondering what their captain was going to do. After a bit, he realized she was crying.

"What's wrong?" he asked.

"Your men . . . on my island."

"What about my men?" Cabrillo pressed.

In an almost inaudible whisper she said. "They're going to die."

"Die! Why?"

"They were foolish. Bad," said Luisa, as she wiped tears from her eyes. "They should not have done what they did."

Cabrillo was aware that many of the island Chumash no longer viewed the strange explorers as friends. The Indians suspected that the Spaniards were filled with evil spirits, which were now invading their island. Various illnesses, previously unknown to the Chumash, were affecting some of their people, which the tribal medicine man was unable to cure. Cabrillo looked compassionately into Luisa's eyes and asked, "What did my men do that was so awful that your people would want to kill them?"

"Your men took a young girl, who is not yet a woman, and forced her to become a woman. That's against our beliefs and is forbidden," Luisa said softly.

"They defiled her?"

"If that's what you call it . . . yes. Now, no Chumash man will want her. She is impure, an outcast. That's not right. The penalty for committing this violation is death. I argued against such a harsh punishment, but my father and the tribal elders would not listen to me."

"And where are my men now?"

"I pleaded with my father to return them back to your ship. But, our people were too angry, and he couldn't agree to that. They are being held in the main lodge guarded by our warriors."

Cabrillo stared over Luisa's head at the island he was so anxious to return to. A few clouds drifted over the island blocking the sun. An unexpected chill ran up his spine. He had, in Mexico, in the war against the mighty Aztec nation on behalf of God, Spain, and the lust of gold, seen hundreds of thousands of natives massacred. Spain was a brutal mistress to Mexico and he'd hoped this voyage, to the Northern Territories would be different. He was tired of killing Indians.

"Luisa, I am so sorry for what my men did to that young girl. But, I will not allow them to die."

"What are you going to do?" she asked.

"I will rescue them. Their families back home would not understand, and would hold me accountable for their deaths. In our country taking an Indian, for a man's pleasure, is not a crime."

Luisa stepped back and stared at him coldly. "Pleasure . . . that's all I am to you?"

Cabrillo did not know what to say. He knew that he had to say something so he said "No," in a sincere voice. But, he knew Luisa didn't believe him. *The real world was not so easy,* he thought. He remembered the butchering of Indian natives, which he supervised, for the sole purpose of using their human fat to make pitch-and-tallow, a substance used to seal their small wooden boats in order to hold in check ruinous sea worms during their campaign against the beautiful floating garden city of Tenochtitlan, on Lake Texcoco, Mexico. Over three hundred thousand Aztecs lived in the majestic city, which was utterly destroyed by the Spanish conquistadors. Cabrillo no longer had a taste for this kind of mission, but yes, he would rescue his men; there was no question about it.

Cabrillo moved away from Luisa. He turned to Ferrer and ordered the assembling of a small rescue party. The men, who were skilled in battle, hurried to gather their war attire and weapons.

For the upcoming conflict Cabrillo was outfitted with a brigandine, a vest made with an outer layer of leather, an inner layer of canvas, and a layer of small, square steel plates riveted in between. Under this he also wore a chainmail neck protector and metal lobster tails' to shield his upper legs. The brigandine and chainmail weighed fifty pounds, but, it would stop a Chumash spear, arrow, or flint knife.

For weapons Cabrillo carried a four-foot-long silver-gilded broadsword, and a gold-plated dagger, sharpened on both sides, its handle encased in emeralds.

Eighteen men were assembled and ready to go in less than thirty minutes. "Release the utility boats," he ordered. Two, twenty foot, oar-powered vessels were lowered into the ocean.

At that moment Luisa stepped in front of Cabrillo—blocking his way.

"I'm going with you," she demanded.

"A rescue party with weapons is no place for a woman," he said in a scolding tone. He gently moved her out of his way.

Without another word, Luisa walked over to the edge of the ship, climbed onto the railing off the main deck, and plunged into the ocean next to her canoe. She immediately surfaced, and using her arms, pulled herself into her craft, untied the ropes, and began to paddle away.

In a high-pitched voice slung over her right shoulder she said, "I'm going. They're my people. I will meet you on the shoreline."

Cabrillo had no alternative but to follow, and in wooden boats a lot slower than Luisa's sleek canoe. After ten minutes of rowing he could see that she was already standing on the shoreline awaiting their arrival. In spite of her willful stubbornness in front of his crew—he secretly admired her spiritedness.

The landing spot was a sandy beach that on prior occasions had proved easy to navigate. Today, however, the tide was extremely low exposing barnacle encrusted boulders and serrated rocks overgrown with bright green eelgrass and brown-tinged bulb kelp. Numerous colorful starfish could be seen feeding upon mussels attached to the exposed rocks. The rolling sound of the surf slapping against the stones ricocheted like a cannon shot. Luisa's small canoe was designed to easily traverse the boulders through watery channels. But, the Spaniard's larger utility vessels, each with nine battle-ready men weighing them down, would prove much more problematic.

Francisco de Vargas, who was a member of Cabrillo's vessel, was in charge of guiding their boat through the maze of rocks and pounding surf. Vargas, with his oily brown hair waving in the wind, grew up operating small fishing boats, and therefore was a skilled navigator in tight circumstances. While the men rowed, he stood in the rear of the boat operating the tiller, determining their next line of travel.

Vargas waited for a sizeable swell to roll underneath their boat before ordering the men to "row like hell for the glory of Spain, and to the defeat of our enemy."

The extra cushion of water enabled the vessel to slide over almost the entire width of the protruding reef. As they neared the shoreline, however, the precipitous nature of their journey bore fruition as the sickening sound of wood grating against submerged rocks could be heard emanating from beneath their feet. As the sound intensified the middle of the craft suddenly splintered, and a jagged segment of rock thrust itself through the shattered hulk—catapaulting two men into the churning surf. The boat, its middle pinned to the stone, began a gradual turn, exposing its maximum width to the next oncoming swell.

"Captain," said Vargas, "this is not good."

Cabrillo gave Vargas an incredulous look. "Not good! The boat's damaged beyond repair, we're sinking, and that's all you have to say."

"The good news is—we're almost at the beach."

"Almost," was all Cabrillo could muster. In reality he could see that they were not going to sink. The water was less than three feet deep, and their boat had already stopped its descent. Fortunately, the other vessel was safely ashore, and the two men tossed overboard were clinging to a nearby boulder. *No deaths yet,* thought Cabrillo.

"Before the next wave crashes into the boat," he said to the crew, "I recommend that we abandon ship."

One by one the men either jumped or lowered themselves into the ocean, making their way cautiously to the beach as they avoided the perilous rocks. As captain, Cabrillo went last. Stepping out onto the prow he vaulted off the vessel, and into the churning surf.

Landing with a loud splash, his encumbered body sank rapidly through the water, his legs smashing into the rocky bottom, throwing him off balance. As Cabrillo struggled to regain his equilibrium, he realized that his right foot was trapped between two immovable reef rocks. While trying to extricate his ensnared leg a large swell suddenly slammed into his body. The force of the impact twisted his right leg beyond its physical limits causing the right lower tibia bone to splinter completely in half, the fractured bone, dagger sharp, severing nerves, tendons, arteries, and muscles, the bone eventually making contact with the biting ocean water. The sound of the bone exploding was heard by Cabrillo through three feet of water, and the image of the large, sharp rock which just moments before had splintered the boards of his boat rendering it useless came immediately to mind.

For a brief moment, he was too stunned to even utter a sound. However, the pain signals issuing from his shattered leg cruelly and all too rapidly made their way to the nerve center of his brain. At that instant of recognition, a hauntingly loud, agonizing scream burst forth from his lips making every soul on the *San Salvador* and every soul on the beach painfully aware that their leader had suffered a horrifying injury.

Bartolome Ferrer and Francisco de Vargas, who were both already on the beach, immediately charged back out into the ocean to rescue their captain. They found Cabrillo floundering helplessly in the surf; the water surrounding him tinged bright red with blood.

Vargas grasped Cabrillo's brigandine vest, supporting him so that he would not drown.

"Captain, what's wrong?" Ferrer yelled.

"My leg," answered Cabrillo somewhere between a growl and a wail, "my right leg . . . it's broken and my foot's caught in the rocks."

Ferrer took a deep breath and dove beneath the waves to inspect the injury. Blood was flowing precipitously from the wound and he had to wave it away in order to assess the situation. A few small, colorful baitfish were at the fracture site nibbling on protruding flesh. A splintered piece of bone extruded from the gaping wound. The angle of the leg was all wrong, and Ferrer could see that Cabrillo's leather boot was sandwiched between two craggy rocks. He resurfaced for air.

"Your foot is pinned between two rocks. I'll need to pull your foot out," Ferrer advised.

"Just do it," he moaned.

"Your leg is badly broken. It'll be extremely painful," Ferrer warned.

"I will die here if you don't."

Ferrer gave a knowing glance at Vargas. "Hang onto the Captain no matter what."

Ferrer took several deep breaths before re-submerging. A juvenile leopard shark was inspecting the leg, its gray and black spotted fusiform body saturated in the river of blood. Ferrer rammed his right fist into the gill slits of the intrusive creature, frightening it away. He then nervously scanned the surrounding waters, verifying that it was alone. He next examined the wedged foot. Pulling on the broken leg wasn't possible. Ferrer would have to shove it out of its rocky prison. He positioned himself and began gently pushing on the leather boot. It didn't budge. He tried a different angle, again with no success. The third attempt, however, resulted in an involuntary but severe thrashing from Cabrillo, his unstuck boot smashing Ferrer in his face, causing a bloody lip. Ferrer was running out of air. He noticed an area of loose sand underneath the boot. Rather than shoving the foot straight forward, Ferrer first pushed downward into the sand, gaining some extra space. He then began to nudge it outward, the ruptured bone grating against reef rocks—pieces of flesh severing into ragged chunks as the leg slid against knifelike barnacles. With a final, out-of-breath frenzied thrust, the boot was mercifully freed from the rocks.

Surfacing, Ferrer gasped for air, refilling his depleted lungs. He noticed that Cabrillo was unconscious in Vargas' arms.

"He couldn't handle the pain," Vargas explained as he struggled to hang onto the unconscious Captain—the weight of battle gear and crashing waves rapidly draining his strength. Several times already Cabrillo's face had slipped beneath the breakers, allowing seawater to surge down his throat.

"I'll hold his head and shoulders," shouted Ferrer, "while you hang onto his upper legs."

After securing Cabrillo in their arms, they began a slow, awkward, shuffling motion back toward the beach. Though a mere thirty feet away, to the exhausted men it seemed like miles.

When they were approximately ten feet from the shoreline, Luisa and several crew members quickly waded into the water to aid the wounded captain and his equally exhausted rescuers. The ship's doctor was sent for as Cabrillo was laid down near a large rock which was used to prop up his upper torso and head. To lessen the shock to Cabrillo's body, he was wrapped with blankets, and his right leg was tied with a tourniquet to stave the flow of blood. Upon his arrival, the doctor cleaned the wounds and then wrapped them with fresh linen. When there was nothing further that Luisa could do, she left to go locate her father.

While Luisa was absent, Cabrillo regained consciousness just as the ship's doctor was concluding his examination. Although groggy, nauseated, and experiencing waves of intense throbbing pain, he was soon able to talk.

"What's the damage?" he inquired, grimacing, as another round of vexatious pain traveled up his leg.

Doctor Manny Hernandez, a middle-age doctor on his first voyage of discovery, used his pudgy-fingered hand to wipe perspiration off his slightly balding head and onto his pants. He then stroked his silver-gray mustache for almost a full minute before responding to Cabrillo's question.

"The lower bone in your right leg is severely fractured."

"I know that," Cabrillo growled. "Can you fix it?"

"No . . . not completely."

"What do you mean *not completely*."

"I'm not capable of fixing it. The bone is shattered. When it splintered it also shredded your muscles, tendons, and blood vessels."

"What have you done so far?"

"I cleaned out the wound, sewed up some major arteries to stop the flow of blood, and straightened your leg with two wooden braces. That's about it other than wrapping it with clean linens and tying it altogether."

"Will I walk again?"

"Walk! You don't understand; your injury is beyond help . . . it's not fixable."

Cabrillo stared at Doctor Hernandez in shocked disbelief. "So what now?"

"We hope and pray that the wound heals on its own. But . . . I fear infection, and if that happens, then you're in God's hands."

"God's hands," Cabrillo observed, "means God will decide if I live or die?"

"If infection sets in, yes."

"And how long till we know?"

"Days."

"Well then, I guess I had better get my affairs in order," he said ruefully, "since God has a tendency to be unpredictable."

Cabrillo's mind was still trying to comprehend the probability of death, when Luisa appeared with the Chief, and over thirty warriors. *Maybe death would come sooner rather than later*, he thought. As his men congregated around him, Luisa abruptly left the side of the Chief and ran up to Cabrillo. The warriors halted, and the Chief, known as Librado, stepped forward walking deliberately to

Cabrillo's side. He then sat down on a boulder next to Cabrillo. Luisa, along with the soldiers, moved a short distance away in order to honor their leaders with privacy.

The Chief was wearing a sea otter cloak that reached down to his ankles. Around his waist he wore a deer skin belt that contained a flint knife. His long black hair was decorated with the teeth of carnivores, bright seashells, and unique pieces of wood. He was well formed and had many of the same physical features as Luisa. Cabrillo had talked with the dignified Chief on many prior occasions, but never under such dire circumstances.

"Luisa told me you were injured. Is it bad?" Chief Librado asked.

Off in the distance, over the ocean, a brown pelican appeared stationary in the sky as it observed a school of baitfish congregating near the surface. Cabrillo stared at it for a brief moment before answering.

"The doctor just gave me his report. It's not good. He cannot fix my injury. He's afraid of infection and thinks I may die."

After a long pause, Chief Librado responded. "In our culture dying is a natural part of life. But it's difficult when it's sudden or too soon. And my daughter carries your child."

Cabrillo did not know what to say in reference to the future child. He had not considered any long-term responsibility. She was just an Indian native who had provided needed gratification. He would have to think about what the Chief meant.

The brown pelican folded its wings tight against its body, diving like an arrow toward the surface of the water.

"You have many men on my island armed for battle," continued Chief Librado. "They should not be here."

"They're here because you're holding five of my men. We will not leave until they're returned."

"Do you know what they did?"

"Luisa told me. She also said she tried to get them released but you refused."

"Setting them free after what they did wasn't possible. As Chief, I'm responsible for all my people. The young girl, Maria, who is thirteen years of age, is now unclean. She may never find a man who will accept her as a mate."

The pelican hit the water with a resounding whack and disappeared.

"Do you want people to die?"

"Your men started this, we did not."

Cabrillo looked at the Chief for an answer to an impossible situation. His injury was dulling his certainty about what to do.

The pelican surfaced, its large throat pouch engorged, filled with a flapping fish.

"You're right," he agreed, "my men may have started it, but it's up to you to finish it."

Chief Librado smiled knowingly. "There's a way to fix this, but it will depend upon you. My people need to see that you, as their leader, will condemn what your men have done, and you must express remorse."

After a brief hesitation Cabrillo said, "I can do that."

"That's not all," continued Chief Librado, "most importantly, you need to honor the young girl and make amends for what happened. Her status must be raised. This will remove the dishonor. If you do these things—then I can release your men."

Cabrillo's countenance indicated confusion. "How do I go about *honoring* her?"

The pelican lifted its beak skyward. The fish gravitated down its long neck and into the gulf of its stomach.

"Your ship—it contains supplies that we do not have on this island. Choose carefully, Captain, the gifts you decide upon may make all the difference. And when you honor a member of my tribe, you must also honor the Chief. It's our culture."

It was Cabrillo's turn to smile. "I think I can do all that, if I live long enough."

"You're a soldier and a captain. You'll have the strength."

"No battle today?" Cabrillo inquired.

"No," said Chief Librado. "Gather your items from your ship. We will meet in five days on a bluff overlooking the cove west of this beach."

The brown pelican began a running dance on the surface of the ocean, wildly flapping its broad, powerful wings, until it had gained enough momentum to break free of its watery constraints—and reenter its heavenly realm of watchfulness.

Chief Librado rose from his sitting position indicating that their discussion had ended. He signaled for Luisa to join him. They both stood together, silent, in front of Cabrillo. Chief Librado gently touched Luisa's bulge.

"Remember my daughter and *your* future child," he said with a tone that was more command than plea. Chief Librado and Luisa then rejoined their warriors, and headed back to their village.

Cabrillo watched them until they disappeared behind a small embankment. *What was he to do about Luisa*, he wondered. He had five days. He would figure it out. Meanwhile, traveling back to his ship, through the rocks and surf, was something he wasn't looking forward to.

On the second day following his injury, Doctor Hernandez's prophetic warning of infection came true. The wound was festering. Cabrillo could see pus oozing and minor pinkish tissue discoloration where the bone had torn his flesh. The affected area was becoming cold and numb, and his face was flushed with a slight fever.

Though he was expecting it, nevertheless on the fourth day he was alarmed to see a substantial increase in black and purple discolored tissue, swollen flesh, red and blue streaks running up his leg, and an offensive odor emanating from the wound. Brown pus was trickling down his leg, the discharge increasing with each passing hour. He knew that gangrene was setting in—the rotting of his own flesh—which would soon poison his entire body. The smoldering pain had become a searing fire, fanning an unrelenting fever.

Despite his pain, and fever-induced delirium, Cabrillo spent his few lucid moments setting his affairs in order. His Chief Pilot, Bartolome Ferrer, would take over command of the expedition—an easy choice. The more difficult decisions concerned the Chumash. What items to give to Maria, to Chief Librado, and what about Luisa? After four days of wresting with this conundrum—he finally knew what to do—and a peace settled over him.

The very last item on his list was his own burial. Would the Chumash permit his burial upon their island? Because of *what* he planned to have buried with him he trusted only Ferrer and Vargas with the actual assignment, which they agreed to, though they did not look forward to this bitter engagement. But Cabrillo was looking at a future not yet present. A tiny bit of immortality, and why not? He expected Luisa to attend. Knowing that his time on this earth was running out, but relieved that his affairs were settled, he slipped into a fitful sleep.

The next day arrived all too soon. The boat ride from the *San Salvador* to the beach was accomplished at high tide in order to avoid the pitfalls of the previous disaster and to make the passage smoother for the Captain. Once on the beach he was placed on a wooden stretcher and transported by four crew members to the meeting site which was situated on a lofty palisade, covered in bright green grass and colorful flowers, overlooking a stunning cove. A padded chair was set up for him. Prior to the short trip, Doctor Hernandez had supplied him with opium crystals, which Cabrillo gratefully snorted.

From his vantage point, his appalling pain now temporarily dulled, Cabrillo observed the sun reflecting surreally off the ocean. A slight breeze churned the air, and the familiar smell of the ocean—salt mixed with seaweed and fish—permeated the atmosphere. Sea otters frolicked in the liquid forests of giant kelp. Yellow daisy-like flowers of the giant coreopsis plant lined the edge of the bluff. Other flowers blanketed the meadow including Indian paintbrush in vibrant red, and island bush poppy hued sunset-orange. Numerous seabirds straddled the wind currents—western gulls, royal terns, ashy storm-petrels, and a noble bald eagle soared above all. Cabrillo marveled at the beauty of the setting.

"Inspiration Point," Chief Librado said. "It's a special place for us. We come here when we need a fresh vision."

"I can see why," Cabrillo confirmed, grimacing as he said this.

Chief Librado could see the tension and feverish pain in Cabrillo's eyes. Luisa walked over and stood next to Cabrillo, her brow wrinkled with concern. "How's your leg?" the Chief asked.

"It's badly infected. There's nothing more that can be done. I will not live long," he said with little emotion. Cabrillo then lifted up the blood-stained linen that covered the injury. Chief Librado and Luisa let out a collective gasp. Luisa pivoted away. The Chief muttered a short Chumash prayer. A few carrion flies landed on the exposed putrid flesh, black and shriveled, its foul-smelling odor permeating the air. Cabrillo quickly covered it up.

"I've made my peace with my God. As you said, *dying is a part of life.*"

"As is living," Chief Librado assured him. "Your child lives within my daughter. Your life will go on."

"If it's a boy," he said, directing his words to Luisa, "I want you to name him Santiago Cabrillo. Will you do that for me?"

"Yes," Luisa said quietly. "But what if it's a girl?"

"Then you choose the first name."

Luisa tried to smile encouragingly, but could not.

"He or she must never forget their heritage," he added solemnly, "it will be important."

Shifting his gaze, Cabrillo said, "I see you brought my five men."

Chief Librado nodded.

Cabrillo observed that his men were guarded by warriors carrying spears tipped with flint arrowheads. His men appeared haggard and frightened. Freedom was in the balance and they knew it. Also attending the gathering were approximately one hundred Indians, including tribal elders, select warriors, Maria, and her parents. It was Cabrillo's first opportunity to see Maria. She was diminutive, and yet he could see flames of fire in her eyes, conveying an inner strength. Her free-flowing hair was light brown, almost blond, unusual for a Chumash.

Cabrillo raised his voice, addressing the Indians. Luisa interpreted for him. In a contrite voice he began. "What my men did to Maria was wrong. It's not the way of our people. The God we serve does not allow it. I'm sorry for the shame they have brought upon Maria, her parents, and to your tribe. I promise that it will never happen again. I'm here today to correct this terrible mistake."

After a momentary pause to regain his strength, he requested that Maria stand next to him. He then ordered his men forward. The Chumash murmured, nervous as to what Cabrillo intended. They looked at their Chief. Chief Librado gave a solemn nod.

Cabrillo handed a dagger to Maria, its edges razor sharp. He ordered his men onto their knees, in a straight line, directly in front of Maria. Fear tinged the facial lines of each man. Maria held the weapon with familiarity. She no longer appeared as a young girl.

"In a book given to us by our God which we call the Bible, there's a story about the significance of a man's hair. In that story a man's hair represented strength, courage, and his closeness to God. Because of this, my men choose to wear their hair long." He paused for a moment in order to allow the Chumash time to ponder what he had said.

"In your Chumash culture," Cabrillo continued, "your hair, how you wear it, and what's woven into it, establishes your identity and your status in the tribe. Because of what my men did to

Maria I will now have her remove their identity and their status—by removing their hair."

Cabrillo encouraged Maria to begin. To his amusement she did not hesitate and seemed to know exactly what to do. She pulled each man's hair straight out with her free hand, and then with the dagger, severed the hair of each man with one quick wrist motion, right at the hairline. His men endured it without complaining even though a few suffered minor nicks. Cabrillo had Ferrer gather the severed hair, which was then placed into a small, ornately adorned, red cedar box, and presented to Maria. The approving utterances and grunts emerging from the Indians confirmed Cabrillo's hopes that Maria's honor was being restored.

"For a man about to die, you did well," Chief Librado said respectfully.

"Symbols have more meaning than gifts," Cabrillo said, wincing, as a fresh ripple of pain ravaged his body.

"I agree."

"But, it's also nice to receive gifts," said Cabrillo, ignoring the pain.

The Chief nodded.

"I will start with Maria." He signaled to his men and several large wooden crates were brought before him. Ferrer and Vargas would act as his hands at distributing the articles. Deciding on what items to mete out for this ceremonious occasion had been difficult for Cabrillo. In the end practicality won out.

"Maria, on behalf of my crew, and on behalf of Spain, I present to you these gifts as an offering of apology, to forever remove the offense caused by my men."

Out of the crates, Ferrer and Vargas presented Maria with colorful fabrics made of silk and cotton, pieces of jewelry that she could weave into her hair, a necklace made from white pearls, iron cooking pots, wooden cooking utensils, and an oval brass container for storing water. The grin on Maria's seraphic face and the tears in her eyes conveyed her silent thanks.

"Chief Librado . . . what to give to a great leader? Not an easy decision." Before the Chief could respond, Cabrillo turned his head and pointed in the direction of the path that lead back down to the beach. Trotting up the path, with a crewmember straddling its back, was a beautiful chestnut-colored Arabian horse.

"Did you know that our ships also transport horses?"

"I've never seen a horse before," Chief Librado said excitedly. "The inland Indians talk about an animal that you can ride. What an amazing beast." The Chief was duly impressed with his gift.

"It's my horse," Cabrillo said nostalgically. "His name is *Morning Star*. Take good care of him. He's a trusted friend."

"*Morning Star* will be treated as a member of our tribe," he assured him.

"Thank you. He's young in years and will serve you well for many more."

Turning to Luisa, Cabrillo presented to her gifts which included the same type of fabrics he had given to Maria, several wool blankets, a gold necklace, supple skins made from the hides of cattle, and soft, thick sheep skins. Finally, he retrieved a rolled parchment from under his vest.

"This document," Cabrillo stated, holding it up for Luisa and the Chief to examine, "is more valuable than all the gifts combined."

"Why's it so valuable?" Chief Librado asked.

"The words on it."

"Words?"

"What they say. What they represent."

"And what do they represent?"

"This island, your lives, your homes, everything . . ." Cabrillo realized it would take some explaining.

"This document is what we Spaniards call a *deed*. It has my official seal," he stated, pointing to a large round waxen symbol. It conveys this island to Luisa and to her descendants—her children, and their children—forever. It prevents any future explorers from exerting a claim over this island."

"How can anyone claim an island?" Luisa wondered.

"Through force, weapons, death," he responded. "Times are changing. I am the first of many explorers to come. With this deed, which my country of Spain will enforce, this island now belongs to Luisa. It will benefit all Chumash."

"And this document will be respected by all future explorers?" Luisa asked.

"There are three originals. The first I entrust to you. The second to Ferrer. Upon his return to our home port of Navidad, Mexico, Ferrer will then file it with the appropriate Spanish authorities. Once filed, your ownership cannot be questioned. The third I retain."

"Our legends state that the first Chumash people were created on this very island by the Earth Goddess, *Hutash*, and that we have existed here, in peace, for thousands of years. And now you're telling us that your country controls our future?" Chief Librado protested.

Cabrillo felt the heaviness of this reality upon the Chumash. His right leg throbbed with the weight of his own terminal wound. He could feel the effects of the gangrene toxins spreading throughout his body. His time was also rapidly changing.

"Yes, Spain will control the future of this island. However, with Luisa's name on this document," he said waving it in the air, "they will leave you alone. There isn't much on this island they would want anyway."

"And this deed will do all that?" Chief Librado asked.

"Yes . . . That's my hope. You call this place *Inspiration Point* because you come here when you need a fresh vision. Unfortunately, that vision is now tied to this writing for the Chumash people."

"Then we will accept it, and preserve it with our sacred relics, and trust that all future explorers will respect its words." Chief

Librado then signaled for his warriors to come forward. They were carrying basket of supplies.

"You have kept your word and now I will do the same. Your men are set free, but they must never return, or they'll be killed. We also present to you the food supplies that they were gathering."

"Thank you," Cabrillo said. He had Ferrer and Vargas take charge of the five men and the needed supplies.

"Two additional requests," Cabrillo said reluctantly. "As you know . . . I'm dying. I would like to spend my final days here at Inspiration Point, enjoying the beauty of these surroundings, with Luisa at my side, as I pass from this world to the next."

"This is a nice place to die. You may stay."

"And," he continued, "I would like to be buried on your island."

Chief Librado gazed at Cabrillo with a heavy heart. "Only Chumash are allowed to be buried on Capitana—the island of our creation. This soil is sacred. Your men must bury you somewhere else."

"I trust only Ferrer and Vargas to do the actual burial. I cannot have other crewmembers involved. I have my reasons. There must be a way."

Chief Librado shook his head deliberately. "I'm sorry—you'll have to find some other site."

Cabrillo eyes pleaded for a resolution, fixating first on the Chief, then Luisa, and then back again. A flash of knowing crossed Luisa's face and she turned and whispered in her father's ear.

"Yes," Chief Librado said, talking out loud to himself. "I will discuss your proposal with the tribal elders and see if they agree."

Chief Librado walked over to the older leaders. After a brief conference he returned. "Luisa's recommendation for a burial site is accepted. May your God be with you as you live out your final days."

Chief Librado and the Chumash Indians that were with him then turned and went back to their village, leaving Luisa to care for Cabrillo.

꙰

By the seventh day following Cabrillo's injury, the gangrene had spread to his entire lower leg. Necrotic black tissue permeated the gaping wound, and the invasive bacterial infection, carried by his bloodstream, was insidiously and systematically shutting down all his internal organs. Babbling incoherently, at times, Cabrillo also had difficulty breathing, and wailed uncontrollably.

On the eighth day he slipped into a coma as the final stages of decay—putrefaction and decomposition—ravaged the leg. On the ninth day, January 3, 1543, Juan Rodriguez Cabrillo died.

The next day, Luisa, Ferrer, and Vargas used one of the small utility boats to transport Cabrillo's body to the burial site. The trip lasted two hours. Once anchored up, Ferrer and Vargas carried Cabrillo's body, now entirely wrapped in linens, up a steep, rocky incline to a small plateau that overlooked the rich, azure-colored Pacific Ocean. After that they returned to their boat to retrieve a four foot by one foot cast-iron chest that Cabrillo requested be buried with him. The contents were unknown. Cabrillo had packed, sealed, and locked it himself. He had paid Ferrer and Vargas generously to keep quiet about the chest.

Digging the grave in the primarily rocky soil required several hours of hard labor. The smell of bird guano saturated the air. The gravesite was apparently a popular nesting rookery for Brandt's cormorants and western gulls. Luisa sobbed as Cabrillo was laid to rest. The chest was situated along Cabrillo's left side. Cabrillo had requested that Ferrer read only one scripture from the Bible: Jeremiah 29:11 which Ferrer recited: *"For I know the thoughts that I think toward you, says the Lord, thoughts of peace and not of evil, to give you a future and a hope."*

"Not much of a *future* and *hope* that I can foresee," murmured Ferrer in a solemn voice, as he finished packing the grave with the rocky soil. They then spent the next hour topping the grave with stones that ranged in size from four to twelve inches, which would act as a natural lid.

Finally, in keeping with Cabrillo's request that his burial site remain largely anonymous, only a brick-size sandstone slab was used to mark his internment. Inscribed on the stone by Ferrer were a Christian cross, and the first two initials of Cabrillo's name, *JR.*

The journey back to Inspiration Point was made in contemplative silence. Luisa returned to her people, and Ferrer and Vargas returned to their two ships—never to see Capitana again.

Six months later Luisa, with her one-month old infant, paddled her Tomol canoe to the location of Cabrillo's burial site. With the child slung on her back, Luisa ascended the rocks, and at the top knelt down beside the grave. Picking up the sandstone slab, she brought it up to her chest. She sat in quiet reflection for several minutes as tears fell on the rocky soil. Then Luisa spoke to Cabrillo, as if he were still alive and listening. "I present to you your son, Santiago Cabrillo." She held him up for Cabrillo to see. "He's strong, like you. He has your red hair, and your eyes. He makes me laugh. Thank you. He will always know his heritage as I promised you."

She then removed an antler carving tool from her waist belt. Placing the grave marker on the ground she proceeded to carve a human stick figure into it, just below JRs initials. "This is your son," she said, pointing to the stick figure, "he will be with you always." She then returned the stone to its rightful place at the head of the grave.

The trip back in the canoe was graced with a majestic sunset as the descending sun painted the lofty clouds in colors of violet, crimson, tangerine, saffron, turquoise and lavender, bathing Luisa and her newborn child with a celestial anointing—a heavenly promise of the future yet to come.

S.S. WINFIELD SCOTT
DECEMBER 1, 1853

Captain Sean Flannigan cursed silently as he fastened his gaze upon the empty wharf. He tossed his ninth cigarette in less than an hour into the frigid San Francisco Bay. The predictable late night fog, gray and miserable, was already billowing in, and soon it would make navigating the waters of the bay treacherous. He hated the fog. *Where the hell are they?* He wondered. It was 11:00 p.m., and his scheduled departure for Panama City was currently running three hours late. Any delay in the two week long voyage upset his sense of rigid punctuality. If it wasn't for the promised bonus, his steamer, the *S.S. Winfield Scott*, would be long gone.

Captain Flannigan had just reached the metaphorical point of tossing his bonus, just like his cigarettes, into the bay, when the sound of horse hooves echoing off the wooden wharf pierced the night air. Carriages, their wheels kerplunking as they struck each individually spaced pinewood plank, were fast approaching his ship. "Finally," he muttered to himself, as he marched out of the wheelhouse, anxious to to meet his very special, late night guests.

The leading two-axle covered wagon carriage bore the emblem of the presidency of the United States of America, though in actuality, no president was aboard. A second carriage immediately followed. Twelve U.S. Army Calvary soldiers guarded the two stagecoaches. Four additional soldiers handled the leather reins that controlled the eight Clydesdale draft horses. All had .54 caliber breech-loading Hall percussion rifles and .44 caliber Colt Walker repeating revolvers. It was obvious to Captain Flannigan that the cargo they were delivering was not of an ordinary nature. As the presidential carriage came to a stop in front of the gangplank, two immaculately dressed gentlemen stepped out, each man attired in a brand new double-breasted suit.

"Captain Sean Flannigan?" asked the taller of the two gentlemen.

"Yes."

"Nicholas Trist, United States Diplomat to Mexico—and—I'd like to introduce you to Mexican plenipotentiary representative Benito Juarez. He's here on behalf of Mexico's president, Antonio Lopez de Santa Anna." All three shook hands.

"Now that the pleasantries are over," said Flannigan irritably to Trist, "you're three hours late."

"Purposely done. Are all your passengers asleep?"

"Yes, all three hundred and fifty-seven, plus most of my crew. Why?"

"Do you know what your assignment is?" Trist questioned.

"Not exactly—*receive an important delivery. Cooperate fully.*"

"That's correct. It's critical to the success of this mission that the cargo remain hidden from your passengers and crew—hence the tardy arrival. Furthermore, Mr. Juarez is now your three hundred and fifty-eighth passenger. He'll oversee the security of the shipment."

"Welcome to my steamer," Captain Flannigan said to Juarez. "You're fortunate. We had a last minute cancellation in one of our first class cabins. That room is now yours."

"Thank you," Juarez said, "but I must decline. My bed will be next to my diplomatic mission."

"Your decision, but it's a long voyage."

Turning back to Trist, Flannigan asked. "And what exactly are we shipping?"

"Gold," said Trist soberly, "and an important diplomatic treaty. The treaty was recently signed by our President, Franklin Pierce. The President of Mexico, Santa Anna, will rendezvous with your steamer in Panama City; sign the treaty, and then take delivery of the gold. Juarez will accompany your steamer on its return trip, safeguarding the signed treaty. Upon his arrival in San Francisco, he will then deliver it to my office at the United States Consulate."

"Gold and a diplomatic treaty. This should make for an interesting voyage: We already have eight hundred thousand dollars of gold bullion on board recovered by fortune hungry Argonauts. It's stored in our strong room. You can store your gold and treaty there."

"No," said Juarez, "as I informed you, the gold and treaty will stay with me."

"Of course, your diplomatic mission," Flannigan said sarcastically. "And where might that be since you've declined a first-class cabin?"

"Your second strong room," Juarez replied smugly. "The non-existent room on the bottom deck of your ship, located in the upper bow section, used to transport questionable goods. That room."

"Ah ... that room ... I'm somewhat familiar with it. I will have to see if it's still available," said Flannigan indifferently. "Good investigative research on your part. It will be hot down there. Dress lightly."

A black wharf rat abruptly scurried past Captain Flannigan, dashed up the gangplank and onto the deck of the *Winfield Scott*.

"Another non-paying passenger," brooded the Captain. "And my bonus—"

"Paid upon your arrival in Panama City," Trist responded.

"Then I suggest we have a successful passage."

It took the sixteen Calvary soldiers almost two hours to offload nearly fifteen thousand pounds of gold bars and coins. The gold bars were secured in nondescript brass crates. Each crate held three hundred pounds, with carrying handles on either side. The gold coins were stored in heavy duty burlap canvas sacks, each holding seventy-five pounds. The twenty dollar coins were newly minted and bore the 1850 Double Eagle, Liberty Head design.

The United States-Mexico treaty was encased in a thick, water-proof, oval-shaped glass container. It was sealed with an airtight cork-oak plug, similar to those used to stop up champagne bottles. It was then cradled in sawdust—to prevent it from breaking—in its own richly-wrought brass crate, one half the size of the containers that held the gold bars.

Benito Juarez supervised the placement of the gold in the second strong room. To evenly balance out the weight, the entire length of the mid-portion of the twenty foot room was utilized. The crate holding the treaty was safeguarded among the gold crates to provide additional protection. The strong room was then padlocked, with Juarez commanding the only key.

At approximately 1:45 a.m., the *S.S. Winfield Scott* cast off its mooring lines from Valley's Saint Wharf, and began its ocean voyage, destination Panama City. There would be no other stops along the way.

Because the impenetrable pea-soup fog made clearing the San Francisco Bay and all its attendant hazards—rock reefs, islands, sandbars, and other boats—harrowing, Captain Flannigan nursed his steamer at a sluggish three knots. After nearly two excruciating hours, and with great relief, he emerged from the bay and entered the open ocean. He then throttled the engines to their maximum speed of twelve knots, hoping to make up the time lost by the delay.

Able to relax now, Captain Flannigan reflected on the beauty of his steamer. The *S.S. Winfield Scott* was a product of the New York shipyards of Westervelt and McKay, and was launched on October 27, 1850. Under his command it began running the Pacific route between San Francisco and Panama City with the first voyage taking place on July 20, 1853. The ship was owned by the Pacific Mail Steamship Company, and carried passengers, baggage, cargo, mail, and gold. The *Winfield Scott* was a two hundred and twenty-five foot long wooden vessel with a beam of thirty-four feet, and four decks. The ship was built of wood that included White Oak, Live Oak, Locust Cedar, and Georgia Yellow Pine, with double iron bracing. The propulsion system involved two massive Morgan Iron Works side-lever 370 horsepower steam engines. These engines drove two iron and wood paddlewheels located on either side of the ship, assisted by three square sails on the foremast. The steamer had accommodations for up to four hundred passengers, and its main dining salon could feed over one hundred passengers at a seating.

The *Scott* was named for Major General Winfield Scott, commanding general of the United States Army, and hero of the recent Mexican-American War. In honor of her namesake, the *S.S. Winfield Scott* carried a gilded wooden bust of the general on her bow.

Captain Flannigan's reflective mood was abruptly interrupted when a large swell struck the bow of his ship sending a cascade of salt spray over his wheelhouse and onto the main deck. The wind began picking up and was soon screaming like a disembodied spirit. This four hundred mile stretch of sea between San Francisco and Santa Barbara was traditionally brutal. Tonight would be no different. His shift lasted until 8:00 a.m. He rubbed his eyes; it would be a long night at the helm.

The next day, at 4:15 in the afternoon, Captain Flannigan was awakened by incessant knocking upon his cabin's door. The ship's steward was performing his duty as a human alarm clock. "Okay, okay," the Captain said groggily, "I'm awake. Thanks."

His shift in the wheelhouse began at 5:00 p.m. and would end at 1:00 a.m. He had forty-five minutes to perform his sponge bath, dress, and eat. But, being captain had its privileges—his cabin was larger than most and came equipped with its own private sink and mirror. Looking at his image in the mirror his once Irish red hair was now snowy white, along with his beard. A few wrinkles etched his stoic face. Fifty-two years of life, many spent at sea, were catching up to him. Even a month away from his wife of thirty-one years was never easy. His wife loved the small coastal town of Carmel. Recently, he made her a promise; just eight more years as captain, and then they would move to Carmel.

Strolling into the wheelhouse Captain Flannigan was pleased at the *Scott's* progress. In spite of the surly ocean conditions, his ship had made good passage down the coast. During the next six hours he covered another eighty miles passing Point Conception, which was twelve miles north of Santa Barbara. As soon as he was south of the Point the ocean became blissfully calmer, even more so once he entered the Santa Barbara Channel, which ran between the five Channel Islands.

To shave time off the two-week excursion he typically sailed between the Channel Islands rather than seaward of them. His knowledge as to the situs of the various off-shore islands allowed him to implement this measure. By 11:00 p.m., his ship was within a mile of passing Santa Cruz Island. A crescent moon lit the night sky, barely illuminating the island to his immediate right. At twenty-four miles in length it was a sizable land mass. A misty fog was rolling in. The fog enhanced the already eerie silence as nearly everyone on board the steamer had retired for the night. The last thing he expected was Benito Juarez, who cat-like had sneaked into the wheelhouse, dressed in a form-fitting wool coat and dragging a mid-sized travel bag. He noticed a gold pocket watch dangling from Juarez's right coat pocket.

"Evening Captain."

"Evening Mr. Juarez. Trouble sleeping?"

"No. A little warm but bearable."

"Sorry. Are you carrying the treaty with you?" he asked glancing at the travel bag.

"No Captain—a gift of redemption."

"For whom?"

"For you," Juarez said.

"For me . . . I don't understand," he said suspiciously.

Captain Flannigan stared at Juarez for an indication of chicanery, but observed no such non-verbal signs. Since leaving San

Francisco, Juarez had pretty much kept to himself other than taking meals. The attaché was of average height, clean-shaven, with smooth bronze hair cropped close to his head. He was the first full-blooded, indigenous, non-Spanish Mexican diplomat that Flannigan had encountered. His obvious rise to power was extraordinary considering Spain's disdain for national citizens.

"Do you mind if I sit down?" Juarez asked. "This will take some explaining," he said, indicating the vacant co-pilot seat next to Captain Flannigan.

"Go ahead."

As Juarez sat down he coolly retrieved a .44 caliber Colt revolver from under his wool coat and aimed the barrel toward Flannigan. The Captain turned ashen white.

"Relax . . . If I had any intention of firing it . . . you would already be dead."

"What do you want?" the Captain muttered fearfully.

"Cooperation. But, what I want does not directly involve you."

"It sure seems like it does."

"It involves your ship. You're the unfortunate captain."

"What does that mean—unfortunate captain?" Stealing a glance out the wheelhouse window the Captain noticed the faint glow of the lighthouse located on Cavern Point on the southernmost portion of Santa Cruz Island. As they slid by, it became shrouded in a deepening fog.

"Are you familiar with the Treaty of Guadalupe Hidalgo?" Juarez queried.

"Treaty of Hidalgo? What has a treaty to do with my ship?"

"It ended the Mexican-American War. A war instigated by your country. It was signed on February 2, 1848."

Flannigan remained silent—not sure how best to answer.

"That treaty granted your country undisputed control of Texas and ceded to the United States the territories of California, Nevada, New Mexico, Utah, and parts of Colorado, Kansas, Arizona, Oklahoma, and Wyoming. In return, my country received a mere pittance—eighteen million U.S. dollars—squandered by our politicians, including our current President, Antonio Lopez de Santa Anna."

"You lost the war. Your country agreed to exchange land for money." Captain Flannigan replied defensively. *Where was this going?* He wondered.

"That soil was the *sovereignty* of our country. You had no right to *extort* it from us," Juarez said angrily.

Captain Flannigan observed beads of sweat trickling down Juarez's forehead in spite of the chilly December night. Juarez fingered his pocket watch, checking the time.

"I did not personally deprive you of anything. This is between our countries," Flannigan said, attempting to calm Juarez down.

"The Gadsden Purchase. Are you familiar with that?"

"I believe our countries are currently discussing this particular agreement."

"It's more than just a *discussion*; our exalted president has already agreed to once again dispose of our precious soil in exchange for blood money."

"Our countries aren't currently at war," Flannigan corrected.

"Ten million U.S. dollars. Money that President Santa Anna intends to funnel into his own private army. And do you know why? To squash rebellions in our country. To massacre people speaking out against his corrupt regime. That money will ultimately spill the blood of thousands of innocent Mexicans."

"Is not Santa Anna *your* president? Did he not appoint *you* to your current diplomatic post?" Captain Flannigan reminded him.

"I'm foremost a Mexican patriot," Juarez said proudly. "As of today, I no longer serve Santa Anna."

"Who do you serve?"

"The Ayutla Rebellion. Your newspapers will write about us soon."

"And my ship is somehow caught up in your rebellion?"

"It's what's on your ship."

"Ahh—the gold."

"And the latest treaty for additional land," added Juarez.

The island of Santa Cruz was like a shadow as it gradually faded into a diffused background. Juarez once more consulted his pocket watch. A bead of sweat splashed onto the crystal cover.

Juarez continued. "President Santa Anna is starved for cash in order to finance his ruthless army. He recently reached an agreement with President Pierce to peddle a massive amount of Mexican territory for an immediate shipment of gold bars and coins. We will not allow this."

"You are but one person on my boat. How can you thwart it?" Captain Flannigan said skeptically.

"With this." Juarez reached into his right breast pocket and pulled out a one-foot long cord of half-inch sized brown-colored rope-like material.

The Captain stared at it for a brief moment, uncertainty in his eyes. "What the hell is that?"

"Corded black-powder detonation rope."

"Are you insane?" Flannigan said enraged, his face beet red, his breathing labored.

"I assure you—I'm perfectly sane."

Raising his voice, the Captain asked harshly. "Are you going to destroy my ship and kill everyone on board?"

"It's my expectation that no one will die." Juarez stole a glance at his watch. He returned the explosive material to his pocket.

"And how do you plan on accomplishing that?" Flannigan inquired, moving imperceptibly closer to Juarez's seated position, clandestinely slipping a heavy lead paperweight used to hold nautical charts into his right side pocket, his hand clasping it solidly.

"Simple. I surrounded the gold crates with the detonation rope. Nine minutes ago I ignited a delayed fuse before locking the strong room. There is about one minute left. The rope is a directional explosive. In this case, it will explode downwards obliterating the bow hull. The gold and treaty will descend into the black depths of perdition where they belong."

Gazing out the window as a distraction, Flannigan subtly moved another fraction of an inch closer to Juarez, his right hand still clutching the paperweight.

Juarez raised the Colt revolver. He aimed it squarely at the Captain's chest. He pulled back the hammer, loading the gun. "Do not try and alert your crew—and—if you take another step in my direction, I will blow a hole right through your heart." Captain Flannigan stopped in his tracks and released his grip on the paperweight. Juarez checked his pocket watch and said, "Time's up Captain." A faint muffled blast moderately rocked the steamer. The bow of the ship dipped negligibly. The speed decreased slightly.

"That's it!" the Captain said hopefully."

"It was a controlled explosion. But, the locked strong room is not watertight. Your ship will eventually sink," Juarez said with an air of regret. He lowered the revolver.

"Sink? I thought no one would perish?"

"They won't."

"Have you also planned for the safety of my passengers and crew?" Captain Flannigan asked acrimoniously.

"We're coming up on Anacapa Island. The steamer will be piloted full speed into the island. I've chosen an area of impact that will ensure survival, as you will surely be rescued by passing steamers. You can blame the crash on the thickening fog."

"And you expect my company to believe that?—an experienced captain became disoriented in the fog?"

"You will be punished. Fired. Your days as a steamer captain will end."

"What if I refuse?"

"Then you sink. Your five lifeboats hold twenty passengers each. You do the math."

"What about you? You think I won't tell the authorities once were rescued?"

"I'm sorry to disappoint you. I've made alternate plans."

"You have a boat?"

"I have transportation waiting for me. What you say to the authorities is up to you. If it's any consolation here is your promised bonus," Juarez said, stepping off his chair, and shoving the travel bag with his foot over to Captain Flannigan.

"My bonus?" Curious, Flannigan peered inside the bag. There were two burlap canvas sacks. He opened one of the sacks. Gold coins. He opened the other sack. More gold coins.

"One hundred and fifty pounds," Juarez said with a slight grin. "You'll need these coins for your early retirement."

"I can't keep these."

"Think about it. No one will ever know. You've earned it."

A quarter mile to the right of the *Winfield Scott* the blurred silhouette of Anacapa Island morphed into view—a five-mile long stretch of rock broken into three small islets connected by shallow sandbars.

Captain Flannigan was awestruck by the amount of gold—it was more than his agreed upon bonus. *It wouldn't be right*, he repeated to himself. He re-opened one of the sacks to perform another inspection.

With the Captain's attention diverted Juarez quickly unscrewed a small pharmaceutical vile filed with chloroform. He poured a minute amount into a handkerchief. He then furtively grasped Flannigan from behind, his right arm underneath his neck, twisting and bending it backwards. "Forgive me," Juarez said under his breath. With his left hand he then pressed the handkerchief against the Captain's nose and mouth.

Captain Flannigan flailed violently, kicking his legs haphazardly, his arms revolving like an octopus searching for a grip on Juarez. In one last moment of clarity, before the chloroform's sedative effects dulled his movements, he remembered the lead paperweight. Reaching into his pocket he seized it. He then whipped his arm back over his shoulder, crushing the weight against Juarez's skull, who momentarily loosened his grip. Unfortunately, in his weakened state, the impact did not produce the desired effect. He struggled for a few additional seconds before the anesthetic properties of the colorless volatile liquid had accomplished its goal, and the Captain drifted into unconsciousness.

"It won't last long," Juarez said to the unaware captain as he painfully massaged a goose-egg-sized red welt that was mushrooming on his mid forehead. "Five minutes at most. Sleep well my stout captain. You'll be busy when you awake."

Juarez assumed control of the helm, changing course turning southeast, his speed twelve knots. Soon the islets of Middle Anacapa and East Anacapa came into view. A sandbar separated the two islets—a safe haven for a shipwreck. A few protruding reef rocks, however, jeopardized the passage. Fingerling fog also obscured the seascape. The ship's bow, now heavy with saltwater, plunged precariously. The clamor of stirring, fretful passengers filled the ship. The muted hum of a nearby craft's engine pierced the air.

Holding the steamer steady on its collision course, Juarez raced toward the sandbar. An outcropping of rocks, invisible in the swirling fog, raked the entire bow portion of the *Winfield Scott*. Below deck salt water poured through the gaping holes. The ship struck again. The crushing of timbers echoed like a cannon shot. The rudder was suddenly torn away allowing seawater to rush in through a massive breach in the mid-section of the steamer. The ship's stern began to settle underwater. The *Winfield Scott* lurched to its starboard side. Passengers were screaming and crying. The loud booming sound of crashing breakers pounded the ship. Sluggishly, the forward momentum of the steamer ceased, alighting on a shallow rocky reef, one-hundred yards astray of the providential sandbar.

The Captain began stirring as Juarez retreated from the wheelhouse. He hastily made his way to the gangplank entrance where a twenty-five foot, steam powered fishing schooner awaited his arrival. As the schooner disappeared into the opaque fog the faint outline of a Mexican flag—green, white, and red—could be seen fluttering off its stern.

Captain Flannigan and his crew heroically rescued every passenger on the *S.S. Winfield Scott*. Using the five lifeboats, all three hundred and fifty-seven passengers were transferred to the Island of Anacapa. Provisions and bedding were also brought ashore. As predicted by Benito Juarez, within three days of the tragedy the Pacific Mail Steamer *California* arrived on the scene, and removed all the woman and children. On December 10, 1853 the steamers *Republic,* and the returning *California,* removed all remaining passengers and crew. Most of the mail was recovered along with the baggage, as well as eight hundred thousand dollars worth of gold bullion. The steamer, *S.S. Winfield Scott,* was declared a total loss.

The Superintendent of cattle and sheep operations on neighboring Santa Cruz Island sent a barge to the wreck site, his employees stripping the steamer of its valuable lumber—White Oak, Live Oak, Locust Cedar and Georgia Pine. A portion of the timber was used in the construction of a new winery near Scorpion Cove; however, the bulk of the fine-grained hardwoods were stored for future use in a brick warehouse.

As predicted by Juarez, in the aftermath of the wreck Captain Sean Flannigan lost his position with the Pacific Mail Steamship Company. Following his discharge, he and his wife resettled in Carmel, California, purchasing a brand new three-bedroom cottage nestled on a coastal bluff with a spectacular view of the Pacific Ocean.

From January to March 1854 the United States government conducted a clandestine though exhaustive investigation in the waters surrounding Santa Cruz and Anacapa Islands, searching for the treaty and the fifteen thousand pounds of gold. Since the exact location of the treasure trove was not fully known—much of Captain Flannigan's testimony as to its whereabouts was speculative owing to the fact that the incident occurred during a foggy night—the fortune was never found. Unknown to Benito Juarez, and the United States Government, the actual jettison site was in waters less than one hundred and twenty feet. The incident was classified secret and all knowledge regarding it eventually faded as the few government officials aware of the diplomatic disaster also faded away.

In July 1854, United States President Franklin Pierce attempted to renegotiate a similar treaty with Mexican President, Antonio Lopez de Santa Anna. However, Santa Anna's plan to relinquish additional territory for money became public knowledge. His corrupt power struggle garnered many enemies. The Ayutla Rebellion was successful and Santa Anna was ultimately ousted as president on August 9, 1855. Several interim presidents were appointed over the next three years. On January 19, 1858 Benito Juarez consolidated his power and popular support and was elected president of Mexico. He served his beloved country in this position until his death on July 18, 1872.

In the years that followed, the remaining hulk of the *S.S. Winfield Scott* steamer became partially buried in the shifting sands, obscured by thick kelp forests, and years of disinterest.

1

SIX MONTHS BEFORE PRESENT DAY

There are mornings when you wake up where you wish you had just quietly died in your sleep. The accumulation of life's daily challenges, along with your circumstances—whether self-created or externally caused—eventually weaken your emotional reserves to such an extent that an explosive melt-down is inevitable and utter despair is the result. And then, the pendulum swings, and almost miraculously, through the unforeseen events of twelve life-changing hours, the sun regally sets on a new you. Ruben Negrete, ex-gang member and ex-felon, just experienced a day like that.

It began at 5:30 a.m. when Joey Barton, captain of the *Lucky Lady* fishing and service trawler, roused Negrete from a deep slumber by inserting a twelve-inch, putrid-smelling, California squid into his sleep deprived and hangdog gaping mouth. The practical joke nearly cost Negrete his life as he violently choked on the decaying remains, saturating his cabin walls, clothing, and bedding with projectile vomit. But, having to personally clean up the foul-smelling mess with no hope of sweet revenge, *since Barton was the captain*, added to his misery, and nearly sapped every ounce of Negrete's limited self-control.

The *Lucky Lady* was owned by *West Coast Seafood & Aquaculture,* a privately held company controlled by Karl Goebbel, CEO and President of the seafood conglomerate. He was often referred to as the Architect of the sustainable seafood market, resourcefully using decommissioned oil rigs as the foundation for his operations. The converted oil rigs into fish farms—Grace, Gilda, Gail, and Gina—located ten miles off the Ventura and Santa Barbara coastlines, produced vast quantities of protein rich fish and bivalve mollusks.

Sockeye salmon, yellowfin tuna, bluefin tuna, and white seabass were reared in elaborate self-enclosed nurturing habitats, which were attached to the transformed rigs. The massive, floating habitat structures were constructed with mesh-like Kevlar material, impervious to the corrosive qualities of salt water. The platforms enormous concrete and steel pilings were used to cultivate Pacific mussels, succulent oysters, and jumbo scallops.

The *Lucky Lady* was one of seven ships owned by Karl Goebbel that serviced the four oil rigs. She was currently tied up adjacent to Platform Grace, giving her crew a chance to recover from a grueling night netting squid on the backside of Santa Cruz Island. The squid were but one variety of live food harvested for the developing game fish. The crew of the *Lucky Lady* also netted anchovies, sardines, and mackerel. Negrete, and the only other deckhand, Miguel Chavez, a portly chain-smoking, thirty-something, ex-commercial fisherman, were in charge of offloading the squid into the submerged bait barges. The barges stored the squid until needed—like aquariums in restaurants which held viable, breathing Maine lobsters or Dungeness crabs—until their moment of thermal immolation.

"Enjoy your calamari breakfast?" Chavez asked derisively, upon Negrete's arrival topside.

Negrete guided a flexible four-inch diameter vacuum hose into the *Lucky Lady's* squid-filled fish hold and turned on the pump. "Your idea or the Captain's?"

"Actually, the Captain's. But he did ask me to find the right squid," he said with a derisive chuckle." Chavez was at the other end of the hose at the bait barges, directing the watery stream of writhing squid into the barges.

"How old?"

"At least two weeks. Nasty looking thing. I found it on the floor of the engine room."

"Did either of you worthless a-hole's consider the consequences of your actions?"

"No."

"You know . . . I don't forget a personal stunt like that," Negrete said angrily.

"Blame the Captain, not me. Just following orders," Chavez said defensively.

Negrete jammed the hose violently into a mass of squid, causing panic and severing tentacles. He smiled sardonically. "A year on this boat and I still get treated like a greenhorn . . . like—" He spat a large wad of snot in Chavez's direction, just missing. "You think it's all a silly joke—but watch your back, hombre—it's a big ocean."

His voice quivering, Chavez said, "You threatening me?"

Negrete felt empowered hearing the fear in Chavez's voice. "You *know* me . . . you decide," he whispered coldly.

Negrete unconsciously reached up with his left hand and began stroking a jagged, rose colored birthmark on his left cheek that extended to his left ear. Born with a long slender blemish on his skin, Negrete had it enhanced with a tattoo to make it appear as a deadly fer-de-lance viper. His thought, *if your face is disfigured, you might as well make it useful.*

'Saurian', that was his previous gang member name, which meant reptilian. Born in South Central Los Angeles in a predominantly black neighborhood, to a Mexican dad and a Cuban mom, he was the odd kid out. If it hadn't been for the 4th Street Mexican Gang, and the protection they provided, he probably would have died at a young age. The gang became his dad, his mother, his brothers, and his sisters. At five-feet eleven and one hundred-fifty pounds, he had a paper thin but sinewy body. Many an opposing gang member, who mistakenly equated his small frame with weakness, soon learned that his wiry quick, cheetah-like reflexes made him a deadly adversary.

To increase his chances of survival, Negrete frequented a neighborhood underground school which taught a type of karate that was particularly violent and whose teachers had abandoned the usual Eastern ethical codes of behavior. This form of karate was not meant to be viewed as a spectator sport in gymnasiums for the attainment of trophies and ribbons. Its only victory was obtained when the opponent was lying vanquished on the floor dead or severely maimed. Negrete became a master, and knowledge of his ruthlessness soon protected him from all but the most reckless and brainless of challengers.

One such rival gang member, too young to know better, decided to take Negrete on and was swiftly dispatched, and Negrete, at age twenty, found himself in a state prison on a charge of manslaughter. While imprisoned, to the surprise of many, he obtained his high school diploma, acing every class he attended. Apparently, beneath his ruthless façade, there existed a gifted intellect. After serving five years he was paroled. The one thing that jail had taught him—as did his previous gang affiliation— was that you had to know who your friends were.

Upon Negrete's release from prison, his probation officer found him his current job through a special work-furlough program administered by the courts. The employers who participated were paid a substantial stipend by the state if they employed ex-cons for at least one year. Negrete's one-year anniversary had recently transpired, and he bitterly acknowledged that he was still a deckhand, still earning minimum wage—which was certainly not commensurate with the workload.

After an hour of vacuuming, the last squid vanished into its storage tank. Negrete turned off the pump, stretching and flexing his aching arms. He kicked a dead squid back into the fish hold. He noticed a California sea lion lounging in the water next to the bait barge hoping for a free handout, its head tilted, its hazel colored eyes pleading—like a dog begging for a treat. The sound of a rifle shot shattered the air. The seal slipped beneath the surface, trailing a stream of blood.

"Damn seals," Captain Barton said irritably. "Steal our squid and fish. Defecate on our docks. I hate 'em. Like ocean rats." His eyes bulged as he spoke. He continued to aim the 22 carbine rifle in the general vicinity where the seal disappeared. The black synthetic stainless steel rifle glistened in the sun and the smell of gunpowder hung in the air.

"You nearly shot me," Negrete shouted angrily.

"Yea—well, I didn't."

"Want to switch places next time?"

"Don't be a smart-ass. I know how to aim a gun."

"Thanks, I'll remember that . . . if there is a *next* time."

"And what's that suppose to mean?" Captain Barton asked caustically.

Negrete noticed that the gun was now pointed in his direction. His body tensed. Adrenaline flowed. He forced himself to settle down. Although Negrete knew he could easily take on the captain, he also knew that a violent confrontation would violate his probation, resulting in an immediate dismissal and additional jail time. "Nothing—it means absolutely nothing," he said carefully. He began to coil the four-inch flexible hose. The activity helped distract his anger. He stowed it on a metal hanger.

"Good," replied the Captain, "you're not so dumb after all."

Negrete tasted blood as he bit his upper lip. The Captain, a former crab fisherman out of Alaska stood six feet one inch, was in his mid-fifties, had chocolate-colored eyes, a bulbous nose, a face cratered with sun damage, and a personality befitting a man possessed. Negrete swallowed his own blood. Backing down from an opponent violated his internal code of conduct.

"Now," continued the Captain, "finish cleaning up . . . the two of you. We leave in fifteen minutes for the other three platforms. We're already behind in making our deliveries so let's pick it up."

Gilda was the next platform on their delivery schedule. Like the others, it was stripped of anything that had to do with the production of oil and gas. However, the living quarters were maintained and had been recently upgraded. New stainless steel docks were installed, along with metal runways leading out to the fish habitats. The typical workhorse crane seen towering atop an oil platform was retained, and was used for loading and offloading supplies, equipment, garbage, and seafood. Each platform was self-sufficient; housing an electrical generator, solar panels, and water desalinator. To preserve the freshness of the fish, every platform had its own state-of-the art processing plant where the fish were immediately filleted, vacuum packed or stored in dry ice, and shipped that same day. The mollusks were simply packaged whole, in dry ice, and shipped within twenty-four hours.

When Karl Goebbel first purchased the platforms, they were a drab gray-brown in appearance. After hiring professional painters, they now sparkled in turquoise-blue, radiating the beauty of the surrounding ocean. In addition, he hired a famous wildlife artist who created one-hundred foot long murals on each platform, depicting the various game fish he was raising. On Platform Grace, the soaring sockeye salmon, on Gilda, the stately yellowfin tuna, on Gail, the succulent bluefin tuna, and on Gina, the stunning white seabass. All four renderings were visible from the Pacific Coast Highway, the main thoroughfare along the shoreline. At night, the platforms were brilliantly illuminated, sparkling like gems floating on an ethereal sea.

Unlike Platform Grace, which welcomed visitors and the news media, Gilda, Gail, and Gina, were off-limits to the public and news organizations. Bright yellow six-foot high buoys, anchored three-hundred yards off the corners of each platform, warned anyone approaching that they were encroaching on private property, and that trespassers would be prosecuted to the full extent of the law.

As the seventy-five foot *Lucky Lady* slid up to Gilda, Negrete stood on the bow and tossed a two-inch thick nylon mooring rope to a worker on the platform who then wrapped it around a heavy metal cleat, securing it with a clove hitch knot. Chavez did the same from the stern. The supplies they were delivering were stored under tarp-covered wooden pallets located in the rear of the ship.

"Ok boys, let's get to work," Captain Barton ordered.

Working together, Negrete and Chavez removed the tarps. The pallets, each holding twenty one-hundred pound bags of meat and bone meal, were designed to be lifted by the crane. As the crane hook descended, Negrete snagged it with his right hand and fastened it to the first pallet, watching the load as it lifted into the air. Chavez began preparing the second pallet.

Negrete noted the familiar packaging label embossed on the bags: *Meat and Bone Meal, Product of Canada.* Inquisitive as to the food item that they were delivering he had recently researched it on the Internet. The results surprised him.

In a belittling tone he asked Chavez, "Hey homeboy, do you know what meat and bone meal is?"

"Do I care?"

"Take a guess."

"Ground up meat and bones from fish," replied Chavez.

"Wrong—it's *not* from fish."

"What then?"

"Primarily cows."

"Cows?"

"Yes . . . they grind up what's left of cows—what we humans won't eat—and make it into these pellets. They also include other dead animals in the mix." Negrete pulled a few half inch brown pellets from a torn bag and let them slide through his fingers.

"What part of cows don't we eat?" Chavez inquired.

"Organs, fetuses, bones, brain—any inedible part of a cow and downer cows not suitable for human consumption," Negrete answered.

"So, we're feeding nasty cow parts and other pulverized critters to all these farm-raised fish," Chavez laughed cynically.

"Yes, but not at Grace. At Grace they're only fed live food, like the squid we caught last night."

"So, what's your point?"

"Do you ever wonder why these fish are only fed these pellets?" Negrete asked.

"Cheaper. Squid and baitfish are too expensive to serve as feed for the entire stock. Fish need protein to grow. Cows are a good reliable source."

Standing on the *Lucky Lady* and looking out and observing the vastness of Goebbels' seafood operation, Negrete slowly nodded his head in agreement. He normally considered Chavez a moron but had to admit that he was probably correct on this particular issue.

The crane hook returned for its next load. Chavez attached it to the second pallet.

Negrete watched as it ascended to the third-tier level where the pallets were stored in a small warehouse. He thought about Karl Goebbels' seafood empire. An intelligent man, he concluded, and very shrewd. Using Grace as his flagship fish farm, where the public and the news media were welcomed, was masterful. If the ignoramuses knew the real truth—that seventy-five percent of Goebbel's farmed-raised fish were fed resurrected cow meat—they would probably gag on their expensive fish fillet dinners. Negrete desperately wanted to meet this Goebbel and convince him that his services on behalf of *West Coast Seafood & Aquaculture* were definitely being under-utilized.

Four hours later the last pallet was delivered to Platform Gina, and the *Lucky Lady* began making its way back to her home port at Ventura Harbor. At seventy-five feet in length with a beam of twenty feet, the trawler's two Caterpillar 3412 diesel engines could easily propel her at twenty-five knots. Her deck size was twenty-five feet by fifteen feet, with a cargo carrying capacity of sixteen pallets. She was equipped with GPS, two VHF's, one Single-Side Band, Weather Fax, Loran C, forty-eight mile Rastascan Radar, two heads with showers, four double-occupancy staterooms, a kitchen that could feed eight passengers, a twenty-ton live-fish hold, one twelve-foot Zodiac inflatable boat with a Mercury twenty-five horsepower four-stroke outboard engine, and two commercial nets for catching baitfish and squid.

The *Lucky Lady's* home berth at Ventura Harbor was in its own private cove exclusively occupied by *West Coast Seafood & Aquaculture*. The facilities at the inlet included nine boat slips, various storehouses, repair facility, fueling dock, a twenty-five thousand square foot refrigerated warehouse, and refrigerated transportation vehicles.

Upon their arrival, Captain Barton initially docked the *Lucky Lady* at a temporary anchorage where new pallets were being loaded for tomorrow's workday. Chavez was on call to help with the reloading, after which he was dismissed for the day. Meanwhile, Negrete had a half-hour break before he was required to return to the ship to assist with the refueling.

Stepping off the ship, Negrete casually sauntered over to Chavez's older model Toyota Tundra pickup truck. Looking around to make sure he was not being watched, he quickly unscrewed the gas cap. From a backpack he was wearing, he removed a plastic half-gallon milk carton filled with malodorous smelling anchovies and squid. He popped off the lid and carefully poured the contents down the gas-funnel pipe, and then screwed the gas cap back on. He next retrieved a Sharpie black pen from his backpack and in bold print wrote on the milk carton: *I don't forget.* One squid and one anchovy remained in the carton as a sadistic reminder. Finally, with his right foot he shattered the driver's side window. He carefully placed the milk carton on the driver's seat. Satisfied, he left to go have a beer before returning back to the boat.

An hour later the *Lucky Lady* arrived at the fueling dock located at the far end of the cove. After tying up, Negrete jumped over the rail to retrieve the extra-long rubber fuel hose. The two fuel tanks on the *Lucky Lady* were situated in the middle of her deck. Each tank held ten-thousand gallons and each empty tank required fifteen minutes to fill. Negrete inserted the galvanized hose tip into the first fuel tank and began dispensing the ultra-low sulphur diesel fuel. Unlike a public gas station, there was no automatic shutoff valve when the tank was full. Negrete had to listen attentively to ascertain when the tank was nearing its capacity. The Captain, carelessly smoking a cigarette, stepped out of the upper-level pilothouse to rubberneck the process.

The tank was evidently empty when the fueling began since it was taking a long time to fill. A second supply ship, similar in size to the *Lucky Lady*, pulled up to the opposite side of the fuel dock. The late afternoon onshore ocean breeze had picked up making it difficult for the captain to dock his ship. The ship's side to side maneuvering jets, throttled at maximum thrust, sounded like jet engines as the captain struggled to accomplish the docking. Suddenly, a collision horn sounded. Negrete ran to the rail to observe the impact. The captain of the vessel, through long years of experience, or just pure luck, narrowly avoided the expected collision with the wooden dock. There was a long, loud scraping sound—wood against metal—but the damage was insignificant. Disappointed, Negrete looked over to see that his captain also stood mesmerized by the unfolding drama.

The geyser-like sound of erupting gas and fluid interrupted Negrete's reverie. He knew instantly what had happened. A ten-thousand gallon depleted fuel tank contains an expansive amount of residual gas vapors; if you overfill a once empty tank too quickly, the gas vapors become compressed, eventually bursting forth like an Old Faithful Geyser.

Negrete immediately reached over and yanked the fuel hose out of the tank, grabbed the nozzle handle and moved the *on* button to the *off* position, shutting down the flow of diesel fuel. Unfortunately, the damage had been done. Approximately twenty gallons of foul smelling diesel fuel saturated the boat deck coating everything in a slick, gel like scum. The Captain's heavy footsteps could be heard echoing off the aluminum steps as he swiftly descended from the elevated pilothouse.

"What the hell happened?" Captain Barton bellowed his face flushed red, his breathing rapid.

Setting down the fuel hose, Negrete replied in a voice edged with sarcasm, "Perhaps I slightly overfilled the fuel tank—no big deal."

"You've created one heck of a shitty mess."

"Things happen, I'll clean it up."

"Out of your paycheck you will," Captain Barton said firmly.

"I'm an employee—you can't do that," Negrete countered.

"Now you're telling me what I can and cannot do."

"I'm just saying—"

Moving closer the Captain interrupted, "You just shut your mouth, you worthless *Beaner*, before I fire your pathetic little ass. Hiring prison garbage like you was never my idea—"

"*Un culera hijo de puta*," Negrete said angrily.

"Hey Wetback speak English," Captain Barton demanded.

"You want to know what it means—"

"I'm waiting."

"Asshole, son of a whore," Negrete said slowly enunciating each syllable.

The Captain's balled up right fist hammered Negrete's right temple at the exact moment he uttered the last word. Negrete flew backwards, whacking his head against the teak wood railing.

Dazed, he attempted to stand up. Slippery fuel coated his rubber work boots causing him to lose his balance and fall sideways, landing on his back at the Captain's feet.

"How convenient," growled Barton, stomping down, impelling the right heel of his leather work boot into Negrete's chest, fracturing ribs.

What's the matter brown boy," taunted the Captain, "can't handle the heat? No gang members to back you up?"

As Negrete attempted to roll away, his Levi jeans, flannel shirt, and wool jacket became imbued with diesel fuel. A steel-toe boot found its way between his buttocks, drilling his groin, and sending nauseating shock waves throughout his body. A second kick walloped his lower back, slamming his body into a storage rack.

Violent rage burned within Negrete. He painfully struggled to his feet. Captain Barton approached him lugging a six-foot long fishing gaff crowned with a razor sharp curved iron hook. The gaff was normally used to land large fish.

Negrete looked for some type of protection. On the storage rack he noticed a two-foot long dead-blow club, also known as a shark bat. It was designed to subdue thrashing sharks accidentally caught in their fishing nets. Made with a tough durometer urethane outer shell, aluminum rod core, polycarbonate internal shell, and filled with one pound of lead shot, it was a deadly weapon. He picked it up. It felt solid. He rotated it between his hands. He liked the feel. He was once again back with his former 4th Street Mexican Gang. He knew what to do.

"You want some of me?" he chided with a devious grin.

The Captain hesitated and then smiled. He rushed forward. He thrust the tapered gaff forcefully into the left sternum area of Negrete's chest. He twisted it upward, endeavoring to drive the barbed hook into Negrete's heart. The tip began to penetrate Negrete's skin. Blood oozed out. As Captain Barton shrieked triumphantly, Negrete intentionally leaned backwards, causing the Captain to stumble forward. It was a fatal move. With seething ferocity Negrete whipped the shark bat forward as if he was hitting a home run out of a four-hundred foot baseball park, brutally smashing it against the Captain's skull, fragmenting the bone. The Captain staggered a few steps before collapsing onto the deck.

Negrete tossed the shark bat in the direction of the storage rack. His senses were on heightened alert. His nostrils flared, seeking air. He felt alive, powerful. His ribs hurt, and there was a tiny puncture wound below his left nipple. He started shaking. Not from fear or pain, but from the suddenness and shock of it all. Awareness penetrated his brain. His first thought: *Any witnesses?* He did a complete three hundred and sixty degree turn. There did not appear to be any. The dock was empty. Fortunately, no crewmembers on board the other docked vessel shouted, or offered any help. No police sirens split the air. *Good*, he sighed with relief.

He next checked the Captain, though he was certain that he was dead. Too much blood. The skull crushed, misshapen, a smattering of brain tissue, the Captain's eyes rolled back in their sockets, the whites showing. Negrete's heart raced. He had to come up with a plan, and fast. He studied the pilothouse where the Captain had descended. The stainless steel stairs were narrow, steep. Diesel fuel coated a majority of the steps. Captain Joey Barton was old for his years, his coordination questionable. He had his plan of action.

Negrete unclipped the cell phone from his belt and popped it open. Searching through his stored 'contacts' he located the corporate telephone number for *West Coast Seafood & Aquaculture*. He double-tapped it with his right index finger highlighting the number. One more tap and it dialed automatically. He had a tragic accident to report. The corporate offices were only five minutes away, off Victoria Avenue. Whatever individual they sent to investigate the incident didn't concern him. Negrete figured his street and jail smarts would serve him well, and that he could deceive anyone. However, he would need to change into a new set of clothes, and bandage his wound. Fortunately, in his cabin, he had a change of clothing, plus the ship carried a fully stocked first aid kit. In addition, other rearrangement work involving the accident scene had to be tactfully engineered.

Fifteen minutes later a black H-2 stretch limousine pulled up to the fuel dock. A sizable man exited the driver's door. Another bulkier man exited the rear door and together they stood expectantly, surveying the surroundings. Each man was dressed in black slacks, black wing-tip shoes, black pullover cardigan sweaters, and black sunglasses. From their bulk and demeanor, Negrete recognized them as bodyguards. A few minutes later, the larger of the two men opened the rear door. A distinguished-looking gentleman stepped out. He was tall, about six-foot three, lean with broad shoulders, and square jawed. His salt and pepper-colored hair was worn long and tied in a stylish ponytail with several gold bands. His clothing was all leather—black leather pants, black leather jacket, black leather gloves, and black leather cowboy boots. His eyes remained concealed behind black Chanel sunglasses. Clearly, this was the Big Boss.

With his men leading the way, they quickly walked toward the *Lucky Lady.* The two large men stopped and stood watch at the entrance to the fuel dock. The Boss man continued walking and Negrete noticed he was carrying a manila folder. Thirty seconds later Karl Goebbel stepped onboard the *Lucky Lady.* This was not what Negrete anticipated. His mouth was suddenly dry. He needed a drink.

"Ruben Negrete?" said the man without a hint of malice in his voice.

Feeling more diminutive than his five-foot-eleven frame Negrete responded, "Yes."

"Karl Goebbel."

Goebbel extended his hand and Negrete awkwardly shook it.

"David at corporate," continued Goebbel, "who you *calmly* spoke to about twenty minutes ago, informed me that Captain Joey Barton had an accident." Goebbel stared at the limp body lying in diesel fuel next to the storage rack.

Trying to disguise the tremor in his voice, Negrete responded: "I overfilled one of the fuel tanks," he said pointing toward the middle of the deck, "and diesel fuel shot up everywhere. Some landed on the stairs going up to the bridge."

"And what happened next?" Goebbel asked.

"He slipped and fell—I mean he slipped off the stairs—I mean he was coming down the stairs, and then he slipped. He smashed his head on the galvanized storage racks."

Negrete strolled over to the storage racks and pointed to the top of a two-inch tubular bar. "He hit here," he said.

Goebbel examined the bar. There was blood on it, a few pieces of bone, and what appeared to be strands of off-white tapioca pudding. "What's this?" Goebbel asked, indicating the white stuff.

"His brain," Negrete replied.

Goebbel re-examined the bar. "A lot of blood for a millisecond impact."

Negrete had not thought about that. "Hard to know," was all he could muster.

Goebbel smiled broadly. "Yes, hard to know."

Negrete watched in growing apprehension as Goebbel continued to examine the scene. He felt like a mouse in the crosshairs of a cat. He suppressed the urge to urinate. Goebbel scrutinized every detail on the storage rack. He inspected the deck. He peered at the fuel tank. He opened it up. He could see that it was full. He even probed the Captain's head wound using a Mont-Blanc pen. He removed Captain Barton's wallet and keys and pocketed them. He next cautiously walked up and down the pilothouse stairway—repeating the procedure several times—each time gazing intently into Negrete's eyes. Negrete could not see Goebbel's eyes because of the lifeless sunglasses. He was on the wrong side of a two-way mirror.

"Which stair did he slip off?" Goebbel asked.

"The one near the top," Negrete assured him.

"Not much diesel fuel on the upper stairs."

"Then—a little lower—perhaps."

"Perhaps," Goebbel repeated.

Negrete did not like to hear his words being replayed. It did not sound comforting. Goebbel descended the stairs. He walked to the stern. He appeared to be taking in the entire picture. A sardonic grin materialized on his face. He carefully walked back to the storage rack, reached under it, and came up with a shark bat. Negrete died inside. Urine flowed down his legs. *Stupid Beaner* entered his brain.

Goebbel examined the bat, turning it around, peering at all sides. He was like a microscope in his probing. He passed it to his right hand. He looked down at Captain Barton. He then swung the bat with all his strength as if he was the perpetrator. He ceased his swing right at Barton's hairline, bending down to place the barrel of the bat in the cavity, which now had congealed blood replacing the void. It fit. He stood up. He flung the bat into the cove where it landed with a pleasant splash, and rapidly sank out of sight.

"You need to be more careful next time," he said.

He wiped the blood off his gloves with a rag retrieved from the storage cart, and also tossed that into the cove. He waved to his men guarding the entrance to the fuel dock. Negrete assumed it was some sort of signal.

"We have business. I require a small snack and prefer to sit. Do you mind if we take this into the kitchen area?" Goebbel asked politely.

Negrete speechless, barely nodded his head. Like a chastised puppy he obediently followed Goebbel into the *Luck Lady's* kitchen and sat rattled as Goebbel prepared a tuna fish sandwich on rye bread. Negrete's stomach churned at the smell of the food.

Between bites Goebbel spoke.

"Captain Barton was as you say in Spanish, *un guey*, an idiot."

Though Negrete agreed, he said nothing.

Goebbel, wiping a crumb from his lower lip continued, "Have you ever been afflicted by greed, Ruben . . . and demanded more than what was appropriate?"

Negrete knew that this was a pivotal type question and that he had to be very careful in his response. "Yes," he said.

Goebbel raised his eyebrows, "How so?"

"From individuals that are under my control."

Goebbel roared with laughter. After a few moments he calmed down and said, "Honest answer and one that I agree with; but, how about from a superior?"

Negrete could hear the sound of men working coming from outside on the boat deck. He assumed it was Goebbel's two men. "Never," he said.

"Wise. Now take the late Captain Barton, he had difficulty grasping this very sensible business concept. I pay well—there are nice perks and occasional bonuses—especially for those captains who perform certain discreet assignments."

"So—his death was not a disappointment," Negrete said cautiously.

With a sardonic grin, Goebbel said, "No son, but a little messier than an accidental drowning."

"You know . . . it was self-defense," Negrete said. He lifted the sweatshirt he was wearing exposing a chest painted black and blue with bruises and crimson abrasions. He peeled off a large bandage, revealing the iron hook lesion.

Goebbel momentarily glanced at the injuries. "I'm glad you had a worthy fight," he said.

"What about the body, police investigation, and autopsy?" Negrete asked concerned.

Popping the last of the sandwich into his mouth Goebbel said, "You picked a good captain to put the kibosh on. His parents are dead. He has no siblings. He's never been married and he has no kids. No one gives a crap about him."

"Now what happens?"

"Fodder for the fish. He quit working without giving notice, and we have no forwarding address. Simple."

Changing the subject Goebbel unclasped the manila folder he was carrying. It was Negrete's employee and criminal file. Goebbel briefly scanned the documents. "Manslaughter conviction for the death of a rival gang member. Nothing wrong with that. Academically—while incarcerated—you successfully obtained your high school degree, obtaining all A's. Now that's impressive for an ex-gangbanger! Your file also indicates that your dad is deceased."

"Yes."

"From what?"

"Hit by an eighteen wheeler while jay-walking across El Segundo Boulevard on my tenth birthday. He was drunk and left us with no life insurance. We incinerated his body. My mom had to pay for the damage to the front-end of the truck."

"No love lost?"

"He was a worthless alcoholic."

Sounding emphatic, Goebbel said, "Did you know—I lost my wife?"

"No," Negrete said.

"Scuba diving off Catalina Island at ninety feet."

Curious, Negrete asked, "What happened?"

"Her air regulator went into free-flow. She panicked and attempted an emergency ascent."

"Were you there?"

"Yes—right by her side the entire time."

"She didn't make it?"

"She failed to expel air from her lungs as she neared the surface. Her lungs kept expanding. They turned into a bomb."

"A bomb?" Negrete inquired.

"Her lungs exploded—massive air embolism." Goebbel pantomimed bursting lungs with his hands. "The final thirty feet she was like an upside down ketchup bottle. I was worried about sharks."

"Did you ever discover why her regulator went into free-flow?" Negrete asked.

"That's the beauty about scuba diving accidents—they're so hard to verify. When you're a novice diver, things happen."

Negrete was about ready to offer his condolences when it struck him. This story was not about an unfortunate tragedy it was a testament as to what Karl Goebbel was capable of. "I assume you eventually recovered from her death?" Negrete said warily.

"Six months and five-million dollars later. The beauty of non-taxable life insurance. As they say, the living must live."

Goebbel closed the folder that summarized Negrete's life. He reached into his pocket and removed the wallet and keys that he had acquired from Captain Barton. He dumped the wallet's contents onto the table. Out spilled over a thousand dollars in cash, numerous credit cards, a security card, business cards, receipts, and miscellaneous hand-written notes. He made two piles. In one pile he placed the cash, a *West Coast Seafood & Aquaculture* Visa credit card, and the security card. He added the keys. The other pile he slipped back into his pocket.

"You ready to do business, Mr. Negrete?"

Not exactly sure where this was going but piqued, Negrete said, "I'm listening."

"For ten years I've managed a very profitable company. I've amassed a small fortune and intend to make a whole lot more. Captain Barton's ill-fated demise left a vacancy. Are you interested in filling that void?"

Negrete swallowed hard. Ex-gang members and ex-felons didn't receive many breaks in life. He knew that Barton's old job had strings attached, those seen and those unseen. He also knew Goebbel was not a big believer in charity. "What's required?"

"Unconditional devotion to the company. Do as I order. Bend some rules on occasion. Don't disclose any company secrets. Make the enterprise money. Don't pull a Captain Barton on me."

"What's the actual job?"

"Three jobs: "Captain of the *Lucky Lady* after you've completed five months of intensive training and become Coast Guard Certified. My Personal Assistant at the platforms; you will be my eyes and ears monitoring the fish farms. Finally, an Enforcer—if anyone gets in my way, or disregards my requests—then you step in."

Like a fish, Negrete could feel the hook being set. "My pay?"

Goebbel smiled. He set the hook. He pushed the pile of items obtained from Barton's wallet over to Negrete. "One thousand-plus dollars, as your signing bonus. A company Visa credit card. It will be changed into your name. The keys to Barton's brand new Dodge Ram pickup truck, which my company owns. A security card that unlocks the door to a company owned two-bedroom townhouse located at Port Marluna in Oxnard. The Captain has untimely ended his stay. It's yours to enjoy as long as you remain in my employ. A starting salary of sixty-five thousand dollars, medical and dental benefits, and participation in the company's 401k retirement plan."

Stuttering, Negrete said, "I don't want Miguel Chavez on my ship."

"He'll be reassigned. Anything else?"

"No," Negrete said.

"Good—your training begins tomorrow. A temporary captain will be assigned to the *Lucky Lady*. Your first task at sunrise—besides cleaning up the fuel spill—will be an early morning excursion to a six thousand foot abyss known as Santa Cruz Basin. There's a barrel that desires a visit to Davy Jones's locker."

As they walked out of the kitchen and onto the boat deck Negrete noticed that Barton's body was missing.

"Where's Barton?" Negrete asked.

Pretending to play drums on a brand new fifty-five-gallon metal barrel marked Food Supplies Goebbel said, "Human Sardine. Poke a few holes in it and make sure that it sinks fast."

Arriving at the parking lot, Goebbel departed in his limousine. Negrete located Barton's pickup truck. He liked the red color. The sage-colored pure Corinthian-leather seats looked inviting. His days as a transit bus passenger had ended. When he started the turbo-charged 5.7 liter Hemi engine, the digital clock displayed 5:25 p.m. It had been an incredible twelve hours. He was anxious to see what goodies existed in Barton's townhouse. Through the front windshield he observed the *Lucky Lady* gently swaying in her dock slip. Her two-toned coloring, sapphire-blue up to the deck rail, and ivory-white on the upper deck, blazed radiantly in the final prisms of sunlight.

As Negrete turned onto Harbor Boulevard, heading east toward Oxnard, he reflected on the changing tides of fortune. His *luck* had certainly changed, and his devotion to Karl Goebbel was now absolute—he had found his new gang leader.

2

Half a mile from Scorpion Cove, Kurt Nichols turned the ignition switch to the off position, shutting down the flow of diesel fuel into the stern drive Volvo Penta, 260-horsepower turbo engine. The twenty-five foot Davis Rock Harbor fishing and diving vessel, christened *Serenity*, came to a complete stop and then began leisurely drifting in the two-mile per hour ocean current. Giant bladder kelp, yellowish-brown in color, slipped beneath the ship. The early afternoon sun, its seasonal path nearly overhead, was illuminating the ocean aquarium, whose crystal-clear water was alive with immense schools of silvery topsmelt, blue halfmoons, olive opaleye, and bronze-colored calico bass. A gregarious garibaldi, so resolutely orange, glowed like an incandescent bulb in the watery depths.

"It's time Dad," Mischa Nichols said softly. At age sixteen, Mischa was the mirror image of her mother, Tessa. But, unlike her mother who had wavy coral-brown hair, Mischa's hair was an exquisite platinum blond. Her usually alert cobalt-blue eyes were now beacons of love and warmth. At five feet ten inches, she was an inch taller than her mom.

"Here you go Dad," Jake Nichols said, as he somberly handed his dad a polished cherrywood urn, decorated with a pure white dove. Seventeen years of age, Jake was tall and slender, six feet three inches, naturally tanned like his dad, with clear deep-green eyes that sparkled with mirthful intelligence. His light-brown hair was worn in a ruffled surfer *I don't care style* that was rarely graced by a comb. Jake had just concluded his senior year at Malibu High School, his sister Mischa, eleventh grade.

Kurt Nichols hesitated. Moisture glistened off his cheeks, and it was clear that his children were equally distraught. He had rehearsed this precise moment numerous times, especially in his dreams, but the actual reality was worse than imagined. *I will never know the reason why*, he thought. Tessa, his precious wife, had died almost three years ago on what had begun as a lovely Memorial Day weekend. It was Saturday, and Tessa, Jake, and Mischa were at Paradise Cove in Malibu, enjoying a relaxing day at the beach. The weather was perfect—a classic Chamber of Commerce day—sunny and warm, the ocean tranquil.

Kurt had purposely skipped the outing, choosing work over family. A professor of Marine Biology at the University of Malibu, he had set aside the holiday as an opportunity to finalize an internal memorandum that was long overdue. It concerned the dismal failure of an experimental relocation program that involved transplanting one hundred and forty endangered sea otters from Monterey Bay to San Nicolas Island. Unfortunately, nearly all the displaced mammals had either died or swam back to Monterey, with only eighteen choosing to remain. He was in his office drafting the melancholy report, when the telephone call came in. Tessa, while standing on the beach and lifeguarding their two children who were screaming with delight as they rode boogie-boards in one-foot surf, had suddenly collapsed. Emergency crews arrived within minutes; fire department, paramedics, police, and several Los Angeles County lifeguards, but all heroic measures failed that day. Tessa had apparently died within seconds. The autopsy report stated the cause of death as a massive brain aneurysm—the morbid bursting of a major artery in her brain.

The loss to Kurt, Jake, and Mischa, went beyond grief—it was devastating. In the twinkling of an eye a devoted mother, and loving spouse, had simply vanished from their presence. Terminal cancer would have—at a minimum—given them years, or months, of mental and emotional preparation; an exploding aneurysm provided no such opportunity.

Unknown to Kurt, Tessa had recently affixed an addendum to her Living Trust and Pour-Over Will, which specified cremation rather than burial. Furthermore, the document instructed that within six months of her death, half of her ashes were to be scattered at sea, and half on Santa Cruz Island. The legal codicil ended with a brief personal note that tormented Kurt for months following her passing. It was as if she knew that she would die young: *Kurt—I love you more than you can imagine—so I'm releasing you. You are not to be bound to a tombstone or an ash urn. That is not your destiny. When you look upon Jake and Mischa, you will see and remember me. I live within them. Love them unconditionally as I know you will. Dispose of my ashes within six months—and move on—for the benefit of our children. I order you to experience love again. I know you so well, my wonderfully faithful husband, and that is why I changed this document. I will see you face to face soon enough, so cherish our earthly memories, honor my requests, and continue on with your life. Love Tessa.*

To help bury his grief during the first year following her death Kurt became immersed in his work, essentially ignoring his children who were cared for by a full-time nanny. The second year, when parental guilt re-entered the picture, he fired the nanny and poured his life back into his attention-starved children, oftentimes missing work. At the start of the third year he finally learned from his past two years of pendulum-swinging excessiveness, and a life of balance re-established itself between work and family. Throughout those thirty-six months, well-meaning friends often encouraged him to date. But he was not emotionally ready, and his children's psychological welfare was of more importance to him than his own selfish desires.

Kurt hadn't intentionally meant to ignore his wife's request that he dispose of her ashes within six months, but parting with her ashes meant permanently releasing Tessa, and he wanted to hang onto what physically remained for as long as possible. It was only in the last five months that the heartrending burden veiled deep within his soul had begun to lift, allowing him to tentatively move on. "Letting go is never easy," he muttered under his breath, but Mischa, his always perceptive daughter, was right: It was time.

Kurt unscrewed the lid from the wood urn. From the stern of the boat he set free half of the ashes into a delicate breeze. The lighter particles ascended heavenward, but the majority cascaded to the surface of the sea, dissolving into grayish filaments. He watched transfixed until the last remnants of Tessa's ashes disappeared. "Good-bye Tessa," he whispered, "we will always love you—we will never forget you." He screwed the lid back on. The remaining ashes would grace the countryside of Santa Cruz Island, Tessa's ancestral home, and where he was now relocating his family. The boat ride over and the distribution of Tessa's ashes was the ending of one chapter in Kurt's life, and the beginning of a new one, his teenage children rising to the occasion and agreeing to dad's disruption of their mainland lives for an island existence.

Kurt rubbed the sleeve of his shirt against his eyes, cleared his throat, inhaled deeply, wrapped his arms tenderly around his children, and said, "Your mother loved these waters in the same way she cherished Santa Cruz Island. This is where she belongs— it's her final resting place." Pausing to steady his voice, he continued: "But, *knowing* your mother, her heavenly soul is maintaining a vigilant eye on our lives, forever, no matter what we do."

"Do you truly believe that?" Jake asked, wiping a few tears from his eyes.

"Absolutely," Kurt said with a grin.

"So, she's observing us now?" Mischa questioned.

Gently stroking Mischa's hair, Kurt said, "Yes . . . I can feel her spirit in my heart. It was that same presence, speaking to me in a still quiet voice, which prompted my decision to move our family to Santa Cruz Island."

"Mom is behind our relocation?" Jake asked.

"In a way. Like the changing seasons, I felt released to begin a new chapter in our lives, so a year ago, when the University offered me the position of Senior Project Scientist, I knew that I had received my answer."

"Why did you wait a year before accepting the position?" Mischa wondered.

"Your schooling, your friends, my need to be certain that you were both emotionally ready, and my secret surprise, which required time," Kurt said in a conspiratorial tone.

Jake and Mischa simultaneously wiggled out from under their dad's embrace. Stopping four feet away, they both gazed suspiciously. Mischa spoke first: "What's the surprise?"

Smiling smugly, Kurt said, "I made the assumption that dorm life at the Marine Lab was not a win-win situation for our family. The conditions are somewhat cramped, sparse communal bathrooms, small kitchen, and a complete lack of privacy." He paused for effect. "You remember the island winery that was constructed in 1854?"

"The dilapidated winery on the bluff overlooking Scorpion Cove?" Mischa answered.

"That winery," Kurt replied, "it's not so old anymore. I had it renovated. For the last nine months artisans of every craft, using island-burned brick and stockpiled wood from the wreck of the *Winfield Scott*, transformed that dingy winery into a lovely island house, complete with all the modern amenities."

"What kind of modern amenities?" Jake asked.

"Satellite television, high-speed Internet, solar electricity with lithium-ion battery backup, the usual appliances, stocked kitchen, family room with a fireplace and library, multimedia home entertainment room, and your own private bedroom and bathroom. How's that sound?"

"Like heaven," Mischa said, with the first smile she had shown that day.

"Cool," Jake confirmed.

"Unfortunately, the caretaker's adobe house next door is still the same," Kurt complained. Adam Timbrook said 'no' when I suggested a remodeling of his rustic 1830 house—so—we have a tiny eyesore. Apparently he likes it just the way it is."

"It's no big deal," said Mischa, "I've always wanted to meet Adam—he's a fixture on the island."

"He's been the island caretaker for at least sixty years," Kurt said, "hired by your grandfather. Adam's in his early eighties, 100 percent Chumash Indian, and probably the last of his kind. Most Chumash are now mixed."

"Is it true that only Chumash Indians are legally allowed as caretakers and guides on Santa Cruz Island?" Jake asked.

"That's correct. In 1822, when Spanish Missionaries relocated your mother's Chumash ancestors to the Santa Barbara Mission, and the island was leased out to cattle and sheep ranchers, the lease agreements specified that *only* Chumash Indians were authorized as caretakers and guides. That policy has continued to this day."

"Do you know why?" Jake asked.

"To protect the hundreds of ancient Indian sites is my best guess—or life-long employment for the Chumash."

"Call it a young woman's intuition," Mischa countered, "but I suspect there's something else."

"Ask Timbrook—he's a walking encyclopedia on anything having to do with the island, and especially on Chumash history. But, enough talk; if we want to observe the 1:30 p.m. underwater broadcast of *Live from Scorpion Cove*, we'd better crank up the engine and shove off. Dr. Eva Chen moderates the dive today. She's new at the lab, and I'm anxious to meet her."

Kurt Nichols restarted the engine and piloted *Serenity* toward Scorpion Cove as Jake and Mischa, standing ceremoniously at the stern, scattered multi-colored rose petals in the boat's wake, creating a procession of scented floral patterns as a final tribute to their mother. The sudden appearance of two striped dolphins, light gray on top and pinkish underneath, performing acrobatic somersaults alongside the boat, added a magical touch to their mother's eulogy.

As he entered the anchorage, Kurt marveled at the natural ingenuity and artistry of Scorpion Cove. The harbor was not only picturesque, but functional, its u-shape with protruding granite rocks on either side, provided shelter from the harsh elements. Scorpion Cove was designated a State Marine Reserve, which assured that all fish and invertebrate life were—for all time— protected from commercial or recreational fishing. As a consequence, the abundance and quality of sea life exploded; lobsters for example, typically one to two pounds outside the reserve, averaged four to ten pounds within.

Scorpion Cove's pier, constructed out of stainless steel and pinewood, extended out a hundred yards. The *Serenity's* assigned docking niche was at the mid-point. The landing pier was erected upon immense concrete blocks—remnants from a wharf originally built in 1938 for hauling cattle and sheep.

While approaching the dock, preparing to tie up, Kurt chuckled at the oversized sapphire-blue and pearl-white, twelve by six foot aluminum sign which brashly proclaimed: *Private Property— University of Malibu, Marine Biology Laboratory—Santa Cruz Island.* The property was private in salt-spray encrusted words only. No person was ever refused admittance to the lab inasmuch as the public was always welcomed.

Once docked, Jake immediately announced that he was going to explore their new residence, and to verify the download speed on their new satellite Internet connection. Kurt suspected that Jake was primarily interested in the status of his multi-player on-line war game involving nefarious alien races, which never seemed to end.

Meanwhile, in preparation for the underwater spectacle, Kurt and Mischa changed into their swimsuits. Next, they slowly slipped into their seven-millimeter thick neoprene wetsuits and booties—a wrestling contest, as any diver can attest to. Kurt's wetsuit was raven black with blue trim; Mischa's pink and light gray like the dolphins she loved. The wetsuits and booties provided insulation against the sixty-degree water. The *Serenity's* forward cabin came equipped with a petite kitchen, a marine head, and a queen-sized bedroom, which also functioned as their changing room. The *Serenity* also housed their skin and scuba diving equipment, fishing gear, and two eleven-foot, sandstone-colored Ocean Kayaks. Prior to exiting the boat they each strapped on a weight belt and a six-inch titanium dive knife. Kurt packed a mesh dive bag with their neoprene hoods, dive masks, snorkels, and fins.

The production, *Live from Scorpion Cove*, was filmed at the end of the pier, in fifty feet of water. A stainless steel staircase led down to a large teak wood platform, with two aluminum swim steps that permitted easy access in and out of the ocean. The once weekly exploratory program was carried live by the Wilderness Channel and the Internet, and was transmitted via a wireless uplink to a surface transceiver connected to an Apple computer with a 32-inch LED display, which was then uplinked to a satellite. The host diver was outfitted with a Guardian Full Face Mask which was equipped with a state-of-the-art digital through-water microphone system that allowed crystal clear, two-way communication with either the surface, or with a fellow diver. The diver was both camera operator and moderator. The time was 1:20 p.m.

"Ten minutes to show time," Kurt said, as they casually strolled toward the end of the pier, their booties making mild squeaking sounds on the warm wood. The sun, angled slightly west, cast ten-foot shadows, which ceased at the dock's edge. A slight breeze agitated the air. A solitary California sea lion swam haphazardly through the steel pilings.

"Do you see Dr. Chen?" Mischa asked.

"I've never actually met her. I know she's Asian."

"Brilliant dad—did the last name, *Chen*, give you a clue?" Mischa joked.

"No, but the photograph attached to her resumé did—Miss Know-It-All—and I don't think she's all Asian."

"If not all Asian, then what?"

"Eurasian . . . a mix of European and Asian, with an abundance of intelligence blended in."

"What colleges did she attend? Mischa asked.

"Three different universities," Kurt answered. "She obtained her BS Degree from the University of California at Santa Barbara in Organic Chemistry with a minor in Marine Biology. She then attended Stanford University and picked up her Master's Degree in Marine Biology with an emphasis in Environmental Conservation, Marine Animals, and Fisheries Protection. Eva was awarded her Ph.D., in Marine Biology from the University of California San Diego, in affiliation with the Scripps Institution of Oceanography. Her doctoral dissertation involved studying the effects of red tide on marine organisms. After receiving her Ph.D., at age twenty-six, she was hired by the Scripps Institute of Oceanography as an expert in Marine Biodiversity and Conservation. She continued in that position until recently—when lured away by our illustrious marine lab."

"Smart lady," Mischa affirmed.

"That's definitely true; every degree was bestowed with 'Honors' and 'Distinction.'"

As Kurt and Mischa reached the end of the dock they observed two young men gathered around a LED display, engrossed in the on-screen visuals. Kurt interrupted one of the viewers. "Where's Dr. Chen?"

"Underwater," said a curly-haired technician whose eye's remained glued to the screen.

"Daniel Petersen?" Kurt asked.

Turning to see who was interrupting, Petersen said, "Oh—Dr. Nichols—it's so good to see you. Sorry. You know me . . . I get caught up in my work."

"Yes you do," Kurt agreed, "and that's why I hired you." Daniel Petersen was in his second year of his Master's program in Marine Biology, and was proving to be a prodigy in all types of underwater technology. Kurt introduced both men to his daughter Mischa. The second man, Jason Slater, was interning for the summer after having completed his freshman year at the University of Malibu. He held Mischa's hand a little longer than necessary as his eyes roved up then down. Mischa's face flushed red. *Boys will be boys* Kurt mused, suppressing mild irritation.

"It's just the two of you?" Kurt asked.

"That's all it takes," Petersen said, "modern technology eliminates unnecessary bodies. Slater runs the satellite uplink, and I handle the sound and camera feed from Dr. Chen."

"Is Dr. Chen scuba diving alone?" Kurt questioned, staring at the images on the display.

"Yes," Slater reported. "She stated that less bubbles in the water equates to a greater tally of fish. More fish creates a first-class panoramic seascape. She likes her audience to remain riveted in their cushy seats."

"I admire her enthusiasm, but I'm not a big fan on scuba diving alone," Kurt said concerned.

"She's experienced and knowledgeable about her dive gear," Petersen assured him. "I could tell that by the way she meticulously planned her dive."

"And besides, if anything goes wrong, we're all suited and ready to go," Mischa chimed in.

"That's true," Kurt agreed, "but we're only skin diving."

Checking his watch Petersen announced, "One minute to show time."

All four gathered around the LED screen. The image appeared stationary, the camera not yet moving. A ten-foot underwater granite archway filled the screen. The rocky outcropping was painted with red and green marine algae and undulating yellowish-green eelgrass. The rocks were adorned with purple, black, and ruby-red spiny sea urchins, and vibrant red corynactic anemones as well as the more common green variety. In the outlying area soared amber-colored giant kelp fronds, creating a cathedral-like canopy. A school of golden-tinged sardines sailed through the arch, while a three-foot black and red-orange male sheepshead hung greedily in the background.

"This is her opening," Slater explained. "Eva's pre-positioned the camera so that she'll be in the initial scene."

A petite female diver swam into view. She situated her body in the middle of the archway. The effect was dramatic. Kurt observed that she was wearing a peacock-blue wetsuit trimmed with violet that fit her slender figure perfectly. Her Guardian dive mask, lavender in color, highlighted her tanned face and fawn-colored eyes. With the water temperature at sixty-two degrees, a gaudy neoprene hood was almost mandatory. Eva, however, wore none; her long, silky black hair swirled in the caressing ocean current. Kurt had to admit, Eva understood what a camera craved. She was also equipped with a Scubapro sky-blue Bella BC—buoyancy compensator—with Air-2, Guardian first and second stage regulator that was connected to her tank and face mask, Mares Icon HD wrist dive computer, 100 cubic-foot high-pressure steel tank in glossy black, and Scubapro twin jet max open-heel split fins in salmon pink.

"Dr. Chen, ten second warning," Petersen advised.

"Thanks Daniel," Eva replied with a calm and soothing voice.

"Great clarity," Kurt said.

"The best undersea communication equipment on the market," Petersen boasted, "with a range of over four thousand feet in calm seas."

"Impressive technology," Mischa admitted.

Eva smiled expansively, her pearl-white teeth perfectly aligned, and addressed the camera and her audience, "Good afternoon, and welcome to the most awe-inspiring marine environment in the world. My name is Eva Chen. I have a Ph.D. in Marine Biology, and the distinct honor of leading today's ocean tour. We will be travelling through one of the most biologically diverse ecosystems on our blue planet. We are presently in fifty feet of water off the east side of Santa Cruz Island. We are in luck today—the water is amazingly clear—and the fish life is incredible. Are you ready to begin?" She then, unexpectedly, withdrew two dead squid from a pouch on her BC. She placed one on her right shoulder, the other she kept in her left hand.

"What's she doing?" Mischa wondered.

"No idea," Slater answered.

"Fish food," Kurt said.

"Dr. Chen," transmitted Petersen, "what's up?"

Eva did not respond. She briefly glanced over her right shoulder, and then sat very still. From a small cave in the archway, a five foot long green moray eel slowly slithered out, its mouth opening and closing, revealing large fanglike teeth.

"Are you crazy?" Petersen shouted into his microphone.

Eva ignored the panicked comment. "Moray eels have a far worse reputation than they deserve," she began. "They are not vicious, or dangerous, if treated with dignity. If managed properly these wonderful creatures are quite docile and will eat right out of your hand like a little puppy."

"That's no friendly pooch," Petersen said.

"Maybe a pit bull puppy," Slater added.

The serpent-shaped eel, its beady eyes flame-red, silently glided to Eva's right shoulder, its needle sharp teeth plucking the squid and devouring it whole. The eel then slyly snaked its way down her shoulder, Eva's right hand tenderly stroking its cylindrical body while it descended. It then approached her left hand, its canine teeth clearly visible. She opened her hand revealing the second squid. The eel nuzzled the squid and gently removed it, consuming it with one quick shake of its pointed snout. It next drifted back up her upper torso, circled her neck, and then slowly made its way back to its darkened den.

"As you can see," Eva continued in a triumphal voice, "the moray eel is not an evil monster; it's a magnanimous fish simply trying to survive, as all sea-life is. And now—let's continue our *hike* through the rich kelp forests of Santa Cruz Island. Let me retrieve my camera, and together we'll begin our journey of discovery." Eva swam directly toward the camera lens, her face filling the entire screen, a strikingly pretty picture.

"I like that lady," Mischa said enthusiastically, "she has my kind of spunk."

"She forgot to say 'only do this if you are a professional,'" Kurt said with a weak smile.

Eva's camera panned the surrounding area, its high definition images stunning. She narrated as she coasted through the exquisitely rich seascapes.

"The Giant kelp is the fastest growing algae plant in the world—adding up to two feet per day," Eva said, focusing the camera on a dense grove of swaying vegetation. "The kelp beds, in their opulence, have been compared to lush tropical rain forests on land, or the magnificence of our northern redwood forests." Like a glider, Eva gracefully sailed through a thick strand of kelp—warm rays of sunlight filtering through the canopy, mixing light and shadows, creating a mystical affect. Schools of silvery anchovies, blue rockfish, and frosted topsmelt, added to the magical quality. Football-sized calico bass—so named because of the calico white spotting on their back and sides—darted among the baitfish, gulping down any too slow to avoid their predatory jaws.

Eva maneuvered downward, the camera pinpointing a light gray entity with dark gray blotches, hovering in the midst of thick kelp fronds. "Now, this is a special treat," Eva said excitedly, "a Pacific electric ray, at least four feet long. Gorgeous, isn't it! But beware; it can pack a whopping 260-volt charge for any aggressor foolish enough to challenge it. Do you know how the ray kills its prey? It stuns a fish with an electrical discharge before eating it—sort of the microwave of the ocean," Eva said with a small devious laugh. She maintained a safe distance from the ray as she drifted deeper in the direction of a rocky reef that was sculpted with numerous holes, nooks, and crannies.

Eva leveled out her descent at five feet above the reef. In an animated voice she continued: "As I soar with the current, watch carefully to see what the camera picks up. You will be amazed to discover the diversity of life on just one tiny section of an extensive reef system."

Eva's camera lens initially focused on the surface of the rocks capturing dazzling strawberry and glow-white anemones, huge yellow sun stars, blood stars, five-legged canary yellow sea stars, purple hydrocoral, tangerine tinted sponges, red sea fans and thickets of jade-green sea grass weaving in the current as well as colorful small reef fish flitting here and there.

Eva next aimed the camera at individual species—wavy turban snails clamored over a rocky shelf, joined by a small contingent of armor coated rock crabs. A timid octopus, the ocean's master illusionist, altered its colors as it searched for a fissure to hide in. An orange-and-purple Spanish shawl nudibranch—its garish coloring acting as a neon warning sign to potential predators of its foul taste and toxicity—nonchalantly inched its slug-like body along the reef. In the crevices, and attached to rocks, were dozens of savory rock scallops as well as opalescent red abalones. Delectable spiny lobsters, their foot-long antennas oscillating, ventured forth from their craggy lairs, curious as to the noisy intruder.

"And now," Eva announced reverently, "I have the privilege of introducing you to the Miss America of marine fish, the loveliest of all California reef fish—the brilliantly orange garibaldi!" Eva's camera zoomed in on two brightly colored fish swimming with a sculling motion above a rocky outcropping; the cavorting pair occasionally zipping in and out of a small grotto, their sanctuary in a dangerous sea.

Eva continued: "The garibaldi fish is fully protected by law, and is the California State Marine Fish. Adults average fourteen inches in length and are fiercely territorial. If you look closely you'll observe that one of the garibaldis is a juvenile. Juveniles outdo their parents visually, and are absolutely gorgeous. Notice the shimmering orange-red coloring and iridescent blue spots and trim," Eva said breathlessly. Eva's camera followed the juvenile as it chased after the adult. A California sea lion maneuvered into view. Her camera tracked the sea lion as it entered into the picture.

"It appears," Eva said, "that we have a furry visitor—a California sea lion. It's obviously a female because of its modest size, and light tan coat. Males are much larger and have darker coats. She looks to be about one hundred and thirty pounds, a little skinny, since her ribs are showing." The sea lion banked and dipped in the distance, steadily making its way closer to Eva's position.

"Sea lions are playful and intelligent rascals that love to intimidate divers," resumed Eva. "They have been known to swoop down on an unsuspecting diver, and then veer off at the last second—sort of their cat and mouse game. Let's see what our friend has in store for us today."

Eva's camera followed the sea lion, which initially spiraled to the surface, resupplying its lungs with fresh oxygen. It then propelled itself downward at a high rate of speed intercepting the two frolicking garibaldis, blocking their escape route, giving the impression of playing a game of tag. Within a split second, however, the seal mischievously accelerated—performed an inverted barrel roll—and materialized underneath the two startled fishes, biting the head off the adult, and swallowing the juvenile whole. The decapitated adult plunged in a neurotic circle, its lifeblood gradually draining away.

"Oh no . . . " Eva said demurely, "this is not what I was expecting. I'm so sorry you had to witness this, but sea lions do love to eat, and besides squid, fish are their favorite food." Eva continued to watch the lifeless body until it touched bottom, unaware that she was recording the entire sequence.

"Are you okay, Dr. Chen?" Petersen asked.

On a separate communication channel, Dr. Chen answered, "Yes, I'm fine, but a little irritated at a stupid sea lion for destroying two beautiful fish—hold on—" Eva squealed loudly, her camera providing a visual display of what was transpiring.

The sea lion had returned and latched its inch-long canine teeth onto Eva's right fin, its dog-like head gyrating back and forth, thrashing Eva's leg as if it were a garment in a washing machine. In the confusion, Eva had switched back to the public communication channel.

"The sea lion is trying to steal her fin," Mischa gasped.

"Look at its eyes," Kurt said, "they're glazed over."

"That's one abnormally aggressive sea lion," Petersen said nervously.

The first fin was ruthlessly ripped from Eva's foot, and like a crazed animal, the sea lion reappeared, violently tearing the second fin away. Eva struggled to maintain her equilibrium, shrieking and flailing her arms at the beast, begging that it leave her alone. Without her fins, she was akin to an overweight and out-of-water duck, and she dropped like a lead weight to the sea floor, her feet landing on a sandy patch. The sea lion began circling, moving surreptitiously closer with each pass—exhaling bubbles in a frenzied manner—its jaws snapping loudly.

Eva tracked the sea lion with her camera transmitting evolving snapshots of the unfolding drama. When the sea lion had shaved the circle to less than seven feet, it launched a rogue attack, jack-hammering its rigid body directly into Eva's head, neck, and back, sending her tumbling across the sand, the pitching momentum flinging her into a solid granite rock imbued with thousands of mussels. Miraculously, Eva held onto the camera, its lens aimed straight out—broadcasting a sea lion manifesting as if in the throes of an epileptic seizure, thrashing and contorting its body, raging against the sea, uprooting giant kelp with its double-edged teeth, and pouncing upon any fish foolish enough to venture into its demented domain. For a few seconds the foursome on the pier watched in silent horror at the sea lions bizarre behavior. But it only took a few moments before they realized that the camera hadn't moved at all and they called out to Eva. When she failed to respond they feared that she was either seriously hurt or unconscious.

"Dad, do something," Mischa shouted "before that freak of nature kills her."

"She may already be dead," Slater whispered.

"She's not, I know it" Petersen said confidently, "she has a full face mask, so she's still receiving oxygen."

Kurt glared at the location where Eva laid incapacitated fifty feet below. He turned, speaking urgently to his daughter; "Mischa—I'll need my speargun—now! Without a word Mischa removed her cumbersome weight belt and sprinted for the *Serenity* where their spearguns were stored.

Retrieving his dive bag, Kurt removed his neoprene hood, dive mask, snorkel, and fins. He swiftly pulled the hood over his head, and then tucked it into his wetsuit, which he zipped up. To prevent his mask from fogging up, he spat into it and smeared the hot saliva over the interior glass then rinsed it out. Finally, he strapped on his dive fins just as Mischa, out-of-breath, returned with two Riffe Mid-Handle, fifty-inch spearguns.

Kurt scowled. "You brought your own speargun?"

"I thought you're not supposed to dive alone," Mischa reminded him.

"You're *not* going into that ocean with that insane sea lion—end of discussion—do you understand that?" he said with great finality.

"No—but I understand what you're saying."

"Good," Kurt said as he jumped off the platform and into the water, where he immediately loaded his speargun. The Hawaiian model teakwood speargun came equipped with three 9/16 x 24 inch rubber power bands, a 5/16 x 55 inch spearshaft tipped with a razor sharp two-barbed detachable spearhead, and a vertical reel filled with two-hundred feet of six-hundred pound Spectra line. The powerful speargun had seen action against halibut, yellowtail, and white seabass, with the largest fish speared weighing sixty-five pounds. Spearing a sea lion was not something that Kurt wanted to think about. He was trusting that his imposing physical presence, along with a menacing-looking device, would frighten the sea lion and keep it away. At six feet two inches, and one hundred and eighty-five pounds, he would appear more formidable than Eva, or so he hoped.

Swimming stealthily, he approached Eva's position. Through the clear water he observed her laying obliquely, her back against a rock, a steady stream of air bubbles escaping from her regulator. Fortunately, the regulator was still coupled to her full face mask. *She's alive* he realized with a sigh of relief. Her camera was now pointing straight up. Thankfully, the sea lion had mysteriously disappeared. At a depth of fifty feet, he could hold his breath for about one minute. Drawing in several deep breaths, he dove. On the way down, he pinched his nose several times to equalize the ambient pressure change. He covered the distance in less than ten seconds.

As soon as he arrived at Eva's side he set his speargun aside and immediately inspected the dive computer located on Eva's right wrist to ascertain the status of her air supply. A 100 cubic foot high-pressure steel tank, when filled to capacity, holds 3400 pounds of air per square inch. Eva's computer registered 650 psi, an air supply of approximately eight minutes, which meant that he would have to act swiftly. His next priority was performing a cursory assessment of Eva's overall condition. Fortunately, she had no broken bones, bleeding, or any discernable injuries. There were a few nicks in her wetsuit, a missing bootie, and a mid-sized welt on the back of her head—the probable cause of her concussion. Peeking at Eva's countenance he was surprised at how serene she appeared. He was also a little nonplused by an emotional stirring that he had not experienced in years. His lungs finally screaming for air, he shot like a missile toward the surface. On the way up, he solidified his rescue plan.

Attached to Eva's BC was an Air-2—an emergency regulator that provided an alternative air source, which was linked to Eva's own air supply. By buddy breathing, and securing Eva in his protective arms, they could ascend as one. The primary difficulty involved their rate of ascent. To avoid Eva sustaining an air embolism, the rupturing of blood vessels in her lungs, he had to carefully time their ascent. The major drawback to his scheme was her limited supply of air—buddy breathing would reduce that amount by half—the eight minutes had just become four.

Holding his breath again, he quickly plummeted the fifty feet, coming alongside of Eva. A hasty three-hundred and sixty-degree revolution revealed no sign of the sea lion. Approaching the wounded diver, he cautiously lifted her body off the ocean floor, rotating her so that she was facing him, and inserted the spare Air-2 regulator into his mouth. The intoxicating flow of oxygen was invigorating. Next, he briefly depressed a small red button located on Eva's power inflator, which added a tiny amount of air into her BC. The nominal amount of air lifted them off the sandy bottom. With his two arms securely holding Eva, he was unable to retrieve his speargun or Eva's camera.

His intent was a controlled ascent of fifteen feet per minute, which required close monitoring of Eva's wrist computer. If their speed increased too fast, he would vent air from her BC. If too slow, he would add a puff of additional oxygen. After two minutes they were twenty feet from the surface. He could almost taste the refreshing air, a mere seventy-five seconds away. The air in Eva's tank was down to 235 psi. They would make it—narrowly. And then they were attacked. The ambush was masterfully executed.

The placid ocean erupted as the sea lion, with torpedo-like accuracy, swooped down at their location from an elevated position. It then executed a ninety-degree power dive turn—scarcely inches from their upper torsos—creating a backwash of surge that catapulted them end over end. In the millisecond prior to the billowing impact, Kurt was able to delve into the creature's eyes, which were vacant and devoid of any life force.

During the seething confusion, Eva was torn from his embrace. As a consequence, the Air-2 regulator was abruptly torn from his lips. Air turned into salt water as his autonomic reflex for oxygen kicked in, his muddled consciousness failing to distinguish liquid from air. Coughing underwater, regurgitating sea water mixed with vomit, and expelling what little air he had left, he knew that drowning was but a breath away. *Eva—where was Eva?* Logically, he scanned the depths. *No Eva.* Panicking, he searched left, then right, pirouetting like a dancer. *No Eva.* His time was up. He could literally sense his brain shutting down. *He had to get to the surface*—his subconscious drive for self-preservation took over—submerging all other emotions. He kicked vigorously with his fins, driving his frame forcefully upwards, his head unexpectedly slamming into Eva's feet. She had been floating above him the entire time. Crawling up the front side of her body he desperately lunged for the Air-2, thrusting it into his maw, gorging on the cool, revitalizing air.

Relieved he was no longer drowning; his attention again was turned to saving Eva. He glanced at the computer. The tank was down to 125 psi; their depth, ten feet. He gazed skyward. The sun beckoned, the ripples on the surface visible, a brown pelican languished above their heads, its webbed feet delicately stroking the water, propelling it forward. A few minor dolphin strokes with his fins and their daytime nightmare would be ancient history. His brain told his legs to end this ordeal, but they did not respond as expected. They were frozen as if cemented in concrete.

Looking down to ascertain the problem, his line of sight was interrupted by the malevolent eyes of the sea lion, its tenacious jaws fastened onto his fins. Incubus was back. Frantically, he pulled on one leg and then the other, attempting to forcibly extract his fins, but the effort proved futile. The death grip was unshakeable. He stole a brief glimpse at the computer: Psi 103. It was then that he felt it; movement, not upward, but downward. The sea lion was dragging them into deeper water—the tug slow, steady, calculated—the realization terrifying.

Weights, *I must get rid of our weights*, he thought. He unbuckled his weight belt, dumping eighteen pounds. He unsnapped Eva's BC integrated weight system, scrapping another twelve pounds. He added air to Eva's BC, increasing their buoyancy. His superficial efforts accomplishing measured success; they were no longer descending, but they also weren't rising. The computer informed him that they were stationary at eleven feet, psi 72, 71, 70. It was dropping fast.

He stared hatefully at the invidious sea lion, the corners of its muzzle turned up, smiling, if that was possible. He thought about his children—their dreams and aspirations. He thought about Eva, and what a disappointing hero he had turned out to be. Sacrifice—before the air supply was totally depleted—he would release his grip on Eva, sending her to the surface. Alone, he would face the sea lion. Withdrawing his titanium knife he prepared for the deadly encounter. The eyes—he would first go for the eyes.

He turned cursing the sea lion, ready for his revenge, when the jaws suddenly sprang open, disgorging his fins. Without weights, and with an overly inflated BC, he and Eva rocketed toward the surface. As they soared upwards, he noticed a large bronze spear-shaft jutting out from the mid-portion of the sea lion's oval head. It had been a perfectly aimed shot that had incapacitated the creature instantly. Bursting forth from their watery domain and into the bright sunlight, his last visual image was of an elegant skin diver in a pretty pink wetsuit, ascending at a controlled rate, with a discharged speargun in her hands.

3

Kurt let out a breath of relief when Eva's flickering eyelids indicated that she was waking up from her trauma-induced stupor. Though it seemed like hours, a mere ten minutes had elapsed since their tumultuous ordeal had ended.

When Eva and Kurt shot to the surface the shared scuba tank was down to its last whiff of oxygen, and the new asphyxiation emergency demanded immediate action. Within seconds Kurt was able to uncouple Eva's potentially suffocating full-face mask, and although she was still unconscious, he was encouraged when he heard a rasping sound escaping from her mouth, confirming that she was breathing on her own. With his heroic daughter Mischa on Eva's left side, and Kurt on her right, and her inflated BC functioning as a life preserver, they had cautiously escorted her senseless body back to the teakwood platform located at the end of the pier, where Petersen and Slater helped to gently lift Eva out of the water. Her bulky and constricting diving equipment was then carefully removed.

Eva was now lying peacefully on a canvas stretcher, cocooned in a soft woolen blanket. Kym Snyder, a thirty-year veteran of the UCLA Hospital Trauma Center, and the marine lab's resident nurse, chuckled after competing her in-field assessment.

"Other than a mild concussion and a few contusions," Kym disclosed, "she's one lucky lady. She'll wake up with one hell of a headache, slightly nauseated, and in need of some extra sleep, but she'll be okay. Once we're at the the clinic, however, I'll have her undergo a few precautionary x-rays to rule out any skull fractures, but my cursory examination indicates no such injury." Kym, after thirty years of treating horrendously injured patients at UCLA, was not one prone to exaggeration, nor excessive sympathy.

As Eva's eyes fully opened, a melancholy cry of despair involuntarily burst forth from her lips, and her arms lashed out as if assailing or blocking an imaginary enemy. After a few seconds of erratic movements, Eva calmed down, the tormenting nightmare apparently over.

Inclining protectively, Kurt spontaneously reached out, his fingers tenderly touching her cheeks, his countenance edged with compassion. "It's okay . . . you're safe now . . . nothing is going to hurt you," he said soothingly.

Responding, Eva blinked her eyes several times, moved her lips as if to speak, swallowed, focused intensely on Kurt's eyes for what seemed like a minute, and then, to everyone's surprise, smiled.

"Emerald-green, or early spring-green?" she asked.

"What?"

"Your eyes—they're amazingly captivating—especially up close."

Blushing vibrant red, Kurt promptly stepped back, enduring an ensemble of tension-releasing laughter. "For your information, 'Romeo and Juliet' royal green," he said, in a mock attempt at restoring his dignity.

"I know that I know you," Eva said, as she continued staring at Kurt, "but there's a gong clanging inside my brain, so I'm somewhat befuddled at the moment. What's your name?"

"Kurt Nichols or Dr. Nichols for college students like Petersen and Slater; and this is my daughter Mischa, who is the actual hero of the day."

"How embarrassing," Eva said, "you hired me, but we've never actually met, so I'm hopefully forgiven. And your daughter—she's my champion? I need to hear her story."

Mischa gently held Eva's hand. "Truthfully, my dad was also pretty amazing; he just needed a little extra help toward the end. And the feeding stunt with that moray eel snacking right out of your hand—I loved it. The next time you go scuba diving—you and I are doing that daredevil act together."

"It's a date," Eva replied.

Interrupting, Kym said, "Sorry, but all these niceties have to wait until after x-rays, so say your farewells, and save your stories for later." Asserting her medical authority, nurse Kym commandeered an electric golf cart that was parked on the pier, and had Eva's stretcher loaded onto it.

Before it departed, Kurt impulsively asked Eva. "How about dinner tonight at 7:00, at our winery house," and then thoughtfully added, "if you're up for it."

"That sounds wonderful," Eva answered, "assuming nurse Kym gives me the green light."

Nurse Kym's plummeting facial scowl instantly conveyed her professional opinion of the idea, but softening said, "We'll see."

"Thank you," Kurt said, making the assumption that the answer was yes. "Our Chumash Indian caretaker, Adam Timbrook, will be preparing a traditional Chumash dinner in honor of our homecoming. So, at the very least, it will be an epicurean night to remember."

"Sounds nice—see you at 7:00 p.m.," Eva said, as her golf cart began advancing down the pier.

Turning back to Mischa, Kurt said, "We need to go for another swim. We left behind some expensive dive gear and a dead sea lion."

While Petersen and Slater packed up the production equipment, Kurt and Mischa re-entered the water. Swimming leisurely on the surface they arrived at the exact spot where their lethal encounter with the sea lion occurred. Kurt intuitively perceived an anomalous condition at the dive site; the normally prolific seas now empty of any marine life. He removed his snorkel so that he could talk. Mischa did likewise.

Straddling water, Kurt said, "You notice anything strange?"

"No sharks." Mischa replied.

"Not just sharks. Take a closer look."

Mischa replaced her snorkel and re-examined the ocean floor, the kelp canopy, algae coated rocks, caves, sea grass beds, and the dead seal lying on the bottom. She spun around slowly taking in the entire panoramic scene. She spit out her snorkel.

"Nothing," she said, "no fish, no sign of life, no anything."

"Bingo—a complete absence of any marine life in the area surrounding the seal's body."

"Why?" Mischa asked.

"The smell of death."

"But death is an integral part of the ocean environment. Fish eat fish. Sharks eat seals. Almost every creature in the sea nibbles on something dead. I don't get it," Mischa said perplexed.

"My hunch involves your spear shaft which apparently dislodged an odious chemical embedded deep within its mangled brain that disseminated a different *type* of death. Sea life can smell it."

"I think I know about that aroma," Mischa said excitedly, "it's the same death scent that scientists have documented involving great white sharks off of the Farrallon Islands—"

"Precisely," said Kurt butting in, "when a killer whale slaughters a great white shark the odor of its death permeates the water, resulting in white sharks vanishing from the killing zone—the ghost-like disappearance lasting up to twelve months."

"But—I've never heard of it happening because of a deceased seal," Mischa said.

"Therein lies the mystery," confirmed Kurt. "Since this sea lion was obviously peculiar, a necropsy may help solve the riddle."

"What do you want me to do?" Mischa asked as she reinserted her snorkel.

"I'll pick up and unload my speargun, retrieve Eva's swim fins, and rescue the camera. You make sure your spear tip is secure, and then unwind Spectra line from your speargun reel as we swim back to the platform. Once on the platform we'll simply reel the sea lion in. I'm sure Eva and her team will want to dissect it as soon as possible."

After hyperventilating to fill their lungs to capacity, Kurt and Mischa dove straight down, stopping only briefly to clear their ears. Kurt first recovered his speargun and immediately unhooked the three elastic rubber bands attached to metal notches on the bronze spearshaft, disarming the underwater weapon. He next recovered Eva's swim fins and finally the HD camera. At the same time Mischa was verifying that the detachable spearhead was buried deep within the skull of the sea lion. Towing a hefty sea lion through salt water required a firmly fixed spearhead. Satisfied, she began to unravel line from the reel as she ascended to the surface. Together they swam back to the platform. Once on the wooden platform—like fisherman catching a fish—they reeled the sea lion in. As they were about to hoist the dead mammal up onto the pier, Jake showed up.

"My wonderful brother," Mischa said derisively but with a smile, "it's so good to see you, and just in time to lend a helping hand."

"Skip the flattery," Jake said, "do you guys know that you are celebrities?"

"What are you talking about?" questioned Kurt.

"YouTube. There I am, immersed in my riveting on-line alien war game, when I receive a text from a friend regarding a radical sea lion attack that was streaming live. A viewer had the foresight to record it; then immediately uploaded it to YouTube. I placed my game on hold to check it out and just about died—it was my own flesh and blood. Of course, I see that it all turns out favorably so naturally I finished out my game before rushing down here to congratulate you on your new superstar status."

"But what does YouTube have to do with what your friend saw streaming live?" Kurt inquired.

"Dad, sometimes I think you're a dinosaur. Your misadventure with the seal was instantly uploaded to YouTube. As of eight minutes ago over twenty thousand people have viewed the clip. I bet by tomorrow morning there will be over a million hits. They're already a half-dozen e-mails from boys wanting to date Mischa. I guess spearing a sea lion is a sexy thing."

Tossing her hair around like a movie star Mischa asked. "Are any of them cute?"

"Don't forget the letters that will most certainly arrive from PETA supporters," groaned Kurt. "Anyway, we're on an island, so the press will hopefully leave us alone. In a few days our fame will be replaced with the next Internet sensation. And as far as *cute* goes, Mischa, I don't allow dating by computer. I may be a young thirty-nine-year-old dad, but I'm old fashioned when it comes to Internet dating."

"Old fashioned is being kind," Mischa whined.

Changing the subject, Kurt said. "Glad you're here Jake—we'll need your muscle to wrench this deplorable creature out of the ocean and into this cart we found. Once you've completed that task please transport it to the pathology lab, but make sure they refrigerate it—we need to preserve her remains until the necropsy takes place."

"And, we don't want a stinky sea lion on our hands," Mischa added.

"Conan the Barbarian at your service," Jake said gallantly.

Jake resourcefully tied a nylon cord around the sea lion's hind flippers and then utilizing his six-foot three inch frame, broad shoulders, and youthful exuberance, simply dragged the approximately one hundred and thirty pound sea lion out of the water and into the cart.

"What about the spearshaft?" Jake asked. The bronze spearshaft with its detachable spearhead was still imbedded in the sea lion's skull.

"Yank it out," Mischa suggested.

"Okay," Jake said. Using both hands, Jake rotated the spearshaft back and forth, expanding the entrance wound. When the hole appeared wide enough, he tried pulling it straight out, with no success. Not willing to cater to defeat, Jake renewed his efforts. He first planted his feet firmly on the solid pier. Next, he counted out loud—"One, two," and at "three," he jerked the spearshaft with one massive tug, the instrument of death exploding from its bony prison, a popping sound accompanying its exit, the double-edge spearhead saturated with stringy pieces of bloody-white tissue. Grinning victoriously, Jake then dipped the spearhead into the water, removing the grisly remnants. He next bowed like a Knight of the Roundtable as he proudly handed the spearshaft back to Mischa.

"Thanks Jake," Mischa said as she patted him on the shoulder. "You're the greatest, see you in a bit."

"Remember—dinner at 7:00—and we have a female guest," reminded Kurt, as Jake embarked on his short journey of conveyance to the pathology lab.

Kurt and Mischa next rinsed off their dive gear with fresh water in order to remove caustic salt residue, then draped it over a wooden railing to dry in the wind and sun. Finished, they casually wandered down the wooden pier in the direction of the marine biology facilities.

"Are you thrilled with your appointment as Senior Project Scientist?" Mischa asked.

"Thrilled—more like electrified," laughed Kurt, "it's a culmination of a life-long dream."

"Did Mom's donation help?"

"I would like to think not—that my selection was based upon merit. Her contribution of nine million dollars from her Santa Cruz Island Trust Fund was granted with specific instructions that it remain anonymous. Certainly the deeding of fifteen acres for the lab site is common knowledge, but that's about it. As far as the public knows—and for that matter marine lab employees—the various buildings were constructed with University of Malibu endowment funds, and matching corporate grants. No building is named after our family, not even a toilet. Because of my affiliation with the University, and its marine biology program, your mom wanted to avoid even the appearance of favoritism. People will talk of course, especially after I renovated the old winery, but that's to be expected. If you walk in true personal integrity, even the critics will eventually be silenced."

"That sounds like a rehearsed speech," Mischa chided.

"I guess I've thought about it for a long time. But you're right; it does ring of a prepared monologue."

Walking toward the lab structures, Mischa said, "I like the fact that the buildings are nestled into the island itself, blending in with the natural landscape."

"That was architecturally mandated when the property was deeded over. A majority of the exterior walls are fabricated with native stone, and any external paint tones are in harmony with the pigmentation of the coastal bluffs."

"What's in all the buildings?" questioned Mischa.

"You want the tourist version?" Kurt asked.

"Yes," Mischa said, "since you're so good at giving lengthy speeches."

"Thanks for the back-handed compliment," Kurt laughed. "I will try and keep it succinct."

"The University of Malibu Marine Biology Laboratory consists of six main buildings and one suite-style housing unit that is home to fifteen residents," Kurt said, pointing to each selected building. "Four of the buildings are equipped with running seawater facilities. The structures provide offices, laboratories, specialized equipment, computers, and various sized aquariums—for the study and research on the biology, biochemistry, physiology, molecular biology, genetics, and ecology of marine animals, marine invertebrates, fish, plants, algae, and microorganisms. One building contains four large saltwater tanks designed for captive breeding and reintroduction into the local environment of blue and yellowfin tunas, white seabass, yellowtail, and the severely endangered red and green abalone. The building you see over there," he said, pointing to a quaint building with an imposing ocean view, "is our research library containing a vast collection of marine science materials in oceanography, marine biology, fisheries, zoology, and marine ecosystems. Electricity is provided via solar panels and lithium-ion batteries, with a diesel generator backup for cloudy or rainy days. For heating and cooking we use natural gas, which is also plumbed into every lab. Fresh water is supplied by means of a twenty-thousand gallon per day desalination plant; and, to top it all off, we have our own miniaturized, state-of-the art, tertiary sewage treatment plant that produces potable water. It's watering our vegetation even as I speak."

Avoiding the fine-mist spray emitting from the garden sprinklers located next to their crushed granite walkway, and stifling a pretend yawn, Mischa asked, "Need a breath, Dad?"

"No."

"Okay—next topic Mr. Chitchat: What's the *Purpose Statement* of the lab?"

"Good question," Kurt replied. "Basically our laboratory's primary purpose is to study how biodiversity affects marine ecosystems including the restoration of marine habitats, fisheries, and the elimination of environmental toxins in the ecosystems. In fact, one of Dr. Chen's areas of expertise is the study of neurotoxins in marine animals and oceanic systems. Analysis of that deranged sea lion will no doubt be her first priority."

"And what is your first priority, Dad?"

"Ensuring the tranquility of my two exceptional children."

Smirking, Mischa asked again, "And your *honest* second priority?"

"Overseeing all marine lab research projects."

In a matriarchal tone of voice Mischa said, "I will hold you personally accountable for priority number one, and occasionally allow you to dabble in priority number two."

"Will you also be in charge of signing my paycheck?" laughed Kurt.

"Of course not, but I will race you up the knoll to our house since my body is craving a well-deserved shower."

As she sprinted away like a spry gazelle, Kurt knew that he had already lost the race, so he simply enjoyed watching his spirited young daughter bound up the ridge. So much boldness and confidence in a mere sixteen-year-old never ceased to amaze him, but he also knew that she dearly missed her mother, and their seemingly endless motherly daughter chats—a discourse that, as a father, he was incapable of duplicating.

Mischa's senior year at Malibu High School would commence in early September, as would Jake's freshman year of college at the University of Malibu. Jake, seventeen years of age, was a wonderfully protective brother of his junior sister that only deepened after Tessa's passing. The death of their mother had instilled in his two children just how precious life and family were, and forever solidified their love for one another.

Kurt smiled as he thought about their upcoming summer on Santa Cruz Island. Memories—that's what he was creating, which was something he was profoundly looking forward to.

4

The house, or as Kurt preferred to call it, the winery, was situated on top of a promontory, in a grassy field, that had a stunning view of the ocean. The perspective from the family room's large custom-made plate-glass window included Cavern Point, Scorpion Cove, the western end of Anacapa Island, and the Marine Lab. The caretaker's archaic adobe house was set further back in the field, and was adjacent to a small horse stable. A crushed granite walkway wound its way from the pier to the house, and was wide enough to accommodate a four-wheeled vehicle. All the single lane roads and trails on the island were constructed with earth-toned crushed granite, which was aesthetically more pleasing than cement or asphalt.

Mounting the final steps to his front porch, Kurt was proud of the hard work involved in converting the old winery into a beautiful and loving home while preserving the rich history of the landmark structure. The wreck of the steamer, *S.S. Winfield Scott*, was the source of the timber utilized in the initial construction of the winery. Additional lumber essential for the remodel was secured from a dilapidated brick warehouse, where the bulk of the *Scott's* one hundred and sixty-year-old purloined hardwoods were stored. The fine-grained durable hardwood planks—Live Oak, Locust Cedar, Georgia Pine, and White Oak—had easily withstood the test of time, requiring minimal sanding and polishing before being fully restored to their original unblemished condition.

The *Scott's* Live Oak, yellowish-brown in color, heavy, and very dense, was used for the structural beams. Locust Cedar, carved from the heartwood portion of the tree, russet brown with prominent straight grain, was availed as structural posts throughout the house. Georgia Antique Heart Pine, burnished red and knotty, refined in its beauty, was utilized for the stairs, crown molding, door casings, window casings, and paneling in the family room, library, and multimedia room. White Oak, the sapwood nearly white, exquisitely warm and inviting, was employed as flooring in the bedrooms. The rest of the flooring throughout the house consisted of multi-sized, tumbled, ivory travertine tiles, with historical Catalina Island decorative paver tiles' enhancing all passageways and step-offs. Embedded in the wall above the family room fireplace was a colorful panel depicting toucan birds designed by Catalina Tile, with other multicolored tropical birds and resplendent reef fish deco tiles gracing the kitchen and bathrooms.

The façade of the winery was constructed from quarried Santa Cruz Island stones that were then sandblasted to highlight their diverse hues. Blue flagstone rock was utilized on the ramps, terraces, and viewing deck, and came from the north side of the island.

The landscape consisted of Santa Cruz Island endemic plants and trees and included the Santa Cruz Island ironwood, coastal sagebrush, yarrow bush in both the pink and white variety, giant coreopsis with dazzling yellow daisy-like flowers, northern island morning glory with its livid pink, white and cadmium yellow creeping blossoms, and the Santa Cruz Island silver lotus. Two oak trees provided shade at the rear of the house. The only nonnative plant was the climbing wisteria vine with pendent flower clusters in opalescent purple that draped the Locust Cedar trellis which circumvented the redwood viewing deck located outside

DALE KORNREICH

the family room. Kurt considered the wisteria flower one of
God's paradisaical gifts to mankind and imagined that heaven
had to be adorned with such elegant vines.

The entryway embodied a work of art—two eight by three foot
beautifully restored French copper-clad doors salvaged from the
wreck of the *S.S. Winfield Scott*. The ancient copper had acquired
its characteristic greenish-blue patina from oxidization. Kurt
marveled at the antique doorways which once beckoned passengers into the *Scott's* elaborate dining saloon.

Stepping into his house, Kurt could hear the sound of running water, which meant that Mischa was luxuriating in her well-
deserved shower. While waiting his turn, he flicked open his
cell phone to check the time—5:00 p.m. Two more hours until
dinner, he frowned as his stomach growled, protesting for an
earlier start time. A small snack would have to suffice. Strolling
into the kitchen he chose a Mackintosh apple, its fruity flesh
crisp and succulent. After a few delicious bites he hummed
a satisfied tune. Gazing out the kitchen window he observed
Adam Timbrook, their Chumash Indian caretaker, hunched
over a roasting pit, white smoke suffused with savory aromas
wafting out. Dinner, cooked underground Chumash style, excited Kurt's gastronomical juices. Knowing Timbrook, it would
be a meal to remember.

Silence—Mischa had finished her shower. He tossed the
core of the apple into a stainless steel trashcan wedged underneath the sink. Looking at his image in the reflective glass of
the KitchenAid microwave he introspectively realized that he was
oddly nervous about the evening. *Was Eva a date, or what?* His
impetuous invite undoubtedly created the impression of a date.
What to wear? Mischa would know. Daughters instinctively understood those sorts of things. Suddenly, it looked like the two hours
of lag time was not enough. He was a teenager all over again with
pathetic prom night jitters. A nice, comforting, drawn-out very

96

hot shower would pacify his butterflies—or maybe even a bath. Either way, he swiftly bolted from the kitchen and down a narrow hallway, anxious to reach the pseudo-sanctuary of his master bedroom. He had an evening to prepare for.

5

The last of the fifty-five gallon metal barrels, their removable lids secured with locking rings, was finally loaded on the rear deck of the *Lucky Lady*. Each of the sixteen barrels was dark-blue in color and designed for storing and transporting hazardous waste, although these particular barrels had been re-labeled as Food Supplies or Diesel Fuel. It was 4:30 a.m. and the heavy mist, which still hung above the water, had transformed the adjoining ships into indistinct and vague shapes.

"Fog—God how I love it," Karl Goebbel said to Captain Negrete. The owner of *West Coast Seafood & Aquaculture*, had unexpectedly arrived at the shipping dock, just as Negrete was about to cast off.

"You're up early," said Negrete.

Stepping onto the *Lucky Lady*, Goebbel said, "Nothing better than a nippy curtain of misty vapors to wake a man up. This your third trip with the barrels?"

Negrete was sure that Goebbel already knew the answer, but he responded anyway. "Yes."

"Any problems so far?"

"No," Negrete replied truthfully.

"Good! And always under cover of fog?"

"There's no delivery without the soupy mess," Negrete assured him, "although navigating through that white shit is a pain in the ass."

Laughing, Goebbel smacked Negrete on his right shoulder. Negrete twisted slightly from the not so subtle impact, and with difficulty restrained himself from responding in kind.

"You're a good man," Goebbel said. "I knew I could count on you, and congratulations on obtaining your Captain's license."

"Thanks," Negrete said, rubbing his shoulder.

Goebbel next snapped open a lavish, anaconda-skin briefcase, and extracted a bulging envelope. "Your bonus for the barrels," he said. "As I informed you at our first meeting, if you take care of me, I'll take care of you. In the future, one of my men will periodically deliver these payments. It's your decision as to how you distribute the cash among your shipmates."

Negrete watched as Goebbel stepped off the ship, disappearing into the nebulous haze. He ripped open the envelope. It was filled with fifty, crisp and shiny, one hundred dollar bills. Five thousand dollars for dumping a few barrels oozing with hazardous waste—it was a supplemental stipend that he could easily become accustomed to. His two crewmembers would each receive one of the bills.

Negrete recruited his new deckhands from his prior connections with the 4th Street Mexican Gang. Both of these individuals had committed enough crimes that if apprehended, they'd spend the rest of their lives in prison. Their malfeasance included drive-by shootings, assaults, drug trafficking, extortion of local businesses, carjacking, home-invasion robberies, human smuggling, prostitution, robbery, and vandalism.

The attribute Negrete most appreciated about his new deckhands was that 4th Streeters abided by a strict set of rules. Any violation of the code of conduct, would subject the member to severe discipline. The most egregious breach was the failure to obey the command of a gang leader, or failure to show proper respect, which would result in a brutal beating. Negrete, as an ex-gang leader, incorporated and applied these same rules to his ship. As Captain his word was law and any infraction would be met with a raging rebuke, or worse. His first enlistee was a gang member nicknamed Pancho, after the Mexican revolutionary, Pancho Villa.

In his mid twenties, Jose Pancho Diaz was five feet eight, two hundred and twenty pounds, and a build like a dump truck. His deep-set brown eyes, scarred reddish-brown skin, shaved head, and seemingly endless tattoos, helped further the impression that he could and would flatten anything, or anybody, in his path. The tattoo on his back depicted a savage pit bull eviscerating a rival gang member. Serpents slithered down his arms, and tarantulas and black widows crawled up his legs. His chest was inscribed with a seven-inch number 4, in Gothic-style lettering, in reference to his 4th Street gang affiliation. His shaved head was engraved with the image of a heinous and ghastly Grim Reaper wielding a scythe.

The second deckhand, Raul 'Shade' Alvarado, was a wraithlike opposite to Pancho. Whereas Pancho was solid, Shade was emaciated with cadaverous pale grayish-colored eyes. Twenty-seven years old, Shade was six feet one, a hundred and fifty pounds, with tar-colored greasy hair, narrowed nose, sunken face, and cocaine blemished teeth. He was as devious and shrewd as Pancho was physical. From the corners of his ears dangled two silver Christian crosses, intentionally worn upside down, in disrespect to his mother's devotion to the Catholic Church. As a seven-year-old altar boy he had experienced first-hand the conniving charm of a pedophile priest—and then the awful stigma of being called a liar by both his mother and the church—which then required personal confession of his slanderous sin before the exact same priest that had violated him.

After casting off the mooring ropes, Captain Negrete guided the *Lucky Lady* through the gentle swells marking the harbor entrance and out into the open ocean, his ship ghost-like in the misty whiteout. His intended destination was Santa Cruz Basin, an ocean canyon over six-thousand feet deep, located off the southeast corner of Santa Cruz Island. The early morning marine weather advisory stated that the three-thousand foot layer of fog would not burn off until noon. He had plenty of time. Cruising at twelve knots, he would arrive at his private underwater rubbish site within two hours.

Negrete was aware that the barrels contained biological and nonbiological waste obtained from two corporate entities: A financially strapped biotech research company headquartered in Ventura County, its waste crammed into barrels labeled Food Supplies, and a less than scrupulous local hospital, its discards in the containers stamped Diesel Fuel. Huge cost-savings cinched the deals with these companies as proper disposal of hazardous waste was prohibitively expensive. A shell company owned by Karl Goebbel offered a budgetary option. At a fifty-percent reduction in cost, his disposal company, *Eco Friendly, Inc.*, would handle all their waste issues. Neither company balked, nor asked any questions.

Goebbel warned Negrete, that if he valued his health, he would avoid any actual contact with the hazardous waste. Although curious as to what he was dumping, he had yet to open a barrel and investigate. The normal procedure involved twisting off two small silicone plugs affixed to the removable lids, which then allowed sea water to pour into the barrels, causing them to sink. Today would be different. He would unlatch the bolted rings and unseal several barrels. The potential environmental damage from the toxic mass spilling out into the ocean did not concern him. What he cared about was knowledge, information, and hard facts, which one day might prove even more beneficial than his current pay-out. In this business covering your ass was important.

The twenty-five mile journey to the Santa Cruz Basin was completed in less than two hours. The depth meter, backlit in sky-blue, displayed the seafloor at five thousand two hundred and forty-eight feet. Not quite six thousand, but deep enough. Negrete killed the Caterpillar engines letting the boat drift in the slow-moving current, the ocean serene, scarcely a ripple upon its surface. The rising sun barely penetrated the gray fog, and the early morning light refracted in strange ways, casting ghoulish shadows. Santa Cruz Island, three miles off the port side, remained hidden behind a vaporous mist. A crashing sound broke the silence off the starboard side, followed by a subdued hush. Then a thunderous splash rocked the boat, followed by an eerie swooshing sound, as if a large object was sliding beneath the sea. *Probably a humpback whale,* thought Negrete.

Speaking to his crew by their gang names, he announced, "Pancho, Shade, today we're going to examined the barrels contents before sinking them."

"All of them?" Pancho asked quickly.

"A few, we'll see. Bring one barrel at a time onto the swim-platform, and then unlatch and remove the lid. As you dump out the items, I'll take photos. Wear the nitrile-coated Kevlar gloves. They're cut-resistant. We'll start with the barrels labeled Diesel Fuel, which contain medical waste."

Pancho and Shade maneuvered the first 200-pound barrel onto the reinforced fiberglass swim-platform. Because the *Lucky Lady* was a commercial boat, the platform was substantial—measuring eighteen by six feet—and could support over twenty-five hundred pounds. Using a pipe wrench, Slade unfastened the one inch galvanized nut that held the locking ring. A hissing noise escaped as the ring was loosened. The device was then lifted off the barrel as one complete unit. A metallic iron-like aroma filled the air, intermixed with a powerful disinfectant-type stench.

"Remove the lid," Negrete ordered.

Slade gripped it on both sides, wiggled it to make sure that it was loose, and then popped it straight up. After that he tossed the metal lid into the sea, like a Frisbee, where it skipped one time before sinking.

The surface of the open barrel was draped with a red medical bio-hazard waste bag emblazoned with a black skull and cross-bones. "Dump it out on the platform," Negrete commanded. "After I take my photographs use the bristle scrubbing brooms, and just shove the shit into the ocean."

Pancho and Shade positioned themselves on opposite sides of the barrel, cautiously tipping it until the contaminated medical refuse tumbled out. They worked their way backwards, creating a line of perilous medical garbage. When the last item spilled out, they jettisoned the barrel into the sea, where it twirled in a circle for a brief moment before enough water sloshed in, drowning the waste cylinder.

"The beauty of modern medicine," explained Negrete, as he snapped photographs of urine soiled bedding, vomit coated gowns, plastic bedside urinals, cotton dressings, syringes, ma-rooned-stained bandages, latex gloves, swabs, large gauze ban-dages saturated with coagulated blood and rancid body fluids, and surgical gowns drenched beet-red from bloody surgeries.

Looking like he was about to add some of his own vomit to the mix, Slade asked, "Are you done Captain?"

"Yes, get rid of this shit, and then open one additional medi-cal waste barrel."

Cleaning up took several minutes after which they wrestled the next barrel onto the platform. After Pancho and Shade dumped out the contents, Negrete yelled, "Jackpot!"

The second barrel contained pathological waste, tissue, or-gans and infectious components. Globs of yellow fat from lipo-suction surgeries, parts of spongy lungs, kidneys, an oval-shaped spleen, a liver covered with fiber-like tissue caused by cirrhosis, rubbery segments from colons, numerous afterbirths, sections of marble-white skin, and a severed female foot horribly discolored from advance diabetes—the toenails painted livid pink. In addition, there was a plethora of unrecognizable bits and pieces of human tissue from countless surgeries, long stringy nerves, flexile bands of ligaments, tubular blood vessels, lumps of rose-colored striated muscles, fragments of bones, and, finally, numerous glass vials of tainted blood.

"No heart," Negrete said disappointed as he finished taking his digital photographs. Continuing, he said, "Okay, sweep the human scraps overboard. Next type of container—a Food Supplies barrel—let's see what delicious goodies the biotech research company has for us."

Pancho and Shade hurriedly swept the pathological waste into the arms of the ocean and then positioned an extremely heavy Food Supplies barrel upon the platform. Removing the lid as before, they dumped the mass of grisly items onto the platform. Shade vomited. Pancho dry heaved a few times, but managed to avoid chumming the ocean with his breakfast. Disgorged along the swim-platform were an aggregation of laboratory primates and rodents—a gruesome mass of diseased and tormented creatures—several decapitated, others surgically altered, and many appeared as if segmented through an industrial meat shredder. The stench was beyond nauseating. It was the odor of fear, mixed with unrelenting pain, agony, and abuse, fused with decaying flesh, spiritless blood, unwholesome bodily fluids, and putrid excrement.

"Forget jackpot, we just won the lottery," Negrete said ecstatically, as he feverishly snapped dozens of shots depicting the macabre scene. Lying cold and motionless were the trunks of albino rats and mice—their heads guillotined off—an efficient and inexpensive way to end their laboratory lives; pint-sized mahogany-colored guinea pigs, their eyes melted into their sockets, the end result of product testing. Primates—macaques, spider monkeys, squirrel monkeys, and one chimpanzee—laid frozen in time, terror etched on their dead faces, their bodies sliced, carved, and divided, experimental beacons of hope for the human race, their demise necessary for the advancement of modern science.

Pancho and Shade waited impatiently for Negrete to finish his photographic journal. Upon completing the task, Negrete signaled for them to proceed with cleanup. Using the bristle brooms, and a fire hose, they began cleansing the platform of the animal waste. The clarity of the water was incredible, and they were able to observe the bodies of the animals recede into the dark void. Kicking a fresh batch of rats, mice, and guinea pigs into the water, they stood transfixed by the spectacle. Suddenly, the floating carcasses disappeared from their field of vision, and at the same time they noticed an undulating snake-like behemoth darting among the remaining corpses.

Pointing his right index finger in the direction of the meandering serpent, Pancho shouted, "What the hell is that?"

"Sea monster," Shade said warily, as he made an upside-down sign of the cross on his chest.

Upon hearing Pancho's piercing shout and Shade's comment, Negrete swiftly joined them.

Approximately thirty feet below the surface of the water a slender leviathan at least fifty-five feet in length swam with a rhythmic wave-like motion. The sea creature's scaleless body was covered with silvery blue skin, its flanks garbed with irregular bluish to blackish dots, streaks, and squiggles. Its body was topped with a rippling crimson-colored dorsal fin that ran the entire length of its oar-like body, ending at a tapered tail. Ten to twelve elongated cardinal-red fins formed a cockscomb-like plume near the animal's head, creating a magnificent waving crest. The beast had a small mouth for its size and seemed to be inhaling the small rodents rather than tearing them apart like a shark. Negrete estimated its weight at seven to nine hundred pounds. He had no clue as to what it was, but was cognizant of the fact that a sailor's superstitious belief in legendary dragon-like sea monsters had become a reality, as one of the ocean's own denizens of the deep was furtively devouring bio-hazardous waste beneath his ship.

"Toss it the chimpanzee," Negrete ordered. "Let's see how hungry it is."

Using the bristle broom Pancho shoved the four foot, one-hundred pound female chimpanzee into the water. As it spiraled downwards, the chimp's gangly arms gave the impression of embracing them, its pink face, hands, and feet turned upwards, a stoic grimace burned into its human-like coutenance.

Once the chimpanzee had descended approximately fifteen feet, the sea creature's interest was piqued, and it changed direction to intercept the anthropoid ape, its sinuous body graceful as it ascended, its full length silhouetted against the inky blackness. Upon reaching the chimp it first explored its dark coat, starting with the hindquarters, rubbing its small oblique mouth against the coarse fur. It then worked its way up, to the top of the arched forehead, and then over to the ape's face, hovering less than twenty-four inches from the animal's closed eyes, flat nose, and protruding jaws which were clamped shut. As the serpent continued to inspect the ape, a lurching-type swell struck the seaward side of the *Lucky Lady*, moderately rocking the ship, the invisible tentacles of the oceanic swell impacting the chimpanzee, shifting it to within inches of the sea creature, startling it, its movements erratic, fearful.

Laughing derisively Pancho said, "Look, the beast is afraid of a little-old monkey."

Within seconds of Pancho's remark, a second more powerful swell pounded the ship, the ape, and the sea serpent. As the forceful swell struck the chimpanzee, its eyelids sprang open, revealing opaque, vacant eyes. At the same time, the chimp's lower mandible slid downward, exposing rows of sharpened canine teeth, glistening white in the transparent water. The sudden gargoyle-like appearance of the ape immediately changed the sea serpent into a prismatic, shimmering monster, flashing iridescent blues, greens, chartreuse, and purple, its ophidian form now coiled around the ape, its behavior obviously defensive in nature.

"What the hell is it doing?" asked Negrete to no one in particular, while at the same time getting down on his hands and knees for a closer look. Pancho and Shade did the same.

The kaleidoscopic manifestations of the sea serpent appeared to be reaching a crescendo, the intensity of the luminous rainbow colors wavering, entering into a point of climax. It was at this juncture that a dazzling white light pulsated outward from the creature's body, zapping the potentially menacing ape, and impacting all three men stationed on the metal swim-platform—the voltaic discharge temporarily paralyzing all voluntary muscular movement—splaying them out like zombies.

After several minutes Negrete and his coworkers remained stunned, unable to move their limbs as tingling, numbness, and pain radiated to their four extremities. Five minutes later a majority of the discomfort had subsided, and Negrete was able to crawl back onto the rear deck of the *Lucky Lady*, with Pancho and Shade dragging themselves in his path. It would take an additional three minutes before anyone was capable of speech. Pancho, a singed dump truck of a man, lying on his side, spoke first.

"What the hell happened?" he asked weakly.

"The beast that you thought was intimidated by that ape almost killed us," Negrete said, shaking his arms and hands to restore circulation.

"I feel like I was hit by lighting," Shade added.

"You were," Negrete confirmed. "That sea monster is clearly electrogenic, like an electric ray. We were jolted with over two hundred volts."

"How come we're not dead?" Shade asked.

Pulling his superficially seared body onto a deck chair, Negrete answered, "Because the animal's weapon is designed to stun its prey or enemies. The discharge is a one-time event, thank God, since a steady current would have certainly fried us."

Pancho stood up, shaky on his feet, walked to the rear railing, and glanced down into the azure water. "That son-of-a-bitch is gone," he said. "I don't see it anywhere. If it comes back, I'll blow the sucker's brains out." He removed a Smith & Wesson .44 magnum revolver from a holster strapped to his side, hidden underneath his jacket. He feigned a few pretend shots into the water.

"You better get close," Negrete advised, "since shooting a projectile through salt water is like blasting a hole through solid wood. The bullet loses its lethal punch immediately."

"How close?" Pancho wondered.

"Within eight feet," Negrete answered.

"You can always use a speargun," Shade offered.

"And be towed to hell, while being electrically charred, no thank you," Pancho replied.

Turning serious, Shade asked: "What was that creature? I've never heard of such a thing."

"Research on the Internet should answer your question," Negrete said. "I suspect it's a rare, deep water fish. Our dumping ground is apparently located atop its home turf. Hopefully, the shit it ate today will end its pitiful life." Negrete then spat a drippy wad of spittle out into the ocean to emphasize his point.

"What about the thirteen remaining barrels?" Shade asked.

"Dump them—let's pile on as much hazardous waste as possible on that serpent's hood—may he rest in peace," Negrete said with a grin.

Shade and Pancho spent the next half hour hauling overweight barrels onto the swim-platform, twisting off the two silicone plugs, rolling the barrels into the ocean, and then verifying that they had sunk. The last thing they wanted was a metal container filled with noxious waste washing ashore on Santa Cruz Island raising suspicious eyebrows. The final barrel, stuffed with medical waste, proved uncooperative, and failed to sink. It drifted alongside the ship, bobbing like a champagne cork, seven feet off the starboard side. Pancho tried to use an eight-foot long bamboo fish gaff in a futile attempt to manhandle the barrel down to its watery grave. After several minutes of frustrating effort, he gave up, ranting and raving at the stubborn container.

Laughing, Shade said, "Pancho, give me your gun."

"Why?"

"Target practice—blast a few holes—and that barrel will sink like a rock."

"Fine," said Pancho, "but you'll owe me for the bullets." Pancho handed his revolver to Shade and then stepped back. The double action revolver was filled with six, 240 grain jacketed hollow-point cartridges.

Holding the gun with both hands, Shade lined up the red dot aiming sight on the mid-portion of the barrel, which was an inch underwater. Pulling back the hammer and cocking the gun, he then gently squeezed the trigger. The explosion was deafening and the gun's powerful recoil forcibly propelled Shade backwards two steps. The bullets mushrooming impact produced an eight-foot geyser of water mixed with metal and pulverized medical waste. When the cascade of debris ended, the barrel was still afloat.

"You idiot, you can't even sink it," berated Pancho.

Ignoring Pancho's snide remark, Shade repositioned his body against the boat railing, and leaned forward, which allowed him to get a few feet closer to the barrel. He fired the gun five times in rapid succession, discharging all the bullets. The thwack of the expandable projectiles ripping into the barrel was thunderous— the 1200 cumulative grains of fragmented lead liquefying vials of contaminated blood and human tissue—creating a violent blowback of pureed medical waste that inundated Shade. The drenching fluids, tainted with the Hepatitis C and HIV virus, penetrated his eye sockets, naval cavities, and his widely agape canker-sore inflamed mouth. Unbeknownst to Shade, his future life expectancy of fifty-one years had just taken a substantial hit.

Watching the noisy ruckus, Negrete merely shook his head in utter amazement. Pancho, on the other hand, was rolling on the deck, clamoring with ridiculing laughter. Fortunately, the obstinate barrel, with a few last gurgling sounds, slowly sank into the blue depths, the beady yellow eyes of a slithering sea serpent following its five thousand foot plunge.

"Clean yourself up," Negrete ordered, "and especially the damn boat."

Negrete then sauntered back into the wheelhouse, started the engines, entered the GPS coordinates for Platform Gina, plugged his Smartphone into the ship's audio system, throttled the engines to ten knots, and sat back and enjoyed the onslaught of heavy metal music. The fog was lifting, and the first rays of sunshine were beginning to peek through. The time was 9:35 a.m. He still had ten pallets of meat and bone meal to deliver to Gina before his working day was complete. After that, he would go back to his townhouse for an afternoon siesta, and then head up the coast to the Chumash Casino in San Ynez for an evening of Texas Hold 'Em poker. He had five thousand dollars to gamble with, and like the name of his boat, he was feeling uncommonly lucky.

6

"**D**ad," Mischa hollered in a piercing voice that easily resonated down the narrow hallway and into the master bedroom, "its 6:50 p.m.—you ready?"

"One more minute," Kurt replied.

While Kurt finished dressing, Jake and Mischa set the dining room table for five. The oval-shaped table and set of six chairs, manufactured from eco-friendly plantation-grown teak wood, fit nicely in the dining room, which was angled so that it faced Anacapa Island. A six-inch diameter sandalwood candle glowed radiantly from the middle of the table, its sweet woody scent infusing the whole room.

"We're done!" Mischa declared, and then noticed a minor faux pas. "The little fork goes to the left of the big fork," she said, scolding Jake on his table-setting etiquette. "You have it backwards."

"Sorry Ms. Martha Stewart, I'm not a girl," Jake said curtly.

"Maybe in your next life, if you're lucky," she said smugly, switching the forks as she spoke.

Kurt could hear the good-natured banter between his son and his daughter as he walked into the dining room. Their amiable mood and excitement reflected his own.

"So . . . how do I look?" he asked.

Giving him an appraising once over, Mischa said, "Do a slow steady turn, like a model."

"Ok," Kurt said, as he strutted in a circular pattern, exaggerating his masculine qualities.

"Good Lord Dad," Jake said, "TMI—Too Much Information."

Laughing, Mischa said, "My debonair dad, some day you'll get it. But of course you look absolutely dashing, especially since I chose your outfit."

"Is the word humble in your vocabulary?" Jake pressed.

Ignoring Jake's comment, and walking around her dad, Mischa pretended to be a high-fashioned runway announcer. "Our next model is wearing a Tommy Bahama long-sleeve washed-linen shirt, Polynesia blue. The pants—Lucky Brand distressed-vintage straight-leg jeans, medium-blue wash with light fading on the legs. The footwear—expresso-colored classic Vans skate shoes. It's called understated flamboyance, not too young, and not too old."

"A shirt, pants, and shoes, no big deal," Jake quipped.

Giving his daughter a thankful embrace, Kurt said, "Mischa, pay no attention to your brother. I thank God for my style-savvy daughter."

"Any time," beamed Mischa.

Inspecting the dining room table, Kurt said, "It looks great . . . Thanks. The only item missing is Riedel wine glasses for the adults."

"What type of wine are you serving?" Jake inquired.

"I have a nice bottle of Opus One. It's a red Bordeaux—a blend of Cabernet Sauvignon, Cabernet Franc, Merlot, and Malbec grapes. It's also referred to as a Meritage."

"Can I see the bottle?" Mischa asked.

"I opened it earlier, to let it breathe, so be careful," Kurt said, as he retrieved the bottle from a hutch located next to the table.

Mischa cautiously examined the dark colored 750 ml, slightly dusty bottle. "This wine is old," she complained. "Vinted and bottled in 1997. Don't you think you should serve something a little newer rather than getting rid of your old stock? I thought you wanted to impress Eva."

"What's your age?" Kurt asked with a big grin.

"Why—what has that got to do with your stuffy old wine?"

"Will you promise me that you'll stay young and innocent forever?"

"I think," Jake said, enjoying the moment, "that Dad appreciates your lack of knowledge concerning alcohol. For your information, the older the wine, the better it is, assuming that it matured gracefully."

"Now who's Ms. Martha Stewart?" jested Mischa.

"Maybe I should keep a closer eye on my son," Kurt said, meaning that as a compliment "—you spout facts like a French connoisseur. But your brother is right; the flavor of aged wine is richer, more focused, and much more complex, than a younger wine. I doubt Eva or Timbrook will be disappointed."

"Whatever," Mischa said.

"Doorbell," Jake announced as the classical sounding chimes reverberated throughout the house.

"I'll get it," Kurt said, as he ambled to the entryway. He opened the copper-clad doors by turning an ornate brass doorknob. The doors swung inward.

"Adam," Kurt said, "welcome to our house." He wrapped his arms around Adam Timbrook, who immediately reciprocated, and a mutual bear hug was exchanged.

"It's been a long time . . . too long in fact," Timbrook said wistfully, as the hug ended. Timbrook was in his early eighties although physically he appeared as a man in his early sixties. He was short and stocky, five feet nine inches, one hundred and ninety pounds, with large bones, and solid muscles from constant outdoor use. His hair, cocoa-brown with age appropriate silver streaks, was worn in a long ponytail which today was intertwined with colorful strings of fabric and symbolic decorations, including teeth from an extinct Pygmy mammoth and saber-toothed cat, olivella shell beads, and tail-feathers from a bald and golden eagle. His winsome and compassionate smile enhanced a dark, earthy countenance etched with deep wrinkle lines caused by too much sun. His normal, everyday clothes were simple and practical: work boots, leather sandals, Levi jeans, assorted tee-shirts, and various sweatshirts for colder days. For tonight's dinner party Timbrook was dressed in a newer pair of Levi jeans, a Quicksilver t-shirt, and leather sandals.

"My children, Jake and Mischa," Kurt said, formally introducing them. Timbrook shook their extended hands, but Mischa also insisted upon a friendly embrace.

Addressing Jake and Mischa ceremoniously, Timbrook said: "Welcome back, descendants of Juan Rodriguez Cabrillo and Luisa Librado—to the Island of Limuw—the ancestral home of your Chumash forefathers."

"Thank you," Jake said, "but what island is Limuw?"

"Limuw is the Chumash name for Santa Cruz Island. Translated it means *In the Sea*. The name is thousands of years old."

"The name Limuw certainly makes logical sense," Mischa said. "The island is literally '*In the Sea,*' since it is surrounded by the Pacific Ocean on all four sides."

"Your interpretation is correct, but only applies to one part of the meaning," Timbrook said. "The exact significance of the Chumash name is multi-faceted, and like a good mystery, it has multiple layers."

"And what manifold layers of Chumash cuisine are you serving tonight?" Kurt asked, salivating at the bouquet of flavors emerging from several succulent dishes hidden beneath aluminum foil. The platters of food were neatly arranged in a large Chumash-made wicker basket that Timbrook had temporarily placed on the porch for the greeting.

"I will explain my dinner menu once everyone has arrived. It's my understanding that one guest is still missing."

"Not any longer," Eva said, stepping through the doorway. "And it smells absolutely delicious."

After another round of quick introductions, Timbrook carried his basket to a buffet table situated next to the dining room table, and began unloading. Jake and Mischa lent supporting and curious hands.

Kurt could not help but admire Eva's selection of clothing. Her petite body was adorned in a lavender-silk floral-print dress with ruffled details, a long lightweight turquoise colored twisted cotton cardigan sweater, beige platform sandals with white leather straps, and a sterling silver and marcasite pendant with luster abalone. Her glossy jet-black hair flowed in a wavy waterfall pattern to her lower back. She wore light pink lipgloss, shimmering face powder, and iridescent eye shadow. She was carrying a python-embossed cross-body bag, with a short strap, in peacock blue.

"And I thought you looked good in a neoprene wetsuit—nice transformation," Kurt remarked, and instantly blushed beet-red after realizing what he had said.

"I'll take that as a compliment," Eva said with an amused smile. She then set her purse down on a natural slate and iron table located at the entryway.

"How are you feeling?" Kurt inquired.

"Thank you for asking," Eva said. "I'm still a little sore. I had a slight headache which two Aleve pills took care of, and I suspect I'll have a few ugly bruises by tomorrow morning. Overall, Nurse Snyder was very pleased with my recovery. The x-rays showed no fractures. She allowed me to attend tonight's dinner as long as I drove the electric golf cart. *No strenuous walking for twenty-four hours*, were her final command words," laughed Eva.

"That's wonderful news," Kurt said.

Turning serious, Eva said. "I watched the sea lion encounter on YouTube. I was astonished at how much the camera captured. You and Mischa saved my life. It'll take a long time to pay off that debt . . . if ever."

"Did I hear my name?" Mischa said, stepping into the conversation.

"I was just informing your dad how amazing you two were today. I owe you a debt of gratitude for rescuing me."

"Are you kidding?" Mischa exclaimed, "Today was almost fun. You owe me nothing other than our agreed upon Scuba diving trip back to that moray eel. Sorry—got to run—have to go finish helping Jake."

Mischa returned back to the dining room and began filling the water goblets with Pellegrino water. Jake added slices of lemon. "That's one special child," Eva said.

"I know," Kurt agreed.

"Who's hungry?" Timbrook announced.

"Starving," Eva said, as a chorus of famished voices echoed a similar testament. They gathered around the buffet table.

"What's for dinner?" Mischa asked.

"Before we begin," Timbrook said, "I need to say a few words. I promise to keep it short. Tonight's dinner is a celebration for the island of Limuw and for the Nichols family. In 1822 your ancestors were forcibly removed by Spanish Missionaries and relocated to Santa Barbara. For the first time since that date, offspring of the Cabrillo bloodline mixed with Chumash blood have been restored to their ancestral home—an island that has stayed within the Cabrillo legacy since 1543 and now is entrusted to the Nichols lineage. In recognition of this symbolic reunion, and to honor this historical occasion, a traditional Chumash banquet has been prepared."

Timbrook paused to clear his throat before continuing: "Please bow your heads," he politely requested. "Lord . . . we thank you for this special day . . . a day you predestined long ago. Thank you for allowing an old Indian to play a part. Bless this food, bless the Nichols family, and bless Eva. Amen."

"Thanks for your warm reception and your prayer," Kurt said kindly, "and now for us ignoramuses, you need to describe what it is we're about to eat."

"Yes, of course," Timbrook said. "In an outdoor roasting pit, filled with super-heated rocks, covered with layers of grass, and topped with soil, I baked halibut, quail, and wild hyacinth bulbs. The process takes twelve hours. The halibut was cooked wrapped in fresh seaweed, butter, ocean salt, lemon juice, parsley, paprika, and pepper. The quail was roasted in its own natural juices garnished with olive oil, ocean salt, pepper, wild rosemary, sage, and thyme. The hyacinth bulbs were simply steamed and are an excellent side dish with your fish."

Timbrook briefly halted his description as he circumspectly removed the aluminum foil covering the dishes. "The acorn mush was prepared from a mixture of acorns gathered from black and tan oak trees, which produce the best quality nuts. They were collected in the autumn, hulled, dried, and stored. This morning I ground the acorns into a fine powder with a stone mortar and pestle. The flour was then leached using cold water and a cheese-cloth, to remove the bitter tannic acid. It was next mixed with water and then cooked using red-hot stones placed into the liquid. Finally, I added some butter, cornmeal, dried currants, and a little salt for flavoring. It has a sweet nutty taste which goes well with your quail, or your fish. The indigenous salad is a mixture of sweet clover, miner's lettuce, watercress, and mustard greens, seasoned with salt and pepper, and garnished with a honey-mustard salad dressing. The hot tea was brewed from wild rose petals. The Opus One Bordeaux is graciously provided by our host, Kurt Nichols. So, as the French say, *Bon Appétit*, or as the Chumash say, 'go for it.'"

Go for it, was an understatement, as everyone plunged right in, heaping their plates to overflowing, the stress of the long day having magnified their appetites. Very few words were spoken initially as each person blissfully concentrated on each and every tantalizing bite. The halibut, imbued with spices from both land and sea, and infused with a small dash of hyacinth bulb, simply melted in their mouths. The fall-off-the-bone quail, when smothered in acorn mush, exploded into a profusion of gamey flavors that harkened their modern taste buds back to an earlier hunter-gatherer experience. Finally, the local salad, embellished with a contemporary salad dressing, surprised everyone with its crisp, moist, organic savoriness.

Raising his wine glass, Kurt said gallantly, "A salute to the greatest Chumash chef in Southern California—our very own—Adam Timbrook." The clinking of glass against glass pervaded the atmosphere along with a vociferous outcry of contented Yes's and Amen's.

"Thank you," Timbrook said, "and a special thanks to Kurt for sharing an exquisite bottle of wine. It's a rare treat to sample twentie[th] century's most prestigious vintage."

"Anytime," Kurt said. "An exceptional wine is meant to be relished among good friends."

"My compliments to all," Eva added, "for a wonderful culinary experience."

"That was delicious," Jake agreed.

"Just curious," Mischa asked, "were the halibut and quail fresh, or frozen?"

"Mischa!" scolded Kurt.

"It's okay," Timbrook said, "the food I serve is always fresh. Yesterday afternoon I went spear fishing and impaled a fifteen-pound California halibut in twenty feet of water off of Potato Harbor. The fish was so well camouflaged—lying partially buried in the sandy bottom—that I almost missed seeing it. The quail I shot two days ago with my Remington Sporting 410 shotgun, about one mile up Scorpion Canyon."

"The next time you go food gathering I'm tagging along," Mischa said, "and not as a spectator."

"Me too," Jake added.

"A little company sounds good to me," said Timbrook.

"I did not know that quail existed on Santa Cruz Island," Kurt reflected.

"About twenty-five years ago a sizeable flock was blown out to sea by an extremely powerful Santa Ana offshore wind event, and miraculously landed on the island," Timbrook explained.

"They traveled over twenty-two miles?" Kurt asked skeptically.

"A little manna from heaven—more or less the same as what God provided for the Israelites in the wilderness."

"But these quail," Kurt continued, "were nice and plump, similar to mountain quail, not petite-sized like their smaller coastal cousins."

"Benevolent of God to send the big ones," Timbrook replied with a thin smile.

"Did God have any island help?" Kurt asked with a twinkle in his eye.

"As you know," Timbrook said reverentially, "God works in mysterious ways, and he sometimes requires the assistance of human ingenuity."

"As you said, it was gracious of God to stock the island with corpulent quail."

"I thank him every time I sit down to dine on one of his fine-feathered friends," laughed Timbrook, whose warm-hearted laughter quickly spread to everyone at the table as the absurdity of his story sunk in.

As the last of the snickering died down Eva said to Timbrook, "Do you mind telling me a little about yourself? I've never met a Chumash Indian before, and after such an opulent meal, I'm fascinated to learn a few additional details about the man behind it."

"I'm eighty-three years of age, how far back do you want me to go?"

"Short story version . . . family . . . how you ended up on this island," Eva suggested.

"Not an easy request," Timbrook said. "Family history: my parents were among the last surviving remnants of the Chumash nation at the beginning of the twentieth centry. The tally—less than several hundred pure Chumash remained. As you probably know, European viruses and diseases decimated my ancestors. We once numbered over twenty-five thousand strong at the time Juan Rodriguez Cabrillo first discovered our tribal villages. My parents spent their entire lives residing in a small adobe house on the Santa Ynez Chumash Indian Reservation which is located just north of Santa Barbara. They each worked very hard and saved enough money to send me to UCLA, where I obtained a BS degree in Psychology, a degree I never utilized. But, it has helped me in my dealings with people. At age twenty-two, and one year out of college, I met my future wife, Maria. We were married that same year. Maria was seventy-five percent Chumash and twenty-five percent Spanish. I loved her very much. Within a month of our marriage I was offered the job as caretaker on Santa Cruz Island by James Cabrillo—Tessa Nichols' grandfather—almost sixty years ago. Maria encouraged me to accept the position, which I did. We looked forward to returning to the ancestral birthplace of the Chumash, and to raising our family. As it turned out, Maria was infertile, due to endometriosis. Nonetheless, we had a great life together. We cherished being the guardians of this marvelous island, acting as tour guides, replanting native vegetation, securing the Chumash historical sites, ridding the island of non-native animals such as goats, sheep, feral pigs, and golden eagles, restoring the population of island foxes, reintroducing bald eagles, taking care of the facilities, kayaking, fishing, diving, hiking, having friends over, vacationing on the mainland, and loving each other in a way that only isolation and absolute dependency upon one another could produce. She passed away almost seven years ago, and I still miss her immensely. Maria is buried on Santa Cruz at a sacred Chumash site located on Montannon Ridge. As a Christian, God helped me to overcome my intense grief and sorrow. Part of my comfort was the Bible's assurance that Maria and I would someday be reunited in heaven. Since her death, I've continued to do what I have always done, passionately taking care of this unique island. Finally—a word to the Nichols family—I'm ecstatic that my insular life has now come to an end. I look forward to spending quality time with my new island neighbors, and fellow adventurers." He said the last three words while staring at Jake and Mischa.

"Sorry about your wife," Eva said softly.

"Thank you," Timbrook said.

"Do your Christian beliefs conflict with your Chumash identity?" Kurt asked.

"No, I've reconciled the two. Spanish missionaries, beginning in the sixteenth century harmed my people's cultural way of life in the same ruthless manner that their foreign diseases essentially wiped us out. Forgiving them was emotionally arduous. But, the Bible commands forgiveness of one's enemy—so after much soul-searching—I forgave them for their horrendous acts of misplaced piety. Throughout my life I've had no difficulty retaining my Chumash identity, heritage, and culture, while embracing the tenets of Christianity. Today's modern missionaries would hopefully not make the same terrible mistakes."

"Where do you go to church?" Jake asked.

"Inspiration Point just North of Scorpion Cove. There's a nice sitting rock that overlooks the ocean. I bring my Bible, read from it, talk to God, and pray. Best church on earth. The congregation is made up of seabirds, dolphins, whales, sea otters, and seals. We've never had a church split," chuckled Timbrook.

"I have a question," Mischa said, "but not about religion. I was wondering—why are only Chumash Indians allowed as caretakers or guides on Santa Cruz Island?"

"Good question Mischa. It's been that way since 1822 when the last of the Cabrillo family was relocated by Spanish missionaries to the Santa Barbara Mission. Even though absent, ownership of the island continued in the Cabrillo lineage. At that time the island was leased out to cattle and sheep ranchers. Ever since 1822 all agreements, or contracts, or bill of sales, concerning the island have required Chumash Indians as caretakers or guides."

"Thanks for the insightful history lesson, but why?" Mischa persisted.

"I really don't know why," Timbrook said cautiously. "It was never clarified in any of the original documents. Possibly it was done to protect the island's numerous Chumash archeological sites, or a familial connection because of the mixed blood line. Who knows, but I'm happy for the job. You're a descendent, what do you think?"

"I think," Mischa said suspiciously, "that the same reasons that existed in 1822 exist today."

"Why do you say that?" Timbrook asked.

"Because the grounds were never enumerated—think about it—one hundred and eighty years of signed contracts. The absence of any defining words in any agreement clinches the deal for me."

"Are you a conspiracy-theory type person?" Timbrook teased.

"I've watched my share of television and surfed some intriguing Internet sites . . . so maybe," Mischa grinned.

"Nothing improper about seeking the truth," Timbrook said.

"Speaking of the truth," Jake said, "any idea where Captain Cabrillo is buried?"

"Sixty years and I have yet to discover his grave. I've explored every probable gravesite on this entire island, searching for his tombstone, and zilch. The historical records state that he was buried on the island of Capitana, which is meaningless information. In the early exploratory days the Spaniards called all the various Channel Islands Capitana. So, which one is it? There are a total of eight offshore islands. A monument honoring Captain Cabrillo's life was placed above Cuyler Harbor, on San Miguel Island in 1937, but I doubt San Miguel is the right island. Too cold, too windy, and the surrounding waters are exceptionally treacherous. My gut tells me that this is the actual island, but after sixty years of searching, I'm probably wrong."

"We'll help you," Jake declared.

"Thanks, maybe your genetic bond, your spiritual roots, will aid in the search. That is one prayer that God has not answered—revealing the final whereabouts of Captain Cabrillo."

"In almost all unsolved mysteries," Mischa commented, "the obvious is usually overlooked."

"You may be correct," Timbrook replied, "maybe your young eyes will have a better chance of seeing the obvious. Anyway, it's conversation break-time for this old Indian, and time to clean up. What's say you and Jake and I do the dishes, and let your dad and Eva relax in front of the fireplace?"

"No," Eva said, "you made the dinner, the least I can do is clean up."

"You want me to call Major General Nurse Snyder?" Timbrook threatened with a devious smirk.

"But—"

"No more buts—go, it's a cool evening, enjoy the fire, and remember—no business discussions. We'll put you to work cleaning dishes at our next dinner event."

"He's right," Kurt said, "you'll have plenty of future opportunities, and arguing with an Indian elder is a violation of the house rules."

"I concede," Eva said reluctantly, "show me the way."

Kurt led Eva into a combination family room and library. The library housed a collection of approximately one thousand volumes on marine sciences and marine biology, with a computer work station. The room, paneled in knotty Georgia Antiqued Heart Pine painted pearl white, was enhanced with an ivory-colored travertine tile floor. It was decorated with South Sea rattan furniture, including a sofa, loveseat, two chairs with ottomans, two end tables, and a rectangular coffee table. The tables were topped with beveled glass etched with snowy white egrets. The South Sea furniture was characterized by a rolling rattan construction with criss-crossing framework, antique finish, and plush cotton fabric in a tropical foliage pattern with a sprinkling of pink and white hibiscus flowers.

The room's east view presented an unobstructed view of Scorpion Cove with Anacapa Island framed in the distant background. The north wall contained the fireplace which was surrounded by a white marble mantle over which was positioned, in a recessed space, a sixteen by twenty-two inch Catalina tile mosaic portraying colorful Toucan birds. The west wall featured a colossal oil painting by marine artist, Robert Lynn Nelson, and depicted the undersea world of Catalina Island off of Casino Point. Marine artist Robert Wyland's bronze sculptures of bottlenose dolphins, humpback whales, and endangered green sea turtles, finished the room's ocean decor. Silk plants, including bird of paradise with its bright orange and purple flowers, sword bromeliad with its lavender and pink flowers, enchanting orchids in every hue of the rainbow, and lofty banana palms with their brilliantly red, yellow, and green flowers, dotted the room.

"Is this paradise?" Eva asked upon entering the room and settling down in the loveseat.

"I'm glad you like it. I designed this room as a vacation-style retreat."

"For a male interior decorator you did quite well."

Laughing, Kurt said, "We males do get it right on occasion." Kurt then walked over to the fireplace, turned on the natural gas, and tossed a lit match into the vapors igniting the wood. Turning back to Eva he said, "As your host for the evening I have a special treat for you. Relax and I'll be right back."

He quickly left the room for the kitchen, where he opened the freezer and removed two frosted crystal liqueur glasses and a bottle of Lemonel Limoncello. He returned back to the family room.

"Ever tried the Mediterranean nectar called Limoncello?" Kurt asked. "It's made from full-flavored lemons and vodka."

"No—not yet," Eva replied.

Kurt poured the ice-cold liquid into the slender liqueur glasses. "A toast," said Kurt, "to a day that began like no other, but ended delightfully." Smiling, they both delicately clinked their two glasses, creating a high-pitched musical sound, and then leisurely sipped the golden-yellow liquor.

"This is extraordinary," Eva said. "The ambrosial quality is delicious—a sweet, tart, lemony flavor—with a nice bite to it." Eva drained her small glass, which Kurt promptly refilled. Noticing that the wood was now burning radiantly, he walked to the fireplace and turned off the gas. He then sat down in a chair adjacent to Eva's loveseat.

"How does it feel to receive warmth from east coast wood over one hundred and sixty years old?" Kurt asked.

"You imported old wood for your fireplace?"

"No, it's wood from the wreck of the *S.S. Winfield Scott* steamer which crashed into Anacapa Island on December 2, 1853," Kurt explained. "Wood from that wreck was salvaged and used to construct the original winery, with the bulk of the wood stored for future use. Most of that old wood was utilized in the building of this house. However, some of the planks were severely damaged in the shipwreck. The carpenters throughout the construction process had to saw off the damaged portions. I instructed them to save all the irregular pieces as future firewood. Nothing burns better or hotter than fine-grained hardwoods."

Setting her glass down on the coffee table and rubbing her hands together Eva said, "As a relatively thin woman I do appreciate a blazing hot fire—so keep the wood coming."

"A lady who is easily chilled, what a rarity," Kurt teased. "Don't worry," he said as he pointed to the round copper firewood bucket adjacent to the fireplace, "it's filled to capacity, and stored in the backyard is an additional cord of wood. I think you'll stay moderately toasty."

Reveling in another sip of her Limoncello, Eva said, "I know Timbrook said no work talk, but tomorrow morning I plan on performing the necropsy on the sea lion and was wondering if you wouldn't mind attending?"

"What time?"

"Around 10:30."

"I'll be there."

"Thanks, I know its dead, but it still spooks the hell out of me."

"It will be interesting to see what the post-mortem reveals. That was one deranged sea lion."

Eva suddenly shook her head as a tormented person would do when attempting to physically rid their psyche of a nefarious memory. "You okay?" Kurt asked concerned.

"Yes, and no," Eva replied, wiping a few tears from her eyes, "That YouTube video was intense. I realized I almost died today. We need to discover the cause of the sea lion's maniacal behavior. What if there are others? That thought turns my stomach."

Kurt retrieved a box of Kleenex tissue and removed several for Eva. "Tomorrow we should know," Kurt said optimistically. "At least it will be the beginning of our investigation. In all probability that sea lion was a solitary aberration."

Dabbing her eyes with the tissue Eva said, "Yes . . . we can certainly hope." She then generated a weak smile. "Enough shop talk. Timbrook would be angry. Can I ask a personal question, which if you don't want to answer, I'll understand?"

"Be my guest," said Kurt.

"I know your wife, Tessa, once owned Santa Cruz Island, but I am a little foggy on the historical details regarding the island, and when everything changed. I was wondering if you wouldn't mind providing me with a brief overview. There's not much in the public records."

"You did say brief," Kurt laughed.

Eva nodded her head.

Kurt indulged in a sumptuous sip of Limoncello, before he began. "Tessa's maiden name was Cabrillo. She was the last Cabrillo in a long line of descendants going all the way back to the Spanish explorer, Captain Juan Rodriguez Cabrillo. In the year 1542 Captain Cabrillo had an affair with a Chumash girl by the name of Luisa. Captain Cabrillo died from gangrene shortly before the child was born. Prior to his death, he deeded the island of Santa Cruz to Luisa and to her heirs. Luisa bore a son and named him Santiago Cabrillo. When Luisa died the island passed to Santiago. When Santiago died the island passed to his progeny. The long line of succession continued unabated for generations. In fact, it was a miracle that the Cabrillo bloodline even survived. There was never an overabundance of Cabrillo children, especially with the scourge of European diseases, but somehow the lineage persisted."

"No one ever challenged ownership?" Eva asked.

"No—never contested. The island itself was considered worthless. The waters surrounding it were valuable, filled with fur seals, sea otters, fish, abalones, and lobsters, but that resource was exploited by anyone who owned a ship. When the United States acquired California following the Mexican-American War of 1848, the U.S. government and the State of California continued to recognize the Cabrillo's' ownership over the island."

"They were fortunate," Eva opined.

"Probably so," Kurt agreed. "In 1822, as Timbrook referenced earlier, all the Chumash Indians were removed from the Island, and relocated to cramped villages next to the Santa Barbara Mission. The Cabrillo's—all three that existed at that time—were also removed. Unlike most Chumash who had absolutely no assets, the Cabrillo's still owned Santa Cruz Island. Destitute and needing money, they leased the island out to cattle and sheep ranchers, using the income to purchase a beach house in Malibu. Regrettably, those were the dark decades of the island as thousands of cattle and sheep literally denuded Santa Cruz of its native vegetation.

"That's terrible," Eva acknowledged sadly.

"In 1854 a working winery was also constructed on the island. Over two hundred acres of grapes were planted: Zinfandel, Riesling, Burgundy, Muscatel, and Grenache grapes. That old winery is now our house."

"What happened to the Cabrillo's?" Eva wondered.

"Their house in Malibu was located on a strip of land that to-day is called Paradise Cove. That house, rebuilt and modernized several times over, still exists. After 1822 the Cabrillo's severed any relationship with their Chumash brethren, and intermarried with other races. Unfortunately, they never produced much of any offspring. Tessa's dad, Logan, was an only child of James and Martha Cabrillo, Tessa's grandparents. Logan married Ashley, Tessa's mom. Logan and Ashley had only one child, Tessa."

"When did you and Tessa marry?" Eva asked.

"In college," Kurt said. "We met when Tessa was nineteen and a sophomore. I was twenty and a junior. We were both attending the University of Malibu. The circumstances were not ideal. She had just buried her parents, killed in an automobile accident. A wrong-way drunk driver on Pacific Coast Highway had abruptly ended their lives, leaving her alone in the world. Rather than collapsing into depression or bitterness, Tessa faced the world with renewed vigor, anxious to make a difference. Her incredible spirit so captivated me that I instantly fell in love with her, plus, she was cute. We were married within a year and moved into her parent's house in Paradise Cove, breathing new life into it. The infertility curse that had followed the Cabrillo clan for centuries ended, and Tessa became pregnant immediately. Nine months later out pops Jake. Thirteen months after Jake's arrival, Mischa shows up. We finally explored the benefits of birth control, fig-uring that two children in two years had pushed the limits as to what a young couple in college could handle."

"How did being married with two children affect your college studies?" Eva asked.

"It was difficult, but we had an edge—financial wherewith-al. As an only child, Tessa inherited her parent's entire estate, which included a substantial sum of money and numerous as-sets. Plus, she received a sizeable wrongful death settlement from the drunk driver's insurance company. My parents were

SANTA CRUZ, THE ISLAND OF LIMUW

not wealthy, but they had the fortitude to set aside sufficient funds to cover my college education. With monetary resources, we were able to hire a nanny, which allowed us to complete our studies. I obtained my Bachelor of Science, Masters Degree, and Ph.D., all in Marine Biology, from the University of Malibu, and was hired by the university as a research scientist upon completion of my Ph.D. In the years that followed I was promoted to Assistant Professor, then Full Professor, and now my current position, Senior Project Scientist. Tessa's major was English, with an emphasis in Classical Literature. Being married, pregnant, and having children, made the process extremely onerous, but she never complained, and the University worked with her. After obtaining her Bachelor of Arts Degree in English, she then devoted the ensuing two years to acquiring her Secondary Teaching Credential, and Masters Degree in Secondary Education. She then dedicated the succeeding five years to being the finest full-time mom on earth, spending quality time with our children, and nourishing them during their early formative years. Once they were in elementary school she applied for and was accepted as an English teacher at Malibu High School, which position she held, and treasured, until the day of her death. Her students at the memorial service brought tears to every attendees eyes in their laudatory adulations."

"Tessa was definitely a remarkable person," Eva said graciously.

"Thank you—she was a loving wife, faithful friend, devoted mother, and awesome teacher—who is daily missed." Changing the subject by rising to his feet in order to check on the dying fire, Kurt snatched several pieces of wood from the copper firewood bucket. As he was about to chuck the fragments into the ebbing fire he suddenly hesitated, and instead spent a few seconds closely examining the cuttings, eventually deciding to set the segments aside. He subsequently found other scraps that were suitable, tossed them into the fireplace, rekindling the fire. After that, he returned back to his chair.

After a respectful pause in their conversation Eva said, "If you don't object to me asking, what happened to Santa Cruz Island after Tessa's parents passed away?"

"I don't mind," said Kurt. "The centuries of sheep, cattle, and pig ranching, along with man's destructive activities, had wreaked havoc on the ecology of a once pristine sixty-two thousand acre island, and something had to be done. A national, non-profit environmental group called The Nature Conservancy had expressed an interest in the island. They promised to preserve, protect, and restore the natural ecosystems of the island, at their own expense, if Tessa transferred legal ownership to the Conservancy. In addition, The National Park Service had also expressed an interest in purchasing the entire island. After lengthy and time-consuming consultations involving lawyers, environmentalists, and government bureaucrats—Tessa made her decision. Three-quarters or approximately seventy-six percent of the island was donated to The Nature Conservancy. One-quarter or roughly twenty-four percent was sold to the National Park Service for twenty-eight million dollars. Twenty-five million of that money went into the non-profit, Nichols Foundation. Both agreements contained the historical or usual provision that only Chumash Indians could serve as caretakers or guides. Lastly, two hundred acres, however, were never sold or donated, and to this day remain in the Nichols family. Those two hundred acres comprise the area that the Marine lab is currently situated upon, the old winery, Cavern Point, Scorpion Cove, and all land that encompasses the ancient Chumash village of Swaxil including Scorpion Anchorage. Swaxil was personal to Tessa, since this ancient island site was the heart and soul of the Chumash nation. When Tessa died, her entire estate passed to me. I continue to honor her memory in the operation and distribution of her assets through the Nichols Foundation. And that, in a nutshell, covers it," Kurt said, as he drained what remained of his lemony liqueur.

"That's a lot of information," said Eva. "Thanks for being open and candid and for your willingness to share intimate details of your life. I hope you don't mind, but in a funny way I now feel closer to you and your family, knowing your history, and what you've been through. The other day I turned thirty years of age and was immersed in my own self-pity party, foolishly thinking that I would stay twenty-something forever. Single and thirty years of age—it will cause any woman to become depressed. Your outlook on life, the trauma you've endured, your exceptional children, your passion for excellence, places a new perspective on what's important."

"Don't be too hard on yourself," Kurt laughed. "I turn forty in a few months, and was dreading my own turn of the decade thirties-to-forty transition. My reality check is to always consider the alternative, and when I do, I zealously appreciate every birthday."

"You are trim, fit, physically active, and have a natural outdoor beauty about you. In addition, your fairly long hair implies a subtle rebel streak—which I like—and you have an engaging smile, so I wouldn't be too distressed about turning forty," Eva said appreciatively.

"You forgot, 'intellectually stimulating', in your assessment," Kurt said, slightly embarrassed.

Smiling cat-like, Eva said, "I thought the focus was on aging. Intellect can follow you to the grave."

Laughing, Kurt said, "I stand corrected."

Mischa's voice echoed from the kitchen, interrupting their conversation. "Dad, Eva, we have two unusual guests we want you to meet. They are special friends of Timbrook. Wait there, we'll come to you."

Kurt and Eva heard the sound of giggling as they approached. Timbrook entered the family room first. "It's okay," Timbrook cautioned, "they're harmless." Kurt and Eva exchanged puzzled glances.

"You ready," Jake announced as he entered the room." "Our first guest is Charlie, whose date tonight is Elizabeth, local residents in need of an evening meal."

Mischa, with a guilt-like grin on her face, marched into the room, followed by Charlie, an Island fox, and Elizabeth, a spotted skunk.

"Oh my God—"

"It's okay Eva, they're harmless," Timbrook said quickly, "Charlie is perfectly tame, and Elizabeth is oblivious to being a skunk. I failed to put out their kibble tonight, so they came searching for me. I thought I would introduce you, inasmuch as you're now neighbors."

The Island fox had a gray back, with reddish-brown sides, white underside, and distinctive black, white, and rufous markings on its face. The spotted skunk had black and white spots on its forehead, with interrupted white stripes over its back and sides. The pint-sized creatures were each being hand-fed doggie kibble by Mischa and Jake.

Gently stroking the skunk's fur as she fed it Mischa said, "Elizabeth's fur is so fine and silky soft . . . you should give it a try."

Bravely masking her timidity, Eva first caressed the skunk and then the fox, with Kurt joining in the fun.

"Wow, they're amazing," Eva said. "Sorry for being startled. But, you have to admit, they're not your typical house pets."

"On this island they are," Timbrook said. "They have no natural predators and no fear of man. And now—I think it's time they skedaddled back outside since they also have no fear of soiling your brand new floors."

"Jake . . . Mischa," Kurt said, "would you be the perfect hosts and kindly escort our furry guests outside, and then it's time for bed. Say your goodbyes."

Jake and Mischa each said adieu, and then formed an entourage of humans and animals, marching toward the great outdoors.

Yawning, Eva said, "It's been a long day, it's time for me to go too."

"And this old Indian," added Timbrook.

"One moment," Kurt said, "I have something I want to show you first." Kurt snagged the scraps of cut planks that he had set aside next to the fireplace. "Take a close look at the atypical damage to these three pieces of hardwood that originated from the *Scott* steamer."

Timbrook and Eva each scrupulously examined the marred lumber, inspecting each one as if under a microscope.

"Burst damage from impacting the reef rocks?" Eva offered.

Timbrook probed one specimen in particular, carefully rotating it in his hands. The edges were ripped apart as if by an explosion, and there were black scorch marks on many of the splintered fringes.

"Looks seared, as if by fire," Timbrook observed.

"If my memory serves me right, there was no fire on board the *Scott* the night of the collision," Kurt said.

"Not that I can recall," Timbrook agreed.

"Are you thinking a fire caused the sinking?" Eva asked.

"There is no record of any fire—so no—but the timber is singed, which indicates a combustible heat source, albeit temporary. A fire would char the wood, rather than generate superficial discoloration. The pulverized inset dark matter is also peculiar."

"How do you know all this? I thought you were a Marine Biologist." Eva asked in awe.

"My dad was a captain in the Los Angeles Fire Department. One of his duties was arson investigation. He taught me a lot about fires and ignition sources."

"So, we have a one hundred and sixty-year-old mystery," laughed Timbrook.

"It appears so," Kurt said with a twinkle in his eye.

After saying good night to Eva and Timbrook, Kurt returned to the family room, retrieving the last piece of *Scott* wood held by Timbrook. Using a Buck knife, he scraped off tiny fragments of blacken material onto a Kleenex, depositing the specks into a Ziploc plastic bag.

Tomorrow, after the sea lion necropsy, he would begin a forensic odyssey back in time, employing sophisticated twenty-first century lab equipment to help solve what now seemed a maritime riddle—the real reason for the sinking of the *S.S. Winfield Scott.*

7

Matthew Sedrak, M.D., was thirty-five, a tad under six feet, one hundred and seventy pounds, with curly blond hair, eyes the color of spring bluegrass, tanned squared face, delicate hands, and an upbeat temperament. His sunny disposition was partially due to his early morning ritual of riding the waves at Surfer's Point in Ventura for at least an hour before heading to work—the curling waves his tension releaser—nature's gift to a stressed out hospital neurologist. Single for five years, the product of a failed marriage doomed from day one—doctors should never marry doctors—fortunately kid-less, he lived in a two-bedroom condominium directly across from Surfer's Point, considered one of the premier surfing spots in all of Southern California. Instead of one insanely crowded point break it had upwards of seven—strung out over a half-mile of coastline—which mercifully thinned out the crowds for each peak. Today the conditions had been pristine, with a pumping overhead south swell generating gut-wrenching hollow tubes. For a surfer, life could not get any better.

Returning back to his condominium refreshed and relaxed, Dr. Sedrak quickly showered, shaved, and then slipped on his hospital garbs—starched white pants and a light blue wrap-around gown—his name embroidered in black free-style script on his upper left pocket. He then jumped into his Fuji white, super-charged Range Rover, his indulgent reward after his divorce, and travelled on winding side streets to Ventura County Community Hospital, the short jaunt just minutes from his house, stopping first for his pick-me-up coffee on the way. A 60's era rock and roll song surged through the Harman/Kardon 720 watts digital surround sound system, the haunting melody concerning a 'nightmare come true' still stuck in his head as he sauntered through the front foyer of the hospital.

His ten-hour shift began at 7:30 a.m., and his *nightmare come true* was a wacked-out patient that lay sedated and horizontal in room 302, his arms and legs tightly bound by soft restraints affixed to his sanatorium bed.

Dr. Sedrak was Board Certified in Neurology through the American Board of Psychiatry and Neurology, with an added qualification in Clinical Neurophysiology and Neurorehabilitation. His college education began at the Massachusetts Institute of Technology. He double-majored, obtaining a Bachelor of Arts degree in Biology, and a Bachelor of Science degree in Chemistry, graduating Summa Cum Laude. He next attended Medical School at Harvard University, graduating Cum Laude. He then returned to his home state of California, performing his Residency in Neurology and Psychiatry at UCLA Medical Center. In addition to his medical work at Ventura County Community Hospital, he also moonlighted two nights a week as an Assistant Clinical Professor of Neurology at UCLA School of Medicine.

The twenty-nine-year-old male patient identified as Keith Merkel, arrived at the hospital two days ago. He was transported by ambulance after having been tasered by a police officer, his spouse of five years fearing for her life. The normally mild-mannered, laid-back, peace-loving manager of the local *Organic Garden's* health food store, had, over a period of six weeks, become increasing psychotic, culminating in an attack upon his wife, snarling and baring his teeth, like a rabid dog infected with end-stage rabies. Fortunately, the astute spouse had a container of pepper spray, which she emptied into her husband's face, sufficiently disorienting him until the police arrived. In spite of the disabling pepper spray he still had to be tasered—his uncontrolled ferocity almost bestial in nature.

During the past two days, Dr. Sedrak had subjected Keith Merkel to a litany of tests, starting with a comprehensive neurological exam, then x-rays and a CT scan to rule out any potential skull fracture or subdural hematoma. He then underwent a full-body bone scan to look for invasive cancerous tumors, an EEG to measure any abnormal electrical brain activity, an MRI cross-sectional study of the white and gray matter of Keith's brain, and a spinal tap with a large gauge needle to withdraw cerebral spinal fluid. As an afterthought he also ordered a tonsil biopsy. The numerous tests had produced some very interesting, and disturbing, results. Unfortunately, during the shadowy hours of the night Keith Merkel had lapsed into a coma, his breathing labored, his blood pressure dropping rapidly, his prognosis bleak.

Dr. Sedrak was scheduled to meet with Keith's wife, Desiree, at 9:00 in the morning to discuss the various test results, his diagnosis, and now with the change in Keith's condition, to convey some dismal news. The one piece absent from the perplexing medical puzzle was the patient's prior medical and personal history. The complexities of dealing with the initial emergency, along with Desiree's involvement in a potential spousal-abuse criminal probe, had temporarily delayed gathering the pertinent background information. He now planned on reviewing the missing historical data in chronological detail, particularly since the National Center for Disease Control, located in Atlanta, Georgia, wanted it peformed as soon as possible.

Desiree entered the hospital conference room wearing a 70's era fish-net white cotton dress which hung to her calves, her foot-wear, psychedelic hued flip-flops. Her neck was adorned with a showy bluish-green jade necklace, carved in the image of a fiery sun, her wrist and ankles also arrayed with jadestone set in polished silver, the jewelry jangling as she walked. She was twenty-seven, attractive in a down-to-earth way, with golden-brown eyes, five foot three, one hundred pounds, with unkempt long blond hair decorated with pink and white Hawaiian plumeria flowers, whose heady fragrance filled the room. She worked as a masseuse, specializing in deep-tissue Swedish-style massages. As Desiree sat down in a beige, fabric-covered accent chair, she patted her eyes with a Kleenex. Dr. Sedrak noted that her eyes were streaked red from crying so he waited patiently for her to begin. He sat across from her behind a Rosewood writing desk, a yellow legal pad at the ready for note taking. Desiree spoke first.

"He didn't know what he was doing," she said tearfully. "That's what I told the police officer. It's obvious . . . something is terribly wrong with him. That's not the man I married—he's completely changed—something dreadful has happened to him."

"I know," said Dr. Sedrak sympathetically, "the test results validate your suspicions."

"And what do they reveal?" she asked, leaning forward, concern written into her furrowed brow.

Squirming in his chair, Dr. Sedrak said, "Before I divulge the findings, I first have to ask some background questions."

"Why?"

"It's important for my final diagnosis. What you know about Keith will hopefully resolve some relevant medical questions related to his unusual condition."

"What do you want to know?"

"To start—when did you first notice any peculiar symptoms?"

"About six weeks ago," she said. "My husband believes that the earth is bathed in celestial energy, and that your positive attitude reflects the amount that you are tapping into. It's a New Age spiritual thing—keeping your Karma filled to capacity. When he exhibited signs of depression and anxiety, I knew something was wrong."

"Did you ask what was bothering him?"

"Yes. Was it work? Was it me? Was it money issues? He had no answer. He then started having memory lapses. He'd forget where his car keys were, what day it was, why he went to the grocery store, what to buy, things like that. At work, it was even worse. As manager of a health food store, people relied on him. He neglected to order stock, double-booked employees, failed to pay bills, and even left the store unlocked one night in addition to not setting the burglar alarm. Two weeks ago his employer forced him to take an involuntary leave of absence. I tried to take him to a holistic doctor, but he refused to go, becoming verbally angry at the suggestion."

"In the last month-and-a-half," Dr. Sedrak asked softly, "did he physically abuse you?"

"Thank God, no!" Desiree said firmly. "Two days ago, even in his maniacal state, he did not actually strike me. Violence was not a part of his genetic makeup. He abhorred war, despised the death penalty, and was a life-long member of PETA. Rather than having children and burdening the earth, we chose to adopt unwanted dogs destined for a cruel death. So far we've rescued three mixed breeds from the county animal shelter."

Dr. Sedrak wrote as she spoke. "What other symptoms did you observe?"

"Social withdrawal from all his friends; refusing to leave the house, and living like a hermit. He became clumsy, his balance way off. He ran almost blindly into objects, fell several times, stumbled over household steps, had difficulty shaving, and basically couldn't do anything that involved hand-eye coordination. In the last week he had bizarre mood swings, involuntary muscle contractions, was fatigued in spite of ten hours of sleep, slurred his speech, and was incontinent. In the final days he seemed to be hallucinating—seeing things that didn't exist, and accusing me of all sorts of sordid behavior."

"Why didn't you call an ambulance, or take him to a medical doctor?" Dr. Sedrak wondered.

"Because everything happened so fast," Desiree said defensively. "And he deteriorated so quickly—and our holistic beliefs—we're not big fans of modern medicine and drug-toting doctors."

"I can understand," Dr. Sedrak said kindly, "too many people take too many drugs. There is wisdom in exploring natural remedies."

"Thank you," Desiree said with a thin smile.

"Now—regarding Keith's medical history," Dr. Sedrak persisted, "I have a series of questions that I need to ask."

"I'll tell you what I know."

"Has your husband ever had brain surgery?"

"No."

"Ever received human growth hormones?"

"No—"

"Blood transfusion?"

"No—"

"Organ transplant?"

"No—"

"Injected bovine insulin into his body at any time?"

"No—not that I'm aware."

"Travelled to England or France?"

"No . . . wait a minute . . . Yes."

"Which country?"

"What difference does it matter?—England—when he was a kid."

"How old?"

"Nine or ten."

"How long was he in England?"

"About two weeks, he was on vacation with his parents. I've seen the pictures. He loved that country. Why are you asking these types of questions?"

"You'll understand shortly. Did he eat English beef while on vacation?"

To Dr. Sedrak's surprise, Desiree laughed hysterically. After a minute or two she calmed down, blowing her nose into a Kleenex. "Beef, you want to know if Keith ate beef while in England. Number one, why would I know? Number two—I do know— Keith and his parents are hard core, dyed-in-the-wool, Vegans. They've been vegetarians their entire life and raised Keith in the same beliefs and practices. My husband wouldn't touch any animal-based food product. The only exception is fish, much to the disapproval of his parents. He's somewhat anemic, and needed the extra iron that fish provides. He eats only humanely raised fish that is never tortured by a hook. As for me, I hate the smell and taste of fish, and won't have anything to do with it."

"You're certain about this?" Dr. Sedrak inquired with a bewildered tone.

"Absolutely," Desiree confirmed.

"How often does he eat fish?"

"Probably four times a week. His store sells it. *Organic Garden's* health food market is Ventura County's exclusive distributor of farm-raised fish from *West Coast Seafood & Aquaculture.* You've heard of entrepreneur Karl Goebbel—the oil to fish-platform's guy? It's his offshore based business that my husband acquires his fish from."

"So—no hot dogs, no burgers, no prime rib, no steaks, no tacos, and no beef-related products—ever?" Dr. Sedrak asked again.

"I already told you—No. Why do you care so much about beef?"

"Variant Creutzfeldt-Jakob disease."

"What the hell is that? Is that what my husband has?" said Desiree anxiously.

"You've heard of mad cow disease? It's the same disease, different name," Dr. Sedrak replied gravely. "And yes, I'm sorry to say, that's what your husband is suffering from. The battery of neurological tests has regrettably confirmed that diagnosis."

"Is he dying?" Desiree asked nervously.

"I don't know." Dr. Sedrak lied.

"What did the tests reveal?" Desiree asked hopefully.

In a sterile-like voice, Dr. Sedrak responded. "He has no skull fracture, no subdural hematoma, and no signs of cancer. The EEG showed a characteristically abnormal electrical brain pattern. The MRI irrefutably found spongiform encephalopathy throughout the gray and white matter of his brain. This sponge-like or Swiss cheese appearing condition occurs when the brain is severely riddled with holes. The spinal tap found the presence of prion proteins in the spinal fluid. These defective proteins don't exist in a healthy individual. Immunostaining of the tonsil biopsy also revealed the presence of prion proteins. Your husband is unequivocally suffering from mad cow disease, probably caused from his consumption of English cuisine laced with bovine spongiform encephalopathy, albeit, unknowingly. Perhaps it was in his soup, or stew, or chowder, or in a spicy sauce. The possibilities are endless. At the time he was in England the disease was spreading rapidly throughout the entire country."

"But that was over twenty years ago," Desiree observed bitterly. "Are you telling me that it can lay dormant for decades?"

"In certain cases, yes," Dr. Sedrak said professionally.

With a sudden look of panic mixed with dread and in a quivering voice, Desiree whispered, "Is it contagious?"

"No—there are no studies which suggest that it is communicable," Dr. Sedrak assured her. "You have to eat the actual flesh of an infected animal before you can acquire the disease."

Looking relieved, Desiree stood up. She walked toward the only window in the small conference room and stared at a large number of people entering and exiting the hospital: adults, children, hospital staff, and even a golden retriever therapy dog. She spun around in a tight circle scanning the blank walls. She nibbled at her fingernails. She ran her hands through her golden locks, fluffing her hair. She straightened her dress. She noticed a pen on the floor, picked it up, rolled it between her fingers, and then placed it upon Dr. Sedrak's desk. She checked the time on her watch. She gazed at the closed door, her constitution suddenly changing.

"I want to see my husband, *now*," Desiree demanded.

"Of course," said Dr. Sedrak compassionately.

They entered the hallway. The corridor was narrow, the walls painted sky blue, a color purposely chosen to convey hope. Nurses, doctors, staff, patients, and family members all wandered by, speaking in hushed voices, careful to avoid disturbing the occupants cloistered in cell-like rooms. Keith Merkel's room was at the far end of the hallway.

As they approached the room, Desiree noticed the change immediately. The perpetually opened entryway to Keith's room was now closed, its façade plastered with infectious disease warnings, admittance limited to authorized medical personnel only. Dr. Sedrak was the first one to reach the door, and like a gentleman, opened it for Desiree. She stepped into the sanitized room. An alarm abruptly sounded. Loud, mournful, a wailing pitch to its feverish melody, disconcerting in its affect. Dr. Sedrak sprinted past Desiree, stopping in front of both the heart and brain monitors, the green-backed LED screens flat-lined, the pencil thin black oscillations morbidly straight against the equator of each machine.

Other medical personnel bolted into the room. Two nurses, an older man who loudly announced that he was a cardiologist, a resident physician, and a strikingly tall, all white clad surgeon.

Desiree found a corner and hid. Medical confusion reigned. Orders were barked. The soft restraints were removed from Keith's arms and legs. An AED machine was rushed into the dwindling space. The electrical sizzle of it powering up pervaded the room. The 'All Clear,' and then the flopping dead fish motion as it discharged its energy directly into Keith's heart. Two more times it fired up, each time more electrically robust than the last, and two more times Keith spasmodically convulsed upon his hospital bed. After the third vain attempt, a calming, pensive voice arched itself above the hum of the machines. "It's okay—we've done all that we can—let's close it down." A psychological shift occurred. No more nervous tension. Machines were turned off. A dispirited silence settled over the area. A cotton white sheet was drawn over Keith's body. As quickly as they arrived, like lemmings, they darted back out into the sanctity of the hallway and down the meandering passageways of the hospital. Only Dr. Sedrak remained. He noticed Desiree hiding in the corner, drawn up into a fetal position, moaning a sorrowful whimper.

He ambled over to where she laid curled up like a little child. He tenderly lifted her off the floor and into a standing position, and then wrapped his arms around her. "I'm so sorry," he said, and meant every word. Sobbing, she held onto her comforter, a tiny light in a darkening room, a momentary pause in a day that had only just begun. Dr. Sedrak's cell phone rang. He checked the number. The CDC was calling. They would have to wait. A patient was in need of care.

8

The fifteen-inch diameter wall-mounted clock located on the south side of the Pathology Lab, with its lush tropical rainforest luminescent background, displayed the time as ten thirty-three.

"Are you all ready to slice and dice?" Kurt said aloud as he approached Eva from her blindside. Eva was decked out in a white lab coat over her Levi straight-leg blue jeans, and had her hair pulled tightly back in a ponytail. She was bent over and visually assessing a female sea lion carcass that lay sprawled out on a shiny stainless steel examination table.

"You're three minutes late," she scolded, "and since when does a Ph.D. in Marine Biology, and the Senior Project Scientist, refer to a necropsy as a Freddie Kruger *Nightmare on Elm Street* slash event?"

"When the subject of our investigation aspired to make a victim of today's resident pathologist," replied Kurt chivalrously.

"Thanks," said Eva, "for your support. This is one postmortem I'm not overly sentimental about. With some departed animals, I feel guilty about putting a knife to their lifeless bodies, especially when I look into their desolate eyes, but our rogue demon here, I think not."

"That's what I wanted to hear," Kurt said. "I assume yesterday's malignant sea lion spooks have all been expelled?"

"Yes—they've all left," laughed Eva. "Fortunately, I'm one tough lady who's always been successful at quickly working through my mental bruises."

"I have no doubt," Kurt admitted, as he proceeded to the opposite side of the three-foot high examination table. The door into the Pathology Lab suddenly swung open, and a young man with a two-day old beard, loose-fitting polyester pants, and a Hawaiian shirt, moseyed in.

"Good morning Dr. Nichols," the man said.

"Hi Brandon," Kurt answered, and then introduced Brandon to Eva as neither had met. Continuing Kurt said: "Brandon Kagan is our in-house cerebral chemist with two Ph.D.'s in chemistry. The first doctorate he achieved in Organic Chemistry and the second in Physical Chemistry. The wiz kid earned his degrees from Stanford University and all before the age of twenty-three. We were lucky to snag him."

"The promise of unlimited scuba diving solidified the deal," Brandon said with a slight grin.

"A vow we intend to uphold." Kurt then slipped his right hand into his front pants pocket retrieving a small Ziploc baggie, which he passed to Brandon.

Gawking at the minuscule quantity of black material, Brandon commented. "So this is what you called me about—that you wanted analyzed, *el pronto*."

"Is it enough?"

"Are you kidding," said Brandon, "a pin-head amount would be sufficient. You're talking Mr. Chemist here. Any thoughts on its composition?"

"No clues from me," said Kurt. "I want your own independent analysis as to its elements."

"With my avant-garde scientific machines, not a problem," Brandon said boastfully.

"How long will it take?" Kurt asked.

"Less than two hours."

"That's great! We'll still be here—so return back to the Pathology Lab when you're finished."

"Sounds like a plan," Brandon acknowledged. As he exited the lab he said to Kurt and Eva, "Have fun dissecting your seal."

After a brief pause, Eva said to Kurt. "What was that about?"

"Remember the charred pieces of *Scott* wood from last night? After you and Timbrook left I scraped a tiny portion of the blackened substance into a Ziploc. Upon waking up this morning I immediately texted Brandon asking if he could run some tests on it, and he said Yes. One of my leisurely pursuits is the love of a great mystery. The *Scott* wood fits that category. I'm curious to see what Brandon's investigation reveals, autonomous from any external enlightenment."

"Based upon his scholarly credentials, and his avant-garde scientific machines," Eva said putting her hand on her hip and smiling, "you'll have your answers by twelve-noon."

"I hope so. It's either something exhilarating—or boring coal dust or black dirt that somehow became embedded in the wood after the accident."

Redirecting Kurt's attention back to their subject matter, Eva asked amusedly. "Well, Mr. Sherlock Holmes, since you love enigmas, do you think it would be incumbent on us to ascertain what mysterious secrets our beloved sea lion is concealing, or is that too mundane a topic?"

"No—not at all—haul out the chainsaw and start ripping."

"Sorry, no chainsaw today," said Eva with a devious smirk. "We'll first start with a comprehensive surface examination, then measurements, and finally the dastardly scalpel, hacksaw, and meat scissors, which should satisfy your lust for carved-up flesh."

Listening to Eva, Kurt had to smile. His daughter was right; she was a lady with a lot of spunk. *Nothing wrong with that*, he thought. "I'm here to help," he said congenially, "tell me what to do." He knew that those nine special words were like music to a woman's ears.

"You can begin by donning your latex gloves and slipping into a lab coat," Eva commanded, taking charge immediately. "I would hate to see your stylish clothing stained with sea lion juices."

"So would I," Kurt said, as he obediently followed Eva's instructions.

Eva then pushed a black button attached to the examination table, which activated the overhead high-definition camcorder. All necropsies were digitally recorded. To Kurt and to the camcorder, Eva said, "Prior to the lab employees positioning the sea lion on the examination table, I had them weigh it. The roughly five-year-old tan-colored female California Sea Lion tipped the scales at one hundred and thirty-eight pounds. A healthy adult should weigh approximately two hundred and twenty-five pounds. The subject sea lion was severely underweight, gaunt, with thinning blubber, and penetrating ribs."

Using a waterproof fabric measuring tape, and with Kurt helping, Eva continued. "The body length is four-feet-six inches with a girth of two-feet-eight inches."

Eva then strapped on a headset with a LED lighted magnifying loop. "Employing a 5x magnifying loop the exterior carcass is systematically inspected for injurious lesions, hair loss, or scars. The mid-portion of the skull contains a singular puncture wound created by a large diameter spear shaft."

Utilizing a pencil-thin stainless steel measuring device, Eva first checked the depth of the perforation before continuing with her evaluation. "The gash is four inches deep. The cause of death is presumed to be traumatic brain damage. Further exploration of the sea lion corpse reveals patches of pink skin, indicating substantial hair loss. A cursory appraisal of the entire carcass does not demonstrate any other visible scars, trauma, or external signs of infectious diseases."

Interrupting Kurt said, "You missed a minor nick." He then pointed to a tiny rent in the fur located near the left shoulder area.

"You're right," Eva said. "Good eyes." She then nudged her measuring device into the slanted rift. "Wow, this injury goes deep." The device stopped at eight inches. She tapped it several times against whatever object was impeding its forward movement.

"What do you think?" Kurt asked.

"Something solid is definitely down there," Eva insisted. "Hand me my scalpel." She then made an incision following the path of the descending fissure, until she arrived at its termination point. Decomposition fluids and blood exuded into the cleaved flesh, obliterating her view. With her gloved right hand she probed the open gash, her fingers foraging blindly, squeezing tissue, rummaging through muscle, searching stealthily, until with a victorious smile, Eva said "Yes," and then quickly withdrew her hand.

"What did the Easter egg hunt elicit?" Kurt mused.

"This," Eva said proudly, holding up a blood-soaked, marble sized lump of lead. She wiped it off with a paper towel.

The object was deformed on one side, like a miniature mushroom cap. "A bullet," Kurt said surprised.

"Small caliber," Eva confirmed, "probably a fifty-grain, .22 caliber projectile."

"Glad you know your ammunition."

"Blame it on a forensic class during my undergraduate studies. We conducted research on all types of ammo and their deformation properties after impact."

"Could the bullet wound be the smoking gun behind the sea lion's aberrant behavior?" Kurt suggested.

"Cute metaphor," Eva said. "But no. It only pierced the blubber and muscle tissue. It never impacted any vital organs. Although painful and clearly uncomfortable, it was not life-threatening."

"So—an angry fisherman shoots a marauding sea lion—a familiar spectacle in California coastal waters," Kurt postulates, "injuring the animal, but not provoking its lunacy."

"Excellent summation of the facts thus far," Eva concurred. "However, as they say in meditation classes, *the answer lies within.* Our explanation still lies concealed within this lumbering beast. It's time to do some serious cutting."

Quickly and efficiently, Eva carved open the carcass with a nine-inch scalpel along the ventral midline. Internal organs were inspected methodically for lesions and infectious diseases. Tissues were sampled for virology, parasitology, bacteriology, the blubber for toxicology, and the skin for genetics. The reproductive tract was dissected out and examined grossly. The uterine horns were opened and sifted for signs of pregnancy, which were negative. The mandible was dissected out using the hacksaw, tagged, and macerated to remove the teeth, which were prepared for an exact age determination. The meat scissors were then used to open the stomach, with the fetid contents flushed into a 1 mm sieve for straining. Relatively undigested material was set aside. Eva was startled at what they discovered.

"For an emaciated creature, her stomach was amazingly full," Eva reported.

Surveying the complement of partially dissolved sea critters, Kurt said audibly, "Dismembered squid bodies, squid beaks, fish heads, fish eyeballs, fish bones, red tuna crabs, and numerous juvenile fish, some swallowed whole, and others shredded into indistinct chunks. And lastly—an adorable adolescent garibaldi still vividly orange and the mutilated head of its precious mother—torn off by our feisty sea lion on live television."

Remaining strong, Eva said, "It's odd for a sea lion to be feasting on a mixed variety of young game fish, particularly since their normal diet consists of squid, mackerel, sardines, and anchovies."

Utilizing a small water hose, Kurt rinsed off the digestive mucous from the unscathed juvenile fish. "I'll be damned," he said, "you're right—fingerling white seabass, immature tuna, and ten-inch salmon fry—a smorgasbord of seafood. This seafaring gourmet had expensive taste."

"Where in the world would a sea lion devour such an assembly of delicacies in our localized ocean environment?" Eva wondered.

Chuckling out loud, Kurt exclaimed—"Oil platforms! She was dining on hatchery raised fish from our nearby fish farms. That also explains why she was shot. They're not too fond of seals stealing *their* fish."

"*Their fish,*" Eva declared, "apparently did nothing toward improving her scrawny physique. I think I'll have the farm-raised fish tested for anything virulent."

"Like what?" Kurt asked.

"Human introduced diseases, toxins, or pathogens that might have neurologically affected the sea lion."

"Interesting path; what's next with our eviscerated sea lion?"

"Removal of what's left of its brain and then we're done," said Eva. "You're daughter's borehole has complicated the process."

"Next time I'll tell her to miss," Kurt said mischievously.

"That's okay, I'll work around it," Eva said with a thin smile.

Utilizing the fine-tooth blade of the hacksaw, Eva gingerly sawed through the thick bony structure, completing a circular one-quarter inch deep cut. She then lifted the skull cap off as one complete unit, exposing the grayish-white spaghetti brain. Wielding a petite scalpel she severed the fibrous spinal cord, freeing the brainstem, cerebellum, and large cerebrum from the spine. Cupping her hands, she then slid them underneath the unfettered brain, and gradually raised the gray matter out of its protective cradle, gel-like slime oozing from her gloves, and placed it in a round plastic Tupperware food container.

"Ceviche anyone?" Kurt joked.

Ignoring Kurt's attempt at humor Eva remarked, "Peculiar looking brain. The texture is all wrong. It should be nice and firm. It's too cushiony, too springy."

"Hand me the 100x magnifying loop," Kurt requested. After strapping the headset on, and turning on the LED light, Kurt meticulously examined the brain, particularly the right and left cerebral hemispheres of the cerebrum.

"What do you see?"

"Lesions," Kurt whispered, "lots of porous lesions. It looks like sponge cake. The structural changes are certainly abnormal, consistent with a disabling degenerative disease. You need to take a gander at this." Kurt then removed the headset and handed it to Eva.

Eva took her time, scrutinizing every square inch of the brain. "Wow," she said, and then added, "this is amazing, awesome," and then in a hushed tone she concluded, "this is unnatural, awful, and dreadful." After completing her examination she removed the headset.

"We now know why the creature was deranged," Kurt explained, "a brain garbled with pestilence."

"Any idea what it is?"

"Off the top of my head—no. I've never seen or heard of a sea lion with this type of brain-wasting malady."

"What do you mean by *wasting*?" Eva questioned.

"The brain is enfeebled—the condition obviously requiring time to develop—especially with the amount of debilitated tissue."

"What about a neurological infirmity known as Chronic Wasting Disease, which is presently afflicting deer, elk, and moose in fourteen of our states—is that something we should consider?" Eva proposed.

"Are you suggesting Chronic Wasting Disease as the cause of the sea lion's dementia?" Kurt said incredulously. "Those are land animals. They're all members of the deer family, not sea creatures. Inter-species transmission is farcical. I'm not aware of any sea lions comingling with deer, elk, or moose, where the likelihood of transmission might even occur."

"Just a thought," Eva said shrugging her shoulders.

"Is there a test that can irrefutably resolve the issue?" Kurt asked conciliatorily.

"Yes," responded Eva, "a histopathological brain tissue microscopic study. It will unequivocally answer the question. In addition, it'll provide a definitive diagnosis of whatever scourge was tormenting our sea lion."

"How long does it take?"

"A few days," Eva replied.

"Patience was never my best virtue," Kurt lamented. "Please keep me updated. Hopefully, whatever the diagnosis, it's not contagious, and our wayward sea lion was the only harbinger of this crippling disorder."

"That would be gratifying news," Eva agreed, as she turned off the camcorder, the necropsy having reached its conclusion.

Eva and Kurt then began the tedious task of cleaning up, separating out those items that required further testing, from those items that would be carbonized in the two thousand-degree incinerator, including the bulk of the sea lion carcass, which would be reduced to a cupful of ashes in the infernal heat. At precisely twelve noon Brandon Kagan re-entered the Pathology Lab, carrying a folded piece of paper.

"How goes the Necromanglers?" Brandon asked with a sardonic smile.

"Necromangler," Eva repeated quizzically, as if it were a term derived from ancient Babylon.

"Someone who abuses a corpse," Brandon replied. "It's from a delightful song. I assumed you've heard it."

"A sea lion is not a human corpse, it's an animal," corrected Kurt, "and our *abuse* was for scientific purposes only. And no, I haven't had the privilege of suffering through it."

"Fortunately, neither have I," added Eva.

"Remind me to text you the link so that you can have that opportunity," said Brandon.

"The e-mail is on its way," quipped Kurt, and then asked, "Are those the test results?" referring to the solitary piece of paper that Brandon was carrying.

"This," said Brandon, who shot a fleeting glance toward Kurt, and then irritably refolded the document. "Interesting test results; it would help in my brilliant analysis if I knew where the substance originated from."

"You do like your job?" Kurt teased.

"I anticipated that type of pithy response," Brandon said dejectedly. "However, if you require my enlightened expertise in the future please do not hesitate to grovel."

"You're number one on my list," Kurt said. "So, what did you find?"

"Before I can answer that question," Brandon replied, "I have to briefly explain the complexity of the chemical extraction process so that you can appreciate my drudgery."

Kurt sighed. "I'm all ears."

Brandon addressed Kurt and Eva as if they were his students. "The black residue sample that you provided was analyzed using the latest technology currently on the market. It's called solid phase micro-extraction combined with gas chromatography, which focuses on the chemical compounds present in the material. Every residue particle, no matter how small, contains signatures of every element in that specimen, which the extraction process can detect. After extraction, the gas chromatograph coupled with a nitrogen phosphorus detector is then used to separate and identify the analytes. If everything is functioning properly, the signature elements are identified, which then allows us to put a physical name to the mysterious substance."

"And was everything operating correctly?" Kurt asked.

"Of course," Brandon bragged. He casually flipped open the folded piece of paper. "The test identified four signature elements in your residue sample, which were then broken down into their actual percentage amounts. The four chemical compounds were—seventy percent potassium nitrate, fourteen percent softwood charcoal, sixteen percent sulfur, and a trace of potassium sulfide."

"I'm a Marine Biologist not a chemist," Kurt reminded Brandon, "please illuminate."

"Black powder," replied Brandon smugly, "used as gunpowder or blasting powder. And for your inquiring mind, potassium sulfides are *only formed* when black powder is burned. Your specimen was derived from a fiery explosion. I would love to know the source of your sample, but I humbly leave that titillating bit of information to your discretion."

"Thank you for your excellent work," Kurt said, "and thanks for respecting my need for confidentiality, but I'll handle it from this point forward." Kurt was about to dismiss Brandon, when Eva interposed.

"Brandon," began Eva in an alluring voice, "I have another wonderful mystery for you to delve into, very perplexing and unimaginably formidable, which will require all of your wisdom, expertise, and acumen. The question is . . . are you up for it?"

Kurt's eyebrow's spiraled upwards. *Talk about butter and flattery*, he thought. This woman knows how to massage a man into action through manipulation of the male ego.

"You know I'm a pushover for honest adulation, puffery, and excessive fawning," Brandon said whimsically. "I see that you speak the truth. My services are therefore at your command." He performed a half-bow in Eva's direction.

Laughing, Eva said, "Much obliged kind sir." She then handed Brandon two Tupperware containers. The first held the sea lion's brain, the other, juvenile white seabass, tuna, and salmon. "Please run a histopathological tissue microscopic study on the brain. We need a diagnosis of its neurological disorder as soon as possible. With the fish—please test for viruses, parasites, bacteria, toxins, poisons, unusual chemicals, diseases, and contagions."

"I know the fish came from the sea lion's stomach—why the interest?" Brandon asked.

Responding, Kurt said, "The fish, in all probability, originated from the fish farms located at the converted oil rigs. The sea
lion was feasting on hatchery-raised fish. Apparently the young
fish had either an escape route, or the sea lion had access to the
massive grow-out pens. Eva wonders if there's a connection between the sea lion's sickness and the farm-raised fish. It's a wild
hunch, but worth a shot."

"Sounds intriguing," Brandon said. "I'll run the tests and let
you know. Time-wise, it should take about three days. I'll upload
the conclusions into the lab's mainframe computer." Brandon
then said his goodbyes and exited the Pathology Lab.

Once Brandon was out of hearing range, Eva said excitedly,
"Black powder on the *Scott*, with an explosion, splintered planks,
and no official word in any of the history books or maritime records. I'd say your leisurely pursuit of a good mystery has miraculously sprouted wings and taken on a life of its own."

Kurt grinned adventurously as he listened to Eva. The wheels
were already churning within his subconscious. Tomorrow he
would begin to put those rotating discs into exploratory motion.
He turned to Eva, "Tell me about that black powder again?" Eva
smiled as she reached out and tenderly squeezed his hand, "If I
were you," she began, "I would commence my investigation by—"

9

"It's time," shouted Mischa to Jake, urging her semi-slumbering brother to speed up the preparatory process. "One more minute," Jake replied irritably, which Mischa knew from past experiences meant at least three. Teenage boys did not wake up quickly. The time was 7:05 a.m., which meant that they were already five minutes late for their agreed upon rendezvous with Timbrook at the horse stables.

"He'll leave without us," Mischa warned, although she knew her statement was false. Timbrook would wait. She just loved irking her brother. The night before they had pre-packed for their adventure, so all Jake had to do was dress, gobble down a quick bowl of cereal, and brush his teeth. At the moment he had accomplished two out of the three. She could hear the vibrating hum of the electrical tooth brush and knew that he was close to being done. He always saved his teeth for last. The door finally opened and out walked her droopy-eyed sibling.

Mischa admired her brother who was unique in a special way; he was gifted with both left and right brain attributes—scientific and creative—which was unusual for a man.

"Did you make our lunch?" Jake asked hopefully as he wiped a modicum of white toothpaste off the corner of his right upper lip.

"Maybe . . . does smoked turkey, provolone cheese, sliced to-matoes, wedges of avocado, alfalfa sprouts, on nine-grain bread, lathered with spicy chipotle mayonnaise, with two chocolate chip energy bars, an apple each, and a Snickers bar for dessert sound yummy?" Mischa replied smugly.

"You bet, and thanks," said Jake, "early mornings and I don't get along. I owe you one."

"One! That's being overly optimistic," laughed Mischa, as they exited the rear door of their house. On the back porch Mischa had placed their supplies for their day's adventure.

Jake was about to respond when the impatient whine of an agi-tated horse reminded him of the time. "I think Timbrook, and the horses are waiting," Jake said contritely.

They each quickly wiggled into backpacks specifically de-signed to hold their diving equipment, and to which had been added, one towel, lunch, and several water bottles. Today they intended to skindive at Yellowbanks, a reef located on the south-east side of Santa Cruz Island. Yellowbanks was famous for its thick kelp, abundant eelgrass beds, rocky pinnacles, and sandy shoals—a perfect habitat for the California halibut. Mischa and Jake were on a hunting expedition for the tasty flatfish, trusting Timbrook's assurances that the location was prime real estate for the fish. In addition to the backpacks, they each carried a Riffe Mid-Handle, fifty-inch speargun.

Walking at brisk pace, they made their way across a pasture flourishing with brown and green stalks of Mediterranean canary grass, past Timbrook's adobe house, and to an adjacent horse sta-ble, where Timbrook had two mustangs tethered to a bronze hitch-ing post. The larger of the two horses was a powerfully built male, smoky black in color, and clearly eager to get out on the trail. The petite female, standing calmly next to her agitated companion, had the golden coat, luxuriant white mane, and tail of a palomino.

"Say Hi to Gabriel and Aiyana," Timbrook said. "Gabriel was named after a biblical archangel, and Aiyana is an Indian word for Everblooming."

"Hello beautiful," Mischa said softly to Aiyana. She then reached into her pants pocket and retrieved eight sugar cubes. She gave four to Jake. Palms up and flat, with their fingers held close together, they fed the special treats to the horses, Mischa choosing Aiyana, and Jake, Gabriel. The animals snorted in euphoric delight, an equine's version of purring, as they nibbled on the sugary crystals.

"Smart idea," Timbrook confirmed, "you're now friends for life."

"I know nothing about horses," Jake said, "but these animals are magnificent."

"Gorgeous aren't they," said Timbrook. "I rescued them from the high deserts of New Mexico, where the Bureau of Land Management intended to euthanize them unless adopted. Mustangs are as original as our country, and are deserving of life, not a shameful death. The spiritual bond between mustangs and Indians runs deep. Santa Cruz has now become their island of salvation, and every day, in subtle ways, they communicate their appreciation for their redemptive existence."

"They talk to you?" Jake asked with a hint of sarcasm.

"Of course," grinned Timbrook, "as do the birds, trees, flowers, the wind, the waves, and all the inhabitants on our planet, both in the water and on the land, if you'll only listen. Each has its own special language."

"And that's in your Bible?" queried Mischa.

"Genesis 1:26, where God gave man dominion over every living thing that moves on the face of the earth. All animals and fish move, as do the plants, the wind, and the ocean waves; however, man's sovereign authority over all living things—that wonderful endowment by God to the human race—has been selfishly used by man as an excuse to rape and plunder our planet, which was never God's intent."

"Sounds like God should extract His heavenly paddleboard and give man a good spanking," joked Jake.

"Someday He will," said Timbrook in a barely audible whisper. After an awkward moment of silence, Timbrook continued. "I've said enough about a difficult subject. It's too early to be discussing eschatology. Hand me your backpacks and spearguns. Aiyana will be your packhorse for today's journey."

Aiyana was outfitted with a sawbuck packsaddle with two heavy duty side-by-side rectangular canvas saddlebags. The packsaddle rested on a wool saddle blanket and a saddle pad, which helped disseminate the weight of the load. Timbrook stowed the backpacks in the large canvas saddlebags. The spearguns were situated on top of the packsaddle and affixed with leather pack cinches. Jake and Mischa would be walking while Timbrook rode Gabriel. Gabriel was outfitted with an antique-looking natural-leather western saddle, two nylon hornbags, and two heavy-duty nylon saddlebags. Each nylon bag was filled to capacity; the contents unknown.

Yellowbanks was a four-mile journey from Scorpion Cove. It involved traveling southwest along Smuggler's Trail to Smuggler's Cove, and then following a rarely used footpath north to Yellowbanks. The excursion was expected to take an hour and fifteen minutes. Timbrook was their escort for the first two miles, after which he would veer off, taking an unmarked trail to Montannon Ridge, where a sacred Chumash site existed, and where his wife was buried. Jake and Mischa would continue onto the coast. At 2:00 p.m. they would meet up at the same junction, retracing their route back to the stables.

Like the veteran horse rider that he was, Timbrook mounted Gabriel as if he was twenty years of age and with a chucking sound assumed the lead while Mischa and Jake walked either parallel to Gabriel, or slightly behind the stallion, depending upon the width of the trail. Aiyana obediently brought up the rear. The pace was slow and steady, with a slight uphill incline. The morning was crisp with a chilly marine layer enveloping the island, cloaking it in obscurity.

"It should burn off by 8:30," Timbrook said aloud, referring to the dense, vaporous gray fog that clung voraciously to the earthen island.

Shivering from the sodden air, Jake murmured, "I hate the fog."

Laughing, Timbrook countered, "I appreciate the misty soup. It's one of nature's greatest blessings. It's what bathes the island in life-giving moisture when there's no rain, sustaining the flora, and all life that is dependent upon it."

"I suppose," Jake mumbled.

"Now, if you're out in a boat," added Timbrook, "it's a different ballgame, and I'm with you."

For the next ten minutes they walked in silence, the only sound the hoof beats of the plodding horses and their own footsteps. The path continued inland, cutting across the island, cleaving to an upward grade.

The trail then approached a major zigzag as they encountered ancient igneous rock that obstructed a straight passage. Clinging to the vesicular textured rocks in basketball-sized voids were Santa Cruz Island lotus plants, with light yellow flowers protruding from a base of dull-green succulent-like petals. In an area of deep shade, several spectacular Humboldt lilies bloomed, the flowers orange-yellow with dark red blotches, the sepals and petals rolled back and under, a natural ornament worthy of decorating the White House Christmas tree.

The trail then entered into a long curve as it wound its way toward the cross-point where Timbrook would then take his own route to Montannon Ridge. At 1800 feet, Montannon Ridge was the second highest mountain peak on Santa Cruz Island. At the end of the bend, they came to a flat area filled with lush green grass and an artesian spring. Timbrook halted their progress to give the horses a brief rest, a nibble of grass, and a drink of water.

Mischa sat down on a flat rock. She sipped water from a stainless steel water container. She then began picking at a small wart on the ring finger of her left hand.

Observing what she was doing, Timbrook said, "Do you want to see that wart wither and die?"

"This ugly thing," Mischa scowled, "most definitely."

"Today's your day," Timbrook said. He ambled over to a near-by ravine and disappeared into a thick clump of bushes. Within a minute he returned with a freshly cut one-foot-long stem. "It will take several applications," he advised, "but the juice from this plant will eventually kill the wart. In a week's time the wart will die and fall off." He grasped Mischa's hand, re-cut the stem, and dribbled several colorless drops onto the unsightly virus. The juice turned black upon contacting the wart.

"What type of plant?" Mischa asked.

"Poison oak."

Mischa instinctively withdrew her hand from his clutch. "Is it safe?" she asked nervously, slightly embarrassed at her timidity.

"Absolutely," Timbrook assured her. "The Chumash ethno-botanical knowledge of plants, including their medicinal value, spans thousands of years. The only pharmacy during those years was nature's own herbal remedies. Our medicine men discovered long ago that the juice from the poison-oak plant was uncommonly effective against skin cancers, warts, and other persistent sores."

"Okay, Dr. Timbrook, I'm placing my trust in you," said Mischa, as she cautiously slipped her left hand back into his grip allowing him to finish applying the oozing toxins.

Following an additional five-minute respite, and after wolfing down their energy bars, they resumed their trek. Mischa noticed that the curtain of hazy fog was incrementally dissipating, the benevolent sun dissolving the flimsy-white vapors. The trail opened up and Mischa was able to tread next to Timbrook, her new angel in the war against repulsive viruses.

"Do you ever miss the mainland?" she asked.

"Yes and no," Timbrook answered. "Certain fast food I dream about. An In-N-Out Burger is a must when I go ashore. Traffic and crime I can live without; however, the one thing that I dearly miss is the raucous howl of a pack of coyotes. Their animated out-cry of mingled feral voices makes me feel alive, and reminds me that the world is still wild and untamed. Plus, a Chumash legend asserts that a coyote named Sky Coyote is our actual father—that he watches over us, giving us food and protection. Of course that's just a myth, an interesting legend, but it does illustrate the nexus between our two species."

"Why don't you simply import a couple of coyotes like you did with the quail?" Mischa asked.

"I thought about it," said Timbrook, "but they would ultimate-ly destroy the wildlife on the island. The foxes wouldn't stand a chance nor would the thousands of nesting seabirds."

"No coyotes then," Mischa confirmed.

"Yes, only in my dreams," laughed Timbrook.

Mischa smiled at Timbrook's dream remark. In the last few days she had learned much about the Chumash way of life; its unique culture, enchanting myths, love of nature, and use of dec-orative symbols—like the teeth interwoven in Timbrook's flowing locks. "Are the teeth, braided in your hair, real?" she asked.

"Of course," Timbrook said.

"From an extinct Pygmy mammoth and saber-toothed cat?"

"Yes, but the saber-tooth cat was also a pygmy."

"I've never heard of a dwarf saber-toothed cat," Mischa said distrustfully.

"The Chumash discovered such creatures when they began populating the islands thirteen thousand years ago. The Pygmy mammoths and saber-toothed cats lived on three of the Channel Islands—Santa Cruz, Santa Rosa, and San Miguel. The genetic mutation that miniaturized the Columbian mammoths affected the saber-toothed cats in the same way, causing eventual dwarfism.

Unfortunately, the early Chumash tribes indiscriminately hunted the defenseless mammoths for food, decimating the populations on all three islands. The cats were killed by young Indians as proof of manhood. It's a disgraceful blemish on our history; as such, it is one of the main reasons why the outside world has never heard of the Pygmy saber-toothed cats that once roamed these islands. I wear their teeth out of respect and honor of their memory."

"Midget-sized saber-toothed cats—that would have been an amazing sight." Mischa said mournfully.

"Indeed," Timbrook agreed.

Jake, who had been hanging back, joined Mischa and Timbrook. At that moment Gabriel snorted loudly, with Aiyana responding in-kind igniting a one minute back-and-forth soliloquy of vociferous snickering between the two beasts. "Horse communication," said Timbrook.

When the horse clamor abated, Jake said to Timbrook, "At our dinner party the other night, you stated that you've explored every probable gravesite on this entire island searching for the tombstone of Captain Cabrillo, and I was wondering, is that really true?"

"Mainly true," Timbrook admitted. "Obviously, I've not covered every square inch of the island."

"Where have you looked?" Mischa wondered.

"In all the logical locations."

"And where are those?" Jake inquired.

Gabriel's right front horseshoe caught on an exposed root causing him to stumble. Fortunately, the horse regained its balance quickly, and continued as if nothing was amiss. "I love sure-footed mustang's," Timbrook said thankfully, as he rubbed the horse's muscular neck. "As far as locations, I've searched every square foot of every prominent promontory, headland, and spit of land that juts out to sea. If I was Captain Cabrillo and knew that I was dying, I would demand that my final resting place occupy the most prestigious and panoramic bluff over-looking the azure ocean."

"And you've scoured all of those?" Jake asked cynically.

"Yes—every possible burial site within five miles of the Chumash village of Swaxil. Swaxil is now called Scorpion Cove. Swaxil was the center of the Chumash nation. It's where Chief Librado resid-ed and where his daughter Luisa, Cabrillo's mistress and the moth-er of his son, your ancient grandfather, dwelt. Assuming Cabrillo died in Swaxil, he had to be buried nearby. I've even taken into consideration the Chumash's disdain of the Spaniards, and the re-ality that they would insist that Captain Cabrillo's grave occupy a situs a significant distance from their village."

"How unhappy were the Chumash with the Spanish?" Mischa questioned.

"The Chumash despised them at that point in time," re-sponded Timbrook. "Their foreign maladies were beginning to decimate our people. The Spanish treated the Chumash as be-neath them, raped our woman, and claimed our ancestral lands as theirs. Captain Cabrillo had worn out his welcome prior to his death."

"If what you say is correct, why would Chief Librado even per-mit Cabrillo's interment on Limuw Island?" Jake mused.

Timbrook smiled at Jake's use of the word Limuw. "Because of Luisa's relationship with the captain, and her unborn child, who was half Chumash."

"If your assumption is correct," Mischa said seriously, "then you've either failed to discover Captain Cabrillo's true where-abouts, or he's not buried on Santa Cruz Island."

"As always your logic is impeccable," Timbrook agreed.

Smiling warmly at the compliment, Mischa skipped a few steps along the trail, and then turned reflective, as a new ques-tion surfaced within her. "It's my understanding that there is a Chumash legend that states that the very first Chumash people were created on Santa Cruz Island—"

"There is," interrupted Timbrook, "it's called Rainbow Bridge."

"Okay," said Mischa thinking out loud. "Is the island of your creation—Limuw as you call it—considered holy ground, especially back in 1542?"

"In 1542...yes...the soil of Limuw was esteemed as hallowed."

Her voice edging up a notch with lucid excitement, Mischa asked, "If Limuw was deemed consecrated, set apart for the Chumash nation—would the Chumash give permission for an alien, a hostile foreigner—to be buried on their sacred island?"

Timbrook sat on his horse in contemplative silence for a short period of time before responding. "I honestly don't know. You've asked a terribly good question and one that I've not considered. All these years of searching, for a potentially non-existent grave, that's hard to swallow."

"It's just a whimsy notion," Mischa quickly added after seeing the pain on Timbrook's countenance. "Luisa and the child— those are valid reasons too."

Ignoring her remark, Timbrook said, "It may explain a lot. Maybe the folks who erected a memorial to Captain Juan Rodriguez Cabrillo on San Miguel Island were correct. Perhaps he was interned there—definitely worth investigating—I've plainly exhausted the probability of Santa Cruz Island as his final place of repose."

Gabriel suddenly came to a halt in the middle of the trail as did Aiyana. Timbrook dismounted from his horse and approached Aiyana. He unwound a ten-foot long nylon tether attached to her packsaddle.

"What's going on?" Jake asked.

"Parting of the ways until 2:00 p.m.," replied Timbrook. He handed the lead tether to Jake. "You'll need to escort Aiyana for about a quarter of a mile to prevent her from following Gabriel. After that she'll obey you without hesitation."

"I don't see any other trail for you to take," Mischa said perplexed, as she stared intently into the coastal sagebrush plants that lined the path searching for any tell-tale sign of an opening.

"The trail is purposely hidden—it's not open to the public," Timbrook said solemnly. "It is seldom traversed and takes many twists and turns before ending at Montannon Ridge, the location of a very sacred Chumash Indian site. My wife Maria is buried there as are all the former Chumash Chief Headman, going back thousands of years. If the public became aware of the site, vulture-like grave robbers would descend upon it, defiling sanctified ground, and confiscating historical treasures."

"We won't tell a soul," Jake promised. Mischa nodded her agreement.

"Thanks," Timbrook said, "you are now part of a select minority. Only a handful of individuals even know of its existence." He then eyed something on the ground and stooped down, picking up a three-inch long transparent sparkling rock, pearly white in color. "Mica," he said, "not valuable, but special in its own way. I like collecting it and creating picturesque art deco motifs from it." After showing it to Mischa and Jake he dropped it into his pants pocket.

"Is there anything else that we need to know or do before we embark on our dive adventure?" Jake asked Timbrook.

Addressing his comments to both children, Timbrook said, "Yes, when you arrive at your dive site please remove Aiyana's pack saddle and allow her to roam free." He then handed Mischa a tiny, tubular whistle. "When you're finished diving, blow this whistle, and Aiyana will magically reappear. She's been trained to respond to its piercing sound. Good luck and good hunting." He then remounted Gabriel and disappeared through a section of sagebrush that appeared as solid as an English hedge.

Mischa noted the exact spot and marked it with a flat, darkly pitted, volcanic rock. "You never know," she said to Jake, "but I trust my woman's sixth sense."

Jake gave Mischa a sarcastic *oh really* type grin while shaking his head. He then secured Aiyana's rope tether, leading the mare toward Smuggler's Cove and Yellowbanks, and a spearfishing odyssey that neither Mischa nor Jake could have anticipated.

10

It's been four days, thought Eva, *where are the test results?* Brandon Kagan had promised to upload his findings into the lab's mainframe computer within seventy-two hours. The fact that Brandon said it *should* take approximately three days was irrelevant. Her patience was wearing thin. For the fifth time in two hours Eva used her laptop computer to once again log onto the lab's Pathology website. Highlighting the *Lab Test Results* icon, Eva brought up its registry of documents, noting the most recently added items to the menu.

"Hallelujah, thank you Brandon!" she shouted, her effervescent words echoing off the cream-colored walls of her meager ten by twelve foot lab which doubled as an office. Two coral-red Lipochrome canaries, asleep inside their rainforest decorated birdcage, flitted nervously at the unexpected outburst. "Sorry," Eva said in a soothing voice, calming the songbirds down, who rewarded her with a forgiving chirp.

The report was divided into two sections. The first was titled *Sea Lion Histopathological Brain Tissue Study*; the second, *Test Results for Aquaculture Raised Fish*. The introduction contained a brief explanatory note from Brandon. "I apologize for the delay in posting my findings. I completed my investigation yesterday morning, but in an abundance of caution, and deeming it necessary to obtain a second opinion, I e-mailed the test results along with my assumptions, to a medically qualified Pathologist at the Ventura County Medical Center. His review naturally agreed with my conclusions."

Eva smiled at the use of the word *naturally*. Dr. Brandon Kagan was not one lacking in confidence. Gently touching the LED screen with her right index finger Eva quickly scrolled down to page two and the histopathological findings. Brandon's summary was concise and to the point.

"The brain tissue was processed into histological sections and placed onto glass slides where they were then examined using a light microscope and an electron microscope. Both microscopic studies confirmed the diagnosis of the sea lion's neurological disorder—a prion disease called spongiform encephalopathy. In the bovine community it's also known as mad cow disease. In deer herds it's referred to as Chronic Wasting Disease. Note: The sea lion's variety of abnormal proteinacious particles was a ninety-nine percent match to bovine spongiform encephalopathy, an epidemic that has decimated the cattle herds of Europe. In North America there are a few published reports that the brain-wasting malady has acquired a sporadic foothold in the beef industry, especially in Canada. Finally, a quick perusal of prestigious scientific journals indicates that the transmission of spongiform encephalopathy in non-ruminant livestock, such as our California sea lion, is considered genetically improbable. The primary reason: the significant lack of homology, which creates a species barrier effect preventing infection. Obviously . . . the theoretical supposition against cross-species transference is patently false."

Brandon's concluding sentence sent shivers up Eva's spine as she visualized an ocean crawling with psychotic sea lions. "Unfortunately, the more pressing question is how that transmission occurred, and how widespread is the infection?"

Visibly shaken, Eva scrolled to the next page to assess Brandon's analysis of the aquaculture game fish. "Organic fish they are not," began the chemist's critique. "The salmon, tuna, and white seabass were all infested with sea lice, undoubtedly caused by overcrowded fish pens and unsanitary conditions. Tissue examination revealed trace amounts of Emamectin Benzoate, an ingredient found in the pesticide Slice, used to treat sea lice infestations. The salmon were also suffering from a debilitating viral disease known as Infectious Salmon Anemia, which makes the flesh mushy and unappetizing. Furthermore, if this wasn't enough, I detected the colorant Canthaxanthin, a red-dye additive fed to salmon to make their flesh pink."

As Eva continued to read from the report she could feel bile rising within her esophagus at the very thought of consuming any of the tainted fish. "A sampling of the muscle meat disclosed high levels of two antibiotics—Flumequine and Oxolinic Acid—antibiotics that are not permitted in American aquaculture. Finally, histological assessment of the brain tissue on all three species, tuna, sea bass, and salmon, divulged no defective proteinacious particles, ruling out the juvenile fish as the source of the sea lion's spongiform encephalopathy. Of concluding interest were the stomach contents: a blackish brown sludge that smelled awful, like fecal matter. This paste-like mush piqued my curiosity. What were they being fed? To answer that question I performed a DNA analysis. To my surprise the predominant genetic fingerprint of the food substance was good old-fashioned beef, along with other animal-based proteins, which I haven't had time to sequence. The farmed-raised fish were therefore primarily feasting on ground-up heifers, and secondarily on bits and pieces of other unknown animals. Now, isn't that a hoot? Anyway, I thought you should know. I, for one, will never gorge on game fish cultivated by *West Coast Seafood & Aquaculture*." Eva unconsciously nodded her agreement, Brandon's insightful epicurean pronouncement ending his report.

Eva gazed intently at the computer screen, percolating Brandon's findings. She sent an e-mail thanking Brandon for his report and then forwarded it to Kurt Nichols. The severe muscle spasms radiating between her neck and shoulders meant that her emotions were in a raw state. She sat perplexed, mystified, frightened, and angry. The very likely prospect that other sea lions may be infected haunted her. She was incensed at the manner in which the aquaculture fish farms were being operated and the condition of their food product. Karl Goebbel's national media campaign had assured the consuming public that his seafood was as natural and as wholesome as the wild-caught variety. *What a fraud*, thought Eva. *How does he get away with it?* She wondered. *Where are the USDA inspectors?* She seethed. Eva was certain that a nexus existed between the aquaculture farms and the transmissible spongiform encephalopathy. A foreign prion had accomplished the impossible and crossed the species barrier. *But, what that connection was, and how it had occurred, eluded her at this precise moment.*

On a hunch she Googled *West Coast Seafood & Aquaculture* and studied their home page. A brilliantly lit turquoise-colored oil platform named Grace sparkled in a radiant glow cast by the setting sun. A one hundred foot long mural of a sockeye salmon adorned its mainland side. Eva examined numerous photographs depicting the four converted oil rigs. She sifted through the specs on each individual fish farm. She found it interesting that Gilda, Gail, and Gina were off limits to the public. Grace was their flagship operation and allowed visitors. All four oil rigs were within ten miles of Santa Cruz Island. After an hour of on-line research she smiled jubilantly. She had formulated the semblance of a plan. It was time to pay a surprise visit to Goebbel's offshore fish farms. She picked up her office telephone and speed dialed the marine lab's equipment specialist; she had a boat to reserve.

11

Kurt leaned back in his ergonomically designed tan-colored leather chair, rubbing his exhausted green eyes, coaxing them to refocus, and then sipped from a mug of coffee two hours old. Hot or cold, the liquid stimulus did its job, and awakened his cloudy brain. For the last seven hours he had cemented his derriere to his computer workstation located in the library of his house, researching every known article, report, or commentary on the wreck of the *S.S. Winfield Scott*. Looking beyond his thirty-inch computer screen and out the eastern plate glass window, Anacapa Island rose portentously from the sea, its three interconnected islands clearly visible in the late afternoon sunlight despite five miles of separation. Middle Anacapa Island, with its tangled mass of protruding volcanic rock, was the *Scott's* graveyard.

His exhaustive fact-finding mission involved sifting through numerous websites on the *Scott* incident which included the Channel Islands National Marine Sanctuary, S.S. Winfield Scott Vessel History; National Park Service, U.S. Department of the Interior, and State of California Marine Shipwreck Database; Wikipedia, the free Encyclopedia; California Diving News, which featured a lengthy article on the shipwreck; a myriad of newspaper articles circa December 1853 regarding the disaster, and of particular interest, several eyewitness accounts.

One frequently quoted passenger, Edward Bosqui, testified: "At midnight I was suddenly awakened from a sound sleep by a terrible jarring and then crashing of timbers. I hurried out onto the deck where my attention was fixed on a wall of towering cliffs, the tops of which were hidden by the fog and darkness and appeared about to fall and crush us. All around was the loud booming of angry breakers surging about invisible rocks."

Edward Bosqui's first-hand observations were typical of all the eyewitness accounts, and helped established the *official* version of the incident. That authorized rendition as understood by Kurt concluded that shortly before midnight on December 2, 1853 Captain Sean Flannigan, after having navigated the *Scott* into the Santa Barbara Channel in an effort to save time, ill-fatedly entered into pea-soup fog. The captain, believing that he had passed Anacapa Island, turned southeast in the impenetrable mist, a tragic miscalculation. The ship, within minutes, crashed bow first into an outcropping of rocks off of Middle Anacapa Island at approximately twelve knots. It then ran aground on a shallow reef tearing off its rudder. Seawater poured into the vessel's hold through two gaping fissures, causing the *Scott* to list precariously. The captain gave the order to abandon ship and the *Scott* was successfully evacuated in less than two hours. Fortunately, every passenger and crewmember survived the ordeal. Salvaged from the wreck—$800,000.00 in gold bullion, nearly all the passengers' luggage, and sacks of U.S. mail.

Infuriating to Kurt was the glaring reality that none of the informative websites or eyewitness testimonies alluded to any fire or detonation, which added to the bedeviling mystery. Even his own extensive marine library harbored a small book, twenty pages in length, on the history and demise of the *Scott*. Written by James P. Delgado, *Water Soaked and Covered with Barnacles—The Wreck of the*

S.S. Winfield Scott, the well-researched, succinct treatise, was bereft of a single word concerning any fiery explosion or conflagration on the steamer.

Kurt swiveled his chair in a half-circle and stared at the remnant pieces of charred and scorched wood that remained next to his fireplace. That wood revealed a one hundred and sixty-year-old hidden truth—confirmed by Brandon Kagan's chemical analysis—the perplexing enigma still resting in obscurity.

In a humorous follow-up telephone conversation initiated by Brandon, the sagacious chemist informed Kurt: "Oh . . . by the way . . . I believe I failed to mention during our dialogue at the necropsy lab that my analysis also revealed trace amounts of sodium chloride, commonly referred to as sea salt, and that the blacken lumber was White Oak, a timber often used in the construction of sea-going ships because of its cellular structure, which is waterproof and rot resistant. Are any of these particular facts of interest to you?" Kurt could detect Brandon's accelerated breathing through his earpiece and knew that the scientist was on a fishing expedition for additional details, the *failed to mention* purposely done, necessitating a future discussion about his findings. Kurt's only reply was, "Thank you Brandon, those supplemental facts might be of help." He then hung up. As it turned out, his marathon hours of research had revealed an interesting nugget; that White Oak, during the 1800's, was the lumber of choice for forging a ship's hull, and that the *Scott's* hull was fabricated from White Oak. Brandon's gratuitous information had proved extremely valuable; he now knew the situs of the incendiary explosion—the ship's inner hull.

Kurt, dog-tired, was about to end his Internet quest, when a revelation occurred to his enervated psyche. *The company that owned the S.S. Winfield Scott . . . does it still exist? And, what about its own internal investigation which certainly must have taken place?* With the passing of one hundred and sixty years he figured that any secrecy surrounding an onboard explosion would no longer be an embarrassment to the seagoing enterprise, and that access to its internal files would be allowed.

Through his previous studies, Kurt was aware that the *Scott* was owned by the Pacific Mail Steamship Company. For the next hour he learned all that he could about the company. His web search revealed that in 1925 it was purchased by Sydney Baron & Company. Regrettably, in 1937 the Great Depression sank the company into bankruptcy, with The United States Maritime Commission assuming control of its assets. In 1952 the remaining assets of the company were then sold to a group of investors who renamed the company, Transpacific Shipping Corporation, or TSC. In 1997 TSC merged with Singapore-based Global Asian Lines Limited, a subsidiary of Poseidon Holdings. To Kurt's pleasant surprise TSC still maintained a regional office in the city of San Francisco. The antique-looking, red-brick building pictured on the screen was located near the Port of San Francisco, at 2 Union Street—which just happened to be the identical office address as the original Pacific Mail Steamship Company—a minor miracle in Kurt's opinion, considering the passage of time. Unfortunately, TSC's home webpage failed to list any telephone number, nor was Kurt able to unearth one, even with operator help. He noted that the TSC website was last updated eight days earlier, verifying that it was still a viable business entity.

Kurt sat back in his leather chair, contemplating the color image of the TSC office. A face-to-face meeting was always more productive than an out-of-the-blue telephone call, particularly with the nature of his inquiry; besides, he was due for a mini-vacation. He loved *visiting* the city of San Francisco. The colorful ambience, the odd assortment of people, the eclectic mix of stores squeezed together along the Embarcadero, the aromatic flower boxes that silhouetted the store fronts, but most importantly, the exotic seafood at Fisherman's Wharf. Kurt envisioned feasting upon a piping hot tureen of clam chowder served in its own sourdough bread bowl, then moving on to a whole Dungeness crab steamed in its own natural juices and drenched in lemon garlic butter—all washed down with a chilled bottle of Sierra Nevada pale ale. Dessert, of course, would involve decadent morsels of San Francisco Ghirardelli chocolate, accompanied by a warm cup of frothy cappuccino, spiked with Amaretto liqueur.

Kurt shook his head, erasing his food-lust daydream. He then pulled up the Southwest Airlines website and booked a short-haul flight from Los Angeles International Airport to San Francisco International Airport, leaving at 10:00 a.m., four days hence. He next arranged for a mid-sized Hertz rental car, acknowledging by e-mail that a Ford Focus hybrid would be acceptable.

Arising from his chair the thought suddenly struck him—he had not a clue as to what he was going to say or do once he arrived at the TSC regional office—the cat-like skills of an investigative detective absent from his genetic makeup. A frown briefly sullied his visage, but then just as quickly dissolved into a presumptuous smile. He was a talented marine biologist; he would figure it out.

12

D r. Sedrak switched off the engine to his Range Rover, the front of his SUV pointing due west. He was parked in a dilapidated asphalt parking space at Surfer's Point. The car's cobalt blue digital clock blazed 5:41 a.m., the sun's warm rays just beginning to caress the ocean. He leisurely munched on several small handfuls of Trader Joe's Tropical Forest Granola, vanilla and coconut the predominant flavors. He sipped strawberry kefir from a six ounce plastic bottle. Granola and kefir, breakfast Southern California style, especially if you were a surfer.

A northwest groundswell, which had originated off the Aleutian Islands, was beginning to impact the reef–currently head high—with long period forerunners offering some larger sets, the clean workable lines allowing for some exciting corners. The shape was still a little sectiony and soft owing to the extreme high tide courtesy of a full moon. The surf would improve as the tide dropped. The winds were calm to light, flowing offshore, causing the waves to feather as they crested over. He counted five other surfers already out at the point, carving up the waves. To be number one in the line-up required paddling out at the first hint of early light, a devotional ritual he had practiced on many prior occasions. A young girl, perhaps nine, with drenched blond hair, was astride an eight foot foam surfboard in the inner splash zone, her dad positioned in the water next to her, guiding her in the fine art of surfing.

Dr. Sedrak had one hour and fifteen minutes to surf before the reality of work dictated that he exit his salty domain. Surfing purified his mind, renewed his body, and infused his internal spirit. He quickly finished off the granola and kefir and stepped out of his car, retrieving his surfboard from the surf rack attached to the roof of his vehicle. His Al Merrick designed and shaped *Big Willy* surfboard was his board of choice for today's waves. Made from a rigid polyurethane foam core layered with fiberglass cloth coated with polyester resins, seven feet in length and twenty inches wide, it provided solid flotation, paddling capability, and incredible ripping speed, allowing him to sculpt the waves with intricate twists and turns.

The beach report indicated that the water temperature was a chilly fifty-eight degrees, necessitating the wearing of a wetsuit for thermal protection. His O'Neill Psychofreak black neoprene wetsuit was state-of-the-art, providing air-firewall insulation and water wicking, keeping him warm and comfortable. It took several minutes to wiggle into his form-fitting wetsuit, and another minute to slip on his neoprene booties. Using a bar of Sticky Bumps Original Cold Surf Wax, he applied a thin layer of the tacky wax to the surface of his surfboard—the adhesive texture permitting his feet to stay planted every time he dropped down into a wave, or executed any radical turns.

After checking to make sure that his car was locked, he next crossed over a sidewalk that ran alongside the beach, down a tangle of granite boulders, and onto the sandy beach. The ocean laid fifty yards distant. Before entering the water he paused to stretch his muscles, performing various range-of-motion exercises, the therapeutic calisthenics essential at preventing cramping and muscle strains. While executing the movements he noticed that the Three Stooges, Moe, Larry, and Curly had joined the lineup.

The Three Stooges were three Pacific bottlenose dolphins. Moe was the only male, accompanied by, Larry and Curly, his twosome harem. Moe was about thirteen feet long and twelve hundred pounds. The females were significantly smaller, approximately ten feet, and eight hundred pounds. Their territory included Surfer's Point, Ventura Harbor to the South, Santa Barbara to the North, and the nearby Channel Islands. The local surfing community considered them honorary celebrities— riding the ocean swells with their earthly brethren almost every day of the year. A newspaper reporter initially coined their nicknames, writing a front-page article on their raucous vaudeville act of hobnobbing with the Ventura surfers, sliding down the waves with obvious glee, and performing aerobatic feats worthy of a circus act as they exited a crashing wave. Highly intelligent, with a brain second in size only to a human's—Moe, Larry, and Curly were extraordinary representatives of the cetacean species. Having the trio at your particular break was considered a positive omen.

The last step before Dr. Sedrak entered the ocean involved attaching an eight-foot long surf leash to his right ankle using interlocking Velcro. The leash prevented an unpleasant swim in the event he lost his surfboard in a wipeout. The leash ran from his ankle to an attachment connected to the rear portion of his board. As he was reaching down to Velcro the leash to his right ankle, the rowdy antics of Moe stopped him in mid-action.

The robust dolphin, bluish-gray, with a whitish underside, had separated itself from the females, and was catapulting its sleek, streamline body through the sea at a hell-bent rate, attempting to catch up with a surfer who had caught a shoulder-high wave. In the past, as personally experienced by Dr. Sedrak, the dolphin and the surfer would become as one with the wave, the creature bow-riding the precise movements of the surfboard, ending the harmonious ride with a spectacular twisting somersault, at times vaulting right over the surfer. Today, however, something seemed amiss, off, distorted—the sound had changed.

Moe was a tremendous communicator. His squeaks and squeals were well known. They were notes of pleasure, passionate, fervent, and full of energy, an animal in rapturous bliss, particularly when pursuing a wave. But not today; the sounds this time were high-pitched, piercing, intensely harsh, and laced with rage.

Dr. Sedrak watched as the gap between surfer and dolphin rapidly narrowed. Within a split second the surfer and dolphin became inseparable. At first everything appeared as normal, Moe weaving alongside the surfer, each mutually surfing the swell, animal and human in perfect unity. Moe then abruptly disappeared, diving beneath the wave, resurfacing a short distance behind the surfer. He then accelerated to catch up, its thick and powerful tail pummeling the water, creating its own whitewater. Twenty feet from the surfer, with a flick of its tailfin, Moe once more dove underwater, vanishing from sight.

Dr. Sedrak began silently counting the seconds awaiting Moe's reappearance and was interrupted at four. The Discovery Channel had inadvertently prepared him for this horrific point in time—a great white shark viciously attacking a seal from below—hurling the unsuspecting pinniped skyward, and clutching it in its razor-sharp teeth as it fell.

The surfer, like the pinniped, was oblivious to his fate. Moe's twelve hundred pounds of stoutly built muscle, stampeding at roughly twenty-two miles per hour, ruthlessly walloped the underside of the surfboard, launching both board and man fifteen feet straight up, the surfboard disintegrating upon impact, the man a ragdoll as he gyrated through the atmosphere like a shot bird, hitting the surface of the ocean with a sickening thud.

The four remaining surfers started shouting, screaming for help, their agitated state apparent even to Dr. Sedrak. Bravely, two surfers began paddling in earnest, in the direction of their stricken brethren, traveling side by side. The other two, perhaps fearing that a shark attack had occurred, began paddling shoreward, anxious to catch the next wave in. Unfortunately, they were in-between sets, with no significant swell on the horizon.

Dr. Sedrak stood frozen in the sand, his years of dealing with medical emergencies temporarily short-circuited, his psyche still trying to comprehend the inexplicable and sadistic assault. Fortunately, the pause in professional discipline was brief, and he began to run toward the ocean, lugging his surfboard, anxious to participate in the rescue, when the situation tragically mutated.

The two Samaritan surfers, paddling swiftly in the direction of their fallen friend, were fifty feet away when Moe began an acrobatic display—unparalleled to anything that Dr. Sedrak had previously observed. Spiraling through the air, executing somersaults one right after the other, leaping ten, fifteen feet out of the water, landing with a thunderous splash, and then repeating the same dynamic maneuvers, each time moving surreptitiously closer to the two surfers—Moe had become a dolphin on steroids.

Like déjà vu in slow motion, Dr. Sedrak foresaw what was about to occur, but was impotent to prevent it. Moe's definitive aerobatic ascent was staggering, at least twenty feet; the inverted spin, theatrical; the ear-piercing shriek, preternatural; the splashdown, villainous. Dr. Sedrak tried to scream a warning, but nothing came out. The illusion was now real. Thirteen feet of horizontal dolphin, with gravity as its benefactor, demolished the unsuspecting surfers, pulverizing them into the depths of the ocean, like a flyswatter scoring a direct hit.

Dr. Sedrak, although not religious, hastily whispered a prayer for safety. He then scoured the area of impact and noticed that the surfboards had splintered into chunks of floating debris, the two surfers' part of the flotsam, their black neoprene wetsuits buoying them up, the awful stench of silence. Moe, however, had moved off, heading north, on a trajectory that would intercept the two remaining surfers who were desperately struggling to reach the shoreline, their rapid arm strokes indicative of their desire for survival.

Dr. Sedrak stood helplessly in the sand, riveted to the unfolding spectacle. It was akin to a typical Los Angeles County high-speed police chase broadcast live—voyeuristic eyes glued to the screen, authentic death and destruction possibly seconds away, the ultimate reality show. Dr. Sedrak, with his fatalistic medical practitioner's mind had already scored another victory for the dolphin, when the Roman god of the sea, Neptune, interposed, delivering an enormous swell. Both surfers paddled furiously, catching the breaking comber, the miracle wall of water conveying the auspicious duo into the inner sanctuary of the beach. Dr. Sedrak breathed a thankful sigh of relief, surprised to discover that he had been holding his breath.

Moe, incensed at this deprivation, whipped his cylindrical body into a churning frenzy, creating his own backwash of turbulent waves, a washing machine gone haywire. Within thirty seconds he ceased his rampage and spy-hopped, using the muscles of his powerful tail to thrust his upper torso completely out of the ocean, allowing him to visually browse his immediate surroundings.

Dr. Sedrak watched fascinated, amazed by the display of bizarre intelligence. To his horror, the rotating scan ceased when the only moving, splashing, cavorting object, thrashing around in the nearby ocean, came into view—a young girl and her dad. The two were still immersed in their own world, chasing waves in the surf zone, perilously ignorant of the marauding dolphin. In the split-second that Dr. Sedrak had taken to shift his gaze from

Moe to the child, and then back to Moe, the dolphin had slipped beneath the waves, a sinister torpedo on a new mission.

Dr. Sedrak's logical brain instantly estimated the separation distance at about three hundred and fifty feet. A dolphin cruising at twenty miles per hour would travel a little over twenty-nine feet per second, taking roughly twelve seconds to swim the expanse. He had eleven seconds left. Grasping the only weapon available, his surfboard, he scrambled toward the girl and her dad, screaming, "Get out of the water! Get out of the water!" his words falling on deaf ears, the roaring thunder of the crashing beachcombers easily drowning him out.

13

Karl Goebbel hungrily smacked his lips, anticipating the predatory moment, his carnal senses blazing lustfully, savoring the sight of the curvaceous newscaster cautiously descending the gang plank from the *Lucky Lady* and stepping onto Platform Grace. He had daily fantasized about his illusory television mistress, Rachel Knox, KCLA 9's newest field journalist. His personal invitation for an exclusive interview and a private tour of his aquaculture facilities was instantly agreed to by the attractive reporter.

Rachel Knox had recently relocated from a small Miami-Dade, Florida television station to metropolitan Los Angeles, anxious to enhance her newscasting career. A former men's magazine centerfold—who astutely realized that her occupation as a nude would be short-lived—wisely embarked on a second career by majoring in Broadcast Journalism at the University of Miami. The newscaster was thirty-three years old, five feet ten and a hundred and twenty-five pounds, with platinum blond hair that swept past her shoulders in lavish curls down to her mid-back. Flawless skin, a sensuous face, sapphire blue eyes, and a mouthful of pure white teeth topped off her striking good looks. Rachel's current position as a field reporter was a necessary step toward her ultimate goal of becoming an anchorwoman. In the highly competitive

L.A. market the attractive journalist was willing to do just about anything in order to nail down an A-list story that would help advance her career.

Accompanying Rachel was a strapping man shouldering a high-definition camera, and a timorous looking soundman. Both men were dressed in casual clothes; Levi jeans, flannels, and tennis shoes. The cameraman was sporting a blue Dodger baseball hat, and the soundman was wearing a red beanie emblazoned with a Mammoth Ski Resort logo.

Rachel's outfit, however, was anything but casual. Her apparel was specifically designed to titillate the testosterone-driven male audience, feeding their insatiable appetite for seductive lady newscasters, which had a positive effect on advertising revenue.

Goebbel was aware that he was panting and salivating like a brutish dog as he watched Rachel stroll across the landing platform and up a flight of galvanized stairs. She was dressed in premium butter-soft, sleek lamb-leather pants glistening moonlight white, which fitted her like a glove emphasizing every luscious curve of her exquisite figure. Her upper body was adorned with a pout-pink sleeveless low-cut silk blouse that left nothing to the imagination. For added warmth she donned an asymmetrical lamb leather jacket designed by Elie Tahari, honey-wheat in color. Her feet were decked out in Italian Christian Louboutin tall black leather boots, with the signature red leather sole. Around her neck sparkled a necklace of sequins—exotic wood, resin, turquoise, coral, and semiprecious stones.

Rachel was poised and confident, obviously ready for the interview. Walking straight up to Karl Goebbel she said in the sweet husky voice he was accustomed to, "Good morning Mr. Goebbel. Thank you for this unique opportunity to interview a true pioneer in the sustainable seafood market. I'm still deciding on how best to reward you for our time together," she said with a wink, "so let me know if you have any ideas." She then shook his hand, letting her sensory touch linger longer than customary, a delicious smile also in the offering.

"Forget formalities," Goebbel said with a laugh, "please call me Karl. And, by the way, I admire your choice of clothing."

"Leather, or so I'm told," Rachel said coyly, "is in vogue when standing in the presence of entrepreneur, Karl Goebbel." She then stared up and down at Goebbel's own ensemble of lamb leather clothing, her gaze lingering on his custom made tailored pants that sheathed him like thin veneer.

"Birds of a feather, I like that," Goebbel said with a devious smile, reciprocating with his own suggestive stare. "Ready to begin our interview and tour?"

"All primed," Rachel replied. "My camera and sound men will follow us like unobtrusive shadows, capturing our dialogue exchange, and filming anything of interest that you direct them toward."

"We're presently standing in a captivating setting," Goebbel advised, "with the *Lucky Lady*, the blue Pacific, and Santa Cruz Island as our backdrop. It's a great location for any introductory remarks, or preliminary questions."

"Sounds good to me," said Rachel. Without the need to utter a word, her cameraman and soundman automatically positioned themselves for the shot. She then situated Goebbel to her immediate left, holding the wireless microphone in her right hand. Finally, she angled her body in such a way as to accentuate her feminine features, finishing her preparations by shaking her head up and down, creating a candlelit tossed-hair bedroom look. "You all set?" she asked.

Goebbel nodded his head.

Flashing a radiant smile, Rachel began. "Good morning, this is KCLA 9 field reporter Rachel Knox, standing on Oil Platform Grace ten miles off the coast of Ventura County with the CEO and President of *West Coast Seafood & Aquaculture*, Karl Goebbel. Mr. Goebbel is respectfully known as the Architect of the sustainable seafood market, having converted four decommissioned oil rigs into massive fish farms, producing vast quantities of farm-raised fish and bivalve mollusks." Rachel then paused, allowing the camera to pan the oil rig structure and then the surrounding waters, giving the audience a bird's-eye view of Goebbel's enterprise. She then continued. "Mr. Goebbel, or should I say Dr. Goebbel, obtained his Ph.D. in Marine Biology from the University of San Diego graduating Magna Cum Laude, his doctorate thesis on the viability of converting oil rigs into fish farms, a visionary dream that became a reality ten years ago. And now my first question for Dr. Goebbel, or Karl, as he prefers to be called, is this: What exactly are bivalve mollusks and what types of game fish do you cultivate?"

"Bivalve mollusks," Goebbel chuckled, "are incredibly tasty and at the same time dangerous to eat, producing an aphrodisiacal effect and reputedly arousing sexual desires, especially the mussels and oysters that we nurture. The jury's still out on our jumbo scallops, but they're worth the risk. As far as game fish, our gorgeous one hundred foot murals, on the mainland side of each oil rig, graphically depict our various seafood fares— sockeye salmon, yellowfin tuna, bluefin tuna, and white seabass."

"Your aphrodisiac comment will undoubtedly cause a male induced run on the local fish markets," laughed Rachel.

"As a wise professor once said, 'never waste a good opportunity for free publicity or product endorsement.' Besides," Goebbel said, looking directly into the camera and flashing a Cheshire grin, "I'm a walking testimonial, having personally tested our oysters and mussels and their stimulating effects on numerous occasions."

Taking a second to recover from Goebbel's disclosure and with her cheeks slightly flushed, Rachel said, "I think I'll pass on expounding on that enlightening revelation and move on to my next question: Do your industrial-sized fish farms harm the nearby ocean environment? As you know, in many parts of the world, fish farming has destroyed the local ecology."

"That's a valid question, and one that I'm glad you asked," Goebbel said with a fatherly tone. "As you know, marine aquaculture is the production of aquatic life under grower-controlled conditions. The problem throughout the world is that most aquafarms are located in near-shore facilities—in waters less than fifty feet, which are extremely detrimental to the local environment—versus our deep-water facility. As you can imagine, thousands of fish discharge tons of waste. Fish defecate just like humans, and in shallow seas, the feces and uneaten feeder food leads to eutrophication of the nearby waters—lower oxygen levels—decimating the local eco-system, wiping out marine life, and spreading diseases. That is not a good thing . . . not at all." Goebbel suddenly stopped speaking, slightly bowing his head, his face a mirror of sadness.

Ignoring Goebbel's feigned contriteness, Rachel pressed, "So, Karl, what differentiates your operation from the poorly run fish farms?"

"Everything!" Goebbel declared, lifting his head and smiling expansively. "It's the difference between night and day. Do you mind if I take your audience on an exploratory tour of our facilities? I think it will help in answering your questions."

Realizing that she had been set up, Rachel replied, "No that would be great."

Goebbel then escorted Rachel and her crew to a safety railing that circumvented the oil rig. "Let's start by peering over the edge of the platform."

Fifty feet below, the ocean was a swirling mass of choppy seas as deep ocean swells slammed against the rig's hulking circular pontoon legs, each leg creating its own miniature whirlpool. The barking cry of a lone sea lion could be heard echoing off the structure's criss-crossed metal beams. "The seafloor," continued Goebbel, "is three hundred and twenty feet below us. Notice the incredible clarity of the water, with visibility easily exceeding ninety feet. The seas this far out from the mainland are purified by powerful ocean currents which daily cleanse the water of any possible impurities." As everyone stood transfixed by the sight, marveling at the vague outlines of countless numbers of fish cavorting in the depths, Goebbel silently retrieved a pre-positioned five-gallon bucket of water dyed golden-yellow, and dumped it over the railing, the waterfall of tainted liquid turning the surface of the ocean into an undulating sunflower.

"What are you doing?" Rachel yelled.

"Watch," Goebbel said, "demonstrations are more potent than words." Within seconds the sunflower had evolved into filaments of yellowish strings, which then dissolved into nothingness, the tendrils carried away as if transported by an unseen tsunami, the entire illustration taking less than thirty seconds.

"And the significance of your colorful exhibition is . . . ?" asked Rachel.

"That sustainable aquaculture farming in the deep ocean can be accomplished with zero repercussions on native species, or the nearby environment—satisfying Americans' growing appetite for abundant, affordable, and wholesome seafood. As demonstrated, the dispersing effect of vigorous ocean currents eliminates any negative impact on the local ecosystem.

"Do we just accept your word," Rachel said skeptically, "or do you have any further proof?"

"As the criminal justice system mandates, 'you need evidence beyond a reasonable doubt,' which fortunately for us is just around the next corner." Goebbel had the threesome follow him a short distance, leading them into a spacious rectangular room where one of the walls was covered with eight one-hundred-inch, ultra-high definition screens. The room was darkened, with a sophisticated computer station adjacent to the screens; it looked like a war-room in a modern warship. Goebbel sat down in a contoured black leather chair opposite a computer monitor. Rather than touching anything, he spoke audibly to the computer, his succinct commands providing instant results, the computer responding in-kind with its own enchanting feminine voice.

"A voice-activated system, how nice, and how very pricey," Rachel commented.

"Quicker than typing," Goebbel confirmed, "and not too expensive. The fish are worth the extra change."

"And how is this room connected to the additional *evidence* that you're providing?" Rachel asked.

"Patience," Goebbel chided, "the system takes a few minutes to come on-line. For your viewers' information, you're standing in our main operations center. From this venue I can exercise control over the entire Platform Grace fish farming activities. I now direct your attention to the eight, wall-mounted screens." Goebbel then uttered a final instruction, the consoles promptly blazing to life, each displaying a specific underwater scene.

Rachel's eyes moved from one visual display to the next until she had viewed all eight, the green-hued scenery constantly changing as if watching a slow-motion movie, the panorama breathtaking. This is amazing," she murmured, and then asked the obvious, "You have underwater cameras?"

"Eight at three-hundred feet—the ones you're presently viewing—another eight at sixty feet, four cameras on the inside bottom corners of each Kevlar mesh fish structure, and four cameras situated within every fish habitat at a depth of five feet," Goebbel explained. "The cameras are high-definition and can pivot three-hundred and sixty degrees. During any given hour we can survey the quality of the ocean depths as well as inspect the health of our game fish, allowing us to instantly know if our enterprise is adversely affecting the surrounding ecosystem."

"Can you describe what the consoles are exhibiting?" Rachel asked.

"Even with LED strobe lights attached to every camera, the water appears as a greenish haze because of a lack of penetrating sunlight," Goebbel clarified. "Furthermore, the aquatic life at three-hundred-feet is a bit sparser than at sixty feet, as you'll soon observe. Along the sandy bottom and swimming among the pillars you'll notice various deep water rockfish, including several big uglymouth boccaccio's, redbanded rockfish, calico rockfish, canary rockfish, a huge yelloweyed rockfish, and a couple of California scorpionfish whose spines are mildly poisonous although their flesh is quite tasty. If your eyes are really sharp you'll also perceive some accidental trash, a large wrench, one severely rusted Mag-Lite flashlight, aluminum cans, glass bottles, and a barnacle encrusted diver's mask. Once a year we use a remote-controlled submersible to retrieve as much garbage as possible."

"Generous of you."

"We do our best," Goebbel assured her. "I will now switch to our cameras located at sixty feet."

Rachel and her two crew members all let out an audible sigh. The contrast in marine life between a depth of three-hundred feet, and sixty, was overwhelming, the seascape now grandiose, and the ocean teeming with thousands of elegant creatures, the water azure-blue.

"My God!" Rachel exclaimed.

"I knew you would like it," laughed Goebbel. "The platforms vertical framework acts as a marine life oasis attracting thousands of species. Over the years the enormous skeletal structures have been transformed into a vibrant and prolific artificial reefs pulsating with life. The labyrinth of pillars and cross-beams are coated with strawberry anemones, milky-white matridium anemones, layers of filter-feeding sponges, hundreds of plate-sized scallops, and thousands of foot-long ebony mussels. Occupying every additional nook and cranny are millions of pink jewel-like corynactus californica along with millions of plankton-feeding acorn barnacles. If you look closely you'll observe numerous exotic critters slowly advancing across the beams including pencil-thin rainbow-hued brittle stars, oversized orange and purple sea stars that are feasting on the hapless scallops and mussels, a myriad of fluorescent nudibranchs, and a contingent of armor-plated rock crabs."

"I'm impressed by your marine knowledge," Rachel said. "Could you please continue describing for my audience the extraordinary diversity of species that inhabit this man-made structure?"

"On the interconnected crossbeams," resumed Goebbel in a professor-like voice, "are several bug-eyed marbled cabezons and numerous multi-colored petite gobies. Milling about in close proximity to the beams and pillars are three familiar residents: the easy-to-spot bright orange garibaldi known for its gregarious personality, the elusive checkered calico bass, and the puppy-dog friendly bucktoothed sheepshead. Pulsing through the fluid space are fist-sized jellies whose two-foot long stinging tentacles are the bane of all divers. Floating in dense thundercloud like formations are countless blacksmiths whose perch-shaped violet-blue bodies sway to the rhythmic movements of the ocean currents, their territory shared with grayish throngs of softball-sized halfmoons. The legions of shimmering silvery fish weaving harmoniously throughout the silhouetted supports are John Steinbeck's famous Cannery Row sardines—the primary food source for most game fish off the southern California coast. Stealthily stalking the jellies and sardines is a rare open-water passerby, an ocean sunfish, also known as mola-mola or swimming head, a docile giant that can easily exceed one-thousand pounds. Our specimen, however, is an adolescent, at about two-hundred pounds."

"I feel like I've slipped into an aquarium," squealed Rachel. "All the radiant colors and the multitude of living creatures are beyond belief, and all this in the midst of a commercial venture."

"It certainly negates any argument that our industrial-sized fish farms are harming the local environment," Goebbel said, reminding Rachel of her prior comment.

"I agree," said Rachel, "apology appropriately bestowed."

"Apology accepted," Goebbel confirmed, and then added: "As a special treat it's feeding time for our game fish, so you'll have the privilege of witnessing the procedure." Goebbel then voiced an order, the computer instantly responding, shifting the perspective to the cameras located in the yellowfin tuna grow-out pens which were the size of a football field, and forty feet deep.

Swimming in a leisurely circle was roughly one thousand yellowfin tuna, or ahi, by their Hawaiian name. The dark metallic-blue tuna were two years old, thirty-six inches in length, and close to fifty pounds, with bright yellow dorsal and anal fins—the reason for its common name.

The four cameras positioned at five feet captured the spectacle from above, and the four cameras mounted on the underside of the enclosed net filmed the scene from below.

"That's a lot of fish," Rachel said excitedly.

"Actually our stocking density is less than fifty-percent of the norm for saltwater game fish," said Goebbel.

"Why?"

"Because overcrowding seriously stresses the fish which often leads to parasitic infections, viral infections, fungal infections, and sea lice infestations. Sea lice are the ticks of the ocean, sucking the lifeblood out of an infected fish. Severe congestion, like that which occurs in our densely populated cities, also causes abnormal behaviors such as increased aggression, widespread injuries, and high mortality rates."

"Who would operate an aquaculture fish farm like that?" Rachel asked disgusted.

"Primarily big European firms who run factory-style salmon farms in Chile, Norway, Scotland, and Eastern Canada," Goebbel replied. "All their farms have frequent sea lice infestations and have suffered from a devastating viral disease known as Infectious Salmon Anemia, which makes the flesh mushy and tasteless requiring its destruction. Millions of fish have died as a result. These infections have necessitated the use of large amounts of antibiotics, anti-bacterial, and anti-parasitic drugs, which are banned in the United States."

"That's awful," Rachel said. "I had no idea."

"I promise you this, *West Coast Seafood & Aquaculture's* philosophy and operations are exactly opposite of the sloppy European farms," Goebbel said reassuringly, "so please inform your audience."

"Another attempt at free publicity?" asked Rachel smiling.

"Maybe," said Goebbel, "but it's your decision. Right now, however, it's time for our show. You've never lived until you've experienced yellowfin tuna gorging at the dinner table. They are voracious eaters, pigs of the ocean, vacuuming everything in sight, sucking it straight into their bottomless stomachs. We harvest the tuna at two years of age, so these fusiform beasts are enjoying one of their last meals before they succumb to the mechanical death chamber. In addition to the cameras, we have sensors built into the bottom portion of the nets that electronically inform us if any of the feeder food slips through. If the food is eaten quickly, and none falls through the nets, then we know that the tuna are still hungry, so we feed them more. But, if even the slightest amount begins to sneak through, triggering the sensor alarms, then we feed them less. It's the perfect solution to an age-old problem— successfully calculating the optimum amount."

"What exactly do they eat?" Rachel wondered.

"Squid, sardines, anchovies, and green mackerel, sliced into two-inch sections," Goebbel explained. "Their food is native, natural, and free of antibiotics, netted by Captain Negrete within the last twenty-four to forty-eight hours. A five-inch rotating feeder tube extends out over the grow-out pen, spewing the diced sea fare from one end of the pen to the other. This system evenly distributes the segmented morsels over a wide area spreading the tuna out and preventing unnecessary collisions. No one wants bruised sashimi."

Laughing, Rachel said, "That's the gospel truth."

"I'm all set to initiate the feeding frenzy," Goebbel advised, "is your film crew ready?"

"Locked and loaded and anxious to record the food orgy."

"You won't soon forget," Goebbel insisted. He then issued a brief verbal order triggering the process, and immediately the feeder tube began disgorging its bloodied contents into the arena, inflaming a super-pack of ravenous oceanic wolves, their stream-lined physiques rising feverishly for the gluttonous massacre.

Rachel stared stupefied, her mouth slightly puckered, her breathing shallow, her eyes stitched wide open, hypnotized by the graphic display of passionate disorder.

A thousand famished tuna went ballistic at the same time, chasing dismembered prey with reckless abandonment, pursuing each delectable fragment with lighting bursts of speed, busting out of the water and then crashing back, churning the surface into a whitish froth, all the while greedily inhaling every shred-ded chunk within their predacious path—the fanatical need to devour everything in sight, the only evolutionary impulse operat-ing within their untamed brains.

The first sensor alarm sounded three minutes into the car-nage resulting in Goebbel shutting off the food spigot. Within five minutes nothing remained of the chopped sushi feast other than thousands of silvery scales, the twinkling remnants gently drifting into the ocean depths, the fragments too small to trip a sensory warning.

Rachel closed her eyes, breathed deeply, and used her silk sleeve to wipe a few specks of moisture from her forehead. "That was almost sexual," she whispered, momentarily forgetting that she was being recorded. She immediately checked with her team, *giving them the look,* which meant that her aroused outburst would be summarily edited, both crewmembers smirking as they per-formed their expunging tasks.

"You too," said Goebbel bursting out in laughter, "and I thought I was the only one." He took pleasure in Rachel's mortified look of embarrassment, the Freudian admission priceless.

"We all say things we regret," Rachel said defensively, "and it probably won't be the last time."

"I won't tell a soul," Goebbel vowed.

"Thanks," Rachel said. "And I believe we're almost done. We need some external footage of the actual fish pens, but otherwise it's a wrap."

"Great!" Goebbel said. "When your crewmembers have completed their final footage have them mosey on over to our Grace dining room and partake of a delicious, on-the-house, seafood lunch. It's not the mainland, but it's pretty darn good. I've asked our chef, who also double's as a platform engineer, to prepare anything they want; however, I highly recommend our coconut-crusted California sea bass, hazelnut-crusted sockeye salmon, yellowfin tuna tataki sashimi, or fresh shucked oysters Rockefeller."

Walking over to her team Rachel informed them of their final assignment and lunch. Strolling back to Goebbel, Rachel asked: "What about me?"

"As a reporter, you're a member of a privileged class," Goebbel said, "and will therefore be my personal guest of honor for a lunch extraordinaire in my own private suite, which is blessed with an alluring view of Santa Cruz Island."

"And what if I say no," Rachel said coquettishly.

"Not in the equation," Goebbel countered.

"In that case, lead the way."

Platform Grace had four levels with the lower three devoted exclusively to the operation of the aquaculture enterprise. Level four was Karl Goebbel's own private domain, serving as a deluxe office and personal overnight bungalow for lengthy stays and special guests.

Goebbel guided Rachel to an internal elevator that led directly to his suite. When the doors slid opened a distinctive looking, middle-aged gentleman wearing white overalls and a USDA cap, stepped out. He was carrying a small, insulated cooler, and his plastic nametag read Tom Ashley.

"Howdy Tom," said Goebbel, "I'd like to introduce you to Rachel Knox, a field reporter, and future anchorwoman, with KCLA 9. She's hosting a news story on *West Coast Seafood & Aquaculture.*

While shaking hands, Rachel said, "Pleasure to meet you," whereupon Tom said, "Nice to meet you." He then excused himself and strolled down the metal corridor.

Goebbel and Rachel then entered the elevator, but prior to the doors closing, Goebbel called out to Tom. "How's your new sporty BMW 335 performing?"

"Wonderfully."

As the doors closed, and the elevator began to ascend, Rachel asked, "Who's Tom?"

"United States Department of Agriculture Seafood Inspector; it was on his cap. Once a month he collects random fish samples, which he then takes back to his lab for testing. He's searching for antibiotics, parasites, infectious diseases, or any harmful chemical residues. That's why he's toting a cooler. To date we've never failed a test."

"Congratulations," said Rachel, "it's good to see our tax dollars at work; on the other hand, I do have a problem with a low-level government bureaucrat being able to afford a 3-Series BMW worth at least fifty thousand dollars. We're obviously overpaying. No wonder our country is broke."

"You are undoubtedly correct," Goebbel said, "a terrible waste of money."

A pinging noise indicated that they had arrived at level four. As Rachel exited the elevator she said with a grin, "Anchorwoman, now that's a happy thought."

"Only speaking what I see. You continue to interview important persons, or obtain choice assignments, and your television station won't have a choice—they'll have to promote you."

"How about a tour of Platforms Gilda, Gail, and Gina?" Rachel suggested. "In my preparatory research I did not come across any meaningful news stories regarding those facilities."

"They're off limits to the public or any news organizations," Goebbel replied quickly. "Way too dangerous. Only Platform Grace was modified for visitors. The other platforms have none of the safety features that were incorporated into Grace's conversion. It was our way of minimizing start-up costs. A good personal injury lawyer would destroy us in a court of law."

"Just inquiring," Rachel said apologetically.

The entrance to Goebbel's suite was only a few yards from the elevator. Goebbel entered a security code, and the doors swung open, revealing a combination office and summer cottage, with decorations as lavish as any office or house located in Beverly Hills.

Rachel stepped through the doorway but ignored the décor. She faced Goebbel, her eyes riveted onto his. "You said just a few moments ago that you're willing to help advance my career. What exactly are you willing to do?"

Goebbel reciprocated with a pleasant smile. He understood the script. "Wealthy people," he said, "have lots of friends, some that are acceptable, and some that are worse than leeches. In the end, however, everyone scratches each other's backs because that's the nature of the game, with the few pathetic holdouts always willing to deep six their righteous morals for a check. It's a wonderful world that we live in, and one that I thoroughly love."

"And that world of influential contacts would enthusiastically assist me with my professional ambitions?" Rachel asked. She removed her Elie Tahari jacket and draped it over an elegant antique French baroque-styled chair.

"You want interviews with politicians—I know them all— whether Democrat or Republican, it doesn't matter to me, they're all the same. Men or woman of consequence, just tell me who you'd like to question, and I'll place the call. Movie stars, they're the easiest since there's hardly a camera they don't love. They do, however, have one egotistical requirement, a proper introduction, which I can handle. I don't mean to brag but I can open doors that you can only dream about."

After a brief silence, Rachel asked calculatedly. "The Governor will be in town in four days. Can you arrange an interview?"

"Consider it done," Goebbel said without hesitation. "I'll let you know the time and location. Will a half hour be sufficient?"

"It will do," Rachel said, hardly able to mask her excitement. "Thank you, thank you." She then flirtatiously fingered the top button to her silk blouse, casually sliding it open, tauntingly moving to the second, but leaving it intact after a few breathless seconds of effort. Rachel then sat down in the French chair. "Help a lady with her boots?" she asked.

"Most definitely," Goebbel said, first sliding off one boot and then the other, the present view more tantalizing than the one out his window. After situating the boots next to the door he asked Rachel, "Care for an appetizer before lunch?"

"Yes, I'm starving," she said, "the ocean air seems to have stimulated my appetite."

Goebbel left the room, returning within a few minutes with a silver tray of hors d'oeuvre, which he placed on a Mediterranean crafted cedarwood coffee table adjacent to an alabaster-colored leather couch. He waived Rachel over and she joined him. "The seafood was prepared by our chef, the additional items I chose."

Rachel laughed after glancing at the contents of the tray: raw oysters on the half shell with a cucumber Mignonette sauce; steamed mussels in white wine flavored with tarragon, shallots, and butter; grilled French bread, two glasses of bubbly Champagne, and two snow-white lines of crystal coke. She acknowledged the message with a knowing look and a luscious smile. "I guess I know what's for dessert," she said playfully, and then feasted on a succulent oyster.

14

Within three seconds Dr. Sedrak was at the water's edge. Another two seconds and he was knee deep. One more second and the surging seas were lapping against his waist. Five seconds remained on his internal clock. He was less than fifteen feet away. The young girl was lying atop her surfboard waiting for the next wave, her feet dangling over the side, a surf leash attached to her right ankle. Her face was radiant, flashing a big enthusiastic grin, excited to be out surfing. Her father was standing behind her—holding onto the rear of the surfboard—preparing to launch his child once the next rolling swell arrived. He was encouraging his daughter with words of affirmation. "You're doing incredibly well . . . a natural surfer . . . you own the waves."

The man was tall, at least six feet four inches, the ocean barely up to his waist. He had long wavy brown hair and jet-blue eyes. The lively eyes were the same color as his daughter.

Dr. Sedrak hollered, "You need to get out of the ocean now!" It was the first time in his life that he had ever yelled so loudly at a fellow human being. His voice was harsher than he expected. The man and the girl both stared at him as if he were a drug-crazed wacko.

"Why?" The man yelled back suspiciously.

"A dolphin. It's gone nuts. It's attacking surfers." Dr. Sedrak replied quickly. "And it's heading toward you." He anxiously surveyed the surrounding waters.

"You're also a surfer," the man said, glancing at the surfboard that Dr. Sedrak was carrying, "so you should know that dolphins are our friends." The man's tone was somewhat deprecating, as if he were speaking to a landlubber who knew nothing about the ocean's creatures.

Dr. Sedrak was about to respond when he spied a hooked dorsal fin twenty feet away heading in their direction, accompanied by a roiling volume of displaced water, the animal unable to hide its bulky presence in the shallow water.

"It's here," Dr. Sedrak announced his voice barely above a whisper.

"Your loony dolphin?" the guy joked. "Where?"

"Behind you" Dr. Sedrak replied. The man suddenly jerked his head downward, peering intently into the silty water, shifting his stance while nervously inspecting his feet.

"Something large just bumped my legs," he said, his voice quivering with uncertainty.

"Dad," squealed the girl, "why are you yanking on my leash?" The twelve–foot long surf leash, made from tough urethane, had been lying in the water, the safety line drifting in the current.

Perplexed the father asked, "What are you talking about?"

"Daddy," she screamed.

Dr. Sedrak watched in horror as Moe surfaced with the leash clamped within his short beak. He then dove, pulling the girl right off the surfboard and dragging her underwater. The father, who had been at the rear of the surfboard, lunged for the board, wrapping his elongated arms around its midsection—engaging in a human versus beast surreal tug of war—the spoils much more precious than the usual dunking in the muck.

Within a few seconds it became obvious to Dr. Sedrak that Moe was toying with the man, relishing the life and death game.

Swimming in a tight circle he would intentionally cease pulling and allow the girl to crawl back to the surface, suck in a few breaths of air, shriek for her daddy, and then he would begin the sadistic scenario all over again, wrenching the two-legged terrestrial being once more beneath the waves.

After the fourth time it was apparent to Dr. Sedrak who would win the battle, and whose life would be sacrificed. The child had become noticeably weaker, the choking, gasping struggle for oxygen torturous—the dolphin's lust for amusement unrelenting. His hope that Moe would unilaterally release the girl had turned into a pipedream. The speed and incomprehensible actions of the dolphin had rendered both the doctor and the father momentarily helpless—the father precariously clinging to the one item that was keeping him connected to his child.

With the completion of another revolution the man's panicked eyes pleaded with Dr. Sedrak, "*Do something . . . please!*"

Sedrak snapped out of his delayed reaction. *But how do you defeat a twelve-hundred pound homicidal dolphin?* He asked inaudibly, and shuddered. His singular weapon was his bulky surfboard. *What tactic to employ?* He desperately needed a plan. *Human shield* entered his mind, which he instantly dismissed as suicidal. A half-ton dolphin would plow right through him like an M1 Abrams tank. But, the predictability of Moe's circular route did make the Kamikaze idea plausible. If he hindered its path the crazed dolphin would have to slow down, creating an opportunity to whack the creature with his surfboard, and maybe, just maybe, inducing him to let go of the surf leash, freeing the girl. Not much of a plan, but it's all he had.

With the dolphin already halfway through its compact spherical loop, Dr. Sedrak hurriedly sloshed his six-foot frame to the cutoff point, situating his body and surfboard for the inevitable onslaught. As Moe approached his location the animal slowed down as expected, its precise echolocation, normally used for hunting down prey, now revealing the doctor's exact position and size.

When Moe was less than eight feet away he stopped. This was not anticipated. The girl floated to the surface, soundless. Moe then elevated his bulbous head, the surf leash wrapped around its inch-long interlocking conical teeth—the dolphin's eyes probing, inspecting Dr. Sedrak, an eerie clicking noise resonating from the deranged mammal.

The eyes were what shocked Dr. Sedrak. Dolphins have irises like a cat that are spectacularly shiny, the mid-sized orb rich black in coloration. But Moe's eyes were opaque, dull, and lightless. As a physician he knew that he was staring into the visual aperture of an unhealthy and diseased dolphin.

In his many years as a neurologist, Dr. Sedrak had learned to expect the unexpected, that a patient's medical condition could deteriorate in a fraction of a second, requiring an on-the-spot response. A sickly animal, with its primordial instincts still intact, would be even less predictable. As a result, Dr. Sedrak quietly repositioned his surfboard, changing strategies. When Moe abruptly thrashed the ocean with his twin flukes, accelerating out of the water, jaws agape and emitting a diabolical wail—the doctor was intuitively prepared for the confrontation, his defensive reflexes on hyperdrive.

Dr. Sedrak held the surfboard as he would a colossal javelin, his right hand clutching the tail end, ready to launch it, his left hand steadying the board, the tapered front end a formidable projectile. His attention was directed at Moe's unhinged jaws, each lined with a row of glistening white teeth, their intended objective his neck and head. Reacting in self-defense, he forcefully heaved the surfboard into the gaping orifice and then ducked, the psychotic cruise missile barely missing his upper torso.

Miraculously, Dr. Sedrak's aim was exemplary, the polyurethane harpoon finding its mark, cleaving the surf leash and obliterating dozens of teeth. Splintered enamel spiraled like white shrapnel through the air as the surfboard fortuitously continued its destructive path, dissecting the dolphin's tongue in half, sliding deeper into the throat, and blowing out the esophagus. A fine mist of crimson fluid spewed forth as the board finally lodged in the base of the animal's gullet, its forward momentum exhausted.

Relieved to be alive, Dr. Sedrak watched transfixed as Moe's unrestrained inertia conveyed his ponderous mass beyond his position. With the red-stained surfboard jutting out of its jaws, the dolphin plummeted into three feet of water, the sandy bottom solid, the dynamic impact cataclysmic—impaling the seven-foot surfboard straight through the dolphin's stomach, gutting the upper and lower intestines, shattering the spine, severing the spinal cord, ravaging large quantities of insulating blubber, and lastly, punching a ragged hole through the outer layer of its thick skin, eighteen inches aft of the dorsal fin.

Moe's skewered, moribund body then experienced violent, involuntary muscular contractions, the spasmodic activity spewing forth volumes of iron-rich blood, discoloring the surrounding waters— the twitchy, jerky convulsions ending almost as quickly as they began—Moe's lifeless carcass a floating lump of tormented flesh rising and falling in the surf. A few gluttonous Western seagulls, nosily arguing among themselves as they jockeyed for position, were already alighting upon the corpse, desirous for an easy meal.

Ignoring the gory scene, Dr. Sedrak thought: *What happened to the child?* And then he heard it—a voice.

"Help . . . please help me . . . can anyone help me," wailed the father. He was cradling his unconscious daughter in his arms; tears curled off his cheeks, the salty drops mixing with the salt water on his child's upturned face.

Dr. Sedrak immediately forged a watery channel to the man's side arriving within seconds, acutely aware that the man was clueless on how to save his precious little girl. There was no time for niceties. "I'm a medical doctor, give me your child," he commanded, reaching for the girl.

The man hesitated, unwilling to release his daughter. "She's dead," he said softly, his right hand tenderly stroking her forehead, a moaning cry escaping from his lips.

Dr. Sedrak knew that one of the symptoms of extreme shock was the inability to process logical information. Another sign was being delusional. Time was of the essence. The young girl's life was at stake. Trust needed to be established before the man would likely relinquish his child—necessitating a different approach. "What's your daughter's name?" Sedrak asked quickly.

After a brief moment he replied, "Reese."

"R-e-e-s-e, as in Reese Witherspoon, the actress?"

"Yes—we always loved that name."

"That's a beautiful name."

"How old is Reese?"

"Nine."

"What's your name?"

"Ryan."

"Ok, Ryan, now who am I?"

"The man who killed the dolphin."

"Yes, and what else—what did I tell you a few moments ago?"

"You called yourself a doctor."

"Yes, Ryan, I'm a very good doctor. I've saved hundreds of lives, and I can save your angelic Reese, if you'll just let me."

"She's not dead?" he asked skeptically.

"She's drowning Ryan. I have to remove salt water from her lungs, blow air back into them, and then she'll be just fine. It's called CPR." Dr. Sedrak prayed that he could deliver on his optimistic promise.

"What do you need me to do?" Ryan asked.

Dr. Sedrak sighed inwardly. He had gained the man's confidence. It had taken twenty cherished seconds. "Do everything I request of you Ryan."

"Okay," he replied

"First . . . hand me Reese, and I'll also require her surfboard as a medical platform. The beach is too far away, and time is critical to Reese's survival."

Ryan reluctantly surrendered Reese to Dr. Sedrak, and then rushed off to retrieve the foam surfboard that fortunately was drifting nearby.

While Ryan was recovering the surfboard Dr. Sedrak began CPR, embracing Reese as he would a baby, his sense of balance wavering, the current tugging at his legs. He first gently shook Reese's shoulders while loudly calling out her name, but received no response. She was definitely unconscious. He next tilted her head back, lifting the chin up, and checked her airway. Thankfully, it was not clogged with suffocating vomit. With his left fingers he then pinched Reese's delicate nose shut, inhaled deeply, sealed her mouth with his own, and slowly emptied his lungs until her chest rose approximately two inches. After disengaging his mouth, he watched as the air escaped, seeing the chest go back down. He then repeated the rescue breath a second time, just as Ryan arrived with the surfboard. He placed Reese on her back on the bobbing surfboard, removed his neoprene booties, and arranged them under her shoulders. The makeshift rubber pillow helped in keeping her head tilted back and the airway opened.

"Ryan, you *must* make the surfboard immovable. I can't do my job if the waves are jostling Reese. Can you do that?"

"Absolutely," Ryan assured Dr. Sedrak. Moving to the back of the board Ryan secured the side rails with his muscular arms, stabilizing the platform. He also utilized his six feet four inch physique as a human seawall, blocking the incoming swells.

With Reese stationary, Dr. Sedrak began exigent chest compressions, pumping the pectorals, attempting to restore circulation. Placing the heel of his right hand directly on Reese's breastbone, he first pushed straight down compressing the chest about two inches, paused, allowed the chest to recoil, and then began anew, performing the same procedure thirty times in eighteen seconds. During the process he could tangibly feel and hear the bones in her chest popping and snapping, like frozen tree branches on a bitterly cold winter night, the unsettling twang normal with CPR. After thirty compressions he switched back to rescue breaths, delivered two, and then back again to compressions, repeating the life or death scenario every twenty-two seconds, silently praying for a providential resurrection of an innocent little girl.

Following three complete cycles of CPR, Reese remained motionless—her eyes shut tight, her skin pallid, her lips bluish from lack of oxygen—her body deathlike. Dr. Sedrak felt warm beads of sweat trickling down his spine in spite of the icy water, the first nuance of professional panic on his part. He knew that Reese's brain was close to self-destructing unless oxygenated within the next sixty seconds. He began round four with dwindling optimism, once again covering her mouth with his own, and pinching her nose shut. He was about to exhale when a breaking wave plowed into his makeshift gurney, the surging whitewater smothering them in a churning mass of tumultuous water—his right arm locked around Reese's waist restraining her from sliding off the surfboard—his next saving breath exchanged underwater. Gratefully, the turbulent swell passed within seconds, allowing the board to re-emerge from the drenching, the doctor and Reese still yoked in their struggle. As a veil of saltwater cascaded off Dr. Sedrak's frame, he finalized rescue breath number two, and then switched back to compressions.

"Doctor I'm so sorry." Ryan said apologetically, "I couldn't block it; the swell was just too big."

"It's okay, we're fine, don't worry about it," Dr. Sedrak said reassuringly. He then spoke ultimatum-type words over Reese, his voice authoritative, his sense of impending doom evident. "Come on Reese, wake up! Wake up! Breathe child, breathe!" Reese, however, ignored his orders, her demeanor stoic, lifeless, the additional thirty compressions having zero effect.

Off in the distance Dr. Sedrak heard the familiar whine of approaching emergency vehicles, their piercing sirens clogging the airwaves, the sound becoming louder with each passing second.

Shifting back to rescue breaths, Dr. Sedrak delivered the first one, and was about to transfer the second when he sensed a gurgling, rumbling clamor deep within Reese's thorax, the convulsive racket like an erupting geyser—the marvelous sound of life. Removing his mouth he immediately turned Reese onto her side to prevent aspiration, and watched with tears in his eyes as she vomited into the ocean—distasteful saltwater, pink sputum, stomach fluids, and today's breakfast, the brown frothy deluge the most enchanting puke he had ever seen. After heaving, Reese began coughing, discharging whatever remnants remained, and then she started crying. Dr. Sedrak gently picked her up. When he was satisfied that she was breathing on her own, he presented Reese to her father, whose bearish arms encircled his cherished bundle, and a mutual healing chorus of weeping ensued—the bond of love between father and child immeasurable.

After a respectful waiting period Dr. Sedrak said to Ryan, "Reese needs to undergo a full medical examination at the hospital as soon as possible, and she appears hypothermic. The emergency personnel will have nice warm blankets, and the ambulance will be toasty hot. We need to get going."

Ryan acknowledged his understanding by nodding his head. Dr. Sedrak retrieved the surfboard and his booties and together they made their way to the shoreline where a crowd of onlookers had already assembled. Dr. Sedrak noticed that a number of heroic surfers had already paddled out and were attending to Moe's victims, the rescuers patiently awaiting lifeguard assistance.

The mournful squeaks and squeals of Larry and Curly temporarily distracted Dr. Sedrak. The two females were beyond the breakers, cruising along the surface, calling out to Moe—the distress shrieks in the vernacular of dolphins. Fortunately, whatever had caused Moe to go ballistic, had apparently not affected the females. Subsequent to one long sorrowful lament, the two mistresses ceased their high-pitched wailing, executed a histrionic tandem somersault, and then proceeded west, in the direction of the Channel Islands.

Reese, with her dad accompanying her, was transported by ambulance to Ventura County Community Hospital.

The first surfer, whose board had been attacked from underneath was deceased, the exact cause of death massive blunt trauma. The other two surfers had survived. One surfer had a broken femur, cracked ribs, and multiple abrasions, and was taken to Ventura County Community Hospital. The other sustained life-threatening injuries; a burst lumbar fracture, comminuted fracture of the right hip, and a serious concussion, requiring helicopter transport to UCLA Medical Center. Moe was hauled out of the ocean, placed in the back of an old pickup truck, and shipped to the Santa Barbara Zoo where a necropsy was scheduled to be performed, the surfboard still an integral part of his anatomy.

Dr. Sedrak watched nostalgically as his surfboard disappeared around a bend in the road. He would miss that board, but figured shopping for a brand new one would be extremely therapeutic—a prescription that a wise doctor would certainly write.

He then spent three protracted hours at Surfer's Point answering mundane questions from animal control, fish and game, police officers, and newspaper reporters. He even conducted several uncomfortable television interviews, his hair a disheveled mess. During a lull in his sudden popularity he escaped, rushing to the hospital, eager to see a very special patient. When he arrived it was wonderfully clear that Reese was none-the-worse for her calamity—her sun-bleached blond hair was washed and combed, her cheeks rosy red, her eyes sparkling, and her laughter infectious.

Reese was obviously a survivor, having made an amazing recovery, ostensibly suffering no ill effects from her brutal ordeal. A comprehensive medical examination, including numerous x-rays, revealed no residual trauma. The hospital staff treated her like a famous actress, the news of her misfortune spreading like wildfire, the outpouring of well-wishers phenomenal. Soon candy, flowers, and stuffed teddy bears inundated her room, the overabundance graciously redistributed by Reese to other deserving patients.

Dr. Sedrak, however, received the best gift of all—a patient who wrapped her thankful arms around his neck, hugging him like a daughter would a dad, shedding a few tears, speaking soft words filled with gratitude, a young girl eternally indebted to a courageous stranger who had risked his own life to save hers. She made him promise that the next time she ventured out into the surf he would accompany her, surfing the waves together, and that afterwards, it would be her treat at a local In-N-Out Burger. He readily agreed to Reese's proposal and provided her with his personal cell phone number, excited for their watery date.

Later that same day, as Dr. Sedrak was sitting at his desk in his cubicle of an office engaging in administrative work, Nurse Dee Radcliffe, strolled into his office. She was one of the nurses assigned full-time to the neurology department. Known as a perfectionist, a trait sincerely appreciated by the department personnel, she insisted on wearing her shoulder length, auburn tinted hair in a fifties-style bun.

"Dr. Richardson thought you would be interested in these reports," she said, depositing a thin stack of laboratory test results on his sandblasted pine wood desk. Dr. Richardson was a first year resident neurologist in charge of the graveyard shift.

"What are these?" Dr. Sedrak asked.

"Around 11:30 last night," began Nurse Radcliffe, "a twenty-seven-year-old female patient was admitted to the emergency room in a comatose state, her physical and mental condition—according to her roommates—freakishly deteriorating within the last month, totally crashing in the last couple of days. They originally thought she was doing hard drugs. She was dead by 3:00 a.m."

The use of the word *mental* instantly captured Dr. Sedrak's attention. He quickly perused the laboratory findings. "This is incredible," he whispered, "she died from Variant Creutzfeldt-Jakob disease?"

"Yes," the nurse replied. "Dr. Richardson was aware of your prior male patient that expired from the same condition and realized that you would want to examine these test results as soon as possible."

"That's an understatement," Dr. Sedrak said. "She's the second patient to die from mad cow disease in less than two weeks. It's more than random coincidence. Have you interviewed her family?"

"Not yet. They've been notified. Her parents live in Boston, Massachusetts. She was an only child. The parents are flying out today."

"What did her roommates have to say about Sandy's condition?" Dr. Sedrak questioned, referring to the girl's first name.

"Not much. It wasn't exactly a close-knit group. Sandy moved into their house a little over three months ago. She rented a room, which was virtually the extent of their relationship. She occasionally ate her meals at the house, but spent most of her time working as a waitress at Poseidon's Grotto, or hanging out with her fellow employees."

"I'm not familiar with the Grotto," Dr. Sedrak said.

"You need to get out more often," scolded Nurse Radcliffe. "It's our newest seafood restaurant, serving only locally raised, environmentally-friendly, fish and mollusks. The food is quite delicious."

"Any idea if Sandy ever travelled to Europe?" asked Dr. Sedrak, changing the subject.

"Dr. Richardson discussed that possibility with the two room-mates, but the conversation went nowhere. Sandy's past life was never discussed. She had a real job and paid her rent, that's all they cared about."

"Life in the big city," Dr. Sedrak acknowledged. "I'll make the final assumption that the non-meddling roommates knew noth-ing about her dietary habits?"

Smiling, she said, "On that issue you're wrong. Apparently Sandy loved seafood. When she cooked at home it stunk up the house. Neither of the roommates appreciated that fact. They were not aficionados of fish."

"What about beef?"

"Unknown. Foul-smelling fish was all that they could remem-ber."

"Well—that's a start," Dr. Sedrak said, and shrugged. "When the parents arrive, either Dr. Richardson or I will have to inter-view them at length regarding their daughter's globetrotting and culinary history. Thank Dr. Richardson for the reports, and thanks Dee for personally delivering them." He then dismissed Nurse Radcliffe.

Leaning back in his wooden swivel chair, Dr. Sedrak thought, *what a day this has turned out to be.* Mercifully, it was nearing completion, the fatigue factor settling in. He was in dire need of a scorching, soaking bath, infused with Dead Sea salts, the mineral bath rejuvenating and soothing. A glass of chilled Far Niente Chardonnay, coupled with French Ossau-Iraty Vieille Cheese, sweet and nutty, served on sourdough bread, with dried fruit as a side dish, would make the refreshing dip even more luxuriating.

Preparing to pack up for the day, he noticed that his MacBook Pro was still displaying his Internet Explorer web site, the multicolored Google search engine catching his attention.

He wondered what the World Wide Net had to say about the dolphin confrontation. He was always astounded at how rapidly a news event, or even gossip, was instantly disseminated throughout the entire planet. He typed in *deranged dolphin* and then hit the Google search engine button. Within seconds the search parameters brought up fifty-seven probable results. He scrolled through the listings, opened up several of the more promising websites, reviewed journalistic quality articles on the encounter, waded through the blog comments, peered at a number of photographs, and suffered through three of his television interviews, vowing to comb his hair—if there ever was a next time.

Search result number fifty-five was unrelated to his incident, but something made him look. It was an eleven-minute YouTube video of an attack by a California sea lion on a marine biologist. Curious, he clicked on the video—and for the next eleven minutes sat pasted to his chair—mesmerized by the brutal antics of an irrational sea lion as nightmarishly loco as his own bottlenose dolphin. He then viewed it a second time. He was blown away by the bravery of a young girl in a pink wetsuit. If he had an eligible son he would insist on a prearranged marriage.

The introductory caption to the video stated that the marine biologist was Eva Chen, Ph.D., employed with the University of Malibu, and currently stationed at the Marine Biology Lab located on Santa Cruz Island.

Dr. Sedrak calculated that the marine lab was approximately fourteen miles straight out from Surfer's Point, which for a Pacific bottlenose dolphin was a leisurely swim of less than one hour. Given the eerie similarities and ferociousness of their attacks, he was certain that the sea lion and the dolphin were afflicted by the same neurological abnormality.

Using his computer he brought up the University of Malibu website, and jotted down the main telephone number for the marine lab. He dialed the number, a receptionist picking it up on the third ring.

In a casual, moderately pitched voice, he heard a woman say, "University of Malibu, Marine Biology Lab, Dora speaking, how can I help you?"

"I'm calling for Dr. Eva Chen. Is she available?" he asked.

"And whom shall I say is calling?"

"Dr. Matthew Sedrak," he said, "Chief Neurologist with Ventura County Community Hospital."

Rather than receiving an immediate response, there was a slight pause, as if the woman on the other end of the line was evaluating his request.

"Are you the same Dr. Sedrak who saved that poor little girl from that psychotic dolphin?"

"Yes . . . one and the same," he replied.

"And stuffed your surfboard down its throat?"

"A lucky shot," he said truthfully.

"Well, I'll be damned!" she declared. "I'm sure glad that you're more than just a stuffy old doctor, hold please."

Dr. Sedrak smiled, making the assumption that he had just received a compliment. After a reasonable wait a well-groomed feminine voice came back on the line.

"Hello, Dr. Sedrak, this is Eva Chen. You've had quite a day."

"Not much different from your own sea lion encounter," he said. "I viewed your skirmish on YouTube. Over three million hits. You're quite famous."

"The insatiable lust for live-action carnage has its unfortunate devotees," Eva admitted.

Laughing, Dr. Sedrak said, "You're probably correct on that one."

"I know I am," agreed Eva, "and it was an experience I would rather forget. Tell me about your day. I know some of the particulars, but would love the unedited version."

Taking the next ten minutes, Dr. Sedrak recounted in vivid detail his engagement with the dolphin, chronicling its aggressive behavior and attack upon the surfers, its sickly eyes, the dolphin's death and pending necropsy, and ending with the rescue of Reese.

"Wow," Eva said laudably, "you were definitely Reese's guardian angel. I can't imagine anyone else who could have saved her under those circumstances. Makes you wonder if it was all a colossal coincidence or you were a saint sent by God."

"I doubt I'm a saint," Dr. Sedrak said humbly, "simply the right man, in the right place, at the right time, doing the job that he was trained for. If that makes me a messenger of God, so be it."

"Are all doctors trained in the art of hurling a surfboard like a spear?" Eva asked facetiously.

"That may be your one legitimate stab at a divine miracle," chuckled Dr. Sedrak. He then heard Eva also burst into laughter through his earpiece, presumably enjoying his play on words. She had a pleasant laugh.

"Doctor," said Eva turning serious, "concerning the necropsy on the dolphin, please have the pathologist at the Santa Barbara Zoo perform a histopathological brain tissue study. The microscopic studies will divulge if there are any defective proteinacious particles. The histological assessment on our demented sea lion confirmed that she was suffering from a prion disease known as spongiform encephalopathy. From your accounting of the incident it sounds like your dolphin may have the same neurological disorder."

Dr. Sedrak suddenly felt emotionally broadsided, the implications of Eva's sea lion necropsy findings staggering, his stomach queasy, twisted in knots, his brain racing, digesting the data. He dropped the telephone into his lap, found it, brought it back up, but remained speechless.

"Doctor . . . hello, you still there?" Eva inquired.

After a few additional seconds, Dr. Sedrak said, "Yes," his voice stifled.

"What's wrong?" asked Eva.

"The spongiform encephalopathy diagnosis . . . I've had two patients die from that exact same malady in the last nine days. Two humans, one sea lion, and now possibly a dolphin—what the hell is going on?"

"The beginnings of an all-inclusive epidemic," Eva replied dryly.

"How? What's the connection between sea mammals and humans? What's the source of the transmission? What about species barrier protection? This is Mother Nature gone bonkers."

"I do have a theory," Eva said.

"And that is—?"

"Karl Goebbel's *West Coast Seafood & Aquaculture* fish farms," Eva interjected. "We found a significant number of their fish fry in the sea lion's stomach. In addition, we discovered that the juvenile fish were being fed beef byproducts, probably in pellet form, as their primary food source for protein."

"Did you test the fish for mad cow disease?" asked Dr. Sedrak.

"Yes and the answer came back negative."

"Doesn't that pretty much squelch your theory?"

"As to those fish . . . maybe . . . but my gut tells me otherwise, and I usually trust my visceral instincts."

"I may be breaching doctor patient confidentially by telling you this," Dr. Sedrak said carefully, "but both deceased patients were big-time consumers of fish. One patient in particular ate fish fillets exclusively from *West Coast Seafood & Aquaculture*. The other I don't know yet. That person just died . . . last night in fact."

"I'm sorry," Eva said.

"I work at a hospital where death is a regrettable component of each and every single day. I cannot let it become too personal. But, back to your gut—how are you going to transition your intuition into hard evidence?"

"Spying plus field work," Eva confirmed. "I've reserved a marine lab watercraft. I plan on visiting Goebbel's aquaculture fish farms. One is open to the public and three are off limits. Guess where I'm going? I suspect that the *No Public Allowed* fish farms are the probable source of our spongiform encephalopathy."

"Sounds professionally stimulating," Dr. Sedrak said. "Mind if I join you? The CDC is looking for answers, you may have them. But come to think of it, why don't you just report your suspicions to the CDC and have them investigate?"

"Goebbel is a very wealthy man with powerful connections," Eva answered, "I'm sorry to say but I'm not sure I could trust their findings."

"Good point," said Sedrak, "I've lost two patients to the disorder and I certainly want to find out the truth about what's going on; besides . . . I always enjoy delving into a good medical mystery."

"A dolphin killer like you, a rescuer of damsels in distress, on my ship—the answer is unequivocally yes. The lab, however, will require that you sign a Release of All Liability form before you're allowed to set foot on one of our vessels. I assume that's okay?"

"It depends . . . who's driving the boat?" Dr. Sedrak quipped.

"Me, so wear your life jacket and a helmet."

"Okay, but please note in your ship's log that I'm a reluctant passenger."

"You'll survive," Eva teased. "I was planning on casting off at 8:30 in the morning, in three days. Island Packers has a daily ferry service to our island at a reasonable price. They depart from Ventura Harbor at 7:00 a.m., and generally arrive at our pier around 8:15 a.m."

"I'll be there."

"Sounds great—see you in three days," Eva said, and then she terminated the call.

Dr. Sedrak held the telephone in his right hand for about a minute before placing it back into its wireless cradle, his logical mind questioning whether he fully understood what it was he was rushing into. He decided he didn't care. He shut down his MacBook Pro computer, stood up and closed the mini blinds to his office, switched off the overhead lights, and finally walked out of his office, locking the door as he left, anxious to abscond home—it was time for that glass of chardonnay, French cheese, and a sultry bath.

15

J ake, Mischa, and Aiyana, after parting company with Timbrook and Gabriel, continued on Smuggler's Trail, and soon arrived at the white-sand and cobblestone beaches of Smuggler's Cove. A smattering of eucalyptus trees hugged the shoreline, their outstretched branches providing shade for several National Park Service pinewood picnic benches, the timber sun-bleached and stained yellowish-white, the cheesecake discoloration caused by Western gull and brown pelican guano. On a nearby hillside an ancient grove of olive trees blossomed with oval drupe fruit, the oil-rich crop no longer expressed for human consumption. Island scrub jays and Yellow-billed magpie's were the current beneficiaries of the neglected trees. Scurrying among the smooth cobblestones were two-inch purple shore crabs, scavengers of the intertidal zone, their white-tipped pincers excoriating bite-sized morsels of sea lettuce, green algae, or an occasional dead marine organism. As forecasted by Adam Timbrook, the early morning fog was gradually diffusing allowing sunshine to filter through, the radiant light causing the surface of the ocean to sparkle like a million diamonds.

Arriving at Smuggler's Cove, Mischa, Jake, and Aiyana then turned north and began following a footpath that paralleled the beach. The trail hugged the shoreline and then veered inland, with an upslopping bent, as it circumvented an impenetrable portion of the seashore that was blocked by sheer cliffs and tractor-sized borders. After ten minutes of strenuous hiking the path descended into a narrow canyon lined with cypress trees, seaside pink and yellow daises, northern island bush poppies, and island grasses. The canyon was their turn-off point to Yellowbanks. A seasonal creek, now a mere trickle, meandered down the middle of the ravine, the Yellowbanks trail mirroring the contours of the streambed. At that moment Aiyana insisted on a water break dragging a tethered Jake to a small rock-lined pool. She slurped noisily, taking her time at the water hole, her internal storage tank obviously empty. Once back on the pathway it was only a matter of minutes before they arrived at Yellowbanks—aptly named because of the yellowish coloring of the surrounding sandstone cliffs. The ocean was smooth and glassy, the sun blazing, the fog a distant memory. Mischa and Jake immediately removed Aiyana's bulky pack saddle, allowing her to roam free.

Not wasting a second, they each donned their dive equipment—wetsuit, booties, hood, neoprene gloves, and heavyduty nylon weight belt with accessory clips. Attached to the clips was a five-inch titanium dive knife in its own locking sheath, and a stainless steel fish stringer with quick release—just in case an unwanted visitor stopped by. The dive mask, snorkel, and fins would be slipped on once in the water. The speargun would be held pointed outward or downward the entire duration of the dive. Prior to heading out they snacked on chocolate-chip energy bars and consumed a sixteen-ounce bottle of vitamin-enriched water—proper hydration all-important when skin diving in order to avoid disabling leg cramps.

"Wanna bet on who'll spear the largest fish?" Jake asked.

Mischa smiled, she loved competition as much as her brother. "What's the wager?"

"Money . . . ten dollars."

"Ten-minute back massage," Mischa countered. Her brother hated the very idea of giving his sister a back rub. He would rather part with his own money than endure such a painful ignominy.

"Five dollars," he rebutted.

"No—it's a ten-minute rubdown or I'm not betting."

"Fine," Jake said somewhat perturbed, "but I'll want it the instant we arrive home." They then shook on it, sealing their agreement.

Mischa grinned at her brother's presumptuousness; at a minimum it was a coin toss. She then gazed at the waveless, translucent ocean, the conditions ideal for a day of spearfishing. Her attention was momentarily diverted by a snowy egret flaunting a magnificent veil of white plumes on its head, foreneck, and back, its princely body clothed with snowy-white plumage. The medium-sized heron was foraging in the tide pools for small fish, crabs, sea urchins, and octopuses, its darting black bill a formidable lance similar to their own spearguns. If Mischa could choose a pet bird, the snowy egret would be at the top of that list, its stately beauty hypnotic.

Yellowbanks, mused Mischa—according to Timbrook's verbal sketch—had a variety of reefs; some were parallel reefs with sandy shoals in between them, some were low-lying rocky reefs, and others were large rocky outcroppings with modest walls that descended into the depths. The expansive area was covered in lush kelp forests, ribbon surfgrass, and billowing eelgrass beds, all intermixed with spits of sand—ideal habitat for the California halibut and occasional white seabass. Mischa's goal was a savory flatfish, but she would not hesitate to spear a luckless seabass.

"What's the dive plan?" Mischa asked. Every responsible diver formulated a blueprint of their dive prior to entering the water.

"We'll work the various reef structures from west to east," answered Jake, "swimming a snake pattern, rendezvousing every seven to ten minutes as the loops converge. Since I'm primarily interested in a white seabass, I'll work the deeper waters, drop-offs, and edges of the kelp canopies, while you concentrate on the interior reefs for halibut. If you spear a fish, or if you have a problem, signal the other person by blowing your safety whistle." Jake and Mischa each had an orange-colored mariner's whistle attached to a six-inch cord, stored in a small pocket located on the upper right hand corner of their wetsuits.

"Sounds like a workable plan," Mischa confirmed. Walking side by side they entered the ocean, stopping when the water was knee deep, to strap on their fins and rinse out their dive masks with spit, which prevented condensation.

Jake then reached out and touched Mischa's shoulder, "Good luck sister," he said.

"The same to you," Mischa replied with a smile. "Shoot a big one."

"Always," said Jake as he slid into the water, his swimming strokes purposely slow and methodical so as to minimize his noise signature. Game fish, particularly white seabass, spooked at any unfamiliar sound.

Mischa watched her brother silently glide across fifteen yards of quiescent ocean before immersing her own body into the cool Pacific, the icy sea seeping into her wetsuit, her internal furnace immediately heating the thin membrane of seawater, creating an additional layer of thermal protection.

When the water was six feet deep Mischa loaded her speargun—the arduous process of stretching three thick power bands across the entire length of her fifty-five inch spearshaft a daunting task.

As Mischa made her way out, she once again marveled at the panoramic beauty of the island's underwater landscape, its artistic symmetry masterful as if painted by Van Gogh. She loved drifting above the unfettered work of art, a foreign world of liquid space teeming with exotic plants and creatures—every square yard its own Garden of Eden.

Mischa followed Jake's route, ceasing her forward momentum when the water clarity began to diminish. She estimated the depth at about twenty feet. At this distance the ocean floor was still clearly visible, a necessity when hunting halibut, which were bottom-dwelling camouflage experts. California halibut, in late spring, moved into shallower waters to spawn, a fact that Mischa intended to exploit. Her sinuous pattern would take her from twenty feet into five, and then back out, continuing the circuitous search until she either speared a halibut, or fatigue set in. Jake's course ran from a depth of twenty feet to fifty. Their irregular easterly circuit allowed them to strategically cover vast stretches of the ocean floor—increasing the likelihood of success.

Halibut were the Houdini of the seas, the extraordinary fish capable of perfectly matching its skin coloration with whatever sandy or pebbly bottom it rested on, and then hiding its body further by burying itself in the sandy seafloor with only its eyes or rear tailfin visible, making the tasty flatfish extremely difficult to detect. Mischa cherished the underwater Easter egg type hunt, the thrill of victory much the same as discovering a treasured-filled golden egg.

Mischa gradually worked her way toward the shoreline without spying a halibut and then executed a drawn-out right turn moving ten feet beyond her prior course. After that she leisurely threaded her way back to the twenty-foot mark, where she encountered her brother. Treading water, she removed her snorkel and asked, "See anything of interest?"

Jake, after spitting out his snorkel replied, "I wish, but nothing yet, although there's lots of positive signs; a strong current and huge schools of baitfish, so a white seabass should be lurking nearby. It's only a matter of time. What about you?"

"Sightseeing thus far, but I agree the conditions are promising."

"Then let's go get 'em," Jake said encouragingly. He reinserted his snorkel, and with a muffled splash, continued his stalking.

On her return voyage, Mischa circumnavigated a fingerling reef, and continued weaving in and out of dense eelgrass beds, rocky protuberances, and pockets of tannish-white granular sand. A small docile horn shark slumbered in a deep crevice, its abode shared with a trio of spiny lobsters. Non-game fish zigzagged among the reef structures; orange senoritas, olive opaleye, zebra perch, yellow sargo's with their defining black stripe, giant kelpfish, blue rockfish, rubberlip surfperch, black and yellow treefish, and tons of baitfish—sardines, anchovies, and topsmelt. A portly sea cucumber ambled sluggishly across a rocky ridge, its path on a collision course with a solitary octopus whose miniature cave was proudly decorated with pilfered sea shells and bony remnants from its prior meals of hapless crabs.

Green eelgrass meadows, intermixed with craggy reefs and narrow bands of sand, were irresistible to a halibut—like marshes were to ducks. The trick, as Mischa knew, was spotting the deceptive flatfish as it lay buried in the sand or hidden among the waving fronds. The closely packed strands of eelgrass were the ocean's version of extra-long fescue grass, the turbo-charged aquatic turf easily exceeding five feet in height.

As Mischa drifted over an exceptionally large tract of eelgrass, she peered deeply into the foliage, hovering soundlessly as the minimal wave action parted sections of the grass, providing brief glimpses of the sandy bottom. Years of spearfishing had innately clued her to the fact that the sand underneath this section of eelgrass was the right color and consistency preferred by sizeable halibut. The sand was soft for effortless burial, and multicolored—pearly white with a smattering of tan and light brown pebbles—just the right camouflage hue that halibut favored for their ambush blitz on unsuspecting baitfish.

Suspended above the scene Mischa could sense an increase in her heart rate. Intuitively, she knew that halibut were in the vicinity. Gazing intently into a yawning gap she recognized a five-foot-long Pacific angel shark partially nestled in the sand, gray-brown in color with dark spots on its back. Suppressing a yelp of excitement, Mischa was ecstatic at the discovery since the passive shark primarily preyed on halibut, fortifying her opinion about the area's prospects.

Energized, Mischa glided over the entire site, skillfully examining every trace of agitated sand, searching for any hint of her hidden prey. When she had just about given up hope she was rewarded with the vague outlines of a halibut, ensconced in a fine coating of sand. The discovery ignited a hunter's adrenaline rush. Keeping her distance in order to prevent the fish from spooking, she calmly aimed her speargun, targeting a spot just aft of the gill-slits. Prior to discharging the gun Mischa mentally calculated the size of the fish, California Fish and Game Regulations requiring a minimum length of twenty-two inches. After a few seconds of analysis, she concluded that the flatfish was probably legal, but not wanting to take any chances of shooting a short, she lowered her speargun. Mischa had great respect for the size limits, which ensured that every halibut would birth future generations before being harvested. Disappointed, but jubilant at having seen a halibut, she continued her quest.

Coasting across a granite plateau Mischa was captivated by the polychromatic life that clung to the rock—green and strawberry anemones, purple and black-crowned sea urchins, hundreds of orange-freckled yellow brittle stars, stands of gold, red, and purple gorgonian sea fans, and a variety of sponges including the bright yellow-mustard sponge, deep blue-cobalt sponge, and orange puff-ball sponge. Mischa was breathless at the dream-like beauty. The God of creation, she surmised, had saved His most artistic handiwork for the ocean's flora and fauna.

At the end of the underwater mesa, a three-foot long expanse of bespeckled sand wound its way through a compact section of eelgrass, the path leading into deeper waters. Following it, Mischa had a hunch that her moment had arrived. Twenty feet further she came to an abrupt halt—the only features detectable were the eyes—two right-sided ebony irises pointed skyward. She estimated the depth at eighteen feet. She descended to ten feet, and then leveled off, careful to avoid startling the halibut. At this distance Mischa was able to make out the protruding jaws and half-inch needlelike teeth. The jaws were thickset and imposing. *Oh my God, thank you, thank you,* she silently whispered, her psyche reeling with anticipation, knowing that she was staring at a monster halibut. She sank another foot for a closer-up view and noted that the fish was solidly buried, with at least ninety-five percent of its bulk concealed beneath the sand. She searched for its forked caudal fin, and to her amazement discovered its leading edge three feet *beyond* the jaws. *Oh my God,* she thought again, *don't let me miss.*

Mischa quietly repositioned her body slightly off-center to her quarry. With the speargun in her right hand she extended her arm bringing the large two-barbed detachable spearhead within five feet of the halibut. Sighting down the spearshaft she aimed for the kill spot located behind the gills. After murmuring a one second prayer she pulled the trigger. Unlike a shotgun there was no kickback, just the tiniest vibration as the rubber bands were released, hurling the spearshaft forward like an arrow. A millisecond later the tapered tip pierced the halibut, producing no discernible sound upon impact. Burrowing deeply into its flesh, and erupting like an exploding bullet out the opposite side, it gouged a linear path into the sand. The three-inch flanged barbs then sprang open and prevented the mortally wounded halibut from escaping.

Mischa watched for a brief second as the veiled creature mushroomed off the bottom, hemorrhaging blood as it lurched convulsively, its intended destination the abyss. Mischa heard the clicking sound of Spectra line peeling off the vertical reel attached to her speargun as she surged toward the surface, her oxygen-deprived lungs wailing for fresh air. Breeching the water she immediately filled her lungs, and then began tracking her prized halibut.

The initial frenzied dash by the flatfish was short-lived. Mischa was pleased to see that her shot was true, hitting vital organs and quickly dispatching her prey. After reeling in the Spectra line, she hyperventilated and then plunged to the seafloor, her dream fish lying sedately on a sandy shoal. The eyed side of the halibut was light brown with white and dark splotches. The blind side was light cream in color. The body was elliptical and stout. It's *huge and beautiful* screamed Mischa, the bubbles from her shriek rippling toward the surface. She estimated its weight at over forty pounds, enough meat for a week of meals. She grasped the spear-shaft and rapidly ascended, anxious to display her trophy fish to her brother, and smugly remind him of their bet.

Once topside Mischa blew her marine whistle, summoning Jake. She waited a full minute and then blasted it again, creating a long screeching note. After a few seconds, she heard a responsive whistle, and then observed Jake swimming in her direction. Upon his arrival he simply floated for a prolonged period of time, his head pointed straight down, gawking at Mischa's halibut, the muted sound of "wow" exhaling from his snorkel. Mischa smiled contently. This was a moment she would always treasure.

After what seemed like several minutes, Jake finally removed his snorkel and said, "That's one incredible fish. I hate to say it, but I'm jealous. You must be doing cartwheels inside."

"I'm feeling pretty good," Mischa squealed. "I can't wait to show it to Timbrook and Dad."

"Don't forget to post a photograph of your giant halibut on Facebook," Jake added. "Along with your famous sea lion video your e-mail fan club will go nuts."

"It's tough being so popular," Mischa said cheekily, and then added, "while enjoying a well-deserved back massage."

"I'm still hunting . . . *little sister* . . . so don't count your chickens before they hatch."

"I'm not a big believer in fairytales . . . *big brother!*"

"That's too bad, because I am. My fantasy white seabass will soon be your nightmare," Jake said boastfully, and then laughed, his laughter cut short as he briefly choked on some droplets of saltwater that had sloshed into his mouth.

"You okay?" she asked.

"Fine, I apparently needed a drink."

Mischa appreciated her brother's sense of humor and playful cynicism, but also knew that he was extremely proud of her. He constantly bragged about his sister, and would be the first to inform his friends of her accomplishments. "I'm heading in to clean my halibut," Mischa informed Jake, "and then I'll graciously come back out and help in your search for your precious seabass."

"You done spearfishing?" Jake asked.

"Yes. I remember Timbrook's admonition the other day, 'the ocean's resources are finite, so take only what you can consume and nothing more.' Fillets from this fish will last us a long time . . . so yes . . . I'm finished."

"Then I'll see you shortly," Jake said, "and bring your camera, I'm starting to feel lucky."

Mischa watched Jake as he proceeded back out, secretly cheering for his success. White seabass were large, easily exceeding fifty pounds, so her brother did have a chance of beating her. She wouldn't mind losing, but if she did, she would use her angular knuckles in massaging his back. As far as any futuristic photograph of his triumphal fish, Jake knew that Mischa did not possess a waterproof camera.

The swim shoreward was onerous, the towed halibut's corpulent body becoming entangled on two occasions with marine plants—giant kelp and surfgrass—requiring Mischa to expend considerable amounts of energy wrestling the fish from the ocean greenery. Fortunately, the flatfish was too massive for her stainless steel fish stringer that hung from her weight belt—that device designed for fish that weighed less than twenty-five pounds.

Once on shore, and after removing her dive fins and weight belt, she dragged her catch onto a smooth rock that was tailor-made as an out-in-the-field cutting board. Using her five-inch titanium dive knife, Mischa first dissected the red-feathery gills, resulting in the halibut bleeding out, which prevented the meat from becoming unpleasant from stale blood. She next slid the blade along the belly line, slicing open the intestinal cavity. Reaching in with her gloved right hand, she twisted out the gut sack, which contained the heart, liver, stomach, and intestines. She then tossed the bloody gills and innards onto a nearby rock where a pair of pillaging seagulls, squawking over the fresh viscera, indulged in a late morning breakfast. Finally, hoisting her halibut, Mischa walked a few feet beyond the shoreline, coming to a stop in a foot of water where she then immersed her fish. Utilizing the dive knife, she scraped the abdominal area clean of any residual tissue, segments of entrails, or veins; the fragments quickly consumed by a silvery hoard of baitfish. Mischa then briefly exited the water to obtain a fifteen-foot nylon cord stored in her knapsack. Returning, she looped the rope through the eviscerated gill plates securing it with a square knot. Leaving the halibut in the chilly saltwater, she then tied the other end to a jagged rock located near the shoreline, the ocean now acting as a refrigerator, preserving the quality of her catch. Mischa would fillet the fish into servable portions once they arrived back home.

Satisfied and eager for a break, Mischa sat down on a chunk of driftwood. Hungry, she nibbled on a smoked turkey sandwich, guzzled a twelve-ounce bottle of mountain-spring water, and as a reward for her conquest, luxuriated in a comforting Snickers bar. Closing her eyes and assuming a recumbent position, she basked in the warm sunlight, ready for a catnap, her mind fading in and out of reality, her body adrift on a lazy sailboat. The sailboat had just entered a tropical cove when the piercing racket of a whistle instantly aroused her from her repose. *Jake!*

16

Springing to her feet, Mischa scanned the surrounding waters, her eyes darting from one section of reef to the next, searching for her brother. She smiled in relief when she spotted a wetsuit-clad hand waving from the outer fringes of a kelp bed a good two hundred feet away.

Retrieving her weight belt and fins, Mischa immediately plunged into the water, itching to know the reason why he had blown his whistle. Whatever the grounds, he obviously desired her presence. Inasmuch as she was unencumbered with an unwieldy speargun, the swim out would take less than two minutes.

Pumping her arms and legs, Mischa arrived at Jake's location within ninety seconds. Struggling twenty feet below their position was a four-foot white seabass, bluish-gray above with dark speckling and silver underneath, its heavyset fusiform body wrapped around several strands of giant kelp, the spearshaft jutting out from its mid-section. Extracting her snorkel Mischa said, "I'm impressed—it looks like I've lost the bet."

"Big time," Jake replied.

"Not the best shot," Mischa commented.

"It was moving fast, I didn't have time to set up a stone shot. Besides, I was slightly distracted. You won't believe what I found. I'll show you as soon as I take care of my fish. Here, hold my gun."

Without waiting for a response, Jake passed his speargun to Mischa, inhaled deeply, and dove straight down.

Mischa had not a clue as to what her brother was talking about. *What could be more exciting than a huge white seabass?* Staring through the crystalline seas Mischa watched as Jake approached his seabass. The fish, sensing his presence, began thrashing the water, twisting the spearshaft and Spectra line once more around the kelp fronds. Jake, to his credit, patiently waited for the fish to calm down before lunging for its gill slits and inserting his glove hands through each slot, manhandling the fish into submission. With his right hand he removed his dive knife and plunged the hardened blade into its brain. Replacing the knife he then used his muscular hands to tear apart the gills, causing the fish to bleed out—the exuded blood appearing greenish—the color red absent at this depth. Finally, Jake swam in a tight circle, unwinding the fish from the kelp, and then rapidly ascended lugging the seabass—his dilated eyes indicative of his need for oxygen.

Bursting through the surface Jake yanked out his snorkel and sucked in copious amounts of fresh air. After a few moments, he said, "Not bad . . . at least fifty-plus pounds. I'm sorry to say but my mighty sister has fallen. I look forward to this evening's soothing massage."

Mischa smiled at her brother's cockiness and then said, "Congratulations; that's one nice fish."

"This beautiful game fish is nothing compared to what I discovered hiding on the reef. Tag along and I'll show you a unique sea-beast that is definitely one for the books."

"Is it dangerous?" Mischa asked concerned.

"No—if it's what I think it is—we should be okay."

"So . . . what is it?"

"I'm not ruining the surprise. You'll have to see it for yourself, and believe me, you won't be disappointed."

"Alright," said Mischa as she handed the speargun back to Jake, "but if you're wrong, no back rub tonight."

"Trust me—it'll be worth an extra five minutes."

Though intrigued, Mischa reluctantly followed her brother as a thousand thoughts rippled through her consciousness. Jake's seabass trailed a few feet behind his dive fins, oozing a trickle of blood. After covering approximately twenty-five feet Jake hesitated, apparently unsure about his underwater bearings. He then speeded up, swimming with renewed confidence, finally coming to a stop over a rocky grotto. Mischa noticed that the sheltered sanctuary was hewed in by rugged granite walls, creating a tranquil refuge in the midst of a turbulent reef system; and, resting in the middle of the thirty-five foot deep lair, was Jake's sea-creature.

Like stationary buoys, Mischa and Jake floated above the behemoth for breathless minutes before either spoke. The elongated beast was curled up, like a slumbering snake, its brilliant colors—silvery blue, pink, crimson, cardinal-red, and blackish wavy markings—clearly visible from their elevated perch. But the most distinguishing feature was its concave head, which was topped with an ornate, reddish dorsal fin that resembled a decorative headdress, the pinkish feather-like filaments undulating majestically in the slow moving current.

Mischa tapped Jake on his shoulder soliciting his attention. She then indicated by opening and closing her fingers that she wanted to talk. Treading water Mischa said, "It's gorgeous, like a humongous eel that's also a fish that looks like a sea serpent. It must be over fifty feet in length. Do you know what it is?"

Smiling knowingly, Jake said, "Giant oarfish."

"You certain?" Mischa questioned.

"Yes," replied Jake, "there was a recent photograph in our local newspaper that depicted an oarfish of leviathan proportions. It was being cradled by nearly forty US Navy Seals. Apparently the fish had become stranded on their Coronado Island training beach. It was the strangest creature I had ever seen. That image is still stuck in my mind."

"I've never heard of such a fish."

"Very uncommon," Jake explained, "and according to the accompanying article giant oarfish are a docile deep-water species that only journey into shallow seas when they're sick or dying."

"That's sad," Mischa said softly. "If it's dying I suppose there's nothing that can be done, but if it's sick, then there must be something we can do."

"Is my sister experiencing motherly instincts?" Jake asked derisively.

"No," Mischa said curtly, "it's just too magnificent a fish to ignore if it's sick."

"I agree," said Jake, "but there's only one way to know—a face to face meeting. Let's dive down and check out our peculiar friend. Look for any skin infections or obvious discoloration. When a fish is dying its colors begin to fade."

"What about your seabass?" Mischa asked.

"I'll suspend it from a thick strand of kelp. That should hold it."

After a couple of oxygenating breaths they descended head-first, coming to a halt about five feet above the oarfish. Upon their descent the sea serpent had uncurled, visibly nervous at their approach. The fish was now stretched out to its full length, a faint slivery-blue glow resonating from its body.

Mischa was fascinated by the creature's iridescence, which quickly faded. During the encounter she had experienced an odd tingling-like sensation on her exposed skin. Mischa instantly dismissed it as her own jittery nerves reacting to an unfamiliar situation. The outstretched fish, however, had made their medical examination easier. Beginning at the narrowed caudal fin, Mischa and Jake gradually worked their way toward its head with Jake inspecting the left flank, and Mischa its right. The widest section was at the midway point, which Mischa estimated at two feet. Several times she gently stroked its brilliant red dorsal fin, or caressed its scaleless bluish skin. The dorsal fin ran the entire length of the fish. Arriving at its furrowed head Mischa was stunned by the regality of the decorative red cockscomb-like plume, the rich jet-black irises, and was mildly surprised at the small protrusible oblique mouth, which was similar in size to hers. It was apparent that this fish was not a high-end ocean carnivore. She stared into its eyes while tenderly brushing the ornate plume, pleased that the creature tolerated her touch. She noticed Jake a few feet away flashing two thumbs up for her cuddly act. Her introspective moment was interrupted by her screaming lungs, which brutally reminded her of the reality of being a land-based animal, necessitating a rapid ascent, with Jake right behind her.

Surfacing, she refilled her lungs, and then said to Jake, "That was unbelievable; we're doing whatever it takes to save this fish."

"That's fine with me," Jake confirmed. "Based upon my once-over it doesn't seem to be dying. Its skin appeared healthy and there were no external lesions. Did you notice anything?"

"No . . . nothing. But its behavior was definitely consistent with some type of illness; allowing me to pet it wasn't normal."

"That's for sure; fish don't behave that way unless something's amiss. I wonder if it's hungry. If it eats that's a positive sign that maybe we can help it."

Laughing, Mischa said, "I think your white seabass is a bit too large for its tiny mouth."

"That's true, dear sister, but that's not what I'm thinking."

"Then what? Dice up your fish?"

"No . . . what my seabass was feeding on. I plan on cutting open its stomach and removing whatever undigested critters still exists. They should be just about the right size for our sea monster."

"My illustrious brother—you never cease to amaze me."

"Yes, I know, but save your adulations for my back massage." Using his titanium dive knife Jake slit open the belly disemboweling the seabass and causing the water to turn iron-red. He located the grayish-white stomach and hewed it free from the other intestinal vitals. Taking the foot-long rubbery blob, he hacked off one end of it, exposing the rancid contents. "I need your help," he said motioning for Mischa to join him. "Hold this sack of goodies while I finish cleaning my fish." Within a minute Jake's fish was expertly scoured of all viscera.

"Nice job," said Mischa.

"Thanks, and now it's time to ascertain what my seabass was feasting on. While you pour I'll gather the recognizable items." Jake then reinserted his snorkel, realigned his facemask, and plunked his head underwater.

Mischa carefully tipped the leathery sack, dribbling out the seabass's final meals. At the outset a fetid-smelling greenish liquid stained the ocean, followed by an assortment of indistinct nuggets of dissolved sea creatures. *So far—nothing of interest*, thought Mischa. She then noticed that the opening had become clogged, requiring her to squeeze it as if it were a jumbo tube of toothpaste. Applying pressure, she slowly compressed it until it exploded outward, spraying the ocean with a purulent glob of squid, anchovies, sardines, and a medley of shrimp-like krill—Jake's gloved hands eagerly snatching up the intact morsels. Mischa happily flung the deflated stomach a good fifteen feet seaward, and then washed her neoprene hands of any residuals.

Raising his head above the water, Jake said, "That went well. I now have a smorgasbord of regurgitated appetizers. It should be interesting to see if our oarfish agrees." Hyperventilating, Jake then plummeted back down, arriving near the head of the fish.

Mischa enjoyed the spectacle from the surface, watching Jake as he cautiously edged closer to its mouth. He had his right arm extended, brandishing a squid, which he then rubbed across its jaws, attempting to entice the fish to eat. Failing at that, he next wiggled it back and forth, simulating an intoxicating fishing lure—and like a striking viper the oarfish responded—instantly devouring the squid. To Mischa's amusement, the sudden disappearance of the squid had resulted in Jake frantically withdrawing his hand—the agitated momentum causing him to tumble backwards. Regaining his equilibrium he then hurriedly inspected his neoprene fingers, verifying that they were still there. It was obvious to Mischa that he was okay. He looked up to see if she had observed his fear-based panicky gestures. Mischa warmheartedly waved back, assuring him that she had.

Determined to restore his dignity Jake gallantly fed the remainder of the disgorged delicacies to the oarfish, which seemed to inhale each item as it was presented.

Food supply exhausted, Jake swiftly glided upwards rejoining Mischa. After a few breaths of restorative air he said, "Thank God our fish is fond of food, although it's funny how it eats, vacuuming the squid or fish right out of my hand like a high-powered slurp gun. And, for the life of me, I could not discern any visible teeth. It must swallow its food whole."

"How are your fingers?" Mischa asked, teasing her brother.

"All there; and, I *doubt* you would have reacted differently."

"I guess we'll never know, but it was amusing, so thanks for the entertainment."

"You're welcome," Jake said irritably.

Turning serious, Mischa asked, "Any thoughts on what we do next?"

"Talk to Dad. He'll know what to do. He's been involved in rehabilitating lots of marine animals—"

Interrupting, and pointing in the direction of an outer kelp bed, Mischa asked nervously, "Will Dad also know what to do about that?"

Jake stared at where she was pointing. A twelve-inch-high, dark-gray dorsal fin was heading in their direction at a fast pace, like a bloodhound on a scent. "It wants my seabass," Jake said. "I'll dump it, which ought to distract it, giving us plenty of time to swim in."

Before Jake could implement his plan the shark quickly closed the gap and then slid beneath the surface. Popping her head underwater, Mischa scanned for the beast. She located it circling twenty feet below, an adolescent great white shark approximately eight feet in length. Mischa breathed a sigh of relief; mercifully, young great whites weren't man-eaters, preferring game fish and large schools of baitfish over mammalian prey. It probably was interested in Jake's seabass, but was apprehensive about approaching because of their imposing physical presence. Contrary to Hollywood's stereotype as a vicious hunter, great white's rarely launched an attack if they thought their own safety was at risk.

Mischa was about to inform Jake of her assessment when she noticed that the oarfish was once again emitting a bluish-white light, but this time there was a phosphorescent glint to it. She assumed the oarfish was aware of the prowling shark and that the shark was conscious of the oarfish—its shimmering glow a dead giveaway as to its whereabouts. Mischa was contemplating the oarfish's odd behavior when it suddenly emitted a low-level pulsating wave of light that enveloped her body, momentarily jolting her senses, causing her exposed flesh to tingle as if galvanized by an electrical current. Fortunately, the disruption of her mental faculties was only temporary. Remembering the predatory shark Mischa swiftly attempted to ascertain its status. Gazing downward, and then spinning like a compass, she was unable to locate it, the great white having mysteriously vanished. Checking on the oarfish she noted that it had lost its radiant luster and was once again resting peacefully in its hidden niche. The garbled sound of her name spoken in Jake's shrill voice caused her to lift her head. She observed Jake straddling the water next to his seabass.

"You okay?" he asked. "I'm still a little light-headed from what seemed like a discharge of electricity."

"Yes, I'm fine, and you're correct; the oarfish has the same capabilities as an electric eel. Its mild shocking of the water certainly scared off the shark besides energizing all my nerves. Thankfully, the effect was transitory."

"I wonder what it could do if it was really angry?"

"I don't think I want to know," said Mischa seriously.

"Amen on that," Jake said. "We'll stay friends."

"You ready to head in?" Mischa asked.

"Yes, but only after we've marked the location of the oarfish for future dives. I plan on doing whatever I can to help it survive."

"I have the perfect item," Mischa reported, "a bright orange fluorescent nylon safety ribbon. I can cut off a small segment and attach it to the kelp overhanging the oarfish."

"That will work," Jake confirmed.

Removing the safety ribbon from her wetsuit pocket, Mischa cut off a three-foot long section, and then tied it to several strands of kelp floating on the surface, tagging the oarfish's recessed ward. After one last glance at their new found friend, Mischa and Jake leisurely made their way to the beach, with Mischa arriving first as Jake's speargun and seabass hindered his progress.

Once on shore they changed out of their wetsuits and back into their hiking clothes. Mischa then summoned Aiyana with the whistle provided by Timbrook, the female mustang faithfully emerging from the surrounding shrubbery upon hearing the piercing sound. As a reward, Mischa fed Aiyana two crisp Mackintosh apples pinched from their lunch supplies, the horse snickering its approval. Jake, who had not yet eaten, quickly polished off a turkey sandwich, an energy bar, and a Snickers candy bar—washing it all down with a bottle of mountain spring water.

Together they re-hitched Aiyana's sawbuck pack saddle and heavy duty side-by-side canvas saddlebags. The saddlebags were stuffed with their dive equipment and speared fish. The fish were wrapped in surfgrass to preserve their freshness. The time was 12:45 p.m. Their rendezvous with Timbrook was scheduled for 2:00 p.m., giving them ample time to cover the two scenic miles at a laid-back pace.

The return trip to Smuggler's Cove was easy-going and peaceful. At the cove they rested a few minutes, which quickly turned into an impromptu contest of skipping scalloped-shaped cobblestones on the surface of the still glassy ocean—Mischa's score of fourteen out-doing Jake's skimming best of twelve.

From Smuggler's Cove they picked up Smuggler's Trail. The four-mile footpath ended at Scorpion Cove, the location of their house. The meeting place with Timbrook was at the halfway point. The hike was uphill initially and then leveled off, curving around an extinct volcanic mountain, Montannon Ridge, the second highest peak on Santa Cruz Island. At over eighteen hundred feet it would occasionally receive a dusting of winter snow.

Aiyana's stoutness as a reliable packhorse made the journey for Mischa and Jake worry free, allowing them to enjoy the many incredible vistas. Arriving at the gathering point ten minutes early, they sat down on the trail, anticipating Timbrook's arrival. While waiting, Mischa squirted a bottle of water into the flapping maw of Aiyana, with at least fifty-percent dribbling out as frothy white slobber onto the soil.

The perked up ears of Aiyana accompanied by an excited whinny-type utterance, alerted Mischa that Timbrook and Gabriel were nearby. The parting of the sagebrush by the sturdy stallion confirmed her hunch, the horse even stepping on the opaque rock that Mischa had earlier used to mark the concealed entrance to Montannon Ridge.

"Howdy strangers," said Timbrook with a wide grin, "are fish on the menu tonight?"

"How about for a month," Mischa happily replied, "we won the lottery."

"The ocean was indeed very generous," added Jake.

"I'll be the judge of that," Timbrook said jovially, "fishermen are famous for exaggerating the size of their catch." Dismounting Gabriel he patiently stood by as Mischa and Jake untied the saddlebags, revealing their respective fish lodged in the damp surf-grass. After staring at each fish he said, "I'll be darned, you guys were telling the truth." He then murmured a short Chumash prayer while gently touching each fish.

"What are you doing?" asked Mischa.

"Giving thanks to God for honoring His children with such an abundance of meat, and thanking the fish for their sacrifice."

"I don't think they care," Jake said impulsively.

"I know . . . but it should matter to us," Timbrook said solemnly. "All God's creatures should be respected, especially when taken for our sustenance. I always give thanks after a successful hunt."

"I think that's cute," Mischa said, and then mumbled her own prayer of gratitude, with Jake appending an 'Amen' upon its conclusion. She then refastened the saddlebags.

"Guess what else God provided on our dive?" Jake said with an ironic smile.

Seeing the same type of whimsical smile on Mischa's face, Timbrook said, "Not a clue."

"It's longer than a bus," Jake hinted.

"And quite shockingly colorful," Mischa said, joining in.

"Moby Dick or its cousin," answered Timbrook.

"Not even close," said Jake, "a giant oarfish."

"A live oarfish?" Timbrook said awestruck.

"Yes, although we think it's sick," Jake explained. "It's curled up in a rocky cavern at Yellowbanks. I fed it baitfish and squid from my seabass's stomach. We plan on doing whatever we can to nurture it back to health."

"That's admirable and terribly brave of you, and finding one as long as a bus, that's very unusual. Oarfish are extremely rare. Throughout the Chumash existence on this island only a few have ever been encountered, making your find noteworthy."

"It even scared off a small great white shark," Mischa said excitedly, "through an electrical impulse. It has the same capabilities as an electric ray."

"An electrical oarfish—the length of several cars—is a discovery that undoubtedly has spiritual significance," said Timbrook gravely. "The Chumash believe that whenever the natural world allows you to experience something truly extraordinary, that it's a sign, an omen of the future. What it portends I have no idea, but I have to think it must be good since your entire day was filled with favor."

"I'm standing on *good*," Jake said confidently. "How else can you describe our incredible six hours?"

"You're right," said Timbrook, "a giant oarfish, a great white shark, a huge California halibut, and a colossal white seabass, you guys had quite an adventure."

"A typical day on paradise island," laughed Mischa.

"And time to mosey on home," Timbrook advised. "We're still two miles out."

The jaunt home was pleasant and passed quickly for Mischa. She loved Smuggler's Trail and its inescapable scenery. Upon their arrival, Timbrook helped with the unloading of their dive equipment and fish, and then returned back to his own dwellings, Gabriel and Aiyana anxious for their evening meal of honey oats and hay.

Utilizing an outdoor cutting board and a special knife designed for slicing fish, Jake filleted his seabass. Mischa was next with her halibut. All told they ended up with forty-eight pounds of pure-white fillets, which they then vacuum-sealed for long-term storage. At a pound per person, per meal, they had a lot of delicious dinners to look forward to. As they were cleaning up, Mischa said to Jake: "When we met up with Timbrook this afternoon the hornbags and saddlebags on Gabriel were empty. When we left this morning they were filled to capacity. Any thoughts on what type of supplies Timbrook's delivering to Montannon Ridge?"

"I have no idea," Jake replied. "I know his wife's buried there as are all the former Chumash leaders. Perhaps he's conveying materials for repairing the graves, or flowers, or offerings for the dead. After all, he's the caretaker of a very sacred Chumash Indian site."

"You may be right," Mischa said cautiously, "but something seems off, and someday soon I want to pay that mountain a visit."

"Timbrook might not approve," warned Jake.

"If we don't ask, then he can't say no. Ignorance is bliss. We'll just assume that it's okay."

"Remind me to never marry someone like you," laughed Jake. "But I'm game; you've definitely tweaked my interest."

Mischa was about to respond when Kurt joined them. "Hi Dad," Mischa and Jake said simultaneously.

"Hello my audacious kids," he declared, rewarding each with a warm hug, and then said, "Rumor has it that you had an unbelievable day."

"You've talked to Timbrook?" stated Mischa.

"Or a bird," joked Kurt. "Yes, he filled me in at the barn. I thought it neighborly to lend a hand with unsaddling and brushing his horses. Based upon my conversation with Timbrook it's my understanding that we won't be buying fish at the market any day soon."

"No," said Jake, "Mischa and I have successfully filled the freezer. Did he also tell you about the giant oarfish?"

"Yes, and he said that you believe it's sick, and that you want to nurse it back to health."

"Absolutely," squealed Mischa, "it's too amazing to let die. Will you help us?"

Pausing to create some drama before answering, Kurt finally said, "Yes . . . I'll aid my benevolent children in rehabilitating a living sea monster." After the screaming died down, Kurt added, "Your creature's probably suffering from a bout of mild domoic acid toxicity, otherwise it would be dead. It's caused from consuming sardines and anchovies that have regrettably fed on toxic phytoplankton. The toxin normally affects seals, sea lions, otters, cetaceans, and occasionally large fish. Your serpent fits the bill."

"What do you recommend?" asked Jake.

"Strong antibiotics and B-12."

"How do we deliver it?" questioned Mischa.

"Pills hidden inside of squid. We have cartons of frozen squid at the lab for just this type of emergency, and of course, lots of medication. You'll need to administer the pills every single day for a period of seven days. Rather than walking or riding to Yellowbanks, you can use the lab's nineteen-foot Montauk Boston Whaler. The ocean route will save you hours and take less than twenty minutes."

"Thanks Daddy, you're the greatest," shrieked Mischa.

"Ditto to that," said Jake, "and we'll name the fish 'Kurt the Sea Serpent' in your honor."

"Skip the name," Kurt insisted, "it's such an unusual fish that it deserves a chance. My only request is that you take some photographs of the beast. You can borrow one of the lab's underwater cameras."

"That we can do," Jake confirmed.

"Good—then I'll see you at seven tomorrow morning. We'll go to the lab, obtain your squid and pills, and arrange for the Boston Whaler. As you know, I'm catching the ferry at 9:00 a.m. for my trip to San Francisco. I'll be gone for a couple of days, so you're on your own. I trust you'll be okay."

"Daddy, we'll be like little angels," said Mischa serenely, "have fun and don't worry about a thing."

Mischa and Jake could still hear their dad's sarcastic laugh as he closed the back door to their house.

17

The one-hour sardine-packed Southwest Airlines flight from LAX to San Francisco International Airport arrived at Terminal 1 without any delays—a minor miracle by today's aviation standards. Even the confusing Hertz rental car paper-work went off without a hitch, the brand-new hybrid Ford Fusion smelling factory fresh as if Kurt Nichol's was its first paying passenger. The upgraded sedan with its voice-activated navigation system was well worth its weight in gold, the GPS system flawlessly plotting Kurt's route through the labyrinth of narrow and congested city streets—the bane of San Francisco's downtown byways—and an absolute nightmare for unsuspecting tourists. Using the Ford Sync voice activated connective system and his MP3 player, Kurt linked to Pandora Internet Radio—creating a personal music station of San Francisco type performers, beginning with the city's most famous band, The Grateful Dead, whose classic rhythm and instrumental melody 'Truckin' from the *American Beauty* album, blared from the Sony premium 390 watts sound system. *While in the City*, thought Kurt, *you might as well enjoy the flavor of its local artists.*

"Bear left at west Broadway Street," interrupted the feminine voice from the Focus navigation system. Operating on automatic, Kurt obediently complied with its request. After traveling one

246

block it issued a new command, "Turn right on north Battery Street, go three tenths of a mile, and then turn right on east Union Street." Motoring north on Battery Street Kurt dutifully turned right onto Union Street, wherein the refined voice then issued its final advisory, "Your destination is on the right at 2 Union Street."

"Modern technology does have its benefits," murmured Kurt as he parked his car alongside a concrete curb in front of a two story red brick warehouse type building with a cast iron façade and two massive iron doors. Bolted onto the doors were three eighteen-inch brass letters—TSC—which Kurt knew stood for 'Transpacific Shipping Corporation.' The structure's four rectangular windows were fitted with fire-proof cast-iron shutters situated between cast iron pilasters with stylized capitals. Other decorative details included exposed anchor bolts and cornices supported on decorative brackets. The architectural style was similar to Greek Revival. Across the street, at 1 Union Street, was a quaint eatery called the Café de Stijl. The sign on the window advertised its eclectic cuisine as English and International. Kurt could hear his stomach growling; his early morning airline fare of an itty-bitty bag of Georgia peanuts totally inadequate at assuaging his appetite.

Stepping out of the rental car Kurt slowly approached the oppressive iron doors. Deciding on *what to say* concerning his interest in viewing TSC's private files regarding a one hundred and sixty-year-old ship wreck had turned out to be an easy decision; he would simply state the nature of his inquiry as professional— on behalf of the university—which was a half-truth.

The black highly polished lion-head doorknob rotated smoothly in his palm as the lofty door swung silently inward. Crossing the threshold, Kurt closed the door and was surprised to discover that he was alone. He was also amazed at the starkness of the interior considering its ornate exterior. The décor of the room was similar to a typical doctor's office. There were a half-dozen fabric-covered chairs and a small oval-shaped beveled glass table with a pile of neatly arranged nautical magazines. Adorning the red brick walls were several framed pictures of ancient and modern transport ships bearing the company's logos. The austere room had a locked door leading into the inner warehouse, and on the rear wall was a four by three foot glass partition with a bank-like sliding window. An inexpensive silver bell sat adjacent to the glass barrier. Using his right index finger Kurt rang the bell, the annoying dinging sound accomplishing its singular job as he heard a muted Asian-accented voice state, "I'll be right there—just give me a minute."

The minute evolved into two then three before a diminutive Chinese man with thinning gray hair, wearing bifocals, dressed in a pair of ill-fitted white overalls, and the name 'Zheng Tian' embroidered on the front, shuffled up to the protective window and said, "Hello—how can I help you?"

"Is this the regional office of Transpacific Shipping Corporation?" asked Kurt.

"Used to be," answered Tian. "It's now the western repository for Poseidon Holdings. In this building we maintain the records on all ships previously owned or leased by Poseidon Holdings, Global Asian Lines, and Transpacific Shipping Corporation."

"Does that include records of ships owned by the defunct Pacific Mail Steamship Company?" questioned Kurt. "It's my understanding that the Pacific Mail's residual assets were purchased by Transpacific Shipping Corporation in 1952."

"Yes," said Tian carefully, "they were . . . why the interest and who are you?"

"Sorry Mr. Tian, I should have introduced myself first; my name's Kurt Nichols. I'm a professor of Marine Biology at the University of Malibu. Recently I was appointed as Senior Project Scientist in charge of the universities' marine facilities located on Santa Cruz Island." Kurt then politely passed his business card to Tian, who after retrieving the turquoise embossed card raised it to within inches of his spectacles. Kurt continued speaking as Tian meticulously examined the two by three inch identification card. "I'm here on vacation and thought it fortuitous to drop by and review any documents that you might have on the wreck of the *S.S. Winfield Scott*. The reason—within a month our university will conduct an underwater mapping survey of the *Scott* debris field. My assumption is that your in-house records probably contain non-public facts on the calamity that might prove useful in our investigative search. My Internet inquiry, in preparation for our scientific study, indicated that TSC acquired the assets of the bankrupt Pacific Mail Steamship Company in 1952, including all their historical documents."

Tian deposited Kurt's business card into the upper left pocket of his overalls. "You realize that the *Scott* shipwreck occurred in December of 1853."

"Yes—I know," Kurt said duly impressed with Tian's knowledge.

"And you're under the assumption that the *Scott* records still exists even after all these years?" Tian laughed.

"I was hopeful," Kurt said dejectedly.

"Well, you're lucky . . . they do exist," said Tian with a sardonic grin. "For your information, in this business, particularly with a ship lost at sea, those records are never destroyed. There's continued liability issues, insurance matters, rightful ownership, rules of salvage, and disputes over anything of value that is eventually dredged up. I'm sure you're aware of the contentious legal battles between countries, companies, and treasure hunters over the discovery of valuable shipwrecks. Some of these finds are hundreds if not thousands of years old—that's why these documents are stored in perpetuity."

It was Kurt's turn to smile. "Thanks for yanking my leg. May I examine the *Scott* file?"

"I don't know why not. Some files are off-limits to the public. I'm not aware of any hold on the *Scott*. Take a seat and I'll be back in a few minutes."

While waiting Kurt pulled up the lunch menu on his Apple iPhone for the restaurant he observed across the street. It was only 10:45 a.m. but he was starving. A quick perusal of the online bill of fare inflamed his gastric juices, instantly solidifying his decision. He always trusted his stomach, which meant that lunch was now only a few steps away. As he was signing off, the locked door swung open, and Tian entered the room, his previous smile replaced with a scowl. He was carrying a faded and cracked leather folder. He sat down in the chair opposite Kurt.

"This is odd," he said as he unclasped the folder. "Please understand, I've never had a reason to personally inspect the actual *Scott* file. Its perilous journey as a gold-rush steamer is well known, but as a shipwreck it's nothing special—particularly since everything of value was eventually salvaged."

"What's anomalous then?" Kurt asked.

"This," said Tian as he turned the folder upside down.

To Kurt's astonishment only two pieces of yellowish paper drifted to the floor. "That's it?" he said incredulously.

"What's left," Tian replied as he bent over and recovered the stationary. "This letter explains the underlying reasons." He handed the document to Kurt.

Kurt noted that the letter was addressed to the President of the Pacific Mail Steamship Company and was dated December 27, 1853. It contained one small hand-written paragraph: "Upon receipt of this letter you are to *immediately* deliver to Nicholas Trist, United States Diplomat to Mexico, United States Consulate offices, San Francisco, ALL files and/or documents pertaining to the *S.S. Winfield Scott*." The letter was signed by Franklin Pierce. "Franklin Pierce?" . . . . *The Franklin Pierce*?" Kurt stammered.

Tian pointed to the very top of the letter. A gilded eagle within a small circle was clutching an olive branch and several arrows with its talons. Underneath the golden seal, in light blue, and in free-flowing script were the words, 'The White House, Washington D.C.'

"President Pierce!" Kurt exclaimed. "You've got to be kidding. Why would a president of the United States care about an ordinary shipwreck and why would a diplomat assigned to Mexico be involved?"

"Good questions," said Tian, "but since the United States Government never returned the *Scott* file that mystery lays buried in obscurity."

"What's on the other piece of paper?" asked Kurt.

"Just a short scribbled note stating that Captain Sean Flannigan was summarily dismissed from his position with the Pacific Mail Steamship Company and that he relocated to Carmel, California."

"Any address?"

"Scenic Road, Carmel, if that's an address."

"I've been to Carmel several times. If memory serves there *is* a Scenic Road—it follows the rocky coastline—the premiere street for exclusive beach-front homes."

"At least the late captain picked a good place to retire," Tian chuckled. "Back then, property on the beach was relatively cheap."

"Can I have a copy of these two items?" Kurt requested.

"I don't see why not. Sorry about the file being gone. It does make the wreck a bit more interesting. When you map the debris field keep that in mind. But, after all these years, I doubt you'll find anything of significance." Tian then left to make the requested copies, returning within a minute.

"Thank you," Kurt said upon receiving the duplicates.

"Good luck with your underwater investigation," Tian said, "and please let me know if you unearth anything that helps explain the missing file."

"I'll let you know," Kurt confirmed, although he was feeling a smidgen of guilt at not informing Tian about his recent discovery of an incendiary explosion along the hull of the *Scott*. That *was* information that would have helped explain the missing file. But his gut told him to withhold this data from anyone who was not a part of his inner circle, even from someone as accommodating as Tian.

After exiting the building Kurt walked across Union Street and straight through the open doors of Café de Stijl, where the maître d' greeted him with a warm smile. Ironically he was seated in a booth that faced the TSC building. Within fifteen seconds a college-aged waiter appeared at his table, who Kurt acknowledged with a friendly hello, grateful for prompt service.

"Care for a drink—coffee, tea, bottle water—or is tap water okay?" he asked.

It was a few minutes past 11:00 a.m. so Kurt was beyond breakfast and technically heading into the lunch hour—which meant that he could justify ordering a glass of wine. "Tap water is fine and I'll have a glass of Malm Cellars Anderson Valley Reserve Pinot Noir."

"Very good," said the waiter who instantly vanished in the direction of the bar.

Having previewed the menu Kurt knew exactly what he wanted, so when the waiter returned, he ordered. Being famished he settled on two courses—a spinach salad with spicy walnuts, gorgonzola cheese, sliced green apples, and frisee lettuce mixed with a walnut raspberry vinaigrette—and a toasted eggplant sandwich on whole-grain bread rubbed with a clove of roasted garlic, pesto sauce, charred sweet red peppers thinly sliced, and provolone cheese.

Kurt had only taken a couple of sips of his wine when the waiter reappeared with his dishes, the presentation intoxicating. Not wasting a moment, Kurt began luxuriating in his meal; the Malm Pinot Noir was excellent with an impressive silky core of plums, blackberries, cassis, and spice. The organic food was equally wonderful, tasty, and blissfully healthy, the last bite as satiating as the first. It was hard to put his fork down.

Over a cup of rich Sumatran coffee, Kurt reviewed what remained of the *Scott* file; a sixteen decade's old presidential order and a note regarding the ending of a man's career. If Kurt was in Vegas he would bet money on the captain's memory as a major key to unraveling the enigma surrounding the *Scott* and the government's intrusion; unfortunately, Captain Flannigan was dead . . . *or was he?* Captains were meticulous record keepers and notorious at covering their butts if a voyage ended poorly. Obviously the *Scott's* misfortune fit that category. *Could a portion of the Scott file still exist outside the brick walls of the TSC warehouse, or the bureaucratic clutches of the United States Government?* Kurt wondered. *Did the Captain withhold any documents—like a journal, or nautical charts, or a ship's log?* Kurt was beginning to suspect that the wine was making him as delusional as a leprechaun pursuing a pot-of-gold at the end of a rainbow. But, on a fool's hunch, he entered the name Flannigan into his iPhone California White Pages, and was shocked to see that there were for over two hundred Flannigan's. He then narrowed his search parameters to Carmel, and had three hits. He opened each one. The first Flannigan was the name of a restaurant, Flannigan's Seafood Bistro. The second Flannigan was listed as S. Flannigan, with a San Antonio Avenue address. The third, E. Flannigan, resided at 26100 Scenic Road, causing Kurt to unleash an involuntary and loud celebratory shriek, momentarily quieting the restaurant patrons. *Could it possibly be the same address as Captain Flannigan's? Is it the same house? Was this a direct relative of the Captain?* The probability of it being a colossal coincidence seemed beyond belief.

He noted the telephone number and dialed it. On the third ring a computer generated digital voice answered and requested that he leave a message after the beep. Kurt hung up; there was no easy message to leave. It would be better to meet in person. He assumed the E. Flannigan was at work.

Draining the last of his coffee, Kurt then checked with MapQuest. It informed him that the house on Scenic Road was one hundred and nineteen miles from 1 Union Street, and that the anticipated drive time was two hours and twenty minutes. Kurt shook his head knowingly, and then added an extra forty-five minutes to his commute. MapQuest time estimates did not exist in the real world, especially when you had to contend with city traffic.

Kurt looked forward to the impromptu excursion. The section of highway between Monterey and Carmel was spectacular, and included the 17-mile drive through Pebble Beach, recognized as one of the most scenic drives in the world. The awe-inspiring vistas and legendary sites such as the Lone Cypress—one of California's most enduring landmarks—would easily fill Kurt's afternoon hours with sightseeing, allowing him to conveniently arrive at the Flannigan house around 5:30 p.m.

Kurt paid the restaurant bill, adding a hefty tip, cognizant of the financial needs of a hardworking college student. He then exited the bistro. As he slid into his car he changed his Pandora personal music station to the Beach Boys—eager for some good vibrations as he began his afternoon of touristy exploration.

18

It was Thursday and harvest day at the *'couch potatoes' fish farms*, mused Negrete, as he thought about the exercised deprived ocean-going athletes who had become flabby caricatures of their wild cousins. It was a degrading term originated by Negrete—and one that he had wisely chosen to avoid employing around Karl Goebbel—who was presently accompanying him on the *Lucky Lady* as they made their rounds. They had already visited Platforms Grace and Gilda, and were now a few hundred yards east of Gail. Negrete throttled back the engines as he navigated past a six-foot high yellow buoy that proclaimed the seas surrounding the aquafarm as 'off limits to the public,' and that 'trespassers would be prosecuted to the full extent of the law.' His two crewmembers, Shade and Pancho, as requested by Goebbel, had taken the day off. Goebbel's reason—his ongoing training of Negrete concerning the disingenuous aspects of his aquaculture business did not require his shipmates.

After tying up at the landing dock, Goebbel and Negrete made their way to the massive sockeye salmon enclosure where fifty thousand individuals jostled for space. Their cramped quarters were equivalent to a bathtub-sized volume of water for each three-foot fish. The two-and-a-half-year-old salmon were in a frenzy—having been purposely starved over the last ten days in preparation for slaughter—their empty stomachs lessening the chance for waste contamination. On a typical Thursday perhaps five thousand adult salmon would be butchered. But this week Goebbel had a major order to fill; a national grocery chain was advertising '*Natural Salmon from the Crystal Clear Waters of the Blue Pacific*' in its upcoming coast to coast ad campaign, and had requested the huge allotment.

At the far end of the salmon pen was a large, seine-style fishing net. Its four corners were attached to four pulleys, which in turn were controlled by four sturdy winches. The net was stretched across the entire one-hundred-foot enclosure. It hung to within three feet of the forty-foot-deep pen and was weighed down by circular lead weights spaced two feet apart. Cork floats, equally situated along the top upper edges, kept the nylon mesh from sinking. The purpose of the meshwork was to prevent the salmon from escaping, and to funnel the immense school into a closely-knit pack. Once consolidated into a jumbled mass, a two-foot-wide pliable hose, hooked up to a powerful vacuum pump, would then be lowered into the writhing mob, suctioning the fish and immediately spewing them out onto a rubber-coated conveyer belt. The still conscious fish would then be transported to a stainless steel separating table. At the table the salmon would be sorted for quality, and then sent down a slaughter line to have their gills slashed—the fish convulsively bleeding to death as they advanced to the next workstation.

Addressing an assembled group of employees, Goebbel commanded, "Initiate the mechanized seine."

While Goebbel and Negrete watched, the colossal net began inching forward, herding the throng of nervous, jumpy salmon into a workable condensed pod. At this point a workman stuck the vacuum hose into the midst of the corralled fish, turned on the pump, and began siphoning the cage of its valuable inhabitants.

"Evaluation time," said Goebbel to Negrete. "Let's see if my over-paid veterinarian has finally earned his money."

Walking at a hurried pace, they made their way to the separating table, where hundreds of salmon were quickly being graded by laborers who were barely recognizable in their yellow-colored waterproof overalls. After a cursory inspection the salmon were then slung into one of two slaughter lines, the chosen path dependent upon the rating they received.

"God-damned quack of a doctor," Goebbel swore loudly, "son of a bitch incompetent asshole." He then shouted an order, sending an employee scurrying on a mission to locate and retrieve the inept veterinarian.

It was apparent to Negrete why Goebbel was angry; approximately seventy-five percent of the sockeye salmon were infected with ectoparasitic sea lice. The small marine copepods were feeding on the mucous, gills, skin, fins, and blood of their hosts, causing abrasion-like lesions, inflammation, skin erosion, scale loss, constant bleeding, and deep open wounds. The nature and severity of the vampirish infestation varied from one fish to another. In the most severe cases the tiny creatures had eaten down to the actual bone on the fish faces, exposing the skull, a condition referred to as the 'death crown.'

The obvious problem with salmon afflicted with sea lice was the market value of the whole fish—the bloody and ghoulish deformities unappetizing to the consuming public. The other reality, which Negrete had learned over the past several months, was that the malaise acted as a vector for the spread of other pathogens, including Infectious Salmon Anemia and the Furunculosis bacterium. Infectious Salmon Anemia turned the salmon's flesh to mush. Furunculosis caused boil-like blisters on the skin and musculature of the fish.

As a result of the quantity of diseased fish, the two slaughter lines were unequally burdened; the pristine salmon, destined as fresh fish fillets or whole fish, sailed down their line. The plagued fish, which, on an ethically managed aquafarm, would automatically be destroyed, were backed up like polluting cars on a congested Los Angeles freeway. Goebbel, however, was not one to allow lofty principles to interfere with profits. He had the unwholesome salmon entirely filleted, his workers diligent at removing any possible signs of ill health. He then had it either smoked, chopped up and formed into salmon patties for grilling on the barbeque, or had the tasteless flesh disguised by having it packaged as gourmet dinners: *Macadamia-Crusted Salmon Marinated in a Thai Peanut Sauce; Herb-Crusted Salmon Flavored with a Pommery Mustard Sauce; Parmesan-Crusted Salmon Fused with Lemon Butter;* or, *Coconut-Crusted Salmon Smothered in a Rum Butter Sauce.* Goebbel, in fact, charged a premium for the designer dinners; he also advertised the salmon patties as rich in Omega-3 and as a healthy alternative to red meat, and sold a majority of the smoked fish during the seasonal holidays.

Negrete grimaced sympathetically as Dr. Alfonso Mendez entered the room. Envisioning Goebbel's unrestrained wrath, he would not want to be Mendez at this moment. Dr. Mendez received his doctoral degree in Veterinary Medicine from the Universidad de Conception School, located in Chile. After graduating second in his class, he was hired by a multinational Norwegian Aquaculture Company as their in-house veterinarian overseeing the health of millions of salmon at their Chilean Aquafarms. The oversized fish enclosures were crammed to capacity, inevitably leading to massive sea lice infestations as well as devastating viral and bacterial infections. In treating the myriad of afflictions, Dr. Mendez pioneered the use of controversial pesticides and antibiotics in an attempt at controlling the chronic outbreaks. When Goebbel's aquafarms suffered the same fate he immediately hired the most knowledgeable person in the business—Alfonso Mendez, D.V.M.

Wearing a white frock and tennis shoes Dr. Mendez entered the butchering room. Five feet seven, a hundred fifty pounds, forty-two years old, with brown hair and brown eyes, and a warm squared face, he smiled respectfully as he recognized his boss. His smile instantly dissolved when Goebbel did not reciprocate.

He walked the final few steps as if he was stepping across a minefield, his expansive eyes glued to a steel table where Goebbel had neatly arranged five exemplar salmon.

Gripping a salmon disfigured by sea lice, Goebbel forcefully rammed it into the arms of Mendez, miring the doctor's unsullied coat with blood and mucus. Raising his voice he said, "I pay you for shit like this?"

Visibly rattled, Dr. Mendez held onto the salmon as if it were an infant child, its 'death crown' inches from his face—the outer flesh picked clean by over a dozen copepods—the ravenous lamprey-like creatures now extracting pinkish tissue deep within the skull's sunken furrows. Calmly placing the fish back on the table, Mendez then wiped his hands clean of its slimy residue, further soiling his coat. Elevating his chin until he was staring straight into Goebbel's irises, the petite doctor somehow found his voice, and with an inner boldness far surpassing his physical height said, "Yes . . . and I earned every damn peso."

Negrete silently laughed, admiring the doctor's bravado or stupidity, their mutual boss not very big on insubordination. Negrete anticipated Goebbel's response. It didn't take long.

Standing six feet three inches, Goebbel was like an ancient Nephilim giant compared to the diminutive Mendez. Towering above the doctor Goebbel reacted violently; using his muscular arms and hands he grabbed Mendez by his mid-section—hoisting the startled man off the ground as if he was weightless, and then, in the same mold as a barbaric Sumo wrestler, body slammed him into the five salmon, the dynamic impact rupturing the fish and ejecting bloody entrails in every direction.

Negrete sensed a fearful hush enveloping the slaughter room as every employee stared at the prostrated doctor—lifeless on the mangled carcasses of his watery patients. For a brief second he wondered if Goebbel had inadvertently murdered the doctor.

"Get back to work!" Goebbel yelled at the rubbernecking laborers. "It's none of your damn business."

Negrete noted that the workers did not require a second warning. He was about to personally assess Dr. Mendez's physical condition when the man suddenly sat up; *he's certainly resilient*, thought Negrete. The doctor then began cleansing his body of gut fragments, ridding the viscera with his index fingers—flicking off each grisly item as if it were a pesky fly. Satisfied with his new state of tidiness, Mendez then spoke to Goebbel, who was standing two arm lengths away.

"Do you want to know the reasons *why* I've earned my money?" Dr. Mendez persisted, apparently none the worse after his harsh encounter.

Negrete was now certain that Mendez had a death wish. Perspiration eked down his boss' forehead and his fists were curled into softball-sized boulders. If tension was tangible, Negrete could have sliced it with a switchblade. But, to his surprise, Goebbel restrained himself—at least for the moment.

"And why is that?" Goebbel demanded.

"For my superior knowledge and expertise—"

"Which sucks," interjected Goebbel.

"—at treating and curing debilitating infections that are ravaging your aquafarms."

"Quite a pathetic success story," Goebbel said derisively, "since sockeye salmon were not exempt from your job duties."

"Five months on the job and you expect miracles?"

"I pay you four times what you made in Chile . . . I expect . . . I insist on results."

"You're as naïve as my prior Norwegian managers. In Chile I experimented with every known antibiotic and pesticide—those legal and those illegal—with limited success at eradicating the sea's pestilences. I agreed to do the same . . . on a temporary basis at your three improperly operated fish farms . . . until the promised changes could be implemented."

"Regrettably current economics don't allow any alteration to our ongoing business model," Goebbel informed him.

"You mean ridiculous profits and to hell with the consuming public," Dr. Mendez countered.

"I've received no complaints from any of our customers nor have you refused a paycheck."

"My compensation doesn't matter to me anymore, and it's only a question of time before an independent lab conducts its own investigation and discovers our illegal use of banned chemicals, or God forbid, a new USDA inspector who's unbribable shows up."

"You threatening me?" Goebbel asked coldly.

"Absolutely not; I've committed my own litany of sins. But you originally hired me for my expertise. Platform Grace epitomizes the ideal aquafarm. Gilda, Gail and Gina are verifiable disasters—just like the Chilean-managed farms, and for that matter, a vast majority of the world's industrial-style aquafarms. You can't cultivate millions of fish in a tiny space and expect vigorous, healthy fish. At best your sockeye salmon grow-out pens should contain fifteen thousand individuals; you have fifty thousand—guaranteeing infestations of sea lice, Infectious Salmon Anemia, and Furunculosis. A month ago I unilaterally decided against the continual use of any pesticides or antibiotics. They're not needed at Grace, and I will no longer administer them at Gilda, Gail, or Gina. You want unadulterated, natural fish like your advertisements boast? Lower the stocking densities—only then will the predictable virus and bacterial plagues cease. Also, for purity sake, stop feeding your fish meat and bone meal made from cows. Those pellets are abnormal fodder and a perversion of the food cycle. It also turns the flesh of salmon a dirty gray necessitating the use of the red dye Canthaxanthin in order to artificially colorize the meat and fraudulently boosts its value."

Leaning toward Mendez in an intimidating manner, Goebbel said, "You finished with your self-righteous sermon? For your information the protein-rich pellets are seven times cheaper than the locally harvested foodstuff. That makes the cost of running Grace astronomical compared to the other facilities. In fact, we're lucky if we break-even on that metal money-pit of a facade. It's the millions of fish at this facility, and the two other platforms, that generate all my profits. Your little stunt of withholding critical medicine and pesticides has unfortunately put a huge dent in my bottom line; higher labor costs, wasted meat, additional packaging, expensive ingredients, and the realistic possibility that some asshole buyer or customer will notice something amiss, contact a local news organization, and essentially shut us down with the adverse publicity and subsequent investigation."

"So . . . nothing's ever going to change?" Dr. Mendez asked discouraged.

Laughing derisively, Goebbel said, "You're an idiot—no reforms were ever planned."

"Then why was I brought in?"

"Have you ever picked a lock?" Goebbel asked rhetorically. "You are our lock, our brilliant pawn, painstakingly picked and manipulated in order to provide *West Coast Seafood & Aquaculture* with the correct percentages and types of pesticides and antibiotics required to successfully operate a congested fish farm— without the need for any troubling modifications. There is, however, one minor revision in the overall management structure of the company that I am pleased to share with you; your services as a veterinarian are hereby terminated. Your return trip back to the mainland leaves in five minutes with Captain Negrete as your special host. Enjoy the boat ride, and, incidentally, there will be no final paycheck."

"You can't treat me this way," Dr. Mendez protested, "I have legal rights."

"The hell you do!" Goebbel angrily replied. "You're on a six-month work Visa and I just cancelled its renewal. Unless you want me to notify immigration I strongly suggest that you shut your damn mouth and immediately remove your ass to the *Lucky Lady*."

Dr. Mendez viscerally reacted to Goebbel's disparaging rant by reflectively opening his mouth to respond in kind, but then

sanely snapped it shut without uttering a word, and in a final dignified huff stalked out of the slaughter room.

"Frikkin' moron," Goebbel said aloud for everyone to hear. And
then in a conspiratorial whisper said to Negrete, "Unfortunately the
doctor knows too much. I'm having an empty barrel loaded onto
your ship. A side trip to the Santa Cruz Basin seems appropriate.
Let me know when he's no longer a threat." Before Negrete could
reply Goebbel slipped out of the slaughter room, his boss purposely
avoiding any collusive eye contact.

Walking unhurriedly and in contemplative silence, Negrete
made his way to the *Lucky Lady*. Murder—of an innocent man—
was his boss's order. On two prior occasions he had ended a
man's life; a rival gang member and Captain Barton. But those
incidents occurred during a life and death struggle, when he was
emotionally enraged, and self-defense kicked in as a legitimate
excuse. To kill someone in cold-blood was different. *And how?*
Use the shark bat as he did on Barton, or stab the doctor with the
boat's twelve-inch fillet knife, or through a simpler and less messy
option, strangulation. Considering the difficult circumstances
of a rocking ship, strangulation made the most sense. He could
easily compress the doctor's windpipe with his two bare hands,
or obstruct the intake of air with a rope, or suffocate him using
a thin wire. He did not own a gun. He had no doubt about the
probability of success. The doctor was all brains and little brawn,
weak and soft, and physically incapable of defending himself.

After casting off from Platform Gail, Negrete gunned the
engines, anxious for this voyage to end. Dr. Mendez was sulking in the ship's kitchen, which was fine with Negrete; small talk
would not have been conducive to fulfilling the task at hand. As
he passed the yellow 'no trespassing buoy,' he noted a relatively new, twenty-six foot cruiser anchored up fifteen feet beyond
the restricted zone, the ship's bow inscribed with the *University of
Malibu, Marine Lab* logo. A lone gentleman decked out in fishing
gear waved as he roared by. In gold lettering, on the ship's stern,

was the vessel's name—*Amber Waves*. Normally he would have stopped to investigate, but not today. His calendar was booked solid. Besides, as was typical with most yachts that anchored up, it was just a fisherman out for the day, hoping to catch escaped game fish. But, being prudent, he radioed Goebbel, and reported the ship.

From the buoy he headed south for three miles and then turned southwest. When he cleared San Pedro Point, situated on the southernmost tip of Santa Cruz Island, he veered due west instead of turning east toward the ship's home port located at Ventura Harbor. At this point even the pouting doctor knew something was up. It wasn't long before he stepped into the pilothouse.

"This isn't the way back home," the doctor insisted.

After a brief hesitation, Negrete said, "Minor detour for sightseeing."

"Sightseeing what—an empty ocean?"

"Whales . . . dolphins . . . seals."

"That's crap, and you know it."

"I guess we'll know soon enough," Negrete said and shrugged his shoulders.

"Why the bullshit?" demanded Dr. Mendez.

Negrete did not answer. Dr. Mendez wasn't being fooled by his cockeyed verbiage.

After a minute Mendez asked nervously, "What have I done to you?"

Negrete noticed that Dr. Mendez was shivering. He increased their speed. On the horizon a flock of Brandt's cormorants were dive-bombing a school of sardines. A few brown pelicans joined in. He ignored the doctor's question. Santa Cruz Basin was less than a tenth of a mile away. With his left hand he nervously fingered a two-foot section of steel wire concealed within his pants pocket. Wire was always quicker.

"What have I done to you?" Dr. Mendez repeated.

Negrete did not want to respond. Communication served no purpose at this point. But he felt the doctor deserved an honest explanation. "My boss fired you. Vengeful people spread rumors."

His voice trembling, Dr. Mendez said, "I'm from Chile. I'll take the next plane out—and tell your boss that I don't hold a grudge."

Too much talking, thought Negrete. A gun would have been ten times easier. Suddenly, the GPS unit attached to the pilothouse roof sounded a musical chime informing him that the *Lucky Lady* had arrived at the mile deep abyss. He throttled back the engines, slowing the craft to a crawl. He then provided Dr. Mendez with one last reason. "Damaging gossip knows no boundaries."

"I won't tell a soul," Dr. Mendez promised.

Negrete shook his head. Though murder was as old as time, the universal use of the Internet had changed everything. This ongoing discussion was going nowhere. He switched off the dual engines, letting the boat drift.

"I have a wife and two young daughters," pleaded Dr. Mendez. "Here, let me show you." Fumbling for his wallet the doctor extracted two small pictures. In his nervous haste they slipped out of his grasp and fell to the deck. Shaking like a palm tree during a violent hurricane, he attempted to retrieve them.

"Leave them!" shouted Negrete. The doctor froze, but it was too late for Negrete. The photos had landed upright, and the pretty faces of the man's wife and two young daughters were instantly seared upon his conscience. The spouse appeared thirty-ish; the girls, five and seven. An attractive widow could always find a new husband, but a daughter never recovered from the loss of a loving and faithful father. Growing up in South Central Los Angeles he had witnessed the deaths of far too many dads. The neighborhood gangs killed indiscriminately, with some of their bullets striking harmless bystanders, including fathers. He was always surprised at how the adolescent girls never fully recovered. Boys seemed to do much better. He had hated his dad, and when he died unexpectedly, Negrete's world actually improved. Dr. Mendez's photos—fortunately or unfortunately—were too much. Too many painful memories. Wearily rubbing his eyes, Negrete sighed. He had made his decision. "What's their names?"

"Who?" Dr. Mendez asked confused.

"Your daughters."

"Maria and Elizabeth."

Common Biblical names, Negrete surmised. Catholicism was strong in Chile. His own mother was named Maria, after Saint Mary, the mother of Jesus. "And your wife?"

"Sharon."

Sharon, concluded Negrete, was another Christian name. He restarted the *Lucky Lady's* engines and cranked the ship's wheel 180 degrees, redirecting the boat east—toward Ventura Harbor. Once the craft was cruising at eight knots, he engaged the autopilot. The return trip would take less than two hours. Dr. Mendez was still standing in the pilothouse, as stationary as a Greek marble statute. Negrete indicated by waving his hand that Mendez was to occupy the co-pilot's seat. The doctor obediently responded.

"My life is now in your hands," Negrete said, educating the doctor on the seriousness of the situation.

"I understand," said the doctor.

"You'll need to disappear . . . on the first plane out . . . and immediately return back to your native Chile."

"I have cash in my apartment, a laptop computer, clothes, and other items that I'll need to obtain—before I can leave."

"Absolutely not," Negrete objected. "You're supposedly dead. The property in your apartment is now mine. Goebbel expects that."

"But—I have four thousand dollars stashed in my unit."

"Where?" asked Negrete.

"Why should I tell you?" Dr. Mendez asked suspiciously.

"Because you owe me." Using a key, Negrete opened a locked console adjacent to the Captain's seat, removed a wad of crisp, one hundred dollar bills, and handed five thousand to Dr. Mendez. "Advance payment for the cash, computer, and whatever else I find of value."

In a choked-up voice Dr. Mendez said, "Thank you. It's in a hollowed-out book—Herman Melville's, *Moby Dick*."

"I'll find it," Negrete assured him. He then took possession of Dr. Mendez's apartment key. "One other thing—you need to lay low for at least six months. No discussing your experiences in America, no Internet blogging, no mass e-mails, no lectures at any universities, no new publications, and take down any personal websites. I don't want Goebbel accidentally discovering you're still alive. In a few months your name won't even ring a bell in his memory. But, in the short term it's important to hide your existence. If he does eventually find out, then I'll have to deal with it; however, the longer that moment is delayed—the better off I'll be."

"I'll be as inconspicuous as a grain of sand on the seashore," Dr. Mendez declared. "Financially, I've done well, so making money is not an issue—at least for the next year."

"Good—then we have an understanding."

"Yes," nodded Dr. Mendez.

Prior to arriving at Ventura Harbor, Negrete halted the *Lucky Lady's* progress long enough to sink a barrel who's intended purpose had been circumvented. While he was engaged in this activity, Dr. Mendez ordered a cab, and arranged passage to his own country via Chile's International Airline, the jet departing from LAX at 10:00 p.m.

On his way home, Negrete deviated from his usual route in order to swing by Dr. Mendez's apartment, and secure a classic novel. The unit was leased by *West Coast Seafood & Aquaculture*. Negrete was pleased to discover that Dr. Mendez's assurances of four thousand dollars cash proved accurate. The laptop computer was also a brand-new Apple MacBook Pro. In addition to the computer there was an Apple iPod and iPad. The doctor liked expensive electronics. The clothes, unfortunately, were not Negrete's size or style. Most everything else was stock rental items—furniture and kitchen appliances. Before leaving, he checked the refrigerator and was pleased to discover an unopened bottle of Don Julio 1942 Tequila, which typically retailed for over one hundred twenty-five dollars. Overall, Negrete came out ahead.

Driving to his townhouse, Negrete's cell phone rang. He checked the caller ID and noted that it was Goebbel. Rather than answering the call he sent back a responsive text stating, "Our mutual friend is chilling out." It was a perfect message; not really a lie but not quite the truth. Goebbel would assume he was referring to the bone-chilling temperatures at the bottom of the sea, while the actual Mendez was *chilling* at the airport. And, as icing on the cake, Negrete was looking forward to his own *chilled* glass of expensive Don Julio Tequila—a perfect way to end an arduous day.

19

Eva Chen stood at the steering wheel of the quietly idling *Amber Waves*, a twenty-six foot Seaswirl Striper owned by the Marine Lab. She had just glanced at her watch when the vessel she was waiting for came into view. *Punctual as usual,* she thought as the sixty-five foot Island Packers ferry pulled up to the Scorpion Cove pier. A waiting crewmember deftly tethered the ship to an aluminum passenger ramp located near the end of the wooden dock. Coffee-hyped and anxious to come ashore, commuters quickly disembarked and made their way up the ramp. Eva scrutinized each passenger, searching for Doctor Matthew Sedrak. In a brief and somewhat humorous e-mail, he had described himself as an 'intelligent looking six foot, blond haired and blue-eyed surfer, who just happened to be a doctor.' As it was the only description Eva had of the man, their rendezvous seemed more like an old-fashioned blind date than a meeting of espionage-minded partners. Eyeing the crowd, Eva concluded that identifying the neurologist wouldn't be overly difficult inasmuch as most doctors were stylistically vogue in their manner of dress, though the surfer identifier might prove this theory invalid.

A curly haired, blond gentleman, dressed in bright red O'Neill board shorts, black Olukai skater shoes, a tight-fitting bluish

Volcom tee-shirt covered by a charcoal gray Billabong hooded sweatshirt, and carrying a tan colored Kenneth Cole leather brief-case, caught her attention.

"Dr. Sedrak?" she asked as the man came alongside her vessel.

Stopping abruptly he replied, "Yes—and I assume you're Dr. Chen."

"Captain Chen today," she said gallantly, "and welcome to my yacht."

"And a beautiful ship that she is," Dr. Sedrak declared, and laughed. He then stepped onboard.

After a quick handshake, Eva said, "Let's skip the Doctor titles since it's just you and I."

"That's fine with me."

Redoing the handshake she said, "Eva Chen."

"Matthew Sedrak."

"That's much better," Eva said with a pleased smile, "formal titles are overrated."

"I couldn't agree more," Sedrak said, and then asked: "Where do I store my briefcase?"

"Cabin area, it'll stay dry in there."

Pointing to his briefcase, Sedrak said, "Before we weigh anchor I have some interesting test results."

"Of what?" asked Eva.

"The Santa Barbara Zoo's histological brain tissue study on that bottlenose dolphin that attacked several surfers at Surfer's Point. Would you like to see them now?"

"Most definitely yes," Eva said enthusiastically, "there's a table in the galley we can use."

Leading the way, Eva opened the door to the interior cabin and galley. She sat down in a cushioned booth adjacent to a small rectangular stainless steel table suitable for four compact adults. Sedrak joined her, occupying the opposite seat. Unclasping his briefcase, he removed a thin folder and handed it to Eva.

After examining the document Eva read its conclusion out loud: "The male, Tursips Truncatus, or by its more familiar name, Pacific bottlenose dolphin, was suffering from an advanced stage of spongiform encephalopathy, a debilitating prion disease similar to Chronic Wasting Disease found in ruminant livestock, or as it's known in humans, Variant Creutzfeldt-Jakob disease. Our research indicates that this is the first documented case of this particular brain-wasting malady affecting a cetacean species. All other cases involve land-based animals. How that transmission occurred—cross-species transference—is genetically unknown. The nature of this disorder requires a priority one investigation to determine if this is the beginning of a devastating epidemic. A copy of this report has been forwarded to the CDC."

"Scary isn't it?" Sedrak commented.

Sliding the file back, Eva said, "If it's the start of an epidemic it goes way beyond that; the probable impact upon all animal species is terrifying."

"Two humans, a sea lion, and a dolphin, all afflicted with the same pathology and all within a short window of time—it's nature run amuck," Sedrak said emphatically.

"And that's what today's investigative trip is all about," Eva replied forcefully, "to hopefully find some answers and possibly end this crisis."

"You're still convinced that Goebbel's aquafarms are the culprit?"

"More than ever."

"Then I suggest we get going," Sedrak said. "The sooner we solve this perplexing medical mystery, the sooner mankind, sea lions, and our dolphin friends, can return to a state of benign normalcy."

"I concur wholeheartedly," Eva said.

While Sedrak jettisoned the mooring ropes and retrieved the elliptical dock shield fenders, Eva warmed up the 310 horsepower

Volvo Penta inboard diesel engine. Once the engine was at sufficient operating temperature, she slowly eased the ship away from the dock and out into the cove. Once free of the speed constraints, Eva accelerated to twelve knots and inputted the GPS coordinates for Platform Gail—their estimated time of arrival less than forty minutes. In her analysis of the three off-limits aquafarms Gail was her first choice; it was the furthest from Grace, which in her logical mind meant it was probably the most poorly managed of the three non-public platforms, therefore making it the ideal snooping place. It was clearly a better option than just tossing a coin.

Walking back into the cabin Sedrak asked, "Where to?"

"Platform Gail."

"What do you have in mind once we arrive?"

"Drop anchor just outside the restricted zone and initially act like casual tourists out for a day of sightseeing and fishing. I borrowed two of the lab's Sunagor Mega Zoom Binoculars which will enable us to examine every square foot of the facility. After that you'll spend the next two hours fishing and hopefully catching several escaped game fish. Any fish hooked we'll have analyzed by the lab. Meanwhile, I'll surreptitiously explore the underside of the aquafarm using a closed circuit Drager Rebreather. The unit produces no bubbles so no one will know I'm there."

"I'm not a scuba diver, so forgive me for asking, but is that a safe thing to do in the open ocean?"

"Honestly—I should have a buddy, especially with a rebreather, but I'm willing to accept the risks. I've never suffered a serious incident."

"I like the word *serious* which ignores minor to moderate. You know . . . if anything happens down under . . . there's not much I can do for you," Sedrak said concerned.

"Thank you, that's sweet," said Eva, "but I promise I'll be beyond careful."

"That's good because you're definitely on your own," he warned. "Now, as for your volunteer fisherman, what bait did you bring?"

"Squid, the lab has lots of it, and the fish love it; it's their version of candy."

"Squid as candy—only in the gastric eyes of a fish," laughed Sedrak.

"You've never had calamari?" Eva asked.

"I hate the very idea of eating a creature that tastes like elastic rubber, has wraithlike tentacles, miniature suction cups, and pisses black ink."

"Where's your sense of adventure?" laughed Eva.

"In free-range organic chicken," Sedrak grinned.

"Not a bad alternative," Eva agreed. She then stole a furtive glance at Sedrak. He was considerably more charming than she had expected. An intelligent, brave, sensitive, compassionate, and comely doctor—a tempting combination—and then there was Kurt Nichols. *Quality men, what a rare treat,* thought Eva.

For the next twenty minutes they rode in silence. Eva spent the time formulating her dive plan and mentally reviewing what she hoped to accomplish while submerged. Platform Gail was situated approximately two miles north, off the western tip of Santa Cruz Island. Skirting the mainland side of the island, she maintained a constant distance of several hundred yards from the craggy cliffs and primordial shoreline, as captivating in its natural beauty as it was a millennium ago. Upon reaching Painted Cave State Marine Conversation Area she turned north, toward Gail. Travelling at twelve knots it would be another seven minutes.

"Is that massive black hole that we just passed a cavern?" asked Sedrak.

"Painted Cave," Eva replied. "It's one of the largest and longest sea caves in the world."

"How big?"

"The subterranean grotto has a 160-foot entrance ceiling, threshold width of 100 feet, and extends 1215 feet in length; it's longer than four football fields."

"Wow! Sedrak marveled. "Have you ever surveyed it?""

"Not yet, but it's a priority item on my bucket list."

"Why's it called Painted Cave?"

"Because of its colorful rocks, rainbow-dyed lichens, and variegated algae."

"You might think I'm being bold—but count me in on that future trip."

"Of course; it would be an honor to have your company. In fact, Jake and Mischa—two adorable teenagers whose dad oversees the marine lab—recently expressed an interest in exploring the cave along with the island's Chumash Indian caretaker, Adam Timbrook, who said he would act as our guide. He's an expert at navigating the labyrinth of bisecting chambers and swirling tidal currents, which occasionally can be quite treacherous. We'll make it a combined date."

"In the not-too-distant future," Sedrak insisted.

"I'll talk with Jake, Mischa, and Timbrook upon our return and confirm a day," Eva assured him.

"Thanks, nothing better than a spine-tingling journey into nature's majesty."

"I'm glad you're a swashbuckler," advised Eva, "because today's perilous adventure begins in seven minutes."

"Your First Mate is ready, willing, and able to serve," Sedrak joked, and then executed a military type salute that was far from polished.

Eva rewarded his boyish attempt at humor with a girlish smile. The doctor was turning out to be an excellent First Mate.

Cruising at twelve knots, the time passed quickly. "Behold the behemoth," Eva said, referring to Platform Gail, which filled the skyline. The ungainly four-story structure sprouted from the sea like a misplaced Goliath-sized erector set. Easing off on the fuel, Eva rapidly decelerated, and guided the ship to a stop within fifteen feet of a six-foot high, yellow-colored No Trespassing buoy. She then had Sedrak undo the anchor lock, which allowed her to drop the ship's forty-eight-pound stainless-steel fluke anchor. It had a long descent before hitting bottom. Eva slowly backed the ship, dragging the anchor, until the flukes dug in, whereupon she shut down the engine.

"That anchor took a lot of rope," Sedrak reported.

"Seven hundred feet," Eva confirmed.

"And you're still diving?"

"Yes. I won't go below sixty feet, so it doesn't matter how deep it is."

"That platform is at least three hundred yards away," Sedrak added, "that's a long swim."

Eva laughed and said, "I'm not a martyr so don't worry; I'll be employing a submarine propulsion device."

"A what?"

"An electric scooter. The torpedo-shaped apparatus will do all the work. I'll just hang on for the ride."

"A Disneyland-type excursion under the sea—towing a pretty mermaid—I should have known," Sedrak said, looking relieved.

Blushing red at the compliment, Eva whined, "Unfortunately a *fat* mermaid in my thick wetsuit," and then changing the subject asked, "Ready to conduct Operation Spy, Mr. Sleuth?"

"Absolutely."

"We'll stay inside the cabin in order to avoid detection," Eva explained, "since two individuals intensely scrutinizing an aqua-farm with binoculars may raise some hackles." She then slid open the boat's side windows inasmuch as the glass had become coated with salt-spray during their forty-minute journey. Using the Sunagor binoculars they began a high-resolution inspection of the imposing structure and fish pens.

After ten minutes Sedrak asked, "See anything of interest?"

"Not much; a docked ship named the *Lucky Lady,* workers scurrying about like pollen-smitten bees, and apparently it's chow time," Eva replied. "Those mechanical feeding tubes are saturating the pens with tons of pellets, which the fish are going nuts over."

"Any idea what those pellets are made from?" Sedrak asked.

"According to our lab . . . cow by-products."

"Did you say *cows?*" Sedrak repeated.

"Well yes, in the sense of the word, but in pellet form. The carcasses are pulverized into meat and bone meal and then formulated into those disgusting pellets which the fish seem to love. Brandon, a chemist at our lab, analyzed the substance and stated it's rich in protein."

"Do you know where they're produced—what country?" Sedrak asked.

"No . . . does it matter?"

"Maybe—if it's fabricated in Europe."

"The workers are dumping additional bags into those feeder tubes—perhaps we can get a read on the manufacturer or country of origin," Eva said optimistically.

Raising their binoculars, they both examined the distant sacks. After five minutes Sedrak lowered his glasses and shook his head. "The writing's too small. We'll need an actual bag. Did you do any better?"

"No," she said grinning, "but I've now modified my dive plan."

"And that would be—"

"Snatching an empty sack. And, from the shiny appearance of the bags they're obviously made from waterproof plastic which means I can drag a sack through the ocean without it falling apart or dissolving."

"Gutsy. What if you get caught?"

"I won't," Eva said confidently. "They're piling the empty bags at the water's edge. Shadowy-like, I'll ascend to where they're being stacked, reach up, seize a sack, and then disappear before anyone notices. I can't imagine they'll miss one bag. They'll just assume it fell into the sea."

Sedrak appeared to weigh his response before offering his opinion. "It's dangerous, but feasible, so please be cautious."

"Always," she said, and rewarded his concern with a warm smile. "It's time to suit up."

Staying within the security of the spacious cabin, Eva first laid out all her dive gear. She then professionally checked and tested each piece of equipment—ensuring that each component was functioning properly before donning a single item. The sole glitch was her Oceanic Mako DPV Scooter. For some unknown reason its rechargeable battery was only three-quarters full. Instead of two hours of electrical juice she had less than an hour and a half. Not good news; it meant that she would have to vigilantly monitor the LED Battery Indicator throughout the duration of her dive. While Eva was suiting up, Sedrak was out on the deck rigging his fishing tackle. He was determined to fill the fish hold. Instead of catch and release, he planned on the exact opposite, catch and decease.

Finished, Eva clumsily hobbled out onto the deck. Encumbered with an odd assortment of equipment she resembled the quirky beast from the Sci-Fi movie, *The Creature from the Black Lagoon*.

"I love your gaudy wetsuit," Sedrak remarked, "you look like a military frogman."

"It's a marine camo, mottled design; the brown green elements alter and obscure my appearance camouflaging me while underwater."

"If an Eva existed in a parallel universe," Sedrak said with wonder, "her dimensional twin would assuredly be a formidable secret agent."

"Now that's a pleasant thought," Eva said with a laugh. She then strolled to the swim platform and immediately submerged her torso into the ocean, anxious to limit her exposure on the open deck. Hanging onto the boat's swim ladder Eva waited as Sedrak retrieved her scooter. Mercifully, the fifty-four pound device became neutrally buoyant once immersed. After a final cursory check, Eva inserted the rebreather mouthpiece between her lips, gave a thumbs up—*I'm okay* gesture to Sedrak—and then slipped beneath the waves.

The change in worlds was immediate—the clear blue sky was instantly replaced with cold, green water, and visibility less than twenty feet. In order to conserve energy, Eva executed a slow downward spiral, allowing gravity to do its job. When her dive computer registered a depth of fifty feet she stopped her descent by adding some air to her buoyancy compensator. Contrary to her bravado topside, being alone in the middle of the ocean was an unnerving experience. Suspended like a piñata in seven hundred feet of murky water, her mind was seduced into believing that every ill-defined silhouette or reflection was a toothy creature lurking in the inhospitable abyss waiting to ambush her. Eva realized that in order to remain calm and focused she had to take control of her psyche. Fortunately, years of training helped: *the ocean is your friend*, she told herself. *Shark attacks in California are extremely rare; you are a professional diver; you've successfully completed hundreds of dives; your rebreather has over four hours of oxygen; the distorted clarity is caused by millions of microscopic plankton; the scooter, travelling at 2.5 miles per hour will take less than five minutes to reach the aquafarm; concentrate on the mission; you can do this; you're a fearless girl; relax and have fun.* Having exorcised her dive demons Eva felt the nervous tension slowly drain from her body. Checking her wrist-mounted compass, she repositioned her scooter so that it pointed due west. Without the simplistic eleventh century invention, Eva would essentially be blind as she attempted to navigate underwater. She then squeezed the throttle trigger, and the Mako DPV was off and running in the direction of Platform Gail.

Eva controlled the Mako's path with just a gentle movement of her arms. By twisting its streamlined nose in the desired direction, it would pitch left, right, up, or down—as easy as manipulating a feather—making the ride smooth and effortless. Cruising at over two knots it was hardly a roller-coaster ride, yet at the same time wonderfully exhilarating as Eva glided through the sea like a winged bird, banking and rolling as if skating on rivers of air. She maintained her depth between forty-five and fifty-five feet, adjusting the variable pitch propeller whenever necessary.

As she sailed through the turbid ocean, Eva noticed that it was uncannily devoid of marine life. She had her suspicions on what had caused this dead zone, but she needed proof. Eva observed a few small shoals of sardines, an occasional Pacific mackerel, and a couple of escaped aquafarm game fish. A half-dozen four-foot California barracuda hovered near the fringes of the sardines. Ferocious predators, these jackals of the seas were capable of swooping in and seizing a mouthful of sardines in one frenzied dash.

Gazing at her dive computer, Eva was exasperated to see that only four minutes had elapsed; it seemed much longer. She had just decreased the Mako's thrust to less than one mile per hour when she crashed headfirst into Gail's metal struts, its greenish color almost matching that of the water. It was an encounter she'd wanted to avoid, but luckily no harm had occurred.

At exactly five minutes and twenty seconds into her dive Eva finally slipped into the skeletal maze that made up Platform Gail. The unearthly setting caused Eva's entire body to stiffen as if temporarily paralyzed by fear. In clear seas Eva cherished diving beneath an oil platform. Today, unfortunately, the ocean below the sprawling edifice was churned up, and diving under an oil rig, when her perspective was obfuscated by cloudy seas, was comparable to strolling companionless through a graveyard on a moonless night, or sleeping alone in a poltergeist-haunted house. As a diver Eva typically appreciated structure of any type—whether a sandy bottom, seaweed, kelp, rocks, oil rig, or even a sunken ship—the familiar objects providing a sense of tactile security.

Eva's pre-planned dive strategies was to first survey the subaqueous operation of the aquafarm, and then pilfer the empty feed sack on her way back to the ship. Gently squeezing the scooter's trigger, Eva began a systematic inspection of Goebbel's vast array of netted fish enclosures.

After a half hour of cruising under and around numerous Kevlar meshed habitats, Eva was shocked to discover the egregious stocking densities of each pen. Every fish sty, whether stocked with bluefin tuna, yellowfin tuna, white seabass, or sockeye salmon, was crammed to capacity with thousands upon thousands of fish—all pitifully jammed together like stop-and-go traffic on a late afternoon Los Angeles freeway—with no relief exit in sight.

Clearly, no room to roam created an environment of unrelenting stress resulting in severely abnormal behavior. Eva observed pent-up aggression antithetical to the four species, with numerous fish ruthlessly attacking their own kind and causing widespread injuries and even death. Many of the fish were missing fins, or had chunks ripped from their bodies, or ulcerated sores, or had developed blinding cataracts, or had become oddly deformed like gnarled hunchbacks of the Notre Dame kind. Millions of sea lice—a parasitic blood-sucking flesh-eating creature—were prevalent in every pen. Unfortunately for the salmon, they were its favorite meal—the tiny denizens nibbling day and night until many of the sockeye were reduced to living zombies. It was a horrifying sight.

Throughout her dive Eva was occasionally visited by a curious sea lion or a wary bottlenose dolphin. The animals seemed apprehensive in their approach as if the noiseless human was somehow in competition for the few escaped game fish. One overly bold dolphin captured Eva's attention, and she began following it. The creature, aware of her actions, took off, soaring in and out through the steel pillars, with Eva in hot pursuit. The chase abruptly ended when the scooter's LED indicator light flashed yellow informing Eva that the battery level was now below sixty percent. Continuing the pursuit for any additional length of time would have guaranteed a drained battery. Her mission still required obtaining a feed sack and traversing 900-feet of open seas.

Checking her compass, Eva reoriented her scooter so that it pointed east—the direction of the empty pellet bags and her ship. Apparently her little romp with the dolphin had taken her to the far side of the oil rig. Coasting beneath the grow-out pens, Eva became nauseated at the amount of fish feces and dissolved food pellets that continuously rained down on her like mummy-brown snowflakes. The nutrient-loaded effluent had led to eutrophication of the waters underneath the nets, creating a dead zone similar to what occurs every summer in the Gulf of Mexico. Flora and fauna, of any type, was unnaturally absent as the tainted excrement from hundreds of thousands of fish along with protein rich food particles suffocated the life out of the nearby ocean.

The sudden vroom of a sizeable propeller churning the seas clued Eva to the fact that the large supply ship, previously seen docked at Gail, had departed. The turbulent swooshing sound of its prop wash was magnified underwater, causing Eva to shudder at the deafening roar, the noise thankfully ebbing as the vessel distanced itself from the aquafarm.

Where is that walkway containing the empty pellet bags? Eva asked herself. She felt certain that she was in the vicinity of the actual fish pen that she and Sedrak had focused upon. She cruised to within five feet of the surface, searching for the metal causeway where the bags were stacked. Before surfacing, she tried staring through the water to see if there were any workers in the area. Being detected or apprehended was not on her itinerary. Regrettably, it was easier to see down into the water than it was staring up through it from below. Underneath she was like a visually impaired person who had misplaced her coke-bottle glasses, where every image was now distorted. Eva realized that she did not have a choice in the matter; she would have to surface and take her chances if she hoped to obtain a sack. Hiding behind a massive beam for protection, she ascended the final few feet.

Peering around the girder, Eva was pleasantly surprised to see that the stack of empty bags was still situated at the water's edge, less than twenty-five feet away, and there was no one in sight. *Hallelujah!* She silently shrieked.

Descending to ten feet, she immediately scooted over to the calculated spot, and began to rise. Breaching the surface with hardly a ripple, she then dog-paddled the final few feet until her body was positioned alongside the bags. Temporarily releasing her grip on the scooter, Eva kicked her fins to build thrust, and quickly launched her body out of the water. On the way back down she latched onto a sack with her right hand, and was beginning to descend into the water when her gloved left hand was itself ensnared by a leather hand as unyielding as the tempered jaws of a cast-iron vise.

Hanging suspended over the ocean like a trophy fish, Eva tried yanking her clasped hand in a futile effort at breaking free from the steadfast hold. Her total weight, which included her dive equipment, was in excess of one hundred and fifty pounds, and yet the man held her as if he was curling a twenty-pound dumbbell weight. The man was as solid as he was tall, towering several inches above six feet, with muscular arms and hands. His clothing was hewed from expensive black leather, and his eyes were concealed behind black Chanel sunglasses. His grayish colored hair was tied in a fashionable ponytail with several gold bands. Eva instantly recognized the man—Karl Goebbel—the exalted owner of *West Coast Seafood & Aquaculture.*

Smiling with absolutely the whitest teeth Eva had ever seen, Goebbel said gloatingly, "My staff had you on radar the entire time. I'll make the assumption that you had a splendid time illegally touring our facilities. You know . . . trespassing is a punishable offense." He then laughed as he jerked Eva's body up and down, dragging her feet through the water, and then as a way to emphasize his point, flailed her body against the metal platform.

Spitting out her mouthpiece Eva screamed, "What do you want?" Mercifully, her seven-millimeter thick wetsuit had cushioned the impact, and she was not harmed.

"Why are you here?" he asked authoritatively. "We've scoped your vessel and therefore know by the name imprinted on its bow that you're from the marine lab. I want to know why the lab has a sudden interest in my facility, and why you're endeavoring to steal an empty feed sack."

Miraculously, Eva still clutched the bag in her right hand. She was about to respond, when she noticed a slight slippage of Goebbel's grasp. Wiggling her fingers and then physically constricting and tightening the muscles and ligaments in her slender hand, she was able to further reduce its actual size. In addition, the oily hydrating lotion that she daily applied to her arms and hands was adding to the slipperiness of her wet neoprene glove. Goebbel, who was also acutely aware of the tenuousness of his grip, attempted to firm up his hold by crushing the delicate bones in Eva's hand, and in so doing accomplished the exact opposite—popping the glove off as if he was squeezing a half-peeled banana.

Tumbling into the ocean with a thunderous splash, Eva instinctively reinserted her mouthpiece, and dove straight down. At fifteen feet she stopped her descent and began searching for her scooter, spotting the prized device adrift in a westward flowing current. Executing a few powerful dolphin strokes she was reunited with her Mako scooter within a matter of seconds. Pointing it eastward toward the direction of her ship, Eva crushed the throttle trigger, instantly accelerating the scooter to its maximum speed of 2.7 miles per hour, while towing the coveted prize; a plastic feed bag.

She had traveled about seventy feet when the first explosion occurred. She knew exactly what it was—a seal bomb—which was a potent underwater firecracker typically used by commercial fisherman to scare off seals. The thrower obviously knew her intended path since the first shock wave almost dislodged Eva from her scooter, and caused an annoying echo-like ringing in both of her ears. Fortunately the blasts were meant to *scare* seals and not *kill* them, although a direct hit had the potential to be lethal. Eva immediately deviated from a straight line to a circuitous course, pushing her scooter to its limits. The next two salvos detonated harmlessly in an area lacking a human target—Eva's erratic track allowing her to successfully elude the lobbed bombs. After another fifteen seconds she was too far away for the incendiary contraptions to have any damaging effect.

Eva breathed a sigh of relief. She was not overly concerned about any above-water pursuit inasmuch as the only ship docked at Gail had recently departed. She knew the platform was equipped with emergency life rafts, but she doubted the rig's hired hands would actually go through the time-consuming process of deploying one. Taking a minute for underwater housework, Eva folded the feed sack, and tucked it into a large zippered pouch that was a component of her rebreather unit. She was just starting to emotionally let down—when the scooter sounded an alarm. Checking the LED indicator light she noted that it was flashing red, which meant that the battery level was dangerously low. As if that wasn't enough, she could sense a steadily increasing westward current that was beginning to hinder her forward progression.

Eva's knowledge of oceanic currents, and in particular, those located off of Southern California, flooded her mind, causing a brief moment of trepidation. She knew that the tidal currents whipping around in the middle of the Santa Barbara Channel were unpredictable and treacherous. Also, knowing that the strongest tidal flow existed in the upper level of the ocean, Eva dove to eighty feet in an attempt to lessen its influence on her eastward journey. Initially it helped, but the flowing watercourse was accelerating, and its effect was significantly interfering with her headway. The scooter's speed was also decreasing with each passing minute as its electrical engine drained what remained of the precious battery juices—rapidly decelerating from two miles per hour down to one, then limping along at a snail's pace, and finally dying with a lifeless sputter. Eva hung onto the scooter even though it was now a worthless piece of machinery—unwilling to part with an expensive piece of equipment, and one that had served her so well. But as the tidal flux increased, the weight of the object began to drag Eva backwards. Reluctantly, she released the Mako, and because it was neutrally buoyant, it slowly drifted in the current, stranded at eighty feet.

Eva then began her own battle with the river of moving water as she resolutely inched her way toward the approximate location of the ship. The beauty of the rebreather was that it still contained hours of oxygen, so running out of air was not a problem. She descended to one-hundred feet, but the tidal surge was as strong at this level as it was at eighty. She then descended to one hundred and thirty feet, the maximum operating depth of her rebreather, and unfortunately discerned no visible change. Physically swimming against the current was exhausting, especially with the chilly Pacific seeping into her wetsuit, numbing her limbs, and further sapping her reserve strength. The ongoing struggle was becoming mentally challenging allowing snippets of panic to enter into her brain. Eva estimated that she had covered about seven hundred feet, with about two hundred to go. Surfacing was out of the question since the current topside would be a raging beast.

Buckling down, Eva summoned every last fiber of stamina left within her, and counted her forward momentum not in yards but in feet, her inner drive unwilling to succumb to defeat. After fifteen minutes of tortuous progress, her flesh and bones had maxed out, and a diver's worst nightmare occurred—an incapacitating cramp struck Eva's right calf—disabling her leg and leaving her functionally lame. Unable to swim, and in excruciating pain with severe muscle spasms, Eva had to surface. Her fear upon surfacing was that she would be swept away in the four-mile per hour current, which was capable of transporting an individual one to two nautical miles in less than an hour. She prayed that Sedrak would fish her out of the ocean before she drifted into oblivion. Filling her BC with tiny puffs of air she began a controlled ascent. On the journey upward she passed the time by massaging her calf, anxious to restore circulation and assuage the involuntary muscle contractions. At forty feet she was met with the surprise of her life, which, but for the throbbing discomfort of her aching calf and the apparatus in her mouth, would have caused her to laugh euphorically.

Dangling in the water, marked with a high intensity strobe light, and weighed down by pounds of heavy fishing weights, was a diver's safety line. The one-inch thick nylon rope, tethered to the boat's stern, was typically deployed as a safety measure when diving in strong currents, sometimes extending out three hundred feet. Normally it floated on the surface and was attached to a buoy, but Sedrak had apparently removed the buoy, added the ultra bright flashing strobe light, and sank it with a consolidated bundle of one pound leaded fishing weights. How he had thought of this, being a non-diver and unfamiliar with hazardous oceanic currents, was beyond Eva's comprehension. Dr. Sedrak, Eva mused, was obviously an incredibly resourceful man.

Not wasting a moment, Eva hitched herself to the line and gave it several strong tugs—signaling Sedrak that she had arrived—and was rewarded with the wonderful sensation of being dragged forward through the water.

The free ride took longer than Eva expected. Several times Sedrak paused for a period of time before continuing with renewed effort. After a while she pitied the poor doctor; reeling in a hundred and fifty pound encumbered lady against a relentless current had to be laborious.

When the fiberglass swim step finally came into view, Eva shouted praises through her mouthpiece, jubilant that her ordeal had ended.

Sedrak helped Eva off-load her dive equipment while she was still treading water, and then lent a supporting hand as she unsteadily climbed up the stainless steel ladder, and into the comfort of a vinyl deck chair. The doctor then handed her a towel and a thirty-two-ounce bottle of orange Gatorade. She drank the Gatorade in less than thirty seconds. The cramp, blissfully, had all but disappeared. After a few additional moments of rest, and with Sedrak seated in the seat next to her, she leaned over and kissed him softly on the cheek, letting her lips linger.

"Thank you," she said.

"Anytime," Sedrak said with a wide grin, and then asked: "Was today one of those, 'I've never suffered a serious dive incident' type experiences?"

"Maybe," Eva said reciprocating with her own smile.

"Thought so," Sedrak replied, "I think I'll stick with surfing."

"Don't forget about marauding dolphins," she joked. She then spent the next ten minutes bringing Sedrak up to speed on the details of her dive. She concluded by asking: "What made you think to deploy the safety line, with the flickering strobe light, and to weigh it down?"

"The surface current," replied Sedrak. "It kept getting stronger. I figured you would try to swim under it. It made no sense deploying a floating safety line, and I had lots of extra fishing weights. At the time it seemed like the logical thing to do. I also wanted you to spot my underwater safety harness. I was rummaging through your dive bag, searching for a waterproof flashlight, when I discovered the strobe light."

"It may have saved my life," Eva whispered, "so thank you for being my champion."

"Do champions deserve a second smooch?" Sedrak said laughing. "My other cheek is lonely."

"Indeed they do," Eva replied, and caressed it with her lips, and then asked: "Anything else?"

"Yes, show me the feed sack that you snitched."

"Borrowed," said Eva, "I'm not a thief." She then unzipped the pouch on her rebreather, retrieved it, and handed it to Sedrak.

After unfolding it Sedrak read the words printed on the packaging label: "Meat and Bone Meal, produced and manufactured at Aspen Packers of Calmar, Alberta, Canada."

"That's not Europe."

"Not at all," Sedrak said disappointed. "But it's not the United States, so I still think it's worth looking into."

"What do you suggest?"

"You like Canada?"

"I've never been."

"It's beautiful, especially Alberta this time of the year."

"You serious?" Eva asked skeptically.

"Definitely; a visit to the manufacturer of *West Coast Seafood & Aquaculture's* meat and bone meal sounds like a jolly good vacation."

"Who's paying?" Eva wondered.

"The CDC. They're very much interested in discovering the source of the mad cow outbreak. I'll let the U.S. taxpayers foot the bill. We're conducting valuable research; they can't say no."

"If it's on their tab . . . I'll join you."

"Our second adventurous tryst," Sedrak said facetiously. "This could be the start of something special. I'll check with the airlines and get back to you within a week with some possible dates."

"I'm ready for a non-dive exploit so it sounds enticing," Eva said, and then asked: "And what about you—while I was Ms. Jacques Cousteau, risking my life—did you catch any game fish?"

"Are you kidding," Sedrak said boastfully, "I slaughtered them."

Opening the Seaswirl's built in insulated fish box, Sedrak proudly displayed eleven exotic game fish—four sockeye salmon, three yellowfin tuna, two bluefin tuna, and two white seabass—each weighing between ten to twenty-five pounds.

"That's one hellacious day of fishing," Eva declared. "It'll keep our chemist busy for hours analyzing these fish for any evidence of mad cow disease."

"Not a bad day of fishing—for both of us," Sedrak agreed. "My only worry was the ship from the rig—when it took off in my direction I was certain that I would be boarded, so I waved a friendly 'hello' like the charming chap that I am, and for whatever reason they raced on by as if I didn't exist."

"That was fortunate," Eva concurred.

As Sedrak and Eva hoisted their anchor and prepared to shove off, a tall stocky man dressed in leather, standing on the highest portion of Platform Gail, angrily powered down his high-definition digital camera. If looks could kill—the *Amber Waves* and its two passengers would be permanent residents of King Neptune's abode—lounging peacefully at the bottom of the sea.

20

The morning sun was just peeking through the clouds as Jake and Mischa rounded San Pedro Point in a small watercraft—destination Smuggler's Cove in order to continue their ongoing mission of mercy to save an ailing giant oarfish. The billowy cumulus clouds occasionally parted, allowing cathedral-like shafts of light to penetrate, illuminating the ocean's surface in brief displays of dazzling radiance. Because of the early hour, and the high dew point, the focused sunbeams were tangibly visible, as if endowed with material form. Sailors loved this moment of intimacy—when the awesome power of creation was both perceivable and touchable.

Mischa's older sibling, Jake, was at the controls of the lab's nineteen-foot Boston Whaler, powered by a 115 HP electronic fuel-injected Mercury Fourstroke outboard engine. The innovative engine purred like a lovable Siamese cat, casting its own unique sound as they motored through the gentle swells. Mischa occupied the passenger side of the same vinyl bench seat as her brother. The legendary Whaler design was supposedly unsinkable, highly maneuverable, and considered ideal for near shore exploration. Cruising at roughly twenty miles per hour, they still had two miles of ocean to cross before reaching their objective. The sturdy vessel was recently acquired by the lab, and had yet to be properly christened—with the honor of naming the ship entrusted to Jake and Mischa.

Today was day three in their crusade at rehabilitating the giant oarfish. Two days ago, their dad had procured from the lab's pharmacy a week's supply of antibiotics. The prescriptive titles meant nothing to Mischa—Phenobarbitone, Dexamethasone, and Penicillin—potent drugs that controlled seizures, cerebral edema, neutralized toxins, and attacked any infection. They also laced squid with vitamin B-12, which helped promote healing. The medications and B-12 were all in gel capsules, which worked well on land, but began to dissolve once submerged in salt water. The solution as Jake and Mischa had learned on day one was to take a whole squid, poke a tiny hole in its thick mantle, insert the pills, and then roll it up into a sushi ball. The technique worked well as long as the oarfish ate the delicacy within three minutes of immersion. Fortunately their dad had anticipated possible difficulties and had provided them with extra capsules.

The first day had definitely proved challenging; the feeble-looking oarfish was coiled deep within its lair, languishing sedately, with its distinctive prismatic skin now lackluster and mottled. After several frustrating attempts Jake finally succeeded in coaxing the creature into ingesting an entire sushi ball filled with therapeutic drugs. Mischa then experienced her own moment of success when she victoriously enticed the oarfish into swallowing two handfuls of twelve-inch squid. For a fifty-five foot beast it wasn't much, but it was a beginning. In order to restore its strength their dad estimated it would have to consume at least twenty pounds of meat per feeding session. At a half pound each that meant forty squid.

The second day results were somewhat similar to day one, with the creature barely moving and lacking any real appetite, although it did polish off a few extra squid. Mischa was hopeful that today's outing—day three—would be different and that the serpent would finally consume enough protein to begin to heal and to rebuild its muscles. Along that line she had purposely doctored the squid, confident that her actions would somehow stimulate its craving for nourishment.

As they entered Smuggler's Cove Jake eased off on the gas, slowing the Whaler. During their prior spearfishing excursion she had come up with the idea of tagging the serpent's sheltered sanctuary with a bright fluorescent orange nylon ribbon to mark its exact location. Within seconds of arriving at the Cove, she spotted the marker. "There it is!" she said triumphantly.

"Your idea has certainly paid off," Jake admitted. He then skillfully brought the boat to a halt within fifteen feet of the orange marker, shut the engine and let the vessel's momentum carry them the final few feet. Being concerned that the iron anchor might accidentally strike and injure their patient or that the sound of lowering it might startle it making it abandon its grotto, they instead secured their craft by tying its bow docking rope to several strands of giant kelp. To further ensure their success in their anticipated seven days of treatment, they had decided to skin dive rather than use scuba tanks, since most marine creatures became nervous and distrustful in the presence of the obnoxiously loud, bubble spewing, apparatuses.

As Jake was packing a slimy squid with the oarfish's daily allotment of curative pills and B-12, he said to Mischa, "Ready for day three?"

"Absolutely," she replied, "whatever it takes, and whatever time is required, that sea monster is going to recover."

"I like your optimism," laughed Jake.

"It ate a little on the first day, it ate a bit more yesterday, and it will eat like a ravenous pig today," Mischa said with determination.

"How do you know that?"

"Because of how I prepared its food; I squirted a tube of anchovy paste into my bucket of squid. It's been marinating all morning. I figured it would enrich the squid's flavor, making the candy bait even more irresistible."

"I feel my stomach growling just listening to you talk," Jake joked as he rubbed his abdominal area and smacked his lips. "When did you become such an expert on an oarfish's dietary preferences?"

"Every creature, including ocean critters likes their food a little spicy. The only seasoning that we had in our kitchen pantry—which I thought might work—was a tube of anchovy paste."

"It's a dumb fish," Jake reminded her, "not some sea-going finicky gourmet."

"That's your own narrow-minded opinion," Mischa said somewhat miffed, "let's wait and see what the oarfish thinks."

"We'll know soon enough," Jake said. He then sauntered over to Mischa's bucket and with a pretentious look dipped his medicinal filled squid into her aromatic concoction, raised it to his nose, sniffed it, and then in a slightly mocking tone said, "Yum, yum, bon appétit."

Refusing to dignify his derisive stunt Mischa said, "I'll see you underwater." She then finished donning her skin diving gear, dumped her scented squid into a nylon mesh sack, and using the dive ladder, slipped into the ocean. Jake immediately joined her.

"I'll go first," he said, "medicine before gluttony."

Jake's persistent sarcasm made Mischa glad she wasn't armed with a speargun; she would have been tempted to ding her brother. "I'll be right behind you," she said.

Plunging thirty-five feet, they found the giant oarfish encamped in its rocky cradle, the same as the prior two days, but with a trace more color to its silvery-blue scaleless skin. It also lifted its head, and followed their movements with disk-like eyes. Mischa watched as Jake edged closer to its oddly shaped, oblique mouth. He held the squid in the palm of his hand. He then extended his hand to within inches of its delicate jaws. To Mischa's delight the oarfish instantly inhaled the squid—the medicated ten-armed cephalopod disappearing in the blink of an eye—causing Mischa to crack a gratifying smile through her facemask. *The anchovy paste seems to be working,* she thought. As Jake ascended, seeking fresh oxygen, Mischa followed in his wake.

Treading water, Mischa said, "That was rather easy."

"It must've been hungry," Jake snapped.

"I'm sure it was," Mischa said playfully. "But even an oarfish appreciates good cooking."

"That was only one stupid squid. Try your bag of marinated ones before crowing like a rooster."

"I'm on my way. You can join me if you get bored being a spectator," Mischa teased.

After several deep replenishing breaths, Mischa quickly descended to the oarfish's shallow haven. Reaching into her mesh bag she extracted a handful of California squid. Cradling approximately eight in her right hand she positioned them beneath the serpent's protrusible mouth. Instead of swiftly gulping them down, the oarfish's decorative red headdress briefly flared bright red as it appeared to 'taste' the water surrounding the food items. It then arched its concave head in such a way as to nuzzle the stack of squid. Apparently satisfied with its investigative foraging, it began vacuuming each individual specimen—sucking them up like a high-powered cyclone sweeper—and after finishing off the final one commenced scrounging around for more.

Shaking with excitement, Mischa opened her mesh bag in order to withdraw additional squid. As she was about to reach in she was pleasantly surprised to find the oarfish intrusively poking its muzzle at the sack's entrance. Curious to see what the creature would do, she enlarged the gap, whereupon the serpent promptly burrowed its head inside, and rapidly plundered every last squid.

Ecstatic at being the proud diver of an empty sack, but desperate for air, Mischa soared toward the surface. At the fifteen-foot level she zipped by Jake, whose pouty demeanor informed her that he had observed the entire feeding frenzy.

Climbing back onto the boat, with Jake right behind her, she was anxious to hear his spin on the oarfish's sudden lust for squid. After removing her dive gear she asked sweetly, "Your eyes working okay today?"

"There's nothing wrong with my vision, little sister, so thanks for your concern. As I said earlier, it's probably starving."

"I'm sure it's famished, my fair-minded brother, but aren't you also willing to concede a few kudos for my anchovy paste idea?"

"A couple—but that's all I'm giving you," grinned Jake as he grabbed Mischa and tossed her overboard. Striking the water headfirst she dove straight down, executed a u-turn at about the ten-foot mark, and then took her time as she slowly worked her way back to the boarding ladder at the boat's stern. Laughing underwater at her brother's silliness—men had such fragile egos—she also knew that this was her brother's way of saying, 'of course you're right,' without actually admitting it. As she mounted the ladder's top rung, Jake flung a beach towel in her direction, which she caught with a "Thanks bro."

"You're welcome. And tomorrow . . . use two tubes of anchovy paste, double the amount of squid, and throw in few frozen sardines. That amount should equal twenty pounds. Let's get this sea monster back to its old self."

Smiling, Mischa said, "Aye Captain." As she wrapped herself in the warm cotton towel Jake prepared the boat for departure.

On day four the oarfish's color had improved substantially with a distinctive silvery-blue shimmer emanating from its skin. The medicated squid and extra food rations were all devoured within fifteen minutes of their arrival. When the last squid and sardine had disappeared, the serpent unexpectedly slithered out from its granite shelter, and followed Jake and Mischa half the distance to the surface, before returning back to its lair.

The fifth day was analogous to the previous one except the oarfish consumed its entire meal outside its rocky niche, and afterwards, tagged along like an obedient dog as Jake and Mischa explored the reef system near its sanctuary. It was also the day that they complied with their dad's request for photographs. Using a Sealife underwater digital camera they captured over one hundred images of the creature. Furthermore, as astutely noted by Mischa, the oarfish's coloration had changed dramatically, becoming more rainbow-like.

Day six was a day of revelation for both Jake and Mischa. Within seconds upon their arrival at Smuggler's Cove, and before they had even anchored up, the oarfish was swimming and thrashing the water alongside their boat, begging for its meal. Allowing the boat to drift, they hand fed their new pet from inside the Whaler, never once having to get wet.

Jake, in trying to fathom the oarfish's strange behavior, had an epiphany: "That fish has evidently linked the unique tone quality or pitch of our outboard engine to us—to our vessel," he explained to Mischa, "that's why it came up as soon as we arrived."

"Definitely *not* a dumb fish," Mischa said sharply, reminding Jake of his rude comment on day three.

"I agree," he said humbly. "I've now altered my perspective."

"Your expression of repentance is hereby accepted," Mischa said with a wink and a smile.

To their surprise and regret, the oarfish did not reappear on day seven. When it failed to greet them at the surface, Jake and Mischa began an underwater search. After confirming that it was not in its rocky grotto, they expanded their search outward—inspecting every possible hideaway within a one hundred yard radius. After two hours of probing, and without a single sighting, it was apparent that the creature had vacated its temporary home. Returning back to their boat, Jake started the Mercury outboard engine, and then made two complete passes across Smuggler's

Cove. Their hope was that the familiar drone of the engine would summon the serpent—the spinning propeller announcing a sumptuous feast topside—but to no avail.

Mischa realized that their 'success' at treating the oarfish had also ended their atypical relationship. Disappointed at its disappearance, but elated at the implication behind the creature's absence, they reluctantly headed home.

Approximately one mile from their home port of Scorpion Cove Mischa cried, "Stop the boat!"

"Why?" asked Jake, who nonetheless immediately complied with Mischa's request and brought the Whaler to a sudden halt.

Staring intently off the seaward side of the boat Mischa said excitedly, "A wavy-like movement just below the surface caught my eye as if a large animal was about to breech."

"A pod of dolphins, whales, a shark, what?" Jake asked annoyed.

"I'm not sure . . . for a second I thought it was . . . but it's no longer there."

"You thought it was—what?—our oarfish coming back to say a proper goodbye," Jake said derisively.

"Maybe," she murmured, and then shouted, "Jake—look out!"

Before Jake could physically respond the ocean erupted in a fountain of exploding water as an anaconda-shaped sea monster launched itself from its watery realm—landing with a loud thud across the Whaler's eight-foot beam—with two-thirds of the creature still submerged beneath the waves, and the upper third intently probing the interior of the ship for its clearly now expected, daily rations.

"It's back!" shrieked Mischa.

"That's an understatement," Jake said dryly.

Mischa quickly obtained her bucket of fermented squid and sardines, and began to hand feed each individual morsel to the exotic deep-water fish, relishing the tender moment. "This is incredible," she squealed.

"Don't forget its final day of pills," Jake advised.

"Thanks Jake," she said, "it completely slipped my mind." Mischa then tossed her brother a squid, which he promptly stuffed with pills. The last medicated cephalopod vanished the second Jake presented it to the oarfish. Within two minutes every last squid and sardine was polished off, and the giant oarfish slithered back into the ocean. As it descended into the abyss it dazzled them with a pulsating kaleidoscopic display, while slowly propelling itself steadily downward with an undulating type motion. They continued to watch it until the iridescent beast faded into nothingness, swallowed-up by the inky blackness of the ocean depths.

"That was amazing," Jake declared.

"Beyond amazing," Mischa repeated, "it's a once in a lifetime experience."

"Not exactly," Jake assured her. "Because I have a feeling this is the first of many such encounters. That oarfish *knows* the sound of our vessel. It's only a matter of time before we meet again."

"I can hardly wait," Mischa said. "From this day forward a bucket of squid is mandatory on all our trips."

"That's for sure," Jake affirmed. "And, one other item; we'll need to post a note at the marine lab warning any employee that captain's this ship that they may be in for the surprise of their life. We don't want anyone dying of a heart attack from a fanciful sea monster confrontation."

Laughing, Mischa agreed. "That would clearly be a drag—which reminds me—our ship's interaction with the oarfish has solidified my opinion as to the appropriate name for this vessel."

"And what name might that be?" Jake asked warily.

"*Nessie.*"

"That's a wimpy girl's name!" Jake complained.

"Yes, but it's also the name of the legendary Loch Ness Monster which is plainly *not* a sissy."

"*Nessie,*" Jake said rolling the 'ssie' off his tongue in a glib manner. It's certainly not my first choice, but I can live with it; however, the next ship that requires christening—I'm in charge of choosing a manly-man name.

"It's a deal," confirmed Mischa.

After shaking on it, Jake then restarted the Mercury engine, and with contented smiles, and the heartfelt satisfaction of a task well done, brother and sister headed home.

21

The drive south from San Francisco to Carmel was exhilarating. Kurt marveled at the variety of geographical treasures: The Lone Cypress prevailing on its craggy perch for over two hundred years; the emerald clarity of Stillwater Cove, and the unrivaled beauty of Spanish Bay. But foremost was the world-renowned Pebble Beach Golf Links, where a mere $495 gave you the privilege of losing your golf ball in the 'water trap' of the Pacific Ocean. At almost $500 for eighteen holes, it was golf for the wealthy.

With the kind help of his navigation system, Kurt turned onto Scenic Road and parked his car across the street from the house designated as 26100. The solitary abode was situated on a coveted rocky promontory on the western tip of Carmel Point with unobstructed views of the Pacific Ocean. Based upon the 'fresh look' of the stately dwelling it was apparent that it had recently undergone a major remodel, the light stone exterior glistening in the fading light. Two wind-shaped cypress trees adorned the front yard and mist from an antiqued-bronze swordfish fountain sparkled in the sunlight. The landscape consisted of plants and flowers native to the coastal climate, their water needs ecofriendly. The pathway to the front door was constructed from crushed shells intermixed with Hawaiian black volcanic sand. *Captain Flannigan's retirement choice was exemplary,* thought Kurt as a dozen brown pelicans, in B-52 formation, glided effortlessly over the ocean bungalow.

The time was 5:45 p.m., and a sixties era powder-blue Mercedes Benz coupe was parked in the granite blend pavestone driveway. "That's a good sign," Kurt said under his breath as he unfastened his seatbelt. The presence of a car indicated the strong likelihood that someone was home.

Locking his car, Kurt hastily made his way to the front entry-way, pausing a moment to admire the restored antique Spanish double doors forged from what he surmised was Honduran mahogany. In lieu of an electric doorbell there was an ornate brass dolphin doorknocker. Kurt banged it twice and then waited. The sound was disturbingly loud, its metallic rasp an unmistakable summons to anyone inside.

After a brief interlude he heard a faint voice coming from the opposite side of the doors, "Who's there?"

"Dr. Nichols from the University of Malibu," Kurt replied loudly, hoping to impress the occupant.

There was a brief pause and then, "Please hold your business card up to the peephole," the person instructed.

Kurt could tell by the feminine tone that the disembodied voice belonged to a woman and he immediately complied with her request. He also voluntarily displayed his California Driver's License. He knew that unless the individual trusted him that she would not unlock the doors. "Anything else?" he asked in a soothing and reassuring voice.

"Yes . . . what do you want?"

He decided to be straightforward: "Information regarding the wreck of the *S.S. Winfield Scott.*" For several suspenseful seconds he waited for a reply—the tension palpable—the only discernible sound the cascading melody emanating from the water fountain.

"Just a moment," she finally said.

Kurt smiled. He could hear the unlatching of the dead-bolt and then the door inching open, revealing a woman who looked like she was in her early sixties, attractive, and wearing a silk tie-waist long dress in painted flowers print, and flat leather sandals with bow detail in blush suede. She was tall, about five feet nine, and thin, but not too thin. Flowing to below her shoulders, her long, wavy snow-white hair was elegantly captivating. "I'm sorry," Kurt stuttered, "are you going out for the evening?"

"No," she laughed, "I just arrived home from a fundraiser at the Monterey Bay Aquarium and you happened to catch me before I had a chance to change. Our group raises money for their Children's Educational Center. By the way, my name's Emily," she said as she extended her hand, "and please come in."

After a quick handshake, Kurt stepped inside, as Emily closed the door. The foyer was lined with polished marble tiles in a rich dark brown, inlayed with the fossilized remains of kosmoceras, orthoceras, and trilobites, the extinct invertebrates clearly visible. Analyzing the uncommon tiles Kurt declared, "These tiles are amazing!"

"They're from Morocco," Emily said informatively. "I feel like I've stepped into a primordial world every time I walk across my own floor."

"You have," Kurt insisted, "an ocean of prehistoric creatures."

"And speaking of prehistoric—why is a professor from the University of Malibu interested in an ancient wreck?"

"Because of a mystery; we recently discovered evidence of an explosion on the *Scott*. But, before I discuss that further—I'm making the assumption that you're a distant relative of Captain Flannigan?"

"He was my great, great, great grandpa. I think that's the correct number of grandpa's. I was a 'Flannigan' until I married in 1971. Unfortunately that marriage only lasted twelve years.

Upon my divorce I reverted back to my maiden name and moved into this house."

"Is this house on the exact same site as Captain Flannigan's original cottage?" Kurt asked.

"Yes, but remodeled of course and upgraded several times. The latest makeover took place five years ago. For lack of a better title, I'm the steward of the Flannigan Estate Carmel Beach House. I manage the property on behalf of all the Flannigan kinfolk, and as such, I'm its only permanent resident. At times, however, it morphs into a crowded vacation home, especially during the summer months."

"May we sit down?" suggested Kurt. "My professional inquisitiveness into the wreck of the *S.S. Winfield Scott* will take some explaining."

"Of course, and I have the ideal place to converse," she said pointing toward a double French door, "our outdoor veranda with its complimentary million-dollar view. It's a balmy night by Carmel standards, plus we have an outdoor fireplace and two overhead heaters, so we should stay warm."

"Sounds perfect," Kurt agreed.

"I'll fetch us something to drink while you become accustomed to the view."

As Emily made her way into the kitchen Kurt found his way out onto the ocean porch, and settled down in a redwood Adirondack chair that was adjacent to a gas-burning copper fire bowl. The metal fire pit was already exuding heat indicating that Emily was able to ignite it from inside the house. The deck was constructed from teak and extended approximately fifty feet out onto the rocky peninsula. The whitewater views, as professed by Emily, were magnificent, with roaring opaline ocean waves crashing on the rocks, the thunderous sounds intermixed with barking sea lions and the high-pitched call of seagulls. Two ivory-faced sea otters floated on the surface of a kelp bed, basking in the sun's final rays of light. Beyond the pounding waves stretched the open sea and the dreams of every mariner. Kurt was so immersed in the untamed natural beauty and the sweeping panoramic seascapes that he failed to notice Emily's arrival.

"Breathtaking, isn't it?"

"It certainly is."

"As is this glass of 2006 Duckhorn Vineyards Napa Valley Merlot, Three Palms Vineyard, paired-up with stone-ground crackers, and slices of cheese. You strike me as a connoisseur of quality wine."

"You are indeed speaking my language, but in all honesty I'm not a big fan of merlot."

"That's because you've never tasted a Duckhorn. Try it; if it's disagreeable with your palate, I'll take a dip in the ocean," Emily said with a wink.

"You're extremely brave, or foolish," laughed Kurt. Lifting the Riedel wine glass he first held it against the sunset, checking the merlot's clarity; he then sniffed it evaluating its bouquet. He next swished a small amount around the back of his mouth before swallowing and assessing its finishing touch. After a moment of meditative hesitation he smiled, and said, "You'll stay dry tonight. I stand corrected; this merlot is definitely full-bodied—delivering vibrant fruit flavors with layers of red currant, raspberry and black cherry underscored by elements of strawberry, and caramel, all leading to a long, jammy finish. I'm now a Duckhorn merlot devotee—so thank you."

"You're welcome, and you clearly know your wine."

"Thanks; years of self-indulgent study," laughed Kurt, and then said, "this is not the reception I envisioned when I first knocked on your door."

"Me either, when I heard the knock. But how often does a mature lady have a good-looking professor rapping at her door and inquiring about a one hundred and sixty-year-old family incident? But tell me—why the interest—after all these years? You mentioned something about an explosion? This is the first I've heard about it."

Kurt had decided on the drive down to be up front regarding his *Scott* investigation. "The University's marine lab recently analyzed wood from the *Scott* shipwreck. Based upon the results a determination was made that an incendiary explosion had occurred somewhere along the hull of the *Scott* prior to its destructive impact upon the rocks of Middle Anacapa Island."

"What led to the analysis being done in the first place?" Emily asked.

"Fragmented and charred White Oak timber from the hull of the ship and traces of black powder residue embedded in several oak pieces made us suspect that a section of the hull was blown apart and scorched by a searing blast."

"How could black powder survive for one hundred and sixty years submerged in the caustic ocean?"

"It didn't. That wood was stored in a brick warehouse on Santa Cruz Island. It was salvaged from the *Scott* within weeks of the incident."

"And how did the marine lab come into possession of this wood, and who brought it to their attention?" Emily pressed.

Kurt had to admit, Emily was as sharp as a carpet tack. "That will take some explaining," he replied, "including my family history."

"The evening's still young," said Emily sipping her wine, "and I'm all yours."

Taken aback a bit from that last remark, Kurt was certain that she had misspoken and had meant to say I'm all ears. He began with Juan Rodriguez Cabrillo and his Chumash mistress Luisa, the deeding of Santa Cruz Island to Luisa and to her heirs including the latest heiress, his wife, Tessa. He next discussed her decision to donate seventy-six percent of the island to The Nature Conservancy and to sell approximately twenty-four percent to the

305

National Park Service for twenty-eight million—with twenty-five million going directly into the non-profit Nichols Foundation. He also clarified that two hundred acres were never sold or donated and to this day remained in the Nichols family, and that the marine lab was built upon a portion of that acreage. He described the unfortunate death of his wife, but that her legacy continues in their two exceptional children. Finally, he pointed out that hardwoods recovered from the *Scott* were utilized in the construction of a winery on Santa Cruz Island around 1854, but that the bulk of the salvaged lumber was held in storage. Further, that over a year ago Kurt had the crumbling winery converted into a modern house using the stored *Scott* hardwoods, and that leftover scraps were set aside as firewood.

Kurt concluded his summary by advising Emily that at a recent dinner party, while he was stoking a fire, he discovered planks with singe marks and burst-like damage. Curious, he scraped off tiny fragments of the charred material and had it analyzed by the marine lab's chemist. The test results confirmed that the substance was black powder residue—which piqued his investigative interest—leading to his trip to San Francisco and the old corporate offices of the Pacific Mail Steamship Company, and concluding with his visit to Emily's home.

"An explosion on the *Scott*," said Emily slowly, "again, you're the first person to ever make that allegation. I'm not aware of any *Scott* crew members or passengers testifying to such an event."

"None in the formal records," Kurt countered. "And that's why I'm here; I'm making the logical assumption that Captain Flannigan was cognizant of the explosion, but for reasons known only by him intentionally withheld those facts during his disciplinary hearing. I'm also trusting that he discreetly retained personal records of the incident. If those records still exist I would love to examine them and see if they contain any clues as to what transpired that fateful night. For some reason the *explosive fire* part of the calamity has been purposely eliminated from the historical records." Kurt then shared with Emily President Pierce's involvement in the aftermath of the *Scott* shipwreck, and the Government's seizure of the entire *S.S. Winfield Scott* file. After finishing his short synopsis Kurt watched Emily's reaction, sipping his wine as he did so. To his surprise she seemed far-away as if strolling on a distant beach.

"When a voice in the future fathoms the deeds of the past, and his heart is pure, only then may disclosure be made," Emily whispered.

After a moment of silence Kurt asked, "Excuse me?"

"A directive from the late Captain," Emily replied, "that was to remain secret for at least one hundred years."

"Why?"

"I truly don't know," Emily said. "Those instructions have been passed down from one generation of Flannigan to the next. When my dad made me memorize the line, I thought it was just a cute Flannigan riddle, but now I'm not so sure. Follow me; I have something to show you."

Arising from his chair, Kurt hurried to catch up with Emily, who had already entered the residence and was striding down a narrow hallway. She stopped in front of a closed door that was on the ocean side of the house. The entryway was apparently locked. She reached above its contoured wood molding and retrieved a skeleton key, which she used to unlock the door.

"Nice security," Kurt commented wryly.

"It works," she assured him as they both walked into the room. Emily paused for a brief second to switch on the overhead lights, which illuminated a bedroom from another era. "Kurt," Emily said respectfully, "Captain Flannigan's private chambers."

Kurt stared transfixed. He felt as if he had entered a time portal or was gazing at a museum quality reproduction of the eighteenth century. "I thought you had the house remodeled?"

"Everything but this space; we've kept it as is, other than having it wired for electricity."

The walls were paneled with Georgia Antique Heart Pine as were the moldings and window casings. The flooring was White Oak. "Is this wood from the *Winfield Scott?*" Kurt asked with wonder just short of awe. "It's seems eerily similar to what I have in my house."

"Yes," Emily confirmed. "Your ancestors weren't the only ones who paid the *Scott* a visit after its demise. The Captain chartered his own ship. Besides the wood, he removed items that had significance for him. Those furnishings continue to decorate this room."

The artifacts included two pine chairs, a pine writing desk, a brass and copper kerosene lantern, an elegant Dome Top sea trunk, pearly white *Scott* china with dark blue striping in a fouled anchor nautical pattern, copper and brass fastenings, a life preserver with the ship's name, and the *Scott's* bronze bell. Hanging on the north wall was a large wooden American eagle with a coat of arms, and perched atop a distressed pine coffee table was the gilded wooden bust of Major General Winfield Scott, commanding general of the United States Army and hero of the Mexican-American War of 1846-1848, and namesake of the *S.S. Winfield Scott.*

Chuckling, Kurt said, "I've always puzzled over what became of the ship's gold-colored figurehead—now I know. The Captain must have expended a considerable amount of effort at sawing the carving from the bow's timber."

Shrugging her shoulders Emily said, "That I don't know. But the Captain did labor at creating a hidden compartment on the rear portion of the bust, and that's where he secreted his enigmatic riddle concerning the *Scott.*"

Kurt watched fascinated as Emily tapped several times on the back of General Scott's head, and a six by two inch section of solid-appearing wood slid out—revealing a small drawer that held an intricately designed silver box. She removed the container and sat down in one of the pine chairs. Kurt joined her.

"That's incredible," Kurt said, "smacks of a James Bond movie."

"Slightly theatrical in my opinion," replied Emily, "but the Captain must have had his reasons."

"What's in it?" Kurt asked enthusiastically.

"The *only* personal records retained by Captain Flannigan of that fateful night. Earlier, you asked if you could examine them. The answer is yes. Captain Flannigan's singular requirement was an unadulterated heart. My own heart testifies to the fact that you meet this criterion. As far as I know you are the first non-Flannigan to ever view the contents of this box. I hope you're not disappointed; the Captain left very little." Placing the box on her lap Emily unhitched a tiny silver clasp, and with her right index finger and thumb she gently lifted the silver lid.

Kurt sat mesmerized as Emily exposed the items. She extracted an off-white piece of paper rolled up like a miniature scroll, and a gold coin. She handed the coin to Kurt.

After carefully inspecting the shiny object, Kurt said, "A twenty-dollar 1850 Double Eagle, Liberty Head gold coin. The quality is extraordinary indicating that it was newly minted. I doubt it was ever circulated."

"My thoughts as well."

"Why the gold coinage?" Kurt asked as he returned the coin to Emily.

"That's your conundrum to decipher." She then passed the scroll to Kurt and said, "The perplexing words on that antiqued paper, as penned by Captain Flannigan, will hopefully provide the answer to your mysterious explosion."

Kurt uncurled the scroll and began to read.

Delays, delays, purposeful tardiness
Gray, gloomy, misty fog
Horses, carriages, soldiers, midnight
Collaboration, covenant, scheming
Trist, Santa Anna, Juarez, Pierce
The Winfield Scott a diplomatic pawn

Precious yellow weight
Opulence and compact, solid and glass
A bow strong room to mask
Panama City—a conspirator's dream
Land, land, land; war, war, war
Brother Hidalgo, Sister Gadsden, Baby Ayutla
Sovereignty, corruption, patriotism
A known path-an inside passage
Beacon of light, Cavern Point, ¼ mile distant in the night
Santa Cruz an ebbing apparition
Anacapa's cliffs an illusory vision
Rolling thunder, a directional rumble
Black-powder horizon, a pierced ship
A deposit upon the sea
Chloroform veiled in cloth
Forgotten minutes
A safe-haven islet, unseen tortuous rocks
Escape and safety, rescue and recovery
A plethora of secrets lie beneath
Impervious to sea or time
Awaiting a man of charity

Kurt re-read the Captain's riddle a second time. "Absolutely amazing," he said. "So much in so few words; it's apparent that something major transpired upon his ship. My educated guess is that the gold coin serves as a clue."

"I agree," Emily said. "But that's just a part of it; as you continue to distill the Captain's words you'll understand that it's much bigger than a piece of precious metal. And now it's your destiny to entangle the web."

"No Flannigan has ever acted upon the Captain's ramblings?" asked Kurt.

"It wasn't even allowed for the first hundred years. After that most Flannigan's thought it was a joke—a dying man trying to obfuscate his guilt for the wreck. Besides, the Captain became wealthy, investing in the communities of Carmel and Monterey. He bought several fishing boats and started the first cannery on what was to become Cannery Row. He was also a builder, and constructed some of the finest Victorian homes along our coast. In Carmel, the oldest restaurant in town still bears his signature—Flannigan's Seafood Bistro—whose manager is yours truly. Inherited wealth, I believe, inhibits entrepreneurship or whimsical pursuits."

"Probably true," Kurt said. "But this I'll promise you—that I'll employ all my skills and talents at resolving the riddle of the *Scott*."

"And perhaps clearing the Captain's name," Emily added.

"Double-dipping—I'm always good for that," laughed Kurt.

Laughing herself, Emily got up from her chair and said, "Your cute metaphor reminds me that it's time for supper and as such, I have a proposal: After I make you several copies of the Captain's riddle, it would be my pleasure to treat you to dinner at a restaurant where I can guarantee a delicious fish meal, excellent service, and delightful ambiance, all delivered at a nominal charge."

Salivating inwardly, Kurt quickly stood and replied, "It's a date."

Emily then tossed the gold coin in Kurt's direction. Acting instinctively he snatched it in midair.

"I think the Captain would want you to have it," she said.

Kurt immediately flipped it back to Emily. "My contribution to the Monterey Bay Aquarium's Education Center; auction it on E-bay. That coin is worth thousands and will bless many a child."

Emily smiled warmly. "I think the Captain has his benevolent marine knight." She then walked over and slipped her arm inside of Kurt's. "Care to escort a lady to a fabulous restaurant?"

Kurt smiled back. "I wouldn't have it any other way."

22

Eva and Dr. Sedrak arrived in the Providence of Alberta, Canada, via an Air Canada Boeing 787 Dreamliner, landing at Edmonton International Airport. The recently modernized airport was constructed on the extreme outskirts of Edmonton, and was actually closer to the quaint city of Leduc than its namesake. The time was 8:45 a.m., and their meeting with the Production Manager at Aspen Packers was scheduled for 10:30 a.m. Eva had earlier Mapquested the drive time to Calmar—approximately sixty minutes—the city where the meat and bone meal packing company was located.

After picking up their Chevy Malibu Hertz rental car—with Dr. Sedrak occupying the driver's seat and Eva acting as their navigator—they quickly exited the airfield by way of Airport Road. They then turned south onto Highway 2, which was also known as the *Queen Elizabeth II Highway*. Twenty minutes later, and a tenth of a mile past Harry Bienert Park, Sedrak turned west onto Highway 39, the main thoroughfare leading into the City of Calmar.

Lounging comfortably in the passenger seat, Eva had time to review the complimentary Hertz Alberta Travel Guide. The touristy brochure highlighted points of historical interest concerning the Canadian Providence, including the fact that the land, which they were now motoring by, was once a vast golden prairie teeming with wild flowers, nutritional grasses, bison, mule deer, elk, wolves, coyotes, hawks, and eagles. Furthermore, that over the last century the lush open fields had gradually been subdivided into agricultural plots, with some tracts producing bountiful crops, while others were now pastureland for thousands of head of livestock—with cattle predominating over sheep, goats, and pigs. The tranquil countryside was also postcard picturesque with numerous fishponds, winding creeks, and Victorian style rustic homes surrounded by beds of late spring flowers.

Two days prior to their scheduled trip Eva had conducted a brief Internet search into the particulars of Aspen Packers animal rendering facility. Her research revealed that the company had purposely located their mammalian recycling factory several miles outside of Calmar, in a rural area, far from the olfactory senses of any nearby human inhabitants. An online disclaimer warned that a tour of its plant was not recommended for the faint-of-heart, or weak-of-stomach.

After driving through the small agricultural town of Calmar, Eva read aloud the names of the county roads that zipped past their vehicle—whose street titles were anything but original—as they searched for the turnoff to Aspen Packers. "Range Road 271 . . . Range Road 272 . . . Range Road 273 . . . Range Road 274 . . . there it is," she announced, "Range Road 275." Sedrak immediately turned left onto a narrowed two-lane road. They traveled about half a mile before Sedrak executed another left turn onto Township Road 494, which was paved with crushed granite. After travelling about one hundred yards they observed an asphalt-coated side street and a nondescript metal sign proclaiming, *Aspen Packers.* Prior to entering the facitie's driveway, Sedrak pulled the car onto an adjacent dirt shoulder, letting the engine idle in the park mode.

Leaning toward Eva, Sedrak said, "Let's go over our cover story one more time."

"Okay—if you want to," she said, "but I'm not overly concerned."

"Forgive me . . . it's the paranoid doctor inside," Sedrak said anxiously. "It's like a difficult surgery, the results can't be guaranteed, so proper preparation is essential in order to avoid critical mistakes."

"No one's going to die," Eva said calmly, "so relax; besides, your role in the façade is easy—you get to play yourself."

"I know—Dr. Matthew Sedrak—majority stockholder in a new start-up aquaculture company located off of Point Loma, San Diego."

"Yes," laughed Eva, "you're the money and I'm the brains behind the enterprise. My newly printed business card states that I'm the CEO of *Coronado Aquaculture Unlimited*, with a Ph.D. in Marine Aquaculture."

Clearly displeased, Sedrak said, "Skip the *brains* self-adulation portion, how about us being co-partners with you serving as the hands-on person."

Smiling Eva said, "I can do that."

"Thank you—and our primary interest in their rendering plant is the Goebbel connection?"

"That's correct," Eva confirmed. "In my conversation with Claude Desbrow, Aspen Packer's Production Manager, I informed him that in my inquiries with the presidents of several aquaculture companies, that a Mr. Karl Goebbel—the renowned owner of *West Coast Seafood & Aquaculture*—had strongly recommended Aspen Packers as a source for 'reasonably cheap, protein rich pellets in lieu of wild-caught, expensive baitfish'—and that's why we're here—to personally assess whether we want to buy the exact same product."

"That story certainly sounds credible," Sedrak agreed.

"Then we have nothing to worry about."

"I know," Sedrak mumbled, "but to be honest, I'm uncomfortable at being deceptive."

"My righteous doctor—stressed at being a little naughty, how pitifully sweet," grinned Eva. "But don't fret—I'll make you this promise—no one at the hospital will ever know."

"Including Facebook?" Sedrak demanded.

"Including Facebook."

"Good, then let's get it done," Sedrak said, finally assured. He maneuvered the Malibu's gear shift from park to drive, moved onto the roadway, and began to accelerate down the asphalt driveway.

After travelling approximately one-third of a mile, the road crested a small bluff, and then slanted downward into a shallow valley. At the bottom of the basin, essentially hidden from public view, was a sprawling structure of interconnected boxed-shaped two-story buildings constructed from inexpensive corrugated steel. Running alongside the exterior walls of each building were industrial strength pipes of various dimensions; some were as small as an inch, while others were immense—over a foot in diameter. Aligned in organized rows against the sides of each structure were massive iron storage tanks and aluminum silos, some exceeding three stories in height. Numerous smokestacks, painted a motley brownish-green and looking like dead redwood trees, protruded from the roofs. Several belched a blackish effluence of smoky ash while others spewed forth a dense cloud of vaporized water. Half a dozen dump trucks, a handful of bin-lifter waste collection vehicles, two refrigerated eighteen-wheelers, and several smaller cargo vans occupied a back parking lot.

Looking over the facilities' grounds Eva was taken aback at the complete absence of any decorative landscaping or inspirational art. In fact, not a single tree, bush, or flower adorned the Aspen Packers property. Instead, the entire steel edifice was surrounded by a sea of grayish concrete, which in some areas was marred with blotchy and irregular stains, reddish-black in color.

As Sedrak pulled into a guest parking stall, a noxious smell infiltrated the car, penetrating their nostrils, and causing bile to rise up in Eva's throat. "What in God's name is that awful odor?" she asked, and gagged violently.

"The aroma of cooked flesh," Sedrak clarified, and then in a soft voice asked, "Are you okay?"

"No, but I'll survive." Eva's attempt to temporarily stave off the fumes by squeezing her nose between her thumb and index finger met with minimal success. Holding her nose, and sounding nasal, she said, "A dead skunk would be preferable over that offensive stench."

"It'll be worse inside," Sedrak warned.

"I know—I just need a couple of minutes to get acclimated to it."

Sedrak gave her five, which was enough time to listen to one upbeat pop song and some meaningless DJ jabber on the car radio. Before another set of songs could start he asked, "You ready?"

"Yes."

As they exited the car, a clamorous rushing sound, along with hissing noises, could be heard emanating from the slew of pipes and valves that circumvented the building. It was obvious to Eva that the factory was in full operating mode. Walking through the front door, which was held open by Sedrak, she felt as if she had entered an oppressive mausoleum. Claude Desbrow was waiting. He shook her hand and introduced himself the instant she stepped into the sterile foyer. Sedrak immediately followed with his own introductions with the Plant Manager, who was in his mid-fifties, slight of build, with thinning reddish-brown hair, and brown eyes. He was dressed in off-white company overalls. *A poor choice of color,* Eva thought as she observed flecks of rust-colored stains.

"Sorry about the smell," Desbrow said, looking directly at Eva. "After a while you'll get used to it. The perimeter security cameras captured your negative response to the invasive odors. I've worked here twenty-seven years and rarely notice it."

"Nice to know there's no privacy while sitting in your own car," Eva said curtly.

"Can't be helped," Desbrow said, somewhat apologetically, "with PETA protestors and animal-rights wackos, we have to monitor all activity on our property. We're not intentionally trying to be intrusive, but we do have to be vigilant."

"We do live in a world with plenty of kooks who will go to any lengths to attain their goals," Sedrak offered, attempting to be gracious, "so we understand your need for cameras." He gave a discreet sideways look at Eva who did her best to keep a neutral façade. Changing the subject, he said, "We look forward to our tour. As you know, your manufacturing facility—and the meat and bone meal pellets it produces—came highly recommended."

Smiling at the compliment, Desbrow said, "Karl Goebbel— he's one of our best customers. It will be an honor to show you around; but, what part of the process do you want to observe?"

"Everything," said Eva, "from the very beginning to completion of the pellets. We want to know exactly how the pellets are made, what goes into them, and, most importantly, inspect your quality control. We will not agree to any major purchases without our own personal assessment—in spite of Goebbel's glowing remarks."

Scratching his chin and looking worried, Desbrow said, "What you'll see—if we start at the initial stage—won't be a pretty sight. My original intention was to just show you the end-stage of production, not the starting point. As you know we recycle animal flesh. Based upon your parking lot reaction, I'm making the assumption that you've never previously set foot in a plant such as ours. If you think the smell is awful . . . the visuals are a hundred times worse."

"Oh . . . I'm now over that foul odor," Eva informed Desbrow. "And, I can assure you as part of my Ph.D. program, and as a marine biologist, I've conducted necropsies on quite a few aquatic animals, with some beyond putrid—so seeing lifeless creatures, or their remains, are a nonissue."

"And ditto as to this doctor," Sedrak advised. "As a specialist in neurology at a major hospital, I'm unfortunately quite familiar with death."

Biting his lower lip, Desbrow searched their expressions for a moment and then said, "It's your tour—so nothing will be off limits. But I'm cautioning you—prepare yourselves; a few dead marine animals, and a few deceased patients, are not the same as what you're about to lay eyes on."

"I understand," Eva and Sedrak said simultaneously.

"I wonder if you truly do," Desbrow murmured, "but in an hour we'll know. Follow me—if you want to see it from the beginning, then that's where we'll start."

Instead of walking through the building, Desbrow lead them back outside, and to a four-person electric shuttle cart. As they moved out he said, "Our starting point is at the back of the factory, where the various delivery trucks are now parked. That's where the raw materials are dropped off."

"By *raw materials* you mean cows?" Eva asked.

Chuckling, Desbrow said, "You'll soon know. Use your Halloween imagination, and maybe you'll get it half right." Two minutes later he parked the cart next to one of the large dump trucks, whereupon they exited the vehicle.

As they were approaching a massive sliding cargo door at the rear entrance to the facility, Sedrak asked: "Why do you own dump trucks?"

"They're commodity transporters—conveying huge quantities of unprocessed livestock," answered Desbrow.

Looking nonplused, Eva asked, "You mean those trucks haul dead animals as if they were topsoil, gravel, or sand, and then dump them at your plant in the same manner as if they were delivering building materials to a construction site?"

"I wouldn't quite characterize it that way—but your description is somewhat accurate, although slightly crude," replied Desbrow. "Every afternoon all our transport trucks and vans head out; some are sent to cattle ranches to retrieve dead livestock, a few to pig and poultry farms for similar purposes, and others to slaughterhouses, supermarkets, veterinary clinics, animal shelters, private farms, our local zoo, butcher shops, restaurants, and lastly, Alberta's highway maintenance department—to pick up road kill. We're a non-discriminatory, full-service, animal recycling center," laughed Desbrow, "which you'll personally comprehend in less than one minute." Grasping the cargo door handle he slid the aluminum door open—its well-greased rollers making the task effortless—revealing a cavernous storage area.

Stepping inside, Eva froze in her tracks, latched onto Sedrak's left arm, and let out a high-pitched, but brief, startled gasp. Heaped into species specific piles across the vast concrete floor were the carcasses of at least a hundred animals. The biggest stack contained approximately twenty-five cows and bulls. Rectangular metal waste bins, and fifty-five gallon galvanized drums were also packed with dead creatures and mostly unrecognizable parts from slaughterhouses. The rancid assault upon Eva's nostrils was indescribable, and it took everything within her to keep from retching.

"Not a pretty sight," Desbrow said sympathetically, "but I did forewarn you."

"I know," Eva said, "it's just more than I expected."

"The disposal and recycling of dead animals and discarded flesh is, by its very nature, a ghastly business; to spin it any other way would be lying."

"So many animals . . . it's overwhelming." Eva said mournfully.

"It's a bit more crowded than usual," Desbrow confirmed. "The collection trucks apparently had an exceptional day." He then handed Eva and Sedrak a white hardhat and a black pair of waterproof work boots. "Please wear the hardhat at all times. I also recommend removing your city shoes and substituting them for these boots; your footwear won't be the same if you don't."

"That's a no-brainer," Eva affirmed, and in less than thirty seconds they had both eagerly complied with Desbrow's advice.

Addressing Eva and Sedrak, Desbrow said, "The first stage of recycling takes place at the giant auger grinding pit—so that's where we'll commence our tour. It's on the opposite side of this storage area, so watch your step as we carefully approach it."

With Desbrow leading, Sedrak and Eva followed, on a path that weaved in and out among the dead animals. In addition to the mound of young beef cattle and dairy cows, there were a few elderly looking horses, a half dozen goats, a silver-haired donkey, an alpaca that appeared to have a broken leg, two llamas, an adult spotted giraffe, a tiny hippo who obviously had died at birth, and a cluster of hogs. One of the hogs was inflated like a hot-air balloon from putrefying gases, and was secreting thousands of white maggots from its orifices.

Situated in its own roped-off section was the road kill, where the traumatically mutilated bodies of three mule deer laid broken on the concrete floor along with a six point bull elk, several skunks, raccoons, opossums, and numerous rabbits.

Assembled along the perimeter were fifty-five gallon drums that were stuffed with animal shelter and veterinary clinic euthanized dogs and cats. Other drums were filled with chickens, turkeys, a couple of white ducks, butcher shop trimmings, and restaurant scraps consisting of leftover meat and fat from fryers and grease traps. Most of the metal waste bins contained inedible cattle parts from local slaughterhouses—heads, hooves, bones, blood, intestines, and internal organs. The smaller bins held spoiled or rejected meat from supermarkets, the moldy contents still wrapped in Styrofoam or plastic trays, surrounded by shrinkwrap.

"Dogs and cats, I had no idea," Eva whispered to Sedrak.

Responding in an equally hushed voice, Sedrak said caustically, "I bet neither Fido the faithful dog, or Fluffy the cuddly house cat, had any idea that their masters would dispose of their remains in such a dishonorable manner."

"I wonder whether their owners are even aware that their treasured pets are now being reformulated into food pellets," Eva suggested.

"You may be right," Sedrak agreed, and then asked: "Did you see that pig with thousands of maggots swarming over its body?"

"Revolting," Eva replied. "How can they recycle a decaying pig that is polluted with bacteria and riddled with vermin?" she asked louder than she meant to.

"I heard that," said Desbrow. "The answer: lots of heat—two hundred and eighty degrees worth—which will destroy any possible germs; and, the writhing maggots, they're just added protein."

"Thank you," Eva said, slightly embarrassed at being overheard, "that makes perfect sense."

As they approached the pit area, Eva observed two employees operating Bobcat mini-dozers, and one employee operating a forklift, loading the 'raw material' into a ten-foot-deep stainless steel pit. A pudgy man, with dirty blond hair, and dressed in a beige-colored company jump suit, was instructing the machine operators as to which product was next-in-line to be bulldozed, or poured out into the gluttonous hole. The dozer drivers, speeding toward the stockpiled cattle, were apparently ordered to retrieve two carcasses. Using the vertical blades attached to the front of their tractors, they rolled the bulky animals across the floor until the creatures tumbled into the pit. Eva was still too far away to see inside the giant auger, but the moment the bovines disappeared she could hear the nightmarish sounds of disintegrating bones, and flesh being squeezed and shredded. The man who was functioning as a supervisor then had the forklift operator dump a barrel of cats and dogs into the rotating crusher. Fortunately, the noise of popping bones from the former pets was imperceptible. Next to go into the pit was a small bin of supermarket meats.

The boss man, suddenly aware of their presence, rushed to intercept them before they reached the edge of the pit. "Howdy Claude," he said, "I see we have visitors."

"Good morning David. Yes—two prospective customers—referred by Karl Goebbel. They're interested in viewing the entirety of our operation before agreeing to purchase any meat and bone meal for their San Diego aquafarm." Coughing unexpectedly, Desbrow paused to clear his throat before continuing with the introductions: "Dr. Eva Chen, Dr. Matthew Sedrak, it's my pleasure to introduce you to Chef David Gietler, chief cooker, and senior mixer at Aspen Packers."

After shaking hands, Sedrak asked: "You're an actual chef?"

"Only in the rendering business," answered Gietler with an uncomfortable laugh. "Our plant works like a super-sized kitchen, and I'm the head chef. The chief cooker or chef, blends the raw materials in order to maintain a certain ratio between the carcasses available, in conjunction with other raw stock, in order to create a balanced meat and bone meal product suitable for our customer's individual needs."

"What's the blend ratio for an aquafarm?" asked Sedrak.

"Eighty-five percent cattle—whole steers, cows, and inedible scraps from slaughterhouses—and fifteen-percent other raw ingredients."

"Does that also include flea collars, pet I.D. tags, the euthanizing drug sodium Phenobarbital, Styrofoam, plastic trays, and shrink wrap?" Eva asked scathingly. "I couldn't help but notice that several of the dogs and cats still had their flea collars and pet I.D. tags, and that almost all the supermarket meats were still within their original packaging. I'm also making the supposition that a majority of the dogs and cats were recently put to sleep with sodium Phenobarbital. As you're probably aware, that potent drug does not degrade—even with the passage of time or heat—and is now a lethal component in your mixture, along with flea collar insecticides."

At first, neither Gietler nor Desbrow offered a response to Eva's question, or follow-up diatribe. After an awkward silence, with both gentlemen staring intently at the other, Desbrow indicated by a subtle nod that Gietler would provide the answer.

"It's the sky-high labor costs Dr. Chen," Gietler said apologetically, "that's the culprit. It's just too costly and time consuming to have plant personnel cutting off flea collars, I.D. tags, or unwrapping thousands of rejected or spoiled meat packs. The grinding, cooking, and sifting process, however, eventually separates out most of the Styrofoam, plastics, and tags. And, as far as any leftover drugs and insecticides, ongoing testing by our quality control department has confirmed that any residual amounts are minuscule and harmless."

"I'll assume those reports are readily available . . . for verification purposes?" Sedrak demanded.

"Absolutely," Desbrow assured him.

"Thank you," Eva said, "please e-mail the last two years of test results to our account as soon as possible, and, if you don't mind, I'd like to continue with our tour, starting with the pit, and then progress through the other rendering stages at a rapid pace. Unfortunately, our plane leaves Edmonton International Airport at 1:00 p.m., so time is of the essence."

"You're certain that you want to inspect the actual pit?" Gietler asked stalling, and then by way of explanation advised: "The grinding of flesh and bones can be quite disturbing."

"We're aware of that," Sedrak replied, and Eva added, "I'm okay with it," and Desbrow said, "Whatever the customers want."

"Alright," Gietler said condescendingly, "you crave a tour of the pit—that I'll give you—but, watch your step, I don't want anyone falling in and ruining my recipe." He smiled at his own joke, revealing teeth stained yellowish-brown, the outer enamel darkened by years of chewing tobacco. "For your viewing pleasure," he continued, "the next raw ingredient scheduled for the pit is a large container of slaughterhouse parts." Gietler then signaled the forklift driver by shouting and pointing, as to which bin to pick up.

After securing the ten by six foot *parts* container, the forklift operator deposited it into a pneumatic cradle situated at the opposite end of the stainless steel pit. Eva estimated the pit's length at thirty feet, its width at eight and its depth at ten.

Climbing down from the forklift, the driver proceeded to lock the bin to the cradle by securing it with four coupling clamps; he then unhooked the container's hinged gates, and lastly, switched on the cradle's pneumatic lift. As the bin was slowly elevated its contents began oozing out—from an initial trickle of gooey sanguine-colored liquid, to a repulsive deluge of decapitated cattle heads, globs of coagulated blood, hooves, hearts the size of small basketballs, pinkish lungs, rust-colored livers, ruby-red kidneys, intestines, stomachs, and entire skeletal systems that were essentially intact, but cleanly excoriated of all edible meat.

Rotating at the bottom of the pit was a giant auger grinder—whose sharp-edged screws began cutting the dismembered chunks into manageable pieces—like an at-home food processor, but on a gargantuan scale.

The crushing, splintering sounds were so unsettling to Eva that after a few seconds she instinctively covered her ears. A moment later she also turned away, disengaging her eyes from the macabre scene. "I'm so sorry," she said aloud, "I thought I could emotionally deal with it."

"Nothing to be ashamed of," Desbrow said charitably, "in fact, several of our own employees can't stomach the pit, and are unwilling to work near it. Mr. Gietler, on the other hand, has a cast-iron potbelly, and has never had a problem."

"Too much Canadian ale," Gietler said with a raspy laugh while patting his bowling ball contoured paunch.

Sedrak, in contrast to Eva, was still staring into the pit, firmly riveted to every revolution of the industrial blades, until the last morsel was chopped into a fist-sized lump. "What happens next?" He asked Gietler.

"It's transported by a twelve-inch diameter pipe to another auger for additional shredding, and from there to a 'crusher' that pulverizes the segments into thumb-nail sized fragments—and that's just the first three stages—"

"Rather than hearing about it from Gietler," Desbrow said interrupting, "let's carry on with our tour, where you can visually examine each step of the process."

"Sounds good to me," Sedrak confirmed. Eva just nodded.

As they resumed their inspection of the plant, out of the corner of her eye, Eva observed the dozer nudge the newborn hippo into the nefarious pit—which she now considered a portal into hell.

Their next stop was the second augur—where they spent a few squeamish minutes gazing at bloody meat and bones being minced into barely recognizable pieces—and then onto the crusher, where the product was pounded down to a fraction of its original size. "From the crusher," Desbrow explained as they continued with their walking tour, "the raw product is then funneled into a stainless steel, 12,000-liter pressurized batch cooker." Standing next to the cylindrical shaped boiler, he said, "The batch cooker functions in the same manner as a pressure cooker in your own kitchen, except ours steams the crushed material for two to three hours at two-hundred and eighty degrees." Desbrow then paused for several minutes in order to allow them ample time to appraise the whistling steamer. "As the product simmers in the hot soup," continued Desbrow "the animal fat melts away producing tallow, which rises to the top and is skimmed off. The cooked meat and bone is then sent to a hammer-mill press, which is the next amazing gadget on our journey."

Stopping in front of the press, his voice almost a shout, he said, "As you can easily perceive, the machine was appropriately named—its one deafening device. This unique apparatus squeezes out any remaining moisture, and also pulverizes the product into a gritty powder. That powder is then transported by conveyor belt to a twelve-mesh shaker screen," Desbrow said, pointing to a rectangular machine just fifteen feet away, "where any unwanted items are sifted out such as hair, plastic, metal, Styrofoam, and large bone chips. The filtered meat and bone meal product is then whisked away in a six-inch pipe," Desbrow explained, indicating an overhead pipe, "and sent to that odd-looking red and yellow contraption that is positioned against the far wall—which just happens to be our final machine."

Eva, anxious for the visit to end, was ecstatic at the news. As they gathered around the *contraption*, Desbrow picked up where he had left off. "This remarkable piece of equipment is called a pellet mill; it's where the meat and bone meal is pressed through ring dies—and then cut to length by rotating knives—producing the half-inch brown pellets that Mr. Goebbel purchases in bulk for his aquafarms." Reaching down, Desbrow scooped up a handful from a holding bin, and dribbled them into both Sedrak's and Eva's hands. Eva allowed hers to fall to the floor. "These pellets," Desbrow continued, "are rich in protein, inexpensive, and will nourish your fish from fingerlings to adulthood . . . and that my friends, concludes our facilities tour."

Desbrow then ushered them into a nearby office, where coffee and blueberry scones awaited them. Eva was unable to eat, while Sedrak appeared famished. She did, however, appreciate the coffee. After everyone was settled into their seats, the Plant Manager smiling amiably asked, "Do you have any questions or concerns?"

Sedrak, munching contently on a scone that generated more crumbs than viable bites, replied, "Yes," and asked: "Is this rendering plant typical of all such factories?"

"Yes and no," Desbrow answered. "We're an independent rendering plant, versus an integrated plant; an integrated plant is located on the actual premises of a slaughterhouse. Our independence, however, allows us to process a wide variety of animal remains—as you clearly witnessed today. But, as a result of our independent status, our facility is only allowed to manufacture non-ruminant meat and bone meal for pigs, poultry, and fish. We also produce non-edible tallow—rendered fat—which is used by a significant number of commercial businesses in their manufacturing processes."

"Why are you prohibited from producing meat and bone meal for ruminant cows and sheep?" Eva asked.

"Because our plant processes downer cattle of all ages—as long as they arrive with a certificate from a veterinarian stating that they died from something, other than mad cow disease; and, we process all cattle that have inexplicably died—no matter what the cause—if they are under thirty months of age. Finally, we handle slaughterhouse waste that contains specific risk materials from butchered cattle."

"What constitutes specific risk materials, and why is that bad?" Sedrak wondered.

"It's any raw material from a cattle's skull, brain, spinal column, intestines, and other nervous system tissues. Specific risk materials, as well as downer cows, and dead cows under thirty months of age, *might* be tainted with the abnormal prion that causes mad cow disease. Although the probability is minimal— we believe it's less than one in a million—it's nonetheless statistical. In any event, all scientific studies to date have shown that pigs, poultry, and fish are not susceptible to the infection because of cross-species barrier protection. That natural safeguard prevents the transmission of spongiform encephalopathy in non-ruminant livestock. The good news from all this information is this: in the end it doesn't matter what types of raw materials our plant uses in producing meat and bone meal for pigs, poultry, or fish—because these creatures are genetically unaffected by the disease."

"Unfortunately," Eva reported, "cross-species barrier protection did not prevent the disease from spreading from sheep to cattle, and from cattle to humans; and, to add to the dilemma, there's even some speculation that sheep originally acquired the disease from wild elk or deer."

"True," Desbrow said, "but that's the extent of it. Pigs seem immune to it, and the species barrier effect is too great to enable infection in non-mammalian, poultry and fish."

"If that's correct," said Eva, "and I certainly trust that it is . . . then my irrational fears regarding the epidemic are mistaken. But, I do have one final issue that I need clarification on. In preparing for today's trip I discovered that Canada slaughters over three million head of cattle each year, and, that only a tiny fraction are actually tested for mad cow disease; further, that in spite of these low test rates, you've had seventeen confirmed cases in the last eight years. The haunting question still residing in the back of my mind is this: Are the feed pellets formulated by Aspen Packers infected with mad cow disease?"

"Absolutely not!" Desbrow said confidently. "And, I can also make you this guarantee—our product is completely safe for all your aquaculture needs. As I said earlier, at most only one cow in a million has the disease, and besides, even *if* it did exist in our pellets—which is purely theoretical—it would have no adverse effect on your farm-raised fish."

"That's a relief," Sedrak said charitably, as he wiped a pile of crumbs off his lap. "The possibility of our fish becoming infected with the disease was a major concern for both Eva and I, and the primary reason for our visit. Your knowledge of the issue, and the manner in which you run your plant, has certainly allayed our worse fears. As a result, as soon as our aquafarm is up and running, Aspen Packers should anticipate receiving a major purchase order from *Coronado Aquaculture Unlimited*."

Flashing a jubilant and successful smile, Desbrow thanked them for their visit, apologized once again for the smell, and assured them that they would not regret their decision. He then cheerfully escorted them back to their rental car and waved a friendly goodbye as they drove off.

Eva and Sedrak remained silent until they had exited the Aspen Packers property. After Sedrak turned right onto Township Road 494, Eva said tearfully, "God that was awful . . . I think I'll have nightmares for years; and that horrid smell—these clothes are probably ruined." She then dabbed her eyes with a Kleenex, blew her nose into the same tissue, and then stuffed it into the car's ashtray.

"It was definitely an effort to maintain my own composure," Sedrak confessed, "plus play Mr. Nice Guy at the same time."

"You were wonderful," Eva gushed, "a gracious customer who wisely sang the praises of their commodity—with a promise to buy—Mr. Desbrow must think you walk on water."

"Just doing my part in the masquerade."

"If I was your teacher you'd get an A."

"Thank you Professor Chen," Sedrak said with a smile.

"You're welcome," and then changing the subject Eva asked, "What's your opinion regarding the pellets?"

"The same as yours."

"Contaminated with mad cow disease?"

"Without a doubt . . . but only an occasional batch," replied Sedrak as he turned right onto Range Road 275, which he would travel on for about a half mile before turning east onto Highway 39. "However, even that small amount," he continued, "is apparently sufficient to spread the disorder."

"If that's true," Eva reflected out loud, "and Goebbel's fish are consuming feed that from time to time is tainted with mad cow disease—why haven't we been able to detect it?" As you know, the game fish previously examined by Brandon were symptom-free, and had no evidence of the malady."

"What about the eleven fish I recently caught?" Sedrak asked. "Those test results should be finalized by now."

Eva's expression lit up, "Only one way to know . . . " She pulled out her cell phone and after converting it to speakerphone so that Sedrak could participate in the dialogue, she dialed Brandon. On the fourth ring he answered.

"Eva," Brandon answered, "I'm glad you called—"

"You're on speakerphone," advised Eva, "Dr. Sedrak's with me."

"Howdy doctor."

"Hello Brandon."

"Let me guess the reason for your call," Brandon teased, "my analysis of Dr. Sedrak's eleven fish."

"You're a mind reader," Eva said, stroking Brandon's ego, "and yes, that's why we're calling—so tell us what you've discovered?"

"Interesting findings," Brandon said with forced nonchalance. "You sure you don't want to wait until you come back? I hear you're up in Alberta, Canada sightseeing at a delightful rendering plant."

"BRANDON," said Eva exasperated, "NOW, I can't wait until tomorrow; and, for your information, the excursion to the plant was anything but a pleasure trip."

"Okay—but you owe me an expensive dinner. You'll understand after I've finished my summary."

"Brandon . . . its Doctor Sedrak . . . I'll spring for the dinner; and, from what Eva's bragged about you, you're obviously a genius in your field—so choose the best restaurant on the mainland, and we'll make it a triple date."

"Deal," Brandon said quickly, "but no seafood."

"No seafood, or beef," Sedrak confirmed. "It's either chicken or vegan." Sedrak slowed to 35 mph as he drove into the City of Calmar. The city was approximately three blocks in length, and would take about two minutes to traverse.

"Histological assessment of the brain tissue on all eleven fish," began Brandon, "revealed no defective proteinacious particles. In addition, my exam of the spinal cord and central nervous system came back with the same negative findings. My initial conclusion—the fish were not suffering from spongiform encephalopathy, or as you refer to it, mad cow disease."

"You've got to be kidding me," Eva said, bitterly disappointed. "That doesn't make sense—that none of the fish are contaminated—especially after our informative tour of the rendering facility. Maybe we just need a larger test sample . . . a hundred fish if necessary. Everything inside of me screams that the fish are infected with the disease. And to think that you had the audacity to con the doctor into a high-priced meal when you knew the results were negative."

"No—I duped you into a dinner because of *this* incredible piece of news," chided Brandon. "Being the brilliant scientist that I am, I went beyond the norm, and tested each individual fish organs—eyes, heart, liver, spleen, pancreas, intestines, swim bladder, kidneys, stomach lining, and ovaries on the female fish—and came up with absolutely nothing. I next tested the muscle meat, and once again came up empty-handed. At that point I was convinced that your fish were devoid of any foreign prions. And then I had an epiphany: I recalled reading a recent USDA advisory concerning the consumption of fish; the bulletin recommended removal of the blood line and lateral line before cooking, because that's where a fish stores its most dangerous toxins."

"What type of toxins, and what's a blood and lateral line?" Sedrak asked.

"DDT, mercury, and PCPs," answered Brandon. "The blood line is the thin layer of brown meat on the outside of a fillet, and the lateral line is the dark brown vein that runs through the middle of the fillet. When cooked it blends right in with the white meat."

Anticipating where this was going, and in voice tinged with excitement, Eva asked, "And what we're your findings?"

"Two out of the eleven fish were carriers of the defective prions—a sockeye salmon and a yellowfin tuna. It's now clear,"

Brandon said confidently, "that Goebbel's game fish are the source of the spongiform encephalopathy."

"Brandon, you're Albert Einstein resurrected," Eva squealed. "Besides a delicious dinner you're now entitled to a decadent bottle of wine and a luscious dessert."

"Just add it to my tab." Sedrak groaned, and then said, "I do have a question: What did you mean by *carriers?*"

Sedrak observed the Highway 2 sign and turned north. In twenty minutes they would arrive at Edmonton International Airport.

"The salmon and tuna are asymptomatic carriers of the disease," Brandon explained. In other words, the contagion thrives within the tissue of their bodies—within the blood line and lateral line—without causing any symptoms or ill effects."

"They're vectors of the disorder?" Eva stated.

"Exactly," Brandon said. "Although the fish are unaffected by the disease, they can still transmit it to warm-blooded animals once their flesh is ingested. The natural world is full of such hosts who unknowingly act as vectors sowing dreadful viruses, bacteria, or parasites. For example, deer ticks are carriers of Lyme disease. Mosquitoes transmit Malaria, dengue fever, yellow fever, and West Nile. Domestic cats are the primary host for a parasitic protozoon that causes cat-scratch disease. Fleas transmit bubonic plague, typhus, and tapeworms. Bats are a natural reservoir for zoonotic pathogens including rabies and severe respiratory syndrome, although in this case the rabies virus will eventually kill its flying host. Even humans can contract an infectious disease, display no ill symptoms, and pass it on to others—"

"Mary Mallon," Sedrak said, butting in, "is a classic case that we studied in medical school. She was better known as Typhoid Mary, and was an asymptomatic carrier of typhoid fever. At the beginning of the twentieth century she worked as a cook for several prestigious families in New York City, and infected dozens of family members without once becoming sick."

"Your Mary Mallon is now personified in Goebbel's game fish," Brandon warned. "We'll have a major epidemic if we don't do something shortly."

"Of course—we must act immediately," Sedrak said. "Please e-mail your test results to my hospital account as soon as possible. I'll need to review your findings before forwarding them to the CDC. In the meantime, Eva and I will finalize our field inspection report regarding Aspen Packers, and their link to the recent outbreak of mad cow disease. I'm sure Canadian authorities will also become involved. It will take some time, but eventually we'll shut down Goebbel's operation. He's a powerful man, with influential friends, so we'll have to proceed carefully."

"I understand, so let me know if there is anything else that I can do. Have a safe flight, and we'll talk soon." Brandon then terminated the call.

"Wow," Eva exclaimed, "we've had one heck of a productive day."

"Yes," Sedrak confirmed, "it certainly has been, and now we need to strategize our future actions. For example: Who do we involve in the matter? Supposing Goebbel is bribing government workers, what official agencies can we trust besides the CDC? And, what outside experts should we consult with? It's a lot to consider." The approaching overhead freeway sign indicated that the airport was seven kilometers away.

"Fortunately, we'll have plenty of time on the plane for that type of discussion," Eva reminded him. Her cell phone suddenly chimed indicating that she had received a text. Checking the sender, Eva said, "It's from Mischa." Tabbing the 'text inbox' she opened it up, and then read it out loud. "We've reserved the boat, *Nessie*, for Monday, for our planned trip to Painted Cave. It's just the right size for maneuvering inside the cavern. Please tell Dr. Sedrak that he's invited. Timbrook will be our guide. Jake's excited. We're leaving at 7:30 a.m. from Scorpion Pier. See you then. XO Mischa. P.S. Tomorrow Jake and I are spending the day exploring the island on horseback . . . Yea!"

"Do you have any plans for this upcoming Monday?" Eva asked.

"Painted Cave," Sedrak replied, "I'll reschedule my patients. I wouldn't miss it for the world."

Karl Goebbel silently cursed as he crushed the printed e-mail in his muscular hands. Claude Desbrow, the Plant Manager at Aspen Packers, had sent him an e-mail thanking him for the new business referral—Eva Chen, Ph.D., and Matthew Sedrak, M.D.— partners in a startup, San Diego-based aquafarm, and further, that he had personally accompanied the pair during their in-depth tour of the Aspen facilities.

Goebbel had not a clue why they were inspecting the rendering plant, but he had his suspicions. A quick Internet search had alerted him to the fact that Dr. Chen was stationed at the marine lab on Santa Cruz Island, and was probably the female diver that he had almost captured at Platform Gail, and who had stolen an empty feed sack.

What really concerned him, however, was a small, innocuous article in the back of the local newspaper regarding rumors of two patients dying of mad cow disease at Ventura County Community Hospital, and that the hospital's resident neurologist, Matthew Sedrak, M.D., was in charge of the investigation in cooperation with the CDC. Unfortunately, according to the article, Dr. Sedrak was unavailable for comment inasmuch as he was on a short vacation in Alberta, Canada.

Dr. Chen, Dr. Sedrak, and the CDC, all in bed together, conducting a clandestine investigation of his aquaculture company. The idea of this being a coincidence did not exist in Karl Goebbel's vocabulary. Clenching the e-mail, he constricted it until it was about the size of a small glass marble, and then with his right index finger, flicked it like a bullet across the room—smiling venomously at the pinging sound it created as it ricochet off a porcelain scale model of one of his prized racing yachts. *This investigation had to end before it destroys his enterprise,* he brooded. Striding to the opposite side of the room in order to retrieve the crumpled e-mail, Goebbel, in a sudden fit of rage, violently stomped on what remained of it—the vibrating impact inadvertently dislodging the delicate yacht from its perch. Crashing against the marble floor, the model splintered into hundreds of indistinct pieces. Scowling at the destroyed ship, Goebbel then began to laugh—the fortuitous incident kindling a plan of action. *Serious mishaps, while boating near the Channel Islands, were fortunately as common in California waters as were fatal scuba-diving accidents—something his ex-wife could easily attest to.* Grinning maliciously, he made an inner vow: *The next time he observed the two doctors prowling the sea in a marine lab boat—it would be their last.* He then placed a telephone call to Negrete; it was time for his enforcer to earn his next paycheck.

23

"You're all set to go," Timbrook said to Mischa, as he finished cinching Aiyana's western-trail saddle with a latigo knot, and then entwined the fingers of both hands to give the teenager a boost up. He had earlier saddled up Gabriel, which Jake was now astride—the amateur cowboy beaming like a teenager who had miraculously won the lottery. "Just make sure and rest 'em after an hour of strenuous riding."

"You don't have to worry about a thing," promised Mischa, "we'll treat your mustangs as if they're family."

"They are," Timbrook assured her. "Enjoy yourselves, and good luck searching for Cabrillo's grave."

"I wish you could join us," said Mischa.

"Sorry, medical appointment on the mainland," replied Timbrook. "The island ferry leaves at 9:00 a.m., my exam begins at 11:00 a.m., so I should be back by 2:00 p.m."

"What's ailing you?" Jake asked.

"When you're eighty-four . . . just about everything," laughed Timbrook. "My body may look strong, but it has its share of age appropriate aches and pains. I'm scheduled for a comprehensive exam and a few diagnostic tests—which I've agreed to—as long as there's no intrusive probing."

"We'll be praying for you," Mischa advised, "so let us know how it all turns out."

"I'll know later today, and thanks for your prayers," said Timbrook. He then spoke a few Chumash words to each horse, massaged their necks, said 'goodbye' to Jake and Mischa, and then, at a slow shuffle, headed toward Scorpion Pier—where he would board the ferry in a half hour.

When Timbrook was out of range, Jake said, "He seems older today."

"He is," Mischa agreed. "He may have laughed about his body aches, but Timbrook's not one to waste an entire day visiting a doctor unless something is seriously wrong."

"Any idea what it could be?"

"No, but knowing Timbrook I doubt he'll tell us. His faith sustains him, and whatever it is, he'll just accept it and move on with his life." She then uttered a short, audible prayer for Timbrook's health, and ended it with a loud 'amen.'

After a respectful moment of silence, Jake said, somewhat cheekily, "That's one hell of a good prayer, my spiritual sister," and then stated, "Our ancestor's grave is awaiting our discovery—are you ready to ride?"

"You bet," answered Mischa, and then added mysteriously, "and who knows what else we just might come across in our search?"

Jake awarded Mischa with a quizzical frown that implied, *what are you talking about?* But, before he could inquire, Mischa kicked Aiyana with the heel of her boot, spurring the horse into a canter. Gabriel, who was not used to bringing up the rear, snorted loudly and without any signal from Jake, bolted into a gallop, zipping past the mare within seconds. Satisfied at having re-established his leadership position, the big stallion then slowed to an easy trot, with Jake ashen white at the reins.

Twisting in his saddle so that he directly faced Mischa, Jake said irritably, "How about warning me before taking off like a crazed lunatic—I almost fell off my horse."

Convulsing with laughter, Mischa said, "Okay greenhorn . . . you have my word . . . no impromptu cantering without a precautionary alert."

Discerning the sarcastic subtlety of Mischa's wisecrack, Jake said, "Thanks, but I won't hold my breath," and then added, "Don't forget I'm a tit for tat kind of brother." Sulking, he turned his back on Mischa, and after a brief interval—where the only sound was the horses' hooves on the dirt trail—shrieked a diabolical cackle, creating the impression that he had decided upon the appropriate pay back. Unfortunately, the sudden and unexpected noise startled Gabriel whose reactive leap nearly unseated Jake for the second time.

This time Mischa thought it best to keep her laughter to herself. Besides, she knew from past experience that her brother's piercing howl amounted to nothing more than windless puffery. Fortunately, for her sake, his temperament did not allow for vindictiveness.

The sound of crashing surf as it exploded against the base of a two-hundred-foot granite cliff indicated that the trail had reached the coastal bluffs situated on the westernmost side of Scorpion Cove. At that point the path abruptly ended and their continued journey would require their blazing their own trail across unmarked countryside. Stopping, and then dismounting, they decided to briefly rest their horses.

In their pre-trip consultations with Timbrook he had recommended skirting the southwest coastline from Scorpion Cove to Smuggler's Cove, and then doubling back by way of Smuggler's Trail. The seaboard route was less than four miles in length. Smuggler's Trail added another four miles. Depending upon how much time they spent searching for Captain Cabrillo's tomb, their circuitous adventure should take about five hours.

The Scorpion to Smuggler's Cove segment was chosen because Timbrook had previously conducted only one cursory search of this expansive area. The reason—it was situated on the 'ocean side' of the island, which in his opinion was a non-desirable burial site. The promontories, palisades, and headlands were constantly battered by ocean breezes, nipping fog, punishing waves, and violent winter tempests, making it less than ideal as a final resting place for a prominent captain.

An analysis by Mischa and Jake of a 3-D topographical map charting this section of the island revealed only five potential burial sites. Each of the prospective areas jutted out into the ocean, was sufficiently ample in size, and had breathtaking panoramic views—necessary requirements for a noble's internment. San Pedro Point appeared to be the most promising, and was at the halfway mark.

Prior to embarking on their outing Jake had volunteered to pack their food supplies. To Mischa's amusement her brother had loaded their saddlebags with two large bags of beef jerky—enough to nourish a carnivore for a week—a sixteen-ounce bag of trail mix, eight apples, two bags of baby carrots, a small box of sugar cubes, and six bottles of Gatorade. When Mischa questioned her brother about the 'excessive amount of provisions' he replied: "Explorer scout training—if something goes wrong, we'll have enough edibles to last us a few days; and the extra apples, carrots, and especially the sugar cubes are for the mustangs." After listening to Jake's explanation Mischa was impressed; her brother's packing logic was impeccable.

After remounting their steeds and walking them to within a few feet of the cliff's edge, they gazed at the ocean. Swimming in the clear, kaleidoscopic waters of Scorpion Cove was a pod of northern elephant seals. The hulking giants, at two thousand pounds apiece, were considered the aircraft carriers of the seal world. Floating along the surface just outside the surf zone, a tangled mat of golden-hued giant kelp stretched out over three hundred yards; finally, abutting the shoreline, opulent beds of emerald-green eel grass, which rose and fell in ever-changing patterns with each passing wave.

Raising her voice Mischa yelled, "Jake . . . whale at 12:00 o'clock!" A quarter mile beyond the shoreline a forty-ton plankton-feeding humpback had breached, thrusting its entire bulk airborne for a fleeting second. The behemoth then splashed down with a thunderous report and immediately vanished into the sapphire-blue sea—leaving behind an immense frothy wake. "That was awesome!" she said excitedly.

"It certainly was," Jake said with a wide grin. "That's a first for me."

"Northern elephant seals and a baleen whale, that's an encouraging sign," Mischa insisted.

"Or," Jake opined, "It's just a typical day on Santa Cruz Island."

"That's probably true," laughed Mischa. She then observed two endangered California sea otters basking on an acre-sized offshore island that was a part of, and yet separate from, Santa Cruz Island. "Do you see those otters?"

"Yes," said Jake, "hopefully it's a mated pair."

"A litter of adorable otter pups, now that would be a sight worth seeing," she said, and sighed. Staring at the otters, Mischa appreciated the fact that the island of Santa Cruz was surrounded by a substantial number of unexplored rocky outcroppings which were essentially off-limits to humans and as a consequence, served as rookeries for all types of seals, birds, and sea otters. Within the extended boundaries of Scorpion Cove she observed five such islets, with one grandiose enough to accommodate a Beverly Hills mansion. The largest of all the individual islets, however, existed on the backside of Santa Cruz. Gull Island was plateau-shaped, two-tenths of a mile in length, soared sixty-five feet above the waterline, and had been set aside as a marine sanctuary for nesting seabirds and underwater flora and fauna.

"It's time to move out," Jake announced breaking the reverie. With a gentle pull of the inside rein, he turned Gabriel west toward their first potential burial site. He headed out at a leisurely trot, with Aiyana bringing up the rear—matching the stallion's every hoofbeat.

The cross-country route chosen by Jake ran slightly inland of the island's craggy shoreline. Fortunately, the hillsides along this section of the coastline lacked any significant vegetation, making it easily passable on horseback. Six-inch Island grasses, mingled with two-foot tall Mediterranean canary grasses, covered the slopes. The grasses were beginning to fade from green to yellowish-brown with the approach of summer. An occasional cluster of giant coreopsis, with vibrant green foliage and resplendent yellow daises, hugged the steep knolls that paralleled the coast. In less than a month the stunning seasonal plant would turn grayish black in color as it entered into its dormant phase during the dry summer months. The once beautiful flowering plant would remain withered and 'death-like' until the advent of soaking winter rains.

After ten more minutes of riding Jake and Mischa arrived at their first destination—a small peninsula that extended approximately fifty yards beyond the shoreline. Dismounting, the brother and sister immediately reached into their saddlebags in order to retrieve a small shovel, a miniature pickaxe, and over a dozen multi-colored marker flags. The twenty-inch wire-masted flags would serve as reference points to indicate already surveyed territory. The last thing they wanted to do was re-inspect the same plot of land. They then set their horses free to graze on the grasses while they searched for Cabrillo's gravesite.

Standing seven feet apart, Jake and Mischa each placed a flag at their starting position, and then began to walk forward; their eyes glued to the ground. In a loud voice Jake said, "Remember what Timbrook said about the burial chamber—that in all probability it would be very crude—a hastily dug hole approximately six to seven feet in length, parallel or perpendicular to the ocean, and packed with earth and pebbles. Further, that the raised mound would be almost indistinguishable from the surrounding soil, especially with the passage of time, though there may be a few larger stones on top, and possibly a tombstone chiseled from island rock."

"He also warned," Mischa added, "with over four hundred and seventy years of erosion, any inscription on the memorial might be imperceptible."

"I know," Jake moaned, "it seems like we're looking for a needle in a haystack."

"That may be true," Mischa agreed, "but don't forget we have Cabrillo's blood running through our veins, and that should give us a familial edge."

"Let's hope you're right," Jake said skeptically.

For the next fifteen minutes Jake and Mischa scoured the protruding spit, marking every turnabout with a flag and verifying that they were still seven feet apart. They then would turn and slowly walk the next leg. In order to save time they agreed in advance to only dig if they discovered a potential surface disturbance or height variation that was equivalent in size to a burial pit. This particular peninsula had only one such patch of land, which they spent several anxious minutes excavating. When Jake's axe struck an object that created a pinging-type sound, their expectations were raised. Further digging, however, revealed an inglorious treasure trove of discarded trash—rusted cans and broken bottles—apparently buried years ago by island cowboys.

"That was a bust," Jake fumed.

"At least it got our hearts skipping a beat," Mischa said with a smile. "There are still four peninsulas left, and the day's still young."

"Always the optimist," Jake said, returning Mischa's smile.

After gathering their tools and picking up their marker flags, Mischa whistled the way Timbrook had previously instructed her in order to summon the horses. The high-pitched sound generated an instant response, and the horses were at their sides within seconds. After repacking their saddlebags, they both enjoyed a few mouthfuls of trail mix, and drained a bottle of Gatorade.

The mustangs also participated in the mid-morning snack, with each equine receiving a crisp apple and three sugar cubes.

The second promontory was twice the size as the first, and twice as disappointing. Their meticulous reconnoitering produced nothing of significance, not even an ancient rubbish heap. The third headland was at San Pedro Point, which Timbrook felt was the most promising. This classic-style peninsula, with its majestic views on all three sides, protruded far beyond the shoreline, and was aesthetically similar to the headlands that the Monterey coastline was famous for. Its distinguishing feature was a trio of Bishop Pines, which gave it the appearance of being sanctified.

Jumping off Gabriel, Jake said, "This has to be the place . . . I can feel it in my bones."

"It certainly *looks* like a suitable burial site," Mischa admitted as she slid off Aiyana. She hurriedly unpacked her tools, and joined her brother as they visually mapped out the area and devised a search. Her brother's contagious enthusiasm was also raising her expectations.

For the next forty-five minutes they carefully probed every square foot that fell within their burial parameters. After thoroughly examining a section, they would mark it with a flag, and then move on to the next favorable parcel. They saved the most auspicious grounds for last—a stretch that bordered a precipitous cliff with a breath-taking view of Anacapa Island.

"This has to be it," Jake said confidently.

"I agree," Mischa said, "this area has an eternal vista, and if I was the dying captain, this would definitely be my first choice."

While Jake walked within five feet of the bluff's edge, Mischa replicated his path, but seven feet further inland. Following one complete pass, they then retraced their steps, but with Mischa responsible for the inside passage. Jake had insisted on a second pair of eyes analyzing the exact same turf—concerned that he might have missed something. Upon completion of the duplicate once-over, Mischa assured him that he had not. They then moved outward an additional fifteen feet, and made two complete passes, switching places as they had done earlier. Unfortunately, their diligence proved fruitless, and the only thing of interest was a large mound of sun-bleached shells.

"He's not here," Mischa lamented.

"I know," Jake said, "just lots and lots of discarded shells. Kicking the pile with the toe of his boot, he muttered, "Abalones, mussels, scallops, and saltwater snails; somebody had a fondness for seafood."

"It's a Chumash Indian midden deposit," Mischa advised. "It's their version of an open dump. This type of organic rubbish heap was usually located just outside a village."

"At least that explains why there's no captain," Jake said, as he now began smashing the brittle shells. "The Chumash would never bury a foreigner next to one of their settlements."

Mischa nodded in agreement as she whistled signaling the horses. After stowing their tools they swung up on their mounts and at a slow trot, headed toward the fourth and fifth sites, which were situated within minutes of each other.

The two side-by-side, almost identical granite promontories, had captivating views, peaceful settings, a smattering of scented flowers, gnarled cypress trees, and plots of land befitting a sea captain's internment—but no such place was found. Frustrated, and with faces etched with disappointment, they left the twin headlands, and made the ten-minute ride to Smuggler's Cove where they knew of a small, fresh-water creek that flowed into the ocean. Remaining perched on their steeds, they made a brief stop in the middle of the stream—allowing the horses a much-needed liquid break.

Sitting astride Gabriel while the stallion guzzled mouthfuls of water, Jake complained, "Three wasted hours!"

"No," Mischa countered, "three hours of elimination. We can now cross off this portion of the island."

"How refreshingly positive," Jake said critically. "At this rate it'll take years. If you hadn't noticed—the island is massive—with hundreds of probable burial sites."

"Very true, brother, but you're primary assumptions are wrong. If he's buried on Santa Cruz, it's on this side of the island, not on the backside, so those sites don't matter. Trust me—someday we'll find him—I just know it."

"Good . . . then you choose the next plausible area."

"I'm already thinking about that," Mischa said musingly. In the distance, rising like a misty mirage, she spied Gull Island, surrounded by a fingerling of fog.

Gabriel suddenly lifted his head and neighed, indicating that he had quenched his thirst. Aiyana, being slightly smaller, had finished sooner, and was already nibbling on shoots of succulent grass.

"Time to move out," Jake said. Using the command word, *giddyap,* and with a gentle nudge of the leather reins, he guided Gabriel to the entrance of Smuggler's Trail. As usual, Aiyana was a few paces behind.

For the first quarter mile the switchback trail climbed about four hundred feet before leveling off and then winding its way around Montannon Ridge. Traveling at a leisurely gait, they enjoyed the panoramic views and the untamed natural beauty of the island. Within a half hour they had reached the midpoint and the turnoff to Montannon Ridge. On their last excursion Mischa had purposely marked the concealed trail with a flat rock.

Knowing that they were nearing the hidden entryway, Mischa prodded the mare with the heel of her boot until it was striding alongside Gabriel. The stallion, agitated by the maneuver, flared his ears backwards and brayed a warning. Scowling himself, Jake turned and asked, "What are you doing?"

"Next adventure bro."

"And what might that be?"

"Montannon Ridge. We're almost at the turnoff."

"My sweet, conniving sister, how cute," laughed Jake, and then asked, "Would Timbrook approve of this detour?"

"Unfortunately, he's not here to ask."

"How convenient."

"I prefer to call it fate."

Mischa's comment resulted in Jake laughing so hard that both horses simultaneously swung their heads and stared at him as if he had gone mad. "So . . . you believe it's our destiny to journey to Montannon Ridge."

Rounding a bend in the trail, Mischa spied the telltale rock, and immediately brought Aiyana to a halt opposite the stone. Jake also stopped. "Absolutely," Mischa said, "that's why I discreetly marked the spot."

"And today's the day? It seems like you've helped fate along a bit," Jake teased.

"The day's still young," Mischa said with a pleading voice, "the horses are in good shape, we have plenty of food and drink, and we deserve something positive after our unproductive search for Cabrillo's grave."

"I have to admit," Jake said eyeing the stone that identified the threshold, "since learning about the sacred site my curiosity has been stirred up—so the answer is yes—but, let's keep this off-trail indiscretion to ourselves."

"My sentiments exactly," Mischa assured him, and then squealed with delight. "This is going to be fun."

"I hope you're right," Jake said, and then added, "but remember, according to Timbrook's own words the passageway to Montannon Ridge is rarely used, which means there won't be much of a trail. But, I figure Gabriel has the route memorized, so I'll just sit back and enjoy the ride."

"Spoken like a wise buckaroo," Mischa said, meaning it as a compliment. "Mustang's are incredibly bright, and as you suggested, since Gabriel's made the odyssey numerous times, it shouldn't be a problem."

Jake positioned Gabriel so that he was centered over Mischa's indicator rock, gave the horse a swift kick, and then held on as the stallion parted the coastal sagebrush and disappeared into the thick foliage. Aiyana obediently followed, vanishing through the same obscure trailhead.

Initially, the bridle path was somewhat recognizable and relatively flat making for an easy start. However, after the first tenth of a mile the trail entered into a series of long, uphill switchbacks, becoming incrementally steeper with each completed loop. Mischa approximated that each segment represented a one-hundred-foot gain in elevation. Montannon Ridge, at eighteen hundred feet, was the second highest peak on the island, and with a starting altitude at five hundred feet, it meant they had an arduous thirteen-hundred-foot climb.

After an hour of steady plodding, they had zigzagged eleven times, and were close to the summit. Any semblance of a path had ceased around the seventh bend, and their reliance upon Gabriel's pre-existent knowledge of the trail had become absolute. Their only rest stop was unplanned; a four foot yellowish-brown nonvenomous gopher snake was sunning itself in the middle of their track, blocking their passage. Gabriel froze and refused to walk around the serpent, forcing Jake to deal with the reptile. Dismounting, Jake silently approached the creature, gently picked it up by its mid-section, and then released it in a nearby rock pile—without once getting bitten.

The final one-hundred-foot climb involved trudging through thick Island manzanita that was so dense that it appeared impassable to a human, much less a massive horse. But somehow Gabriel forged a path—weaving a route known only to him—until suddenly the shrubbery ended, and they were in a narrow corridor of weathered igneous rock. At the end of the fifty-yard gorge was a natural archway, with a gap barely wide enough for a horse.

Approximately twenty-five feet from the impressive gateway, Mischa abruptly reigned in Aiyana, which also brought Gabriel to a halt. "Jake!" she said excitedly, "The arch . . . it's covered with Chumash art."

Decorating the overhanging span were a myriad of colored pictographs; a regal looking coyote crouched on a cumulus cloud howling at the moon; elaborate sun-like circles; a rainbow bridge connecting the island to the mainland with caricatures of stick-like humans falling off the bridge and into the sea where they then morphed into dolphins; sea otters and sea lions at play; a soaring vulture, and other abstract paintings whose symbolic meanings eluded Mischa. The colors, although faded, were spectacular—various shades of black, royal purple, deep red, bright orange, sulphur-yellow, and chalky white.

Needing several minutes to take it all in, Jake finally whispered, "Amazing," and then in a voice filled with reverence, "those drawings are ancient."

"How old?" Mischa asked.

"Hundreds of years . . . maybe a thousand."

As Mischa continued to stare in awe at the intricate artwork, a canine-like apparition suddenly materialized at the entryway, temporarily shocking her consciousness, and overloading her sense of reality. Before she could psychologically process the un-expected data, the unknown entity leaped into the air, landing with scarcely a sound ten feet in front of their horses. There it took up a defensive position, pacing back and forth, uttering a ferocious guttural growl, and baring its pearl-colored teeth. The hair along the creature's entire back bristled, exaggerating its size and making it appear brutish. Mischa noted that the animal had pure white hair mixed with streaks of gray, and that its virulently glaring eyes were arctic blue. The creature's eyes locked onto hers, exploring the very depths of her soul, leaving her feeling powerless. The distant sound of Jake's voice freed her from the animal's hypnotic gaze.

"Is that a wolf?" he asked.

Mischa was too frightened to instantly respond. She required a few seconds before Jake's question stimulated the rational side of her intellect. She then, for the first time, truly inspected the animal, taking her time to analyze its overall structure, and dog-like mannerisms. "No," she said hesitantly, "it's definitely not a wolf . . . probably one of the northern breeds . . . Alaskan mala-mute or Siberian husky."

"It's too small to be a malamute," Jake insisted, "maybe a hus-ky. But what's it doing here?"

As Jake was speaking, the dog continued to snarl and lunge at them, but at the same time kept its ears erect rather than pinned back—an amiable gesture—belying its ferocious demeanor. Finally, it focused its attention on just the mustangs and suddenly and unexpectedly began wagging its bushy tail. Surprised at the change in the husky's behavior, Mischa also observed that the normally high-strung mustangs were perfectly calm; fearless in the presence of a hostile dog and gawking at the pooch as if they were old friends rather than mortal enemies. The revelation was illuminating. She laughed, and by the look in the husky's eyes, she humiliated it, whereupon the animal instantly ceased any re-maining combative behavior and lay down. Mischa slid off her horse.

"What are you doing?" Jake said concerned.

"They're buddies—the mustangs and the dog—I'm confident the husky is harmless." Mischa slowly walked toward the prostrate dog; stopping within two feet, she got down on her knees, and in an act of submissiveness nervously extended her right hand, and allowed the canine to become familiar with her scent. The husky initially emitted a low growl and then, to Mischa's relief, sniffed her hand, and to her complete surprise began licking it, and then to her utter astonishment, moved on to her face, cleaning her cheeks and nose.

"I think you're now an official member of its pack," Jake said, roaring with laughter.

Mischa smiled, pleased at having been accepted into the canine's clan. As she was wiping off the doggie saliva with her sleeve, the animal rolled onto its back so that she could rub its belly. While in that position, she noticed that the husky was a female, and that around its neck was a thin leather collar with an attached circular brass pet I.D. tag. She silently read the name inscribed on the tag: *Journey.* "Jake," she said aloud, "the Siberian's name is Journey." At the mention of her name, the husky jumped up, obviously ecstatic at having her name spoken. Jake then joined Mischa and received his own thorough licking and formal acceptance into the pack.

As Jake was scratching Journey's head, he said, "Don't you find it odd that Timbrook has a Siberian stationed on top of Montannon Ridge?"

"It's probably a guard dog," Mischa answered, "although I've never heard of a Siberian husky serving as a watchdog."

"I think our experience proves it's definitely worthless," Jake insisted with a chuckle.

"I'm not so sure . . . maybe the Siberian's job is to just scare off potential visitors . . . not attack them. I think the mustangs interfered with Journey's trained response; she *knew* who they were, but *not* their riders. If we had hiked in alone I'm positive the outcome would have been different, and we'd be currently hightailing our way back down the mountain."

"Perhaps . . . but thankfully we'll never know; besides, without Gabriel's trail knowledge, we never would have found this place."

"True," Mischa agreed, "and the fact that Timbrook has the entrance protected by a fulltime furry guardian has me chomping at the bit so see what lies beyond the archway."

"We'll know soon enough," Jake said.

Instead of remounting, they walked alongside their horses, with Journey out in front, leading the way. They passed single file beneath the span, and stepped into a sacred Chumash site—one that for thousands of years—had remain concealed from the outside world.

Once on the other side Mischa gasped, felt lightheaded, instinctively inhaled and exhaled, and then rubbed her eyes as if she was waking up from a dream, "Oh my god!" she murmured.

24

Kurt Nichols waved goodbye as the Island Packers ferry pulled away from the Scorpion Cove pier. Adam Timbrook, standing on the ferry's bow politely tipped his baseball hat, acknowledging Kurt's farewell gesture. Two days earlier Timbrook had informed Kurt that on Friday he was traveling to the mainland for a medical appointment with his family doctor, which Kurt assumed was nothing more than a yearly physical. Ninety minutes earlier he had also said goodbye to Mischa and Jake as they embarked on their own special errand— on horseback—searching for Captain Cabrillo's burial site. He did not think their quest would succeed, but he had wisely kept that opinion to himself. *If Timbrook was unable to discover Cabrillo's grave,* he thought, *what chance did they have?* Nonetheless he wished them luck, and as was typical with his self-assured daughter, she had smugly countered, "The word luck doesn't exist in my vocabulary, but thanks anyway, Dad."

Kurt had arrived at the dock around 8:00 a.m. in order to prepare *Serenity* for his own clandestine adventure—searching for the *S.S. Winfield Scott's* underwater booty. The only people who were aware of his plans were Timbrook, Eva, his two kids, and out of necessity, Daniel Petersen, a student at the University of Malibu who had just stepped onto his yacht. Petersen, who was just a month away from completing his Master's, was a genius at deploying and operating state-of-the-art underwater technology. Prior to disclosing any specific facts to the brilliant techno wizard, Kurt had demanded that he sign a confidentiality agreement, ensuring that their adventure would remain private. Petersen had griped about endorsing the one-sided contract, citing his First Amendment rights, but in the end he reluctantly agreed. Only then did Kurt reveal the substance of their mission. Along with the informative overview, he provided Petersen with three important documents: The chemical analysis by Brandon Kagan of the black substance obtained from the scorched pieces of the *Scott's* wood; President Franklin Pierce's hand-written memo demanding that the entire *Scott* file be turned over to Nicholas Trist, United States Diplomat to Mexico; and, Captain Flannigan's poetic words describing that fateful night. He also told Petersen about the twenty dollar Double Eagle Liberty Head gold coin.

After Petersen had finished his perusal of the documents, he understood the need for secrecy, and apologized for his pigheadedness.

During their preparation time, Kurt and Petersen had loaded the *Serenity* with scuba equipment, lift bags, and high-tech underwater search equipment manufactured by JW Fishers. The first item was a Pulse 12 Towfish—a boat-towed metal detector that scanned the ocean floor for ferrous metals—iron and steel—and non-ferrous metals such as gold and silver. The bright yellow torpedo-shaped device was tethered to the boat by three hundred feet of cable and had a detection envelope that extended twenty-four feet across the ocean floor. The instrument also had the ability to ascertain objects buried in sediment up to fourteen feet. Readout data and GPS coordinates were transmitted via wiring spliced into the cable that was in turn linked to a topside computer and a Pulse 12 Control Box.

The second apparatus was a DV-1 high-resolution-color camera with two high-intensity tungsten-halogen lights, and two hundred and fifty feet of cable. The cable was connected from the camera to a topside video recorder and monitor. The system was deployed over the side of the vessel and then lowered to the bottom. It allowed verification of a suspected target without the need for time-consuming check-out dives.

The third and final gadget was a Pulse 8X; a handheld, underwater metal detector powered by an internal 9 volt rechargeable battery pack. The detector allowed a scuba diver to zero in on a suspected target. The highly sensitive, pulse-induction instrument unearthed all types of metal—ferrous and nonferrous—including gold coins and bars, and had both audio and visual outputs. The audio was provided by underwater earphones that were tucked under the diver's hood, and the visual output was displayed on a large, easy to read meter.

Kurt had purchased the underwater equipment with his own funds in order to avoid any University entanglements. It was also the reason why he was using his personal yacht, and why he was on vacation for a week. Petersen however, was still a student, which created a potential conflict of interest. They had solved the problem by categorizing his involvement as a volunteer intern on behalf of an independent enterprise.

With the ship fully loaded, including their lunch and bottled water, Petersen untied the mooring lines, and Kurt slowly began to ease the twenty-five foot ship away from the dock and out into the cove. Petersen joined him in the wheelhouse and sat down in the co-pilot's seat.

"A fiery explosion on the *Scott*," whistled Petersen, "a presidential cover-up, and a captain who penned a few tantalizing clues— I'd say we have one hell of a nice mystery."

"And with your specialized expertise," laughed Kurt, "we'll have it solved by noon."

"Noon of what day?" moaned Petersen. "It's a huge ocean. According to Captain Flannigan's riddle, the *Winfield Scott* passed within a quarter mile of Cavern Point and then continued with its southerly transit—*Santa Cruz an ebbing apparition*—until it collided with Middle Anacapa Island. For your information, the distance from Cavern Point to the wreck site is nine miles. That's nine miles of seafloor, and that's assuming the *Scott* didn't deviate from its path. The Towfish is a wonderful tool, but it does have its limitations. At best we'll cover less than twenty-four feet of seabed with each pass, and that's *not* a whole lot of acreage. Locating a sunken ship would be a piece of cake compared to searching the shifting bottom for an unknown amount of scattered debris."

"Hey, where's your faith?" chided Kurt.

"As a scientist I'm a realist, and my hope rests in the quality of our equipment and our superior intellect. Which reminds me, did you conduct any research into President Pierce's sudden interest in the *Scott* wreck?"

"Of course, and it turned out to be a great big goose egg. There's nothing in any maritime records, historical writings, books, and zilch on the Internet."

"Did you contact Washington?"

"No. Awakening a slumbering beast seemed ill-advised."

"You don't trust your own government?" Petersen asked with a silly grin. "Speaking of faith, where's yours?"

"Today," Kurt said, "it's in you, me, *Serenity,* and the underwater contrivances from JW Fisher."

"That, Professor Nichols, makes you a pragmatist—just like me."

Kurt's guileless smile belied the truth behind Petersen's platitude. *Spending several days with an astute technologist,* thought Kurt, *might not be so bad after all.* Fortunately for them the marine report predicted calm seas over the next several days, other than in the late afternoon when a slight surface chop was expected. Kurt was cognizant of the fact that a successful treasure hunt was dependent upon a cooperative ocean, and thus far the conditions appeared favorable.

The *Serenity,* chugging along at a notch above idle, had finally passed the cove's five mile per hour speed limit marker; Kurt aimed the boat's bow toward Cavern Point—their starting place—and thrusting the throttle forward, quickly accelerated to ten knots. As they covered the scant half mile to their destination, he noticed that Petersen was re-reading Captain Flannigan's words. "What do you think?" he asked.

"Some passages are relatively straightforward—like the directional movement of his ship, the Captain's involvement in a conspiracy, and the fact that his ship was pierced—yet others are a bit confusing. But, considering the amount of money you've already invested in this project, I'm assuming you've already deciphered the ambiguous phrases, and all I have to do is probe your brain for those answers."

Smiling smugly Kurt said, "In fact, I've analyzed that document *ad nauseam,* so what's your first question?"

"Captain Flannigan mentioned four individuals, Trist, Santa Anna, Juarez, and Pierce. I know who Pierce is, but who are the others?"

"Nicholas Trist was the United States Diplomat to Mexico from 1847 to 1854. Santa Anna was President of Mexico, off and on, from 1833 to 1855. In 1855, Benito Juarez, through the Ayutla Rebellion, successfully ousted Santa Anna from office. In 1858 Benito Juarez was elected President of Mexico. He served in that capacity for fourteen years."

"All politicians," Petersen said with disdain, "no wonder Captain Flannigan used the words *collaboration, covenant,* and *scheming* to describe their actions, and that the *Winfield Scott* was a diplomatic pawn in their conspiracy."

"True," Kurt said, "but Benito Juarez was not your typical politician—he was a beloved leader of his country."

"Okay . . . one out of four."

"And Trist," Kurt added, "successfully negotiated the Treaty of Guadalupe Hidalgo."

"Which leads me to my next question: What's the underlying meaning behind the line, *Brother Hidalgo, Sister Gadsden,* and *Baby Ayutla?*"

"I'm not exactly sure; the Treaty of Guadalupe Hidalgo, which was signed in 1848, ended the Mexican-American War and granted to the United States undisputed control of Texas, California, Nevada, New Mexico, Utah, and parts of Colorado, Kansas, Arizona, Oklahoma, and Wyoming—six hundred thousand square miles—at a cost of only eighteen million dollars. The Gadsden Purchase of 1853 transferred to the United States an additional thirty thousand square miles for a payment of ten million dollars. That transfer of real estate expanded the borders of both Arizona and New Mexico."

"The cost of acquiring territory was getting more expensive," Petersen observed, and then asked. "Was 'Baby Ayutla' another property deal?"

"No," said Kurt, "which makes its literary linkage with Hidalgo and Gadsden a bit odd. The Ayutla Rebellion began in 1854 and eventually resulted in the overthrow of Santa Anna. My research revealed that the Ayutla Revolution had nothing to do with the transfer, or sale, of any tracts of land to the United States."

Petersen shrugged. "Maybe the answer lies at the bottom of the sea."

"Maybe," Kurt repeated.

"But, my favorite part of the riddle," Petersen said enthusiastically, "is the reference to 'Precious yellow weight . . . impervious to sea or time.' The *only* yellow mineral that's impervious to the caustic effects of salt water or to the deteriorating effects of time—is gold. It's my opinion that the gold coin that accompanied Captain Flannigan's riddle was a tantalizing harbinger of what lies beneath."

Kurt nodded while trying to suppress a confirming smile. "We'll know soon enough."

"There's Cavern Point," Petersen announced, "with its dilapidated lighthouse."

Situated on the jagged edge of a steep promontory was a nineteenth century, whitewashed and candy-cane striped lighthouse. Constructed in 1851, the seventy-five foot tower was fitted with a Fresnel lens. The specialized lens used refraction as well as reflection to channel a beam of over 500,000 candlepower that was visible up to ten miles away. Its benevolent function as a beacon of light, however, had abruptly ended at the start of World War II. The oil-lit flame was extinguished in order to prevent the Japanese submarine fleet from using the signal as a navigational tool. After the war the structure was boarded up and abandoned.

Once the *Serenity* was opposite the lighthouse, Kurt headed straight out, setting the ship's GPS tracking device to inform them with a beep once they were a quarter mile from the landmark. In less than two minutes it chimed at which point he shifted the engine into neutral, letting the boat drift in the slow-moving current. "You're now in charge," he informed Petersen.

"In that case—it's Captain Petersen," the graduate student replied with a wry smile.

"First Mate," Kurt countered, "and even that's being generous."

"Alright, but the lowly title will cost you a cold beer."

"If we're successful . . . I'll buy you a pony keg."

"Deal," Petersen said quickly, "but I get to pick the micro-brewery."

After nodding his assent, Petersen flashed a devious smile, which alerted Kurt to the fact that he had probably been duped into purchasing an expensive barrel of beer. Some of the specialty brands had price tags in excess of two thousand dollars. *If he succeeds in our task*, Kurt shrugged, *he'll deserve it.* He returned Petersen's insidious smile—the conniving student wouldn't be drinking alone. "Okay my illustrious First Mate, what's your plan-of-action for our treasure hunt?"

"Obviously we'll commence our underwater search utilizing the Pulse 12, towing the device ten feet off the bottom along a parallel grid pattern. The parameters are based upon Captain Flannigan's last known route—a quarter mile off the lighthouse, to the actual collision site at Anacapa Island. Our initial run will follow the sea path most likely taken by the Captain. If it's unsuccessful, we'll expand outward—twenty feet with each succeeding pass. We'll continue in this northeast direction until we've surveyed two hundred feet of ocean floor times nine miles. If no objects are detected, we'll move the boat twenty feet inside of our original starting point, and repeat the same methodical process, but heading southwest."

"I thought the instrument had a detection envelope that extended twenty-four feet across the ocean floor," Kurt advised.

"It does," Petersen confirmed, "but to ensure that we don't miss the target, we'll want some overlap to compensate for inaccuracy."

"Makes sense," Kurt agreed, "nine miles along an irregular sea lane, twenty feet at a time, this needle-in-a-haystack search could take a long time."

"That's what I tried to tell you earlier," Petersen reminded Kurt. "Besides lots of patience, and a tranquil ocean, we'll also need some divine luck. Even with our GPS tied into the boat's autopilot we're still subject to slight deviations—currents, wind, and rolling swells which have the potential to adversely affect the GPS' pinpoint precision. Over a nine-mile stretch of ocean these miniscule shifts could result in large fingerlings of seafloor being unintentionally overlooked."

"Such negativity," Kurt said as he playfully slapped Petersen's back, "you forget who you are. You're a genius; the probability of failure doesn't exist."

"Tell that to Professor Barnett who gave me an A- in *Aqueous Chemistry* last semester."

"It's still an A," Kurt clarified.

"Yes, but that pathetic little dash on the end hurt . . . my scholastic pride was wounded for at least a month."

"Call your mom."

"I did, and she was about as sympathetic as you are."

Laughing Kurt said, "Sorry, about your mom, but you're welcome to stick it to me by locating the items on the seafloor and earning your month's supply of beer."

"That I intend to do. During your spare moments you might want to look up Crown Ambassador Reserve, it's an Australian beer sold in 750 ml Champagne bottles. I'll want a pony keg's worth—that's about forty bottles at ninety dollars a bottle."

Kurt instantly did the math: *Thirty-six hundred dollars.* "No problem," he said.

"I didn't think so," said Petersen grinning jovially as he began preparing the Pulse 12 Towfish for deployment. After powering up the various components, Petersen carefully checked each unit to verify that they were functioning properly, and in particular, that the Towfish was downloading the *Serenity's* GPS telemetry. The position fix data, which contained both latitude and longitude, was critical for pinpointing the exact location—within feet—of a favorable target. The last item attached to the Pulse 12 was an altimeter that Petersen fastened to its underside. The altimeter measured the Towfish's distance from the seafloor. Without this instrument they would be essentially guessing at its actual operating depth. Since their search was in seas over a hundred feet deep, a downrigger with a fifty-pound ingot of lead was required in order to keep the metal detector directly below the ship. Satisfied with his workmanship, Petersen began lowering the Towfish and downrigger into the water with an electric hoist that was attached to the stern of the boat. When it had descended to within ten feet of the bottom he advised Kurt, "We're all set to go. The *Fish* is at 115 feet and the ocean floor is around 125."

"What tow speed do you recommend?"

"Six miles per hour," Petersen suggested, "otherwise we'll have depth control problems."

"An hour and a half for each nine mile section," Kurt lamented, "It's going to be a long day."

"Long week," Petersen corrected.

"Thanks for that optimistic reminder," Kurt groaned. While Petersen remained at the ship's stern, Kurt returned to the wheelhouse where he imputed the latitude and longitude of their current position as Waypoint 1 into the marine GPS system. Using a nautical chart he repeated the same procedure for Waypoint 2—the actual collision site of the *S.S. Winfield Scott.* Humming the Disney tune, *Pirates of the Caribbean,* he gripped the control throttle with his right hand, lifted its safety locking mechanism, shifted from neutral into forward, accelerated to six miles per hour, and engaged the autopilot. Their treasure hunt had officially begun; from this point forward he would remain primarily in the wheelhouse monitoring their position, speed, and heading. Petersen would shout out a warning if anything significant appeared, either visually or audibly, on the Pulse 12 Control Box. Gazing out the forward cabin window Kurt whispered, "Captain Flannigan . . . it's time to wake up . . . and reveal your secret."

25

Standing on the opposite side of the archway, Mischa continued to stare at the inexplicable scene that had rendered her temporarily speechless. Her brother was responding in a similar fashion, and stood motionless as if in a trance.

Back on familiar turf, however, Gabriel, Aiyana, and Journey took off, running at full speed in the direction of a small rush-lined pond that was located on the western edge of the cathedral-like valley—the husky's rhapsodic yelping, as it nipped playfully at the heels of the two horses, reverberated off the sheer volcanic walls.

The area reminded Mischa of an animal reserve in Africa, Ngorongoro Crater Wildlife Sanctuary, which she had learned about on a Discovery Channel special. The Tanzania preserve was situated in an extinct caldera and was surrounded by impassable cliffs—with only one entryway. The inaccessibility of the enclosed valley had allowed the natural habitat to remain unspoiled and the abundant wildlife safe from human interference.

In a soft voice, barely above a whisper, Jake asked, "What are they?"

Half submerged in the shallow marsh-like pond were over a dozen animals, with an equal number browsing on the succulent brush that fringed the swampland. The creatures were diminutive in size, less than four feet tall, with shaggy reddish-brown hair on top of their heads, upper shoulders, and along their entire back. From their midsection down to their pillar-like legs and broad feet, the exposed skin was grayish in color. Each animal had a flattish head, small floppy ears, short neck, large muscular trunk, and a pair of spiraled ivory tusks that extended two to three feet beyond their mouths. Several of the creatures were engaged in frolicsome sparing battles and were emitting high-spirited trumpeting sounds.

"Miniature elephants," Mischa said in awe, "but, unlike anything I've ever seen in a zoo or on television."

Jake stared intently at the strange mammals for several minutes before he offered his own opinion. "Oh my God," he said ecstatically, "they're Pygmy mammoths!"

"Mammoths!" Mischa exclaimed loudly. "How's that possible . . . when they've been extinct for over ten thousand years?"

Laughing Jake replied, "I suspect the Chumash Indians are responsible for that improbable preservation, which also explains why the Chumash are the *only* caretakers allowed on this Island. It's obvious that our Indian friends didn't exterminate all the mammoths, and have carefully guarded their very existence for thousands of years."

"If you're right . . . and my eyes tell me that you are . . . the implications are staggering."

One of the beasts, with magnificent curved tusks, and whose mass was slightly bulkier than the rest of the herd—began a slow shuffle in their direction, using its trunk to sniff the air.

"I bet it's the leader," Jake said under his breath.

As the creature approached, Mischa quickly removed her Apple i-Phone and began snapping photographs of the majestic animal, trying to steady her trembling hands so that her pictures would not come out as blurs. After taking several images she switched to video, but when the beast was less than fifteen feet away, she pressed the stop button and slipped the i-Phone back into its leather holder.

The mammoth ceased its advance five feet in front of them, raised its trunk, and blasted a deep, resonating sound that filled the air. At that instant the entire valley went silent, and every mammoth's eyes and ears were focused on their leader and its interaction with the two human intruders. Out of the corner of her eye, Mischa spied the husky, moving with rhythmic lopes, rapidly approaching their position. Upon its arrival, it immediately situated its body between Mischa and her brother, and began howling at the mammoth. It continued its ear-splitting baying until the creature ceased its bellowing. During the commotion, Gabriel and Aiyana, who were grazing down by the pond, left their foraging site and at a fast trot, joined their riders. Mischa could tell by their snorting and nervous prancing that the horses were perturbed by the noisy ruckus. She couldn't blame them—it was unsettling for her as well.

In a soft voice Mischa mumbled, "It's nice to have a Siberian protector."

Jake nodded and then added, "I think it's communicating to the chief mammoth that we're okay."

Before Mischa could respond, the mammoth stretched out its trunk and using its lip, which served as a finger as well as its nose, commenced a thorough exploration of her physique. The sensitive lip first touched and smelled the fibers of her hair, then continued down her face, arms, legs, and clothing—lingering longest on the scents contained within Mischa's clothes. It also probed areas that made her feel slightly uncomfortable but she made herself stand perfectly still. The mammoth then focused its attention on Jake, repeating the same sensory inspection. When the animal finished its investigation, it retracted its trunk, and stood stock-still for a moment, as if analyzing the data that it had gleaned. To Mischa's surprise the mammoth then seemed to grin, lifted its trunk, and belted out a melody that sounded Celtic in its origin, and hypnotically soothing. Once the mellifluous ballad had ended, the other mammoths that had until now remained quiet, vocalized their own responsive chorus, filling the natural cathedral with an enchanting ancient song. The serenade lasted for two minutes and upon its conclusion, the valley returned to a state of normalcy.

Holding back tears, Mischa said, "That was definitely special."

"A musical journey into the past—from mammoths that are supposedly extinct—who would have guessed," Jake marveled.

"That performance, especially from their illustrious leader, deserves a nourishing reward," Mischa declared.

"There goes our lunch," Jake said with a knowing smile. He joined Mischa in emptying their saddlebags of the trail mix, apples, baby carrots, and sugar cubes. The only thing left was the Gatorade and two large bags of beef jerky.

Gabriel and Aiyana—acutely aware of the food items they were transporting—were each given an apple, a few carrots, and a couple of sugar cubes, before Mischa and Jake turned their attention to their new prehistoric friend. The chief mammoth, who was also now clearly aware of the feast, had gently nudged Mischa with its tusks while she was feeding the mustangs, eliciting a squeal of surprise from her.

"Patience," she said reprimanding the elephant as if the creature understood English, "our horses first—since they've earned it by working hard—and mammoths second."

Once they began to feed the leader, it was as if they had rung a telepathic dinner bell, and the entire herd—those in the shallow pond and those outside of it—raced to their location, seeking a handout. The husky, sensing the thunderous approach, had wisely scrambled to safer grounds. Surrounded by over thirty pygmy mammoths of all ages and sizes, Mischa and Jake were initially frightened, which feeling was fortunately short-lived, as they soon discovered that the elephants were incredibly sweet-tempered and respectful toward humans. With so many mouths competing for a treat, it didn't take long before their limited supplies were exhausted. The herd then dispersed except for the chief mammoth that stayed by their side.

Mischa had saved a few sugar cubes that she now promptly served to the leader, who returned the favor by allowing her to run her hands through its thick, bristle-like fur. The hair was similar to a horse's mane, except there was also a soft, wooly undercoat. Using her fingertips, she massaged its head, shoulders, and back, which to her delight generated a deep-throated cooing sound. During the rubdown procedure Mischa was able to closely examine the creature's physical features, which lead to her discovery that the leader of the herd was a male. After a moment's reflection, she named him 'Kilimanjaro', after the famous snow-capped volcanic mountain located in Tanzania, Africa.

"I'm sure Timbrook's already named it," Jake reminded her.

"Perhaps, but it's Kilimanjaro until I hear otherwise," she said defiantly. "The premier mammoth should have an appropriate name."

"Is Kilimanjarooooo up for a walk?" Jake asked, purposely slurring the ending of the mammal's new name, "Since we'll need to head back shortly, and there's still a lot to be seen."

"I have not a clue whether he'll follow us," she admitted, "but you're right, time is of the essence."

They recommenced their exploratory mission, this time with the unlikely entourage of a bull mammoth, Siberian husky, and two mustangs. They started at the parameter of the pond, which was about an acre in size, and was fed by an artesian spring. The slope of the land permitted the overflow from the small lake to spread outward across an expansive meadow, perpetually watering the pastureland, and providing an endless source of rich fodder for the mammoths. The grazing ground was filled with grasses indigenous to the island, as well as imported alfalfa and clover. The pond itself was lined with rushes, cattails, and meadow barley, and out in the deeper water—white and yellow water-lilies, lesser duckweed, floating-leaved pondweed, and other aquatic plants—all which the mammoths seemed to relish and were quite capable of reaching in the shallow wash. The backside of the pond was shaded with a row of mature sycamore trees that abutted the steep canyon walls. A lack of symmetry in the façade of the stone walls caught Mischa's attention.

"Are those caves?" she asked, pointing at the dark irregularities at the base of the cliffs.

"Where?" Jake inquired.

"Across the pond . . . on both sides."

"Looks like it."

"Let's check it out."

"Definitely," Jake agreed.

"Race you."

"You're on."

Mischa took off, gaining an early lead, but was quickly passed by Jake, who body-slammed her as he dashed by.

"Cheater," she screamed.

"You're in my way," Jake shouted back.

Mischa knew that Jake would ultimately win, which was okay; her thrill came with the adrenalin of competition. Besides, as she gleefully observed, the husky was outpacing Jake and had already arrived at their goal, which meant that Jake had lost to a dog, something she would be sure to mention. The horses had chosen to sit out the needless exercise, preferring foraging, whereas Kilimanjaro was trumpeting his pleasure at the new adventure, lumbering step-by-step alongside Mischa.

Prior to arriving at the foot of the cliffs Mischa noticed that the entire side of the mountain was riddled with caves, and that animal trails—trampled into the moist earth—made a beeline to each one. Jake had stopped at the largest cavern and was patiently awaiting her appearance.

Panting, and slightly out-of-breath, Mischa joined him. But, prior to saying a word to her sibling, she immediately knelt and lavished Journey with an affectionate hug, congratulating the canine track star on her cross-country victory. Her brother's brooding glare made the demonstrative effort priceless.

"You still lost," Jake reminded her, and then changing the subject said, "This cavern is huge."

"Mammoth in size," Mischa agreed, which caused her brother to groan and then chuckle.

"Cute," he said.

"Any idea how these caves were created?" Mischa asked.

"Since these islands are volcanic in origin, my assumption is that they're ancient lava tubes. There's usually a main lava tube—which explains the larger cavern, and a series of smaller ones—which accounts for the mid-sized caves."

As Mischa was staring at the sculpted contours of the cavern's entrance, Kilimanjaro trudged right in, followed by Journey. Both animals dissolved into wispy shadows as the inky blackness swallowed them up.

"I think this hollow in the earth is their subterranean den," Mischa suggested.

"Probably," Jake said, "but there's only one way to confirm." Without hesitation, he walked straight in, with Mischa right behind him. Once they had traveled about twenty-five feet, they momentarily paused, and allowed their pupils to adjust to the diminished light.

The underground chamber was about the size of a professional indoor hockey rink. The floor consisted of polished rock, soft dirt, and a semi-organized network of circular or rectangular piles of dried vegetation—primarily constructed from bulrushes from the outside pond. The lava tube became narrower toward the rear of the cave, and was blocked by a pile of boulders where the roof had collapsed, providing a natural skylight. Yellowish bacteria coated the walls, along with patches of green moss near the entrance; etched into the sides of the lava tube were defining curb marks indicating former molten-lava flow levels. An occasional Townsend's long-eared bat briefly lifted-off from its upside down perch, and soundlessly glided across the length of the room, before returning to its daytime roost.

Mischa observed that the mammoth had bedded down in the middle of the habitation on a grandiose mat of vegetation, undoubtedly symbolizing its hierarchical status among the herd. Kilimanjaro, however, was not the only occupant. Five other mammoths were also lounging on their flora mattresses, including a female with a calf that had to be less than a month old. The husky, like a cop on a city beat, had initially wandered throughout the entire enclosure, sniffing and probing every niche, checking in with each slumbering mammoth and greeting them with a few licks—before she trotted to the front of the cavern, and unexpectedly disappeared into a side cave.

"Did you notice that connective cave on our way in?" Jake asked.

"No," replied Mischa, "I must've missed it because of the darkness."

Without another word, they both quickly scurried over to where Journey had vanished. The grotto-like entrance was only five feet high necessitating a ducking maneuver in order to avoid smacking their heads. Once past the threshold the interior was a lot roomier; about the size of a small bedroom with eight-foot ceilings. Unlike the main cavern, which had remained unaltered, this rocky shelter had been decorated by man. The husky was curled up in the northeast corner on a plush, rounded sheepskin dog bed that rested on a large bamboo thatched pad. Attached to the east wall was a Quickfeed solar-powered automatic feeder with a 12-volt rechargeable battery. The device held fifty pounds of dog food, and was programmed to dispense fifteen ounces of kibble two times a day. An electrical cord ran from the machine through a hole in the rock wall, and presumably, to an external solar-panel array. Adjoining the feeder was a gravity-fed watering station with a five-gallon plastic holding tank. Covering the entire north wall was a magnificent pictograph of a pure white Siberian husky guarding a herd of pygmy mammoths, with the Pacific Ocean as a backdrop, and with what appeared to be two young mountain lions play-fighting on a mountain ledge. Fastened to the west wall was a rough-hewn redwood plank, with words and dates carved into it.

"Definitely its home," Jake said.

The dog laid with its eyes opened, watching them. Mischa walked over and began scratching Journey's head, which it seemed to appreciate. "I wonder if it ever gets lonely?" she asked. "Plenty of elephant friends," Jake assured her, "plus Timbrook makes frequent visits."

"That's not the same," Mischa said softly. She bent down and gave Journey a loving kiss, rubbed its belly for a minute, whispered in its ear, "*you now have us too,*" stood up, and turned and gazed at the Chumash artwork. "It's stunning . . . I wonder what individual painted it?"

"A very gifted Chumash artist," Jake replied. "It's obviously too old to have been sketched by Timbrook. The realistic quality of the animals, however, is amazing, although the painter's depiction of an actual mountain lion is a bit odd—I've never seen a mountain lion with its canine teeth sticking out like that."

"Maybe the artist was inserting some intentional humor into the mural," Mischa speculated.

"Possibly," Jake agreed.

They next inspected the redwood plank. "I'll be darned," whistled Jake, "the names of every Siberian guardian since 1825, and the years they served."

"Laska," Mischa said, as she began to read the names out loud, "1825 to 1837; Keyara, 1837 to 1851; Shadow, 1851 to 1857; that's only six years," she said sadly. She continued reciting all the names until she arrived at Misty, the name of the husky that served before Journey. "Wow!" she exclaimed. "Misty performed his duties for twenty years, which is a miracle lifespan for a working dog."

She noted that only Misty's name was embellished with gold leaf. Also, according to the plank, Journey's tour-of-mammoth-duty began three years ago. Journey was number fifteen on the list.

"Nice of the Chumash to honor their furry protectors," Jake said sincerely.

They suddenly jumped at the humming sound of an energized motor accompanied by a swooshing noise, and then the pitter-patter of kibble being discharged into a stainless steel dog bowl.

"It's chow time," Mischa said with a chagrined smile. She expected Journey to exuberantly bolt out of her bed, rush the bowl, and essentially inhale the entire contents within seconds—as all dogs do. Instead, the husky just sat up in her bed, yawned as if she was waking up, and then stared fixedly at the entrance to her den with her ears at full attention, and an alert expression on her wolf-like face.

"What's she waiting on?" Jake asked. "She can't be sick."

"Maybe we make her nervous," Mischa suggested.

"What do you recommend?"

"Sit, rather than stand, and no talking."

"Okay."

They settled down beneath the redwood plank, with their backs against the west wall. As the seconds ticked by, Mischa noticed that Journey's facial features had become more animated, and that her tail was beginning to twitch. Turning to Jake she whispered in his ear, "Something's got her excited."

In an equally low voice he said, "Probably a kibble plundering mammoth. It's obvious Journey knows it's coming, which means it's not the first time."

"Shsssss," Mischa said under her breath, "I think I hear it."

Journey's faint growl gave them a final heads-up. "Showtime," Jake said.

Mischa expected a mammoth to march in as if it owned the place; she also anticipated that it would create a fair amount of noise inasmuch as the elephants, although dwarf-like, were still ponderous. But, what unexpectedly leaped into the room and landed in a crouch with scarcely a sound, just a few feet away from them, was the antithesis of a docile mammoth. She instinctively reacted by latching onto Jake for protection, and found herself too terrified to utter a scream. The beast eyed them, but kept slinking toward the food, causing Journey's growl to become more intense. Her brother began to tremble, and her body also began to shake. Journey's fur bristled, inflating her size as she stepped out of her bed, and began stalking the intruder. Unlike the growling dog, the large feline creature was snarling and spitting, its yellowish lynx-like eyes ominously narrowed. Its scimitar-shaped fangs, which protruded four inches from its upper jaw, were surrealistic and portended a painful death. As the beast made its way to the food bowl it lowered its head while at the same time maintaining a wary eye on the dog that was edging closer. Journey waited until the animal was engrossed in consuming her kibble before she attacked. Mischa was certain that the husky would be torn asunder, and that they would be the creature's next victims. What actually occurred, however, revealed the cunning intelligence of the Arctic breed.

She had assumed that Journey would attack with its teeth. Instead, the husky dove between the animal's heavy-set limbs, and like an Olympian wrestler, flipped the creature onto its back, exposing the vulnerable side of its throat. She then lunged for the tender area and clamped her jaws around it. Mischa responded to the grisly scene by closing her eyes—imagining what would happen next—a punctured jugular vein spraying the room with a torrent of syrupy blood. Her body tense and her eyes closed tight, she waited, her mind visualizing horrendous carnage, gore, and mutilation. The cave fell silent and Mischa slowly opened her eyes and saw that, at least in her immediate vicinity, there wasn't a drop of blood. She cautiously cast her eyes about a bit further and to her amazement observed the exact opposite of what she had dreaded: Journey and the creature were still locked in seeming battle, but the atmosphere had changed. The vicious growling and the combative snarling had ceased. To her absolute surprise the upended animal was purring like a house cat, and Journey— the apparent winner in the dramatic skirmish—was wagging its furry tail while *pretending* to be inflicting mortal wounds. *It was all just a silly game!* Mischa suddenly realized, except that the creature that Journey was tangling with was not your typical canine playmate. Jake must have read her mind:

"That mountain lion, or leopard . . . or whatever it is . . . is the same animal depicted in the Chumash pictograph," Jake reported.

Mischa looked at the painting again. "You're right," she confirmed with a tone of awe in her voice. As she was staring at the ancient painting, the two adversaries ended their engagement. She briefly panicked thinking that the contentious clash would begin anew, but she quickly relaxed—the unnamed feline casually got up, lapped up some water, and then settled down on Journey's bed, while the husky unhurriedly ate what remained of its afternoon meal.

"They're obviously good buddies," Jake assured her, "since neither animal had any intent on harming the other, the fight wasn't real, and she doesn't care that it's now occupying her resting place."

Mischa nodded her head in agreement. *What type of creature was it?* She wondered. The strange feline lying peacefully upon Journey's bed began cleaning its smooth coat with a raspy pink tongue, and was performing the task as if it hadn't a care in the world. Its plush fur, which had a golden hue to it, was marked with chestnut-faded rosettes, comparable to those on a leopard, but smaller and more densely packed. Each rosette was made up of three or four black spots on the outside with a yellow-brown center. The fur on the underbelly was lighter in color, almost pale, with rosettes roughly fifty-percent larger. It had long whitish whiskers and claws that were clearly retractable. Earlier, when it was playing with the husky, Mischa saw that the large cat had a bobtail, bulky body, short massive limbs, and a muscular neck. It was certainly more robustly built than a leopard, and had a shape similar to a hyena. It was approximately three feet high, and measured about four feet from snout to rump. Mischa estimated its weight at eighty pounds. But, its most distinguishing feature by far was a set of powerfully built maxillary canines that jutted out four inches from its upper jaw, and were shaped like daggers. The mammal's teeth were eerily similar to a tooth braided in Timbrook's hair, which rekindled a recent memory stored within Mischa's subconscious. She recalled that during their walk to Yellowbanks, Timbrook had stated that Santa Cruz Island used to be populated with Pygmy mammoths and—.

"Jake," Mischa said enthusiastically, "I know the animal's identity."

"You do? What?"

"A Pygmy saber-toothed cat!"

Biting his lower lip, Jake said, "That just blows my mind. Finding a prehistoric saber-toothed cat is even more improbable than the discovery of mammoths."

"The Chumash are obviously the Houdini's of the Indian world," Mischa bragged. "To have successfully hidden these animals from the public for hundreds of years is an extraordinary achievement."

"I think the island's unique isolation, impenetrable cliffs, and enclosed biosphere certainly helped," Jake added.

"And," Mischa said with a knowing smile, "there must be others besides Diego."

"Who's Diego?" Jake asked.

"The name I've chosen for our living fossil. It's the same name as the saber-toothed cat in the Disney movie, *Ice Age*."

"And that's now *his* name," Jake said sarcastically. "How do you know it's a boy?"

Mischa quickly studied the feline's anatomy, "Yep...it's a boy... so Diego stays."

"And is Diego friendly with strangers?" Jake asked.

"Must be," answered Mischa, "since we're still alive." She stood up, and slowly walked toward Diego. "Nice kitty," she said softly, "nice friendly kitty."

"That's not a typical kitty," Jake reminded her.

When she was less than three feet away Diego abruptly rose to its feet. Startled, Mischa attempted to back-track, but the saber-toothed cat was too fast, and before she knew it, the animal was plastered against her legs. Mischa froze, anticipating a perforating bite that would exceed her worse nightmare. Instead, she felt a warm muzzle rubbing against her legs, then a neck, and finally the entire body. The cat then turned around and repeated the same maneuver, massaging its opposite side. Several times Mischa was almost bowled over by the strength of the animal. During the fourth round Diego began vocalizing his contentment by exercising his unique feline vibrato—purring—which increased in volume with each turn. The realization as to what Diego was doing made Mischa laugh; the saber-toothed cat was using her legs as a type of scratching post. She reached down and caressed the sweet spot between its ears, and was gratified when the roar-like purr reached a near-deafening decibel level.

"Tone it down," Jake demanded as he cupped his hands over his ears. His exuberant grin, however, belied his true feelings. He immediately arose from his seated position and joined Mischa, stroking the cat along its upper back. "This is better than a dream," he said.

Journey's loud bark, which was more like a wolf howl than an actual bark, interrupted their special moment. She had finished eating, and was indicating to Diego by her body language—dropping her forequarters to the ground while keeping her hindquarters up, wagging her tail, and giving off short yelps—that it was playtime. Diego needed no additional prompting, and when Journey raced out of the cave, he bounded after her.

Mischa watched them take off. "A Siberian husky and a saber-toothed cat, engaged in a feigned fight and now a childish game of chase, who would have predicted that?"

"No one," Jake replied. "What we are witnessing—if posted on YouTube—would turn the world upside down."

They followed the frolicking duo outside, and watched them sprint toward the pond. Just when it appeared that the saber-toothed cat would overtake Journey, the husky bolted into the pond, and landed with an explosive splash ten feet from the shoreline. Diego, however, came to a screeching halt at the water's edge, and let loose a savage roar.

"Cat's never change," Mischa said, "they hate getting wet."

Journey dog paddled to the opposite side of the lake where Gabriel and Aiyana were still grazing and after a few encouraging barks convinced the horses to join in the fray. Meanwhile, the saber-toothed cat had silently circled the pond—wherein he quickly resumed the pursuit—which now included two horses. With Journey leading the unlikely pack, she made a mad dash back to Mischa and Jake's position, veering off at the last second and disappearing into one of the smaller caves. The saber-toothed cat also vanished into the darkened hollow as did the mustangs.

Mischa and Jake ran to the entrance and promptly stepped inside. The cave was about one quarter the size of the mammoth's cavern, had similar rocky features, slightly brighter, but was shaped like a rounded great room.

Standing in the middle of the chamber were the mustangs, husky, saber-toothed cat, and milling about throughout the entire expanse were duplicates of Diego. Mischa counted a total of fifteen. In a voice brimming with excitement she said to Jake, "Now we know where the saber-toothed cats dwell."

"Simply amazing," he said. "I knew there had to be others, but actually seeing them, gathered in one place . . . that's a whole different story."

Mischa noticed that affixed to the entryway wall were two feeding systems that were the exact, though larger, counterparts to Journey's. She opened one of the attached storage bins and removed a few rectangular pellets. They were three inches long, and smelled like compacted meat intermixed with vegetable protein and a little honey. "Probably nutritious," she commented, "but I think I'll pass." She handed one to Jake.

After a perfunctory whiff, he said, "I agree."

As they were examining the food, a young saber-toothed cat wandered up to them, squatted down, looked them in the eye, and began speaking in a solicitous murmuring tone.

"Is it begging?" Mischa asked.

Laughing, Jake said, "That clearly sounds like a begging voice to me." He tossed the pellet he was holding in the direction of the cat, which ambushed it in midair. "That's a skillful feline."

Mischa did the same, and before they knew it, they were surrounded by fifteen saber-toothed cats.

"The two bags of beef jerky," Mischa remembered, "they would love it."

"I'll get them," Jake offered. He hurried over to the horses, unlatched the saddlebags that held the bags of dried beef jerky, and quickly rejoined his sister.

Parceling out the jerky, they gave each cat its fair share—the process taking less than five minutes. When the last morsel was consumed, it was replaced by the sound of gratified purring.

Hearing the sound of contentment, Mischa couldn't help but smile. "The way to an animal's heart is through its stomach, especially a cat's."

"Or a mammoth's," Jake added. "I think we've made a lot of new friends today."

"Definitely," Mischa affirmed. *Primordial paradise,* she thought, *this place is a miracle come to life.* She looked around the cavern . . . *being a witness to supposedly extinct animals roaming free . . . was awe-inspiring.* She sighed; unfortunately it was getting late. "Jake," she said, "I figure we have less than thirty minutes before we have to depart—otherwise we'll be traversing this mountain in the dark."

Nodding his head in agreement, Jake said, "So much to see, and so little time. But since I'm sure you got some good pictures and video of the mammoth—let me do the same for the cats before we leave." Removing his i-Phone Jake quickly snapped over a dozen photographs before switching to video and recording the saber-toothed cats interacting with the Siberian husky and mustangs.

Reluctantly parting company with the saber-toothed cats, they led the horses out of the cave, and after remounting, headed toward the small lake at a medium trot. Journey, their new faithful companion, eagerly tagged along. They briefly stopped at the pond for a one-minute water break, and then rode across the meadow, past a half dozen browsing mammoths, and then continued alongside the base of the cliffs. In a few moments, they found themselves in a shady oasis of black and tan oak trees. Thousands of protein and vitamin-filled acorns, in their early stages of growth, trimmed the trees, which undoubtedly would be harvested in late autumn by the mammoths. Lace lichen shrouded the oak limbs creating a rainforest effect, and at the base of the trees, vines of Island morning glory, intertwined in the underbrush. Cottontail rabbits seemed to be everywhere, nibbling on the grasses, and scurrying among the trees and low-lying chaparral.

"I imagine those rabbits provide supplemental meat for the saber-toothed cats," Jake said. "The Chumash must have seeded this valley with them eons ago."

Laughing, Mischa said, "A hare's reputation for debauchery has certainly served them well. They won't be going extinct anytime soon." She watched a few plump bunnies scatter as they approached their location. She loved the charming critters, but also understood the natural order of things, and sustaining saber-toothed cats far outweighed the life of a rabbit here and there.

The thicket of oak trees, occasionally punctuated with Santa Cruz Island pine, lofty sycamores, and Bishop Pines, abutted the steep cliffs. After traveling about two hundred yards they came upon a manmade clearing and the horses and husky made an abrupt halt. Native Island oak trees surrounded the one-acre site, and at each compass corner—north, south, east, and west—soared a tapered obelisk of intricately stacked rocks. Mischa estimated the height of the four-sided monoliths at twelve feet. The structures were primarily made from granite and were un-adorned, except the western facing obelisk, which was coated in a ceremonial red-ochre paint.

"What is this place?" Jake asked.

"I don't know," Mischa said softly. She sensed that the land was set apart for a special, likely sacred purpose. Just after re-sponding to Jake, she noticed distinctive stone markers scattered throughout the site. She gasped: "An Indian graveyard!" she ex-claimed. "It's where the Island Chumash entombed their tribal leaders."

"Chief Headman is how Timbrook described them," correct-ed Jake, "plus it's also where he buried his wife Maria."

Sliding off their horses, they both hesitated before venturing in. "I think we should take off our shoes," Mischa whispered, "be-cause we'll be walking on sacred ground."

Jake shrugged his shoulders and replied, "I suppose."

After removing their footwear, they carefully made their way down the rows of burial sites. The older graves were marked with prosaic chunks of granite or volcanic rock. The passage of time—rain, fog, sun, and wind infused with salt crystals—had slowly disintegrated any epitaphs, decorative artifacts, or person-al belongings. "These burial pits must be thousands of years old," Mischa guessed.

"That's a distinct possibility," Jake admitted, "especially since these islands were colonized by the Chumash over thirteen thousand years ago."

Mischa observed that the newer appearing graves had tombstones hewed from sandstone or precious steatite. Surrounding the cinderblock-sized memorials were olivella shell beads, abalone shells, brown cowries, arrowheads, flint knives, obsidian spear points, and deer antler tools. She was surprised that none of the headstones contained a name; the only inscription—a solitary carving of a land or marine mammal, bird, or fish. The creatures were outlined in hematite, a red mineral that highlighted the animal's profile. "Why aren't there any names?" Mischa wondered.

"That's an easy answer," Jake said condescendingly. "The Chumash had no written language."

"Then what's the purpose of the engraved animals?"

"Unknown, but they're obviously significant—otherwise it wouldn't be on their headstones. My hunch . . . it's their spirit guide, or an earth totem, or it epitomized the way they governed, or simply an animal that the Chief had a fondness for."

"My creature of choice would be a snowy egret in shimmering-white plumage."

"Mine . . . " laughed Jake, as he briefly stopped to admire a tombstone that was etched with a majestic broadbill swordfish, "an eleven-ton male orca."

At the very end of the cemetery, in its own rocky niche, they found the grave of Maria. It was marked with a highly polished rose-colored marble headstone in which had been chiseled her name, an elegant pink hummingbird, the month, day, and year of her birth and death, and the words: *"One of God's Special Angel's— the Love of my Life—Rest in His Peace."* The grave was planted with native Indian paintbrush—bright red in color—and the ground surrounding the flowers was moist from a recent watering.

Next to Maria was a smaller plot marked with a narrow rectangular piece of bluish granite. A brass plaque imbedded in the granite depicted a Siberian husky sitting in a regal manner, and the words: *"Misty—Faithful Servant for Twenty Years."* Lastly, on the other side of Maria was a freshly dug burial pit, the size clearly meant for an adult human.

Though disconcerted by the implications of the newly dug site, Mischa maintained a respectful silence for several minutes after which she wiped her eyes with the sleeve of her blouse, and murmured, "There's such sadness in death, especially for those you loved."

Jake cleared his throat and said graciously, "Maria was Timbrook's lifelong soul mate on a secluded island, so her death was huge, as was his dog Misty, a loyal friend, who undoubtedly helped heal his heart after his wife's passing."

"I agree," Mischa said, then pointed at the vacant chamber, "But what I don't understand is why he's already dug his own burial pit."

"That's certainly a bit weird," Jake agreed, "but then again, Timbrook's a highly structured individual; he's in his mid-eighties, and as an Indian in tune with his body, he's aware that his years are numbered."

"Sometimes your pragmatism is a bit annoying," Mischa said raising her voice. "He could easily live to be a hundred."

"You're right," Jake said backing off.

Mischa touched her right index finger to her lips and then planted a kiss on each headstone. "May you both rest in peace," she whispered. She then turned to Jake and said, "It's time to go."

Walking solemnly back to Gabriel, Aiyana, and Journey, Mischa and Jake slipped on their shoes, remounted the mustangs, and quickly made their way out of the valley. At the arch, the husky came to a halt. Reining in her own horse, Mischa reached into a pocket located on the backside of her jeans and retrieved an irregular-shaped slab of beef jerky. "You deserve this more than anyone else," she said as she flung it toward Journey. The husky snagged it before it hit the ground, temporarily dropped it, and rewarded Mischa with a thankful yelp, before picking it back up and making short work of it. "We'll be back soon," she promised.

A few hundred feet down the trail, they turned back and saw Journey silhouetted in the middle of the gateway. A quarter of the way down the mountain they heard a low-pitched howl, *'owooooo,'* rolling across the late afternoon sky—mournful and yet blithesome—the husky purposely wavering and modulating its wail as a professional singer would do with an operaetic aria.

"I think Journey misses her human pack-mates," Jake said.

Mischa just nodded her head.

They arrived at the stables shortly before dusk and were removing the saddles when Timbrook joined them.

"How was your doctor's appointment?" Mischa asked.

"About as expected," Timbrook chuckled. "He didn't tell me anything that I didn't already know. But, who cares about a boring medical appointment; tell me about your day. Did you discover Captain Cabrillo's whereabouts?"

Mischa exchanged a knowing glance with Jake before responding. "No, but we did unearth an ancient dump filled with rusted cans and broken bottles, and a Chumash midden rubbish heap. I think it was trash day on the island. No gravesite yet; but, at least we've eliminated a section of the island, which will help narrow our future searches."

"You were gone a long time," Timbrook said eyeing them carefully. "I expected you back by 2:00 p.m. at the latest. I was beginning to worry about you."

"We're amateurs at this," Jake said with a nervous laugh, "it took us longer than we anticipated."

"That so?" Timbrook said looking at them suspiciously. "The mustangs are worn out and these types of horses don't tire easily.

You obviously deviated from your original plans. Where else did you *Journey*?"

When Mischa heard Timbrook use the word 'Journey' she knew the jig was up. Attempting to deceive an old Indian, she decided, was an exercise in futility. "Montannon Ridge!" she squealed with pent-up excitement. "That place is a modern day miracle . . . why didn't you tell us?"

Timbrook shook his head as if angry, sighed as if disappointed, but then cracked a friendly grin. "I never should have underestimated you two, especially the crafty female. In answer to your question, I had planned to make a full disclosure to your dad within a week. I assume you'll now take care of that for me. But, that's as far as that information goes; no one else is to know about Montannon Ridge until after your dad and I deem it safe to make the facts public. As you are probably cognizant, the preservation of these exceptional animals is paramount. But this island is changing, and the secret of Santa Cruz—carefully guarded by its Chumash caretakers for thousands of years—is ending."

"Pygmy mammoths and saber-toothed cats, I still can't believe its real; and, a Siberian husky as their protector. How did the Chumash accomplish this extraordinary feat?" Jake asked.

"An ongoing labor of love that's endured for thousands of years," Timbrook replied. "The pygmy mammoths, which descended from the mainland Columbian mammoth, once roamed the islands of San Miguel, Santa Rosa, and Santa Cruz. Unfortunately, my ancestors exterminated the herds on San Miguel and Santa Rosa Island. There was, however, a small remnant that had miraculously survived on Santa Cruz by hiding in the valley located atop Montannon Ridge. Also discovered in that same refuge were a few pygmy saber-toothed cats. Thankfully, my forefathers had the wisdom to declare both animals off-limits to any further hunting, and the prehistoric beasts have been under the Chumash aegis ever since. In fact, the creatures are considered coequal to our dolphin brethren—endowed with a spirit—and that upon physical death they will join us in the afterlife."

"Do you believe that?" Mischa asked.

Smiling, Timbrook said, "I'll know soon enough."

"I have a question," Jake said seriously, "what about inbreeding?"

"Very astute of you," Timbrook said admirably. "It *was* a problem. Any mammoth calf or saber-toothed kitten that was born with *any* genetic defect—no matter how slight—was instantly culled. The action was extremely difficult, sometimes cruel, but absolutely necessary in order to ensure the survival of future generations. In the last four hundred years not a single newborn has arrived with any congenital abnormalities, which demonstrates how successful the program was. In addition, the animals instinctively know to limit their numbers, and only a few births occur each year."

"How did the Chumash prevent the saber-toothed cats from preying on the mammoths?" Mischa wondered.

"Separate caves, lots of meat, and Chumash sentries. In less than one saber-toothed generation—according to our verbal history on the felines—the problem was eliminated, and the two deadly enemies had become friends."

"What kind of meat do they consume?" Jake inquired.

"In the days of old they were supplied with seal, otter, fish, and deer from the mainland. Later on, in the last one hundred and seventy five years—when the island was used for ranching—an occasional goat, sheep, or steer was pilfered from the destructive herds," Timbrook said with a sly wink, "along with elk and mule deer from Santa Rosa Island. In the last twenty years they were switched to high-quality kibble fabricated from bison, venison, or wild salmon. They also occasionally snag a cottontail rabbit."

"No shortage of rabbits," Mischa confirmed. "I think the saber-toothed cats have gotten lazy."

"Maybe," laughed Timbrook.

"Why do the Chumash utilize a Siberian husky to safeguard the valley?" Jake asked.

"Yes . . . the *White Ghost* . . . Journey is quite the actress. With the advent of cattle and sheep ranching in the early 1800's, Mexican cowboys, or *Vaqueros* were soon riding all over the island. In order to keep them off of Montannon Ridge, and away from our sacred burial grounds and the exotic creatures, we created a myth—that a wolf-like creature wandered the ridge—viciously guarding the Chumash burial site from unwelcomed intruders. The Vaqueros were extremely superstitious, and even their infrequent encounters with the 'evil' apparition solidified in their own minds that the mystical beast was in fact, real. Over time they avoided the mountain as if it was cursed. The ruse worked perfectly. We imported our first husky from the Alaskan territory in 1825, and they've served us faithfully ever since."

"You've never tried any other type of dog?" Mischa probed.

"No—the Siberian husky is a true Indian dog—having been developed by the Chukchi tribe in Siberia. Plus, the husky is a pack animal that will defend its pack against any unwelcomed trespassers. In our case its pack consists of the mammoths and saber-toothed cats. It can also endure prolonged cold, fog, and wind, and actually relishes it, because of its insulating double coat. Most dogs can't handle such extreme weather. As far as color—we've primarily used silver and gray Siberians because of the ghost myth. Finally, its daily nutritional needs are minimal, making it easy to take care of."

"Journey has already accepted us into her pack," Jake bragged.

"I have no doubt," Timbrook assured him, "she's an intelligent dog."

Becoming solemn, Mischa said, "We saw Maria's grave, Timbrook, it's lovely and we said a prayer over it. We also saw Misty's grave. But, what I wasn't expecting to find was yours! Why did you dig your own burial pit? Are you sure you're all right?"

"Don't worry my young friend," Timbrook answered. "It just that when my day arrives there's nowhere else I want to be buried, so I'm thinking ahead. Besides, upon my death I don't foresee a rush of volunteers climbing Montannon Ridge in order to excavate my grave, so I took the initiative."

"I still have a lot to learn from you," scolded Mischa, "so you had better delay your departure."

"It's up to God," Timbrook said with a half smile, "He's the one who determines my days."

"Then keep talking to Him," Mischa urged.

Jake who had been listening to the exchange said, "I have no desire to string out this morbid subject, but I am curious about one thing. At the Chumash gravesite there were four obelisks, and one was painted red: Why?"

"It's a Chumash custom that the dead are buried in a fetal position facing west. The rocky monolith that you observed—coated in a layer of ceremonial red-ochre paint—is located on the western corner, and therefore serves as our guidepost."

"Interesting," was Jake's only response.

The conversation was interrupted when Mischa and Jake's iPhone's both chimed at the same time indicating an incoming text. Mischa removed the cell phone from its leather carrying case, touched the screen, and opened it up. "It's Dad," she explained. She silently read the message before reading it out loud. "Dinner in five minutes. Where are you? If you're with Timbrook tell him he's expected as usual. Love Dad." She immediately texted back. "At the stables. Starving! We'll be right there. Timbrook said 'of course he'll be there.' XO."

"Go," Timbrook ordered, "I'll finish up with the horses. Inform your dad that I should arrive in about seven minutes, and that I expect him to uncork his finest wine. He'll understand my request once we begin our stories. If my assumptions are correct, it'll be an evening he won't soon forget. There's nothing better," laughed Timbrook, "than altering a man's sense of reality."

Mischa could still hear Timbrook's mischievous laughter as she and Jake walked through the rear entrance to their house.

26

Kurt massaged his eyes in a vain attempt at vanquishing drowsiness caused by tedious repetition; he then quickly moved his right hand over his mouth in order to stifle his third yawn in less than ten minutes. Sensing tightness creeping into his spine he next performed an inverted 'Y' stretch by arching his back as he remained seated in the Captain's chair. The malaise of boredom had unfortunately infused the pilothouse. He once again stared at the digital clock embedded in *Serenity's* teak console. *Five hours without a single hit on the towfish*—it was enough to drive a sane skipper bonkers. Kurt's initial bullish optimism had faded with each passing hour, and his inner psyche now flirted with its evil counterpart, pessimism. As prophesied by Petersen, the search would probably take days not hours, especially when searching for a one hundred and sixty year-old target whose dimensions were unknown. Thus far they had inspected thirty miles of seabed. *Two round trips and nothing to show for it* thought Kurt, as he shrugged his shoulders and shook his head; he was becoming irritable. His body was not designed for sitting like a stoic mannequin for endless hours. His mild case of ADHD—Attention Deficit Hyperactivity Disorder—served him well as an energetic Marine Biologist, but had the opposite effect in his current capacity as a navigator on a methodical boat. He checked the Autopilot; it was functioning perfectly. State-of-the-art GPS systems had slowly replaced the need for gifted helmsmanship, and in the process, had lessened a captain's role. Feeling somewhat useless, Kurt decided to pay Petersen a visit. The tech-savvy student, monitoring a twelve-inch laptop computer and a Pulse 12 Control Box, was sitting in a padded deck chair at the boat's stern.

Peering over Petersen's shoulder, Kurt asked, "Anything?"

"Nada, zilch, diddly squat," Petersen replied in a dead monotone. "It's like a desert out there. You'd think by now we would've stumbled on something—a lost anchor, a sunken fishing boat, pieces of metallic junk, or chunks of discarded trash. But finding absolutely nothing—that surprises even me."

"At least we haven't wasted our time investigating a worthless target."

"Lucky us," Petersen said sarcastically. "At this moment I would almost welcome that. In my opinion treasure hunting is like fishing; the fish nibble before they bite, and that nibbling raises your expectations. An empty ocean scares the hell out of me. An explosion on the *Winfield Scott* must have left a significant debris field. Our Pulse 12 should have detected foreshadowing clues—tiny fragments—with that rubble trail eventually leading to the mother lode. Its absence makes me nervous."

"The ship didn't sink," Kurt said reminding Petersen. "Whatever fell to the ocean floor descended in one jumbled mass. The ocean is shallow in this section—less than one hundred and thirty feet—which means that the objects impacted the seafloor within seconds of the blast and had no time to spread out. My suspicion . . . it's condensed into one small area."

Nodding, Petersen said, "I hate to admit it, but you're probably right."

"Probably?" Kurt echoed with mock haughtiness. "As a distinguished professor I'm rarely mistaken in my understanding of things."

"And that's a narcissistic fantasy," Petersen said with an ironic smile.

Admiring the bravado of Petersen's comment Kurt chuckled silently and then said, "No wonder Professor Barnett gave you an A- last semester."

"Ouch . . . that hurts . . . it's my belief that grades are supposedly based upon merit not sucking up contests—"

Petersen suddenly stopped talking, and his relaxed demeanor abruptly changed. "What's wrong?" Kurt asked.

In a hyped-up voice Petersen said, "Absolutely nothing; in fact, lady luck is finally smiling upon us—we're getting our first hit." He then cranked up the volume on the Control Box from minimum to maximum.

Within a matter of seconds the sound emanating from the speaker modulated from a barely audible low tone, to a piercingly high pitch. At the same time the needle in the meter display swung from a position barely above zero to the three-quarter mark. "Hallelujah," yelled Kurt. "We did it!" Just as he was about to congratulate Petersen on a job well done, the needle immediately plummeted back to zero and the speaker fell silent.

Frowning, Petersen complained, "What the heck just happened?"

"Should I turn the boat around?" asked Kurt.

"Not yet; the latitude and longitude coordinates are automatically stored on the computer's memory, so if we have to turn around, we'll have that position information. It's just weird . . . a major hit should have lasted a lot longer."

"What if the Pulse 12 only glimpsed a tiny corner of the potential target," Kurt suggested, "could that explain it?"

"Possibly," Petersen replied, "but unlikely. A tangible find almost always generates a huge magnetic field that doesn't end abruptly as this one unfortunately did."

"Then what did we cross over?" Kurt persisted.

"Obviously something that contained ferrous or non-ferrous material."

"You mean metal or gold."

"Precisely—but a nominal amount; perhaps the rubble trail that you believe doesn't exist."

"Then why aren't we getting any further hits?"

Smiling broadly, Petersen said, "You're a man of such little faith." He then lifted the Control Box off his lap so that Kurt had a clear view of its electronic panel. Within the meter display the bronze needle was slowly edging upwards. Once it passed the .3 meter reading, the audio once again began sounding off until it became earsplitting, causing Petersen to lower the volume. Staring hypnotically at the device, Kurt stood with a stupid grin plastered across his face. "Captain Nichols," Petersen advised, "now would be a good time to shut off the engines."

"Yes—my thoughts exactly," Kurt said distantly, as if waking up from a dream, and then hurriedly made his way into the pilothouse. As he was preparing to shut down the engines, the ship suddenly experienced a jolting vibration as if on the losing end of a tug of war. Of greater concern to Kurt, however, was the ripping sound of a fishing reel unwinding—except they weren't fishing, which meant only one thing—the cable and downrigger line connected to the Pulse 12 towfish were unraveling at an alarming rate. From the rear of the boat he could hear Petersen yelling; his words muffled by the loud clamor of a piece of machinery whose structural integrity was being severely tested. Kurt knew exactly what Petersen was screaming about. The Pulse 12 had become entangled with an underwater obstacle—a protruding seamount, giant kelp, debris from the *Winfield Scott,* or some other shipwreck. He immediately shifted the engines into neutral and from neutral into reverse, halting the ship's forward progression, and in the process gaining back fifty feet of surface territory. He then killed the engines while praying that the newly installed electric hoist was still attached to the boat's stern. If torn from its mounting it meant that twenty-thousand-dollars worth of equipment—hoist, towfish, and downrigger—was stranded at the bottom of the sea. Recovering the items would require a tremendous amount of time and effort, and would significantly impede their treasure hunt.

Jumping down from the Captain's chair Kurt quickly exited the pilothouse and ran out onto the main deck. At the stern, where the electric hoist was located, stood Petersen, unintentionally blocking his view.

"That was close," said Petersen, who had obviously heard Kurt's approaching footsteps. "Another fifteen feet, and we would've lost everything."

Kurt breathed a sigh of relief; he could now see that the hoist was still affixed to the rail and that Petersen was using the device to haul in the extra cable and downrigger line that had been dragged overboard. "We got lucky," he said quietly.

"That's an understatement."

"Any idea what ensnared our towfish?" asked Kurt.

"As an optimist it's wreckage from the *Scott*; as a realist, a rocky pinnacle or kelp. Speculation aside, we'll have our answer once we deploy the drop-down video system and obtain an actual image of the scene."

They spent the next five minutes retrieving the rest of the cable and downrigger line until the towfish—and whatever it was snagged on—was directly beneath the *Serenity*. Kurt then returned to the pilothouse in order to actuate a switch that dropped the ship's galvanized anchor.

In the meantime, Petersen began readying the DV-1 camera for deployment. The camera came with a fifteen-inch high-definition color monitor and an internal digital recorder. The equipment was powered by the ship's 120-volt electrical system. The camera was capable of both downward and side viewing, and was encased in a corrosion-proof bright yellow PVC housing. After plugging it in, Petersen connected the cable to the monitor, and then ran a brief operational test. Satisfied that the equipment was functioning properly, he handed the camera to Kurt, who had just returned from the pilothouse. "I'll bestow upon you the privilege of locating our expensive towfish."

"Thanks," Kurt replied, "this should be fun . . . searching the ocean depths without getting wet."

"As long as it doesn't include discovering a damaged metal detector."

"If it's wrapped around a pot-of-gold, who cares," laughed Kurt. Leaning over the side of the boat he began lowering the twenty-three pound camera, which thankfully became almost weightless once underwater. Kurt calculated that the one hundred and twenty-five foot descent would take approximately three minutes. As the video camera slipped beneath the waves the monitor sprang to life, unveiling a cobalt-blue sea.

Initially, the only objects displayed on the small screen were the bluish water, a few trailing bubbles, and strands of emerald-green seaweed. At the fifteen-foot mark, however, the camera punched a hole through a vast shoal of six-to ten-inch Pacific sardines. The silvery fish parted at the sight of the mechanism, creating a funnel-like passageway that allowed the camera to safely pass through.

"It's incredible how they do that," Petersen said amazed. "Not a single shimmering scale touched the lens."

Kurt nodded. "Their instinct for survival is powerful, and the intrusive camera—as perceived by their rudimentary brains—looks like a dangerous creature."

"I bet that school has over a million fish."

"Probably," Kurt murmured in agreement. Gazing intently at the video screen, he was watching the last of the writhing sardines when the picture suddenly darkened, as if some object had passed overhead, blocking the sunlight. Within a few seconds the brightness returned, but the screen was bereft of any sardines. "Interesting . . . the sardines seemed to have disappeared."

"Something spooked them," Petersen said anxiously.

"That could be just about anything that swims in the ocean," laughed Kurt. "When you're a gigantic, protein-rich buffet, and occupy the bottom rung of the food chain, it's always open season."

Petersen frowned. "I'd certainly like to know what frightened the little critters."

"If we're lucky," Kurt said, "maybe we'll catch a glimpse of the predatory fish or animal as it passes in front of the screen."

"That's okay by me as long as it doesn't have serrated teeth."

Kurt could tell by Petersen's knitted brow that he was serious. "You've got nothing to worry about," he said, to assure him, "you don't have to get wet since I'm the only one on this boat certified in the use of scuba gear. If a diver's needed—in order to free the towfish—that's my department."

"I'm a techno-scientist, not an underwater person. I love the ocean, but only from the dry deck of a boat, which is why I only operate equipment topside," Petersen said with a nervous smile. "The movie 'Jaws,' and its successors, confirmed the wisdom of that decision."

"And to think you're my sole shipmate . . . remind me to be extra careful while submerged."

"I'll toss you a line if anything goes wrong," Petersen said gallantly, "or call for help on the ship-to-shore radio."

"Thanks—you really know how to make a person feel safe," Kurt said in a slightly derisive tone as he continued to lower the camera. He estimated that it was now beyond the seventy-five foot mark. To change the viewing area he walked up and down the side the boat, at times spinning the cable 180 degrees, his arms and legs functioning in the same manner as a mobile pendulum. An occasional fish darted in front of the lens; opaleye, kelp greenlings, sheepshead, whitefish, halfmoons, calico bass, and a small cluster of blacksmiths, but nothing that would scare an immense school of sardines.

"We're getting close to the bottom," Petersen warned.

At about the eighty-five foot level the camera descended through a thermocline—a transitional zone between the warm surface water and the colder layer below—where for a brief moment the image on the monitor had the wavy appearance of a desert mirage. Beneath the stratified layer, the color of the water had also changed, from a warm blue to a cool green.

"A thermocline" Kurt reported, "is the diver's equivalent to an icy shower on a cold winter day."

"Dress warmly," Petersen advised.

"I plan to," Kurt replied, and then added, "I think I'm nearing the one-hundred-foot mark." He stopped the camera's descent and began twisting the cable in order to give them a 360-degree panoramic view. "Plankton," he mumbled, "just what we don't need." The tiny creatures flourished in the deep cold water, ascending to the surface during the night, only to drift back down at the first hint of light. Unfortunately, the billions of microscopic organisms had the same effect as city smog, clouding the water in a brown haze and obscuring visibility. Kurt eased the camera down an additional five feet.

"Oh my gosh!" Petersen cried out.

Kurt just stared at the monitor, his eyes barely blinking, his breathing controlled—his mind evaluating the unexpected scene. He rotated the camera, changing its viewpoint, and then, with Petersen accompanying him, he walked up and down the entire length of the ship, dragging the camera. Finally, he lowered it five more feet and repeated the same procedure. "That's awful," he whispered.

"How long do you suppose it's been down there?" Petersen asked.

"At least ten years," he replied softly. *A ghost net*, mumbled Kurt to himself, disgusted at the sight. The high-quality synthetic nets lasted for decades, insidiously entangling and killing any creature unfortunate enough to wander into its spider-like mesh. The huge net was hooked between two rocky pinnacles. Apparently the trawler had lost its dragnet when it became snagged on the razor-sharp rocks. Untethered to its surface ship, the nylon meshwork nonetheless continued its deadly assignment. Trapped within its two inch webbing, and in various stages of decay, were dozens of reef fish, rock crabs, lobsters, spider crabs, a bat ray, two white sea bass, three leopard sharks, one soupfin shark, sand dabs, a California halibut, and a young bottlenose dolphin with its flesh still intact. Based upon the condition of the three-foot animal, it was obviously the *ghost net's* latest victim.

"What type of net is it?" Petersen wondered.

"A benthic trawl net," answered Kurt. "A boat outfitted as a trawler drags the funnel-shaped fishing net along the seafloor, sweeping up every living creature within its destructive path. The net is held open by a solid metal beam that is attached to two massive metal plates. These plates slide over the bottom, disturbing the seabed, and scaring up the fish. It's those iron plates that must've generated the magnetic field picked up by our towfish."

As they began reinspecting the trawl net, they discovered their Pulse 12 towfish. The device had punched a large hole through the thickest part of the netting before becoming inextricably entwined. Kurt now had the camera trained on the yellow metal detector.

"I believe you'll be getting wet," Petersen announced.

"I'll be going underwater for two reasons," Kurt said with a touch of anger, "obviously to free our apparatus, and secondly, to end the ghost net's deadly career."

"It must be heavy," Petersen remarked.

"A thousand-plus pounds," Kurt confirmed. "But, once I cut away the metal plates and the dead sea life, its weight should be reduced by half. I'll attach a rope to it and then we'll use the anchor winch to hoist it to the surface."

"How will we haul it onboard? There's just the two of us."

"We won't . . . we'll drag it behind our boat."

"That's brilliant, Dr. Nichols, no wonder I'm just your humble servant."

"If that's the case I could use some help in preparing for my dive."

After performing an exaggerated curtsey, Petersen said, "I'm at your beck and call."

Kurt had Petersen search the boat for a nylon rope that was at least fifty feet in length. Fortunately, stowed away in the forward hatch, was a one hundred foot, 5/8 thick, double-braided nylon rope, which Petersen coiled into a game bag normally used for collecting lobsters. While Petersen was out searching for the rope, Kurt slipped into a Henderson 8/7 mm thermoprene semi-dry wetsuit with attached hood, 5 mm titanium dive booties, and 5 mm titanium gloves. *That should keep me plenty warm,* he thought. Because he was doing a deep dive, he chose a 130-cubic foot, high-pressure steel scuba tank, filled to 3600 psi. The high-capacity tank held enough oxygen to last the entire dive. The rest of Kurt's equipment included an Atomic T2x titanium scuba regulator, Atomic Cobalt integrated dive computer with digital compass, Scubapro KnightHawk weight-integrated buoyancy compensator, Atomic split-dive fins, LED underwater light, dive mask, and snorkel. The last, but most important item—considering the nature of his dive—was a titanium saw knife with built-in line cutter.

"You look like an oversized duck," Petersen said.

"A very obese duck," Kurt added. "This equipment weighs more than a hundred and twenty-five pounds making it difficult to walk on land; however, once I'm in the water, the heaviness is essentially neutralized." He noticed that Petersen was hauling the camera back to the surface. "What are you doing?" he asked.

"Since you don't have an actual dive buddy, I'll be that person via the camera's eye while at the same time filming your adventure."

"I appreciate that," said Kurt, "it'll be nice to have a mechanical buddy."

As Kurt was performing a final pre-dive safety check he heard Petersen scream a five letter word that instantly got his attention—*S-H-A-R-K.*

"Where?" asked Kurt.

"Below the boat," Petersen said, his voice quivering, "and it's as big as Jaws."

Kurt stared into the ocean. He noticed that the seething mass of sardines had returned, but were now corralled into a jumbo-sized baitball that stretched the entire length of the ship. The immense swirling shoal, Kurt realized, was using the boat's hull as a type of refuge. He scanned the water, searching for the alleged shark. Suddenly, a gaping hole appeared in the midst of the tight pack as millions of individual sardines—acting as one—created a circular passageway. Swimming into the vortex was Petersen's shark, grayish-brown in color with a mottled appearance. It was at least twenty feet long, with a three-foot girth and a prominent dorsal fin. Its gigantic and gaping mouth was causing a frenzy of fear amongst the sardines. "That's a big shark," he said.

"Is that . . . a great white?" Petersen whispered.

Kurt watched the magnificent creature for at least a minute before responding. "It might be," he said, knowing that he was lying, but enjoying the look of utter dread on Petersen's face. The shark certainly looked menacing, particularly to someone who had never had an up-close, personal experience with these noble beasts. As for himself, it had been years since he had last glimpsed one of these coastal-pelagic sharks—the second largest living fish in the world. The Latin name for it was *Cetorhinus maximus*—which meant 'great nosed monster.' Its common name was 'basking shark,' derived from its behavior of 'basking' in the warm surface water. The docile giant was a harmless filter feeder, the same as a baleen whale.

"You're not still diving . . . are you?" asked Petersen.

"Absolutely," grinned Kurt. "That shark has gorged on thousands of sardines and I seriously doubt it's in the mood for a human steak. Besides, I have an expensive toy that needs recovering, and a dragnet to destroy. Wish me luck." Without waiting for a reply, Kurt inserted the regulator into his mouth, and stepped off the yacht. He splashed down in the middle of the sardine shoal, scattering the fish to all points of the compass, and creating his own deserted portal. Before disappearing underwater he executed a right thumb up to Petersen, the international signal for 'I'm okay.' As Kurt descended he spewed forth a cloud of effervescent bubbles and then gagged on a mouthful of saltwater. Laughing while submerged, he concluded, was an act of stupidity. Petersen's lingering expression, however, was priceless—shock and disbelief, mixed with a smidgen of awe. The impromptu stunt had certainly been worth it. His only concern was whether the student, upon realizing the charade, had a forgiving heart.

His explosive entry had split the sardine school into four gyrating groups, which were slowly reconnecting into a single, living entity. The basking shark, startled by the commotion, had receded into the depths. Kurt dropped down to twenty feet before leveling off. He then performed a brief safety check—hoping to avoid a diver's worst nightmare—equipment failure on a deep dive. Satisfied that everything was operating properly, he began searching for the towfish cable, which he located in less than thirty seconds. His intent was to simply follow the cable down to the stuck metal detector. As he was moving down the cable line his left shoulder was suddenly thumbed by a heavy object, causing a moment of panic—his mind conjuring up all types of pernicious creatures. To his relief he discovered that it was the DV-1 camera. *Petersen!* He exclaimed to himself with a sense of relief; his robotic dive buddy had arrived.

After a brief pause to wave at the camera, Kurt continued his descent, traveling at a rate of sixty feet per minute. At the eighty-five foot mark he encountered the thermocline. According to his dive computer, the water temperature had plunged precipitously—from a balmy sixty-three degrees to a nippy fifty-four. The water clarity had also decreased; instead of fifty feet of visibility he had less than twenty—the culprit—particulate matter caused by throngs of plankton, which created an underwater snowstorm. *It could be much worse,* thought Kurt. During a red-tide event, the bioluminescent planktons were so numerous that visibility was often reduced to less than five feet.

At the one hundred foot level he decreased his speed to a crawl. Inching forward, Kurt strained his eyes, searching for the ghost net. After a few feet it began to slowly materialize—like a fuzzy apparition on a foggy night—undulating in the deep ocean current, its marine victims, along with their Pulse 12 Towfish, helplessly entangled in the manmade instrument of death. He hated these factory-sized fishing nets which were capable of eradicating an entire localized species within a matter of months. The nets were also nonselective, sweeping up both marketable and unmarketable fish. The undesirable fish were known as by-catch, and were immediately discarded. On many occasions the wasteful by-catch also included marine animals.

Kurt stared at the newborn bottlenose dolphin snared within the mesh. He wondered about its mother, an intelligent creature that must have endured unimaginable agony as it witnessed its calf drowning—and powerless to do anything about it. The brief struggle had apparently been intense; the nylon netting was tightly twisted around the animal's entire fusiform body, and like a wire garrote, had carved deep nick wounds into its tender flesh.

Hovering in front of the dolphin, Kurt decided that the calf would be the first victim he removed from the deadly mesh. Withdrawing his titanium knife from its protective sheath, he began sawing through the netting, which easily parted with each stroke of the blade. Once freed, he cradled the dolphin in his arms. He then swam to a nearby reef where he gently placed the calf on a bed of golden-yellow bulb kelp that hugged the ocean floor.

Swimming back to the net, Kurt spent the next two minutes untwisting and cutting the Pulse 12 Towfish from the mesh, before he continued liberating additional sea creatures—laying them side by side on the sandy bottom. Stopping for a few seconds in order to check his air supply, he noted that he was down to 2900 psi. On a deep dive, safety dictated that you consume no more than two-thirds of the available gas supply on the descent and while at the bottom, leaving at least one-third for the ascent, a two-minute safety stop at sixty feet, another safety stop at fifteen feet, and a little extra in case of an emergency. Being somewhat cautious Kurt had decided to begin his ascent at 1400 psi.

As he began detaching the bulky iron plates from the dragnet, Kurt soon realized that severing the dead marine creatures from the nylon webbing had been the easy part. Each oblong-shaped plate weighed at least five hundred pounds and was attached to a metal beam whose function was to hold the mouth of the net open while it was being dragged across the bottom. Kurt's task involved separating the netting from both the beam and the plates, and leaving the iron structures behind to safely rust on the seafloor.

For the next five minutes he laboriously sliced his way through forty to fifty feet of netting in addition to eight, one-inch thick cords, which fastened the net to the metal hardware. Checking his work, Kurt allowed himself a brief, victorious smile. His mission was going as planned; the metal was now detached from the netting. The next major item involved disentangling the net from the two rocky pinnacles. As he made his way over to the site, he checked his air supply—2200 psi. He would have to work quickly.

Hanging suspended over the pinnacles, Kurt conducted a hurried assessment of the situation. The dragnet's metal beam had obviously slammed into the shafts of stone, breaking off the pyramidal apexes. Most of the net had slid over the busted pillars, but the trailing end of the net, known as the cod end—which at the time of the incident was undoubtedly filled with trapped fish and therefore heavier—had apparently snagged on the sharp edges. The jagged rocks had shredded the mesh, releasing the fish. *Poetic justice* thought Kurt, although the net ultimately had its silent revenge as it continued its lethal harvest year after year—long after its human operators had disappeared.

Kurt swam down to the first column and immediately began unraveling the net. In some sections the mesh was covered by marine plants, chestnut cowries, scallops, or mussels, which he had to first remove before he could strip the netting from the rocks. Whenever possible he promptly returned the creatures back to their original habitats. The tedious process of unwinding the meshwork, Kurt mused, was similar to untangling a rat's nest caused by a backlash on a fishing reel, or unknotting an extra-fine gold chain necklace—a chore he had often performed on behalf of his now deceased wife.

With one strenuous tug, the final tattered section of the ghost net was dislodged from the first column. He then turned his attention to the second column and began peeling off the netting at a rate that surprised even him. But Kurt's good fortune and quick work didn't last. Regrettably, a major segment of the mesh was buried beneath a thick mat of barnacles that were as unmoving as the rock itself. Thousands of the tiny arthropods had cemented the net to the stone. The only solution, Kurt realized, was an old-fashioned trim job. Brandishing his knife, he proceeded to carve an irregularly shaped hole as he dissected the mesh from the entrenched barnacles. After a few precious, oxygen-consuming minutes, he had successfully extricated the net. Resting for a second, Kurt checked his remaining air supply—1600 psi. He *supposedly* had two hundred pounds to work with before he had to ascend, and he still had one important item left on his underwater agenda.

Reaching into the game bag attached to his BC, Kurt removed the one-hundred-foot nylon rope that Petersen had packed. Grasping one end, he began to weave it in and out through different sections of the dragnet until the whole unit was knitted together. He then tied it off with a bowline knot—creating a non-slipping giant loop. Clutching the remaining loose end with his right hand, he made a hasty retreat for *Serenity's* anchor that had impacted the seafloor approximately twenty feet west of the dragnet. As he was dolphin stroking toward the anchor, Kurt assessed his oxygen level; he was down to 1450 psi. *Time was running out,* he moaned. Swimming up to the anchor he was pleased to discover that it had gouged a deep trench into the sandy bottom. As a captain, it was exactly what you wanted when securing a yacht. He quickly threaded the loose end of the rope through the anchor eyelet until a four-foot segment jutted out from the opposite side, which he used to tie a double half-hitch knot—temporarily uniting the dragnet to the anchor. Kurt then snatched a peek at his air supply—1250 psi—one hundred and fifty pounds less than he had planned, but still within acceptable safety limits. With one final glance at his surroundings he immediately began a slow ascent, staying within several feet of the anchor line on his way to the surface.

Kurt's upward rate of speed was one foot every two seconds; the slothful pace was necessary in order to off-load inert gasses and gas bubbles that had accumulated in his bloodstream during the deep dive. If he ascended too rapidly he risked decompression illness—a life-threatening affliction. After what seemed like a long minute he was at ninety-five feet. Seventy seconds later he was at sixty feet and into warmer water. He was glad to be beyond the thermocline. At the sixty-foot mark he halted his progress. It was time for his two-minute deep stop—an essential part of his decompression algorithm—allowing his body to off-gas. For support, and to avoid being carried away by a surging current, he held onto the anchor line. His faithful companion during the long interlude was Petersen's DV-1 camera, which was suspended right beside him. When the two minutes were up, Kurt first inspected his dive computer before continuing with his ascent. His remaining air supply, he noted with a sense of uneasiness, was down to 850 psi.

In an effort to conserve oxygen, Kurt eased his grip on the anchor line and performed a reverse rope slide. Instead of coasting downward, he drifted skyward—by using the air in his BC as a lifting mechanism. Mathematically it was quite simple; a body's thirst for oxygen was directly related to its level of activity; reduce that level and the consumption rate diminished accordingly.

At the forty-foot mark the ambient light suddenly faded as if a pitch-black cloud was obscuring the sun. Curious, Kurt tilted his head back, looking for an explanation. The answer he noted with a sense of wonder was nature in its untamed glory—the endless stream of sardines was back, along with a ravenous horde of predators.

Releasing his grip on the anchor line, Kurt latched onto Petersen's camera and began filming the awe-inspiring spectacle. The seething mass of sardines had quadrupled in size and extended from the surface down to thirty feet. It was the *Mother of all Smorgasbords*, thought Kurt, although there was only one item on the menu—raw sardine.

Creatures of every type were cashing in on the infinite bounty. Descending from the sky, were brown pelicans, Brandt's cormorants, and eared grebe's. Ascending from the depths were white seabass, yellowtail, and calico bass. Attacking the sardines from every conceivable angle were California sea lions, harbor seals, bottlenose dolphins, and seven-to nine-foot blue sharks. The slim dark-blue sharks, their sides flashing iridescent blue, employed a bulldog-type eating strategy; from essentially a standstill they would suddenly plow into the densest part of the shoal—jaws agape—slaughtering and wounding as many sardines as possible, then afterwards slowly engulfing every bloody morsel. Stationed on the perimeters, like military sharpshooters, were several striped marlins that eagerly consumed any fish that dared to venture too far from the safety of the school. With each successful bite, the bluish, lavender, and whitish bars prominent on the sides of each marlin pulsated with luminescent excitement as if infused with electricity.

Forgetting about his own safety, Kurt floated into the midst of the feeding frenzy. Initially, his entire body was battered by hundreds of six-inch living missiles, but then just as quickly as it began the bombardment ended as the sardines, sensing his presence, created a huge oval-shaped cavity. Staring at the millions of fish orbiting around him, Kurt felt as if he was at the center of the universe, and that the sardines were celestial bodies. As the hole expanded, rifts appeared along its margins, and three slow-moving behemoths entered into his space. The small eyes of the immense creatures inspected him as they approached, and in a nonaggressive manner, the massive gray shapes glided past his motionless body. As they cruised by, Kurt was buffeted by powerful swirling eddies which he imagined were similar to the backwash generated by a small submarine. Prior to re-entering the school, the three majestic basking sharks opened their enormous mouths, and with a flick of their caudal fins, disappeared into a boiling mass of frantic sardines.

Checking his oxygen supply, Kurt noted that it was down to 525 psi. Still clutching Petersen's camera, he swam back to the anchor line, and ascended to fifteen feet, where he began his two-minute shallow-water safety stop. The fifteen-foot stop was critical if he wanted to avoid the possibility of decompression sickness since his blood still contained dangerous levels of gases that needed to be expelled before surfacing.

While relaxing on the line, Kurt continued to watch the various hunters devour hapless sardines. The carnivores seemed to be everywhere, and then suddenly, they vanished. Searching for an explanation, he noticed circular rings of bubbles rising from the abyss like a net toward the surface, surrounding the sardines and concentrating them into tightly-packed shoals. Kurt counted four distinct bubble nets, with tons of frightened fish corralled into each one. *A curtain of bubbles,* he thought as he quickly rummaged through his memory, *means only one thing—whales—humpback whales!*

Within seconds of the revelation he sensed a slight pressure change as if an underwater tempest was brewing, and then he saw them—four bulky leviathans rising from the depths, propelled by giant flukes—each individual cetacean strategically positioned inside of its own bubble net. As they approached the sardines, the humpbacks opened their immense jaws and scooped up thousands of the silvery fish, together with large volumes of seawater. After breaching the surface with their upper torsos the whales, as Kurt knew from past observations, would partially close their jaws, and use their massive tongues to force the water out sideways through their baleen—the comb-like structures acting as sieves—filtering the fish from the saltwater, which were then swallowed whole.

Kurt watched as the humpbacks gradually re-submerged, with one of the creatures passing within twenty feet of his position. The mostly black skin was covered with barnacles and colorful blue-green algae, and its scalloped white flippers were as majestic as the wings on a jet aircraft.

Glancing at his dive computer, Kurt realized that the distractions had caused him to overstay his two-minute shallow-water safety-stop by thirty seconds, and that the air pressure in his tank was down to 175 psi. He used another 25 psi ascending the final fifteen feet, and another 60 psi swimming just under the surface until he arrived at *Serenity's* boarding ladder. Treading water, Kurt silently scolded himself; ending a deepwater dive with less than 100 psi was not a boastful accomplishment. But, he thought elatedly, the awe-inspiring underwater show had been worth the risk. At the swim step he was met by Petersen, who helped him offload some of his heavier equipment so that he could climb up the ladder.

Once on board, Petersen looked at him with a silly grin.

"You pulled a fast one on me," he began. "After you descended, that evil shark re-appeared. I photographed it and uploaded its picture to the Internet. Fortunately, a blogger familiar with marine animals instantly identified your man-eater. Surprise, surprise, your fiendish shark turned out to be a teddy-bear type shark that only feeds on krill, copepods, and small fish. Does the name *basking shark* ring any bells?"

Kurt returned Petersen's smile. "I hate the Internet. Life was a lot more intriguing without it."

"It does, however, keep in check the disingenuous scientist," laughed Petersen.

"What about my dive?" Kurt asked feigning hurt feelings and attempting to change the subject. "Aren't you interested in the exciting details?"

"Yes—now that the air's been cleared of any baseless heroics."

Accepting the reprimand with a good-natured chuckle, Kurt spent the next seven minutes briefing Petersen on the particulars of his dive. Approximately half of the information the student was already familiar with inasmuch as he had shadowed Kurt with the DV-1 camera. But, on several occasions he had lost sight of Kurt, so those unknown items were of profound interest.

After Kurt had finished his summary, Petersen announced: "Today's obviously a bust at discovering precious yellow metal, but that's okay, because it's an environmental victory for the deep blue sea. Salvaging a deadly ghost net will guaranteed that innocent marine life will live to see another day, and that's worth a whole lot more than a pot of gold. We always have tomorrow . . . or the next day . . . or as long as it takes . . . but today, it's our gift to the ocean to have removed one of its curses."

Petersen's unselfish words surprised Kurt. Hearing a student value the welfare of the ocean over gold was refreshing, especially coming from an individual whose generation had invented the 'selfie.' "Let's haul up the dragnet, and head home. Tomorrow, at first light, we'll give it another shot."

The anchor winch strained under the heavy load, but eventually the anchor and dragnet were hoisted to the surface. Petersen untied the double half-hitch knot that Kurt had used to yoke the anchor to the net, and lugging the loose end of the rope down the side of the yacht, tied it to two metal cleats at the boat's stern. As planned, the net would be dragged behind the ship rather than lifted onboard.

The journey home ended up taking longer than expected due to the weight of the net and an unexpected half hour stop in order to free it from a clump of giant kelp.

At the dock it required the combined strength of six marine lab employees before they were able to haul the net onto the pier. Kurt then made arrangements with the Lab's sanitation crew to have the net transported to a trash pit and buried.

Arriving home at around 6:00 p.m., Kurt yelled 'hello' to his two children and received no response. Apparently they were still out on their own adventure searching for Captain Cabrillo's grave. After washing up and changing clothes, he began preparing dinner. The evening's hearty fare included herb-roasted chicken, fried rice, and sautéed asparagus. At 7:15 p.m., when they still hadn't appeared, he sent a text to both Mischa and Jake informing them that dinner would be ready in five minutes, and to verify whether Timbrook would be attending. Mischa immediately texted back stating that they were 'at the stables, starving, we'll be home shortly, and that Timbrook wouldn't miss it for the world.'

Kurt set out four plates. He figured the kids must've had a boring and unsuccessful day since Mischa failed to mention the discovery of Cabrillo's burial chamber in her text. He, at least, had plenty to talk about. He opened a bottle of pinot noir that was rated average by professional wine critics. He heard the rear door screech open.

"Dad," shouted Mischa, "Timbrook said to uncork a bottle of your finest wine." He then heard her giggle. "He also stated that your sense of reality was about to be altered."

He looked at the bottle he had just opened. He replaced the cork. Walking to his wine rack he removed a bottle of Napa Valley pinot noir from the upper shelf. It was rated 95 by Wine Spectator. Using a brass antique corkscrew, he pulled out the cork. *An altered sense of reality*, thought Kurt, *that's simply not possible—not for a scientist who deals in down-to-earth facts.* He sniffed the wine's aroma. It was definitely a world class vintage. He filled two Riedel glasses one quarter full. He looked at the first bottle. He uncorked it again. If Timbrook's story or words were found wanting—his second glass would be from the first bottle. "Mischa," he yelled back, "what the hell are you talking about?"

By the end of the evening only the good wine had been consumed; Timbrook and Mischa had been right—the unimaginable had become real—permanently altering Kurt's sense of truth. The news, at first, was so improbable, that he thought it was just a gag. It took Mischa and Jake's cell phone photos and videos, along with Timbrook's straightforward corroboration, before he was convinced that he was not on the butt-end of a practical joke. *There are dozens of Pygmy mammoths and saber-toothed cats within walking distance from my house*, he thought, and that undisputable fact was mind-boggling, and from a rational perspective, extremely difficult to accept. The stunning information had supercharged his brain which began operating like a Formula One racecar engine stuck in overdrive.

Kurt had been eager to describe his own frustrating yet interesting day, thinking that at least it would provide somewhat enthralling dinnertime entertainment. But clearly, his experience paled in comparison to what he had just heard, so when Timbrook politely asked about Kurt's own day of treasure hunting he reluctantly explained how the Pulse 12 had become entangled with a destructive ghost net, his encounter with a massive school of sardines, diving with several large basking sharks, throngs of plankton, and the sudden appearance of a pod of Humpback whales feasting on thousands of sardines. As he recounted the day's events he observed that Timbrook, Mischa, and Jake appeared to relish every word he spoke as if his adventure was as meritorious and exciting as the discovery of Pygmy mammoths and saber-toothed cats, so at least he felt somewhat justified at his offering.

Staring at the bright-red digital clock, Kurt noted the time—1:00 a.m. Since going to bed at 10:30 p.m. he hadn't slept a wink. Tomorrow, he and Petersen would be back out on the ocean searching for the *Scott's* treasure. If the outing was unsuccessful, they would be back at it once again on Sunday, and if necessary, for the duration of the week. His inner psyche, however, was still mulling over the information he had received—*Pygmy mammoths and saber-toothed cats, with the ancient animals being watched over by a white Siberian husky.* Prior to retiring for the evening Kurt had made Timbrook, Mischa, and Jake promise that as soon as he was done with his treasure hunt, whether it was successful or not, that the very next day they would all travel to Montannon Ridge. Enthusiastic nods were seen all around the table.

At 1:45 a.m. Kurt was still counting mammoths and saber-toothed cats. At 2:10 a.m. his eyes began to sag, stuck in the drowsy state of being half opened and half closed. At 2:25 a.m. he finally drifted into the land of make-believe, and dreamed about fossils coming back to life—mammoths and saber-toothed cats metamorphosing out of soil, roaming free on Santa Cruz Island, and rocking the scientific world which had considered the exotic creatures extinct for thousands of years.

27

It had been another long day out on the ocean for Kurt and Petersen. Being Sunday, and the start of a new week, they had begun their morning full of optimism, but had ended the day in disappointment; just as in the previous two days, they had been unsuccessful at locating their primary target. *Three full days of searching*, thought Kurt, *and the Winfield Scott's treasure remained as elusive as day one.* They had broken off their search around 3:30 p.m. inasmuch as Kurt was in charge of preparing the Sunday evening meal, and needed at least two hours of prep time. The special dinner had become a Nichols' family tradition instituted by his late wife, Tessa, and attendance was essentially mandatory. In addition to a satisfying meal, you were expected to discuss the accomplishments of your past week, and the anticipated events in your upcoming week. Tessa had called it family bonding time. Besides his two children, Timbrook, and Eva had become regular attendees. Kurt had also invited Petersen who had to decline because of a beer-pong party he was hosting at the marine lab's rec-room. Kurt was secretly relieved at the response; Petersen, in spite of his invaluable assistance in helping to locate the *Scott* gold, was not yet a member of their inner circle. In his absence they could now reveal to Eva the Chumash secret hidden for hundreds of years behind the canyon walls of Montannon Ridge.

Kurt had decided to keep the dinner menu simple: Costco meat lasagna, Caesar salad, and garlic toast. Dessert would be fresh berries—raspberries, blueberries, and blackberries—served with a large scoop of vanilla-bean ice cream and topped with a dollop of whipped cream.

Using two cotton potholders he removed the lasagna from the middle rack of his Viking convection oven and quickly placed the piping-hot dish on a Birchwood cutting block to cool. He then changed the setting on the oven from 'bake' to 'broil', and slid in a tray of garlic bread. While waiting for the bread to 'toast,' he dressed the Caesar salad with Worcestershire sauce, parmesan cheese, fresh-squeezed lemon juice, crushed garlic, wine vinegar, olive oil, grated egg, freshly ground black pepper, and a dash of sea salt. Deciding that a taste test was necessary, he plucked a piece of romaine lettuce from the acacia-wood salad bowl, and popped it into his mouth. *Perfect,* Kurt moaned. The aroma of French bread bubbling with butter, garlic, and grated Parmesan cheese was overwhelming and the smell almost irresistible. Opening the oven he noted that the bread had turned a beautiful golden brown. He removed the tray and set it alongside the lasagna, covering it with aluminum foil in order to keep the garlic toast warm and soft. He turned the oven off with a satisfied flourish.

The last issue that Kurt had to address before Timbrook and Eva arrived was the most difficult decision of the evening, but one that he absolutely cherished: Which wine to serve? After carefully examining his extensive collection of California wines, he decided upon a fruity Napa Valley reserve syrah, and uncorked two bottles from J.C. Cellars. He poured himself a glass and had a sip. "Excellent," he said aloud. He then poured two additional glasses so that the wine had a chance to breathe before being consumed.

The sound of the front door being opened and closed was almost immediately followed by a similar noise from the rear door.

Eva and Timbrook had arrived. Knocking, or ringing the door-bell, was no longer required since both were considered the same as family. As his guests stepped into the kitchen, Mischa and Jake joined them. After a round of hugs, Kurt announced, "Dinner is served."

"It smells wonderful," Eva said.

"Downright decadent if you ask me," Timbrook said licking his lips.

"Dad's a good cook," Mischa said proudly.

"Costco and Dad," Kurt insisted.

"Costco had nothing to do with the salad and garlic bread," Jake corrected.

"Thank you son," Kurt said with a laugh, and then added, "Ladies first." He watched as Eva and Mischa began filling their plates. Eva was dressed in a sandstorm-colored v-neck cashmere sweater, figure-skimming black denim leggings, and urban-grey four-inch pumps. Her only jewelry was striated gold beam spear earrings. Her form-fitting silhouette easily surpassed the din-ner he had prepared. Mischa caught him staring and mouthed the word '*Daddy!*' Embarrassed, he quickly turned away but not before experiencing the sensation of blood rushing into his cheeks. He opened the refrigerator door and let the cool air wash over his face. After twenty seconds he slowly closed the door. Fortunately, other than Mischa, no one else noticed his actions. His composure restored, he observed that Mischa and Eva had already passed through the serving line and were walk-ing toward the dining room table, while Timbrook and Jake were completely absorbed with loading up their own platters. He was pleased to see that Timbrook's plate was filled to the brim. In the last two weeks the Indian had clearly lost a fair amount of weight resulting in a more worn and weary appearance. Picking up a plate he immediately joined them, and soon his dish, too, was overflowing.

Following a brief prayer by Timbrook 'thanking the Lord for His incredible bounty,' they began feasting on the Italian meal. Jake, eating like a typical ravenous teenager, finished first and then went back for a second helping. Mischa joined him but only for an additional slice of garlic bread. The adults declined a second round, but left room for dessert. Kurt then recommended a fifteen minute pause before he served the ice cream and berries in order to allow for a small amount of digestion. Everyone nodded their heads in agreement.

The dinner conversation had remained casual and light, intermixed with periods of humor. Timbrook, after replenishing his glass of wine, brought the evening back to its intended purpose. "It's my understanding that the kids have been searching for Captain Cabrillo's grave for the last three days, and that Kurt and Petersen have spent a similar amount of time scouring the ocean for the *Winfield Scott's* treasure. Obviously your various investigations have been unproductive since no one has made any exalted announcements. I'm aware of Friday's results, but I'm in the dark as to Saturday's or today's. I would like to hear an updated report regarding the last two days, but let us begin with Friday's adventure since Eva knows nothing about Mischa and Jake's unscheduled and disobedient side trip to Montannon Ridge—the most sacred of all Chumash sites."

Eva, with a wry smile said, "Aren't the children being a bit naughty." She then turned to Mischa and said, "I trust you didn't inherit these fine qualities from your dad."

Laughing, Mischa said, "No, but when we reveal to you what we discovered, you'll completely understand our willful actions, and you'll forgive us our youthful indiscretions."

"Pretty confident, aren't you?" Eva said slightly perplexed. As she looked around the table she noticed that everyone was smiling. "It's obvious that Mischa and Jake's mischievous behavior had no long-term repercussions."

"Well, yes and no," Jake answered mysteriously.

"We only traveled up to Montannon Ridge," began Mischa, "at the end of our day's adventure. Prior to scaling the ridge, we skirted the southwest coastline from Scorpion Cove to Smuggler's Cove, and investigated five potential burial sites. The only thing we discovered was a human trash dump containing rusty cans and old bottles, and a Chumash midden rubbish heap—where we found lots of discarded shells. Not one of the five areas that we explored had a shred of evidence indicating the Captain's gravesite. When we arrived at Smuggler's Cove we began our journey home by way of Smuggler's Trail. The last time we were on that path Timbrook had accompanied us; Jake and I were on a spearfishing trip to Yellowbanks and Timbrook was heading up to Montannon Ridge. The actual turnoff to Montannon Ridge is at the halfway point along the trail. The entrance is strategically concealed behind a thick hedge of coastal sagebrush in order to keep unwanted visitors off the mountain and away from the sacred site. When Timbrook disappeared into the sagebrush, I marked the exact spot with a flat volcanic rock."

Scowling, Timbrook said, "I should've known."

"It wasn't my idea," Jake clarified.

"Jake's innocent," Mischa confirmed.

"He may not have marked the actual entryway," Kurt said paternally, "but he didn't object either, and eventually followed you all the way to the summit."

"Somebody had to keep an eye on her," Jake said in his defense.

"You're a good brother," Mischa declared.

"Enough of the niceties—other than visiting a Chumash graveyard without permission and possibly disturbing the ancestral spirits, what did you discover at Montannon Ridge that has everyone in this room smiling?" Eva wondered.

"Just so you know, "Kurt explained, "their journey revealed secrets that even I was not aware of. In a few minutes you'll know everything."

"I can hardly wait," Eva said somewhat impatiently.

"It's a lot more than just a couple of trivial Chumash secrets kept hush-hush for centuries," Timbrook clarified. "It's a major revelation that once divulged, will impact the world."

"You're pulling my leg," Eva said suspiciously.

"No he's not," Mischa assured her. "While Jake and I were exploring Montannon Ridge we used our i-Phones to snap dozens of photographs and to record several minutes of video. We've uploaded those images onto a MacBook computer. Mere verbal description of what the Chumash have kept hidden from the public eye wouldn't do it justice, so we decided to present it visually, and then answer your questions. Jake," Mischa said looking at her brother, "it's all yours."

Getting up from his seat, Jake placed the computer in front of Eva, flipped open the fifteen-inch screen, scrolled to the file containing the photos and videos, and then clicked the 'play' icon. While Jake was preparing the presentation, Kurt, Timbrook, and Mischa gathered in a tight semi-circle behind Eva's chair.

"Showtime," said Jake.

The first photographs were slightly blurred, but nonetheless showed a creature becoming visibly larger with each subsequent image.

"Sorry," Mischa whispered, "I was overly anxious."

The next series of photographs more cleanly depicted the beast's actual features.

"Is that an elephant?" Eva speculated.

"Yes and no," Timbrook answered.

"It has to be," Eva countered, "it has tusks!"

"Think outside the box," Kurt suggested.

The final images were well-defined and clearly highlighted the animal's shaggy reddish-brown hair that flowed in long curls off its flattish head, shoulders, and entire upper back. The rest of the lower body appeared hairless but grayish in color. When the photos ended the video immediately began playing, which more conspicuously emphasized the creature's diminutive size, floppy ears, short neck, pillar-like legs, muscular trunk, and its glistening two to three foot spiraled ivory tusks.

"Oh my God—this can't be—it isn't possible!" Eva squealed incredulously.

Before anyone could respond, the video ended and the next series of photographs began scrolling across the screen, each picture displayed for a period of five seconds before being automatically replaced with the next image. As each photograph was aired, Eva would utter a short, audible gasp. The photos depicted powerfully built felines that ranged in size from two to four feet in length, with fur golden in color, and marked with light brown rosettes. A majority of the images focused on the creatures' facial features including a few close-ups of the animal's curved, dagger-shaped fangs, which on several of the larger individuals jutted out four inches from the upper jaw. As soon as the slide show ended, the video commenced playing. The ninety-second film began with a sweeping view of the volcanic cave, zeroed in for a few seconds on two feed stations, and then focused on select felines, including a few shots of the mustangs and Siberian husky interacting with the strange cats. The brief video concluded with an intimate shot of Mischa stroking the fur of a heavyset individual that was vocalizing a loud, purr-like roar.

"That's Diego," Mischa advised Eva. "He's my favorite."

"You've already named them?" Timbrook asked amazed.

"Just that one." Mischa answered.

"And Diego . . ." whispered Eva, "has a set of formidable canines that are enormous. As a biologist, I *know* that these types of teeth don't exist in any modern-day carnivores, but were present in beasts that roamed California until their extinction 3000 to 5000 years ago. It therefore appears that Diego—for reasons that

I cannot fathom—has attributes of a nonexistent saber-toothed cat."

"Pygmy saber-toothed cat." Timbrook corrected.

"That's impossible!" Eva exclaimed. "Saber-toothed cats disappeared from the face of the earth ages ago, and besides, I've never even heard of a *Pygmy* saber-toothed cat."

Smiling, Timbrook said, "It may be highly improbable, but, unless your own eyes are deceiving you, their very existence is as real as the people in this room. Santa Cruz Island was their last refuge, and overtime, as occurs with most animals that are separated from a larger gene pool and have to subsist on limited resources, they became more dwarf-like."

"The miniature elephants," asked Eva with a quivering voice, "are they also pygmies—Pygmy mammoths?"

Nodding, Timbrook said, "Descendants of the mainland Columbian mammoths."

"That's what I thought!" Eva said jubilantly. "A breathing fossil that's still roaming the earth . . . it's simply amazing, and to think there are dozens of them coexisting with saber-toothed cats."

"It's certainly an unusual relationship," Timbrook agreed.

"Are there any other de-extinct creatures on this island that you haven't told me about?" Eva asked sarcastically.

Laughing, Timbrook said, "No—just Pygmy mammoths, saber-toothed cats, and one antique Indian."

"You're hardly a relic," said Eva, "a survivor, yes, like the animals that you and your fellow Chumash Indians have loved, and nurtured, for thousands of years."

"It was a task we deeply relished," said Timbrook softly. "But, in the last two hundred years, keeping their existence from the public has been difficult."

Eva sighed, and then suddenly wiped a few tears from her eyes. After a brief pause in order to regain her composure, she said, "Words cannot describe my emotions right now. I feel like

I've been given a gift that I don't deserve, and all I want to do is cry because of the magnitude of what I've received. It's like the best Christmas present imaginable, but instead of just one, there are two. What the Chumash have accomplished in preserving these creatures is beyond measure, and keeping it secret for hundreds of years—that was an absolute miracle. My only concern is for their future; eventually someone in this modern world will discover their presence and then you'll have to deal with the craziness that will surely follow. Have you considered your options when that moment occurs?"

Timbrook's strained expression indicated that he had thought about that day. "The Chumash Tribal elders have wrestled with this issue for decades, and a decision regarding disclosure was finally made six months ago at our winter solstice gathering. After much discussion the council of elders unanimously agreed that the time had arrived to divulge the creature's existence to the public, although a definitive disclosure date wasn't decided upon. Their judgment was based upon several factors, but primarily from information that I provided having lived with the creatures for sixty years. Foremost, the animals deserve their freedom; to once again wander the entire island as they did in the days of old. Secondarily, to reintroduce the Pygmy mammoths and saber-toothed cats to several of the other islands, and eventually—twenty-five years down the road—to secured sanctuaries on the mainland. In addition, in order to satiate the public's desire for a close-up view of these exotic beasts, we've chosen the world famous San Diego Zoo as our partner in exhibiting a male and female of each species. As expected," chuckled Timbrook, "the zoo readily agreed to our proposal. In absolute secrecy they're currently constructing an outdoor enclosure that's similar in design to their island habitat—along with a few extra bonus features—that even the mammoths and saber-toothed cats would approve of."

"It's like a dream that isn't a dream . . . it's so unbelievable it's hard to imagine it's real," Eva declared. "The world will owe the Chumash Nation a huge debt of gratitude. To once again view prehistoric creatures walking the earth will be a fulfillment of every human's most childish fantasy."

"—and then some," added Kurt.

"All true," Timbrook confirmed, "and that day will soon be upon us. But, setting aside Friday's extraordinary discovery, which we could easily discuss for weeks, I would like to hear further from the children regarding their search for Captain Cabrillo's gravesite, and after that, Kurt's investigation into the *Winfield Scott's* treasure."

"Getting back to Saturday and today," Jake began with a deflated tone, "Timbrook's earlier statement about no exalted announcements was unfortunately correct; we weren't successful, even after two additional days of searching."

"What areas of the island did you inspect?" asked Timbrook.

"On Saturday," interjected Mischa, "we began where we ended on Friday, at Smuggler's Cove. We explored every significant promontory adjacent to Yellowbanks, Sandstone Point, and those we thought had potential two miles west of Sandstone. Unfortunately, we only confirmed what you had stated earlier— that the bluffs and cliffs along this section of the island are less than ideal for a burial site. They're cold, windy, and denuded of vegetation. The only objects we found were a few Chumash arrowheads, some broken pottery, and white-washed animal bones."

"I'm sorry for your disappointment," laughed Timbrook, "but it's not entirely unexpected. The burial chamber is either well hidden, at a different location, or on one of the other islands. The animal bones are no doubt from cattle and sheep that used to roam this island. Many a sailor would butcher an animal that strayed too close to the shoreline and then barbeque it where it fell. Rumor had it that the free-range beef and sheep of Santa Cruz Island were mighty tasty," he said with a wink.

"It's good to know that you didn't starve while serving as a caretaker," laughed Eva.

"Not a chance," Timbrook agreed.

"This morning," continued Jake, "we headed in the opposite direction, traveling northeast of Scorpion Cove. We meticulously examined the headlands and peninsulas located along Cavern Point, Potato Harbor, and Coche Point. We ended our journey at the beginning of Chinese Harbor. The highlight of our trip was the discovery of a den of Island foxes. The mother had a litter of four kits and had no qualms about us playing with them."

"The beauty of isolation," Timbrook mused. "They do not fear man since humans do not cause them harm. It's a rare treat in the animal world—to be viewed as a friend and not as a foe."

"Well . . . they actually really, really, love us now," Mischa squealed, "since we shared our sandwiches with them. They're quite fond of nine-grain bread, roast beef, and provolone cheese."

"That was generous," Eva said.

Smiling, Mischa said, "Thank you, it was an incredibly special time."

"Did you discover anything else?" Timbrook asked.

"Not exactly," answered Jake. "Just some old wood, a half-dozen rusty beer cans, and an ancient pair of sunglasses. That's about it."

"Are you now ready to suspend your search?" Timbrook asked.

Before responding, Mischa looked at Jake, who vigorously shook his head back and forth. "Absolutely not!" she replied defiantly. "In fact, we've just begun. But I do have a question: During our three days of wandering I noticed that Santa Cruz is surrounded by numerous islands, with several of them being quite large, like Gull Island. Who owns these individual islands that are detached from the main Island?"

"It depends upon where they're located," Timbrook answered. "If an island borders the National Park Service property, then the

NPS owns it. If it's adjacent to The Nature Conservancy, then they're the legal owners. If it abuts your remaining two-hundred acres, then the Nichols' family is the rightful owner."

"Did the Chumash consider these islands interconnected to the main island?" Mischa asked.

"Good question," answered Timbrook, "but I have no idea. The notion of land ownership did not exist within the Chumash culture and was completely foreign to our way of life. Staking a personal claim to a parcel of land, or an island, was a European concept. Your question, though, has got me curious—what's the reason for your interest?"

"Just thinking about things," Mischa said slyly. "Spending days on a horse, travelling around the island, allows for a bit of contemplative pondering. The picturesque islets captured my attention, which then made me wonder who their legal owners were."

"Now you know," said Timbrook. "And for your information, the five islands off of Scorpion Cove—they belong to the Nichols family—so have fun checking them out."

"That we definitely will," said Jake, "but only after our Painted Cave adventure, which takes place tomorrow."

"The marine conditions look perfect for our big day," Eva said excitedly, "and Dr. Sedrak is thrilled to be accompanying us. He's also ecstatic at having Timbrook as our guide."

Looking slightly piqued, Kurt said, "I didn't know Dr. Sedrak was joining you."

"I'm sorry, I thought you knew," Eva said softly. "Mischa invited the doctor and he responded with a hearty yes, and that, 'he wouldn't miss it for the world.'"

"I bet," Kurt whispered, and then quickly added: "That cave is a complex maze of catacombs; I'm glad Timbrook's leading the tour."

"It's not so bad," Timbrook assured him. "I've explored it on many occasions, and for a sea cave, it's quite safe. In addition, we're timing our arrival at the beginning of an extremely low tide, so that will help by allowing for more headroom."

"I sincerely wish I could join you," Kurt said, "but as you know, Petersen and I will once again be back out on the *Serenity* searching for the *Winfield Scott's* lost treasure—which optimistic statement assumes that it truly does exist. After three long days I'm starting to doubt my initial enthusiasm."

Laughing Timbrook said reassuringly, "I've rarely heard of a treasure hunter having immediate success, so your experience is probably par for the course. If you're on the right trail, you'll eventually discover the *Scott's* treasure, it's just a question of when. However, before you discuss your findings for Saturday and today, Eva needs to be brought-up-to-speed as to what occurred on Friday."

"Friday," began Kurt, "was a complete bust as to finding any gold; however, it was a day when Petersen and I performed a Samaritan act on behalf of the ocean." Kurt then provided Eva with a synopsis of the day's events—the long hours without a single hit on the Pulse 12 Towfish; the towfish becoming snagged on an abandoned benthic trawl net, which unfortunately continued its killing assignment as a mindless *ghost net*. He described the marine life entangled in the net, and in particular, the newborn bottlenose dolphin, which elicited a faint cry from Eva lips. Kurt then chronicled his entire dive, beginning with the basking shark masquerading as a great white shark, the vast shoal of sardines, plankton bloom, his cutting away of the creatures from the net, and finally the arduous task of severing the net from the rocky reef. In descriptive detail he recounted his ascension to the surface where he observed numerous creatures feasting on the buffet of sardines including a trio of basking sharks and the four bubble-spewing humpback whales. He concluded his summary with the journey home, the slow task of dragging the net through miles of ocean, and once at the lab, having it hauled off to the dump.

"That was just day one?" Eva said impressed. "You must've been exhausted!"

"A tiny bit," said Kurt with a warm smile. "But, the thought of gold lying scattered across the ocean floor miraculously keeps the adrenaline flowing."

"What happened on days two and three?" asked Timbrook.

Kurt grinned complacently before responding. "Saturday, on two separate occasions, we thought we had struck pay dirt. The *hits* by our metal-detecting towfish were loud and solid, instantly raising our expectations. The first underwater target turned out to be the commercial fishing vessel *Del Rio*, a purse seiner, which sank in 1952. There wasn't a whole lot to its debris field other than chunks of rusting hardware, a massive diesel engine, propeller, and a few planks of rotting wood. We learned the ship's identity after plugging its GPS coordinates into the National Oceanic and Atmospheric Administration's shipwreck database. According to NOAA's online records the *Del Rio* mysteriously caught fire while fishing off of Anacapa Island, burnt down to its waterline, and then sank."

"Anyone die?" Eva wondered.

"No. The fishermen were lucky. There were two other fishing boats in the vicinity which immediately came to their assistance."

"Thank God!" Eva said.

"What about the second target?" Timbrook asked.

"It also was a shipwreck, but this is the interesting part—its location doesn't exist in the NOAA database."

Timbrook smiled with understanding. "You said, 'its location doesn't exist in the NOAA database,' which implies that you some-how know the identity of the ship."

"I should never underestimate you," Kurt said impressed. "While I was exploring the wreckage with the drop-down video camera, Petersen was combing the Internet for information re-garding shipwrecks off of Anacapa Island that have never been found. There are several, but the one most similar in size to our wreck was the *Steamer Lotus*, which foundered in September 1921 due to a fire in her cargo hold. The steamer was 92 feet from bow to stern, 115 gross tons, and was made out of wood. She originally was built to haul lumber out of San Francisco, but in 1921, the year she sank—and this is the intriguing part—she was operating between Ensenada, Mexico, and San Diego, hauling something much more valuable than timber. Care to guess what that was? Kurt waited for their response, but received only blank stares and shrugged shoulders. He decided to give them a clue. "In 1919 the United States Constitution was amended criminalizing a moral issue." He waited. Timbrook raised his hand like a compliant student. "Go ahead," Kurt acknowledged.

"Eighteenth Amendment," Timbrook answered, "which prohibited the manufacture, sale, or transportation of alcohol and alcoholic beverages."

"Prohibition!" Eva exclaimed.

"Exactly," said Kurt.

"The *Lotus* was a bootlegging ship?" Jake asked.

"No question about it." Kurt replied.

"How did you figure that out?" Mischa wondered.

Kurt laughed. "It really was quite simple—by the vast number of wine bottles, casks, and oak barrels littering the seafloor. A wayward fish could get drunk down there."

"Did you retrieve any of the beverage containers?" Timbrook asked. "From a historical perspective they'd command a hefty price in today's antique market."

"Not yet, but it's on our list of things to do. And . . . considering how well the ocean preserves liquid in airtight receptacles . . . I bet the contents are still drinkable."

"That will also be on our 'list of things to do'," laughed Timbrook.

"What about today?" asked Eva.

"Today," began Kurt, "we detected the watery grave of just one relic—a World War II-era plane. Our unintentional discovery had an added bonus—the resolution of a naval enigma that dates back to 1945."

Mischa's excited facial expression belied her doubts. "Seriously Dad?"

"Absolutely—although the circumstances surrounding the aircraft's demise was tragic. Let me explain: In February 1945 a Grumman TBF Avenger torpedo bomber was involved in a mid-air collision with a second torpedo bomber during a squadron training exercise off the Ventura coastline. The severity of the impact caused the first plane to make an emergency crash landing into the sea near Anacapa Island. The pilot and belly gunner survived, but the dorsal gunner bailed out and was killed. That wreck has been thoroughly explored by divers since the invention of scuba gear.

The second aircraft, with a crew of three, was also extensively damaged, and it too spiraled into the ocean. Unfortunately, its exact crash site wasn't known, and in spite of a thorough investigation by the United States Navy, neither the plane, nor its crew-members, was ever found—until today."

"Are there . . . still bodies?" Eva gasped.

Kurt hesitated before responding. "The plane settled on the bottom in an upright position virtually unscathed except for a severed rudder and damage to its two tail-fins. The Grumman Avenger had an interesting design feature; a large plastic canopy that stretched across the entire crew compartment, which to my surprise, was pretty much intact except for several deep cracks near the pilot's window. When the fifteen-thousand-pound plane slammed into the ocean its interior flooded within seconds. The crew, strapped into their seats, didn't have a chance especially since an 'ejection seat' didn't exist during World War II. This particular Grumman bomber was equipped with three bucket-type seats, which were clearly visible through the plastic canopy. As I ran the underwater camera along its entire length, situated in each individual seat—in a somewhat disorganized pile—was a flight helmet, deteriorating parachute, tattered clothing, and poking through the garments, the skeletal remains of a human being."

"That's morbid!" Jake declared.

"Gruesome," added Mischa. "I'd hate to be a diver down there."

"You'll have to notify the Navy," Timbrook advised.

"I know," said Kurt. "The United States Navy and the National Oceanic and Atmospheric Administration will be delighted by our two discoveries. That disclosure, however, will only take place *after* we've concluded our search for the *Winfield Scott*. The sudden uncovering of two significant wrecks by a private party, within days of each other, might raise more questions than we currently care to answer. They've been down there for decades; a delay of a few more weeks won't harm anyone."

"Next-of-kin from the Avenger might not appreciate that," said Eva.

Kurt looked at Eva, noticed the intensity in her eyes, and slowly nodded. "You're right. If we haven't found the *Winfield Scott* by Tuesday afternoon, I'll notify the Navy first thing Wednesday morning."

"Thank you," she said.

"One other thing," added Kurt, "it's obvious that the plane has remained untouched since the day it crashed."

"How do you know that?" asked Eva.

Kurt smiled for the first time since discussing the Avenger wreck. "Its four Browning machine guns—they're still poised for action. Marine looters are notorious scavengers of the sea especially if the object has intrinsic value. If the plane had previously been discovered—those formidable guns would have been stripped within days."

"Thank God for the silence of the sea," Timbrook murmured. "Disturbing or desecrating a tomb—no matter where it's located—is an unconscionable act." After a short pause, he continued: "The only exceptions . . . legitimate historical research, or its family." He then glanced at Mischa and Jake who looked relieved.

The warbling sound of an incoming text caused everyone at the table to reach for their cell phones. Kurt, the apparent recipient, said, "It's mine; sorry, just give me a second." After checking the message he announced, "It's Petersen but I think he's drunk."

"Why do you say that?" Mischa asked.

"Because he's drinking beer tonight and his text makes no sense." Kurt typed a quick reply: 'Beer affecting your brain?'

"What's in his message?" Jake asked.

"I'll read it," said Kurt. "It's time to order the Crown Ambassador Reserve. I had an epiphany while getting buzzed on beer! I know where the *Scott* gold is. I'm going crazy because I can't tell anyone. P.S. That's 40 bottles in case you've forgotten."

"Is he talking about a bet?" Timbrook asked.

Looking slightly awkward, Kurt said, "Yes . . . I offered to buy him a month's supply of beer if he located the gold."

Laughing sarcastically Eva said, "The University would be proud of you since they're big on professor-student interaction, and what better way to do it than through a beer bet."

"He's over 21 and a graduate student," Kurt said defending himself.

"I think it's a great bet," Jake said reassuringly.

"Thanks son, now I feel much better." An additional incoming text stopped the discussion. "It's Petersen again," Kurt explained. He read it out loud. "I've *only* had three beers so *obviously* I'm not drunk. Tomorrow, you'll see. Two more Corona's and then it's off to the land of Nod. Adios my friend. P.S. Good luck sleeping tonight! Ha, ha, ha."

"Confident chap, isn't he?" Eva said dryly.

"He definitely knows his stuff," Kurt acknowledged. "By tomorrow afternoon—we'll know for sure."

"And by this time tomorrow we'll have explored Painted Cave," Mischa said enthusiastically.

"Which means that it's time to end this evening so that we're all rested come sunrise," Timbrook advised.

"True, but not until after dessert," Kurt insisted. Hearing no argument against it, he got up from the table and walked into the kitchen. As he was about to reach into the freezer for the ice cream his cell phone chimed. It was Petersen; he was sending a follow-up text. "The answer lies in the Control Box data. I reviewed it prior to the party. It all came together after a few beers. I guess I just needed to relax. Anyway, that's how I know. Trust me—I'm brilliant." Kurt stared at the text until the phone automatically closed it out. *Petersen was right,* he thought, *it would be a sleepless night.*

28

It was almost 9:00 a.m. and Negrete was fuming. Goebbel, at the last minute, had insisted on joining this morning's waste disposal trip and as a result of his late arrival, their departure from the dock was a full two and a half hours later than their usual time of 4:00 a.m. It was now almost mid morning—the fog had lifted and the sun was bright—hardly the optimal conditions for a clandestine operation. The three barrels of pathological medical waste and four barrels of biotech animal remnants would take at least a half hour to dispose of, and that was assuming the fifty-five gallon drums sank when shoved overboard. Over time he had learned that one out of seven bobbed like a wine cork, requiring a considerable amount of hands-on effort before the stubborn container succumbed to the effects of gravity and sunk slowly, but surely, to the bottom of the sea. Pancho, his burly crewmember, was down in the engine room, scrubbing the oily floor. Goebbel had ordered him out of the wheelhouse so he could be alone with Negrete. Shade, *Lucky Lady's* other deckhand, was out sick. Negrete's scowling mood was easily picked up by Goebbel who was seated in the second captain's chair.

"It's Monday . . . Mr. Paranoid," Goebbel said bluntly, "we're the only assholes out on the ocean. Southern Californian's are weekend boaters—that's why we dump on Monday. The Coastguard, Harbor Patrol, and Department of Fish and Game, they're all back in port sipping a Starbucks café latte. So relax—besides, we have an important matter to discuss."

Negrete stole a suspicious glance at Goebbel before returning his eyes back to the sea. Now he understood why his boss was onboard. Cruising at fifteen knots the *Lucky Lady* was about four miles north of the western end of Santa Cruz Island. "Like what?" he asked.

"Shade."

Negrete swallowed hard. "What about Shade?"

"Don't bullshit me—you know what's going on."

"He's bedridden."

"I don't give a crap about that . . . it's *why* he's sickly, and what he wants out of it."

"Have you talked to him?" asked Negrete.

"I have his friggin letter!" Goebbel shouted. "The little weasel of a man can't spell, but he's intelligent enough to threaten me with blackmail."

"He has no health insurance; he told me he just wanted *West Coast Seafood & Aquaculture* to pay for his medical care."

"How nice," grinned Goebbel in the same manner as a cat after cornering a mouse. "Imagine that—a former drug-shooting, whore-banging, Mexican gang member who just happens to have HIV and hepatitis C, and is now blaming his misfortune on a righteous American company. I should be honored to pay whatever he asks . . . medical bills, wage loss, pain and suffering, and a shitload of cash in order to take care of all his future needs. Would that be fair?"

Negrete was smart enough not to answer. "What's in his letter?" he asked.

"I'll read it to you—it's short and to the point." Goebbel removed a white envelope from an inner pocket of his black leather jacket. Inside the envelope was a piece of beige stationery.

> 'Deer mr. Goebbl: I got my diszeases from bad blood from a barral on your boat. HIV and Hep C. Im very sick and cant work. I'll need lots of money. I don't want to file a legal claim, but lawyyer said I should. He also said youd get in a lot of trouble if I did. Something about illgal activity. I would like to settle my case without a Lawyyer. Please send check for a million dollars. I give you a weeek. Mail to address on envulope. Sincircly, Raul Alvarado (reel name).'

"I wasn't aware he'd written a letter," Negrete said in an apologetic voice barely above a whisper. "What are you going to do about it?"

Goebbel glared angrily at Negrete as if he was looking at a moron. He then erupted into derisive laughter so loud that it bounced off the walls of the wheelhouse, and which abruptly ended with a bout of choking. After regaining his self-control, he stared with ruthless intimidation into Negrete's eyes. *"What am I going to do about it?* My friend, my precious friend," he said sarcastically as he wrapped a muscular arm around Negrete's right shoulder, "you are so very naïve for someone who has two murders under his belt; I humbly stand here truly amazed. You ask—what am 'I' going to do about it? The answer—absolutely nothing! The real question is this: *What is Negrete going to do about it?* And the obvious answer: 'Whatever it takes boss; just give me two days and Shade will no longer be a problem for the company.' And that, my loyal employee, is the *only* response I expect from you."

"Two days?" Negrete repeated.

"By Wednesday evening," Goebbel hissed. "He's way too dangerous. You're the one that recruited and hired him, which makes the conniving worm your responsibility. If your conscience begins to bother you, just view it for what it justifiably is—mercy-style euthanasia. The man's slowly dying; ending his suffering is an act of benevolence."

Rather than respond and inadvertently say the wrong thing, Negrete just nodded, and was rewarded by an approving smile.

"Good," said Goebbel, "it's always nice to end a business discussion on a positive note, and, as an aside, as soon as we're done seeding the ocean depths with some high-quality waste, I'll have you drop me off at Platform Grace. I have a follow-up interview scheduled later this afternoon with an attractive female reporter from KCLA 9, and that's a question and answer session I would not want to miss—especially the 'After the Show-Show.'"

Negrete understood exactly what Goebbel meant by *After the Show-Show*. A reporter involved in a quid-pro-quo—it wouldn't be the first time, especially in the competitive Los Angeles market. Gazing out the forward cabin window he noted that they were less than a quarter of a mile from Santa Cruz Island, and that his ship was fast approaching a section of the island known for its spectacular sea caves. At that moment, Pancho walked into the wheelhouse.

"Engine room's cleaned," he announced. "What do you want me to do with the oily rags?"

"Toss them overboard of course," Goebbel replied. "They're worthless at this point."

Pancho said, "Okay," and obediently walked back out in order to comply with Goebbel's command.

"We have company," Goebbel warned. He was pointing at a small watercraft located just outside the entrance to a massive sea cave. "Hand me the ship's binoculars?" he demanded.

Negrete opened a cabin drawer and pulled out a pair of Barska 7x50 mm Deep-Sea Marine binoculars, and passed them to Goebbel. In addition, without being asked, he immediately throttled back the engines, decreasing the *Lucky Lady's* speed down to a crawl.

Goebbel spent several minutes focused on the unknown ship that appeared to be at an idle at the cave's entrance. A few minutes later, it slowly began to make its way into the cave's mouth and soon disappeared from view. "What cave is that?" Goebbel asked.

"Painted Cave."

"If memory serves, it goes back a long way."

"Over a quarter of a mile," Negrete acknowledged.

"Hell of place to have an accident," Goebbel said, with a devious grin.

"Did you notice something wrong with their boat?" Negrete asked.

"Not yet. Do you know who owns that ship?"

"No," responded Negrete, "it was too far away."

"University of Malibu, Marine Laboratory. The university's name is stenciled on its transom along with the word *Nessie*."

"The boat's rather small for a research vessel."

"Probably more maneuverable in a sea cave," Goebbel speculated. "Do you know who's on board?"

"No."

"I do. Two individuals who want to destroy my aquaculture business. One's a doctor and the other's a marine lab employee. For the last month they've been conducting a secret investigation that if made public would financially ruin my enterprise. I won't allow that. I made an inner vow—that the next time I observed them prowling the sea in one of their ships—that it would be their last. Today, on my own future grave, that solemn pledge will be fulfilled. Take us in, and I'll get Pancho; we have an operation to plan."

Negrete watched as Goebbel made his way out of the wheelhouse. He gently moved the throttle forward, accelerating the ship to three knots, and then steered the *Lucky* Lady toward the entryway. His stomach was in knots—something that he was not used to. First . . . Shade on a *hit list,* and now two unknown professionals—individuals who probably had not a clue as to the ruthlessness of the person they were investigating. He began to wonder why the prospect of murder was troubling him. It hadn't been a thought process for him when he was back with his gang. First the professor from South America, now Shade and these others. Not normally a reflective person, Negrete tried to think this one through and he realized that his past infractions against humanity were primarily made as a gang member loyally protecting his status and his turf. Kill or be killed was a way of life and that philosophy was never questioned. But he had been away from the gang life for some time now and was in fact enjoying what would be considered by non-gang standards as a 'normal' life. This new existence had had an effect on him—making him more aware of his loss—not only his, but of others. Shade had been a good friend, and these other people he was expected to eliminate were also living everyday normal lives; they weren't expecting, nor did they deserve, to have their lives ended. As the *Lucky Lady* was nearing the cave's entrance, Goebbel and Pancho returned. Goebbel had a smile on his face. It was apparent that they had been talking.

"Pancho's plan is perfect," he said jubilantly. "Either the man's a creative genius or he's one loco Mexican." Both men then burst into laughter.

Negrete tightened his grip on the ship's wheel. Pancho was a self-taught expert on homemade explosive devices. As the ship passed under the cave's rocky threshold he involuntarily ducked. Once inside he observed that the marine lab vessel was less than a hundred yards away, and was slowly inching its way deeper into the cavern. Goebbel, he realized, had lied; besides the two middle-aged adults there was an old man and two young teenagers—a boy and a girl. He could hear their lively chatter echoing off the grotto walls. The knot in his stomach continued to twist until the pain became excruciating. He quickly downshifted into neutral, which brought the *Lucky Lady* to a standstill, and hurriedly ran out onto the deck. At the rail he puked. He watched as his vomit descended into the depths. *What was he going to do?* He had not a clue and immediately heaved a second time.

29

Shortly before 7:30 a.m. the Boston Whaler, *Nessie*, with its five passengers, weighed anchor from Scorpion Cove. Cruising at fourteen knots, the eighteen-mile journey to Painted Cave had taken approximately ninety minutes and Mischa's seafaring duty at the helm was about to come to an end. Throughout the short trip, Jake had vigilantly stood by Mischa's side scanning the ocean for any sign of the giant oarfish. He and Mischa had hoped their unusual friend would still recognize the distinct sound of the boat's engine, as it had done before, and make an appearance. A one-gallon bucket of half-frozen squid still rested at Mischa's feet—uneaten, and now emitting a fishy stench as the cephalopods continued to thaw. Regrettably, the creature had failed to show up, disappointing Timbrook, Eva, and Dr. Sedrak, who had looked forward to their own encounter with the exotic fish. "Maybe on the way back," Mischa had murmured wistfully. She was worried that the oarfish had permanently returned to its abode in the black abyss. Jake nodded in silent agreement and moved forward to find a suitable sightseeing seat.

Arriving at the entrance to Painted Cave, Mischa shifted the Mercury outboard engine into neutral. While the ship was idling, she got up from the Captain's chair, and in a ceremonial voice said, "I hereby relinquish my command," humorously transferring

Nessie's helm to Timbrook who would now guide the nineteen-foot craft into the innermost passages of the second longest sea cave in the world.

"Thank you helmswoman," Timbrook said with a wry smile, "I'm honored to assume command from such a masterful skipper."

"Your compliment is duly noted," Mischa said with a warm smile and a quick laugh, after which she joined Jake in the bow and squeezed into a cushioned sun lounger that was barely large enough for two people.

"Painted Cave," began Timbrook who was also functioning as their tour guide, "stretches 1227 feet inward from its 100 foot-wide, 130 foot-tall entrance. It was formed along a geologic fault that extends throughout the entire cavern. Fifteen thousand years ago the cave began as a narrow fissure that slowly became eroded by the hydraulic impact of battering waves, compressed air, and the abrasive effect of suspended sand, gravel, and rocks carried by the rushing surf. Over time these tremendous forces began to gradually wear away zones of basaltic weakness creating the spectacular sea cave that now looms before us. Santa Cruz Island has approximately 120 wave-cut caves, and neighboring Anacapa has over 135 similar type caves. But, this is the 'Granddaddy' of all such subterranean grottos—Painted Cave—who's natural beauty has been compared to that of an ancient gothic church."

"Why's it called *Painted Cave*?" asked Eva.

"The answer to that," laughed Timbrook, "I'll leave to your own momentary observations." He then re-engaged the throttle.

Mischa felt the boat move forward, but at an almost imperceptible rate, allowing ample time to view the imposing arched gateway. Numerous brown-tinted swallow nests were caked along the overhang, and cormorants nested on the rocky ledges. Santa Cruz Island Live Forever succulents hung from the sheer cliffs. As the boat slipped beneath the irregular and chunky threshold, the reason for the cave's descriptive name became readily apparent: emblazoned into the volcanic walls like a painted tapestry were wavy patterns of vibrant greens, yellows, purples, oranges, blues, reds, and vivid whites; bright hues of red and green marine algae adorned the seawater-splashed walls. "That's incredible!" Mischa said aloud as her voice echoed off the prismatic-colored walls. "It's like an indoor rainbow, but more stunning because it will last forever."

"So many dynamic colors!" exclaimed Eva. "How's it possible?"

"Primarily through mineralization from leeching rainwater combined with the caustic effects of saltwater," began Timbrook, "along with variegated lichen, brilliant algae, and igneous rocks that are deeply-colored."

"The name, 'Painted Cave,' is certainly apropos," Dr. Sedrak confirmed, "and the colors don't end at the entrance, but look to continue into the very heart of the cave."

Pointing at the surface of the water Jake added, "And the underwater scenery . . . it's just as beautiful."

Mischa responded to her brother's assertion by staring into the crystal-clear water. In the intertidal zone she spotted orange, purple, and red sea stars clinging to submerged rocks, delicate golden brittle stars, jumbo rock scallops encrusted in camouflaging moss, ebony-colored mussels, giant green anemones, gooseneck barnacles with bright red suction cups, a smattering of cobalt-blue and pearl-white sponges, and hundreds of purple sea urchins occupying every nook, boulder, and interstitial crevice on the seafloor. "It's definitely on par with the walls," she agreed.

Timbrook stopped the boat when a dozen amiable and curious harbor seals began circling their vessel. The smaller seals were emitting short, high-pitched squeals, while the larger ones were vocalizing deep, low frequency roars.

"What do they want?" asked Eva.

"What do you think?" laughed Timbrook. "They're the dogs of the sea, and they're doing what dogs do best—begging for food."

"Which means," Mischa suggested, "they know we have squid."

"That's a distinct probability," Timbrook assured her, "since harbor seals have a highly developed sense of smell."

"Then we better feed them," she announced, "but only half a bucket—I want to save the rest in case the oarfish shows up on our return trip." Mischa had Jake divvy up the squid—six per person—which disappeared in less than a minute. While they were hand-feeding the seals it became obvious that the little ones were the pups, while the more stocky seals were the parents which explained the differences in the quality of their roars.

"That was fun," said Dr. Sedrak. "It's nice to meet a friendly seal."

"I couldn't agree more," Eva sighed.

"These playful seals are just the tip of the iceberg," Timbrook reported. "Wait until we reach the cave's inner chamber."

With a slightly apprehensive look, Eva asked, "What's in the inner chamber?"

"Hundreds of California sea lions; the creatures inhabit the chamber's rocky ledges and cobblestone beaches. The refuge is almost pitch-black and their tumultuous barking can sometimes be quite eerie. But, we brought plenty of flashlights, so it shouldn't be a problem."

Eva managed a weak smile as she moved closer to Dr. Sedrak. "You're right," she repeated, trying to reassure herself. "It shouldn't be a problem."

"They're loud but harmless," Timbrook clarified as he edged the throttle control lever slightly forward, re-engaging the engine. At an unhurried pace he piloted the boat deeper into the cavern. At the three-hundred-foot mark the walls began to narrow along with a lowered ceiling. "We're about to enter into the temple of the gods," he announced.

Gazing into the depths of the cave, Mischa was awed by the cathedral-like chambers which became progressively smaller the further back she looked. It reminded her of reflected images in opposing mirrors that seemed to go on forever. The walls of each arched chamber were coated in spectral colors—red, yellow, green, blue, indigo, and violet. "It's absolutely stunning!" she said breathlessly. "They're sculpted like individual throne rooms worthy of an earthly king."

"Painted Cave," Timbrook insisted, "is a grotto that certainly lives up to its name."

As they were staring at the cavern walls, the reflected sunlight suddenly dimmed, instantly muting the brightly hued colors and intricate rockwork.

"We're not alone," Dr. Sedrak reported, nodding toward the cave's entrance.

Immediately all heads turned in the direction indicated by the doctor.

"That's a big ship," Jake declared.

Timbrook shook his head and stated cautiously. "That craft is out-of-place; it doesn't look like a tourist or dive ship, and its size suggest that it's a service-type vessel more commonly used for resupplying the offshore oil rigs."

"Blue-collar spelunkers," asked Eva rhetorically, "enjoying an early lunch break?"

"What's a spelunker?" asked Mischa.

"Caver," replied Eva.

Scowling, Timbrook said, "More likely poachers after lobsters since the season closed over two months ago. Painted Cave is famous for its population of sizeable lobsters. The crustaceans thrive in the nocturnal environment which allows them to forage twenty-four seven. Today being Monday, the ocean is typically deserted of watercraft—making it an ideal time to illegally harvest lobsters."

"Assuming your supposition is correct," Dr. Sedrak began, "and they are poachers, can you contact Fish and Game from inside this cave?"

Shaking his head, Timbrook said, "Good question, and the answer is no since *Nessie's* VHF Radio isn't capable of transmitting a signal through this rocky fortress."

"What about the depth of the water—for a boat that size?" asked Mischa.

"This is a deep water cave," Timbrook replied. "The depth ranges from forty-five feet at the entrance to about twenty feet near the back of the cave. There's plenty of water underneath that vessel to keep it from grounding."

"Not wanting to burst your conspiratorial bubble," Eva said interrupting, "but there's the distinct possibility that the ship's crew and passengers may be adventurers just like us, and all your worries and concerns are for naught."

"That may be true," Jake said, "but if they do turn out to be good-for-nothing bad guys, I'll let you know."

"Thank you Jake," Timbrook said in an appreciative tone, "you're now our deputized game warden."

Mischa smiled at hearing Timbrook's emboldening words. Knowing her sibling—who enjoyed receiving a compliment as much as anyone else—he would now scrutinize the trailing ship with eagle eyes. Mischa's own observations of the vessel had not revealed a whole lot; it was definitely a mercantile-type craft versus a private yacht, was two-toned in color—deep blue and ivory white—had a forward cabin, and seemed to be well maintained. It was difficult to obtain an overall view of the ship because her only perspective was of its towering bow section. The name of the boat remained elusive since that snippet of helpful information was stenciled on its stern. The only details about the vessel's actions that raised a red flag were the absence of any obvious passengers or crew, and the disquieting appearance that the ship was shadowing them.

"We're nearing the gateway to the inner chamber," cautioned Timbrook. He asked Dr. Sedrak to pass out a headlamp and a hand-held flashlight to each person and then explained: "The headlamps and flashlights are both powered by lithium batteries and are equipped with ultra-bright LED's with 200-lumen output; that's enough energy to shine a beam of light up to 300 feet.

The chamber is approximately two hundred feet long, one hundred and twenty-five feet wide, and fifty feet high. Obviously your flashlights will be more than adequate."

"From the cave's dripline . . . how far have we travelled?" Eva wondered.

"We've motored almost eight hundred feet," Timbrook confirmed.

"And the inner chamber?" asked Eva.

"It begins around nine hundred feet; but, prior to passing into that section we must first navigate through a narrowed gullet that measure's fifteen feet high, sixteen feet wide, and stretches forty-five feet. Once we've passed through that constricted channel—all daylight will instantly vanish and it will be as if night has suddenly descended—and your flashlights will immediately become your new best friend."

"Is it dangerous?" asked Eva.

"No—it's as safe as a vehicle tunnel on land. Fortunately there's no discernible current and I've piloted through this same passage on many prior occasions." To Jake, he asked, "Any monkey-business with that large ship?"

"Nothing, but its forward progress has slowed considerably."

"That wouldn't surprise me," said Timbrook. "The cave tapers significantly around the six hundred foot mark making for some tricky seamanship beyond that point. That boat is too bulky for the gullet which means it'll have to reverse course shortly."

"How much longer until we pass into the channel?" asked Eva.

"We'll be entering the gullet in less than ten seconds," warned Timbrook. Flipping a switch located on the console he turned on the boat's running lights.

As they neared the entryway Mischa could hear the throaty yelps and ominous groans of hundreds of unseen creatures reverberating from deep within the chamber. The unearthly sound had the effect of making her skin tingle, especially as her inner psyche flooded her consciousness with recent memories of the demented sea lion that had almost killed her dad and Eva. She instinctively shuddered as she quickly relived the deadly encounter. In order to try and erase the painful images from her mind she closed her eyes at the exact moment *Nessie* was propelled into the narrowed gorge. The echoing effect of the confined space amplified the roguish noise from the barking sea lions causing her body to tremble. As the ship drifted further into the gullet she could hear the agitated animals sliding off the adjoining ledges and into the water. After a few long seconds Mischa sensed that they were almost through the connecting cut and she began to relax. Just as she was about to open her eyes the small boat was violently rocked by a resounding thud—an awful primal roar—followed by the vitriolic scream of a terrified woman. "Eva" Mischa shouted as she opened her eyes.

30

"How's the hangover?" asked Kurt.

"I don't have a hangover," Petersen said irritably. "I was late because I forgot to set my alarm—that's all. I *only* tossed down five Corona Lights last night which is almost the same as drinking water considering it has an alcohol content of *just* 3.7 percent."

"What's the alcohol content of a bottle of Crown Ambassador Reserve?"

"10.2 percent . . . and five of those bad boys could easily do some serious damage."

"Are they in the cards today?"

"Absolutely—by mid-afternoon forty of those bodacious bottles will be singing my praises on your platinum credit card."

Kurt smiled; that's what he wanted to hear—an egotistical graduate student who was as confident in his data as he was in the final results. Petersen had arrived at the Scorpion Cove dock almost a half hour late, disheveled, and *looking* disagreeable—the presumed aftereffects of too much alcohol versus waking up late. Kurt was glad it was the latter. He needed a fully functional Petersen for today's outing. It was now 8:45 a.m. and the *Serenity* was approximately two miles from the pier, heading in a northeast direction, and cruising at a speed of twelve knots.

"I'm ready for the Control Box's GPS telemetry," said Kurt.

Petersen reached into the front pocket of his Levi jeans and extracted a crumpled piece of white paper. "I don't trust my memory after last night's drinking binge," he said with a hint of sarcasm. Using the *Serenity's* GPS keypad he punched in two coordinates—latitude and longitude, and then touched the send key—instantly uploading the new information into the ship's navigational system. *Serenity*, which was operating on autopilot, immediately altered its compass direction from northeast to southeast.

Sitting in the captain's chair, Kurt watched the ship's wheel rotate approximately 30 degrees as it responded to the new coordinates. Petersen, who was occupying the co-pilot's seat, had his feet up on the dashboard, and was munching on a chocolate protein bar infused with peanut butter. Reaching under his seat Kurt retrieved a stainless steel thermos that he had earlier filled with Sumatra coffee, a small amount of rich cream, and several tablespoons of organic sugar. Using the thermos lid, which also functioned as a mug, he poured himself a steaming cup of coffee. Cradling the metal cup Kurt could feel the liquid rapidly heating his fingers. Petersen, who despised coffee, was quickly downing a 16 oz can of Monster energy drink that was probably packed with more caffeine than the entire thermos. After a few sips of the warm beverage, Kurt asked, "What exactly was your 'epiphany' regarding the treasure's apparent location?"

"As the unemotional Captain Spock of Star Trek fame would say, 'through logical deduction.' Remember that first hit on the Pulse 12 that came and went like a massive bolt of lightning—"

"Yes—and I was contemplating turning the boat around."

"—*that moment!*" exclaimed Petersen. "But, before we could process its significance, the second major hit occurred, which at the time we thought was just a continuation of the first hit. Unfortunately, the second hit turned out to be an abandoned ghost net that required our attention for the rest of the day. The mistake we made, which I didn't recognize until after I went back and reviewed the Control Box data, was making the assumption that the two magnetic findings were interrelated—the *supposed* rubble trail. The benthic trawl net—as my soused brain suddenly realized—didn't leave a path of debris. When we discovered it, the meshwork and metal plates were entirely intact. In my enlightened state I asked the following question: If the first hit wasn't connected to any rubble trail . . . then what did the Pulse 12 cross-over that created a short-lived but huge magnetic field?"

Kurt's racing brain caught the gist before Petersen was able to finish. "Oh my God, that *is* brilliant, and embarrassingly obvious. You think it's the gold from the *Winfield Scott.*"

"Absolutely," Petersen said exuberantly, and then after a moment of reflection, "at least that's my solemn belief. But, in a few hours we'll know for certain."

Kurt extended his right hand and warmly clasped Petersen's left shoulder. "I'm okay with whatever happens today—whether we find the gold or not. I'm proud of everything we've accomplished thus far; I also realized that without your special skills and expertise this mission would have floundered from the get-go. I may be the head honcho, but you're the reason why this undertaking may actually succeed."

"Or fail," added Petersen softly.

Kurt stole a quick glance at Petersen and noticed that his melancholy word did not match his demeanor. He was actually smiling. "Humble aren't we?"

Laughing, Petersen said, "I've never been modest about my abilities, and right now they're not indicating failure. On a serious note—thank you for the kind words—they mean a lot."

"You're welcome."

For the next five minutes they rode in comfortable silence. Kurt emulated Petersen's casualness by also placing his feet up on the dashboard. He leaned back in his chair, and enjoyed two more cups of coffee. With the ship on autopilot he was able to let the self-acting GPS guide them toward their destination, which was approximately five miles southeast of Cavern Point. Cruising at twelve knots Kurt estimated they were about fourteen minutes from the site. Petersen, after a throat-clearing cough, interrupted the tranquil moment.

"Assuming we find the gold—what's the legal ramifications? From the stories I've read in nautical magazines it would seem that these types of discoveries almost always end up in court."

"It's called the 'Maritime Lawyer's Employment Act,'" joked Kurt, "which unfortunately, isn't far from the truth. But, you've asked a good question. After my meeting with Emily Flannigan in Carmel, I knew that the *Winfield Scott* was carrying more than passengers. Within days of my get-together I hired the most prestigious Maritime law firm in Los Angeles to advise me on this very issue."

"Being proactive—that's a sign of a smart man," Petersen acknowledged, with just a small ironic smile. "What advice did your money buy?"

"That Maritime Shipwreck Treasure Law, the Law of the Sea Convention, Law of Finds, Law of Salvage, and the Abandoned Shipwreck Act of 1987, are still evolving with the discovery of each new shipwreck. In layman terms it simply means that each case is dependent upon its own particular set of facts."

"That doesn't sound encouraging."

"Under our specific circumstances, it's not too bad."

"How's that?"

"There are four factors that a Federal judge considers in awarding salvage rights to the finder of sunken treasure. The first—the location of the treasure trove; second, whether the wrecked ship was owned by a government or a private party; third, whether the owner of the shipwreck has abandoned the vessel; and fourth, whether there has been any dishonest conduct by the treasure hunters."

"Applying those four elements to our situation—what insights did your lawyers provide?"

"Well, their first instruction was to earnestly pray that the treasure exists outside California's three mile territorial limit, or else the state could assert title to the wreck, complicating any recovery efforts. But, if the treasure is where we think it is—in the area near the ghost net—then we are in International waters and the state cannot claim ownership. In regard to the second issue, fortunately the *Winfield Scott* was owned by a private party and not by any governmental entity."

"Why is that important?"

"Because a governmental entity *never* relinquishes its sovereignty over a sunken vessel no matter *where* it's located. In addition, to add insult to injury, neither the passage of time nor lack of any attempt at salvaging the lost ship is sufficient to establish abandonment."

"How long is 'never'?"

"Hundreds and hundreds of years. In February 2009 a salvage company called Odyssey Marine Exploration, found the British warship *HMS Victory*, which was lost in 1744. The ship carried several tons of gold and silver worth an estimated one billion dollars. The British government claimed ownership over the *Victory* and eventually forced the Odyssey to negotiate a sliding scale deal before they could even proceed with salvaging its gold, silver, and other valuable artifacts."

"So, the old adage, 'finders-keepers,' isn't applicable to shipwrecks."

"Not in today's world. Except, as mentioned earlier, if the ship is in international waters, privately owned, and definitely abandoned. So far we are okay with the first two criteria."

"It would seem that the *Scott's* property—lying on the bottom of the sea for over 160 years—has unequivocally been abandoned."

With a knowing smile, Kurt teased, "You're clearly smarter than you look since that's the exact, 'unknown answer to a multimillion dollar question,' put forward by my attorneys."

Laughing, Petersen said, "It's obvious, we don't need a Wall Street lawyer to figure that one out since our salvage operation has nothing to do with the *Winfield Scott*; our search is for just a small segment of its cargo, lost at sea, miles from the actual wreck site."

"Exactly . . . we have no interest in the *Scott* . . . just its jettisoned freight."

"If the cargo is as valuable as we think it is—you'd think someone would have filed a claim for the missing merchandise by now?"

"That's the interesting part," agreed Kurt, "and I had my law firm specifically look into this issue by combing through insurance, public, and private records. After an exhaustive search they were unable to locate a single document indicating that any claim had ever been made or paid to the *Scott* owners, its passengers, or for that matter, the United States Government. Whatever was blown away from the *Scott's* hull, technically speaking doesn't exist."

"Hopefully, by late afternoon, we'll have proved that wrong."

"Hopefully," Kurt repeated.

"What about the fourth factor—dishonest treasure hunters?" asked Petersen.

"That applies to salvage companies that are guilty of fraud, dishonest conduct, or entering a foreign state's twelve-mile territorial waters without permission and consent."

"Do we have permission and consent?"

No, we don't need it, we're United States citizens."

"But, we're still inside our country's territorial waters."

"Yes, by several nautical miles."

"Is that a problem?"

Kurt scowled before replying. "The answer unfortunately is yes, and my lawyers are presently working on that question. Finding the treasure within twelve miles of the coastline means the U.S. will have the legal right to claim a lion's share of the re-covery, but we're still entitled to a Salvor's award."

"How much?"

"If my lawyers are worth their salt . . . twenty-five percent."

"That's terrible; we do all the work and the government get's three quarters."

"Welcome to taxes," laughed Kurt.

The familiar chime of the GPS unit signaled that they were approaching Petersen's coordinates. Kurt immediately disen-gaged the autopilot and slowly brought the ship's speed down to two knots, and then after a moment, to a creeping idle. Keeping an eye on the GPS he maneuvered the *Serenity* until the latitude and longitude lines intersected. "We're here," he announced. Using the ship's docking thrusters Kurt held the ship in position until the anchor impacted the bottom. Shifting the engines into reverse he slowly backed up until he felt the anchor dig into the seafloor. With the anchor properly set he shut down the engines.

"What's our depth?" Petersen asked.

Checking the depth finder, Kurt answered, "One hundred and twenty feet."

"Bottom profile?"

Kurt reviewed the fish finder and sonar unit before respond-ing. "Flat—probably a sandy seafloor."

"No suspicious mounds or unusual structures?"

"Nothing out of the ordinary other than some minor eleva-tion changes."

"How much?"

"A few feet at most—probably caused by underwater currents shifting the sand around."

"That's not what I wanted to hear," groaned Petersen. "I ex-pected a huge mound of gold to magically pop up on your sonar."

"It's never that easy," Kurt reminded him.

"I know," Petersen agreed. "It's my expectations—they're run-ning a bit high."

"As are mine," Kurt confirmed. "It's time to deploy the Pulse 12 Towfish. In less than ten minutes we'll know whether your previous magnetic hit still exists or if it was connected after all to the trawl net."

Petersen required five minutes in order to prepare the Pulse 12 for deployment. Normally, the device was towed behind the ship, but today they would just drop it over the side, lower it to about one hundred and ten feet, and pray for two things—a high-pitched tone to emanate from the Control box, and a wildly swinging meter needle—both indicators of a huge magnetic field.

"Moment of truth," exclaimed Petersen as he began lowering the bright yellow torpedo-shaped instrument from the boat's stern. The altimeter, attached to the underside of the device, kept them informed as to the Towfish's distance from the seafloor. After a minute he announced, "Seventy-five feet."

Kurt stared at the Control box, willing it into action, but was met with cold silence. The sound of falling snow would have been louder.

"Eighty feet," proclaimed Petersen, who had purposely slowed its descent.

After another thirty seconds, "Eighty-five feet."

Kurt could feel beads of sweat forming on his forehead. Instead of continuing to gawk at the Control box he switched his gaze to the surface of the ocean and stared at the path taken by the descending Towfish.

"Ninety feet," Petersen called out.

Kurt wiped the perspiration from his forehead with the palm of his right hand and then noticed that the sweat glands underneath his armpits had suddenly become moist along with an offensive, musky odor.

"Ninety-five feet," Petersen said dryly.

Kurt returned his eyes back to the Control box. He felt like he was staring at a deceased robotic member of his own family. *It's broken*, he thought.

"One hundred feet."

"It's not functioning," Kurt declared. Petersen looked at him as if he didn't understand what he meant. "The Control box," he explained, "it's on the fritz."

Stopping the Towfish's descent, Petersen briefly examined the unit, and then shook his head. "There's nothing wrong with it; it's receiving data from the Pulse 12 but that device doesn't become fully functional until it's barely skimming the ocean floor."

"Thanks—I knew that," said Kurt slightly embarrassed, "I'm just a bit more anxious than I expected."

Petersen laughed. *"You're anxious?* My arms are shaking, my stomach is tied up in knots, and my back is covered in sweat."

Kurt was relieved to hear that his shipmate was as much on edge as he was. "I think our new nicknames should be "Pins & Needles," he said with a nervous laugh. He watched as Petersen continued to lower the Pulse 12 but at a reduced rate— approximately one foot every ten seconds.

After what seemed like a minute stretched to several he reported, "One hundred five feet."

Kurt could feel an anticipatory dread rising up within him; in less than three minutes he would either be crushed emotionally, or launched onto cloud nine. The wait was excruciating. The Control box—an inanimate object with a computer brain— remained speechless.

"One hundred ten feet," Petersen advised, and then added, "Give me a shout when that box comes alive."

Kurt turned away; mentally he couldn't watch the box any longer. If there was a 'hit' he would hear the sound. He fastened his eyes on Santa Cruz Island. He thought about his children. Right now they would be exploring Painted Cave. He missed them. He also suddenly missed his deceased wife, Tessa. *Tessa* he said silently to himself—he hadn't mentioned her name in weeks. It would be nice to have her support. Unexpectedly, an image of Eva slipped into his mind, creating an instant conflict. *Was it wrong to think about Tessa and Eva at the same time?* He asked himself. Gratefully, his attention was diverted by a solitary, American white Pelican, circling the ship. Brown pelicans were a familiar sight, but a white pelican—that was extremely rare. He wondered if the noble creature, with bright white plumage, was a positive omen.

"One hundred and twenty feet," Petersen murmured, "and I have bad news—we've impacted the seafloor."

Taking his eyes off the pelican, Kurt looked at Petersen in shocked disbelief and then shook his head; *it wasn't possible. The graduate student had been so cocksure about the location of the gold that the likelihood of his being mistaken hadn't entered Kurt's mind.* He scanned the skies searching for the white pelican. He turned 360 degrees. *Nothing!* The creature had simply vanished. *A bird as a harbinger of something miraculous—absolute falderal,* he thought disdainfully. *I'm a scientist, not a New-Age kook.* He looked at Petersen and thought the young man was on the verge of tears. "It's alright," he said softly, "unfortunately it was the trawl net all along."

"I was so certain," lamented Petersen. "I don't like being proved wrong."

"It's okay . . . we'll keep searching. We have the rest of the week."

"Yea—I know—but it's still a huge personal disappointment. If you don't mind I just need a few minutes alone in order to collect my thoughts before I retrieve the Pulse 12."

Kurt watched Petersen as he slowly walked to the bow. He felt sorry for the student. The reality of life's disappointments had begun their awful tally. At age 39 Kurt had racked up quite a few. He sat down in a deck chair and waited. He had his own thoughts to deal with. Foremost, where to search next; they had already covered the *Scott's* most likely routes. Expanding the search beyond the initial grid was something he had hoped to avoid. It would be a long, long week. He could feel a headache coming on.

"Hey Kurt," shouted Petersen. "Come check out this bird."

Kurt reluctantly got up from his seat. Birds weren't on his 'most favored list' at the moment. Upon reaching the bow he was temporarily dumbfounded. It was the white pelican.

"That's one whacko seabird," explained Petersen. "When I first arrived at the bow it was sitting sedately in the water five feet off the front of the boat. As soon as it noticed that I was staring at it, it began doing donuts. I've counted seven thus far. I think it's sick."

Kurt didn't say a thing. His earlier thoughts about the aquatic bird came rushing back. *You don't believe in signs,* he told himself. *This is crazy! It's just a stupid bird.* He watched it complete another revolution before it flapped its wings and took off. It circled the ship once before catching a thermal and gliding toward Santa Cruz Island. Kurt immediately ran the calculations through his head. *The Serenity was 25 feet long; the Towfish, with a slight current, struck bottom at least 2 feet off the stern, and if you add the pelican's 5 feet, you have 32 feet. Thirty-two feet—is that enough?* "Petersen," he asked, "what's the detection envelope for a Pulse 12 that's dropped over the side?"

"None until its suspended ten feet above the seafloor, and then it has a range of about twenty-four feet. Why?"

"Do you believe in providence—the guidance of God over the wild creatures of the earth in order to directly affect human affairs?"

"No—why would he do that?"

"I don't really know . . . but I bet Timbrook could answer that question. My best guess—he's a caring God who believes in Holy nudges."

"You're scaring me Professor. What has all this got to do with our search?"

"The white pelican—I think it was a sign."

"A sign of what?"

"Simplistically stated—missing the mark. Humor your Captain and reposition the Pulse 12 approximately five feet off the bow."

"Where the nutty pelican was?"

"Exactly—as if the bird was still sitting there."

"You're the boss, but it's going to take at least ten minutes; I have to retrieve the Towfish."

Petersen required fifteen minutes and two round trips before he was able to transport all the equipment to the bow, and then another three minutes to reconnect everything. "All set," he reported.

"Toss it into the middle of the white pelican's circle," Kurt directed.

Petersen lobbed the thirty-five pound instrument into the imaginary ring, and then began doling out cable at a rapid rate, while keeping a watchful eye on the Control box.

"Thank you," Kurt said, "for indulging your eccentric Captain."

"Any time," laughed Petersen. "But, if we strike gold, I may have to re-evaluate my religious beliefs; in the meantime, I'll still want my forty bottles of beers."

"Jesus turned water into wine—I think God's okay with a few beers."

"A beer-slugging God, I like that. We're approaching ninety feet," warned Petersen.

Kurt's relaxed attitude suddenly evaporated along with his new found faith in divine intervention. It was quickly replaced by the illusion of having experienced a similar disagreeable result only twenty minutes earlier.

"One hundred feet."

Kurt abruptly gagged on a driblet of stomach acid that had risen up his esophagus and into his mouth. *What was he thinking—making a decision based upon the behavior of a seabird?* If the employees at the marine lab ever learned of his critter gaffe, he would be harassed with animal jokes for years.

"One hundred ten feet."

Kurt stopped breathing.

When the Control box siren suddenly erupted with a deafening sound—Kurt fell to his knees, and when the thundering alert caused a throbbing pain deep within his ears, he quickly covered them with his hands. With both ears shielded the intensity of the ringing clamor mercifully waned, but soon another, much louder sound, overpowered the Control box warning signal—the shrill voice of Petersen screaming hallelujah, hallelujah, glory hallelujah—apparently the brilliant graduate student had just found religion.

31

For a horrifying moment Mischa feared she had suffered a catastrophic injury to her eyes until she recalled Timbrook's warning about the inner chamber being pitch-black. *Stop panicking*, she said reprimanding herself. Then immediately the panic returned: "Eva," she shrieked—"Are you okay?" She waited a few seconds but received no response. Suddenly a headlamp was switched on illuminating the boat's aft section where both Eva and Dr. Sedrak were located. Lying prostrate across the rear transom was a large, tan-colored female sea lion that appeared as terrified as Eva. Evidently the ship's passage through the narrow gorge had startled the creature from its resting place, but instead of slipping unnoticed into the opaque water it had accidentally crash-landed on the ship's stern. Within a few seconds of being 'lit-up,' the animal, with a departing grumble and a menacing growl, used its strong foreflippers to propel itself off the fiber-glass transom and back into the sea where it quickly disappeared.

"Anyone hurt?" asked Timbrook who was the only one on the boat with the presence of mind to activate his headlamp. The powerful light was now focused on Eva, whose alabaster complexion conveyed deep shock.

After a moment's hesitation Eva said with a slight stutter, "I'm not physically injured, but it did scare the living daylights out of me." She then offered up a brave smile.

Dr. Sedrak wrapped his arms around Eva and held her protectively. "It was close," he clarified. "That beast almost collided with our heads. Another few inches and I doubt we would have . . . ." The doctor abruptly stopped talking and gave another concerned glance at Eva.

"I'm sorry," said Timbrook. "Nothing like this has ever happened before; if it had, I would have warned you of the possibility. I think it would help lessen our apprehension if everyone turned on their lights; dispelling the darkness is always good for the soul."

"I absolutely agree," said Jake who energized both his headlamp and his hand-held flashlight. Others in the boat quickly followed suit, and soon the entire chamber was ablaze in resplendent light that reflected off the steep walls causing a luminous effect that transformed the dark inner chamber into a natural ballroom of majestic proportions.

"It's unearthly but beautiful," Eva said with a touch of awe, though she found she had to almost shout in order to be heard above the din of the barking sea lions. "Why's this cave so loud?" she asked.

"It's the curvature of the walls," explained Timbrook, "they amplify the sound in the same way as they diffuse the shafts of lights."

"An underground 'Hollywood Bowl,'" said Dr. Sedrak, "with its own refractive light show."

"Exactly," Timbrook confirmed.

"Just how many sea lions are there?" asked Eva.

"It depends upon the season. During the winter months the population swells, but as summer approaches the numbers drop considerably. Right now we're probably down to fifty individuals."

"Remind me to never visit during the winter months," Eva insisted.

Nodding, Timbrook said, "Agreed."

"What other creatures reside within this cavern?" asked Mischa.

"A variety of fish life including rockfish, opaleye, perch, sheepshead, blacksmith, and senoritas, green and black abalone, a great quantity of lobsters, and my favorite—harmless spiny dog-fish and swell sharks which will occasionally congregate in such numbers that they will literally carpet the bottom of the cave," replied Timbrook.

"Are they here now?" asked Eva.

Smiling Timbrook said, "Let's hope so because it's an amazing sight, but first we should begin our nature tour with the cave's most prominent residents—the bellowing noisemakers."

Mischa watched as Timbrook re-engaged the throttle, and at less than a quarter of a knot, steered *Nessie* toward the back of the chamber. After traveling approximately 135 feet the boat came to a stop just shy of two large granite ledges. On the left side of the rocky shelves was a shallow-water cove that terminated with a small cobble beach, and to their right, a much wider and deeper inlet that ended with an impressive cobble and sand-floored beach. The ledges themselves were overrun with a quarrelsome colony of adult and juvenile sea lions whose incessant barking was almost unbearable. *Your estimate was a bit off*, thought Mischa. "*Fifty?*" she said with a hint of sarcasm.

"Fifty times two," said Timbrook correcting himself.

"Why do they like huddling in the dark?" asked Dr. Sedrak.

"It primarily involves safety," said Timbrook. "There are no predatory sharks or killer whales in here; plus, they're not exposed to the elements."

"If you ask me I think they're really just vampires trapped in the body of a seal," Jake joked.

"Cute bro," laughed Mischa, "but it's actually a sign of intelligence when a species takes advantage of its environment in order to enhance its survivability."

"If that's true," said Jake, "where on the intelligence scale do cockroaches fit in?"

"They're bugs," said Mischa in a deprecating tone, "they don't count."

"I'll remember that the next time I squeeze the bejeezus out of one."

"Excuse me," said Timbrook interrupting, "we're not here to discuss the intelligence or value of the orthopterous insect. However, if you have anything to add to our sea lion knowledge I'm all ears."

Mischa mouthed the word no, and Jake just shook his head also indicating no. "Thank you," said Timbrook. "Our next stop is just outside the large passage to our right, where hopefully the bottom will be crawling with a slew of amorous sharks."

"They're mating?" asked Eva.

"That's my belief," said Timbrook as he began to guide *Nessie* toward the passage. "It's the only logical explanation for *why* these normally reclusive sharks would gather in such large numbers in a relatively confined space. They're certainly not foraging for food which leaves only one other option—shark sex."

"There are young children on this boat," Eva said heedfully.

"It's okay," said Jake. "Mischa and I are well-versed on that subject. Our favorite television shows are Animal Planet, the Discovery Channel, and Nat Geo, so whatever hanky-panky these sharks are engaged in will seem tame compared to the content on those channels."

"Well thank God for true-to-life television programs," declared Eva with a smile. "I now feel relieved."

"We're here," announced Timbrook. It had taken him less than two minutes to reposition the boat. Their new location was approximately fifty feet off the beach. "For some reason," he continued, "the sharks like this particular section of the cave. It has a cobble bottom, intermixed with sand, and the water depth is around six feet. The clarity is excellent so the lack of a facemask won't matter. Shine your lights directly into the water, and if the sharks are here, you'll spot them right away."

Leaning over the edge of the boat's rail, Mischa directed her two light sources into the glassy water, elucidating the bottom. After a few seconds she let out a loud squeal; swarming across the seafloor were dozens of small sharks. The slender spiny dogfish sharks were approximately three to four feet in length, deep gray in color with white spots, short snouts, large eyes, and moved in a snake-like fashion. The sturdy swell sharks ranged in size from two to three feet, drab brown with colorful golden-brown mottling, large mouths, short snouts, and catlike eyes. Its common name was based upon the fact that it had the ability to engorge its stomach with water or air to about twice its natural size in order to deter would-be predators. Unlike the gregarious dogfish sharks, the swell sharks were content to lie sedately on the bottom and stirred only if a new shark joined their assemblage. As far as Mischa could tell—based upon her limited knowledge on the mating habits of sharks—none of the creatures seemed engaged in any type of fish shenanigans.

"Do these sharks pose a threat to the sea lions?" asked Dr. Sedrak.

"No," reported Timbrook. "In fact, it's the exact opposite; the sea lions will occasionally consume one of them. These somewhat timid sharks only forage on small reef fish and crustaceans and are about as dangerous to the sea lions, or to humans for that matter, as a detachment of butterflies."

"Shark's—the same as butterflies—that's a first," laughed Eva.

"That might be stretching it," Timbrook agreed, and then changing the subject said: "Many years ago while exploring Painted Cave I discovered a Chumash pictograph at the back end of a deep passage. The drawing was scrawled across a mound of boulders rather than on a flat surface, making the rock painting almost illegible—which is why I believe its very existence continues to remain hidden. Today, as a special treat, I will show you that pictograph whose abstract message still eludes me. It's my hope that one of you will be able to decipher its true meaning."

"That's being overly optimistic," laughed Dr. Sedrak.

"Not necessarily," responded Timbrook. "A fresh set of eyes . . . with their own unbiased perspective . . . you just never know."

"I'll give it a shot," said Jake. "I've always been good at interpreting optical illusions and 3D autostereograms."

"Thanks son," smiled Timbrook, and then to everyone said: "There's one additional item. About five years ago I removed a speck of paint from the pictograph and had it radiocarbon dated. The artwork had me stymied, and as a consequence, I became obsessed with its actual age. The test result, however, was not what I expected. In my own mind I had calculated its age between seven hundred to a thousand years, but the ultimate finding stated otherwise—it indicated an approximate creation date of 1815 to 1825."

"Why is that significant?" asked Eva.

"Because in 1822 the Chumash Indians were involuntarily evicted from Santa Cruz Island and relocated to the Spanish Mission in Santa Barbara, which means," he said slowly in order to give his final words special emphasis, "we have a pictograph that was intentionally sketched during this troublesome time period."

Her countenance brightening with understanding, Eva asked, "Are you suggesting that the rock painting is a message about the Chumash's forced departure?"

"That's my assumption," said Timbrook cautiously, "and that's why I'm interested in your opinions. This boat is filled with insightful individuals regardless of their age."

"I'm ready to take a crack at it," Mischa said helpfully. "But where's the passage?"

Pointing toward the bow of the boat, Timbrook said, "Fifty feet away. The passage lies just beyond that cobble and sand-floored beach."

"I love mysteries," said Eva, "this should be fun."

"In that case, put on your analytical caps," laughed Timbrook as he re-engaged the throttle and piloted the nineteen-foot skiff toward the beach. "I'll be running the bow of the boat up on the sand," he warned, "so hang on to the rails."

Mischa grabbed the stainless steel rails and braced for the impact. She estimated their speed at less than two miles per hour when the Boston Whaler struck the beach. Thankfully, the collision was essentially negligible causing only a slight jarring motion as the sand slowed and then stopped *Nessie's* forward momentum. After Timbrook shut down the engine Mischa, along with Jake, stepped out of the boat. The others soon joined them.

Is the ship secure?" asked Dr. Sedrak who had illuminated the front of the boat. Only three feet of the bow section was on dry sand.

"Yes," Timbrook assured him. "By early afternoon we'll be experiencing one of the lowest tides of the year—a negative 2.1. With this type of extreme tide the water level in this cave will drop by as much as seven feet. In another two hours over half of *Nessie's* hull will be high and dry. This ship won't be floating away anytime soon—that I can guarantee you."

"Thanks—I had forgotten about the low tide," Dr. Sedrak said somewhat apologetically.

"That's okay," said Timbrook. "Nobody in their right mind would want to spend the night in stygian darkness."

"Sea lions would," Mischa quickly chimed in.

"Touché sister," said Jake who rewarded Mischa with a brotherly cuff to her shoulder, and then turning to Timbrook asked: "How far away is the pictograph?"

"One hundred feet beyond the beach. It's a fairly easy hike, and, if everyone's all set to go, I'll lead the way."

Mischa nodded her assent, as did Jake. Dr. Sedrak said "I'm ready," and Eva said, "I can't wait to see it."

Walking in single file, Timbrook guided them up the cove's sandy beach, across twenty feet of layered cobbled stones, and into a cave-like passage that was eighteen-feet-high and fifteen-feet-wide. *A cave within a cave within a cave,* thought Mischa. The floor, she noted, was composed of irregular dark igneous basalt, which contrasted nicely with the white-colored gypsum walls. As they continued further into the cave they had to circumvent several breakdown blocks—huge chunks of stone that had fallen from the ceiling. *Not today!* She prayed silently. With a total of ten light sources—five flashlights and five headlamps—the entire subterranean tunnel was as bright as a summer day. The passage maintained its large dimensions until it abruptly ended at a wall composed of twelve to thirty-six inch boulders. The pictograph was painted across a vast number of individual boulders.

"All these powerful lights really help bring forth the various drawings," Timbrook said excitedly. "On my prior trips I only had a small flashlight."

Mischa found a large stone with a flat surface and sat down. She figured it would take some time to properly analyze the different images. While she pondered the artwork she listened to the ongoing discussions and opinions.

"Red seems to be the primary color used," said Dr. Sedrak, "and then black monochromes."

"There are also touches of blue, yellow, and white," added Eva.

"Is that a rainbow?" asked Jake.

"There are actually two rainbows," answered Timbrook.

"Why two rainbows?" Jake asked.

"That's one of the pictograph's enigmas," replied Timbrook. "The *Rainbow Bridge* legend only speaks of one rainbow. According to the myth the bridge was created by the Earth Goddess, *Hutash,* because Santa Cruz Island was becoming too crowded and the noise was starting to annoy her. She made a bridge out of a rainbow so that some of its Chumash inhabitants could move to the mainland."

"The one bridge is dark—primarily red and black, and the other is light, with blues, yellows, and whites," Dr. Sedrak remarked.

"Do those stick figures represent humans?" asked Jake.

"Yes," said Timbrook.

"On the dark bridge they appear to be walking toward the mainland, and on the lighter bridge they appear to be walking back to the island," said Eva.

"That's interesting," said Timbrook, "I've never noticed that before. That dichotomy doesn't exist in the original *Rainbow Bridge* legend.

"Also . . . at the end of the light bridge—on the island side—is that a coyote floating above it?" asked Eva.

"It certainly is," declared Dr. Sedrak. Turning to Timbrook he asked: "What role does a coyote play in Chumash legends?"

"The coyote is considered the father of the Chumash nation. In our legends he is referred to as *Sky Coyote*. This benevolent animal works on behalf of the Chumash, providing food and sparing our lives. He watches over us from a lofty position. For the Chumash this creature epitomizes the word faith."

"There are lots of animals depicted in the pictograph," observed Jake. "What do they symbolize?"

"Which ones?" Timbrook inquired.

"Bear?"

"Strength, courage, and leadership."

"Eagle?"

"Courage, vision, bravery, and leadership."

"Mountain lion?"

"Power, grace, and stealth."

"Deer?"

"Gentleness, freedom, and agility."

"Owl?"

"Wisdom, poise, and healer."

"Otter?"

"Compassion, playfulness, and laugher."

"Hummingbird?"

"Beauty, energy, and peace."

"And," said Jake, "a pair of dolphins?"

"Loyalty, compassion, and love."

Eva's facial expression indicated a sudden insight. "The artist's choice of animals follows a definite pattern," she insisted. "They all have positive human attributes; none of the animals portrayed exhibit a negative trait."

After a moment of quiet reflection, Timbrook said, "That's an excellent point, and it doesn't end with the animals. The elaborate sun-like circle drawing with twelve pulsating rays exemplifies strength, and the symbols for fertility—water and rain—represent the basic elements for sustaining life. In addition, the other semi-abstract designs depicting squares, circles, triangles, zigzags, crisscrosses, parallel lines, and pinwheels, are spiritual concepts normally crafted by a shaman or medicine man—meaning this site was consecrated—a portal into the sacred realm."

"This was *not* your typical pictograph," Eva declared. "It was drawn for a specific reason and I think I know what that purpose was."

"*What?*" said Timbrook and Dr. Sedrak at the same time.

"Hope."

"Hope?" repeated Timbrook.

"Yes," said Eva, "a message of hope and a prophetic declaration that the Chumash would someday return back to their spiritual roots."

Timbrook looked at Eva and acknowledged her intuitiveness with an understanding smile. "The second rainbow bridge . . . a reversal of the first."

"That's my educated guess," said Eva. "In the dark days of 1822 this perceptive artist had an optimistic vision for the future of the Chumash nation, which he then painted on the stones of Painted Cave."

"Thank you for your thoughtful discernment," whispered Timbrook.

The cave fell silent for a minute as everyone reflected on Eva's revelation. Dr. Sedrak was the first to break the intimate moment. "There's just one painting left that we haven't discussed," he said indicating a drawing that stretched across three boulders. "A wooden canoe, which if my math is correct, is being propelled by twenty-four stick figure paddlers, and attached to its bow, the figurehead of a swordfish."

"That diagram, unfortunately, is a nice piece of Indian fantasy," laughed Timbrook. "The largest plank canoe ever constructed could only seat twelve grown men. The swordfish carving, however, has its own special meaning: only the chief's canoe was outfitted with this type of figurehead. In today's vernacular it would be referred to as the 'royal canoe.'"

"So," quipped Dr. Sedrak, "it was the *Air Force One* or *Presidential Limousine* of the Chumash era."

Nodding, Timbrook said, "That's an appropriate analogy." He then turned to Mischa and said in a soft voice, "You've been as quiet as a mouse which is a bit unnerving since that's not the Mischa I'm used to. Your opinion matters to me and I would appreciate hearing your thoughts on what's been said."

Standing up, Mischa giggled and said, "You don't have to worry about me; it was nice to just listen for a change." She then walked over to the rock wall and stood in front of it. Turning around, she continued: "My thoughts—the same as yours; I agree with everything that's been said regarding the pictograph. But, there's one major detail that bothers me; it's a huge red flag that needs to be addressed." She then purposely paused and enjoyed the questioning looks on everyone's faces.

"That's the Mischa I know," chuckled Timbrook.

After a few more suspension-filled seconds Eva scornfully asked, "*What?*"

"This," she said, waving her arms in front of the boulders.

"The pictograph!" exclaimed Dr. Sedrak. "I thought you were in agreement with our discussion."

"I am," replied Mischa, "but it's the stacked boulders that I have a problem with; they're just too perfectly aligned to be a pile of random rocks."

"It's just a natural-occurring rockfall or cave-in," objected Dr. Sedrak.

"Is it?" challenged Mischa. "For a mass of free-falling rocks they seemed to have miraculously landed one on top of the other, all the way to the ceiling."

"The world is filled with geologic features that are difficult to explain," countered Dr. Sedrak.

"Not this one," insisted Mischa. "I think it's man-made."

"By whom?" asked Eva.

"By the same people that painted the pictograph." Mischa replied.

"The Chumash? For what reason?" argued Dr. Sedrak.

"I don't know," said Mischa.

"If my vote counts in this debate," interjected Jake, "I agree with my sister."

Dr. Sedrak shrugged and said, "Assuming for the sake of argument that what your postulating is accurate, and that the Chumash were responsible for assembling a stone-like tapestry in the rearmost section of a sea cave a quarter of a mile from the open ocean, then it's a major archeological achievement that the scientific community needs to investigate."

Mischa raised her voice and said, "Absolutely not! It was constructed in secrecy—"

Coughing loudly, and then gagging as if he was choking, Timbrook immediately garnered everyone's attention. "I've always wondered about the location of this pictograph," he began in a soft voice. "Why here in the tail-end of a darkened cave? *Why?* It doesn't make any sense. I've asked myself on many occasions— what makes this cave so special that the Chumash were willing to expend their resources, time, and energy in order to create a se- ries of drawings that few people would ever see? Someday I hope to resolve that issue, but obviously not today. In the meantime, based upon my own personal observations, I'm also in agreement with Mischa; this rock wall—for whatever reasons—was built by my ancestors."

Mischa was about to express her gratitude for Timbrook's en- dorsement when she heard the supersonic crack of what sounded like rifle fire. "What was that?" she asked. Before anyone had a chance to respond a bone-chilling explosion occurred followed by a thunderous boom that was instantly followed by a superheated shock wave that rocked the entire cave, hurling Mischa into the stone wall where she slumped to the ground in a dazed condition.

As she struggled to regain her footing, she heard Timbrook scream, "The rock wall—it's collapsing!" Mischa immediately tried to crawl away, but her muscles wouldn't respond to her men- tal commands. *I'm going to die,* she thought. Feeling powerless, she awaited death. "There you are," said a male voice that her confused mind was unable to identify. She then felt two athletic arms encircle her upper torso, after which she was half carried and half dragged a short distance away from the crumbling wall. After a few seconds the person stopped and loosened his grip. "You're safe now," he whispered. As she looked up to see who had risked their life to rescue her, a baseball-sized chunk of rock that had become dislodged from the ceiling crashed into her head, and before she even had a chance to say thank you, she had lapsed into a state of unconsciousness.

32

The tattered brown cotton cloth dangling from the ship's rail was a godsend; Negrete first wiped his lips and chin of vomit splatter before turning the small towel around, blowing his nose, and expelling a wad of gastric mucus. After he had finished cleaning himself it suddenly dawned on him that he had just used one of the oily rags that Pancho had supposedly tossed overboard. He quickly found a fresh cloth and scrubbed his face clean of the engine oil. He then dumped both rags into a five gallon plastic bucket that was used as a waste receptacle. *I need water,* he realized as he tried to swallow—his throat burning from the stomach acids that had scorched the inner lining of his esophagus. Strolling back into the *Lucky Lady's* wheelhouse he was met by the icy stare of Goebbel. Ignoring his piercing gaze, he casually walked over to the ship's refrigerator, opened the door, and removed a 16 oz bottle of mountain spring water. He then re-assumed his spot in the captain's chair, unscrewed the plastic lid, and slowly sipped the cool liquid.

"Why the hell did you just spill your guts?" demanded Goebbel.

Negrete was thankful for the water delay; it had given him time to think. "Food poisoning."

"From what?" snapped Goebbel.

"Raw sushi."

"That's bullshit—I've never heard of a Mexican gangbanger eating sushi."

"*Ex*," Negrete corrected, and then said condescendingly, "there's a few rolls left in my refrigerator; when we get back you're free to sample them."

"Don't patronize me," warned Goebbel, and then in a stony voice asked: "You getting squeamish on me—having second thoughts?"

Putting down his water bottle Negrete paused, took a deep breath, and responded by asking his own question. "So being afflicted with an illness is now a sign of weakness?"

"In my book it is," Goebbel said with a menacing grin, "especially when the individual pukes his cookies at the wrong time and has no other symptoms."

Negrete grunted dismissively. "I guess we're at an impasse. Either you trust me or you don't."

For a brief moment the wheelhouse was filled with an uncomfortable silence as Goebbel appeared to be weighing Negrete's words. "Just drive the ship," he finally said, "and stay at least two hundred feet behind the marine lab's boat. I don't want its passengers becoming anxious over our presence." Goebbel then turned to Pancho and said, "We'll need both cylinders; this cave is bigger than I thought."

Without any additional clarification, Goebbel left the wheelhouse and walked toward the stern of the boat where he disappeared down an external stairwell. There were only two compartments at the bottom of the steps: the engine room and the ship's supply room. Since Goebbel knew nothing about diesel engines, it was a given as to which room he was entering. "What did he mean by 'both cylinders?'" asked Negrete.

Pancho chuckled and replied, "Propane tanks . . . he figures we'll need two in order to accomplish our mission."

"And what *exactly* is that?" Negrete wondered, although he was certain he already knew the answer. The *Lucky Lady's* kitchen came equipped with two 30-pound LP gas cylinders which had only recently been refilled.

"Collapse the cave and create the biggest tomb this side of the Pacific," laughed Pancho.

"There's two young children and an old man on that boat," whispered Negrete, "innocent passengers who have nothing to do with the investigation against Goebbel's company."

"They're teenagers," said Pancho in a dispassionate tone. "Most of my childhood friends were dead by their age. As far as the old man—he's lived long enough; his life no longer matters."

"So . . . you're definitely okay with Goebbel's plan?"

"You're damn right; I don't give a rat's ass about their lives. I'll perform my job duties in the same obedient way that you're supposed to—without hesitation and without a guilty conscience. If Goebbel doubts your loyalty, or if you're foolish enough to challenge his decisions, you'll be shredded into chum and fed to the sharks. It'd be a real shame if I had to suddenly assumed the Captaincy of the *Lucky Lady* because of your unfortunate demise," Pancho said coldly.

Hearing his deckhand's dishonoring words sparked a wave of righteous anger that instantly inflamed every cell of Negrete's body. As Pancho's immediate boss, and especially as his former 4th Street gang leader, his failure to show proper respect was an egregious breach of street etiquette, and as a consequence, was unforgiveable. Negrete was about to respond, both verbally and physically, when he heard Goebbel's plodding footsteps. "We'll finish this discussion later," he murmured under his breath.

Stepping into the pilothouse Goebbel had a look of determination about him that bordered on madness. In his right hand he carried a 22-carbine rifle, and cupped in his left hand, seven orange-tipped bullets which he was caressing as if they were diamonds. "What the hell!" he yelled. "Why isn't this boat moving? And where's my gas cylinders?"

What an asshole, thought Negrete, who tactfully decided to ignore his boss' tirade and instead just focus on getting the ship moving again. He first shifted the throttle control lever from its neutral position to forward, and then accelerated the ship to about one knot—walking speed for a human being, but the only safe speed for a ship the size of the *Lucky Lady* in a constricted cave.

Pancho, who had appeared somewhat taken aback by Goebbel's scolding, mumbled a half-hearted 'I'm sorry' apology before adding, "I'll need my tools before I can begin." He then stomped out of the pilothouse.

Approximately ninety seconds later Pancho reappeared toting a pipe wrench. The ship's propane tanks were located in the wheelhouse galley behind an aluminum cabinet adjacent to a four-burner gas range and convection oven. Pancho promptly popped the cabinet door open, and after shutting off the gas supply, began disconnecting the two tanks. While he was preoccupied with removing the cylinders, Goebbel was busy inserting six cartridges into the gun's star-shaped rotary magazine. After loading the firearm he chambered the first shell. The rifle was now ready to be fired. The seventh cartridge he held pinched between his right thumb and index finger.

Holding the 22-caliber bullet at eye level he asked Negrete, "Are you familiar with this type of ammunition?"

The orange-tipped ammo was a kind of projectile that Negrete had never seen before. "No," he answered.

"It's primarily used by the military. They're built with a small pyrotechnic charge in their base that's made from strontium compounds and magnesium. It's known as a *tracer round* that yields a burning red light when fired, and ignites flammable substances on contact."

"Isn't it a bit small for a tracer round?"

"Not these exceptional babies," chuckled Goebbel. "They were specifically designed for Special Ops forces. These wonderfully nasty, bantam-sized munitions are unfortunately difficult to come by since they're not sold to the public."

Negrete didn't bother to ask the obvious question: *Then how did you acquire them?* His gang experience had taught him an important life lesson: with money, and power, all things were possible. As he watched Goebbel ogle the bullet his stomach once again began to churn. He also observed that Pancho had already uncoupled the first propane tank and was now working on the second cylinder. "What about the children?" he asked.

"What about them?" Goebbel angrily replied.

Negrete knew he had to be careful with his choice of words. "They're not involved. The adults . . . they can be dealt with on another occasion."

Goebbel scowled. "Every single day 370,000 children are added to the world's population. If a couple of juveniles happen to be in the wrong place at the wrong time and suffer an early departure, it won't make a bit of difference in the overall scheme of things. As far as the adults they could spill their guts tomorrow. As a seasoned businessman I don't believe in wasting a golden opportunity regardless of the collateral damage. No . . . we act today; in twenty-four hours it could be too late."

Negrete bit his lower lip in order to keep himself from saying something that he might regret. "What's the plan?" he asked as Pancho finished disconnecting the final tank.

"It's really quite simple; we first have to locate an area of weakness in the cave's ceiling or walls, plant an explosive device, trigger it from a safe distance, and then sit back and watch as the chamber collapses. And, since there's only one entrance into Painted Cave, once that passageway is sealed, escape becomes impossible."

"Won't the authorities suspect foul play?" Negrete asked.

"I doubt it; they'll view it as a naturally occurring event. Caves collapse all the time. Besides, the government is broke, so they won't spend a penny excavating the rubble. In addition, whatever metal fragments survive the denotation will be buried under tons of rock. It's actually the perfect location for an unsolvable crime," laughed Goebbel.

After a moment of reflection, Negrete had to agree; no one would ever conduct a proper investigation. The marine lab would certainly look into it—wondering what became of their ship and the people on board, but they definitely did not have the resources to conduct a full-scale salvage operation. Goebbel was correct; it *was* the ideal crime scene.

"The tanks are all set to go," Pancho reported.

"About time," Goebbel complained, and then said to Negrete. "Take the ship in nice and slow—we need to locate a deep fissure in order to cause the greatest amount of destruction."

In compliance with Goebbel's command, Negrete reduced the *Lucky Lady's* speed to a half knot. The two ships, he noted, were still two hundred feet apart, with the marine lab boat slowly pulling away now that he had throttled down. When he had first entered the massive cave there was more than enough headroom and elbowroom for a vessel the size of the *Lucky Lady*; but, at the six hundred foot mark it was now a different story. The ceiling had dropped to about twenty-five feet and the width was down to thirty-five feet. At least the water depth, at twenty-two feet, was more than adequate. The *Lucky Lady*, with a beam of twenty feet, and a height of fourteen feet, still had sufficient space to maneuver, but it was getting tight, necessitating some skillful seamanship on Negrete's part. There was, however, one thing he knew for certain—it was now impossible to turn his seventy-five foot boat around. When it came time to leave he would have to travel in reverse until he got to within 300 feet of the cave's mouth. At that point the cavern opened up, allowing the ship to pivot 180 degrees.

While Negrete was absorbed with preventing the *Lucky Lady* from sideswiping the rocks, both Goebbel and Pancho were engaged in scanning the ceiling and walls for the optimal fault line or cavity for their improvised bomb. Goebbel, Negrete observed, would alternate between analyzing the cave's structure to keeping a wary eye on the lab boat. As the small craft neared what appeared to be the back end of the cave, its running lights came on. A few seconds later the ship suddenly vanished.

"Where the hell did it go?" asked Goebbel.

Negrete wondered the same thing. He then searched his memory for an explanation. *Painted Cave . . . the second longest sea cave in the world . . . was formed along a geologic fault that extends over a quarter of a mile . . . and has a somewhat secret*—"I know," he blurted out, and then immediately wished he had kept silent.

"What?" Goebbel demanded.

Negrete swallowed hard. He now had to respond to his own reckless admission. "At the rearmost section of the cave there is a narrow tunnel that connects to an expansive inner chamber. It's essentially a whole new cave even though it's part of the Painted Cave system."

"A tunnel," murmured Goebbel with a thoughtful grin. "How convenient; this could be an answer to a prayer. Take us to the entrance—we need to check it out."

An answer to a prayer! Negrete shuddered. Exactly *who* was answering Goebbel's prayers? It certainly wasn't the God of the Bible that his Grandmother used to read to him, or at least he hoped not. For the next three minutes he painstakingly piloted the *Lucky Lady* past walls of volcanic rock that seemed to beg for an opportunity to gouge out huge chunks of the ship's fiberglass siding. After arriving unscathed at the tunnel's entrance, Negrete shook his head in disbelief. With the ceiling barely five feet above the top of the wheelhouse bridge, and the cave's width down to a mere twenty-six feet, it was a minor miracle that he hadn't damaged the ship. He told Pancho to deploy the vinyl dockside mooring fenders in order to protect the *Lucky Lady* from scraping against the rocks. Once the fenders were in place he released the stern anchor. Normally, when anchoring, he would use the bow anchor, but, because of the atypical way his vessel was positioned, he had to employ the one in the rear. With the *Lucky Lady* now safely moored, he reluctantly joined Goebbel and Pancho who were already out on the bow examining the tunnel's threshold with powerful LED flashlights.

"This is too good to be true," said an ecstatic Goebbel.

Negrete followed the two beams of light and then audibly gasped: Goebbel had indeed received an answer to his prayer. Situated several feet above the tunnel's entrance was another cave that stretched across the entire entryway. Its height varied from just inches at its two outer edges to over five feet around its mid-section. The actual depth was unknown, but it appeared to go back at least ten feet.

"It's perfect," said Pancho. "The hollow recess will amplify the blast."

"That's wonderful," gushed Goebbel who had a broad smile on his face, "but it's a weird place for a cave."

"Not really," said Negrete decisively. When Goebbel looked at him with an inquisitive raised eyebrow, Negrete felt it necessary to explain. "A week ago I was waiting to meet with my parole officer and I got bored and picked up the nearest reading material. It ended up being a book about the sea caves on this island. At first I just looked at the interesting pictures then started doing a little reading. "This cave," he said pointing to the one above the tunnel entrance, "is called a Relic Cave. It was carved out by scouring waves prior to the tunnel that now exists beneath it. These double caves occur when the underlying stone is weaker than the rock above it, and with the passage of time, it erodes at an accelerated rate, leaving the original cave—now known as a relic cave—high and dry."

"It seems our Negrete is getting an education along with a conscience," Goebbel said with a tinge of sarcasm. "In a few minutes it'll *truly* be a relic when it's blown to smithereens." He then started laughing at his play on words and was soon joined by Pancho.

Negrete faked a polite smile.

When the laughter died down, the barking sounds of adult sea lions and the high-pitched squeals of young pups could be heard coming from the far side of the tunnel.

"I hate those good-for-nothing creatures," declared Goebbel. "They eat my game fish and destroy the netting around my fish farms. This is a great day—the elimination of two hostile parties at the same time."

"If my statistical numbers are correct," said Negrete referring to the sea lions while at the same time needling Goebbel, "you'll have to exterminate at least 241,000 individuals if you want to wipe out the entire population along the Pacific Coast."

"It's a start," growled Goebbel, who then promptly changed the subject. "That lab boat could reappear at any moment so we need to act quickly. Besides the two propane tanks, we'll also require a ladder. Pancho, you're in charge of transporting the tanks, and Negrete, the ladder. We'll meet on top of the wheel-house bridge. Any questions?"

Negrete shook his head, and Pancho said no.

As Negrete shuffled toward the supply room where the ladder was stored he felt like an unwilling character in a nightmarish dream whose ending had already been predetermined. The word 'impotency' barely described how he felt. *Was he actually going to help in the murder of five humans—two of them children—deaths that would be agonizingly slow? Starvation—what a tortuous way to die; and, assuming they had a supply of fresh water, how long would it take? Two weeks? A month? Who would go first? Probably the elderly man since his internal systems were already in the process of shutting down. The children would obviously be next, and lastly, the middle-aged adults. There HAD to be something he could do. But what?* Dragging himself down the stairway to the supply room was like embarking on his own personal journey into hell; and, when he picked up the ladder and carried it back up the stairs, he knew he had become an accessory to murder. As he passed the door to the wheelhouse he noticed that Pancho had already removed the gas cylinders. The rifle, however, was still on the kitchen table along with the bullet that Goebbel had showed him earlier. Maybe there *was* something he could do after all. He leaned the ladder against the wall and silently stepped inside. Lifting up the gun he examined the rotary magazine. *He'll know,* he thought, *but by then it'll be too late.* Fifteen seconds later Negrete set the gun back down and quickly left the wheelhouse. At the ship's rail he dropped a handful of lethal rubbish into the ocean before retrieving the ladder. He then headed for the ship's bow where there was a set of stairs that lead to the wheelhouse bridge. As he climbed the stairs he could hear Goebbel and Pancho talking, although their words were slightly muffled.

"You're slower than a tortoise," Goebbel complained as Negrete pulled himself up onto the bridge.

Negrete didn't bother to apologize, "It was an awkward item to carry," he said.

"I don't want to hear your BS," Goebbel snapped harshly, "just get the ladder set up."

From the deck of the bridge to the lip of the relic cave, Negrete estimated the expanse at a hair under seven feet—a space that was easily traversed by the twelve-foot extension ladder. After placing the skid-resistant base pads against a metal bulkhead, he proceeded to extend the ladder to a foot above the edge of the cave, giving it shake afterwards to make sure that the interlocking side rails were secure. "All set," he announced.

Curling his lip, Goebbel said, "It's about time . . . now you can help Pancho with the tanks."

The 30-pound tanks—two feet high and one foot wide— each held 7 gallons of propane and weighed 55 pounds when full. Pancho, who was the first to climb up the ladder, used his left hand to grasp the side railing and his right hand to hold the tank. As he slowly worked his way up the ladder it began to vibrate because of the amount of weight and the angle that it was positioned. Pancho froze his progress for a few nervous seconds in order to allow the swaying to die down, and then after a few choice curse words, continued his climb without any further incident. Negrete followed Pancho and essentially duplicated his shipmate's carrying technique. Fortunately, he didn't experience any excessive wobble. Once Negrete reached the cave's rim, Pancho took charge of the cylinder. Because of the cavern's restricted height they both had to stand hunched over.

The relic cave was made up of a singular chamber roughly twelve feet deep, five feet high, and fourteen feet wide, though narrower in some areas. The interior walls were heavily encrusted with gypsum, the floor paved with polished cobbles. A large pinnacle, surrounded by a sizeable pile of angular rocks, jutted up from the middle of the cave. The five foot low ceiling extended seven feet and then tapered to a three foot crawlspace.

Pancho, after scouting out the 'best location,' began gathering flat cobblestones which he used to construct a platform that was situated approximately three feet from the cave's edge and directly opposite the pinnacle. After several minutes of crude masonry work his two foot high rock table was complete. He placed the propane tanks side by side atop the structure, with the cylinder valves directed toward the back of the cave. "You need some height in order to allow for an easier shot," he said by way of explanation, "plus, it helps disperse the gas." After a slight pause he continued: "I've aligned the tanks with the pinnacle and the jagged stones since these natural projectiles will function in the same way as a case of grenades—blasting rocky shrapnel into the ceilings and walls—which will intensify the amount of destruction."

"You honestly think it's going to work?" Negrete asked.

"Absolutely," laughed Pancho. "This cavern is like an empty bomb casing which is harmless until packed with gunpowder. In our case it's explosive gas, and once this cave becomes saturated with propane vapors . . . it'll turn into one hell of a home-made bomb."

"Aren't we lucky," Negrete barely whispered to himself.

Pancho walked over to the cave's edge and yelled down to Goebbel, "Bomb's ready."

"About time!" Goebbel replied. "Tell Negrete to get his ass down here; he needs to get the ship ready to move out. Once we're all set to go, I'll give you the signal to turn on the gas, and then get your butt down here too, or your body parts will end up becoming one with the rubble."

Negrete could still hear Goebbel's sadistic laughter as he stepped off the ladder and made his way into the wheelhouse. After restarting the engines, he waited a few minutes while they warmed up before pressing a button that raised the stern anchor. When the red light on the switch changed to green, he knew that the anchor was secured. As he held the boat steady, Pancho suddenly walked into the wheelhouse and headed straight for the kitchen table where the gun was located. Negrete had expected Goebbel to retrieve the weapon, not his shipmate. Pancho immediately picked up the rifle and before leaving, turned, and with an intimidating smile, pointed it at Negrete's chest.

"The gas is flowing," advised Pancho, who then raised the gun so that it was now level with Negrete's eyes. "Goebbel said," continued Pancho in a teacher to student belittling tone, "you'll need to reposition the ship 125 feet from the relic cave, and that once you're at the new station, to blow the ship's air horn—your signal to Goebbel to commence firing."

Intentionally ignoring the rifle, Negrete replied with a sneer, "Is that all?"

"It must be done promptly," Pancho stammered, "within two minutes."

"Consider it done," Negrete said. "And if I scrape some paint off the ship's hull during the expedited process, I'm sure he'll understand."

"I'll let him know your response," said Pancho who began a measured amble toward the door while still aiming the gun at Negrete's head.

"Oh . . . one other thing," Negrete said in steely voice just as Pancho was about to exit the wheelhouse, "when we get back to the dock, I'd like to walk you to your car."

Pancho's expression instantly changed from one of superiority to dread as he rushed out the door.

Negrete watched him leave and then shook his head as he shifted the throttle lever to reverse, and began piloting the *Lucky Lady* away from the cave. In a few minutes all hell would break loose. Negrete didn't regret his actions though he knew they would come at a huge price. At best, he would lose his job, his company townhouse, and his company truck. At worse, he would lose his life. But Goebbel was right—he was getting a conscience. Admittedly, he was somewhat befuddled by this change in priorities which had come about in the past few months. He didn't know if it was his Catholic upbringing poking its finger at his conscience, or if all the time he had been spending on the ocean, experiencing its beauty and peace, had brought about this change of heart. What he *did* know, no matter what the cost, was that killing the children on the lab boat was not an option.

Piloting the *Lucky Lady* backwards wasn't as difficult as Negrete had initially anticipated. Painted Cave, he noted, was as straight as an arrow; as long as he centered the ship in the middle of the subterranean waterway he was able to avoid impacting the adjoining walls. At the 115-foot mark Negrete prepared to sound the ship's air horn. At this moment he had two choices: he could continue backing up until Goebbel realized he wasn't stopping which would then lead to a major confrontation, or he could just deal with the consequences at the 125-foot mark rather than delay the inevitable. He decided waiting wouldn't accomplish a thing; it was time to let his decision play out and accept the repercussions.

He brought the ship to a halt and then blew the air horn which sounded eerily similar to a train's warning signal.

After hitting the horn, Negrete started counting the seconds. *One . . . two . . . three . . . four . . . five . . . six . . . seven . . . eight . . . nine . . . ten.* By the end of the tenth second he expected to hear Goebbel vociferously erupt with a whole litany of obscene words. Instead, there was only silence. He continued counting. At the sixty-seventh second he finally received his answer—a personal visit by both Goebbel and Pancho. While Pancho stood guard at the doorway, Goebbel stepped into the wheelhouse. In his hands—clenched as if he was carrying a five foot Japanese fighting stick—was the 22 caliber rifle.

"*Why?*" Goebbel shouted, his face red with anger.

Negrete paused before answering as he watched a thin line of drool suddenly detach itself from the left corner of Goebbel's mouth, fall like a raindrop, and then spatter as it impacted the barrel of the rifle. "Didn't Pancho tell you?"

"*Forget Pancho,*" roared Goebbel who edged a few feet closer until he had invaded Negrete's space. "I want to hear it from your own pitiful mouth."

Negrete peered into Goebbel's eyes and said calmly yet defiantly, "I won't allow you to take the lives of those children—"

"—*you won't allow it!*" screamed Goebbel. "You're nothing but a two-bit ghetto scumbag that doesn't have the moral authority to challenge my decisions."

Smiling confidently Negrete said, "I already have."

"You think so," Goebbel scoffed, "then you have the intelligence of a moron. For your information . . . all you succeeded in doing was delaying the explosion by a couple of minutes."

Negrete quickly analyzed Goebbel's facial expressions and body language for any evidence that he was lying and found none. As far as he could discern Goebbel was telling the awful truth. Negrete then glanced at Pancho whose contemptuous look and derisive laughter immediately confirmed his worse fears—the children's lives were still in danger. "God damn you," he shrieked, as he lunged at Goebbel in an attempt to wrestle the firearm from his grip. The mistake he made, which he realized within a millisecond, was that Goebbel had anticipated his move. At the precise moment Negrete launched his attack—Goebbel swung the rifle in the same manner he would a golf club—butt stroking him with the stock of the firearm. The upward motion catching Negrete on the side of his head, knocking him backwards and into the kitchen table, where he dropped like a ragdoll onto the deck. As he lay sprawled on the floor, Negrete sensed that his skull was fractured and that the nerves in his cervical spine had been traumatized. He had a massive headache, blurred vision, extreme nausea, and paralysis below his shoulders. After vomiting, he attempted to stand up, but his damaged body wouldn't respond to his commands.

"Take him below," Goebbel ordered Pancho. "Tie his arms and legs to a bunk bed. I don't want this noble dunderhead causing any more problems. And, while you're taking care of that, I'll reload the gun." Goebbel then started laughing, bent down until his mouth was inches from Negrete's ear, and began whispering: "I'm aware that you can still hear me, and because you're not yet dead I just wanted you to know—I have a whole case of those tracer bullets—that's 100 rounds. When those 40 grains of copper-plated lead projectiles impact the leaking propane tanks at 2000 feet per second, they'll do two things: ignite the escaping gas, and rupture the tanks. The fusion of those two, in a limited space surrounded by hardened rock, will be truly magical. Try to remember all that as you're lying in your comfortable bed; and, when you hear those loud '*pop, pop*' sounds, it's time to kiss your new-found friends *adios*."

Negrete tried to respond but the throbbing pain in his head and neck interfered with his ability to formulate words. After Goebbel left, Pancho grabbed him by his wrists and began dragging him across the floor. At the inner stairwell entrance he hesitated for just a second before continuing. "Enjoy the ride," he said, as he bounced him down the stairway. Mercifully, Negrete's head was kept elevated, but his buttocks and lower back slammed into each aluminum stair. After the eighth step, they reached the bottom floor and a narrow corridor, which led to the sleeping quarters. At the first bunk room, Pancho opened the door, and with a quick lifting motion, scooped Negrete up, and dumped him onto a thick rubber mattress that was atop a built-in platform bed made out of pine wood.

"Wait here," Pancho said as a sick joke, "I'll be right back."

Moments later he returned with a half-inch thick nylon rope which he used to lash Negrete's hands and feet to the bed.

"You ain't going anywhere soon," Pancho said admiring his work. "And, if you have to use the toilet, make sure you ring the service bell. It'd be a crying shame if you soiled your pants . . . which reminds me . . . you won't need this anymore," he said as he lifted Negrete's wallet, and walked out with a slam of the door.

I failed, Negrete thought miserably. *Not only the children, but also myself.* Being a realist, he had zero expectations that he would ever set foot on the mainland again. Once Goebbel and Pancho completed their current task, their next assignment would be Negrete's burial at sea. He hoped . . . prayed . . . that he would be dead before they tossed him into the ocean. Drowning wasn't something he wanted to experience; he had seen too many movies where people had died underwater, and their desperate struggle seemed torturous.

As Negrete lay prostrate on the rubber mattress he could feel a warm tingling sensation flowing from his neck down his shoulders, arms, back, and legs. "Thank God," he said quietly. Whatever the nerve damage was, it apparently was already on the mend, which meant the paralysis was only temporary. *Maybe there was hope after all,* he thought. Just then he heard the unmistakable sound of gunfire followed almost simultaneously by a cataclysmic explosion and shock wave that rocked the ship as if it was caught up in a thundersquall. The clamor of what sounded like large hailstones pelting the ship confused Negrete for a moment until he realized it was debris from the detonation raining down on the *Lucky Lady*. The 'rock storm' lasted for five more seconds before it was followed by a period of profound silence, which was eventually interrupted by shouts of joy—the beginning of a morbid victory celebration which got louder and louder with each passing second.

"I'm so sorry," Negrete mumbled. He closed his eyes as he tried to hide from the disturbing pictures that were scrolling across his conscience. As the images continued—becoming more vivid with each passing frame—he experienced an overwhelming sense of helplessness. Powerless, and truly all alone, for the first time in Negrete's life, he shed tears of compassion for another human being.

33

"Turn it down!" Kurt shouted. The irritating noise emanating from the Control box was beginning to annoy him despite what it portended.

Euphoric over the magnetic hit, Petersen had progressed from screaming 'hallelujah,' to a vain attempt at mimicking the Harlem Shake. He saw more than heard Kurt's request and ceased his bodily gyrations in order to turn the volume switch off. "Happy now?"

"Don't you think those two types of celebratory expressions are incompatible?" Kurt asked.

Petersen shrugged. "If God's okay with a pint of firewater then he wouldn't mind a joyous man shaking his booty."

"The way you spin, bump, and grind . . . I have my doubts," laughed Kurt.

"You may have a point," Petersen agreed, and then after a slight pause asked: "That white pelican—was it a heavenly sign or just a serendipitous moment?"

Kurt could tell by Petersen's tone that it was a thoughtful question. As a scientist, his belief system was based entirely on the empirical evidence gathered through his lab work or by his observations of the natural world. A supernatural event, impacting

DALE KORNREICH

the real world, was by definition outside of that belief system. *Was the bird's guidance just a stroke of good luck or was an omnipotent entity temporarily manipulating its behavior?* That question, at this stage in Kurt's life, was unanswerable. "I honestly don't know," he finally answered. "In my own mind it's a 50/50 split."

Nodding, Petersen said, "Fair enough; but, if there's a pot of gold underneath the pelican's circular tip-off cue, we're upping the split."

Laughing Kurt said, "Agreed."

"What's next?" asked Petersen. "Drop-down video camera or getting wet?"

"Camera—we'll do a quick survey, and then I'll take the plunge."

While Petersen was engaged with recovering the Pulse 12 Towfish, Kurt prepared the DV-1 camera for deployment. Once the Towfish was safely on board, Kurt began lowering the camera from the bow of the boat. After stowing the Towfish, Petersen grabbed a deck chair and joined Kurt on the bow. He placed the chair in front of the monitor, and sitting down, leaned forward so that his face was just inches from the screen, his eyes alert and unblinking. The word 'riveted' understated the degree of fervency. "A little excited, aren't we?" Kurt asked whimsically.

"Oh my gosh!" exclaimed Petersen. "This is like the best chick flick ever—except a hundred times better."

"I don't know about comparing it to that type of movie, but my heart is pounding as if I'd just finished a 5K race."

"It's fear and stress of the unknown," Petersen clarified, "that stimulates our adrenal medulla producing epinephrine, which increases our heart rate, blood pressure, cardiac output, and carbohydrate metabolism."

"You mean we're having an adrenaline rush."

"Exactly."

Anything interesting on the monitor?" asked Kurt.

"A small school of anchovies, a few blacksmiths, and a pair of female sheepheads. Not a whole lot."

"I wouldn't expect much in the way of aquatic life since we're essentially above a sea of sand."

"That's good for our gold search but not for the fish; without any kelp or rocky structures it's much the same as a barren desert down there. What's the camera's approximate depth?" Petersen inquired.

"My best estimate . . . around 80 feet."

"Forty more feet and we'll be on top of the *Scott's* golden hoard," declared an exuberant Petersen.

"Possibly," said Kurt guardedly. After all the false hits he'd decided it best to keep his exuberance under wraps. He gazed at the monitor and was pleased to see that the water clarity was fair to good with twenty to twenty-five foot visibility. Scuba diving in murky conditions wasn't on today's bucket list.

"What's the depth now?" Petersen asked repeating his earlier question.

Kurt grinned. His shipmate was like an anxious child on his way to Disneyland aggravating his parents by repeating the same annoying four words over and over, 'Are we there yet?' "Ninety to ninety-five feet," answered Kurt.

"Thanks," said Petersen.

Kurt slowed the descent rate as he kept his eyes glued to the screen. At the one hundred foot mark the bottom finally came into view, indistinct, like a mirage on a scorching summer day. As he continued to lower the camera, he strained his eyes searching for any odd-shaped object protruding out of the sandy bottom. Approximately ten feet from the seafloor a massive, diamond-shaped, olive-colored bat ray exploded out of the sand—narrowly missing the camera—and stirring up a dense cloud of sediment.

"I can't see a thing now," lamented Petersen. "How big was it?"

"At least six feet wide and close to two hundred pounds."

"That's a monster of a stingray."

"They don't get much bigger."

"Did you spot anything before it fouled-up our viewing?"

"Nothing."

"Likewise," said Petersen, "and that has me worried."

"Only a small portion of the *Scott's* bow was blown away," Kurt said as a reminder. "Any mangled chunks of wood that survived the blast would have disintegrated years ago. If its gold bars and coins we're after—they're probably buried under the sand."

"Then why bother with the camera?"

"Because you just don't know, and the DV-1 provides our first glimpse without jeopardizing anyone's safety."

"I think you're talking about your own precious hide," laughed Petersen, "since you're the only diver on this boat."

"And that particular asset," Kurt said with a smug smirk, "is a lot more valuable than a gleaming mound of gold."

"That's yet to be determined," Petersen joked, and then added: "The water . . . it's clearing up."

Moment's earlier—when the bat ray had unexpectedly sullied the water—Kurt's innate response was to instantly halt the camera's descent. Now with visibility restored, he continued to lower the camera. After dropping it an additional five feet he commenced a slow, panoramic sweep of the seafloor by following the bow's curved deck rail. After one complete pass, Kurt lingered in the area where the pelican had previously performed its circular dance. "See anything?" he asked Petersen.

"Nothing man-made poking out of the sand, but there are some interesting irregularities in the sand patterns that are inconsistent with the rippling effects caused by an underwater current or storm-generated waves."

Kurt stopped and stared intently at the color monitor for a full minute. "You're right," he said enthusiastically, "the sand dispersion is clearly skewed indicating there's something tangible underneath."

"It's either a buried reef—"

"—or gold," interjected Kurt, who despite his earlier convictions to the contrary, now let his guard down and allowed the excitement of the moment to seep in.

"Gold," repeated Petersen in an entrancing voice, "a treasure hunter's gilded dream."

A faint greenish glint in the sand suddenly captured Kurt's attention. "What's that?" he asked out loud. He immediately let down the camera until it was suspended about a foot above the suspicious spot. Highlighted in the middle of the screen, and protruding from the sand, was a half-inch tarnished section of metal.

"Definitely look's man-made," Petersen acknowledged, "but hardly a pot-of-gold."

"It's our first evidentiary clue," Kurt said encouragingly.

"Not much of one."

"It may be quite substantial," objected Kurt. "That metallic item could be the same as an iceberg—not much topside but massive below the surface; once I remove the overlying layer of sand we'll know its true dimensions."

"It sounds like you're about to go for a swim."

"I've been fantasizing about this dive for at least a month," declared Kurt. "I wouldn't miss it for all the tea in China."

"That's an interesting choice of phrases. For your information that particular expression was first uttered in the 1890's and has an Australian origin."

"I wasn't aware of that," Kurt said with a sardonic grin, "so thank you Mr. Trivial Pursuit."

"Anytime."

Turning serious, Kurt said, "While I'm underwater, you'll be in charge of recording the dive with the DV-1. As you know our treasure hunt is essentially an archeological dig, so we'll need to meticulously document our excavation for both scientific and historical purposes."

"And," added Petersen, "for any possible legal entanglements."

"That too," moaned Kurt as he turned over control of the DV-1 to Petersen.

"When digging in the sand," cautioned the student, "try to minimize the amount of obscuring sediment—it won't photograph well."

"I'll be careful," Kurt said reassuringly, though as he walked back to the stern where his dive gear was stowed he knew he had just made an empty promise. The bat ray was Mr. Lily-white compared to the turbid mess he would create once he began churning up the sand.

At the back of the boat, Kurt unpacked his SCUBA equipment which was stored in two large waterproof duffel bags. His selection of gear was the same as for the previous trawl net dive except for three additional items: A commercial grade, handheld, underwater metal detector outfitted with a 10-inch coil; plastic marker flags of various hues; and one bright yellow nylon underwater air lift bag with a hoisting capacity of 500 pounds. The six-inch flags he placed inside a pocket of his BC. The air lift bag came with its own mesh carrying pouch, a 3 cubic foot air tank, and one stainless steel carabiner clip which he attached to a brass ring on the lower left side of his BC. As he was performing a final pre-dive safety check, Petersen joined him.

"I'm all set to film you Boss, so make it a day to remember."

"Thanks for the added pressure," smiled Kurt through the tempered glass lenses of his mask. He then provided Petersen with a brief overview of his dive plan. "I'll begin my hour-long adventure by following the DV-1 cable down to the metal object, place a marker flag at its location, and then spend the next fifteen minutes using the metal detector to sweep the surrounding area for any potential targets, which I'll also mark. After the fifteen minutes are up I'll begin excavating the most promising hits."

"What about the camera?" asked Petersen. "It's essentially stationary. If you stray too far from the underside of the boat I won't be able to film you."

"I'll physically reposition it—if that becomes necessary," Kurt assured him.

"Sounds good," said Petersen. "Best wishes on a successful treasure hunt."

"Thanks," said Kurt, "and your next image of me will be one hundred and twenty feet below the surface." He then inserted the regulator into his mouth, grasped the metal detector with his right hand, and leapfrogged off the boat's stern—landing with a monstrous splash before disappearing into the blue Pacific.

Once in the water Kurt quickly made his way to the ship's bow, located the DV-1 cable, and immediately began following it to the bottom. At the eighty-foot level he passed through a thermocline with a seven-degree temperature drop, which caused his body to experience temporary cold shivers until it adjusted to the rawness. Without the thermal comfort of his semi-dry wetsuit Kurt doubted he'd have lasted five minutes in the icy environment.

Passing the one hundred foot mark he spotted the DV-1 still hovering approximately five feet off the bottom. The sight of the camera caused his pulse to quicken and his breathing to accelerate. *What was on the other side of it? He wondered. Was it just a discarded piece of boat trash—or was it something more?* The answer, Kurt realized, petrified him. It was like asking your sweetheart to marry you when you weren't certain about her response, and possibly setting yourself up for a huge disappointment. He felt his nerves getting all jittery and tingling which caused him to intentionally slow his approach. *This is crazy*, he thought. *For the last several weeks you've lived for this exact moment.* Upon reaching the camera he spun it around so that Petersen could see that he had arrived. He then gave a 'thumbs up' signal informing his shipmate that everything was okay. Kurt felt a slight tug on the camera and released his grip. Apparently Petersen was raising the DV-1 so that he could film the entire scene from a loftier perspective.

Floating five feet off the seafloor Kurt stared at the sand expecting to find the metallic object. He refocused his eyes. He looked up at the camera that was suspended directly above him. *This has to be the right area,* he told himself. He searched again. *Nothing! Where was it?* He yelled into his mouthpiece, and then gagged on a smidgen of salt water that had seeped into his regulator. He began to panic. *Did Petersen reposition the DV-1? Had the boat moved off its anchor? Did the object truly exist in the first place?* Swimming frantically he began scouring the bottom, and in the process deliberately dropped the metal detector so that he could swim unencumbered. After completing an oval-shaped grid search he enlarged it, swam the expanded grid, and still found no trace of the object. Just as he was about to give up he noticed that the camera was behaving like an enticing fishing lure—its topside handler bouncing it up and down off the bottom as if it was a baited jig. *Petersen!* He exclaimed happily. The student's discerning eyes must have found what he was unable to perceive. It took Kurt less than four seconds to reach the DV-1, and then another split second to confirm that the elusive object truly did exist. Elated, he immediately drifted down until his dive mask was only inches from it. The bright light from the camera's strobe illuminated the scene and he could tell that the metal, which was covered in greenish corrosion, had undergone dezincification because of its prolonged salt water immersion. There was only one alloy that Kurt was aware of that changed colors when exposed to the acid in sea water—*brass.*

Brass thought Kurt, the metal alloy preferred by mariner's, especially during the 19th century. In addition, it was also commonly used in the storage of valuables. Seeing the alluring alloy up close caused Kurt to promptly scrap his pre-dive plans of initially marking all promising targets before beginning with any excavations. *It's impossible for a sane man to wait,* he told himself. Using his gloved right hand he rapidly moved it across the metal in powerful sweeping strokes in order to generate a current that would carry the sand away. Kurt's crude method worked but it also brought about an off-white cloud of particulate matter that obfuscated his view. When the sediment finally cleared he audibly gasped and then expelled a jubilant plume of noisy bubbles. He then arched his neck in order to locate the camera, and discovered it hanging just a few feet above his shoulders. Petersen had obviously seen the same thing.

Kurt's sand-whisking procedure had succeeded in stripping an inch of loose silt from around the object, unveiling what appeared to be the corner section of a brass crate. After spending an exhilarating minute examining the rounded corner, Kurt summarily abandoned any pretext of a carefully scripted archeological dig, and began flinging sand as if he was a dog digging out a hole in order to bury its coveted bone. Within three minutes he had uncovered a small crate approximately two feet long, a foot high, carrying handles on either side, and secured with a large corroded latch. Grasping one of the handles Kurt attempted to lift the brass box from its rectangular pit, but despite his best efforts, barely budged it. *It's either stuck or this is one heavy container,* he surmised. He decided to enlarge the opening around the box to see if that would help. He made it wider and deeper, and also removed some of the sand from its underside in order to break up any type of suction. Clasping the handle, he once again tried to yank it out of its sandy prison, but failed miserably—dragging it less than three inches. *This sucker ain't going anywhere,* he concluded. Utilizing the airlift bag was an option, but Kurt wanted to know the crate's contents before committing to its use since the contraption required several precious minutes to properly install.

Eyeing the deteriorated brass latch, Kurt tried to unbuckle it, but the oxidization had sealed it shut. *I can't move it and I can't break into it—you're certainly one lousy treasure hunter,* he chuckled, and then suddenly remembered, *but I do have a tool that might do the trick—my titanium dive knife.* Unsheathing the six-inch blade, Kurt jammed it under the latch. He first twisted it to his left and then to his right in order to try and spring the stuck mechanism. After thirty seconds of effort he reluctantly admitted defeat. With the blade still wedged, he next tried prying the latch open by using his body mass as a leveraging weight. As he slowly elevated his body above the crate—which incrementally increased the pounds per square inch on the fused clasp—the tip of the blade suddenly snapped off, causing him to tumble into the seafloor. Frustrated, but unhurt, Kurt re-sheathed what remained of the knife, and then began searching for a rock to use as an improvised sledge-hammer. After a short swim he found a soccer ball-sized stone that he carried back to the crate. Holding the rock between his two gloved hands he raised it above his shoulders. "Your days of obscurity have ended," Kurt declared prophetically as he began bludgeoning the stubborn latch.

Kurt augmented his impacts between a direct blow and an angled strike, searching for any sign of weakness in the metal's structure. After the fifth round of alternating impacts, he took a momentary break in order to catch his breath. Checking the latch, he was pleased to see that it had become slightly deformed. *A few more whacks ought to do it*, he hoped. With a renewed sense of optimism he began attacking it with an intensity that surprised even him, and halfway through the ninth round—while using a sharp-cornered section of the stone—Kurt sheared off the latch and it dropped to the seafloor. For a brief moment he was too stunned to even move. *I did it . . . I actually did it . . . I severed the latch!* After a few laudatory self-congratulations he set the rock aside and knelt down next to the crate. But, prior to opening it, he turned around to make sure the camera was nearby and almost banged into it with his head. Evidently Petersen was as anxious as he was.

Grasping the lid, Kurt prayed that it hadn't also oxidized like the latch; if it had, the lid would have cemented itself to the box making it almost impossible to remove. As he applied up-ward force—it began to budge. "Thank God," he murmured. Gingerly, he applied additional pressure, and the brass cover, as if on hinges greased with oil, raised up. Holding his breath Kurt peeped inside. After a cursory analysis of the crate's rectangular objects he was overwhelmed with despair—what assailed his eyes was not what he had anticipated.

34

"Mischa . . . Mischa," repeated the concerned voice, "can you hear me?" To Mischa, the 'words,' sounded strange and distant, as if the person was trying to communicate with her through a closed door. She felt something soft placed on her head. It was cool and after a moment she also realized it was damp. *Why was someone putting a wet cloth across her forehead?* She asked herself as a trickle of water ran down the backside of her face causing her to shudder. The voice came through again, but this time the tone seemed more urgent. "MISCHA, MISCHA," it commanded, "open your eyes . . . it's time to wake up." *I'm asleep? And someone's trying to wake me up? How silly of me,* she mused; *I must have forgotten to set my alarm. Just one more minute,* she told herself, but then she heard that demanding voice again, "MISCHA," and this time she reluctantly opened her eyes.

"Thank God!" whispered Dr. Sedrak. "Welcome back."

Mischa stared at him confused. *What was Dr. Sedrak doing in her bedroom shining a flashlight into her eyes? And why did her head hurt so much?* As she painfully turned her head to take in her surroundings, she saw Jake, Eva, and Timbrook, all looking at her with nervous grins. "What's going on?" she asked.

"It'll take a minute," Dr. Sedrak warned. "You've suffered a mild concussion. After the explosion, a rock the size of an orange was dislodged from the ceiling and struck your head. Fortunately," he said with a warm smile, "you're one tough lady."

A concussion? She put her hand up and felt her forehead. *No wonder she had a throbbing headache along with a bump the size of a large marble.* After a moment her short-term memory began reinstalling the details from the last several hours. There was, however, one important piece of information that was still missing. "Who rescued me?" she asked.

When no one responded, Timbrook pointed to Dr. Sedrak.

Mischa smiled at the doctor and said, "Thank you for saving my life—that was incredibly brave."

"I got lucky," explained Dr. Sedrak, "there were eight hands reaching for you, but I managed to get to you first."

"That split second might have made all the difference," said Mischa as she remembered the rock wall collapsing around her, "so you deserve the hug today." She stood up shakily, with Sedrak's help, and rewarded the doctor with an emotional embrace.

"It's my turn to say thanks for being so gracious," said Dr. Sedrak after Mischa finally released him. "But, I do have to caution you; with a blow to the head, you'll be a bit wobbly in the legs, so you'll need to take it easy." He reached into his pocket and removed a small cellophane package which he tore open. "I'm a doctor," he said by way of explanation, "I always carry a few pills with me. These should help mitigate the effects of the concussion."

"What is it?" asked Mischa as Dr. Sedrak placed two white tablets in the palm of her hand.

"Just over-the-counter Ibuprofen," he replied, "but it should help ease the pain."

"In that case I'm all for it," said Mischa charitably as she immediately swallowed both pills.

"Mischa," said Timbrook in a soft voice, "speaking on behalf of everyone—you had us worried for a few tense moments, but thank God you're alright. I also wanted you to know that your analysis of the wall was correct; when the structure collapsed," he said motioning toward it as he illuminated the scene with his lights, "a hidden passageway was revealed on the far side. Why the Chumash created this solid partition, at this particular point, is certainly a mystery. Unfortunately, when the wall crumbled, the pictograph went with it. But, since it's essentially a gigantic puzzle made out of individual boulders, I'm optimistic that some-day it can be reassembled. What lies beyond the cave-in, however, is unknown. It's obvious the passage goes back a long way since our light beams—even after penetrating a hundred feet—are un-able to reveal its true dimensions. Under normal circumstances I would love to explore it, but not today. That baffling explosion has me concerned; it was so powerful that it probably compro-mised the structural integrity of Painted Cave, and now that we know you're okay, we'll need to vacate this section of the cave as soon as possible."

"Any idea what caused it?" asked Mischa.

"I think the other ship suffered a catastrophic explosion," Eva opined.

"That's my theory too," said Jake. "What else could it be?"

"Ships don't normally blow up," cautioned Timbrook, "other than in the movies."

Nodding Eva said, "That may be true, but what if the captain was foolish enough to try and navigate the narrow passageway, and became stuck during the process?"

"Then he embarked on a suicide mission and endangered his entire crew," Timbrook said shaking his head sadly. "That par-ticular ship was so massive that the gullet would have shattered its hull."

"Exactly," said Eva, "resulting in a fire which eventually worked its way to the fuel tanks."

"If those fuel tanks detonated inside the gullet," Timbrook said looking concerned, "then we have a lot to worry about."

"Why?" asked Jake.

Timbrook lowered his voice before responding. "It's the only way out."

Dr. Sedrak frowned. "Then I suggest we board *Nessie* immediately in order to find out if that in fact happened. Timbrook, what's the battery life in our flashlights?"

"About six hours."

"That's what I figured," said Dr. Sedrak. "If the gullet is truly impassable, then we'll need to conserve our energy sources."

"We might as well begin now," Mischa said as she switched off her lights.

"Agreed," said Eva who joined Mischa.

"Jake," Timbrook commanded, "you're in charge of helping your sister back to the boat."

"And I'll escort Eva," Dr. Sedrak volunteered.

"Then let's head out," announced Timbrook, who had kept his light on in order to take the lead.

During their short hike, Mischa held onto her brother's shoulder, while Jake wrapped his arm around her waist. If she began to slip, Jake would tighten his grip, steadying her, until she was able to regain her balance. The most challenging part of the return trip was circumnavigating the additional rock barriers caused by the blast. At one point they had to walk single file around a block of lava that must have weighed at least two tons. As they neared their vessel, Mischa could hear the roar of sea lions, but this time the quality of the sound had changed. Instead of playful chatter, loud barks, and high-pitched squeals, it was like listening to the worst orchestra imaginable, where every instrument was out of tune, and every musician was playing solo. *They're petrified,* she thought, and she instantly felt sorry for them. It was a cacophony of fear and the sound was horrendous. *How many had died?* She wondered. As they approached the boat she saw two carcasses floating on the water—one with its head blown off, and the other shredded, as if it had traveled through a meat grinder. *This is awful* she screamed silently. Timbrook's face, she observed, was ashen white as he surveyed the scene.

"This is a bad sign," Timbrook murmured.

Jake stared at the mutilated bodies for a few seconds before asking, "By *bad sign* are you implying that Eva's assessment was correct?"

Timbrook rubbed his temples before answering. "It's now a distinct possibility. These creatures only inhabit the gullet and inner chamber; their deaths are a bad omen."

"But," said Dr. Sedrak in a measured tone, "until we've viewed the site ourselves we're just speculating as to the amount of damage. In a few minutes—good or bad—we'll know for certain."

"The doctor's right," Timbrook acknowledged, "it accomplishes nothing to presuppose a worst case scenario."

"It's okay," said Jake, "I think we're all a bit anxious—I know I am."

"You're a good man, Jake," said Timbrook with a smile. "And if you don't mind, this old Indian needs your help at getting *Nessie* back in the water. The tide has dropped substantially since putting ashore and now the boat is high and dry."

"I'll also lend a hand," Dr. Sedrak offered.

Between the three men pushing and shoving—with Timbrook and Jake at the side rails and Dr. Sedrak at the bow—they slowly slid the boat back into the water, leaving just a small portion of the forward end of the vessel on the sand. After everyone had safely boarded, Timbrook started the outboard engine, shifted it into reverse, and after gently goosing the throttle, broke free from the beach. Shifting to forward, he set the speed to about three knots, and headed straight for the gullet.

The short journey took less than four minutes. Along the way Timbrook had to carefully maneuver around a half dozen mangled carcasses and several injured sea lions. The water, Mischa noted, was stained red. After arriving at the entrance, Timbrook reduced *Nessie's* speed to half a knot, and guided the ship into the gullet. At what he ascertained was the halfway mark, Timbrook suddenly killed the engine. For a few moments no one said a word as the boat drifted in the middle of the channel. Mischa held her breath as she stared in disbelief at the massive rockfall that totally obstructed the connecting tunnel. When she finally exhaled she could feel the pressure and pulsating pain from the concussion-type headache re-asserting itself just behind her eyes. The silence was interrupted when Eva uttered a cry of despair.

"The passageway . . . it's been obliterated," Eva lamented. "It's like it never existed."

Mischa scanned the enormous pile of rocks that now clogged the gullet for any gap or hole that a human being could possibly squeeze through. She found none. The barrier, she concluded, was impenetrable.

"We're at the dead end of a blind alley," mumbled Dr. Sedrak philosophically, "with nowhere to go, and no way out."

"Can we clear a path through it?" Jake asked.

"I'm afraid not," Timbrook replied. "The stones weigh too much; plus, it appears that this breakdown goes back a long way— at least fifteen to twenty feet. Even with a large Caterpillar tractor it would take days to cut a passage through this mountain of rubble."

"Are we going to die?" Jake whispered.

In the dim lighting, Timbrook looked directly into Jake's eyes and said, "Absolutely not! In my entire life I've never been in a situation that was truly hopeless, and this one certainly isn't. Somehow, we'll find a way out, and if not, then we'll just wait to be rescued. By the end of today . . . when we don't return . . . your dad will move heaven and earth in order to find us, and when he does, he'll employ every expert on the planet in order to free us from this underground prison. He knows we're exploring Painted Cave. This will be the first place he looks. And, when he sees that the gullet has collapsed, he'll logically conclude that we're trapped inside. You know how incredibly smart your dad is;

he'll figure a way to get us out—that I can guarantee you. We may be uncomfortable for a few days, but we'll manage, we'll survive, and someday we'll even laugh at our subterranean adventure."

Jake gave Timbrook a goofy smile and said, "I don't know about 'laughing,' but your optimistic pep talk certainly helps. And you're right, our dad will do whatever it takes to find us. After mom's death, he's been especially protective. He won't sleep a wink until he knows we're safe."

"Thank God for a father like that," said Eva as she wiped a tear from her eye and then added: "I wonder what happened to the people on the other ship."

"I wouldn't hold out much hope," Timbrook said solemnly. "They either died in the explosion or were buried under tons of rock."

"I'm not so sure about that," said Dr. Sedrak. "Think about it . . . if their vessel exploded, why isn't the gullet filled with debris from their ship?" He motioned at the surface of the water. "And something else that's a bit peculiar: smell the air. You'll notice a strong, unpleasant odor, like rotten eggs. There are two gasses that contain that putrid smell—hydrogen sulfide and ethyl mercaptan. Hydrogen sulfide is typically associated with swamps and sewers and is produced from the bacterial breakdown of organic matter in the absence of oxygen. It's also found in volcanic gasses and natural gas wells. Ethyl mercaptan, on the other hand, is a by-product of the petroleum industry, and is mainly added to odorless gasses such as propane in order to impart an obnoxious smell to the fuel."

"Now that you mention it—it does smell like rotten eggs," said Mischa as she sniffed the air.

"What exactly are you saying?" asked Timbrook.

"I wish I knew," replied Dr. Sedrak. "Obviously a very powerful explosion occurred inside the gullet, I just don't think it was the ship."

"Then what?" asked Eva.

Dr. Sedrak hesitated a few seconds before responding. "My best guess—either natural gas or volcanic gases. In the distant past this island used to be an active volcano."

"If what you say is true," Eva said slowly, "what's the ignition source?"

Dr. Sedrak laughed nervously before responding. "It'll sound like a Catch-22, but in all probability it was the other ship, but don't ask me how."

Timbrook started to say something, but then stopped himself. After a few moments he said, "It may have been the other ship, but not *the* ship." After a slight pause, he continued, "By your blank expressions I can tell that my poorly worded statement needs further clarification. Let's assume that the captain knew about the gullet's existence, and that the passengers on his boat wanted to explore the inner chamber. Further, that after anchoring up, he used a shuttle-type craft—probably an inflatable—in order to run the gullet. If Dr. Sedrak's theory is correct, and this tunnel was filled with gas, all it would take was a spark from an inflatable's outboard engine to trigger the devastating explosion."

Nodding, Eva said, "That's definitely a possibility, and if that's what occurred, then we're lucky to be alive ourselves."

"Which means," cautioned Jake, "that extending our stay here could touch off a secondary explosion."

"Agreed," said Timbrook, who immediately swung the boat around.

Within a minute they were back in the inner chamber among the panic-stricken sea lions. The water, Mischa observed, was swarming with the creatures who had apparently abandoned their resting places. Timbrook, in order to avoid colliding into them, lowered the boat's speed to a creeping idle. Seeing the helpless animals, she was overwhelmed with pity. In less than a week the inner chamber, which had been their sanctuary, would become their death chamber—a watery graveyard of rotting carcasses. The sea lions, Mischa realized, needed a rescuer the same as them. However, before they could be helped, her group of five had to first find a way out. *But how?* She asked herself. Timbrook was counting on her dad, and so was she, but that could take days or even a week. Patience, as her father often reminded her, was not one of Mischa's strong virtues. *No situation is hopeless* Timbrook had reminded her brother. Unfortunately, with a pounding headache, trying to think of a solution to their predicament was difficult. Mischa gently massaged the sore spot on her head. The knot was still the size of a walnut. In the last hour she had survived an explosion, a collapsed wall, and a falling rock. *I'm a lucky girl,* she thought, and then it hit her, like the stone that impacted her head, an oh-my-gosh epiphany moment. "There may be an alternative route!" She said louder than she intended.

Jake had seen Mischa rubbing her head and now looked at her as if she wasn't quite right upstairs. "*Where?*" He asked skeptically.

Mischa ignored Jake's tone. "The secret passage beyond the collapsed pictograph; I think the Chumash sealed it prior to leaving the island because they didn't want anyone else using it."

"Is that a realistic possibility?" Eva asked hopefully.

Every eye on the boat immediately turned to Timbrook for the answer. The Indian grinned playfully before responding. "I think Mischa's Chumash heritage is finally asserting itself because I was wondering the same thing—I just hadn't verbalized it yet. However, I don't want to raise any false hopes. Obviously the cave continues a long way beyond the destroyed pictograph. Does it connect to an external entrance? That's a good question. If there's truly another entryway into the inner chamber it's certainly worth looking into. Currently, it seems we have a lot of extra time on our hands so we might as well put it to constructive use. Are there any objections?" Timbrook smiled as he scanned each person's countenance. "I didn't think so, but I thought I would extend the courtesy and ask. And as a reminder, please hang on to the side rails. I'm going to park the boat in the same manner as I did previously.

Mischa was once again impressed with Timbrook's navigational skills as he flawlessly beached *Nessie*. Stepping out of the boat, they made their way across the sandy beach, over the cobblestones, and back into the passage. Once inside, Timbrook had everyone switch on their lights. At the collapsed pictograph they took a short break.

"How are you feeling?" Dr. Sedrak asked Mischa.

Upon exiting the boat Mischa had declined any assistance. "I still have a nasty headache," she reported, "but it's slowly improving along with my equilibrium. If I need any help I'll let you know."

"Please do," Eva insisted. "If you fall and reinjure yourself I'll never forgive myself."

"That's not going to happen," Mischa assured Eva, "and thanks for your concern."

"We're essentially family," said Eva, "of course I care."

Timbrook, who had been sitting down, stood up and said, "If Mischa's good to go then let's head out. I'm anxious to see what exists beyond this artificial wall."

"You don't have to wait on me," Mischa said firmly, "I'm just as excited as you are to set foot in a cave that has remained off-limits for generations."

"That doesn't surprise me," laughed Timbrook. "I knew—in spite of your injuries—that you'd be like a race horse chomping at the bit to see what lies on the other side."

"That would be a Kentucky Derby thoroughbred," added Mischa with a warm smile.

"Remember," Timbrook said to each of them, "these caves have lots of branching passages especially where one fault intersects another. If you see any man-size cleft, fissure, crevice, or crawl space in the wall, please check it out—it may lead to the surface."

As they slowly made their way down the passage, Mischa and Jake carefully examined the walls for any sizable gap, and discovered several promising 'finger fissures' which curved back ten to twenty feet. Unfortunately, every fissure eventually ended at a wall of solid rock. The main passage stayed comfortably wide for the first sixty feet and then began to narrow. After approximately one hundred feet, the width was down to seven feet at which point the passage began a gentle incline for about fifteen feet before suddenly emerging into an aesthetically pleasing dome-shaped room floored with agate cobbles. In the middle of the space was a fire ring made out of sculpted lava rock with flat sitting stones situated around an ancient hearth.

"What an odd place for a campsite," observed Eva.

"It's not a campsite," said Timbrook quietly. "It's a sacred site. Our religious leaders, the shamans, believed that underground locations like these—areas that were truly extraordinary—were portals to the supernatural. It was in these unique settings, while under a drug-induced trance, that they sought out their dream helpers."

"What's a dream helper?" asked Jake.

"In the Chumash belief system it was a personal spirit guide—a celestial being that had the ability to endow a person with real or mystical powers," answered Timbrook.

"What are some examples of *spirit guides*?" Dr. Sedrak wondered.

Timbrook laughed softly. "A 'guide' was whatever appeared to you during your hallucinogenic state. Animals, birds, insects, powerful plants, natural forces, stars, planets—basically anything that could assist a person in their life's journey."

"Do you have a spirit guide?" Mischa asked Timbrook.

Timbrook chuckled before answering. "Yes, his name is Yahweh."

Mischa was about to utter a sarcastic 'I should have known that's what you would say,' but under the prevailing circumstances decided it would be best to err on the side of respect—just in case.

Surprisingly, it was Eva who teased. "Since your spirit guide is supposedly omnipotent, I'm assuming the Grand Poobah has already imparted to his faithful servant a route out of this cave."

"Not exactly," Timbrook said with a whimsical smile. "But then again we haven't yet reached the end of this passage, so there's still time for him to perform a miracle."

"Then lead on," said Dr. Sedrak. "I may be an atheist, but at this moment I'm okay with a divinely-inspired pathway to the outer world."

As they exited the domed room and re-entered the passage, Mischa joined Timbrook, and walked alongside him. In the past weeks the aging Indian had become like a grandfather to her. His knowledge of the island, and of the history and culture of his people, continued to amaze her. With Timbrook at her side she felt secure, safe, as if their current ordeal 'was just a walk in the park,' and that eventually they would find a way out.

"This corridor is incredible!" exclaimed Timbrook. "The vaulted ceilings are similar to arches found in Gothic churches."

"I'm not familiar with that architectural style," Mischa acknowledged, "but I agree it's certainly spectacular."

The passage continued for another thirty feet before it ended at a perfectly arched gateway. On the opposite side of the span was another chamber-type room.

"That room must be massive," declared Timbrook, "since my light beams just disappear into the blackness."

"Massive may be an understatement," Mischa confirmed. Her headlamp and flashlight were also swallowed up by the abysmally large cave.

Approximately ten feet from the doorway Timbrook paused until everyone had gathered around him. "We're about to enter a cavern that is probably similar in size to Painted Cave's inner chamber. Please watch your step since these types of dry caves typically have fracture zones and falling into an unseen chasm is an experience you'll definitely want to avoid."

"I think we're all in agreement on that," laughed Dr. Sedrak. "I know I am especially if I'm the one doing the bandaging."

"Okay then," said Timbrook with an optimistic smile, "if everyone's all set—let's see if this chamber has a doorway to the outside world, and our ticket to freedom."

Timbrook walked into the room first, followed by Mischa, Jake, Eva, and lastly Dr. Sedrak. Once they were inside they formed a semicircle, and with their LED lights, lit up the spacious cavern.

What assailed their eyes wasn't at all what they expected. Timbrook uttered a short gasp and then fell to his knees.

35

For a moment no one said a word as the chamber glowed in resplendent light. Eva broke the silence by emitting a soft squeal. Jake, wide-eyed said, "This is so cool." Dr. Sedrak murmured, "Unbelievable," and Mischa was so wonder-struck that she had difficulty breathing. Timbrook, in a voice choked with emotion said, "Lord . . . thank you . . . now your servant can depart in peace." He then rose from a kneeling position and stood up.

Mischa, after briefly pondering Timbrook's words and looking at him with a quizzical and concerned expression on her face, returned her gaze to the chamber. What she saw brought tears to her eyes, especially the sight of a Tomol canoe that appeared to be at least fifty feet in length, and on its bow, the figurehead of a swordfish. Situated next to it were at least a dozen similar canoes, but at about half the length. "It's the heart and soul of a nation," she whispered, "stored for a future time." *Unfortunately*, she sadly realized, *that moment never occurred.*

"It's a museum of artifacts," declared Dr. Sedrak. "What a treasure trove for historians."

"Is this all from just one village?" Jake wondered.

"Probably a handful of villages," replied Timbrook.

Mischa wiped the tears from her eyes. To personally see the contents of several Chumash communities—their way of life—frozen in time, was a gift beyond measure.

"Did you have an inkling that this place existed?" Eva asked Timbrook.

"There were rumors of its existence," began Timbrook, "that have been passed down from one generation to the next. But, over the years, when its location remained undiscovered, it became the Indian's version of an urban legend—more myth than reality—but a dream nonetheless."

"Why did they hide their most valuable possessions?" asked Dr. Sedrak.

"They thought they would eventually return," continued Timbrook. "In 1822 when the Spanish forced them to leave, they essentially left the island with just their clothing. When the Spaniards searched their abandoned villages they found nothing—all their belongings were gone. A survey of the island failed to locate any of their personal effects, and that's when the rumor began—that the Chumash had hidden their property in a secret location. That spot, of course, remained an elusive mystery . . . until today."

Dr. Sedrak shook his head. "There's a slight problem with what you just said, the Chumash themselves were aware of the site—so how did it pass into obscurity?"

"According to what I've been able to ascertain," Timbrook explained, "only a select number of Chumash elders knew the exact location. Because the Chumash did not have a written language, it was never memorialized in writing. Unfortunately, within six months of their arrival at the Santa Barbara mission, these same individuals, along with their entire families, died after contracting smallpox, measles, or diphtheria—victims of the European diseases for which they had no immunity, and as a result, their knowledge of the site died with them."

"Thankfully," added Eva, "a remnant of the people survived, including our own Adam Timbrook."

"It was a miracle that we didn't go the same way as the dinosaurs," Timbrook said plaintively. "Prior to the arrival of the Europeans there were over twenty-five thousand Chumash living in what are now San Luis Obispo, Santa Barbara, and Ventura Counties; today, there are less than three thousand who share a Chumash ancestry."

"I imagine the discovery of this site will cause quite a stir among your people," Eva said.

"It will be a resurrecting event," Timbrook said quietly.

Jake motioned in the direction of the Tomol canoe. "I'm not trying to be disrespectful, but it appears that our in-house Native American expert was woefully mistaken; that canoe could easily seat twenty-four paddlers."

Smiling, Timbrook said, "I've never been happier to be so wrong. That boat, which is referred to as either a Tomol or plank canoe, was constructed by a special group of men known as *The-Brotherhood-of-the-Canoe,* and was considered to be our most famous invention. The *Brotherhood* disbanded around 1834, which ended the building of any new canoes. Today, it's pure speculation as to how these unique crafts were assembled; the canoes in this cave will help answer that question. As an ancestor to these gifted craftsmen, it would be an honor to show you their canoes along with their other notable wares, while we search for a way out of this chamber."

Mischa again walked beside Timbrook. As they made their way over to the canoe, she asked him the question that had been bothering her. "What did you mean by, 'now your servant can depart in peace?'"

"I'm so sorry if that phrase upset you," said Timbrook, "I was just quoting from the Bible—Luke 2:29—where God promised Simeon that he would not see death until he had seen the Lord

Jesus Christ. The discovery of this chamber is a similar type experience for me. As a young teenager, attending my first tribal
meeting, this very issue—did a secret hoard truly exist?—was
discussed by the Council of Elders. A majority of the Council
thought it was just a myth since no one had ever found it, but in
my own spirit I thought otherwise. When I arrived on this island
I prayed that God would allow me to find it before I died. Today
he answered that request. That scripture was the promise I hung
onto."

Mischa shrugged. "It seems a little morbid if you asked me."

"What can I say," laughed Timbrook, "I've always been a bit
odd."

Nodding, Mischa said, "Sometimes . . . but that's what I like
about you; normal is boring."

As they arrived at the plank canoe Timbrook began describing its characteristics. "This grand ship, which is the largest of
its kind ever crafted, clearly belonged to a Chumash Chief. It
was fashioned entirely by hand with tools made from stone, animal bones, shells, and sharkskin sandpaper, and took two to six
months to build. It was constructed from a massive redwood log
that had floated down the coast from Northern California and
washed up on the island as driftwood. When the canoe was finally finished it was made waterproof by painting it with a mixture
of tar, pine pitch, and red ochre. Its redwood paddles are ten
feet long, with a blade at each end that's shaped like a shovel or a
horse's hoof. As a regal canoe which transported the Chief, it was
decorated accordingly; inlayed in the wood—from its bow to its
stern—are iridescent abalone and olivella shells, and at the front
end of the boat, the carved swordfish."

As Mischa stared at the approximately two hundred-year-
old shells she was amazed at the range of changeable colors that
still shimmered, from silvery white, pink, and red, to deep blues,
greens, and purples. "This ship is truly a work of art," she said
respectfully.

"The other Tomol canoes," said Timbrook pointing, "range in size from twelve to thirty feet. They were used to transport people and goods between the various islands and the mainland, as well as for hunting seals, sea lions, sea otters, and for fishing."

"For hand-crafted ships, built with primitive tools, they're remarkable," declared Dr. Sedrak.

"They most certainly are," Timbrook agreed. "And that's just our ships; the Chumash were also skilled in other areas, as will be revealed in a moment."

As Mischa gazed around the chamber she was duly impressed at how the different types of artifacts were stored—each to their own section of the cavern. It was obvious that the Chumash responsible for organizing the underground facility was a gifted administrator.

After walking around the canoes they arrived at the housewares portion of the cave, which was packed with hundreds of items—bowls and cooking pots made from burl wood and soapstone, wooden trays, ladles, spoons, plates fabricated from shells, and exquisitely shaped coiled baskets that had been made into pitchers, trays, jars, drinking cups, bowls, plates, and storage containers for food and water. Many of the baskets were woven with geometric designs—vertical bars, horizontal bands, zigzags, and stepped lines, all ranging in colors from black, to reddish-brown, white, or light buff.

Timbrook seemed to be at a loss for words as he stared teary-eyed at the vast collection. He uttered a slight gasp before bending down and picking up a globular-shaped basket. "This basket is extraordinary—perfect in every detail," he gushed. He cradled it in his hands as if he were holding a precious newborn. He spent several seconds examining its intricate designs, gently turning the 'jar' in his hands before carefully setting it back down. "You have no idea what this means," he whispered. "In the entire state of California there exists but a few baskets from this time period, and most are far from perfect. The Chumash were renowned for their basketry, and especially their coiled baskets, which were considered outstanding. That skill has essentially been consigned to the past; these baskets represent the heart of our nation, and their discovery will have a profound effect upon my people, and hopefully rekindle that dormant talent." Every member of the group was silent for a few seconds—partly in respect for Timbrook's outpouring of emotion, and partly due to their own overwhelming realization of what the discovery meant.

"What plant materials were used in making the baskets?" Mischa asked quietly.

"Primarily *Juncus Rush*," Timbrook replied. "The plant's slender rods are first wrapped and then sewn together using split strands from the same material. The coiled baskets have over 220 stitches per square inch, and are so finely wrought that they're watertight."

"They're amazingly beautiful," Eva sighed. "They not only served a useful purpose, they're masterpieces of art; clearly the Chumash took pride in their work."

Nodding, Timbrook smiled appreciatively as he continued with their walking tour.

Mischa categorized the next storage area as the 'clothing and bedroom,' section as it contained an assortment of animal skins including deer, bear, seal, sea lions, sea otters, fox, and rabbit. Some of the hides had been made into clothing—buckskin clothes for women and sleeveless capes of various sizes for both men and women. The capes were made from the skins of black bears, sea lions, and the most luxurious, sea otters. A pile of soft blankets came from the skins of rabbits and sea otters. For comfort while sleeping there were a sizeable number of rolled up mats made from the *Bulrush Tule* plant. Finally, stowed in several large baskets was a collection of ceremonial dance skirts for women, bird-feathered headdresses for both men and women, a Chief's bear cape, a shamans' swordfish headdress, and a variety of men's ceremonial clothes that incorporated elements from the earth, sea, and sky in their designs.

Beyond the clothing and bedroom section was an area Mischa laughingly referred to as the 'man cave depot,' as it contained grinding tools, wedges, flakers, awls, drills, hide scrapers, choppers, arrowheads, spears, spear points, knives, bows, arrows, arrowshaft straighteners, wood harpoons, abalone fishhooks, fishing nets, grinding stones, mortars, pestles for grinding acorns, manos, baskets of tar, cordage rope, and ceremonial smoking pipes. According to Timbrook some of the raw materials used in making these tools and weapons included soapstone, steatite, which was a type of soapstone, deer bones, deer antlers, flint, the mineral chert, obsidian, Indian hemp, and wild rye.

The last area of artifacts occupied a relatively small space which Mischa designated the 'monetary, jewelry, musical, and spiritual section.' Arranged in well-ordered piles were shell necklaces, bracelets, and earrings, flutes, clapper sticks, bullroarers, turtle shell rattles, whistles, and carved effigies from steatite—animals, birds, lizards, snakes, sea lions, sea otters, whales, swordfish, and various birds. The final items were a half dozen gallon-sized baskets that were filled with strings of shell beads made from the thick inner shell of the olivella sea snail.

Shining his flashlight into the baskets, Timbrook shook his head sadly. "You're looking at a fortune in Chumash currency. These beads," he said as he picked up a string, "were the same as gold for thousands of years, and were traded for valuable goods. Now they're essentially worthless—just pretty fragments from a common sea snail." Timbrook dropped the strand back into the basket.

"As the saying goes," quipped Jake, "you can't take it with you, so you might as well spend it while you're still alive."

The comment caused everyone to smile in the realization of the irony.

"That's always good advice," Timbrook chuckled. "I think my ancestors needed an Indian Jake."

"And since we're on the pessimistic subject of *not taking it with you*—as we were wandering around this chamber, did anyone happen to notice an exit?" asked Dr. Sedrak somberly. "I for one did not."

After a brief silence, obviously indicating similar observations from the others, Eva said softly, "What now?"

Timbrook's expression was one of strength. "We wait to be rescued; in the meantime, there's food and water on the boat which should last a few days . . . if we're careful. Right now I suggest we head back and enjoy a light lunch and some rest. After that we can discuss our immediate future. Fortunately, the Chumash have provided us with plenty of bedding material if we need to spend the night."

"*IF?*" repeated Jake. "I'm already claiming first rights to the sea otter blankets."

"Ladies first," insisted Mischa, "you get what's left."

"There's more than enough," smiled Timbrook, "even for the able-bodied men."

They returned to the boat in contemplative silence, though Mischa was emotionally still on cloud nine at the discovery of the artifacts. *It will set the Chumash nation on fire,* she realized with a smile. She wondered what they would do with them. Moving the artifacts out of the cavern would certainly be a major undertaking. *And then what?* They'll need to be housed somewhere— perhaps in a brand-new museum. Maybe her dad could help; the Nichols Foundation certainly had the resources to make a generous donation. The thought that she would not have the opportunity to tell him about the treasure never crossed her mind as she had absolute faith in Timbrook and in her dad. It was just a matter of time. As Timbrook said, there was some food and water in the boat, plus they had the ocean, and it was teeming with life. She wondered how long it would take before she was tired of roasted lobster. The thought made her smile. But, as they neared the boat her smile faded as she suddenly experienced an intuitive feeling that something wasn't quite right, and as they walked down the cobble beach that impression—that something was amiss—became even more acute. *I can hear the sound of my own footsteps,* she realized. *Why is that unusual?* The stillness, though peaceful, was discomforting. *Oh my gosh!* "The sea lions," she yelled, "they're all gone."

Every member of their small party suddenly stopped and listened, other than Timbrook, who continued on down to the water's edge where he then stared into the distance. The tide, Mischa noted had dropped significantly, leaving *Nessie* essentially dry-docked.

"Could they be sleeping?" Jake asked.

Eva shook her head. "I highly doubt it. A coordinated group slumber would be next to impossible for these bellicose creatures; being 'neighborly' isn't a part of their loud vocabulary."

"If they're not sleeping and if they're not dead—except for a few—then where did they go?" Dr. Sedrak asked warily.

Timbrook had quietly rejoined the group. "They left," he said matter-of-factly.

"How?" Mischa interjected. "The only outlet is completely blocked."

Timbrook appeared to mull over his words before he responded. "There's a possibility that Painted Cave connects underwater to an adjoining sea cave."

"Why didn't you mention it earlier," Dr. Sedrak said with a hint of frustration.

Timbrook shrugged. "Its existence is purely conjectural; I'm not aware of anyone who has actually seen it, or used it."

"Explain," Eva demanded.

"In the early to mid-twentieth century, a woman by the name of Margaret Eaton—who was married to a sea captain—recounted her Santa Cruz Island adventures in a book titled, *Diary of a Sea*

Captain's Wife. In her memoir she briefly touched upon the possibility of an underwater passage connecting Painted Cave's inner chamber to a nearby sea cave. Her husband and boys had stretched a seal net across an adjacent cave, trapping a substantial number of seals inside, including a large bull seal with unusual markings. At low tide they rowed their boat into this cave with the expectation of finding the cornered seals, but the only sound they heard was the din of rushing sea water; apparently the seals had all disappeared. When they rowed their skiff back to Painted Cave they found the same big bull seal with the unique markings. It was obvious to them that the creature had bypassed their net by traveling through an underground watercourse that linked the two caves."

"Does Ms. Eaton's diary disclose the whereabouts of the cave?" Dr. Sedrak asked.

"No, but there's just two candidates; Little Painted Cave or Seal's Secret Cave. Those are the only sea caves that border Painted Cave."

"My money's on Seal's Secret Cave," declared Jake. "The name itself implies subterfuge."

"We'll know soon enough," Timbrook assured him. "If that alternative route truly exists—today's extreme low tide is a godsend. The precipitous drop in the sea-level means that the water from this chamber will be rushing out, just as it did over half a century ago, which will help facilitate our search for the passage. But, we'll need to get the boat back in the water before we can even begin."

Fortunately, as Mischa observed, the rearmost portion of *Nessie's* stern, which contained the weighty outboard engine, was still immersed in the water, allowing them to easily slide the boat back into the ocean. After everyone had boarded, Timbrook restarted the engine, shifted it into reverse, and then backed the ship off the beach.

Talking loudly over the drone of the engine's noise, Timbrook continued. "Since I haven't a clue as to where the connecting waterway might be, we'll have to survey the entire chamber." He shifted the throttle into forward, and after cruising past the now empty sea lion rocks, he commenced their reconnaissance, beginning with the eastern wall.

Mischa joined Jake in the front of the boat and together they focused their lights on the waterline. *That's where we'll find the opening,* she thought. Timbrook guided *Nessie* on a path that paralleled the rock wall, moving her in and out with every twist and turn, and at a speed that was almost imperceptible—essentially guaranteeing that nothing would be missed. After about ninety-five feet the eastern wall entered into a gradual horseshoe-type turn. At the mid-point of the U-shaped curve they motored past the gullet. The darkened tunnel was eerily silent. A sea lion corpse bobbed at the entrance—a stark reminder that it was now off-limits. Once they were on the other side of the gullet Timbrook announced that they were halfway through their inspection. Within moments of Timbrook's report Mischa heard her brother utter an anxious sigh.

"Don't worry," she murmured to Jake. "The western wall actually abuts the open sea although there is at least a hundred feet of rock in between. If there's a passage—that's where we'll find it. Skirting the eastern side of the chamber was probably a waste of time."

Laughing, but at a level barely above a whisper, Jake joked, "Are you suggesting that Timbrook's an incompetent navigator?"

"No . . . he knows what he's doing," Mischa replied defensively. "He's just covering his bases, and saved the most promising section for last."

"Let's hope so," said Jake. "We've already drifted by a third of it, and it's as solid as the eastern side."

Mischa had to reluctantly agree. The western wall was the same as its eastern counterpart except for the water depth—it was slightly deeper. Mischa shined her lights into the water, which penetrated to the bottom. Scattered along the sea floor were translucent giant white sea anemones with pink highlights. Normally, these flower-like predatory animals were green because of the algae that lived within them, but in the darkened cave they had turned white. *They're beautiful,* she thought, *like all albino creatures, though gorgeous, despite or due to their lack of pigment.* A gurgling sound interrupted her meditative moment. "Excuse me," she said to Jake, "do you need to apologize."

"Not me," he said with a sarcastic grin, "but you can ask the chamber to offer up an apology on my behalf." He then lit up a portion of the wall twenty feet away. "The seal's secret passage," he proudly declared, "is no longer hidden."

Mischa let out a loud squeal as Timbrook carefully repositioned the boat in front of the tunnel.

After studying the entrance for a minute, Timbrook said, "Don't get too excited. It's not as large as I had hoped."

"Why does that matter?" Jake countered. "There's still plenty of room."

"In the beginning . . . yes . . . but fifty feet into the tunnel it may be a different story. Do you see that discolored watermark above the threshold? Timbrook asked as he highlighted it with his handheld flashlight. "It's extends two feet above the entryway. That *mark* explains why this passage has never been discovered— it's always underwater. The only exception is a day like today when we're experiencing an unusually low tide."

"Are you worried about getting stuck?" Dr. Sedrak asked.

Timbrook nodded and then added ominously. "Or capsizing. *Nessie's* bridge clearance is five feet; her beam is eight feet. The entryway appears to be about six feet high and eleven feet wide. In the depths of the tunnel what happens if the ceiling drops down or if the passage narrows? If the height gets below five feet, our bridge will scrape against the rocks. If it gets below three and a half feet, we'll be shoved underwater, and our boat will founder. On the other hand, if the width tapers down to eight feet we're in a similar type predicament. Once we become wedged—the boat will immediately fill with water. If any of these two scenarios occur we'll have to abandon ship and make a swim for it. The concern I have is someone becoming ensnared by the boat or caught up in the current. Drowning is not an easy death."

"What's your estimate on the length of the passage?" asked Eva anxiously.

"At least a hundred feet; this tunnel obviously connects to either Little Painted Cave or Seal's Secret Cave. Once we reach whichever cave it is we'll be okay. Both of them are full-sized sea caves—two to three hundred feet in length with high ceilings."

Mischa spent a few seconds staring at the oval-shaped watery doorway. *What an awful quandary,* she realized. The portal represented either freedom or something much worse. She then searched Timbrook's eyes for a moment before asking, "What do you recommend?"

"If we decide to go, two things—don our life jackets, and lay down in the boat. The life jackets are necessary if we have to abandoned ship; hunkering down is obvious—to avoid impacting our upper torsos against any protruding rocks. Our journey, if successful, will be like a modified roller coaster ride; we'll just let the current carry us through. But, contrary to a captain's prerogative I won't offer my opinion as to whether or not we should go—we're a quasi democracy—we'll vote on it."

"Does it have to be unanimous?" Dr. Sedrak asked.

"I think so," Timbrook answered. "Since our lives are in jeopardy, we have to be in complete accord. I'll give you a minute to think about it and then I'll ask for your decision."

After ninety seconds Timbrook said, "I'll start with the children since they have the most to lose. I'm going to keep it simple—if you answer yes it means we go for it; if you respond with a no it means we wait to be rescued."

"Mischa?"

"Yes."

"Jake?"

"Yes."

"Eva?"

After a slight pause, "Yes."

"Dr. Sedrak?"

"If it's truly a roller coaster ride, which I love, my answer is yes."

Timbrook smiled. "We're an adventurous group—my answer is also yes. However, before we set off you'll need to remove any heavy clothing including your shoes. If you have to go for an unexpected swim you don't want anything dragging you down. Once your life jackets are secured, we'll begin. The entire voyage—based upon the speed of the current and my one hundred foot estimate—should last around three minutes."

Mischa removed a light windbreaker and her tennis shoes before she slipped on an orange colored life jacket. She had Jake tighten the vest's waist belt and shoulder straps—making sure it was snug, after which she did the same for him. They then stretched out in a semi-recumbent position using a seat cushion to elevate their heads. Mischa wanted to see where they were going and lying flat would have prevented that. Once settled, they motioned to Timbrook that they were all ready. When she felt the boat move, Mischa reached over and took Jake's hand. The strength in his firm grip made her feel safe. Whatever happened, she knew that her brother would do all in his power to help her, as she would for him.

As the boat glided past the threshold Mischa immediately understood the import of Timbrook's words. The stony ceiling was just five feet above their heads and dripping seawater would occasionally splash against her face or land in her mouth. It tasted of salt and had an earthy aftertaste that she attributed to the mineral rich rocks. The asymmetrical roof was covered in green moss that glistened when lit up by their headlamps. At about the twenty-five foot mark they drifted under a large colony of black abalones that blanketed the entire ceiling for a distance of fifteen feet. The meat from the edible sea snails was considered a delicacy in many parts of the world. She heard Jake mumble something about being 'hungry' as they passed under the mollusks.

At about the sixty foot mark Timbrook issued a warning about an approaching curve. As they entered the crescent-shaped turn the bow slammed into the angular wall, halting the boat's progress. Mischa immediately tightened her grip around Jake's hand and waited. After a few seconds, the pressure from the surging water, which was piling up against the stern, propelled the vessel forward, and like a car sideswiping a cliff, an ear-splitting grating sound ensued as the ship slowly wrenched its way through the bend.

"Poor *Nessie*," Mischa whispered

"She's definitely suffered some serious scratches," Jake whispered back.

Beyond the curve the tunnel became more constricted and the ceiling appeared to be inching closer with each passing foot. Mischa could also sense a slight acceleration of the current. A banging noise from the ship's rear was quickly followed by a jarring blow to the boat's midsection, and then a reverberating thump to the bow. *Nessie's in the same situation as a metal ball inside a pinball machine,* Mischa realized. But, instead of the ship just ricocheting off innocuous wooden pins and rubber bumpers, it was sustaining knock-out type blows from fists of solid rock. Again, she squeezed Jake's hand and this time he instantly reciprocated.

During a momentary pause in the buffeting, Timbrook yelled, "There's some daylight up ahead . . . I think we're almost through."

"Thank God," murmured Mischa. Using her elbows she elevated her upper torso by about a foot in order to see what Timbrook was referring to. She noticed a glimmer of light at the end of the dark passage and whispered up a prayer of thanksgiving before lowering herself back down.

A sudden heavy jolt caught Mischa by surprise dislodging her handhold. "What was that?" she asked Jake in a panic. Before her brother could respond, a second, more powerful impact struck the bow of the ship, punching a jagged hole through the fiberglass hull. The same unseen object then collided with the outboard engine—temporarily forcing the prop out of the water. A succession of similar hits pummeled the hull and engine, and with each forceful blow Eva would utter a short cry. *Submerged rocks,* Mischa realized, *were playing havoc with the underside of the ship and its propeller; we must be in really shallow waters.* Jake, meanwhile, had gallantly crawled forward and was attempting to plug the leak with a towel that, unfortunately, was not quite large enough to fill the hole. A crushing, grinding sound caused Mischa to immediately look rearward. The ceiling of the passageway had dipped by several inches and the bridge was being shredded by large, jagged rocks. If the ceiling dipped another few inches it would shatter into tiny fragments. She watched in horror as the VHF radio antenna, which was attached to the side of the bridge, was ripped from its mounting and hurled into the sea. She experienced a sudden chill and realized that her clothes were damp from the sea water that now covered the deck. She wondered how Jake was doing. Timbrook, in a voice filled with anxiety warned, "Stay down." Mischa ignored Timbrook's advice and peered forward. The exit loomed just twenty feet away and looked like the end portion of a subway tunnel—a semicircle that appeared to be too small for the size of their boat, but before she could even think about her own safety, *Nessie* had miraculously slipped through.

As the boat drifted in a spacious chamber swarming with barking sea lions, Mischa jubilantly screamed, "We made it!"

Eva tearfully smiled and yelled, "Praise God."

Timbrook nodded and said, "Amen to that." He then added, "Don't forget to switch off your lights."

Jake, who was still struggling with the breach said, "Now I know why the sea lions have shrewdly avoided that tunnel."

Dr. Sedrak, who was still holding Eva in his arms declared, "That was a bit more harrowing than a roller coaster ride." On impulse, he leaned over and kissed her on the lips, and was pleased that she didn't object.

Timbrook, who was watching Jake's losing battle with the sea, said to the young man, "Boston Whaler's are supposedly unsinkable, so do the best job you can to stem the flow; there are plenty of hands on board to help bail out the boat." Addressing the group, he said, "A little water is the least of our problems. As you can all see, *Nessie* has sustained a lot of damage, but she's well made so I'm sure she'll manage to get us back to port. We can't call for help because our ship-to-shore radio is useless without its antenna, and our cell phones won't work because we're in a dead zone. On a lighter note, Jake won his own bet—we're in Seal's Secret Cave."

"That's not surprising," Jake bragged.

"This is an L-shaped cave with two large entrances," Timbrook continued. "The northern entrance is somewhat closer, so that's the route we'll take." He then tried shifting into forward which caused the outboard engine to vibrate strangely. "Uh-oh," he mumbled, "we may have a problem." Timbrook reached behind the engine, flipped a latch, removed the engine hood cover, and began a careful inspection of the motor's internal parts.

After a couple of anxious minutes Dr. Sedrak asked, "What's wrong?"

Timbrook scowled, "It's my fault—I should have lifted the engine out of the water as we made our way through the passage. Those underwater boulders did a number on the gearbox—it's cracked."

"Is that bad?" Eva asked concerned.

Timbrook appeared grim. "The simple answer—yes, it's very bad. At most, I'll be able to run the engine at a notch above idle, and that's if we're lucky since it could quit at any moment. And here's the bad news—it'll take an hour to travel a half mile."

"Scorpion Cove is eighteen miles away—we'll never make it home before dark!" Eva exclaimed.

"*Nessie* won't have to take us home," Timbrook said quietly. "Once we're a third-of-a-mile off the island, we'll be out of the dead zone and our cell phones will once again become operable. At that point we'll obviously call for help, either to the Coast Guard or the Marine Lab, or both."

"Then we better get going," Eva advised, "since its already early afternoon."

"My thoughts exactly," Timbrook confirmed. "Hang on," he joked as he carefully shifted out of neutral into forward. The boat moved forward at a sluggish pace as if was being towed by a land turtle.

Ever observant, Mischa noted that Seal's Secret Cave was small in comparison to Painted Cave—about one fifth its size. It did have an impressive, deep-water main chamber, but it lacked the striking colors or cathedral-like arches of its neighboring cave.

As the boat slowly crawled its way toward the entrance, Mischa kept herself occupied by using a plastic bucket to rid *Nessie* of its unwanted water, while Jake continued his battle with the leak. In the end her brother was only moderately successful, and after ten minutes she gladly handed the bucket to Dr. Sedrak, who continued bailing.

When the boat finally reached the open ocean, Mischa's inward spirits soared. She looked forward to a home-cooked meal, a warm bath, and a comfortable bed. Being somewhat restless, she pulled out her cell phone and checked the signal bars. *No service yet, but we're only a hundred yards out. Patience,* she told herself. She held the phone in her lap and waited.

A loud clanging noise coming from the engine instantly changed her upbeat mood; plus, hearing Timbrook curse for the first time in her life didn't help.

"What now?" Dr. Sedrak asked.

Timbrook looked embarrassed. "I want to first apologize for my inappropriate word, but sometimes a man just reaches his limit. The engine, unfortunately, is freezing up. I've shifted it back into neutral in order to allow it to cool off, but I doubt it'll last much longer. I'll try again in about five minutes, but I'm not overly optimistic. I also know we're still too close to the island for cell phone reception so hopefully—when I re-engage the engine—it will last long enough to get us to that magical spot where communication is possible."

"I don't think that will be necessary," said Eva excitedly as she pointed toward the east. "There's a large ship headed our way."

"They must know we're in trouble," said Jake, "they're coming at a fast clip."

"A little too fast," Timbrook said concerned.

Mischa stared at the commercial vessel. Its outlines seemed vaguely familiar. "Is that the same ship that was shadowing us in Painted Cave?"

"If it is," replied Eva, "it certainly didn't explode, although they may have lost a shuttle-type craft. They knew we were in the cave—I wonder if they've been trying to find us and now they want to ask us some questions regarding it."

"That's possible," said Timbrook, "and while we're answering their questions they can tow *Nessie* back to Scorpion Cove."

Mischa watched as the massive boat bore down on them. *Why isn't it slowing down or altering its course?* She wondered. Not being a seasoned mariner she wasn't quite sure whether its current speed bordered on recklessness. At the last second she heard the engines throttle down as the ship executed a hard sideways turn less than thirty feet from their vessel. Because of its size the rapid maneuver caused a small-scale tidal wave to form which forcefully slammed into the side of their boat and almost swamp it.

"What idiot is in charge of that ship?" Dr. Sedrak angrily snapped.

The answer ended up being worse than his question. Standing at the ship's rail was a heavy-set man covered in hideous tattoos, carrying a rifle, which he aimed at *Nessie's* occupants. Approximately a minute later another man joined him—a tall, distinguish looking gray-haired gentleman, who was dressed in rich black leather.

"Oh no," Eva squealed tearfully.

The man dressed in leather laughed—a sinister laugh that conveyed a message of evil.

"What's going on and who is that man?" Timbrook asked Eva.

Eva looked up but was unable to respond. After a tense moment Dr. Sedrak answered on her behalf. "That man is Karl Goebbel . . . and the explosion in the gullet . . . it wasn't an accident."

36

Not a single gold coin! Kurt mumbled to himself. Disappointed, he let out his breath with a heavy sigh. Stored in the container were a stack of small bricks covered in a thin film of grayish silt. *Bricks—they packed building bricks in a brass crate—what was that all about!* He scowled. And then it hit him like, well, a ton of bricks; using his gloved right hand he quickly wiped off the silt that coated the first layer of . . . *gold bricks. Oh my God!* Kurt yelled at the top of his lungs—turning the sea into a miniature cyclone of effervescent bubbles.

After cleaning off the first gold brick, Kurt held it up for the camera, smiling broadly as he did so, for he knew exactly what it was he was holding—a standard gold bar with a minimum purity of 99.5%, 7 inches long, 3.58 inches wide, 1.75 inches thick, and weighing 400 troy ounces or 27.5 pounds. At today's commodity market prices each gold bar was worth approximately $528,000. Even underwater the molded ingot felt wonderfully heavy.

Placing it back in the crate Kurt counted the total number of bars: *Eleven.* At 27.5 pounds apiece that came to 302.50 pounds—plus the weight of the brass container. *No wonder he hadn't been able to move it.* Thankfully, the air lift bag had a 500-pound hoisting capacity.

After one last gratifying look, Kurt reluctantly replaced the lid on the crate, and then swam over to where he had ditched the Pulse 8X metal detector. Picking up the metal detector, Kurt excitedly continued his survey of the seabed surrounding the brass crate. *Where there's one box of bars there has to be others,* he logically rationalized. Besides, he still hadn't found any gold coins, and their existence was a major clue purposely left behind by Captain Flannigan.

Checking his air supply he was at 2725 psi. Kurt still had three-quarters of a tank, enough for twelve minutes of further exploration, sixteen minutes to excavate and rig the air lift bag, and ten minutes to ascend, including the mandatory two minute decompression stops at 60 and 15 feet. Presumably, at the end of the dive, he would have a seven-minute safety margin of oxygen left.

The state-of-the-art metal detector Kurt was using had both audio and visual target indicators. The audio was provided by dual underwater earphones, which he tucked under his diving hood. The visual output was displayed on a large, easy to read meter. The detector worked by transmitting a continuous stream of high-energy magnetic pulses through the seafloor. When the transmitted pulses struck a piece of metal, an electro-magnetic field was induced in the object causing 'eddy currents to flow in the metal,' which in turn generated a second electro-magnetic field. This second field was then picked up by the detector's coil that triggered the audio alarm. The meter displayed the strength of the signal, the approximate size of the object, and the depth of the target.

Kurt began his search using the brass crate as the center of his circular grid. Upon finishing a revolution, he would then expand outward two feet. Initially, the circles were extremely tight, but after the third ring the circumferences increased dramatically. Halfway through the fourth circle he had his first hit, which he immediately marked with a plastic flag. Looking at the meter, the subject generated a strong signal indicating a sizable object. The depth was less than a foot. The temptation to dig was almost overwhelming. *Just nine more minutes,* he said to himself, *stick to your plan.* At the start of the fifth circle he detected another noteworthy object buried in eighteen inches of sand. He posted a flag, but prior to continuing his search, Kurt relocated Petersen's camera so that he would remain within its visual range.

The sixth ring produced no hits, and the seventh was as barren as the sixth although he did manage to accidentally spook a five-foot Pacific angel shark that was partially buried in the sand. Upon completion of the seventh ring Kurt began to worry. *Was this the extent of the treasure?* He wondered. He had four minutes left as he began the eighth wheel of his search pattern.

At the start of the eighth ring Kurt's earlier exuberance had all but disappeared. At the halfway point he picked up a nominal hit along its outer edge, which instantly revived his gold fever. As he continued to press forward the warning sound quickly faded and then vanished. Executing a u-turn he swam back to where he had first detected the hit, and immediately picked it up again. Sweeping the bottom, Kurt observed that the signal strength increased as the coil was moved in a southerly direction. Following the audio trail, he slowly headed south. With each additional foot the high-frequency pitch became louder. As he crossed over a slight bump in the sand, the audio began to wail, and the needle on the meter went ballistic. *Thank you, thank you, thank you,* he whispered in a voice bristling with emotions. Coming to a stop, he attempted to pinpoint the origin of the intense signal, but it seemed to have no definitive source—as if the entire southwest quadrant was one massive target.

After three minutes of additional sweeping, and marking all significant hits, Kurt paused in order to admire the rectangular-shaped layout that stretched across the seafloor. Staring at his glorious map—fifteen feet long and four to five feet wide and littered with plastic flags—Kurt began uttering the Greek word and California state motto made famous by the California gold rush miners: "Eureka . . . Eureka . . . Eureka . . . I've found it." He then shook his head in utter disbelief; he had discovered the motherlode of the *S.S. Winfield Scott*.

Checking his watch, Kurt noted that he was ninety seconds beyond the twelve minutes he had allocated for exploration. His air-safety margin had just slipped to five and a half minutes unless he shortened his excavation time. *That's not going to happen,* he decided. *There's just too many tempting sites to even think about cutting back.*

Nervous with anticipation, yet slightly stunned with the number of flags, Kurt asked himself: *Which flag do I even start with?* Staring at the assortment of colorful flags reminded him of his childhood days at the local ice cream parlor. The Malibu shop carried thirty-one different types of ice cream—all lined up in parallel rows behind a thick panel of frosted glass, and he was limited to just one flavor. It was an agonizing decision for a youngster, and today's choice was just as difficult, though admittedly, with completely different rewards. And since he had no inkling as to which flag to begin with, he decided to ignore them all and started digging in the middle of his marked-out plot.

At first glance it must have appeared to Petersen via the DV-1 camera that Kurt was excavating in a helter-skelter fashion, when in actuality he had devised a commonsense plan—to scoop out a shallow trench that would eventually run the length and width of the entire site. Kurt's intent was to quarry as much sediment as possible in ten minutes, and then concentrate his efforts on the most promising targets. He'd have plenty of time over the next several days to finish excavating the motherlode as well as unearthing those hits found outside the mapped area.

As Kurt 'sand plowed' the grains of sand with his gloved hands, he created a tornadic cloud of silt that rose at least six feet off the bottom, blocking Petersen's view. *Sorry my friend,* he reflected, *not much I can do about that.*

After eight minutes of continual digging he had removed approximately a foot of sand over a seven-foot section. As he began excavating below the one-foot mark, the moment of triumph that Kurt had longed for finally arrived; initially, he saw just the top portion of a brass crate, similar in size to the one that he had previously uncovered. But, after stripping away some additional sand he was pleased to discover that it was lodged on top of an identical crate, and next to it, gold coins—hundreds and hundreds of radiant coins—and situated next to the coins, another matching crate, and amassed alongside that container, a prodigious mound of yellowish coins that were so concentrated that it appeared as if a slot machine had split open disgorging its entire contents. "Oh God . . . oh God . . . thank you, thank you for your bountiful generosity," Kurt mumbled in gratitude and then realized, with surprise, that he was becoming slightly religious. Picking up one of the coins between his right index finger and his thumb, he raised it to his mask, and was amazed at its mint-state quality. "You're a familiar sight," he whispered. The last time he had handled a twenty dollar 1850 Double Eagle Liberty Head gold piece was at Emily Flannigan's Carmel house. After inserting it into a nylon compartment located on his BC, he proceeded to scooped up two more handfuls, which he deposited into the same pocket, and then zipped it closed. *Three more minutes of excavating and then it's time to deploy the airlift bag,* Kurt said silently as an advisory to himself.

One hundred and eighty seconds later he had exposed nine additional crates, a princess's dowry in gold coins, and a brass crate that was remarkably distinct from the eleven others. One of its more salient features was its lack of weight since Kurt was able to easily free it from its century's old resting place. He then set it on the sand in front of him for a closer analysis. *You're certainly an aberration from the norm; but, most importantly,* he wondered: *Why are you so different?* The crate was half the size of the others, crafted from a richer colored brass, with more refined workmanship, and the lid was inscribed with an intricate drawing. The illustration or artwork, Kurt noted, was actually an engraving, embossed into the hot metal when it was cast. A layer of green silt filled the carving, obscuring its finer details. Taking a few seconds to wipe the grime off, Kurt leaned back a couple of feet in order to enhance his viewing perspective. After a moment's reflection, he exclaimed: *You've got to be kidding me!* Etched into the brass was a bald eagle with its wings outstretched, holding a bundle of 13 arrows in its left talon and an olive branch in its right talon. A coat of arms in the form of a flag shielded its body. In its beak the eagle was clutching a scroll with the motto *E Pluribus Unum,* which Latin phrase meant, 'Out of Many, One.' Over the eagle's head appeared an illuminated 'glory' with 13 stars arranged in five rows. Kurt knew exactly what the image was—The Great Seal of the United States of America—used by the federal government to authenticate their documents. Why the seal had been embossed onto a brass crate was definitely an enigma. *What valuable artifacts are you holding?* He mused. Unlike the other crates this one was padlocked. Hoping the salt water had dissolved the internal locking mechanism, Kurt spent a few seconds applying pressure to the bronze lock by pulling and twisting it in several different directions, but it remained as unyielding as the day it was latched. *I'll need a hacksaw if I want to pry open this one's secrets,* he concluded. Fortuitously, he had such a tool stowed on the boat. Gazing at the elegant crate Kurt made an easy decision: It was definitely going topside along with one container of gold bars.

Checking his dive computer, Kurt now had about four minutes left before he had to ascend. Fortunately, attaching the airlift bag to the handles of one of the three-hundred-pound crates would be the smoothest part of his dive. As far as the ornate crate, it was light enough for Kurt to tow all the way to the boat.

After detaching the airlift bag from his BC, Kurt unraveled it next to one of the crates. The open-bottom parachute-type bag was made out of a sturdy urethane-coated nylon material with a single-point attachment. Connected to the single-point attach-ment were four heavy-duty canvas lifting straps. Kurt clipped two of these straps to each handle, creating a multi-part sling. Using the 3 cubic foot air cylinder, he began inflating the bag with oxygen. As it ballooned out the straps became taut, assert-ing lifting force on the crate. When the strain became 'palpable,' Kurt immediately cut the air flow to short bursts. His goal was to have the object break free of the bottom without it entering into an uncontrollable ascent. *One more twist of the valve ought to do it,* he reasoned. Keeping an eye on the brass crate, Kurt released a pint-sized jet of air which had no effect whatsoever. *Stubborn, aren't you?* He scolded. Throwing open the valve he allowed a gush of air to surge into the swollen parachute and was imme-diately walloped by a soaring brass knuckle the size of a small suitcase. Luckily, the gladiator-style impact was to his steel scuba tank resulting in no physical injuries, but it did knock him off his feet and onto the seafloor wherein he sustained a bruised ego. Sitting helplessly on the sand he watched as the runaway lift bag made a beeline for the surface. Kurt suspected that Petersen was now laughing hysterically—assuming his botched maneuver was captured by the camera. But, his biggest concern was whether the young student would know what to do once the parachute erupt-ed out of the water since the wayward device would undoubtedly capsize and then deflate within a couple of minutes. Petersen would have to retrieve and then secure the lift bag to the ship within that short time frame or else the crate would once again find itself embedded on the seafloor.

Checking his dive computer, Kurt had enough air left for a lei-surely ascent. Grabbing one of the handles on the mystery crate, and holding the metal detector with his other hand, he began a slow but steady ascension, traveling thirty feet per minute. At the 60-foot mark he stopped for two minutes in order to off-load nitrogen from his system. He repeated the same procedure at the 15-foot level, but stayed a total of five minutes, allowing some extra time in order to avoid the possibility of decompression sickness. He then swam the final feet just beneath the surface. As he approached the back of the boat he had to laugh—his previous fears instantly vanishing; roped to the ship's stern was the lift bag and its precious cargo. *You're a worthy shipmate, Mr. Petersen,* he thought with a smile. He surfaced within a foot of *Serenity's* boarding ladder, and the student was already at the bottom step waiting to lend a supporting hand. The most important item that Kurt needed help with—the crate—which he handed to Petersen; the metal detector, though it had done its job admirably, would have to settle for second place.

Once on board Kurt slowly stripped off his equipment until he was down to his swimsuit and then became preoccupied with drying himself off with a beach towel. At that moment Petersen excused himself and ducked into the ship's forward cabin. The student returned with a 1.5 liter magnum bottle of Dom Perignon Brut. Kurt had just given his hair one last going over and was pulling the towel away from his eyes when he was suddenly drenched in French champagne—from a bottle that they had both previously agreed would *only* be opened upon the discovery of the *Scott's* gold.

"That's expensive wine!" Kurt protested, as he wisely licked what dripped into his mouth.

"I'm not a complete fool," replied Petersen, "I only wasted a quarter of a bottle."

"Well, I guess sousing the ship's captain is not a total *waste* of good wine," Kurt teased as he again licked his lips, and then burst out laughing.

Petersen joined in the laughter, pouring a small amount over his own head. He then produced two elegant fluted glasses, and filled each one to the brim. "To a highly successful mission," he said in a satisfied tone.

"Amen to that," said Kurt, "and to an absolutely brilliant and wonderful assistant." They clinked their wine glasses together, creating a bright falsetto sound, then each quickly downed their glasses which Petersen promptly refilled.

After a moment of quiet reflection, Petersen said, "There's a lot of gold down there. If each crate holds eleven bars . . . and you've found thirteen thus far . . . we're talking about extraordinary wealth, plus the thousands of gold coins, plus what's stored in the locked crate that's currently on board."

"Each crate," said Kurt with an overly expansive grin, "has a market value of six million dollars, and the gold content of each Double Eagle is worth at least twelve hundred dollars, but as a historical coin prized by collector's—its face value increases exponentially—perhaps four thousand dollars."

"That's hard to fathom," said Petersen, "the incredible opulence that you'll now have to deal with."

"It's only money," said Kurt, "you can either use it to benefit humanity, or it can be a torturous noose around your neck. As you know a lot of rich people are quite miserable."

"True," Petersen agreed, "but a lot of poor people wouldn't mind trading places."

"The key," said Kurt somberly, "is using your wealth wisely. The real value in the *Scott's* gold is that it will open doors that are now closed—to effect change in a positive way. The government will obviously squander its majority share, but what's left—and thankfully it's still substantial—will be used constructively."

"It will be interesting to see *how* you spend your money and on *what*," Petersen said as he set down his flute. "But right now, I'm more interested in what's inside that locked crate."

"I'm just as curious as you are," said Kurt who also set down his wine glass. "But, we'll need a hacksaw to cut through that bronze padlock. Fortunately, we have that tool on board—it's stored in the utility box on the starboard deck."

"I'll get it," said Petersen as he headed in the direction of the saw.

Kurt picked up the crate and the towel he had used to dry himself, and carried them into the forward cabin. He spread the towel over a teak dining table hoping to protect it from any damage that might be caused by their efforts to open the crate, and then placed the crate on top of it. Petersen returned with the hacksaw, which Kurt was pleased to see was almost brand new. Cutting bronze with an old blade would be a laborious task.

"Your pleasure or mine?" Petersen asked.

"Yours," said Kurt, "I'm still somewhat exhausted from the dive."

"It shouldn't take too long," Petersen declared. "The blade is made out of the newfangled molybdenum high speed steel and should cut through bronze without any problems. Holding the two-inch u-shaped hinged padlock with his left hand, and sawing with his right hand, Petersen began driving the blade with deliberate back and forth strokes. In less than a minute he had sliced through one side of the sliding shackle, and without taking a break, began on the other. Within fifty seconds the final shackle was severed, and with a dull thud, the ancient padlock fell to the table.

"I'm impressed!" gasped Kurt in amazement.

"Ancient bronze didn't have a chance against our modern alloys," Petersen said with a victorious smile.

"In honor of your swift success—I'll let you have the pleasure of raising the cover and revealing the crate's contents."

"In that case we'll need a drum roll," Petersen said anxiously. Placing his hands on each side of the brass lid, he slowly raised it until it was at ninety degrees. "See anything?" he asked.

"Probably the same as you—a crate filled with tannin-stained water," replied Kurt, "that's hopefully hiding a treasure trove within."

"Then it's time for my hands and fingers to go on their own diving adventure," announced Petersen, who immediately plunged them into the reddish-tinged water.

Kurt carefully watched Petersen's expression, which went from questioning scowl, to knowing smile within a matter of seconds;

however, it was the superficial laughter that totally rattled his nerves. "What's so funny?" he asked concerned.

"This!" said Petersen as he quickly extracted a light green oval-shaped glass container from the crate. "A wine bottle from the days of old."

For a brief moment Kurt was taken aback. *A wine bottle . . . locked in its own special receptacle . . . the captain's personal stash in a Federal crate? That's ridiculous!* He briefly examined the bottle and declared incredulously, "There's no wine in it!"

Petersen placed the bottle on the table and spent some time assessing it up close. "You're right," he confirmed. "But," he continued, "unless my eyes are deceiving me—it contains a scroll."

"A message in a bottle—how nice and how quaint, but that's definitely not what I was expecting," Kurt said slightly disappointed.

"It's certainly not filled with sparkling gold or diamonds," Petersen said empathically, "but whoever sealed this glass container with a champagne type oak plug did an excellent job. That official looking document is bone-dry."

"It does make you wonder why they went to so much trouble to safeguard it."

"Only one way to know," said Petersen. Using the same corkscrew wine opener that he had employed on the Dom Perignon, he twisted the cork plug out, and handed the bottle to Kurt. "The captain of the ship should be the first to read this historical communiqué."

"A chivalrous offer," said Kurt, "which I readily accept." He tipped the bottle upside down and a three-page document made from thick cotton fibers slid out. He began straightening the rolled pages by flattening them against the table with his hands, and as he was doing so, noticed that the wording was written in two different languages—English and Spanish. Fortunately, he was as proficient in Spanish as he was in English. He glanced at its title.

Northwestern Mexican Territories and Baja California Peninsula
Purchase Treaty: November 15, 1853
Treaty Between
The United States of America
And The Mexican Republic

The exact same title was then set forth in Spanish. Kurt re-read the title several times before asking Petersen: "Are you aware of any negotiations in the mid-1800's between the United States and Mexico regarding the potential purchase of Mexico's Northern Territories and Baja California?"

"No, but that kind of agreement would have solved the immigration issue," joked Petersen.

Kurt smiled at Petersen's inane response and then continued reading, but this time out loud.

IN THE NAME OF ALMIGHTY GOD:
The President of the United States of America and the President of the Mexican Republic, on behalf of their people, have agreed upon the articles following:

ARTICLE I
There shall be firm and universal peace between the United States of America and the Mexican Republic, and between their respective countries, territories, cities, towns, and people without exception of places or persons.

ARTICLE II
The Mexican Republic desiring to give to the United States a strong proof of its friendship doth hereby cede to the United States in the name of the Mexican Republic forever and in full Sovereignty the following Mexican States with all its right and appurtenances: Baja California,

Baja California Sur, Sonora, Chihuahua, Coahuila, Nuevo Leon, and Tamaulipas.

"Wow—this is incredible!" Kurt said loudly. "If this agreement had become law this would have been a major game changer for our individual countries. Those states represent about forty percent of Mexico's entire landmass. Imagine what our respective countries would look like if this re-drawing of the boundaries had actually taken place."

"The Mexican Government was either desperate for cash or the United States was about to invade their country and forcibly annex their land. A bad deal is still better than a resounding defeat," Petersen speculated.

"Maybe," said Kurt who then picked up where he had left off.

ARTICLE III

In order to designate the boundary lines with due precision, the two Governments shall each appoint a commissioner and a surveyor, who, before the expiration of one year from the date of this Treaty, shall meet at the port of San Diego, and proceed to mark the said boundaries. The boundary lines established by this Article shall be religiously respected by each of the two Republics, and no change shall ever be made therein, except by the express and free consent of both nations.

ARTICLE IV

Mexicans now established in States previously belonging to Mexico, shall be free to continue where they now reside, or to remove at any time to the Mexican Republic, retaining the property which they possess in their respective States, or disposing thereof, and removing the proceeds wherever they please.

Those who shall prefer to remain in the said States may either retain the title and rights of Mexican citizens, or acquire those of citizens of the United States. Those, however, who shall remain in the said States after the expiration of a year from the date of this Treaty, without having declared their intention to retain the character of Mexicans, shall be considered to have elected to become Citizens of the United States.

ARTICLE V

In consideration of the extension acquired by the boundaries of the United States, as defined in the second Article of the present Treaty, the Government of the United States engages to pay to that of the Mexican Republic the sum of five million dollars which amount shall be immediately transferred after the Treaty is dated and signed by Mexican President, Antonio Lopez de Santa Anna.

The sum of five million dollars shall be summarily paid to the Mexican Government by that of the United States, in gold bars and gold coins in the following amounts: forty brass crates each carrying eleven bars of gold and weighing 302.50 lbs apiece; and, 40 canvas sacks each filled with 75 lbs of gold coins. Total gold weight: 15,100 lbs.

"Fifteen thousand pounds of gold!" interrupted Petersen with a shout. "Sitting beneath our boat just waiting for us to retrieve it; that's a bloody fortune. How much is that in today's dollars?"

Taking a few moments Kurt calculated the amount in his head before answering. "At $1200 an ounce x's 241,600 ounces—about two hundred and ninety million dollars—plus or minus a few million."

Petersen responded by mumbling, "That's unbelievable . . . this is crazy . . . the press, or at least the historians, are going to go nuts," and then said, "what else is on the document?"

"Concluding paragraph," said Kurt as he resumed reading.

ARTICLE VI

The present Treaty shall become effective upon the date and signature of Mexican President, Antonio Lopez de Santa Anna.

In good faith whereof, the President of the United States, Franklin Pierce, has signed these Articles in the English and Spanish languages this fifteenth day of November, in the year of our Lord one thousand eight hundred and fifty-three.

President of the United States, Franklin Pierce

President of the Mexican Republic:_____

Antonio Lopez de Santa Anna

Dated:_____

"That's it," said Kurt.

"Did President Pierce actually sign it?" Petersen asked.

"Yes—unless it's a forgery, but it definitely appears to be his actual signature; however, Mexican President Santa Anna apparently never signed it, which explains why this Treaty wasn't implemented and why its very existence hasn't been acknowledged by either government."

"The Mexican people still resent the Treaty of Guadalupe Hidalgo and the Gadsden Purchase which ceded vast tracts of land to the United States; it's certainly understandable why the two governments have kept it a secret."

"But now we have the original," said Kurt philosophically, "which opens up a Pandora's Box as to what to do with it. Its very disclosure could have severe and far-reaching consequences."

"What are you going to do?"

"Meditate on it for a while, but my gut tells me that the public, along with historians, have the right to examine it, plus it explains the gold."

"And," added Petersen, "it also sheds light on the probable reason for the explosion on the *Scott*—sabotage—to prevent the Treaty and its shipment of gold from ever reaching Mexico."

"*Sabotage*," repeated Kurt, "that's an interesting hypothesis; a saboteur will typically resort to the destruction of property in order to undermine the actions of its government that the revolutionary strongly disagrees with. The elimination of a loathsome Treaty, and the gold destined for a despised regime, clearly fits within that definition."

"So . . . does that mean you agree with my theory?"

"In this case," Kurt said with a broad smile, "yes, but don't let my affirmation go to your head."

"I'll stay as humble as the day I was born," promised Petersen.

"That's what I was afraid of," laughed Kurt.

"Along that same line," said Petersen, "you lost the bet."

"That's one bet I'm thrilled to lose."

"That's good because I've already ordered the beer."

"How?"

"On your platinum credit card."

"You lifted it from my wallet?"

"I *temporarily borrowed* it. You left it on the cabin table in plain sight. After you discovered that crate packed with gold bars I thought, 'why wait.' However, I do want to apologize; instead of ninety dollars a bottle they now cost niney-nine. I figured you wouldn't object."

"Have you replaced my credit card?"

"Yes."

"Well, pull it right back out and order another two cases; I'm in the mood to celebrate, especially with my favorite graduate student."

"Consider it done," said Petersen with a warm smile. "And," he added, "that Providence question involving the white pelican—I've upped the split to one hundred percent—it was definitely a heavenly sign."

Kurt watched as Petersen opened a small drawer where he had apparently stashed his wallet after using it earlier. He still wasn't at the one hundred percent level, but he was getting closer. However, there was one thing he had already decided upon, his next art purchase; a sculpture of a white pelican hand carved from rich basswood.

While Petersen was busy placing the new order, Kurt left the cabin and walked to the boat's stern, where he stared with wonder at the brass crate attached to the airlift bag. *You're living a dream,* he said to himself, *enjoy it.* As he was waiting for the student to join him and lend a hand at hoisting the heavy container onto the deck, Kurt emptied the gold coins from the pockets of his BC. He counted fifty-seven. *That's a favorable start,* he thought. *Just 47,943 more and then we'll be done, plus the 39 brass crates.* He chuckled when he realized the enormity of it all. He then began whistling, 'We're in the Money,' the opening song by Ginger Rogers from the 1933 film *Gold Diggers;* his life as a successful treasure hunter had just begun.

Over the next five days, with the help of four trusted diving friends, Kurt and Petersen recovered all forty brass crates, and 45,580 Double Eagle coins. Approximately 2,420 gold coins were never found—the equivalent of two canvas bags.

Once the recovery efforts ceased, Kurt's lawyers began secret negotiations with the United States Justice Department over the amount of the Salvor's reward. They also provided a copy of the treaty to both the United States and Mexican Governments. The discussions, according to the lead attorney, were going well, and a favorable decision was expected any day. Kurt's intent, following a successful agreement, was to schedule a major press conference, and reveal to the world, his amazing discovery.

37

Karl Goebbel leaned against the ship's railing and stared at *Nessie's* passengers with obvious disdain. From his lofty vantage point—both physically and psychologically—he fixed his gargoyle-like gaze upon Eva and Dr. Sedrak, and in a voice filled with loathing said, "Dr. Chen, Dr. Sedrak . . . what a pleasure to see you again. From the information I've gathered you've both been incredibly busy the last thirty days: treating medical patients with unusual diseases, scuba diving on my fish farm at Platform Gail, conducting a number of interesting tests whose results were quite intriguing—yes, hacking your computers was child's play—talking to the CDC, and an exploratory trip to Alberta, Canada. I imagine your tour of Aspen Packers was especially informative unless you had an overly sensitive stomach."

"You're correct about Aspen Packers," Dr. Sedrak said in a defiant tone, "we learned a lot at that repulsive plant. Foremost, that only an insane person would feed rendered cow parts infected with bovine spongiform encephalopathy to farmed-raised fish when there was a high probability that the tainted fish would transmit the deadly disease to human beings. Does Creutzfeldt Jakob disease, or by its British name, mad cow disease, ring a bell, or do you even care?"

"Death is an inevitable part of life, like the rising and setting of the sun," Goebbel hissed. "A few casualties—before their appointed time—what difference does it ultimately make?"

Raising his voice, Dr. Sedrak said, "Because they're preventable, and corporate profits should never be elevated above human life."

"That's where we disagree," Goebbel said condescendingly. "I'm a venture capitalist, and every novel investment involves a certain amount of unpredictability, especially an ocean-based aquafarm. The upside in our situation . . . the world's hungry for nutritious meat, and I provide a reliable supply. The downside—a few people experience a disagreeable reaction. One can't exist without the other. From a cost-benefit analysis it's simple—the need for a steady source of protein-rich fish outweighs any potential risks."

Dr. Sedrak scowled. "Would you like to make that same pathetic speech to Desiree, or to Sandy, or to the parents of a surfer who was killed, or to his two friends that sustained catastrophic injuries, or to a young child by the name of Reese?"

"Who the hell are they?" Goebbel asked derisively. "If they're the names of your patients I don't give a shit."

Dr. Sedrak was appalled—clearly Goebbel was a sociopath. "You may not, but I definitely do. Desiree's husband, Keith, suffered a tormented death from eating your contaminated fish, as did Sandy. The surfers as well as Reese were attacked by an infected bottlenose dolphin. I'm sure a competent personal injury lawyer—in front of a local jury—would enjoy eviscerating your cost-benefit analysis. How many millions of dollars is Keith's life worth, or Sandy's, or the surfer's? What's the value of injuries that will last a lifetime? One, two, three million? Plus, let's not forget the additional millions in punitive and exemplary damages that a jury will gladly assess because of your willful and wanton disregard for human life. What kind of verdict would it take to bankrupt your company? An incensed jury just might do that."

Goebbel stared at Dr. Sedrak in the same way an enraged bull would a red cape. He wrapped his fingers around the stainless steel rail and began squeezing it as if it was a person's neck. His face turned bright red and his facial features became distorted as his brow muscles moved inward and then downward, accompanied by barred teeth, flared nostrils, and loud breathing. After a few moments he relaxed his grip and his expression returned to normal. In a controlled voice he said, "You're clearly not only a skillful doctor, but you're also a good orator. Unfortunately for you, your legal prognosis will never occur. Your boat looks as though it suffered its own perilous journey through hell, and that will shortly be your future too. Somehow, you made it out of that cave; when I'm through, you'll wish you'd never left it."

Timbrook rose to his feet. "What about the children? I don't fully understand what's going on, but obviously they had nothing to do with this investigation against your company."

Goebbel sneered. "They're intelligent eyewitnesses, the same as you. As the cliché goes . . . you're all in the same boat."

Eva joined Timbrook. "You would harm them?" she gasped.

Goebbel smiled. "Absolutely not," he replied sweetly, and after a short laugh added deviously, "but Mother Nature might."

"What do you mean by that?" Eva asked warily.

"You'll know soon enough," Goebbel snapped. "But first, I have a few simple requests that if not properly carried out will result in my sadistic friend, Pancho, reacting accordingly. For example, if I demand that you toss your life jackets into the ocean, and you fail to comply, my loyal employee, who despises disobedience, will respond as follows."

Pancho quickly sighted the rifle and without any warning fired off six rounds in two seconds which punched six, one inch holes through *Nessie's* fiberglass hull. One of the bullets grazed Timbrook's left shin. Timbrook grimaced but said nothing. A thin stream of blood ran down his ankle and pooled at the bottom of the boat. The six bullet holes instantly became miniature geysers as fountains of water gushed into the boat. The sudden and violent assault immediately silenced *Nessie's* passengers. Eva noticed the pinkish fluid mixing with seawater, and was the first to regain her emotional sensibilities, "Timbrook's been shot!" she shouted.

"I'm okay," Timbrook said reassuringly as he sat back down. "The bullet only nicked my left leg."

"But you're bleeding!" she insisted.

"All cuts bleed," he said dismissively as Dr. Sedrak summarily checked the wound. "But what really concerns me," he pressed, "is the amount of water accumulating inside the boat. Even a Boston Whaler will eventually sink."

Dr. Sedrak finished his brief exam, "You were lucky," he said to Timbrook, "the projectile only gouged your skin and a thin layer of muscle; another half inch and it would have shattered your tibia." He then turned and with scorching eyes glared at both Goebbel and Pancho. "Why?" he asked.

"*Why?*" Goebbel repeated in a mocking tone. "For a brilliant doctor your feigned naiveté is almost comical. From my biased perspective the total destruction of a man's livelihood is an extremely serious matter warranting drastic measures. My sanity would definitely be in question if I just sat on the sidelines and allowed you to accomplish your ruinous goal. You've made your own bed by your current actions and now you must live—or in this case, die—with the consequences. Your female accomplice and your hapless companions are merely collateral damage."

Mischa, who had purposely remained silent during the verbal exchange, leaned over to Jake and whispered, "His sanity is already in question, try plugging the holes." She then carefully positioned her cell phone on the bow cushion before standing up. In a voice quivering with trepidation she said to Goebbel, "Whatever you're planning you'll never get away with it. For your information my dad's in charge of the marine lab on Santa Cruz Island. Jake, his only son, is also on board. If you harm his children, or for that matter any of the passengers on this ship, you'll have to deal with his wrath. So far, nothing too bad has occurred. If you turn your boat around and head back to port, at most you'll only be charged with recklessly discharging a firearm, and that mistake can be blamed on an irresponsible employee." She then sat back down and quietly retrieved her cell phone.

Goebbel looked at Mischa and laughed. "I'll grant you this; you're brave for a young girl, but your immaturity also makes you ignorant as to the ways of the world. A pitiful little heroic speech, filled with veiled threats, doesn't change a thing." He then motioned to Pancho who quickly fired off two shots. The copper-tipped slugs smashed into the hull within inches of Jake's right hand, which he had just used to stuff a wad of cloth into a bullet hole. Jake uttered a startled cry even though he hadn't been shot. "Tell your foolish brother," Goebbel added coldly, "to leave the holes alone or else the next salvo won't miss."

"He's not deaf," Mischa replied just as cold-hearted, "he heard you."

"Good—then your brother won't mind obeying my next demand—unplug the leak he just stopped up, plus that nice big one that appears to be of recent origin. Submerged reef rocks," Goebbel chuckled, "can be so brutal on a ship's integrity."

Jake gave Goebbel a hate-filled scowl but responded as directed and removed the fabric corks.

Seawater poured through the eight bullet holes and the large gash, filling the bottom of the boat. *Nessie will be totally inundated and capsize in less than a half hour,* Mischa estimated. With no one actively bailing, the water was already four inches deep.

"It's time to empty the boat," announced Goebbel. "We'll begin with your lifejackets; toss them into the sea."

"Are you serious?" asked Eva.

"Absolutely," Goebbel replied. "Do it or my gangster friend will enforce the order with a barrage of merciless bullets."

Mischa removed her lifejacket and dropped it into the ocean watching as it slowly drifted away. Eva, in a show of contempt, was the last to comply.

"Now," ordered Goebbel, "dump everything into the ocean that's not permanently affixed to the boat—seat cushions, tools, buckets, ice chest, beverage containers, food items, towels, emergency kit, flares, backpacks, and whatever else that's laying around or hidden inside a storage locker."

After five minutes the boat was mostly empty except for its human occupants. The final, 'unattached' item near Mischa was the bucket that contained the squid. It was half full. The sea lions had eaten the other half. The remainder had been set aside for the giant oarfish. *That's not going to happen,* she sadly realized. The oarfish seemed like a distant memory. As she reached for the bucket she accidentally knocked it over and the squid fell out. *Who cares,* she thought. She retrieved the bucket and hurled it into the sea.

Goebbel paced the rail and grinned like a successful prize fighter. "One final piece of equipment," he bellowed. "Your cell phones. It's time for their burial at sea."

Mischa let out a frightened gasp. "Jake," she whispered, "I need your help."

"With what?" he asked under his breath.

"My iPhone—"

"It's replaceable, Mischa," he said slightly irked. "If we get out of this alive, dad will obviously buy you a brand-new one."

"No Jake, that's not it. When that ship showed up I hit my video app. I have footage of everything that's been said. What I've recorded could be used as evidence in a court of law. I don't want to lose that critical information."

Jake paused a few seconds before responding. "I wish I had thought of that," he said with a proud smile. "But, you don't need to worry—your iPhone—it's waterproof. After its last accidental dunking, dad bought you a cell phone with a waterproof case. It'll survive the plunge, but for how long—that's a different story."

Mischa nodded. "I'd forgotten about that. At least there's a chance at recovering the data as long as I can find it again."

"You will," Jake said confidently. "It won't be the only thing down there. We've tossed a lot of objects. Our debris field should be easy to locate."

"Then let's enhance my future search by dropping them together," suggested Mischa. "Two rectangular devices should be easier to spot than just one."

"Excellent idea," Jake agreed.

Holding their arms parallel to one another, Mischa and Jake let go at the same time. As their phones disappeared into the watery depths, Mischa felt like an actual limb had been torn from her body. An iPhone was more than just an electronic instrument—it was her life's story—all her friend's information was stored in its digital memory, along with thousands of e-mails, texts, photos, songs, books, games, movies, and videos, plus hundreds of useful apps. She prayed that the actual separation would be brief. When the phone was no longer visible she looked up and was surprised to see that the two men were gone. She then heard the other ship's engines powering up. *Maybe they're leaving*, she thought hopefully. Unfortunately, her momentary optimism was short-lived. Instead of the ship moving out, the operator had repositioned the boat so that its stern now faced their vessel. Stenciled across its rear were two words, *Lucky Lady*, and lined up on its deck were seven, fifty-five gallon drums. Mischa noticed that the lids had been removed. *Lucky Lady*, she thought, *was an inappropriate name; Devil Lady would be closer to the truth.*

"What are they doing?" asked Jake.

"I have no idea," Mischa responded, "but it can't be good." Mischa checked the water level inside the boat. It had risen another three inches.

After a moment the tattooed man reappeared and wrestled one of the barrels onto the swim platform.

"Whatever's in it must weigh a lot," said Mischa.

After he had the barrel situated, the man Goebbel called Pancho looked at them and laughed.

"What's so funny?" Eva demanded.

"It's dinner time," he replied, "and you're the main dish." He then tipped the barrel over.

What spilled out caused Eva to gag.

Mischa also experienced a wave of nausea. The bloody mess looked like leftovers from a slaughterhouse. The water quickly turned ruby-red.

Jake seemed to be struggling for air, and Timbrook mumbled something about it being unholy.

Only Dr. Sedrak seemed unaffected by the gory scene. "Its pathological medical waste," he clarified, "obviously from an unscrupulous hospital trying to save costs. This type of bio-hazardous material is supposed to be incinerated, which explains why it's being dumped into the ocean—it's a lot less expensive."

"What's in it?" asked Mischa.

Dr. Sedrak appeared to weigh his words before responding. "All types of human tissue; each barrel holds the equivalent of several hundred surgical procedures."

"That's awful," said Eva, "and a dishonor to the patients."

Once the drum was empty, Pancho pushed it down until it filled with water and sank. He then secured a second barrel and repeated the process. With the third drum the ship started moving. At a leisurely pace the *Lucky Lady* entered into a tight pattern around *Nessie*. As the ship circled their vessel Pancho carefully tilted the barrel so that its contents slowly oozed out. After one complete revolution *Nessie* was surrounded with human chum—luring thousands of silvery baitfish and a few dive-bombing seagulls, who gorged on the fleshly remnants.

Timbrook was the first to verbalize what everyone was thinking. "They're trying to attract sharks. When our boat sinks we'll be the next item on the menu."

"They've already succeeded," Jake said as he pointed at a two-foot high dorsal fin slicing through the water.

"That's a large shark," Eva confirmed.

"What type?" Mischa asked.

"Either a great white or a mako," Eva guessed.

The fourth barrel served as the spark that ignited a feeding frenzy. Animal remains—some whole, some surgically mutilated, and some with their heads chopped off, slid out of the barrel.

"Oh my God!" lamented Eva. "Who would intentionally kill so many innocent creatures?" She looked at Dr. Sedrak for the answer.

Mischa also turned to Dr. Sedrak and waited for his response. A majority of the animals, she noted, were albino rodents—rats, mice, guinea pigs, and rabbits—adorable when alive but horrible in death, especially as their white fur was now stained bright red. She uttered a loud gasp when a few piglets tumbled out along with a disemboweled spider monkey.

After a deep sigh Dr. Sedrak said, "You're not going to like my answer, but every member of the human race. Each year millions of animals are sacrificed in the name of science—whether for bio-tech research, medical testing, or in the quest for a new product. In the end we're all somewhat guilty."

"That may be hypothetically true," acknowledged Jake, "but right now mankind's not going to pay the ultimate price—we are—those bloodstained critters are attracting a hoard of savage predators."

Mischa followed Jake's gaze. Instead of one fin there were now four, and those were the ones on the surface. Just beneath their boat was an assortment of grayish blue to deep blue torpedo-shaped sharks. The more robust sharks she assumed were great whites or makos, and the slender ones, blue sharks. Ordinarily she would be thrilled to see so many sharks in one area, but not today. The water was now up to their seats. Another six inches and the boat would founder. She involuntarily shuddered as she thought about what would happen next. A great white's teeth were etched like serrated carving knives, and a mako like curved daggers. Blue sharks had small teeth, but they were triangular and razor-sharp, and once the rather docile sharks were agitated, they attacked like a pack of voracious piranhas.

As the *Lucky Lady* continued to circle *Nessie*, Pancho, in rapid succession, unloaded the fifth, sixth, and final barrel—flooding the ocean with a banquet of meaty corpses, which further aroused the bloodthirsty sharks.

Once the last barrel was emptied out the *Lucky Lady* came to a stop, and Goebbel joined Pancho at the stern's rail. Goebbel then ogled *Nessie's* passengers as he would a girly magazine and Pancho leered at them with a ravenous look.

"Why are they staring at us like we're entertainment?" asked Jake.

"Because we are," Timbrook replied. "The most sickening type of voyeurism involves watching a member of the human race suffer a violent death. The ancient Roman Empire specialized in this type of brutal entertainment with their fight-to-the-death gladiator contests and by their use of wild animals—lions, tigers, and bears—to tear apart criminals or Christians. Right now we're in the same position, and the wild beasts are the sharks."

Eva shook her head. "We can't just sit here and let it happen. Isn't there anything we can do?"

Timbrook and Dr. Sedrak looked at each other—each seeking an answer from the other. After a moment Timbrook spoke, but in a hushed tone. "We only have two options—try to take over the *Lucky Lady*, or make a swim for it."

"How is either one feasible?" moaned Eva.

"I don't see the rifle anymore," said Timbrook, "so it's possible we could overwhelm them with our superior numbers. The ship is only thirty feet away. In spite of the damage to our outboard engine it's still idling, and assuming I can shift it back into forward, maybe we can reach their vessel, and after a brief scuffle, force them to surrender their ship."

Eva eyes teared up. "Have you seen Pancho? He looks like a smaller version of the Incredible Hulk. And Goebbel . . . he looks like a Nazi SS guard. No offense, but either one of those two brutes could single-handedly take out our entire group—not to mention that the rifle may actually be nearby and as soon as we make a move, Pancho would start shooting. You're other plan—making a swim for it—what's the likelihood that any of us would survive that gauntlet of predators?"

Timbrook took his time before he answered. "Pretty good," he said quietly. "The island is less than four hundred feet away—about a fifteen-minute swim. The only impediment, of course, is the sharks; the obvious solution is to keep them distracted. If their attention is successfully diverted . . . then you won't have a problem."

Mischa shivered when she heard Timbrook's words. The lower half of her body was soaked from seawater, but that wasn't the source of her goose bumps. "What did you mean by . . . *you won't have a problem?*"

Timbrook shrugged. "I've been shot, I'm bleeding, and I'm old. I've enjoyed a good life, and to tell you the truth, I look forward to seeing my wife again. I'll be the diversion. My blood will be the bait."

Eva was almost hysterical. "That's crazy—sacrificing your own life for us? I couldn't live with myself if I allowed you to do that."

"Nor could I," Mischa quickly added.

"We may not have a choice," Timbrook whispered. "In about ten minutes this boat will sink, and then it's every man or woman for themselves. At least my plan offers hope."

Jake, who was on the verge of tears, said, "We need to stay together. If the engine's still somewhat functional why can't we just point the boat toward the island and make a run for it. Every foot closer to the island gets us beyond the feeding frenzy."

"Jake does set forth a valid alternative," said Dr. Sedrak, "I vote we give it a try."

"That's our vote too," Eva and Mischa declared together.

Timbrook stared at their faces for a few seconds before responding, "Okay, but if Jake's idea fails, then it's back to my original proposal, which means I'll be the first to abandon ship. Once I'm in the water I'll swim toward the *Lucky Lady* while you immediately head in the opposite direction. Any delay in executing my plan could be costly. No matter what you hear . . . promise me this . . . you'll keep swimming. Is that understood?"

Dr. Sedrak, Eva, Mischa, and Jake reluctantly nodded their agreement.

"Thank you," said Timbrook. "We'll know in a minute if the gears are totally shot."

As Timbrook fiddled with the shifting mechanism, the boat was suddenly rocked by a jarring underwater impact in the exact area where everyone was sitting. Mischa and Jake instinctively lifted their feet. After a brief respite a second collision occurred, but this time at the ship's stern.

"Another impact like that and we'll be upended," Timbrook warned.

In a shaky voice Jake asked. "Why are the sharks attacking the boat?"

"They know the end is near," Eva answered, "and they're trying to accelerate the process."

Mischa uttered a frightened cry when she spotted three huge sharks approaching their vessel. As the creatures began circling *Nessie* a loud, triumphant cheer erupted from the deck of the *Lucky Lady*.

"Unbelievable!" Dr. Sedrak said angrily.

"Ignore them," Eva advised.

"It's useless!" exclaimed Timbrook, "it's stuck in idle. There's nothing more I can do."

"Try again." Dr. Sedrak ordered.

"We're out of time," Timbrook shouted back. He reached down and ripped open the bullet wound, releasing a torrent of fresh blood.

"Watch out!" yelled Mischa as the three sharks collectively plowed into the midsection of the boat, shoving the ship sideways, and causing a wave of water to engulf the interior. The additional deluge swamped *Nessie*. Mischa could feel the boat settling beneath her. In another two minutes they would be treading water.

From the deck of the *Lucky Lady* came ecstatic shouts of joy as if their football team had just won the Super Bowl.

Timbrook stood up. "It's now or never," he screamed.

As Timbrook was preparing to leap, Eva shrieked "*Noooooo.*"

Timbrook suddenly hesitated. Eyes wide. His countenance a picture of death.

38

Nessie, Mischa observed with a horrible sense of foreboding, was now surrounded by over a dozen sharks, rendering any chance of escape impossible. It no longer matter how fast they could swim—they couldn't out swim a pack of sharks. Timbrook's plan had failed. "Jake," she cried. Her brother wrapped his arms around her. She held him tight. "I love you," she whispered. As she snuggled against his chest, the ship's center of gravity suddenly changed. *Nessie* was beginning to slip beneath the waves. The outboard engine abruptly sputtered and finally died as water was drawn into the air intake valve. She looked over at Timbrook to say goodbye and was startled and confused by what she saw. His expression of fear had changed into one of bewilderment. She let go of Jake and looked out over the water. *The sharks . . . they've disappeared! That's impossible,"* she told herself. She gazed into the depths. Not a single beast lurked below. "Jake" she said tearfully, "they're all gone."

"Not all of them," Jake countered. "Something massive just buzzed the ship's bow and is now heading for the *Lucky Lady*."

Mischa stared into the water. *Nothing.* Whatever animal had spooked her brother had already vanished. "Jake—" and then her jaw dropped.

"Oh my God!" Jake mumbled.

A massive eel-like creature had suddenly exploded out of the ocean and was now soaring across the *Lucky Lady's* stern. Mischa had never seen the serpent in such a state of agitation—its three-dimensional skin glowing—reflecting light in a prism of colors, all of which were resplendent in their spectral brilliance. As the giant oarfish glided over the ship's rail its midsection came into contact with the metal deck resulting in the discharge of a bolt of energized light which instantly lit up the entire structure. Fireworks-type sparks flared from the end points of metal objects, and a small blaze erupted in a pile of oily rags. Two, high-pitched, bloodcurdling screams began and ended within a split second of each other, followed by an eerie silence. The smell of ozone and nitric oxide, similar to the odor produced after a severe lighting storm, permeated the air.

Mischa watched breathlessly as the oarfish's momentum carried it across the entire width of the stern. At the opposing rail the creature hesitated for a moment before it slithered back into the ocean—its polychromatic coloring having rapidly faded to a silver-gray. "Jake . . . the oarfish," she began, and then was interrupted when the floor beneath her feet suddenly disappeared. *Nessie's* journey to the bottom of the sea had begun. After enduring a brief immersion, Mischa managed to keep her head above water by dog paddling. She performed a 360-degree spin to make sure that her companions were okay, especially Timbrook. She counted four bobbing heads. *That's everyone,* she murmured to herself, relieved, though she realized they were still in peril.

Dr. Sedrak, who was stroking the water furiously in order to remain vertical asked, "What do we do now? The sharks could return at any moment."

Timbrook, who was having the most difficulty staying afloat said, "I don't think I can make it to the island. Let's try to board the *Lucky Lady*. I think the oarfish stunned its passengers. If we're fortunate they'll still be disabled which will allow us to hog-tie their arms and legs before they fully revive."

"Then we better hurry," Eva insisted. "Even in an anesthetized state those two monsters could be dangerous."

Mischa was about to head toward the boat when she noticed some squid drifting on the water. *The oarfish food!* She quickly nabbed a small handful and stuffed them into her pants pocket.

The thirty-foot swim took less than a minute. Once they reached the swim platform Timbrook boarded first, followed by Dr. Sedrak, Jake, then Eva, and finally Mischa.

As Mischa was climbing up the aluminum ladder she expected to hear scuffling type sounds—men struggling with each other— or words of profanity. Surprisingly, it was relatively quiet except for some indistinct mumbling. Once she stepped onto the rear deck she understood why. The two men were still unconscious. *The oarfish must have really zapped them,* she thought with a smile. She couldn't imagine two individuals more deserving of an electrical shock. Taking in the scene, she saw Timbrook acting as Dr. Sedrak's bodyguard while the doctor was on his knees checking the prone men's vital signs. Jake, was occupied with putting out the small fire. Mischa was stunned that no one seemed overly concerned about what might happen once the bad guys woke up. "You want me to look for some rope?" she asked.

Dr. Sedrak stood up, rubbed his forehead, and then said in a detached tone, "That won't be necessary . . . they're dead."

"They're dead!" Eva repeated, her tone indicating a lack of sympathy.

"Totally lifeless," said Dr. Sedrak apathetically, "like fish in a seafood market."

"How?" asked Eva.

"Their hearts stopped beating," explained Dr. Sedrak. "All it takes to electrocute a human being is seven milliamps for 3 seconds. Electricity kills you by interrupting your heart rhythm— causing it to go arrhythmic. If left untreated, even for a few minutes, it can lead to cardiac arrest or sudden death. In my professional opinion that's what occurred here. That oarfish must pack the voltage of a thousand electric eels, which reminds me—we need to remain on its good side."

"It'll never hurt us," Mischa said defensively.

"Maybe," said Dr. Sedrak carefully. "I know it located our ship by the sound of *Nessie's* engine, which is why you brought the bucket of squid, but why did it attack the *Lucky Lady?*"

"That's a good question," Mischa acknowledged, "I can only hazard a guess."

"Which is?" Dr. Sedrak asked.

"It knew we were in trouble," Mischa postulated, "and that we needed its help. Animals seem to have a sixth sense when it comes to that sort of thing."

Timbrook spoke quietly. "Giant oarfish are very rare and the possibility of Jake and Mischa not only finding one, but befriending it, and that it would eventually save our lives—that sounds like the hand of providence to me."

"An intelligent fish with a heavenly connection—that's a first," admitted Dr. Sedrak.

"Speaking of the oarfish," said Jake, "its back."

"Where?" asked Mischa.

"By the swim step," answered Jake.

"Well, I hope it's not here for an encore performance," said Dr. Sedrak anxiously.

Mischa ignored Dr. Sedrak's cautionary words and quickly made her way down to the swim platform. "I saved some squid for you," she said to the fish as she removed several mangled cephalopods from her pocket. Upon hearing her voice the creature immediately raised its head out of the water and began plucking the squid out of her hand. While it was eating, Mischa gently caressed its decorative red headdress by running her fingers through its feathery plume.

Leaning over the stern rail, Dr. Sedrak said, "That's a sight no one would believe."

"A girl and her serpent," laughed Eva. "That could be the title to a book."

When the last squid disappeared, Mischa rechecked her pocket and found one more. "Unfortunately," she said apologetically, "this is all I have for you today, but the next time we meet I'll have buckets of squid." As the oarfish inhaled the final cephalopod, Mischa bent over and kissed its royal-appearing head. "You're my hero," she whispered, "I'll see you in a few days."

As Mischa was climbing back up the ladder she suddenly realized something: *I haven't named the oarfish.* She silently scolded herself; the fish deserved an appropriate title. *But what?* When she saw Timbrook she knew—it had to be an Indian name. "What's the Indian word for savior?" She asked him.

"That's an odd question," Timbrook chuckled. "Why?"

"I need to name the oarfish," she replied. "It saved our lives, so that's the name I want to give it."

"I suppose it does deserve an honorary title," Timbrook agreed. "The Chumash don't have a word for savior, but the Sioux do. Their word is *Wanikya*."

After a contemplative pause Mischa shook her head. "That won't work. Are there any other Indian words for savior?"

"There may be," he said, "but I'm not familiar with them; however, I do have some additional titles that might work. The Sioux word for brave is *Ohitekah*."

Mischa frowned. "What else?"

The Navajo expression for 'he fights' is *Ahiga*."

Mischa shrugged. "That's a possibility. Any others?"

This time Timbrook laughed out loud, "*Hania*—it's the Hopi word for Spirit Warrior."

Mischa shrieked her approval. "That's it! *Hania.* The giant oarfish is definitely a Spirit Warrior who ascends out of the abyss and into the light. Thank you . . . it's perfect."

"I'll let the Hopi know," smiled Timbrook.

Hania, thought Mischa, would also work as the name for the Marine Lab's next Boston Whaler. *Nessie,* she assumed, was a total loss. Resurrecting the name of a sunken ship seemed blasphemous; besides, a brand-new ship deserved its own unique name. Mischa and Timbrook then joined Dr. Sedrak, Eva, and Jake, who were gathered around the bodies.

"I took the liberty of going through their pockets," explained Dr. Sedrak. "Mr. Goebbel was carrying a wallet, cell phone, and a set of keys. The tattooed man had two wallets in his possession, plus a set of keys."

"Did I hear you say two wallets?" Timbrook inquired.

"Yes," Dr. Sedrak replied. "We found his wallet plus a second billfold, and knowing his unsavory character, it probably was stolen. Both wallets carried identification. According to the two California Driver's Licenses, the dead man's name is Jose Diaz, and the other gentleman, Ruben Negrete."

"The police can contact Mr. Negrete once we're back in port," said Timbrook, "and return his wallet. Meanwhile, we should probably cover their bodies. In addition, some warm clothing would be nice—my wet garments are beginning to give me the chills. I suggest we spend a few minutes searching the ship for a change of clothing and for a suitable shroud."

"We'll check out the staterooms," said Jake volunteering Mischa and himself.

"They're below deck," Timbrook advised, "with the entryway most likely in the wheelhouse. And while you're inspecting the crew quarters we'll search the rest of the ship."

The entrance to the staterooms was exactly where Timbrook predicted—inside the wheelhouse. After walking down a small flight of aluminum stairs Mischa and Jake arrived at a narrow corridor which extended about fifteen feet. Situated on either side of hallway were four cabins, numbered 1 through 4. At the far end of the passageway was a cubicle with the word 'Loo' written on it—British slang for toilet. The door to the bathroom was slightly ajar—allowing the unmistakable odor of raw sewage to fill the hall. After sneaking a quick peek, Mischa slammed the door shut. "Remind me to use the ocean," she gagged, "it's beyond disgusting."

"Marine toilets aren't known for their cleanliness," Jake said informatively, "especially when the ship's only crewmembers are cantankerous men who don't place much value on a spotless potty."

"I suppose," Mischa agreed, "which also explains why most seafarer's are bachelors. But, what really concerns me is whether the stench has permeated the staterooms and infused the clothing with noxious fumes."

"We'll know soon enough," said Jake as he opened the door to room number 4 and stepped in.

Mischa followed Jake. The light coming through a porthole revealed a tiny room. Against one wall was a six-foot bunk bed. The mattress was covered with what appeared to be white cotton sheets, though their present coloration indicated that they hadn't been cleaned in months. The sheets had earthy type stains that exuded a faint fishy scent. A nylon blanket was draped across a portion of the bed. Along the other wall was a pine-lined closet with four drawers. The flooring was off-white linoleum with black speckles. "A cruise ship it's not," Mischa quipped.

After situating the blanket so that it covered the entire mattress, Jake pulled out the drawers and began emptying their contents onto the bed—ankle high socks, Speedo-type underwear, flannel shirts, and Levi jeans. He then unlatched the closet and removed several water-proof jackets and a pair of black rubber boots. One of the jackets was embroidered with a name—Raul 'Shade' Alvarado. "Whoever this Alvarado character was," Jake reported as he held up the jacket, "he was certainly skinny. This room may be dirty, but fortunately his clothes smell fresh."

Mischa inspected a few items. "They're not designed for a fashionista, but they'll keep the ladies warm."

Using the blanket, Jake wrapped up the clothes and handed the bundle to Mischa. "Since they'll only fit a woman you get to carry them."

"I wouldn't expect anything less, especially from my brother," Mischa said with a touch of friendly sarcasm.

The door to room number 3 was bolted shut. A brass name-plate with the inscription *Negrete* was attached to the door just below the room number. "That's a drag," Jake complained. "Should we try busting the lock?"

"Not yet," Mischa replied. "There's still two more cabins."

Cabin number 2 was unlocked, and was arranged the same way as cabin 4. It was obvious that this space belonged to the dead crewmember, Jose Diaz: Soiled clothes, large enough for a burly gorilla, laid scattered across the floor. "He clearly liked his weed," said Mischa as she examined a gallon-sized storage bag that was packed with the hemp plant. An abalone shell, used as an ashtray was overflowing with the leftover butts, and the room reeked of the pungent aroma.

Jake slid open the drawers and closet. After examining the contents he shook his head. "The man didn't wear underwear, and his clothes smell like marijuana smoke." Using an unexpectedly clean pillowcase he began filling it with several plus-sized jeans, white t-shirts, socks, a variety of hoodies, and two pairs of size-thirteen tennis shoes.

"At least you'll be nice and comfortable in your new clothes although you'll probably be mistaken for a pothead," giggled Mischa.

Jake just glared at her. "One more cabin," he said, "and then we should have plenty of clothes." After setting the pillowcase on the floor just outside the room, he opened the door to stateroom number 1, which was designated as a 'guest' cabin, and stepped inside. Mischa placed her bundle next to Jake's and followed him in.

For a moment Mischa was too paralyzed by fear to utter a sound.

Jake said, "What the—"

—and then she screamed.

Within seconds the sound of footsteps bounding down the stairwell could be heard.

Timbrook burst into the room carrying a rifle—the same one that had earlier been used by Pancho. Dr. Sedrak had discovered a fillet knife, which he held tightly in his right hand. Eva had found a small aluminum club. All three had their weapons at the ready. Timbrook, upon observing the unknown man in the room yelled, "Who are you?"

Mischa held up her hands. "It's okay. He's tied up; he's not a danger to anyone." Mischa had ended her scream the moment she realized that the person did not pose a threat. The thin, olive-skinned man had a hideous snake-like tattoo engraved into the left side of his face. Coagulated blood from an obviously deep gash covered the right side of his head. He was lashed to the bunk bed by half-inch thick nylon rope and whoever had secured the knots knew exactly what they were doing—the captive would die a slow, horrible death before he ever escaped. Repeating Timbrook's words Mischa asked, "Who are you? And why are you on this boat?"

The man tried to sit up but was immediately pulled back down. He turned his head and spent several moments staring into each of their eyes. A look of awed disbelief came over his face, "You're all alive . . . and in control of this ship? How's that possible?" he mumbled.

Timbrook lowered the rifle. "At the present time, we'll ask the questions," he said sternly, "until we know who you are. What's your relationship with Goebbel and Diaz, and why are you being held as a prisoner?"

The man nodded his understanding. "My name's Ruben Negrete—captain of the *Lucky Lady*. My position was forcibly terminated a few hours ago when I tried to prevent Goebbel and Diaz—whose nickname is Pancho—from setting off an explosive device inside Painted Cave. As you know I failed. The bomb was so powerful that I'm surprised anyone lived through it."

"We were fortunate—we were exploring a passage deep within the inner chamber when it went off; otherwise we would all be dead. Nonetheless, we still felt its effect. Mischa," Timbrook said indicating, "suffered a concussion from a dislodged rock."

"I'm sorry," Negrete said sincerely.

"We also found your wallet," Dr. Sedrak reported, "it was on Pancho."

Negrete raised his eyebrows. "Pancho let you search him? That man isn't known for being compliant; he stole it after tying me up."

"Both Pancho and Goebbel are deceased," Dr. Sedrak stated. "Electrocuted by a giant oarfish that attacked this ship. And from what I can see, it was an odd stroke of luck that they strapped you to this bed. When the massive energy surge occurred—your rubber mattress acted as an insulator, keeping your body safe from the lethal current."

"They're truly dead?—that's wonderful news," Negrete said with a sarcastic chuckle. "I can't imagine anyone wasting any tears on them. And that bizarre creature . . . it's not the first time the *Lucky Lady's* encounter it. About four weeks ago, as part of my job, we were out at the Santa Cruz Basin disposing of biotech animal remnants when it struck my ship with a wave of electricity. I was knocked out for several minutes as were my two crewmembers. I don't think that sea serpent likes this boat."

"Maybe it's not the actual ship, but your illegal activity—dumping bio-hazardous waste into the ocean that it doesn't appreciate," suggested Jake. "That's what happened today—Goebbel and Pancho were engaged in the same task when the oarfish launched its attack."

"I only did it because it was part of my job. Besides, with Goebbel dead, my dumping days are definitely over with," Negrete assured them, "so I expect the oarfish to leave me alone."

"It's more than just that," said Mischa, "it's our friend. A few weeks ago we found it curled up in a shallow water cove. It was sick, probably from ingesting bio-hazardous waste, and my brother and I spent a week nursing it back to health. We still see it on occasion. It knows how to find our ship by the sound of our outboard engine. Its favorite food is squid, and when it surfaces, we're able to hand-feed it."

"Just remember," Negrete warned with a slight laugh, "to never tick it off."

Mischa smiled. "Dr. Sedrak said essentially the same thing." *She didn't really know this person, but he seemed okay.* "Thank you," she said, "for trying to help us. I can see by your injury that it came at a painful cost."

"It was worth it," said Negrete. "Goebbel butt-stroked me with his rifle and probably fractured my skull. In addition, the nerves in my neck were also temporarily traumatized. But, don't worry—over the years I've endured worse wounds so I know I'll heal up within a matter of days."

Timbrook motioned to Dr. Sedrak. "It's time to set him free."

Using the fillet knife, Dr. Sedrak severed the nylon ropes, and after briefly examining Negrete's head, stated, "He's correct—he'll be fine in less than a week." He then helped Negrete sit up.

"Thank you," Negrete said as he rubbed the circulation back into his wrists and feet.

Putting his hand on Negrete's shoulder, Timbrook said, "This ship needs its Captain, and so do we—assuming you're feeling up for it."

Negrete didn't hesitate. "Where to?" he asked.

"Two destinations—the Marine Lab on Santa Cruz Island, and then over to the mainland. The Sheriff's Department,

Coastguard, and National Park Service, will probably have a ton of questions, and knowing the process, I figure we'll be there a few days, so we'll need to pack a small suitcase."

Mischa gasped. "I almost forgot; we can't leave without my cell phone," and began explaining why it had to be recovered.

Dr. Sedrak shook his head. "It's sitting at the bottom of the sea; it's worthless."

"But its waterproof," Mischa clarified.

Eva asked, "How deep is the water?"

"At least seventy feet," Timbrook answered.

"Too deep to free dive," said Eva, "we would need scuba gear and unfortunately we don't have that equipment."

"We can't just leave it!" Mischa protested.

"I'm sorry," said Timbrook, "there's nothing we can do."

Negrete abruptly stood up. "I'd be dead," he began coldly, "if that piece of garbage had succeeded with his plans." After a brief pause he continued. "A videotaped confession would be the icing on the cake at destroying Goebbel's reputation." He then looked at Eva. "What exactly do you need?"

"An 80 cubic foot scuba tank, regulator, dive computer, buoyancy compensator, 7 millimeter wetsuit, gloves, booties, weight belt, mask, snorkel, fins—the usual stuff," Eva replied.

"This ain't a dive store, but I do have a 19 cubic foot pony tank with a shoulder harness, a regulator with a pressure gauge, a 3 millimeter wetsuit, a six pound weight belt, and a dive mask. Every once in a while something gets wrapped around the boat prop—rope, drift nets, fishing line, kelp, plastic bags, and even clothes. When that happens we have to get into the water to remove it. It's all I got. Will that work?"

Eva laughed. "No BC, no computer, no fins, no gloves, no booties, a warm water wetsuit, and a tank with enough gas to last 3 minutes at 70 feet—why not—it will certainly be a quick dive."

"You sure?" Dr. Sedrak asked concerned.

"I'll be careful," Eva assured him, "I just hope the sharks are all gone and that I can locate Mischa's cell phone with what little bottom time I have."

"While you're getting suited up, we'll change into some dry clothes," said Timbrook.

"You can also check out my limited selection," said Negrete as he walked out the door and unlocked cabin number 3. "My shipmates weren't overly trustworthy," he explained as he opened the door. After laying out his clothes, he left with Eva.

Mischa chose a pair of Levi jeans, a green-colored sweatshirt, and a pair of knee-high rubber boots. Jake was dressed in similar attire, but opted for a black 'hoodie' because he felt it made him look cool. They then joined Negrete, Eva, Timbrook, and Dr. Sedrak in the wheelhouse. Negrete had restarted the *Lucky Lady's* engines and was moving the boat in a slow circular pattern. Eva was already dressed for the dive. Her wetsuit, though, was designed for someone twice her size.

"You look cute," Jake joked.

"No photos," Eva said to everyone, though her expression was whimsical as she knew no one on board possessed a phone.

"Exactly *where* did you toss your cell phone?" Negrete asked Mischa.

"My brother and I dropped ours together—right over the side of the boat. They're both Apple i-Phones. Mine is gold in color and Jake's is black."

Negrete suddenly brought the boat to a stop. "Recognize that," he said pointing at a large elliptical object depicted in the colored fish finder.

"It looks like a blob," Jake replied.

"A fiberglass blob," said Negrete. "That's your boat, resting on the ocean floor. The cell phones should be nearby. Let's hope your vessel didn't land on them. The fish finder also revealed something that I think Eva might appreciate—I don't see any sharks. However, you're sea serpent is still hanging around. See that long squiggly line on the screen—that's your friend."

"*Hania,* squealed Mischa, "that's great. Oarfish and sharks don't mix."

"Let's hope your right," Eva said with a nervous laugh.

"You're all set to go," Negrete said to Eva, "just jump over the side. We'll meet you at the swim step when you're done."

Eva walked out onto the deck. "Wish me luck," she said just before putting in her breathing apparatus and stepping off the boat.

Mischa watched her descend—like a determined arrow—straight down. At about the forty foot mark Eva was no longer visible and the only thing marking her whereabouts was a trail of bubbles.

"How long until she returns?" Jake asked.

"Six . . . seven minutes," answered Mischa.

They decided to wait in the wheelhouse where they could monitor Eva's location by staring at the digital lines scrolling across the fish finder.

"She's definitely on the bottom," Negrete confirmed, "scouring the sea floor near the boat along with your puppy-dog oarfish, which appears to be following her."

"Protecting her," Mischa said with a bit more confidence than she felt. *Hania* hadn't met Eva yet. If the oarfish zapped Eva she wondered if she could ever forgive herself.

"That's a bit odd," Negrete reported, "Eva and her fishy companion are no longer inspecting the sea floor; it looks like they're now exploring the inside of the boat."

"Why would they do that?" Dr. Sedrak asked.

"I wish I knew," said Negrete. "At the moment they're both stationary. Unfortunately we don't have a video feed."

After what seemed like an eternity, Timbrook whispered, "It's been three minutes, and Eva hasn't budged an inch—something's not right."

When another thirty seconds elapsed, Dr. Sedrak began pacing the floor. "Isn't there anything we can do?"

"At that depth, I'm afraid she's on her own," murmured Timbrook.

In frustration Dr. Sedrak shouted at the screen, "EVA . . . MOVE!" He then turned away and buried his face in his hands.

Mischa wiped a tear off her cheek. Dr. Sedrak wasn't the only one filled with a sense of dread. The moment Eva entered the boat Mischa hadn't taken her eyes off the display. The fish finder, as she understood the gadget, was able to see underwater by bouncing sound waves off of targets, and then analyzing the return data. If anything within the unit's electronic window stirred, the graphical images on the screen would instantly change. Mischa was greatly relieved when she observed a gray mass lift off the sunken ship and suddenly accelerate toward the surface. In a jubilant voice, Mischa yelled, "Doctor . . . she heard you . . . Eva's on her way up." Looking again at the screen, Mischa saw an irregular blimp drift off the boat and begin making its way into deeper water. *"Hania,"* she whispered.

After Mischa's announcement a foot race to the swim step quickly ensued, with Dr. Sedrak leading the way. When Eva breached the surface they all cheered and then clapped. Once she was out of the water and safely on the platform, Eva removed her regulator and face mask.

"Oh my God," Eva gushed with a big smile, "diving with an oarfish—what an extraordinary experience. That creature is like a mythical beast from the legends of old. It's so gorgeous, and awesome, and its coloring—just like a rainbow. When I passed over *Nessie* I noticed some squid on her floorboard. I wondered if Hania would eat out of my hand, and I decided to give it a try. I quickly collected every last squid, and to my amazement, that oarfish consumed every morsel! I was so excited I temporarily forgot about the passage of time. Fortunately, I had enough air left to make a hurried ascent. So I apologize if I caused any unnecessary anxiety. It was just so much fun."

Mischa looked at Eva and was genuinely happy to see her friend so passionate about the oarfish. She also looked at Eva's hands and saw that they were empty. *The oarfish must have side-tracked Eva from her original assignment,* she thought. "No cell phone?" she asked.

"Mischa, I'm so sorry, I completely forgot about it." Then with an impish smile, stuck her arm down the front of her wetsuit and pulled out a gold colored i-Phone. "I found it the moment I reached the sea floor . . . as if the device was waiting for me. I placed it inside my wetsuit so I wouldn't lose it," she explained as she handed it to Mischa who anxiously received it.

Mischa checked her phone. The screen was blank. She immediately pressed and held down the power button. "Speak to me," she whispered to the phone. A second later the Apple logo appeared on the screen. "It works," she shrieked. She then gave Eva a victorious hug. "Thank you," she said.

"Find me some warm clothes and we'll call it even," laughed Eva.

"I'm way ahead of you," replied Mischa, "I've already picked them out. They're laid out in cabin number 3."

"Then it's my turn to say thanks," Eva said with a grateful smile as she made her way toward the room.

While Eva was changing, Timbrook located a blue tarp which he used to cover the bodies of Goebbel and Pancho. Dr. Sedrak also returned Negrete's wallet. According to their new captain the journey back to Scorpion Cove was expected to take about forty-five minutes. Because the *Lucky Lady* was a working ship, the only sit down spot on the entire vessel was at the kitchen table located inside the wheelhouse. Timbrook, Dr. Sedrak, Mischa, and Jake were already seated around the table when Eva walked in, dressed in a boyish outfit.

Frowning, Eva said, "Just like the baggy wetsuit, no photos, particularly Mischa, who I know now has a camera."

Mischa giggled. She had already snapped a shot the moment Eva stepped into the wheelhouse.

Eva squeezed in next to Dr. Sedrak. The table, with bench seats, was barely large enough for four adults. Situated in the center of the table were an assortment of beverages that Negrete had procured from the ship's refrigerator, a block of cheddar cheese, and a variety of crackers. Eva chose a diet coke. "Thanks for the snacks," she said to Negrete.

From the Captain's chair Negrete said, "You're welcome."

Timbrook stared at the young man with a reflective look. "Have you thought about what you're going to say to the authorities once we're back in port?" he asked Negrete.

Negrete turned toward Timbrook and with a poignant laugh stated, "Hopefully as little as possible, although we both know that's not going to happen. As you've probably surmised, I'm not exactly an innocent bystander. In the last year I've essentially been Mr. Goebbel's right-hand man, which means my hands are dirty. I've delivered bribes to a corrupt USDA Inspector, I'm aware that our bone meal is tainted with mad cow disease, and I even have photographs of our illegal dumping in case I needed to blackmail Goebbel. My boss may be dead, but I'm certainly not. The public will need someone to crucify, and I'm the perfect scapegoat. Besides, as of today I no longer have a job, so prison being my home for the next twenty years sounds about right."

After Negrete's disclosures, silence filled the room for several moments, the only sound being the rumbling roar of the diesel engines.

Dr. Sedrak was the first to break the silence. "There's no reason why you have to be the fall guy. Are you familiar with the term, 'To Turn State's Evidence'?"

Negrete shook his head.

"In high-profile cases," continued Dr. Sedrak, "the government will typically offer a key witness—a person with insider knowledge regarding the criminal enterprise—immunity from prosecution as long as that individual agrees to testify against his former boss, especially where that witness has exhibited a change of heart. In our situation you unselfishly risked your own life to save ours, and that's the type of character evidence that a judge will look at. Further, as a somewhat renowned doctor, I happen to know a large number of influential people, and a few of them are involved in these types of cases. When we get back to the mainland I'll be more than happy to discuss your unique set of facts with them. I'm pretty certain . . . by the end of my conversations . . . an offer of immunity will be on the table."

With a voice choked with emotion Negrete mumbled, "Thank you."

"And, about finding a new job . . . I'm sure that can also be worked out," Dr. Sedrak said encouragingly.

"I like being a ship's Captain," said Negrete, "and the freedom of the open sea. The *Lucky Lady*, despite her ignoble past, has been good to me. I'll miss this ship."

"As far as I know you're still its Captain," Timbrook said softly, "until someone says otherwise. Throughout the years I've learned a valuable lesson . . . expect the unexpected, that way you're never disappointed. Which reminds me, we need to check in with another captain, Captain Kurt Nichols—Jake and Mischa's dad. He's currently out on his own ship. And assuming we can reach him, I suggest we refrain from mentioning any of the worrisome details of our day. We'll see him soon enough."

"What's the name of his ship?" Negrete asked.

"*Serenity*," replied Jake

"Can you route the call through a speakerphone?" Timbrook wondered.

"Yes," said Negrete, "we're set up for that." Holding the microphone in his hand, he pushed the transmit button. *"Lucky Lady calling Serenity, please respond."*

After a moment, Timbrook said, "Maybe they're no longer at sea."

"Let me try again," said Negrete. *"Lucky Lady calling Serenity, please respond—it's important."*

"This is *Serenity*, how can we help?"

"Dad!" Yelled Mischa and Jake together.

"I'm now switching to Channel 8," Negrete informed *Serenity*.

"Why are you changing channels?" Jake asked.

"Once contact is made on Channel 16—which is the frequency band that all ship's monitor—you then have to switch to a ship-to-ship channel. Along the west coast that's Channel 8," answered Negrete.

"Did I hear the word *Dad*?" the voice asked, confused.

"Yes," yelled Mischa and Jake. "We're on a different boat."

"Everything okay?" he asked concerned.

"We're fine," said Timbrook. "We're just paying a social visit."

"That's rather neighborly," Nichols acknowledged. "We've just pulled into the dock, and once *Serenity's* secure, will begin unloading. Did you guys have fun touring Painted Cave?"

"It was a blast," said Jake with a wry smile.

"And we saw lots of sea lions and sharks," added Mischa.

"Don't forget the oarfish," Eva chipped in. "That was electrifying."

"That creature is certainly amazing," Kurt agreed.

"How was your day?" Dr. Sedrak asked.

"Probably a little bit more exciting than yours; when you get in, we'll discuss it further. But, it was magical. Petersen and I had a day that was golden . . . and then some."

"That's great news!" Mischa said excitedly, and then blurted out. "Because we need to buy a new *Nessie*." Once the words had left her lips Mischa gasped; she knew she had said too much, and immediately covered her mouth with her hands.

"Buy a new *what?*" Kurt asked. "What's wrong with your ship? Is that why you're on the *Lucky Lady?*"

"As I informed you, everyone's fine," Timbrook assured him. "Our ship's parked nearby, so don't worry."

"*Parked where?*" Kurt asked, emphasizing each word.

For a brief moment, no one answered. "Neptune's Net . . . Dave Jones's Locker . . . the briny deep, take your pick," Eva answered.

The long static-filled pause was almost as unnerving as any words.

When Kurt finally responded, it wasn't what they were expecting. Laughter—though of a wild, nearly maniacal type, lasting for approximately ninety seconds. When it ended they could hear Kurt clearing his nose. "You guys are topnotch . . . you almost had me. What do they call that on MTV—being Punk'd. Sorry, but I'm not some empty-headed celebrity. I'll see you shortly. Petersen needs my help at unloading the ship. Love you." He then clicked off.

Negrete held the speechless microphone in his hand. He then looked at Mischa and Jake. "That's your dad?" he asked rhetorically, "I like him."

Mischa and Jake both laughed. Their dad was in for one heck of a surprise.

39

Mischa smiled as she inspected the brand new nineteen-foot Boston Whaler that was tied up to the Scorpion Cove pier. It had just arrived the day before. *It's perfect in its sameness,* she thought. *It has to be an exact replica of Nessie,* she had informed her father, *right down to her signature sounding 115 HP Mercury Fourstroke outboard engine, if they ever hoped to see the oarfish again.* Mischa's dad joked that she was being a little melodramatic, but in the end allowed her to order a similar-type boat. The *only* noticeable change was to the transom. Instead of *Nessie* stenciled across the stern it was now *Hania,* written in bright iridescent letters, in honor of the sea serpent's unique coloring.

Mischa lifted her head and fixed her gaze upon Montannon Ridge, which was enveloped in a layer of dense fog. She had hoped to spot the mustang horses, Gabriel and Aiyana, who were transporting Eva and her dad up the mountain. It was the first time that either one of them had journeyed to the prehistoric sanctuary, and like children on Christmas morning—their level of excitement was palpable. Timbrook was supposed to lead the trip, but bowed out at the last minute due to severe flu-like symptoms. "You don't want to know," he said referring to his illness. Mischa had helped pack their saddle bags with various treats for the animals they would encounter—ten pounds of beef jerky for the saber-toothed cats, sugar cubes, apples, and carrots for the mammoths and horses, and a large rawhide bone for Journey, the Siberian husky. "This food," Mischa promised, "will guarantee your acceptance as a member of the pack or herd."

Refocusing her attention on the new boat Mischa wondered where her brother was. Unfortunately, he was running late for *Hania's* maiden voyage. Minutes later she heard the sound of quick but heavy footsteps echoing off the wooden dock. *It's about time,* she thought. In his hands were two buckets of squid.

"Ready for *Hania's* shakedown cruise?" he asked without apologizing for being late.

Mischa laughed. *Well, he did volunteer to get the squid, a chore that had obviously taken longer than anticipated.* She immediately forgave him for his tardiness. "I doubt we'll find anything wrong with the boat. The Boston Whaler is a time-tested design. If anything goes wrong it will most likely be our fault."

"Human error—evolution's dark side," Jake chuckled in agreement.

Mischa helped her brother load the squid onto the boat. Their plans for *Hania's* inaugural trip involved two objectives: surveying the islands owned by the Nichols family, and then a short trek out into the ocean in hopes of attracting the giant oarfish. It had been fourteen days since their last encounter with the strange creature. *Would the oarfish remember them?* Mischa wasn't sure of the answer, but she was hopeful.

Once they cast off, it only took a minute for them to arrive at their destination. There were a total of five islands within the Scorpion Cove archipelago, but only two lent themselves to exploration. The three smaller islands barely had enough room to accommodate a few sea birds or a sunbathing sea lion; the two larger islets, which ranged in size from a quarter of an acre to almost an acre, and soared forty to fifty feet, were much more inviting. A ten-foot wide channel separated the two islands.

Jake, who was skippering *Hania,* nudged the boat between the islands and then cut the engine. Once the ship came to a stop, Mischa released the anchor, which hit bottom almost the instant it left her hand. She glanced over the side of the vessel and saw that the water depth was less than fifteen feet. "Which island first?" she asked.

"The smaller one," Jake replied, "you always save the biggest and best for last."

Using a six-foot wooden paddle, Mischa pushed against the water, slowly moving the ship until the bow contacted the steep rocky shoreline. While she held the boat steady, Jake carefully stepped off the vessel holding the bow rope in his hand, which he then wrapped around a jagged boulder—keeping the boat tight against the island. Once the boat was secure, Mischa joined him.

"Our own Robinson Crusoe Island," she said dreamily, "this should be fun."

"I hate to pop your paradisaical bubble but it's just a mound of volcanic rock."

"I can always pretend," Mischa said slightly miffed.

"Then welcome to Fantasy Island," teased Jake with a grand sweep of his hand and using a voice that mimicked actor Ricardo Montalban's opening line in the television show with the same name.

Ignoring Jake's attempt at sarcasm, Mischa began climbing up the bell-shaped basalt structure, with the goal of reaching the summit ahead of her brother. Contrary to popular belief, scaling a moderately steep rock formation didn't require great upper body strength, but agile footwork. The trick was finding the appropriate nooks, edges, and ledges to wedge your shoes into, along with good balance. When Mischa reached the apex she sat down and enjoyed the elevated view. Ninety seconds later Jake plopped down next to her, breathing hard. "A little slow aren't we?" she asked facetiously.

"I didn't know it was going to be a footrace," he complained.

"It's those fattening donuts," she said with a grin, "they're weighing you down."

"Hardly—it's having an overly competitive sister."

Mischa laughed. "You're right—I plead guilty as charged." After a brief pause she asked, "What do you think of the view?"

"It's not bad . . . this mountain top allows you to take in the entire cove, the marine lab, and even our house. It certainly gives you a panoramic perspective on our section of Santa Cruz."

"This islet—it's like our own little country, and we get to make all the rules."

Jake laughed. "You're definitely on Fantasy Island."

Mischa smiled. She felt special. Possessing title to a parcel of land was one thing, but owning an actual island—that was a level of ownership that few individuals got to experience. *The next time,* she thought, *I need to pack a picnic lunch.*

"Are you ready to check out country number two?" asked Jake.

"Lead the way," said Mischa as she followed her brother back down the rock and to their boat. After Jake untied the bow rope, they pushed off and then repeated the same docking maneuvers for the larger island.

This island, Mischa noted, was five times the size of the first one. A rather strenuous climb up a sloping cliff revealed a relatively flat plateau-like summit. The eastern side of the island was covered in a thick layer of guano and apparently was a nesting site for a variety of sea birds including ashy storm-petrels, western gulls, Xantus's murrelets, and brown pelicans. The accumulation of excrement had turned the stone pure white as if it was covered in a blanket of snow. Mischa and Jake stayed clear of the birds for two reasons—to avoid disturbing the rookery, and because the pungent stench smelled like decaying fish.

After exploring roughly half the island, Mischa said, "This rock's big enough for a vacation house."

"The odor could be a problem," Jake warned.

"You'd get use to it."

Shaking his head Jake said, "Only if you're old and your nose doesn't work anymore."

"Well, maybe not a house," Mischa agreed, "but someday I'd like to pitch a tent, spend the day observing the nesting birds and their cute fledglings, watch the sun set, and at night stare in wonder at the vastness of the Milky Way."

"Sounds a bit too romantic for my taste—you'll need a boyfriend if you want someone to join you."

"JAKE!" Mischa declared, and then smiling shyly said, "Although that's not a bad idea—an outdoorsy type man would be a nice addition. And I know the perfect spot for our campsite," she said pointing with her index finger, "that scenic promontory overlooking Scorpion Cove."

Jake laughed. "Then we had better check it out; we wouldn't want to disappoint your imaginary suitor."

"Suitors, and they certainly exist; you should see my Facebook page. It's just a question as to *whom?*"

"Keep dreaming," said Jake as he wandered out onto the bluff. As they neared the cliff's edge he stopped with a jolt. "Oh my gosh!" he exclaimed. "That's an unexpected sight."

Mischa was equally amazed. It was huge—perhaps the biggest skeleton she had ever seen—other than in a museum. The creature's bleached skull was just two feet from the precipice, its empty eye sockets still focused on Scorpion Cove. Extending back from the skull, the animal's bony framework—neck, spine, ribs, and the bones from both its front and hind flippers. The jaws still contained the animal's upper and lower canine teeth. She estimated its length at over eleven feet. "What type of seal is it?" she asked.

Jake spent a short time analyzing the skull and the animal's bony anatomy before he answered. "My best guess—a California sea lion, although it's in a class by itself."

"Why do you say that?"

Jake motioned toward the beast. "Just look at it. A mature sea lion is typically six to eight feet in length and weighs between five to eight hundred pounds. This specimen is around eleven feet, which means it weighed at least fifteen hundred pounds. This creature must have dominated its environment during its lifetime. In essence he was their King—until the day he died."

Mischa stared at the perfectly lined up assemblage of bones. Even in death the creature had been left alone. "It must have known that it was dying," said Mischa sadly, "and purposely chose this island as its final resting place."

Jake nodded. "You're probably right; scaling the angled rocks in order to reach this site must have been physically challenging, but since the sea lion knew it was a one-way journey, he endured it."

"It's certainly an ideal setting for a King," Mischa confirmed.

Jake laughed. "What animal, or human for that matter, wouldn't mind spending their final hours atop a beautiful island with a gorgeous seascape? This creature obviously died on its own terms while enjoying a lofty view of its territory. None of that would have occurred if he had passed away on the shores of Santa Cruz."

Mischa looked sharply at her brother as if he had just proclaimed something profound. She mumbled the final sentence out loud. "None of that would have occurred if *he* had passed away on the shores of Santa Cruz." Mischa's mind was racing: the 'he' could also be a person. She remembered her conversation with Timbrook. *If you're unable to be buried on the island of Santa Cruz because the ground is considered sacred—the birthplace of the Chumash nation—then what's the alternative?* The answer was obvious. *On a detached piece of land . . . an island that's not an island!* "Jake," she whispered, "I think I know where Captain Cabrillo is buried."

Jake's jaw dropped. "Where?" he asked.

"Gull Island."

"Why do you say that?"

Mischa quickly explained her reasons. When she had finished she was pleased to see an enthusiastic grin on his face. She had worried that her brother might think her idea was preposterous. "What now?" she asked.

"That's easy," Jake replied, "we check out your hypothesis and see if it's true. The fuel tank's full, there are a few small digging tools in the mechanics box, and we have the entire day to ourselves. I say we head out immediately. Gull Island is only fifteen miles away, which equates to a forty-minute boat ride."

Mischa could barely contain her excitement. *What if I'm right,* she thought. *Have I actually solved a four hundred and fifty-year-old mystery? Timbrook would be ecstatic.* Her optimism was quickly replaced by doubt. *But, I could also be wrong. Then what? Her brother would certainly tease her. She could already hear his words, 'another worthless rabbit trail.'* "Jake," she said, "I'm too nervous to skipper the boat. You drive and I'll keep an eye out for the oarfish."

Jake gave her a funny look. "That was my job today anyway."

Mischa smiled. "Sorry—I'm just feeling a bit giddy over the possibility of finding the gravesite."

Jake laughed. "I understand. I'm almost as anxious as you are."

The brief hike back to their boat seemed like a blur to Mischa. The real possibility of actually discovering Cabrillo's grave was almost too much for her to ponder.

After boarding *Hania,* Jake advanced the throttle control lever to its maximum setting and ran the vessel at full speed for thirty minutes. When Gull Island came into view he reduced the rpm's by twenty percent. "I don't want to burn-out the engine," he informed Mischa.

"That's something dad would certainly appreciate," she confirmed. Despite her excitement, Mischa was a little disappointed that the oarfish hadn't appeared. *We were probably traveling too fast,* she reasoned.

At two-tenths of a mile in length—soaring 65 feet above the waves—Gull Island was the largest of Santa Cruz's satellite islands, and was a nesting site for thousands of endangered sea birds. As part of the state's marine system there was a prohibition against taking or disturbing any of the marine species both above and below the water. Landing on the island was definitely off-limits.

Once they arrived at Gull Island, they spent several minutes navigating its circumference in order to find a suitable place to weigh anchor and disembark. Beds of giant kelp hindered their progress and several times Jake had to shift the engine into neutral in order to untangle kelp strands from the prop. Having viewed all possible landing areas, Jake declared, "The only favorable entry point is on the ocean side, unless you're a mountain goat. Fortunately, the sea is in a calm mood today so anchoring up shouldn't be a problem."

"I'll prepare the anchor," said Mischa, "just let me know when to drop it."

Jake pointed the bow of the boat toward a sloping tongue of rock that jutted out from the main island. When he was approximately seventy feet from the rock's edge he called out, "Release the anchor."

From the front of the ship, Mischa slowly let the nylon anchor line slip through her fingers until the Danforth-style anchor impacted the seafloor. "It's hit bottom," she yelled back.

Jake shifted the engine into reverse and slowly backed up until he felt the flukes dig into the seafloor. "We're good," he informed Mischa. With the anchor 'set' he had his sister release additional rope until *Hania* was situated just a few feet off the island. "Let's hope she doesn't drift into the rocks," said Jake, "but just in case let's deploy the docking fenders."

Mischa and Jake then repeated the same maneuvers they had employed at their previous landings. Once Jake was safely ashore, Mischa handed him their tools—a compact folding pick and shovel combo, hammer, gloves, pliers, and two screwdrivers. She then tossed over a small backpack she had brought along to hold their water bottles. Jake stored the tools in the pockets that were empty. Mischa then leaped from the ship to the large rock that Jake was already on, lost her balance, and rolled. Jake grabbed her before she fell into the ocean.

"You alright?" he asked as he helped his sister to her feet.

After a brief examination Mischa said, "I'm fine other than a few ugly bruises and a wounded ego."

Jake appeared relieved. "Being an explorer can be brutal," he said with a soft laugh.

Scowling, and smiling at the same time, Mischa said, "I'll remember that the next time you get hurt."

Jake nodded. "Fair enough."

Mischa glanced at their potential route up the cliff and noted the modest incline. "You definitely picked the best spot," she said reassuringly. "Now we just need to avoid being seen by anyone in authority. It would be a drag to get an expensive ticket for trespassing in a bird sanctuary, plus I would never forgive myself if I accidentally damaged a nesting site."

"We'll tread carefully, "Jake assured her. "And in regards to any possible ticket, I wouldn't worry about that, I think Professor Nichols could easily fix it."

"Maybe," Mischa said cautiously, "but that's a favor I would hate to call in. To be indebted to our dad, for an extended period of time, that might be worse than the actual citation."

"That's a good point," laughed Jake. "If we see any patrol boats we'll hide behind some rocks." He then picked up the backpack and slung it across his shoulders. He next turned to Mischa and bowed. "Since you're the mystery solver," he said in a formal voice, "you deserve to lead our expedition."

Mischa laughed at her brother's antics. "We'll know soon enough whether I'm correct, and as your obedient sister, I hereby accept your offer."

"Plus," added Jake, "I can catch you if you fall again."

"True, but only if you can keep up with me," she said over her shoulder as she began jogging up the slanted hillside. To her surprise Jake passed her just before they reached the top.

"It's those donuts I ate earlier," he said as he zipped by, "they gave me extra energy."

"Touché," Mischa responded. A few seconds later she climbed over the rim and joined her brother

"This is a big island," observed Jake. "It'll take a while to search it."

"Hopefully not; its length may be over a thousand feet, but we don't have to analyze every square inch, just those sections where you'd expect a prominent captain to be buried. Primarily, the location has to be scenic—not that it matters to a dead person, but it does to the individuals that dug the burial chamber. Our biggest obstacle, however, will be the centuries of scouring weather which will have obliterated any evidence of a gravesite other than a slightly raised mound and a smattering of rocks that seem out-of-place."

"And a small headstone," added Jake, "carved from indigenous rock."

"If we find just one piece of the puzzle—we've found the grave," declared Mischa.

"It'll go faster if we split up," suggested Jake.

"Great idea," Mischa agreed. "If either one of us stumbles across anything tangible just shout. The island's only a stone's throw at its widest."

"I'll start on the western side," Jake offered. "And, unless I hear from you, we'll rendezvous at the other end."

"Good luck," she said. As Jake began his search, Mischa veered east. The terrain along the eastern ridge ranged from flat to moderately hilly and was made up of crushed volcanic rock with very little topsoil. *Digging a burial pit must have been arduous,* she thought. Mischa chose a path that paralleled the bluffs, but about eight feet back. She allowed logic to play into her decision: *If there's a grave, it won't be located on the edge of the cliff, but will be set back at least a few feet, which means I should cross right over it.* As she walked Mischa kept her eyes peeled to the ground looking for any telltale signs of a tomb. Occasionally she would pause for a few moments as she shifted her gaze to the panoramic vistas—the azure ocean, the sweeping views of Santa Cruz Island including Punta Arena Point and Laguna Harbor, the colonies of nesting seabirds, and the dramatic cliffs of Gull Island that dropped straight down to the crashing waves. The scenery was breathtaking. Every fiber inside of Mischa sensed that Captain Cabrillo's remains were on the island. It was a powerful feeling, which flowed deep within her, and one that she had learned to trust. Was it woman's intuition? Maybe. A sixth sense? Possibly. Whatever it was, Mischa never doubted it. After reaching the halfway mark she mumbled to herself, "But where are you?"

The final five hundred feet was a huge disappointment—no impressions in the earth, no discernible marks, and no unusual rock formations—not even a molehill-sized mound. If the Captain's tomb was on the east side, it certainly wasn't in plain sight. When Mischa reached the endmost section of the island Jake was already at their meeting spot. As she walked up to him she asked, "Any luck?"

"No," he replied, "and from your own dour expression I'm betting your experience was similar to mine—no burial chamber."

"No *conspicuous* grave," she said in a frustrated tone. "Any glimmer of hope on the western side of the island?"

"No . . . unless I'm blind to any obvious signs."

"Let's swap routes; maybe you'll see something I missed."

"And vice versa."

Jake failed to notice the grave site, she surmised, *because he rushed his search.* She, however, hadn't. *If it wasn't on the eastern side, then it had to be on the western portion, and her brother had simply overlooked it.* She wouldn't make the same mistake.

Applying the same 'common sense' approach as before Mischa continued her search by maintaining a distance of eight to nine feet from the cliff's edge. This time, however, she kept her eyes focused on the ground, not wanting to miss a single clue. She also slowed her gait to a leisurely saunter in order to avoid passing over any subtle variations in the earth, or irregular grouping of stones. After carefully surveying the first hundred feet she told herself, *patience, it's just around the next bend.* After exploring a number of additional twists, dips, and overhanging bluffs, she was beginning to panic. *Could I have been wrong?* She wondered. *Is it on another islet?* When Mischa was just a hundred yards from their starting point she broke into a cold sweat. *Jake,* she realized, *was probably more thorough in his search than she had given him credit for, particularly since she hadn't discovered anything of interest.* A loud 'thunk' and 'splash' caused her to look up. Jake, she observed, had just tossed a large rock into the ocean and was about to throw a second one. Rushing over to him she yelled, "What are you doing? We're supposed to remain incognito in order to avoid detection from any park rangers, and you're out making lots of noise. Besides, these are sensitive habitats and lobbing large stones into the water not only disturbs the land but also the underwater marine environment."

As Jake turned toward her, Mischa could see the frustration on her brother's face and realized that their search had been harder on him than he had let on. Her anger turned to sympathy as she held out her hand and Jake sheepishly handed her the rectangular stone. Mischa bent over to gently place the rock back on the ground when something about it caught her attention. Although a good portion of it was covered in bird droppings, she could see what appeared to be carvings on the side of the stone—a cross, the letters *JR*, and a human stick figure. *That's odd,* she thought. *What's the probability of finding an inscribed stone on a desolate island?* She quickly analyzed the engravings. *The letters, JR, must be someone's initials. But the cross, what does that mean? And the stick figure—it's something a child would draw. Whoever JR was—he wasn't much of an artist.* Suddenly, a revelatory light went off inside her subconscious. *Could this be Juan Rodriguez Cabrillo's gravestone?*

"Where did you get this?" she asked nervously. Jake pointed to an area just below the ridge and at the side of the trail where they had ascended in order to reach the plateau. Mischa stared at the spot; there was a slight indentation on the ground where the rock had been, but nothing else. She looked up, and just above where Jake had found the stone she observed a rocky outcropping covered in bird guano.

"What is that?" she asked, pointing toward the overhang.

"I didn't look into it," Jake answered, "it's all covered with bird poop and it just looked like a ledge of rocks. Did you check it out on your way back?"

Mischa realized that in her haste to reach Jake she had run right past that area. "No," she answered excitedly, "but I think we should do that right now."

Mischa and Jake hurried up the path and began studying the pile of rocks. Despite some having fallen away, and bits of brush around the area, they were able to ascertain that this was not a single ledge, but a pile of rocks approximately four feet in width and seven feet in length, the perfect size for a grave. There was also a space for the oblong stone that Jake had found. Mischa placed it into the spot; it was obvious that it clearly belonged.

"Oh my gosh," said Mischa putting her hand to her mouth, "we almost missed it. This stone that you were about to hurl into the ocean is unquestionably Cabrillo's gravemarker. The two letters, *JR*, are the initials for *Juan Rodriguez,* and the cross most likely symbolizes his Christian faith, something the Spanish were proud of."

"What about the human stick figure?" Jake asked.

"I'm not sure on that one."

"Maybe it represents his soul," said Jake.

Mischa nodded. "That's a good answer. Life after death—what every Christian hopes for."

After a brief pause, Jake said, "It's time to put our digging tools to constructive use. Jake removed the mini pick and shovel combo from his backpack. After unfolding the device, he began shoveling rocks at a rapid pace.

"Wait!" Mischa demanded. "You're dismantling it too fast."

"That's a problem because—"

"Because we don't want to accidentally destroy Captain Cabrillo's bones which are undoubtedly brittle after lying in the earth for hundreds of years. There's also an issue of respect as we excavate his remains. Further, once we actually verify that it's his tomb, we need to immediately rebury him. My conscience won't allow me to desecrate a grave or bring dishonor to a distant relative."

"Fine," said Jake. "If that's how you want to proceed then I'll need your help since it'll now take longer to unearth."

Mischa removed a pair of gloves from the backpack and slipped them onto her hands. "I'll work one end while you work the other, and since we'll need to refill the pit, let's stack the rocks nearby."

"Aye, aye Captain," said Jake in a derisive tone as he reluctantly complied with her request.

Mischa laughed silently. Fortunately, her brother's grumbles were short-lived since he had a forgiving heart. In less than a minute their little disagreement would be forgotten.

For the next half hour they worked as a well-oiled team as they systematically relocated the top layer of four to twelve inch stones to a new rectangular pile a few feet away. When they were through, the burial pit was now level with the surrounding land. Both Jake's shovel and Mischa's gloves smelled of bird excrement.

"Bird poop sure does stink," said Jake.

"The odor of rotting fish, mixed with intestinal acids, a pinch of salt spray, all sautéed under a warm California sun—does create a bouquet of nauseating aromas."

"You make it almost sound edible," laughed Jake.

Smiling, Mischa said, "Almost, as long as you're a fly."

Jake motioned to the ground. "We're down to rocky soil. I'll shovel until I get tired and then you can take over."

"This island's pretty solid, so the grave has to be shallow."

"I doubt it's deeper than three feet," Jake agreed. "I'm sure that's why they had to pile on a ton of rocks."

"Go slowly," Mischa said as a reminder.

"Don't worry; you have me totally spooked about marring any of the bones." Using the shovel, Jake began scooping out the soil, which was a blend of crushed volcanic rock, granite, sandstone, clay, and a smidgen of top soil. The gritty material was heavy and within a short period of time he was sweating profusely. After fifteen minutes Jake had carved out a hole that was seven feet long, three feet wide, and six inches deep. "You're turn," he said as he handed the digging tool to Mischa. He then reached into the backpack and extracted a sixteen-ounce bottle of water that he downed in less than ten seconds.

Following Jake's outline, Mischa lowered the trench by another four inches. After twenty minutes of scooping dirt she was also drenched in sweat. Stepping out of the hole she said, "I'm obviously not as muscle-bound as you, but I'm proud at what I've accomplished." She passed the shovel back to her brother. "It's my turn for a water break."

Jake smiled. "Not too bad . . . for a girl."

"I'll take that as a compliment," said Mischa as she unscrewed the cap from a plastic water bottle.

Jake, refreshed, approached the task with renewed zeal. "My goal," he announced, "is to lower it by another foot." Beginning on the northwest corner he dug down an additional twelve inches, creating a ditch that he could then work off of. When he was approximately eighteen inches beyond his starting point, the tip of the shovel unexpectedly struck a hard object that sent powerful shockwaves up the handle and into his hands, elbows, and shoulders. "That stung," Jake complained.

"What did you hit?" asked Mischa.

"I'm not sure, but it felt like hardened steel." Using the pick side of the shovel, Jake began scraping the loose dirt in the area where the blade had penetrated—releasing small fragments of soil, which he then scooped out. Moving cautiously, he eventually reached the point where the impact occurred. As he ran his pick over the spot, it produced a harsh, grating type noise.

"That sounds like metal on metal," Mischa said excitedly.

"My thoughts exactly," said Jake as he used his hands to wipe away a thin layer of dirt that had built up between the tip of the pick and whatever it was touching. "Oh my, oh my God," he shrieked, "it looks like some kind of treasure chest." Jake's exuberant groans grew louder as each shovelful revealed an object larger than previously expected or hoped for. In order to widen the hole, he began digging in a new area just to the right of the chest, but abruptly stopped working and uttered a loud gasp. Protruding out of the ground was a long white bone. Using the edge of the blade Jake carefully scraped off an additional inch of soil which unveiled even more bones.

"I think those are leg and hip bones," advised Mischa.

Jake stepped out of the pit and stood next to his sister. "It's creepy exhuming a body," he said softly, "unlike the iron crate which I don't have a problem with."

"Technically speaking," Mischa clarified, "were not exhuming a body, we're just uncovering a skeleton for a brief moment and then reburying it. But that treasure chest—it may not be flesh and bones, but we'll definitely exhume it."

"It will be interesting to see what it contains."

"Riches beyond measure," laughed Mischa.

Nodding Jake said, "Maybe," and after a brief pause added: "Assuming this is the Captain's grave, and I suspect the items in the chest will confirm that . . . do we have to unearth the entire skeleton?"

Mischa looked at her brother and saw that he was serious about his question. "I think we have to," she replied, "since that metal box might not be the only artifact buried with him, plus I want to photograph an intact skeleton."

Jake shrugged. "I thought you might say that."

"But, we only have to expose the bones, not remove them."

"I wasn't planning on handling them," Jake revealed. "Besides, I doubt there's anything concealed beneath the body, especially when they had a metal crate to store things in."

Mischa sensed her brother's discomfort. The bones had gotten to him. "I'll make you an offer," she said tactfully. "Since you're considerably stronger, why don't you work on extricating the treasure chest while I finish digging out the skeleton, but I get to use the shovel."

Jake rewarded Mischa with a grateful smile. "Thanks sister, I'm agreeable to that."

Jake completed his side of the deal in less than thirty minutes. The chest turned out to be approximately four-feet long, one-foot high, and a foot wide. After hauling it out of the pit, Jake spent the next fifteen minutes trying to bust open an iron padlock that had rusted shut. The only tools he had at his disposal were a hammer, pliers, and two screwdrivers. The pliers were essentially worthless, but he was able to use the screwdrivers as wedges. Mischa could hear him still struggling with the lock as she wrapped up her portion of the dig. The skeleton, she was pleased to see, was almost complete. *About ninety percent,* she estimated, although some of the smaller bones from the hands and feet—carpals, metacarpals, tarsals, metatarsals, and phalanges were still missing, presumably hidden under inches of dirt. Removing her cell phone she snapped several images from various angles. *I'm witnessing an historical event,* she realized, *and I need to preserve it.* Furthermore, these photos would serve as proof that they had actually found the skeletal remains of Captain Juan Rodriquez Cabrillo. The only unknown was the contents of the chest; it would either corroborate their discovery, or disprove it. As she was putting her cell phone away she heard her brother utter a triumphant shout—the moment of truth had arrived.

Jake waited a few seconds for Mischa to join him before he lifted the lid. "I'll do it on the count of three," he warned. "One . . . two . . . three." As he began exerting upward pressure, the ancient hinges—dormant for centuries—creaked as he slowly raised the iron cover. When it reached a ninety degree angle it ceased moving.

Mischa, her eyes unblinking, stood transfixed as she gazed into the opened treasure chest. After a few seconds she began crying. Her brother hugged her. "Jake," she whispered, "we actually did it."

Jake laughed as he broke off his embrace. "I think you deserve most of the credit, but I won't refuse my share of the booty."

Mischa glanced into the chest again. It was almost full. "Should we check it out now, or wait until we get back to Scorpion Cove?" she asked.

Jake didn't even hesitate. "NOW," he replied.

Mischa smiled. "I guess that was a dumb question."

Jake just nodded.

Mischa felt goose bumps rising on her skin as she stared into a chest that was in essence a time capsule containing sixteenth century artifacts. *It's unbelievable,* she thought. The relics included a sword that was sheathed in a silver-gilded scabbard, a gold-plated dagger whose ivory handle was encased with emeralds, a finely woven vest of chain-mail armor, a silver cross inlaid with rubies, gold necklaces slung with warrior-like figurines, a gold-colored Aztec style disc framed by two circular bands of encrusted jadeite, gold coins, and several ten-inch long gold ingots that appeared to weigh about four pounds each. Of particular interest to Mischa was a rolled parchment that, according to her high school archeology class, was made from the skins of either sheep or goats, and if kept dry, could last for thousands of years. While Jake was busy examining the gold pieces, she selected the parchment. Fortunately, the animal skin was in excellent shape; she had worried that it might disintegrate the moment she touched it. Sitting down, she held the document in her lap and unrolled it. It was the equivalent of a page in length, and the words were in Spanish as she expected—a language that she had studied since elementary school though it still took a moment for her brain to switch from English to Spanish. The document was titled, *Instrument of Conveyance*, and contained only one line of text. *Grantor, Juan Rodriguez Cabrillo, hereby conveys ownership of the Island of Capitana or by its Indian name Limuw, to Luisa Librado, Grantee, and to her heirs and their heirs forever and ever.* The document was dated *December 28, 1542* and was signed by *Captain Juan Rodriguez Cabrillo* with an official looking waxen seal located next to his name. In addition there were two witnesses—*Bartolome Ferrer* and *Francisco de Vargas*.

Mischa reread it a second time. *Is this the original deed?* She asked herself. After the third reading she was trembling with excitement. *It's real!* She concluded. According to their family genealogy, Luisa had a son which she named Santiago Cabrillo—their great grandfather going back almost fifteen generations. "Jake," she announced gleefully, "we now have undeniable proof that this is the actual gravesite of Captain Cabrillo."

"I know," he replied, "the items in the treasure chest."

"No—it's more than just that," she said as she handed him the parchment. "You need to read this; you'll be surprised at the author."

Jake was as fluent in Spanish as his sister. He quickly reviewed the document, chuckled, and then read it again. "The Captain himself," he said with a sense of awe. "This is definitely the smoking gun of evidentiary proof."

"I know," she squealed, "that's what makes it so valuable."

"As an authentic historical record, it's probably priceless," he said as he handed it back to Mischa. "We'll need to make sure it doesn't get wet."

Mischa carefully re-rolled the deed and placed it inside the chest. "For almost five hundred years this metal container has kept the elements out—this parchment will certainly survive an hour-long voyage across the ocean."

"It's probably the safest spot on the ship," Jake confirmed. He then repacked the chest with several golden artifacts that he had been examining and closed the lid. "It's getting late and we still have to refill the grave, transport the chest down to the boat, and motor home."

Mischa stood up. "At least backfilling the hole will be a whole lot easier than digging it out."

"If you do the shoveling," Jake offered, "I'll replace all the stones."

Mischa compared the mound of dirt with the pile of heavy stones and said "Okay." Most of the soil was located alongside the pit, which allowed her to just bulldoze the material in. She started at the head of the grave and slowly worked her way backwards. Once she completed a one-foot section, Jake would begin piling on the rocks. Their cooperative system ran smoothly, and within forty minutes they were done. After carefully replacing the headstone, Mischa asked Jake to wait a few minutes so that she could run a quick errand. "Potty break," he chided as she headed inland. "No," she yelled back. When she returned she was carrying a small bouquet of island flowers. "It seemed appropriate," she said as she placed the flowers next to the headstone. "Should we have a moment of silence?" she asked.

"Maybe a minute; he's been dead a long time."

After sixty seconds, Mischa said in a soft voice, "Thank you Captain Cabrillo for leaving us a legacy—Santa Cruz Island, the generations of Cabrillo's, and the extraordinary artifacts. I want you to know . . . your memory lives on."

Jake laughed and said, "Amen to that, especially the artifacts."

Mischa scowled as she looked at her brother. "Have you ever heard of the word *reverence?*"

"Of course—I may have laughed but I wasn't being disrespectful, and I think the Captain honored my heart because during our quiet time I thought of a way of transporting the treasure chest down to the boat."

"How?"

"It's actually quite simple. Gravity. I'll be in the back letting the iron box down, while you're in front guiding it. Fortunately the chest has handles on each end. We'll just slide it down the hillside."

"I won't get squashed?"

"It's not too heavy, just awkward. I figure it weighs around a hundred pounds. It'll be like lowering a toboggan—we'll just have to take it nice and slow."

"You promise you won't let go?"

"I give you my solemn word."

Mischa laughed. "Talk about trust, but since I don't have a better strategy, I have to agree by default."

After verifying the safest and quickest route, they proceeded with Jake's plan, and began working their way down the hillside—performing their respective tasks in the same manner as a ski-patrol rescue team. At about the halfway point the rocky soil became more sand-like which lessened the friction under the chest and caused an increase in downward pressure. In order to compensate, Jake used the heels of his shoes to dig in, and assumed a crouched position. The final thirty feet proved to be the most difficult, and when Jake started losing traction and the object accelerated, he yelled at Mischa to get out of the way. He barely managed to hang on—dry skiing on the soles of his shoes—until the iron sled came to a gliding stop just five feet from the water's edge.

"That was cutting it close," he said, and shuddered.

"Are you kidding—that was radical!" Mischa declared. "What an awesome display of athletic skills. It's too bad I didn't film it."

Smiling, Jake said, "Maybe next time, and as compensation for my Gold Medal performance, you're required to lend a hand at loading the treasure chest onto the boat."

Laughing, she said, "I think we're both bringing home the gold—and then some." Grabbing a handle, she helped her brother stow the chest on the ship's rear deck.

While Mischa retrieved the docking fenders, Jake hauled up the anchor. Once it was secured, he started the outboard engine. "You ready to head home?" he asked.

"Absolutely; it's been an incredible day, but unfortunately there's still one thing missing . . . Hania. Hopefully, the oarfish will pay us a visit on our way home."

"Hopefully," Jake repeated as he moved the throttle control to the midway mark. "I'll keep our speed down just in case."

Traveling at reduced rpm's meant the journey back to Scorpion Cove would take over an hour. Mischa donned her polarized sunglasses and began scanning the ocean surface. For some reason—whenever the creature appeared—it typically breached slightly ahead of their vessel, as if it sensed their likely path.

After forty minutes of searching, without a single ripple disturbing the surface, Mischa was ready to call it a day. The oarfish was obviously not in their section of the ocean. They were also now within range of the Scorpion Cove cell phone tower. "I think I'll text dad and Timbrook and give them a heads up."

"Don't tell them everything," Jake suggested. "Just pique their interest."

"Good idea," said Mischa. She created a text, and then read it to Jake for his approval before transmitting it. "You might want to meet us at the dock in about twenty minutes—we've had a very interesting day. See attached photo." The image was of a skeleton.

"That's perfect," laughed Jake. "Send it."

Mischa pushed the 'Send' button. "It's on its way."

Five seconds later she received a response. It was from their dad. She read it out loud. "Is it real? Eva and I just got back from Montannon Ridge." Four seconds later she received a second message. It was from Timbrook. It contained only one word. "Cabrillo?"

"Timbrook's certainly perceptive," Jake attested.

"What should my reply be?"

Jake thought for a moment before responding. "Just text the word 'grandpa.' That's a huge clue."

Mischa giggled. *This was fun.* She sent the message.

"They'll definitely be down at the dock," Jake said confidently. He then moved the throttle control to maximum. "Hania's a no-show," he explained.

"Unfortunately," she said. Mischa then closed her eyes and reclined her seat. It was time for a short sunbathe. "Let me know when we're almost there."

When they were less than a mile from Scorpion Cove, Jake suddenly killed the engine. "He's here," he whispered.

"Where?" said Mischa sitting up.

"About twenty feet in front of the bow."

"He must have gone back down . . . I don't see him."

"He'll come back."

Mischa handed Jake a bucket of squid and kept the other for herself. "Let's cover both sides of the boat—you look west and I'll look east." After almost a minute she began to worry. *Where are you?* She wondered.

"There he is!" They both said simultaneously. The oarfish immediately swam up to Mischa and started inhaling squid like it hadn't feasted in weeks."

"What's wrong with it?" asked Jake. "It's acting nervous and won't approach the boat."

"Are you blind," Mischa said sarcastically, "it's eating like a ravenous pig."

"Eating?" Jake mumbled, and then a few seconds later started laughing hysterically. "Yours maybe, but its twin is a bit indecisive."

Mischa spun around. "Oh my God! "There's two?"

"Yes—unless we're being tricked by a mirage. Hania's obviously on your side of the vessel since he's familiar with our ship, but I must be entertaining its mate."

"Try tossing the squid," Mischa advised. "It's going to take a while before it's comfortable with us."

Jake followed his sister's recommendation and soon both buckets were empty. With no more squid, the creatures began their journey back to the abyss. Mischa watched as they disappeared—undulating shadows in the watery depths.

"That was like ice cream on top of ice cream with a dollop of whipped cream," Mischa said with a satisfied grin.

"The food analogy works for me too," said Jake, "particularly since I'm starving." He then reengaged the engine and pointed their vessel toward Scorpion Cove.

As they entered the inlet, there were three individuals standing next to *Hania's* berth—their dad, Eva, and Timbrook in spite of his illness.

"This will be one of those moments we'll never forget," Mischa said proudly.

Jake looked at his sister and smiled. "I can't wait to see their expressions when we open the treasure chest—that's a memory I will cherish forever." He then tooted the boat's horn. It was time to celebrate.

40

Kurt Nichols smiled as he gazed at his hand-picked audience—less than a dozen individuals. He had purposely limited the number of people invited to the event in order to avoid a media circus. A slight sea breeze ruffled his hair. *Inspiration Point,* he couldn't imagaine a more scenic location for the news conference. Sitting in the front row were his two children, Jake and Mischa, Dr. Eva Chen, Dr. Matthew Sedrak, and Brandon Kagan the chemist. There was also a seat for Adam Timbrook who evidently was running late. The second row included Zheng Tian from the San Francisco offices of Poseidon Holdings, Emily Flannigan, granddaughter to the late Captain Sean Flannigan, Alfonso Mendez, DVM, and Ruben Negrete. Daniel Petersen was also present, but not as a spectator. He was in charge of the PowerPoint presentation that would take place during the press conference—displaying the images on a sixty inch Sony 4K Ultra HDTV, which they had appropriated from Kurt's house. The electricity needed to run the equipment was provided by a portable Honda generator. The only news organization invited to the event was KCLA 9—the largest independently owned television station in the greater Los Angeles area. To Kurt's surprise, they sent a journalist by the name of Rachel Knox, who looked more like a contestant in a beauty pageant than a serious reporter covering an important news conference. But, after visiting with her for a few minutes, he realized that she was as sharp as she was pretty. When at one point she said something slightly flirtatious, Eva, who was listening to their conversation, stepped in and situated herself between Kurt and the newswoman. Later, as he thought about that awkward moment he laughed inwardly; a jealous Eva was certainly flattering.

The conference was scheduled to begin at 10:00 a.m., just three minutes away. *Where's Timbrook?* Kurt wondered. The discovery of the artifacts in Painted Cave was one of the topics he intended to address. Besides, as the Island's representative on behalf of the Chumash Tribe of Indians, he had something special planned for Timbrook. *It's that illness that he won't talk about,* thought Kurt, *that's why he's running late.*

Rachel Knox's team consisted of a cameraman and a soundman. The broadcast was being recorded, and after some minor editing, was scheduled to air on the five o'clock news. Approximately a month earlier, when Kurt initially contacted KCLA 9, there were only two subjects on the agenda—the *S.S. Winfield Scott,* and the prehistoric creatures. In his conversation with the station manager, the only item he mentioned was the discovery of a historical shipwreck with some intriguing cargo, and would Channel 9 be interested in covering the story. The manager immediately said yes, and that the station would send a film crew out to the island. Kurt hadn't revealed the second more improbable news item—the 'discovery' of Pygmy mammoths and saber-toothed cats, since he wanted their existence to remain hidden until the very last moment. Following his discussion with Channel 9, three other stories had developed: Karl Goebbel's mysterious death and subsequent rumor regarding the sale of *West Coast Seafood and Aquaculture* to an anonymous buyer; the unexplained explosion in Painted Cave; plus the unearthing of Captain Cabrillo's gravesite. As a low-level field reporter, Rachel Knox had fortuitously scored the interview of the decade, and in less than eight hours her astonishing footage, and her captivating face, would light up the entire world.

Rather than talking 'off the cuff,' Kurt had prepared a script, although Rachel was allowed to interrupt his presentation with relevant questions. As far as Rachel knew, the subject matter for today's news conference involved a shipwreck; she was unaware of any other topic. Kurt had also converted his script into a press release, with hundreds of attached photos, exhibits, and short videos, all of which would be e-mailed to all the media outlets after KCLA's 5:00 o'clock broadcast.

Standing behind a simple acrylic lectern with a built-in microphone, Kurt observed Rachel give the prearranged ten-second warning signal. He quickly scanned the audience and then beyond—to the path leading up to Inspiration Point. *Still no Timbrook.* Regrettably, he'd have to start without him. Rachel held up 3-2-1 fingers and filming began.

"Greetings from the Island of Santa Cruz, or by its Chumash name, Limuw," he began. "My name is Kurt Nichols, Senior Project Scientist for the University of Malibu, Marine Biology Lab, located on this beautiful island off the California coast." Wiping a bead of sweat from his brow, he continued. "What I say today I say as a private citizen, and not as a spokesperson on behalf of the university. In the last two months this island has revealed some of its secrets, both on land and underwater, which will have an impact far beyond its coastline. Unfortunately, I must also deal with a darker issue . . . Karl Goebbel, and his offshore fish farms. On each topic I will be as brief as possible. For an in-depth discussion, with accompanying photographs, video clips, and exhibits, please visit KCLA 9's website, which will contain the full press release."

Kurt saw Rachel mouth, "What press release?" Kurt smiled back. She would get her copy at the conclusion of the news conference.

"Marine historians are familiar with the wreck of the *S.S. Winfield Scott*, which struck an outcropping of rocks off of Middle Anacapa Island shortly before midnight on December 2, 1853. All four hundred passengers and crew survived, and most of its cargo was successfully recovered including a million dollars worth of gold bullion, but the steamship was a total lost. The wreck was blamed on pea-soup fog, and its Captain, Sean Flannigan, was summarily dismissed from his position with the Pacific Mail Steamship Company. That, in a condensed form, is the official version of the incident. One of Captain Flannigan's heirs is here today," Kurt motioned toward Emily, who stood up and waved before sitting back down. "I would also like to introduce Zheng Tian, Archivist with Poseidon Holdings, where the records of every ship previously owned by Poseidon or its subsidiaries are stored, including the S.S. *Winfield Scott's*." Tian just nodded his head at the introduction. "I made a promise to both Emily and Tian, that I would employ all my talents and skills at unearthing the truth behind the *Scott* wreck, and if possible, clear Captain Flannigan's name. Based upon my investigation I can unequivocally state that the Captain was an unintentional pawn in a diplomatic plot involving two countries—the United States and Mexico, and that Captain Flannigan was actually a hero: unlike the Titanic disaster, this Captain made sure that every man and woman aboard his ship lived to see another day."

"Those are pretty serious allegations," Rachel interrupted. "Do you have any evidence to back up your assertions?"

Kurt laughed. "In a criminal case, in order to obtain a conviction, your evidence must prove guilt beyond a reasonable doubt. In our situation, based upon everything that we've gathered, we could easily meet that standard. Daniel Petersen, who's in charge of today's PowerPoint presentation, helped collect that proof. Our first piece of evidence comes from the *Winfield Scott* itself—its wood. As a quick history lesson, the *Scott* was constructed out of fine-grained hardwoods, and when the wreck occurred, its wood was salvaged. Some of the recovered planks were used in constructing a winery on Santa Cruz, but the bulk of it was stored on the island in a brick warehouse for future use. In the last year I used some of that lumber in building my house on Santa Cruz, and the scraps were set aside as firewood. Approximately two months ago, while stoking a fire, I noticed that a couple of the pieces appeared fragmented, as if ripped apart by a blast, and that several of them contained scorch marks. The seared wood mystified me as there was no record of any fire on the *Scott*. Being a scientist I was curious as to what the substance on the wood might be, so I removed several small slivers of the blackened material and had it analyzed by our lab. Our Chemist, Brandon Kagan, who's seated in the front row, performed that testing. His tests results are now up on the television screen. His conclusion: Black powder—which in the mid-1800's was used as gunpowder or as blasting powder. In our case, Kagan also found potassium sulfide, which only forms when black powder is burned. The singed lumber turned out to be White Oak, which was another important clue since only one section of the *Scott* steamer was made from this type of timber—its hull. Based upon these facts we made a preliminary determination that an incendiary explosion had occurred somewhere along the *Scott's* hull *prior* to its destructive impact upon the rocks of Middle Anacapa Island."

"How do you truly know that?" Rachel asked. "Maybe the impact caused the fire."

"That's a reasonable assumption," Kurt acknowledged. "Violent collisions can ignite a conflagration, but that's not what occurred in this case since none of the survivors reported any fire aboard the *Scott*. After reviewing the test results I realized I was dealing with a maritime mystery, and like Sherlock Holmes, I began to investigate. The first thing I did was research every known article, report, or commentary on the wreck. In my studies I learned that the corporate offices of the Pacific Mail

Steamship Company, which owned the *Winfield Scott,* still had a branch office in San Francisco, but were now a part of Poseidon Holdings. I immediately booked a flight to San Francisco and traveled to their headquarters, where I met Zheng Tian. After a brief discussion about the ship, he informed me that they still had the *Scott* file, which he agreed to produce. Tian revealed that whenever a ship is lost at sea, because of legal issues that could last for centuries, its records are kept in perpetuity. However, when he returned with the folder he had to apologize; it was empty except for two pieces of stationary. The first document was a brief note stating that Captain Flannigan had relocated to Scenic Road in Carmel, California, and the other a short letter, which is now up on the screen." Kurt paused a few moments to give Rachel and the general audience a chance to read the document. Clearly it made an impression as the attendees began murmuring to each other.

"Is this a joke?" Rachel quipped. "Why would the 14th President of the United States care about securing the *Scott* records, and why would a diplomat assigned to Mexico be involved? I assume this letter helps bolster your conspiracy theory."

"It certainly adds to the mystery," answered Kurt. "How often does a sitting president become embroiled in a small-time shipwreck, especially when no one died, and everything of value was recovered? My guess is never. After I left Poseidon Holdings I acted on a wild hunch, and checked the Internet White Pages to see if any Flannigan still resided in Carmel. To my surprise I found a listing for an E. Flannigan with an address on Scenic Road, the same street that Captain Flannigan had relocated to. I immediately wondered if this individual was a direct descendent of the Captain, and if so, whether this person still possessed any of the *Scott* records. I tried calling, but no one answered, so I did the next best thing—I drove down to Carmel, and that's where I met Emily, who confirmed her Flannigan ancestry."

"Was your trip a success?" asked Rachel.

Kurt smiled. "Emily didn't have any *official* records, but the Captain did leave behind two important items—a twenty dollar 1850 Double Eagle, Liberty Head gold coin, and a riddle penned by the Captain himself regarding that fateful night. Petersen has now posted that riddle for your viewing." Kurt paused as Rachel read the words. He could see by her demeanor that the enigmatic message was having an impact.

"No wonder you believe the Captain was a diplomatic pawn," she said softly. "He makes that assertion in his own poem." She then read several verses out loud, *"Collaboration, covenant, scheming . . . Trist, Santa Anna, Juarez, Pierce . . . The Winfield Scott a diplomatic pawn.* It seems his accusations are against Nicholas Trist—an American diplomat; Franklin Pierce—the President of the United States; and two Mexican Presidents, Santa Anna and Benito Juarez. In those days these were powerful people."

Impressed with her historical knowledge, Kurt stared at Rachel with greater respect. "They certainly were," he agreed. "In his riddle the Captain also mentioned two treaties—Guadalupe Hidalgo, which ended the Mexican-American War, and The Gadsden Purchase. Both agreements required Mexico to transfer to the United States vast tracts of land in exchange for millions of dollars in gold bars and coins. The poem also references a possible third treaty, *Ayutla*, which isn't the title to any known agreement, but the name of a Mexican rebellion that eventually ousted Santa Anna from power. The more intriguing parts of the riddle—from a treasure hunter's perspective—are the verses that indicate what the *Scott* was carrying: *Precious yellow weight, opulence and compact, solid and glass . . . a plethora of secrets lie beneath, impervious to sea or time.* How the ship was damaged: *Rolling thunder, a directional rumble, black-powder horizon, a pierced ship, a deposit upon the sea.* And hints at its route at the time of the explosion: *A known path—an inside passage, beacon of light, Cavern Point, ¼ mile distant in the night, Santa Cruz an ebbing apparition, Anacapa's cliffs an illusory vision."*

Rachel looked at Kurt and smiled—the kind of warm, seductive smile that finalists in a beauty pageant reserve for the judges. "I assume your search was successful," she said, then cutting to the chase asked. "How much did you find?"

Kurt laughed inwardly. *She's certainly beautiful,* he thought, *but like a viper I bet there's fangs behind that smile.* He smiled back. "In answer to your question—yes, but on many different levels. On day one of our treasure quest, our boat-towed underwater metal detector became snagged on an abandoned benthic trawl net, which was still killing large quantities of marine life. We immediately suspended our search and spent the next six hours recovering the destructive ghost net. On day two, our metal-detecting towfish found two different wrecks: The first, a commercial fishing vessel named *Del Rio,* a purse seiner, which sank in 1952. This wreck is part of NOAA's shipwreck database, and its location is well known. The second wreck, however, doesn't exist in NOAA's database."

"Why don't they have a record of it?" Rachel asked.

Kurt shrugged, "Like most shipwrecks, once they've capsized and disappeared beneath the waves, their final resting places are generally unknown. Fortunately, we now have that information on this ship, which we'll eventually turn over to NOAA. After analyzing the debris field we were able to put a name to the ship, *Steamer Lotus,* which foundered off of Anacapa Island in 1921 due to a fire in its cargo hold."

"What was scattered across the seafloor that allowed you to make that determination?" Rachel wondered.

Kurt laughed. "Wine bottles, casks, and oak barrels; the *Steamer Lotus* was a bootlegging ship. And, in the near future we plan on salvaging its cargo, which is probably still suitable for drinking."

"Invite me to the party," Rachel said and winked.

Kurt stole a quick glance at Eva whose face sported a distinct scowl. "The next day we made another important discovery, and in the process solved a 1945 naval mystery; the whereabouts of a Grumman TBF Avenger torpedo bomber that had crashed into the waters off of Anacapa Island. Our underwater camera revealed a plane that was still pretty much intact, having settled on the bottom in an upright position. Unfortunately, its three crew-members didn't survive the impact, and their skeletal remains were still visible through the aircraft's plastic canopy. We prompt-ly notified the Navy of our findings, and they've already recovered the bodies. It's our understanding that the site's GPS coordinates will be released to the public within the next month so that family members, divers, and boaters can pay their respects."

"These other shipwrecks and the crashed naval plane are cer-tainly interesting," Rachel acknowledged sweetly as she playfully tossed her hair, "but I'm primarily interested in the *Scott*. Why else would you have invited me to your island?"

Kurt shifted uncomfortably. Rachel's double entendre wasn't subtle. He wisely avoided Eva's eyes. "On the fourth day, thanks to an epiphany that Petersen had, we decided to go back and re-visit a section of the ocean that we had already examined and dismissed as a possible site. Upon reaching the coordinates, we immediately deployed the towfish. At first it appeared to be a dead end, but after repositioning the device to a new area just forty feet away, the meter within the unit's topside control box suddenly went ballistic—indicating a large expanse of ferrous and non-ferrous metals on the ocean floor. As it turned out . . . we had found the *Scott's* debris field."

"And what exactly did you dredge up from the bottom?" Rachel asked.

"With apologies to Captain Flannigan, how about a few clues of my own," Kurt grinned. "It's a metal that all societies cherish, it's listed on the stock exchange, it endures forever, it symbolizes love, and it's a ladies second favorite mineral after diamonds."

"Gold!" said Rachel.

Kurt nodded. "Excellent guess. Over a period of six days we recovered almost fifteen thousand pounds—."

"—Fifteen thousand pounds . . . of gold?" She interrupted in a voice barely above a whisper, sounding excited, but weak. "Seven and a half tons?"

Kurt wasn't surprised to hear the collective gasp from the audience and chuckled at their reaction. "You heard correctly. For your information I still have trouble sleeping at night when I think about it. We unearthed 440 gold bars and 45,580 Double Eagle gold coins. The gold bars were in brass crates that were approximately two feet long and a foot high. We found a total of forty crates. Each container held eleven gold bricks, and each brick weighed 27.5 lbs. The coins were clumped in piles, making their recovery easy. The Double Eagles had originally been stored in canvas sacks, which had obviously disintegrated with the passage of time."

"Do you have any pictures of the gold bars and coins?" Rachel asked.

"Yes, they're included in the press release, but for today, I have a special treat for you. You've probably all noticed the table to my left, which is shrouded in a black cloth. The cloth is covering one of the crates along with a small bag of coins. The crate is packed with eleven golden ingots, the same number as when we found it. Both the bars and coins, however, have undergone extensive cleaning." Kurt removed the velvet cloth. "Feel free to touch, handle, and film them, but please, no souvenirs."

Rachel pouted for the camera, but did as requested. She grunted while extracting two of the bars. "They're wonderfully heavy," she said into the camera as she pretended to be exercising with the most expensive weights on earth. She then opened the bag of coins, and while they slid through her fingers, she uttered a sensuous moan. She counted the Double Eagle's as she slowly refilled the canvas sack. "Exactly one hundred," Rachel said with a sinful smile, "you would know if I took one." As she was walking away from the table she asked, "So, what's the value of your discovery?"

Kurt paused before responding, allowing for a bit of drama. This was the multi-million dollar question that Rachel's audience would remember for the rest of their lives. "On the commodity market gold is currently priced at $1200 an ounce. We recovered approximately 241,600 ounces. Multiply the two numbers and you arrive at a figure that's truly extraordinary—two hundred and ninety million dollars. But, the coins are actually worth double their face value, and as you know we found a lot of coins. Appraising each Double Eagle at $3000 adds another sixty-four million. Total approximate value: three hundred and fifty-four million dollars—plus or minus a few million."

Rachel appeared flustered by the answer and required a few seconds to pull herself together before she was able to ask the next question. "And what percentage do you get to keep? Maritime law typically places a limit on that amount."

"That's true," Kurt replied. "No treasure hunter is entitled to 100%. The gold must be shared with the original 'owner' whether it's a country, company, or private party. In our case we were dealing with the United States of America since it was their gold that the *Scott* was transporting. Under Maritime Shipwreck Treasure Law I'm entitled to a *Salvor's Reward*, which is a percentage of the total amount."

Rachel smiled, displaying a mouthful of perfectly aligned teeth that were as white as Tahitian pearls. "I know you must have hired the best lawyers that money can buy, especially with so much at stake—so what percentage did they negotiate?"

This was the one question that Kurt didn't want to answer, but he also knew that if he didn't answer it now, he would be hounded by the press until he did. "Twenty-five percent."

Rachel laughed—a soft, warm laugh that implied something more. "You just won the lottery! And assuming my math is correct—that's over eighty-eight million dollars, enough to cause any woman to swoon."

Kurt was shocked, not only by the blatant come-on, but also as it was a tactless remark against herself and her gender. He looked at Eva. She was shaking her head. Ignoring Rachel's eyes, he directed his words to the camera, "I appreciate money the same as anyone, but a huge portion of my share will be going into the non-profit, Nichols Foundation, where it will be used to benefit society. In fact, the Foundation just recently made some major decisions which I'll be discussing shortly."

Rachel's bubbly smile quickly dissolved into a frown, and in a condescending voice said, "That's awfully nice of you, although I wonder if someday you'll regret it. From my perspective your decision seems a bit foolish, especially when you haven't given yourself enough time to think about it."

Kurt was appalled by Rachel's selfish response. As a reporter she was supposed to be professional, and this personal observation was certainly out of the realm of professionalism. He peered at Eva for support. For the first time she was smiling. He turned back to Rachel and sternly said, "As an investigative reporter I'm surprised that you haven't asked some obvious questions: Why was the *Scott* carrying so much gold? What was its destination? And foremost, why was the United States involved? Since you don't seem interested in the historical value, I will answer these questions unprompted. As it turned out, gold wasn't the only item buried in the sand. We also uncovered a three-page document—stored in a waterproof glass container inside a diplomatic brass crate—that was a thousand times more precious than the *Scott's* yellow cargo. That document is now posted on the television screen." Kurt watched Rachel's expression as she carefully reviewed each page. By the end of page three her cheeks, which had flushed red at his rebuke, had changed to an ashen color, her eyes had dilated, and her lower jaw was slightly ajar. Kurt silently chuckled; she had grasped the political implications of their discovery.

"This Treaty would have profoundly altered the relationship between our two countries if it had been implemented," she murmured. "I can't believe that a Mexican president would subdivide his nation for a payment of just five million dollars."

"Approximately 40% of their entire land mass."

"What happened to the Treaty? Apparently President Pierce signed it but Mexico's President, Antonio Lopez de Santa Anna, did not. Was this the only copy?"

"It's my belief that this was the *only* copy, and that it *never* reached Panama where Santa Anna was waiting to sign it. The *S.S. Winfield Scott* was sabotaged on its way south."

"By who—and why would they do such a thing?"

"Again, it's speculation on my part, but by either a detachment of Mexican patriots, or a squad of misguided individuals, although it would appear that history has favored the former. In their minds their destructive act was justified in order to prevent an offensive Treaty, and a shipment of gold, from ever reaching Mexico. During this time period President Santa Anna was fighting an uprising in his country known as the Ayutla Revolution. Santa Anna was desperate for cash and was willing to trade land for gold in order to finance an army that could quash the rebellion. In all probability it was members of this rebel group that caused the explosion on the *Scott*. Without the gold, Santa Anna's days were numbered. As it turned out, the Ayutla Revolution succeeded, and Santa Anna was removed from office."

"This Treaty," Rachel warned, "has the potential to open up old territorial wounds. Has our government been notified of its existence?"

"Yes, we provided a copy to both the United States and Mexico. And in regard to territorial wounds—I also struggled with that issue, but decided to release it anyway. As a historical document it's extremely important and therefore deserves to be seen by the public. The next step was easy—I donated it to the Smithsonian Institute."

"You stated earlier that the Nichols Foundation has already decided on how a portion of the money will be spent. Exactly what did you mean by that?"

"I assume you've heard of *West Coast Seafood & Aquaculture*, and the recent death of its owner, Karl Goebbel?"

Rachel laughed uncomfortably. "As a matter of fact I knew him quite well; I recently conducted an in-depth interview regarding his aquaculture business. The question and answer session took place on Platform Grace and included a personal tour of the facility. I found the man to be quite charming. I'm sorry he died."

Kurt observed Rachel brush a tear from her eye. He felt sorry for her—not for her loss, but because she was about to learn the truth about the 'charmer'—Dr. Jekyll was actually Mr. Hyde. "Platform Grace was Goebbel's flagship aquafarm. It was a state-of-the-art facility, environmentally friendly, ethically managed, and produced wholesome game fish raised with natural food—squid, anchovies, sardines, and mackerel. Grace was so well run that it silenced any naysayers and epitomized the ideal fish farm. Anyone who toured the facility walked away impressed. Unfortunately, Goebbel's three other offshore aquafarms, Platforms Gilda, Gail, and Gina, were at the opposite end of the spectrum, which also explains why no one was allowed to visit them."

"That's not entirely true," Rachel said, butting in. "According to Goebbel, they were off-limits because they hadn't been modified for visitors like Platform Grace. Without the added safety features, he was concerned that someone might get hurt and file a personal injury lawsuit."

"Did you ever independently verify that assertion?" asked Kurt.

"It wasn't necessary," Rachel said raising her voice, "I trusted his word."

"That's too bad," Kurt said gently, "because he lied to you. For the last two months the United States Public Health Service, through its agency the Center for Disease Control, Dr. Matthew Sedrak, and Dr. Eva Chen, have all been involved in an investigation of Goebbel's seafood enterprise. Recently, they've also had the invaluable cooperation of two ex-employees, veterinarian Dr. Alfonso Mendez, and Ruben Negrete. All four of these individuals are with us today." Kurt paused for a brief moment as he had each person stand up. "At Grace," he continued, "each underwater grow-out pen was stocked with only ten to fifteen thousand tuna, salmon, or white seabass, which left plenty of space for vigorous, healthy fish. At the three questionable farms, however, the stocking densities typically exceeded fifty thousand, resulting in sickly fish that were oftentimes infected with ectoparasitic sea lice, anemia, and Furunculosis. And, according to Dr. Mendez, in order to treat these outbreaks, massive amounts of imported pesticides and antibiotics were used—imported because these chemicals are banned in the United States. In addition, Goebbel was feeding his fish a type of fodder that no other aquaculture farmer had tried before—protein-rich pellets derived from inexpensive meat and bone meal made from pulverized cows. The pellets were formulated from dead or diseased cows including slaughterhouse waste that contained specific risk materials such as brains, spinal columns, intestines, and other nervous system tissues. The pellets were imported from a region in Canada where mad cow disease still exists."

"Are you implying that Goebbel's game fish were suffering from various maladies including mad cow disease? Rachel asked. "I met the USDA Inspector while I was out on Platform Grace, and according to Goebbel, they had never failed a tissue sample test."

"That's because the *only* fish tested were from Grace," Kurt answered. "Goebbel paid the inspector huge sums of money . . . bribes . . . as long as he ignored the other farms. That person was recently arrested by the FBI and will be tried in Federal Court on corruption charges. Unfortunately, it's too late for Keith or Sandy, two individuals who died from mad cow disease after consuming game fish raised on Goebbel's aquafarms. Furthermore, the disorder affected other animals besides humans. For example, dolphins and sea lions that ate tainted fish also suffered from the deadly disease. Approximately two months ago, a crazed bottlenose dolphin attacked a group of surfers off of Ventura, killing one and injuring three others, including a young girl. Dr. Eva Chen, while filming an underwater show, was viciously attack by a deranged California sea lion which was also afflicted with the brain wasting disorder."

"Do you have any proof to back up your allegations?" Rachel demanded.

"Of course—please refer to the television screen where various test results are now being uploaded. As you've probably heard, my daughter killed the demented sea lion with a speargun, and the dolphin was dispatched by Dr. Sedrak using a surfboard as a type of javelin. Each animal underwent an extensive necropsy including a histopathological brain tissue exam. As it turned out both studies confirmed that the creatures were suffering from mad cow disease. Dr. Kagan, the chemist at our marine lab, also conducted tissue studies on eleven of Goebbel's game fish. His findings confirmed our worse fears—that the fish were asymptomatic carriers of the defective prions that cause mad cow disease. As Dr. Kagan explained the 'contagion thrives inside the tissue of their bodies—within the fish blood and lateral lines— without actually harming the hosts. As vectors of the disorder they were immune to its neurological effects, but were still capable of transmitting the disease to warm-blooded animals once their flesh was consumed.'"

In a voice trembling with uncertainty, Rachel argued, "Maybe Goebbel was ignorant of his internal problems; as you know, employees typically hide this type of damaging information from their bosses in order to avoid losing their jobs; especially if that person happens to be the President and CEO of the corporation."

Kurt nodded. "In certain situations that's true, but not in this case. Goebbel controlled *West Coast Seafood & Aquaculture* with an iron fist, and as a result, was aware of everything."

"How do you truly know that?" Rachel pressed. "He's dead, and I doubt you're able to communicate with his spirit."

"That's true," Kurt replied, "I'm certainly not a medium. Fortunately, we have something that's much more trustworthy; approximately forty-five minutes before Goebbel died he made several incriminating statements that were surreptitiously record-ed by my daughter on her Apple iPhone. Petersen will now play that twelve minute clip."

Kurt carefully watched Rachel's demeanor as she viewed the short video. Mischa had started her recording the moment Dr. Sedrak had mentioned that the explosion in Painted Cave hadn't been an accident. Pancho was the first person to appear on the screen. In his hands was a rifle, which was pointed toward Mischa's iPhone. Seconds later Karl Goebbel came into view, which resulted in Rachel uttering an audible sigh. The journalist, like a moth drawn to a light source, unwittingly moved a few steps closer to the TV as she listened to the vitriolic diatribe between Goebbel and Dr. Sedrak regarding mad cow disease. Rachel gasped when Goebbel acknowledged that his fish were the source of the infection, cringed at Goebbel's cold-hearted attitude to-ward those who had died or suffered catastrophic injuries as a result of the disorder, screamed when the gun was fired, briefly closed her eyes at the sight of blood pouring down Timbrook's leg, gazed sympathetically at Mischa as the young girl pleaded for their lives, and shook her head in disbelief as Goebbel ordered that the boat be emptied of all non-attached items including their lifejackets. The last scene depicted a ship inundated with water followed by distorted images as the cell phone sailed through the air and then descended into the depths.

Rachel's reactions had been closely echoed by the rest of the viewers, and once the video was over, Kurt had to put out his hands in a downward motion in order to quiet the group.

After a moment of silence Rachel, looking contrite, whispered, "I'm so sorry . . . he obviously was a narcissistic psychopath who was able to hide the neurosis from me. After viewing that video it's a miracle that anyone survived. What happened? And why were your friends on board a small boat?"

"They were using the Marine Lab's nineteen-foot Boston Whaler to tour Painted Cave," Kurt answered, "which is a massive sea cave located on the northwest corner of this island. While they were inspecting the main section of the cave they noticed that a large commercial vessel was following them. As they learned later, it was Goebbel's ship. Painted Cave is divided into two major segments; the main cavern and an inner chamber. These two caves are connected by a narrowed forty-five foot long gullet which is so constricted that only the small Marine Lab boat could squeeze through it. Once on the other side, they began exploring the inner chamber that included viewing a Chumash pictograph located at the back end of a deep passage. As they were studying the pictograph, the inner chamber was rocked by a powerful explosion. Fortunately, no one was seriously injured, although Mischa did sustain a concussion from a falling rock. The blast, as they soon ascertained, occurred at the entrance to the gullet, collapsing the connecting tunnel and blocking their only way out. As they subsequently discovered, Goebbel had triggered the explosion in order to kill both Dr. Sedrak and Dr. Chen and thereby end their investigation against his company."

"If this was the only way out, how did they escape?" Rachel asked.

"By sheer luck; there's one additional passage, but it's only navigable during an extraordinary low tide; fortunately, that type of negative tide was taking place that day. But, in using this dangerous exit they ended up damaging their outboard engine on a submerged rock which reduced their speed to a crawl. As they were slowly motoring home, they were intercepted by Goebbel's ship. Mischa's video clip captured the initial interaction between the two vessels."

"What happened after the cell phone was tossed into the sea?" Rachel asked.

"As you saw on the video," Kurt continued, "the Boston Whaler was sinking, which was exactly what Goebbel wanted. On board his ship were seven, fifty-five gallon drums, which were packed with pathological medical waste—human tissue from surgeries, and dissected animal remains from a biotech research firm. Apparently Goebbel was earning extra cash by illegally disposing of bio-hazardous waste into the ocean. As you can imagine, each barrel contained vast amounts of blood."

Rachel let out a horrified shriek. It was obvious by her expression that she had grasped the meaning of his words. "They used the gore to attract sharks?"

"Yes . . . they dumped out all seven barrels, creating a circle of chum around the Boston Whaler. By the time Goebbel and Pancho were finished, the ship was surrounded by over a dozen sharks—great whites, makos, and blues. Escape was impossible, and death seemed all but inevitable."

"But," said Rachel as she surveyed the audience, "It's apparent that everyone survived. How was that possible?"

"By an improbable friendship," Kurt said smiling for the first time. "Over six weeks ago Jake and Mischa nursed a giant oarfish back to health."

"What's an oarfish?" Rachel interrupted.

"It'll take too long to explain," laughed Kurt. "Take a look at the screen; Petersen's posted several pictures of the creature."

After viewing the images for several moments, Rachel exclaimed, "That's incredible!" And it's real?"

"Yes," said Kurt. "They're rare, but they definitely do exist. They're also known as the sea serpents of the ocean. My children found the sick oarfish at a local reef and began treating it with vitamins, antibiotics, and squid. Within a few days the creature made the connection between the sound of their boat's engine and food, and would anticipate their arrival. After it recovered, the oarfish would continue to seek out their craft whenever they crossed over its territory. Jake and Mischa encouraged this unusual behavior by rewarding it with a bucket of squid each time it made an appearance. And as they discovered during their interactions, the animal was endowed with an interesting trait."

Rachel shot Kurt a quizzical look. "What?" she asked.

"It was electrogenic, like an electric eel, and its charged aura repelled sharks. During their first encounter with the oarfish a shark approached, and it responded to the menace by discharging a bolt of electricity that scared off the shark. Fortunately, Jake and Mischa were far enough away that they only suffered a mild electrical shock. That experience, however, did make them wonder what would happen if the creature became truly angry."

Rachel squealed with understanding. "That's how they survived their ordeal—the oarfish showed up, frightening off the sharks."

Kurt smiled. "Exactly, but it also did something that was totally unexpected; it attacked Goebbel's ship, propelling itself out of the water, and landing on the vessel's rear deck. And, as the serpent's body grazed the metal structure, it discharged an enormous amount of electricity causing the entire rear portion to become electrified. Goebbel and Pancho, who were situated in the stern and leaning against the metal railing, both received a fatal dose of electricity stopping their hearts."

"So that's how Goebbel died," Rachel murmured, "he was electrocuted . . . like a common criminal . . . by a fish."

"Certainly an ignominious death," Kurt agreed.

In a somewhat angry voice Rachel said, "After what I've learned today, he clearly deserved it."

Kurt nodded but didn't respond. "Earlier you asked a question that I'm now prepared to answer more fully—how the Nichols Foundation intends to spend its money. As you know, *West Coast Seafood and Aquaculture* was recently sold to an anonymous buyer. That purchaser, I'm pleased to announce, was the Nichols Foundation."

"Why?" Rachel asked in amazement. "With all their diseased fish?"

"Prior to the acquisition, my board and I personally inspected Platform Grace. We left impressed with the quality of its product, which allowed for an easy decision. Our goal is to produce the same grade of nutritious seafood at all four platforms. Platform Grace is a resounding success, while the other three aquafarms are a disaster. In the near future they'll undergo extensive remodeling in order to make them the same as Grace. The diseased fish at these aquafarms will be humanely killed and their carcasses incinerated. Dr. Alfonso Mendez, who came highly recommended by Ruben Negrete, is now the new Director of Operations, and will be responsible for revamping the facilities. Mr. Negrete will be in charge of the ships that supply the natural food and will occasionally help out at the Marine Lab on special assignments. As a private, non-profit company, we don't have to worry about satisfying shareholders or paying dividends. In addition, besides cultivating reasonably priced, protein-rich seafood, the company will provide good paying jobs. Karl Goebbel was correct about one thing—the future of farming lies in offshore aquafarms since the earth has exhausted its arable acreage. If managed properly, in harmony with the local marine environment, these farms will be a blessing, not a curse, and will help meet the demands of a hungry world."

"What responsibility does the new company have to those individuals that died or suffered serious harm as a result of the tainted fish?" Rachel inquired.

"That's a good question," said Kurt, "and I'm glad you asked it. The Nichols Foundation had a non-negotiable demand when it agreed to purchase *West Coast Seafood and Aquaculture*—that all the funds would go into a special trust, and that Goebbel's heirs would not receive a single penny until every family that lost a loved one, or those that were injured, were properly compensated, including an employee by the name of Raul Alvarado who is currently disabled because of a work-related injury."

"How much is in the trust?"

"Fifteen million dollars."

"Hopefully that's enough," Rachel said softly.

"The Nichols Foundation has also hired a marine salvage company to clean out the tons of rubble inside of Painted Cave. That project is expected to take about three weeks. Inclement weather, wind, or swell conditions, could delay the clean-up efforts."

Coming to the close of this portion of his presentation, Kurt scanned the audience for Timbrook. *Where is he?* He wondered. At this point in the press conference he was dealing with issues that primarily involved the Chumash, and he was looking forward to his friend's reaction when he heard what Kurt had to say. After another quick look he sadly realized that he would have to continue without him.

"When the explosion occurred inside Painted Cave the wall containing the pictograph collapsed, revealing a hidden passageway and a possible exit to the outside world. Obviously it turned out to be a dead end, but at the time they didn't know that. The passage terminated at a huge cavern about half the size of Painted Cave. As the group stepped inside it they were instantly transported back in time—to the year 1822. Timbrook immediately fell to his knees, overwhelmed by what he saw, which in his eyes was more valuable than all the gold on the *S.S. Winfield Scott*."

Rachel laughed. "That must have been quite a sight—we're talking fifteen thousand pounds of precious yellow metal."

"For Timbrook it was the discovery of a lifetime." Kurt assured her. "In 1822 the Chumash were involuntarily removed from Santa Cruz Island—departing with little more than just their clothing. When the Spaniards searched the island for their belongings, primarily looking for gold, they found nothing—almost as if the island had never been inhabited. The Chumash, in the weeks prior to their forced exodus, had shrewdly hidden their most valuable possessions believing that they would someday return. Regrettably, that day never came. Because the Chumash did not have a written language, the location of these items was never recorded. Eventually, the few members of the tribe that knew of its whereabouts, died, and that knowledge died with them. The site's exact location remained a mystery until just a few weeks ago—when a deadly explosion meant for evil fortuitously opened up a sealed gateway, bringing great joy, instead."

Rachel smiled. "I imagine they found more than just a few arrowheads, beads, or animal hides considering Timbrook's emotional reaction."

Kurt chuckled. "Indeed they did. If I had some photographs, I could show you a portion of what they found, but unfortunately none were taken, and it will be at least another two weeks before the stones are cleared from the passage. But, to give you an idea as to the magnitude of the discovery, the implements of entire villages were stored within that cave, making it the largest repository of Chumash artifacts known to man."

"What types of artifacts?" Rachel pressed.

Kurt smiled. "It'd take an hour to describe everything, so I'll just provide a brief summary. The Chumash were renowned for their redwood planked canoes, and stashed in the cave were over a dozen Tomol canoes, including a fifty-foot masterpiece that once belonged to a Chumash Chief. There were thousands of other items as well—exquisitely crafted coiled baskets that had been made into pitchers, trays, jars, drinking cups, bowls, and cooking pots; plates fabricated from shells; utensils made from wood or soapstone; an assortment of animal skins that had been made into clothes, capes, and blankets; ceremonial clothes; all types of tools including wedges, flakers, awls, drills, hide scrapers, arrowheads, spears, knives, and arrows; and personal items such as shell necklaces, bracelets, and carved effigies from steatite. There were also baskets filled with Chumash currency—strings of shell beads made from the thick inner shell of the olivella sea snail." Kurt paused for a moment, and in a quieter voice said, "This is just a partial listing of the objects discovered. As Timbrook exclaimed a few evenings ago, 'it's the type of find that archaeologists only dream about, but more importantly, it represents his people's past.'"

Rachel's countenance turned serious. "What decisions have been made regarding the artifacts? They're obviously valuable, and once the passage is cleared out, the cave will be swarming with looters."

"We're certainly aware that by publicizing the discovery we've also alerted potential plunderers," Kurt acknowledged. "Fortunately, they'll never get near the site since a heavy metal gate will be installed across the entrance the moment the passage is reopened."

"A locked gate should take care of the problem," Rachel concurred, and then asked. "Who's the rightful owner of the artifacts? From what you've described they're easily worth a small fortune."

Without hesitating Kurt said, "The Chumash—who were promptly notified the day after their discovery. Its Tribal Government, in consultation with its members, agreed to secure the site as soon as possible, and devised a plan for the eventual removal of the artifacts including the collapsed pictograph, which they hope to have restored. In order to properly display the various objects, the members voted to allocate funds for the construction of a museum."

"Where?" asked Rachel. "The building, from an architectural perspective, would have to be stunning in order to house such a notable collection. I imagine several cities would love to host it."

Kurt frowned, not because he was angry at Rachel's question, but because he was worried. This conference had gone on for over 45 minutes, and his Chumash friend was still a no-show. Without Timbrook here, his surprise announcement would lose some of its luster. He, Mischa, and Jake had made a decision regarding this—one they agreed was long overdue. But this time Kurt's disappointment turned into alarm. He leaned forward into the microphone and asked for a brief time-out. He signaled Eva to come up to the lectern and putting his hand over the microphone, explained his concern and asked if she wouldn't mind going down the path and checking on Timbrook's whereabouts. Eva immediately looked concerned, nodded, and walked away. Turning back to the audience, Kurt said, "The museum will be built on Santa Cruz Island, in the village of Swaxil, the ancestral home of the Chumash . . . on land which they now own." He held up an official looking piece of paper before continuing. "This document is a quitclaim deed. It's a gift from my family, and conveys the ancient village of Swaxil back to its rightful owners, the Chumash Tribe of Indians." Kurt briefly paused as he glanced toward Timbrook's house and sadly shook his head. This was supposed to be an emotional and historical moment as he handed the document to Timbrook, finalizing the transfer. Kurt then looked back at the camera. "The cost of building the museum will be split 50/50 between the Nichols Foundation and the Chumash."

Rachel, ever mercurial in her reactions, seemed genuinely touched this time. She smiled warmly, and then regained her professional demeanor. "How much land are we talking about?"

"Approximately eighty acres," Kurt answered. "This entire section of the island," he said with a wave of his hand, "was once occupied by thousands of Chumash. The ancient village of Swaxil was located in a valley just west of Scorpion Cove. Our donation includes this sacred site, and it's on this land that the museum will be built, along with a new Chumash village."

"What about the Marine lab and its operations? Rachel asked.

"They'll continue as normal," said Kurt. "We'll just have some new neighbors, and with the museum, a few more visitors."

Rachel laughed at Kurt's reply. She then turned and had a brief conversation with her sound and cameraman. Turning back to Kurt she said, "This has been the most incredible day of my journalistic life, but my crew is getting concerned about having enough time to edit the material before tonight's broadcast. Personally I'm not worried because I'm certain that once my station views our footage that I'll be on the nightly show for at least a week. The images we've obtained are too explosive for just one night, especially when it comes to the all-important viewer ratings. So my question is this: Anything else?—and I'm hoping you say yes."

It was Kurt's turn to laugh. "Just two more items; one I'll keep short, but the other I make no promises on. By the way," he said looking at Rachel and then the audience, "after we've completed our press conference, everyones invited to remain for some refreshments. We're serving appetizers and beer, but not just any beer—one of the world's most renowned and expensive—flown in from Australia as payment on a bet."

Rachel checked with her crew. "We're in," she said. "It's hard to pass on good beer."

The remaining guests smiled and nodded and there were a couple of thumbs-up added.

"Thank you, you won't regret it," Kurt smiled in return. He then signaled Petersen who clicked a key bringing a picture on the screen that brought an audible reaction. "What you're looking at," he explained, "is a human skeleton that is just twenty-five years shy of being 500 years old. My children, Mischa and Jake, recently discovered it in a remote area of Santa Cruz Island.

After unearthing it they took several photos, and then reburied it. Because of the potential for grave robbers, I won't disclose its exact location. The person in the grave just happens to be one of their ancestors—Captain Juan Rodriquez Cabrillo—the first European to explore the California coast. He died in 1542 and his famous last name, *Cabrillo,* is well known in California, appearing on banks, streets, parks, hospitals, commercial buildings, and schools. It was thought that he had died on San Miguel Island, but we now know that's not true. In the grave, buried beside him, was an iron chest. Stored within that treasure chest were the following items: a dagger, chain mail, a silver cross, gold necklaces, a golden Aztec disc, gold coins, and gold ingots. The artifacts, as it turned out, were the Captain's inheritance which he had cached for a future member of his bloodline."

"Why do you say that?" Rachel asked.

"Because included with the relics was an animal skin parchment titled *Instrument of Conveyance*—transferring ownership of Santa Cruz Island to Cabrillo's mistress, Luisa Librado—my children's grandmother going back sixteen generations. The parchment is proof that the artifacts were meant for his offspring. The words on the document are in Spanish, and Petersen has it up on the screen."

After staring at for a brief moment, Rachel said, "I don't understand Spanish, but I trust your interpretation. What plans do you have for the artifacts?"

"None," laughed Kurt. "They belong to my children. They found them, they're legitimate heirs; it's now their responsibility."

Rachel smiled. "That's a nice problem—they're welcome to call me if they need any help. By the way, where did they go? They were sitting up front just moments ago."

"They're preparing the final item in today's news conference, which is better suited for a *Ripley's Believe it or Not* episode since we're talking about something that truly has to be seen to be believed."

Rachel raised her eyebrows at Kurt's statement and in a mocking tone stated, "Well, admittedly, it's been a surprising day, but as a seasoned reporter I'm used to hearing exaggerated puffery, I just didn't expect it from you."

Kurt grinned, the kind of grin an amateur poker player is unable to suppress when he's holding four aces. "There are moments when the spoken word is inadequate when attempting to explain the unimaginable, and when that occurs, it's best to just go ahead with the visual. See that wooden shed over there?" He said pointing. "Inside are some creatures that I'm sure most of you are *not* familiar with. My children will now bring them out. And for your information, they're tame, so you don't have to be afraid." Kurt watched as Mischa and Jake entered the shed. After a long minute Jake reappeared, accompanied by two Pygmy mammoths. He had two apples in his hand and walked straight toward Rachel. When he was five feet away he stopped and allowed each animal to munch on the fruit.

"I've *seen* baby Indian elephants before," Rachel said with a hint of sarcasm, "they're definitely cute, but they're hardly *Ripley's* material."

"They're not babies," said Kurt who was still smiling, "they're adults, and they're not Indian, they're Columbian. They're also known as Pygmy mammoths—descendents of the mainland Columbian mammoth. And, according to National Geographic, they've been extinct for 10,000 years."

"That's impossible!" Rachel exclaimed sharply. "This must be a gag!" She then let out a startled scream as Mischa had suddenly emerged from the shed holding the leashes of two eighty-pound saber-toothed cats, which had been specifically chosen because of their extra-long, scimitar-shaped fangs.

"Those felines," said Kurt in a voice loud enough to override Rachel's scream, "are Pygmy saber-toothed cats. They've also been extinct for 10,000 years."

Using a hand for each cat, Mischa began scratching the sensitive spot between their ears, eliciting a soft, vibrant purring sound . . . *Mmmmm.* She then fed each saber-toothed a thick piece of beef jerky, which resulted in loud, contented roars. After they had finished their snack, she unhitched their harnesses and set them free. Jake also released the mammoths, and the four prehistoric beasts, seemingly oblivious to their human spectators, or the hum of a movie camera, entered into a game of chase, feigned battles, and contests of strength.

Rachel, who had quickly regained her composure after her initial shock, was now enjoying the spectacle. "How's this possible?" She asked. "I see them, but I still don't believe it."

"I wish Adam Timbrook was here," Kurt said. Almost as if on cue, Eva returned, and walked into Kurt's view. She raised her hands, palms upward, shrugged her shoulders, and shaking her head, mouthed the word no. Kurt was surprised—he expected that Eva would have found Timbrook in bed sick. But evidently, there was no sign of him at all. "As I was saying, if my Chumash friend was here I would let him address that issue since but for the Chumash these incredible creatures would not exist. As Timbrook explained, 'It was a labor of love that endured for thousands of years.' The actual story goes back almost 13,000 years when the Chumash first arrived at these islands. On the islands of San Miguel, Santa Rosa, and Santa Cruz, they found herds of Pygmy mammoths along with their nemesis, saber-toothed cats, which had also become dwarf-like. Unfortunately, within a short period of time—on the islands of San Miguel and Santa Rosa—the animals were hunted to extinction. On Santa Cruz, however, a small remnant managed to survive by hiding out in a small, isolated valley surrounded by impassable cliffs, and with only one narrow entryway. The Chumash, upon discovering these creatures, and suspecting they were the last of their species, declared these animals off-limits to any further hunting, and the valley became their sanctuary. The area was blessed with its own supply of fresh water, provided by an artesian spring, whose outflow also produced an abundance of lush vegetation. Under the protection of the Chumash, the animals thrived in this environment. And here's a fact your viewers might find interesting: within one animal generation the Chumash had successfully integrated the two species, and the saber-toothed cats no longer viewed mammoths as prey."

"If the mammoths were no longer a food source, what did the saber-toothed cats eat? They obviously didn't become vegetarians."

Laughing, Kurt said, "That's definitely true. The Chumash did two things: they seeded the valley with cottontail rabbits, which as you know are prolific breeders, and they also provided supplemental meat."

"What types of meat?"

"It varied depending upon the time period," explained Kurt. "Primarily it included seals, otter, fish, deer from the mainland, and with the advent of ranching on Santa Cruz, goats, sheep, and cattle, and from Santa Rosa Island, elk and mule deer. In the last twenty years the cats were switched to a high-protein kibble made from bison, venison, or wild salmon."

"Earlier you said they're tame, which I assume means they don't bite?"

"They're as gentle as your own pet." Kurt assured her.

"In that case I would like some footage of me interacting with them."

Kurt watched as Rachel first approached a mammoth and then a saber-toothed cat and spent time caressing each one. *She's certainly not stupid,* thought Kurt. These images would quickly travel all around the world via the Internet making her an instant celebrity. When Rachel returned she was smiling from ear to ear.

"That was awesome," she gushed. "But I wonder . . . once the word gets out, what's to become of these amazing creatures?"

"In one word—freedom—it's time for the Pygmy mammoths and the saber-toothed cats to exist outside their Santa Cruz sanctuary and to begin the process of truly propagating this island. Once Santa Cruz has a stable population we intend to reintroduce them back to the San Miguel and San Rosa Islands, and eventually to secure wildlife reserves on the mainland. In addition, the four individuals that are with us today are being shipped out by the end of this week. We're obviously aware that the public deserves a close-up view of these prehistoric beasts, and with that in mind, our new partner, the San Diego Zoo, has agreed to exhibit a male and female of each species. The zoo, I'm pleased to announce, just recently finished an outdoor enclosure that's almost an exact replica of their island habitat."

"I imagine they *readily* agreed," laughed Rachel. "It's a gold mine. Ticket sales alone could be worth millions."

"It's more than just some extra cash from ticket sales," Kurt added. "It's also their expertise. As a world famous zoo they specialize in breeding endangered animals. The mammoths and saber-toothed cats are definitely on that list. With their help, and with their knowledge, it's our expectation that these magnificent 'little' creatures will continue to walk the earth as long as there's air to breathe."

"Let's hope so," Rachel said and then asked facetiously, "anything else?"

"No," Kurt replied with a smile, "I think we're finally done unless you have some additional questions."

"I'm good for the moment," said Rachel, "but by tomorrow morning that may be a different story, so to speak. Right now, though, I'm ready for a glass of cold Australian beer and a plate of appetizers."

"I think we're all in agreement on that," laughed Kurt. "Our chef from the Marine Lab has prepared a variety of tasty hors d'oeuvres including," and here Kurt picked up a printed list, "jumbo shrimp stuffed with cilantro and chilies, crab cakes with celery-root aioli, seafood stuffed avocados, Asian-glazed chicken wings, grilled asparagus drizzled with aged balsamic vinaigrette, and spring rolls with carrot-ginger dipping sauce." He then put the list down. "The Australian beer is Crown Ambassador Reserve, one of the finest beers made. It's packaged in 750 ml Champagne bottles, and according to their website, it's aged in French oak barrels for 12 months, and on the palate, it has a rich, caramelized malty flavor, balanced by citrus aromas."

Rachel licked her lips and smiled gamely. "Both the food and beer sound luscious."

"Luscious is certainly an apt description," Kurt confirmed. "And you can thank Petersen for the beer selection. I fortunately lost a bet to him—forty bottles worth, and decided to order two extra cases for today's party. So enjoy it—at nearly one hundred dollars per bottle it's a lot more expensive than most wines." Kurt then asked Mischa and Jake to return the mammoths and saber-toothed cats to the shed, and for Petersen to help him load the crate of gold bars and bag of gold coins onto an electric cart. After the cart was loaded, he looked at Petersen and said, "This gold needs to be stored in a secure location as soon as possible—can you do that for me?"

"I suppose," said Petersen who appeared uncomfortable with the assignment. "Where do you want me to take it?"

"Your place," Kurt replied.

"My place?" He repeated, surprised. "It's hardly a vault."

"Then you'll need to do something about that. You may need to order a strongbox or rent a safe-deposit box from a local bank. It would be a shame if the items were stolen."

"It's not my responsibility," Petersen complained, alarmed. "I don't mind helping, and I'll store the gold overnight—God knows I won't get any sleep, but first thing tomorrow morning you'll need to pick it up."

"I'm not going to do that," Kurt replied, and began to walk away. He heard Petersen yell 'hey what's going on?' and then he heard him gasp, and then an incredulous, 'oh my God,' and then a barely audible sobbing started. *He finally got it,* thought Kurt. He turned around, and in a soft voice said, "After you're done, please hurry back; we need to share a treasure hunter's beer together."

Petersen tried to respond, but was emotionally overwhelmed, and the only words that came from his lips were, "Thank you . . . thank you," as more tears rolled down his cheeks, "you know I wasn't expecting this."

As Kurt made his way over to the canopy tent where the food and beer were being served he smiled—a deeply satisfying smile as he reflected on Petersen's reaction. "You've earned every penny," he said out loud as if the student was walking beside him, "I would've failed without you."

At the tent Eva made Kurt sit down at the head of the table while she got him a beer and a plate of appetizers. "At least two crab cakes," he suggested as she headed toward the food line, "they're my favorite." She brought back four.

"No sign of Timbrook?" Kurt asked her.

"I didn't see him and there was nothing unusual going on," she replied.

Kurt was perplexed—at least his friend wasn't sick, but he couldn't help feeling a sense of dread.

Approximately ten minutes later Petersen showed up and they toasted their success as treasure hunters. Neither he nor Petersen said a word about what had transpired earlier. On another occasion he planned on telling his children, but not today.

After about an hour, Rachel and her crew excused themselves. "Thank you," she said prior to leaving, "for everything—for an incredible interview, for a delicious meal, and for your friendship. Give me a call next time you're in Los Angeles and I'll buy the next round of beers." She left her business card on the table. Scribbled in blue ink just underneath her name was a personal cell phone number. On the reversed side of the card she had written a brief message: "Let's get together soon."

Eva promptly picked up the card, scowled as she read it, and then put it in her purse. "It's safer here," she said by way of explanation, "you'll just lose it."

Kurt chuckled, but didn't say anything.

During the next hour Kurt made sure that he spent a little time with each of his guests and thanked them for coming. At about 2:00 p.m. everyone said their goodbyes, and began heading home. The last ferry of the day was scheduled to depart from Scorpion Cove around 3:00 p.m.

After the final guest left Kurt said to Eva, Dr. Sedrak, and his two children, "I think we should go over to Timbrook's place. I'm worried about him; today was so unlike him—he always keeps his commitments." As they were rounding the corner to Timbrook's house they heard the sound of a horse neighing and snorting, as if in distress.

"I think that's Gabriel," Mischa reported, hurrying her pace. "What's wrong with him?"

Before anyone could respond, Gabriel galloped into view, his nostrils flaring and his skin soaked in sweat as if the stallion had just completed a long journey. He came to a halt directly in front of them, reared up on his hind legs, and let loose an enraged roar that was a mix between a neigh, and a guttural squeal, sounding as if he was in the throes of a life and death struggle.

"I've never heard a horse scream before," whispered Eva as she covered her ears.

Mischa grabbed the bridle and attempted to calm Gabriel.

Kurt stared at the horse. It wasn't the unearthly sound that unnerved him, but the empty saddle. A rider-less horse, exhibiting bizarre behavior meant only one thing—Timbrook was in serious trouble.

41

"**D**ad . . . Gabriel and Aiyana are all set to go," Mischa called with a sense of urgency. She had delivered the message through an opened back door.

Kurt was sitting at his desk in the library gazing at a dark cherrywood container adorned with a white dove. He had excused himself from the search party preparations in order to attend to what he thought would be a brief personal errand. The container had been in his possession for three years and he was now contemplating how best to fulfill a promise made regarding its contents. Mischa's solicitous tone, however, had its desired effect—snatching him from his sentimental reverie. *It's the perfect location,* he told himself again, *although not the perfect occasion.* After a poignant sigh he made a decision; he picked it up and placed it inside a backpack. "Thanks Mischa, I'll be right out."

As Kurt was walking toward the stables he saw that Dr. Sedrak was already astride Aiyana and that Mischa was straddling Gabriel. Both horses were outfitted with a pillion-type saddle that was specifically designed to hold two riders. Eva and Jake had agreed to stay behind for three good reasons: number one, the horses could only carry four people; number two, a doctor was an indispensable member of a rescue team; and number three, because Dr. Sedrak hadn't been to the sanctuary yet. And, assuming

Timbrook was healthy enough to ride a horse, he would join Dr. Sedrak on Aiyana.

Kurt quickly made his way over to Gabriel, and after mounting and assuming control of the reins, waved goodbye to Eva and Jake. Mischa, who was seated right behind him, had her arms locked around his waist.

Kurt checked his watch; at most they had just six hours of daylight. If they pushed the horses they could reach the summit in about ninety minutes. Gabriel, after a refreshing hose down and sponge bath along with a handful of alfalfa oat cubes, seemed eager to get under way, perhaps sensing the nature of the outing. *Mustangs*, thought Kurt, *are one tough breed.*

The path to Montannon Ridge began with Smuggler's Trail. After an easy two-mile ride they would then take an obscure side trail that zigzagged its way up the mountain. Based upon Kurt's prior experience he wasn't looking forward to the grueling switchbacks. For the next twelve minutes, however, he could relax. As he listened to the rhythmic plodding of the horses hoofs, he had a moment to reflect on the last thirty minutes. *Organized pandemonium* is how he would describe it. Gabriel's sudden appearance had instantly transformed their small group into a search and rescue team. Dr. Sedrak was in charge of putting together an emergency medical kit. Eva, extra clothing, blankets, and a day's worth of food and beverages just in case they had to spend the night on the mountain. Mischa and Jake were responsible for getting the horses ready, especially Gabriel, who was in need of a liquid cool down in order to reduce his internal heat and lower his heart rate so that he could be ridden again. Kurt's assignment, which he found somewhat disagreeable, was to snoop around inside Timbrook's adobe house looking for any clues that might explain *why* their friend had travelled to Montannon Ridge or if that was where he had indeed gone. As he walked through the house he was surprised at its condition—it was immaculate—as if the occupant had moved out. The kitchen was spotless, there were no dishes in the sink, the garbage can looked as if it had never been used, and the refrigerator was empty except for a few items in the freezer. The living room, den, and bedroom were also in excellent condition. Kurt then checked out the bathroom, which looked as though it had recently been scrubbed. Popping open the medicine cabinet he noted that it was filled with the usual items—Band-Aids, toothpaste, mouthwash, dental floss, Q-tips, tweezers, a bottle of aspirin, a package of over-the-counter sleeping pills, and a sewing kit. The only thing out-of-the-ordinary was a small medicine bottle whose main ingredient was morphine. The prescription attached to the container was dated two weeks earlier and listed the quantity at twenty, the dosage 200 mg, and the amount to be taken each day, one. Kurt carefully poured the medication onto the counter—nineteen pills. Only one of the oval-shaped, green-colored tablets was missing. He quickly refilled the container and placed it back inside the cabinet. When he informed Dr. Sedrak of his finding the doctor's face turned ashen. "These types of powerful opiates are only prescribed for severe pain," he stated professionally, and then in a soft voice added: "And usually for end-stage cancer." Kurt was still thinking about the doctor's discomforting words when they reached the trailhead to Montannon Ridge.

"You'll need to hang on tight," he warned Mischa. "This uphill climb is going to be tough without your own saddle."

"If we slide off try not to land on me," she joked.

"If that happens," said Kurt with a nervous chuckle, "then you'll need to fall to the right and I'll fall to the left."

"As long as there's no cliff on the right," she said dryly.

Kurt dug his knees into the horse's muscular shoulders and tightened his grip on the reins. He wasn't about to squash his daughter. Gabriel seemed to sense his anxiety and chose a route that helped lessened the gravitational tug. *So this is what cowboys call 'horse sense',* Kurt realized as he analyzed the animal's irregular path. After fifty minutes of arduous climbing they finally reached the summit.

"Thank God," said Kurt under his breath. His death grip on Gabriel had caused the muscles in both his hands and knees to become spasmodic—a sign of cramps. He instinctively flexed and shook his fingers and stretched out his legs, which immediately relieved the symptoms.

"You okay?" Mischa asked concerned.

"Yes—just some mild cramps, but they're gone now."

The last obstacle they had to navigate before they reached the entrance to the valley was a narrow gorge that was half the length of a football field. At the end of the constricted corridor they came to an arched doorway. As they were passing through, Mischa asked, "Where's Journey? The last time Jake and I were here she was guarding the gateway."

"I wouldn't worry about her," Kurt said reassuringly as he brought Gabriel to a halt just beyond the entryway. "She's probably with Timbrook, especially if he's hurt. That's what dogs do— they watch over their Masters until help arrives."

Mischa appeared troubled by her dad's answer and in a soft voice said, "That means Timbrook's in bad shape."

Kurt was about to respond when Dr. Sedrak and Aiyana joined them. The doctor had obviously overheard their conversation.

"Mischa don't equate Journey's absence with something tragic. Dog's love companionship, especially with a member of the human race; and, until just a few minutes ago, Timbrook was the only human in this valley. Once she hears our voices or the sound of the horses, or picks up our scent, she'll undoubtedly bolt to our position, and like all dogs, she'll probably lick the skin off our faces. And if Timbrook is truly in need of medical care, she can lead us to his location." Dr. Sedrak then changed the subject. "So this is the secret sanctuary I've heard so much about. It's certainly beautiful—the impenetrable cliffs, the flowering landscape, the lush meadow, and the sky-blue pond, but where are all the mammoths and saber-toothed cats?"

Kurt quickly scanned the valley. He looked at Mischa to see if she had an answer. She shrugged indicating that she didn't know. "That's a good question," said Kurt, "and unfortunately I don't have a clue. On my prior visit—standing at this exact same spot—I observed dozens of animals milling about. It's definitely weird that we can't spot a single creature."

Mischa stared at the canyon wall just beyond the pond. "Maybe they're all huddled inside one of the caves."

"Why would they do that?" Kurt asked.

"Because of Timbrook," she replied. "He must be in one of them, and for some reason they want to be near him."

Kurt nodded. "That's a distinct possibility, and one we need to explore right away." He turned and looked at Dr. Sedrak. "At the base of the cliff, on the other side of the pond, there are a number of old lava tubes which the animals use as their dens. If I was Timbrook, and I was struggling with a medical issue, that's where I would be holed up."

"I agree," said Dr. Sedrak. "When you experience an emergency in a wilderness-type area proper shelter is vital to one's survival."

Kurt prodded Gabriel with the heel of his boot, spurring the horse to a moderate trot. Within a few minutes they were at the entrance to a large cave that served as the living quarters for both the Pygmy mammoths and Journey. At the exact moment Gabriel came to stop Mischa immediately dismounted and rushed into the cavern, shouting at the top of her lungs the names of Timbrook and Journey.

As Kurt was hitching Gabriel and Aiyana to a small oak tree he could still hear Mischa's shrill voice echoing off the volcanic walls . . . *Timbrook . . . Journey*. When it became distant and more urgent he knew she was in the rearmost section of the cave. He looked at Dr. Sedrak. "That's not sounding good." When they walked in Kurt understood why. The underground chamber was vacant. He gazed into Journey's side cave. It too was empty. Mischa sprinted to where they were standing. She was visibly shaken and a few tears trickled down her face.

"Where are they?" she asked.

Kurt tried to look strong. "This is just one of several lava tubes. They could easily be in the next cave. Obviously we'll need to check them all out, especially the saber-toothed cat's subterranean den."

Using the sleeve on her right arm Mischa wiped her eyes. The dust on her face had mixed with the tears leaving her cheeks smudged. She smiled weakly. "I bet they're in the cats' chamber," she said, and then took off at a fast clip.

"I hope you're right," Dr. Sedrak murmured to Kurt, "or she's going to be an emotional wreck."

"She's more stout-hearted than you think," said Kurt defensively, "she'll manage . . . no matter what she finds." They then walked outside. As they were nearing the saber-toothed cats' den an anguished cry erupted from deep within. Kurt and Dr. Sedrak started running. At the entrance Mischa almost crashed into them. She shook her head. Her countenance was like an open book. Kurt didn't need to ask. Mischa then ducked inside the next cave, but was out in less than a minute. *Only two more caves,* thought Kurt. If he was in Vegas he wouldn't like the odds. When Mischa exited the last cave she was sobbing. She dropped to her knees. Kurt gave her a moment before he walked up to her, got down on his own knees, and held her tight.

"We'll find them," he whispered. "They didn't just disappear."

Mischa buried her head into his chest, and squeezed him until he could barely breathe. After a few moments her crying changed to a despondent moan. When Mischa finally looked up her eyes were filled with profound sadness. Kurt silently wept for his daughter. Unfortunately, Dr. Sedrak had been right.

In a soft voice Mischa said, "It's not just Timbrook and Journey I'm worried about, but also the mammoths and the saber-toothed cats." She then paused for a few seconds, and in a still softer voice asked, "Did somebody kill Timbrook and then massacre all the animals?"

Kurt gasped. Mischa's question had caught him by surprise. He quickly analyzed the available evidence and found nothing to support her hypothesis. "Absolutely not!" he exclaimed firmly. "Have you seen any blood? If what you have suggested had occurred there would be blood all over this valley, and as far as I can see there's not a smidgen anywhere." He then leaned over and planted a kiss on her forehead and in a quiet voice said, "They're here, Mischa—Timbrook, Journey, the Pygmy mammoths and the saber-toothed cats—we just haven't found them yet."

"But where?" she asked weakly. "Timbrook has seemingly disappeared; the animals aren't in their dens, or by the pond, or grazing in the meadow, which leaves just the oak forest or the Indian graveyard."

"Then that's where we'll find them," said Kurt confidently as he helped Mischa to her feet.

Mischa shook her head. "It makes no sense. Why would they suddenly abandon this area? And for what purpose?"

"We'll know soon enough," Kurt replied as they made their way back to the horses. Dr. Sedrak, who had gone ahead, had already unhitched them, and was allowing the mustangs to graze on the wild grasses. When they were within a few feet of Gabriel and Aiyana both horses abruptly raised their heads, pricked their ears forward, and stared into the distance.

"What are they looking at?" Mischa wondered.

Kurt strained his eyes trying to get a glimpse at whatever creature or object had piqued their interest. "I don't see a thing."

"It's not what they're seeing," Dr. Sedrak insisted, "but what their ears perceive. Horses are blessed with acute hearing."

Within a few seconds of Dr. Sedrak's remark, Kurt heard a modulating sound that cascaded from a high pitch down to low rumble, and then back up again. The mournful sound sent shivers up his spine. "That sounds like a wolf that's lost its mate," he said.

"It's Journey!" Mischa reported. "And you're right; it definitely sounds awful, as if she's in distress."

"I didn't know Siberian huskies could howl like that," said Dr. Sedrak solemnly.

"Maybe she's hurt . . . we have to help her," Mischa said urgently.

Kurt and Dr. Sedrak both nodded, and without any further discussion immediately remounted the mustangs. Before heading out Kurt turned and looked at Mischa. "Where do you think she is? I'm having difficulty pinpointing the source of Journey's howl."

"I think it's coming from the far side of the valley," she began, and then hesitated as other strange sounds joined Journey's. After listening for a moment she murmured, "Oh my God!"

Kurt was also shocked by what he heard. Journey's howl was now mingled with a multitude of voices—sustained bellowing wails, loud trumpeting, and prolonged deep guttural roars. The sorrowful melody rumbled across the entire valley and was amplified by the volcanic cliffs. *Are they singing?* Kurt wondered. It sounded more like a mournful ballad—sung by the strangest choir he ever heard, Pygmy mammoths, saber-toothed cats, and a Siberian husky.

"Oh my God . . . please no," Mischa whispered in a voice filled with trepidation. "I now know where it's coming from . . . the Chumash burial grounds."

Kurt motioned to Dr. Sedrak that they were about to take off. He gave Gabriel a slight nudge with his right heel, and the horse went from standing still to a canter within a matter of seconds. Aiyana snorted at their sudden departure, but quickly matched Gabriel's pace.

Kurt tried to control Gabriel's movements, but after a few attempts realized he needn't bother—the mustang knew exactly where they were going. Within minutes they arrived at the graveyard. As soon as Gabriel came to a halt Mischa leaped off the horse and started running, heading for the far end of the cemetery, which was surrounded by mammoths and saber-toothed cats. Journey's high-pitched howl was centered deep within the prehistoric pack. Kurt slid off Gabriel and also started running. Dr. Sedrak, he observed, was right behind him. As Mischa neared the creatures they did something Kurt wasn't expecting—immediately ceased their mournful noise and intentionally moved out of her way—creating a path for her. Without hesitation she ran into their midst. A few seconds later he heard an anguished scream. "Mischa!" Kurt yelled. He received no response—only silence. He slowed down as he moved through the animals. "Mischa!" he yelled again, his tone now more desperate. "Where are you?"

"Daddy," she cried, "its Timbrook . . . I think he's dead."

Kurt rushed to Mischa's side. She was in a crouched position, staring into a grave. Tears tumbled from her eyes and spilled into the pit, landing on a person that at first Kurt didn't recognize as Timbrook. He was dressed in what appeared to be a grizzly bearskin cape that reached down to his ankles. On his head was an ornate feathered headdress. The feathers were from eagles—white tail feathers from a bald eagle, and chocolate-brown feathers from a golden eagle. Around his neck was a leather necklace with two, four inch teeth—canines from a saber-toothed cat. Situated at his side was a worn Bible. Kurt noted that a white envelope was tucked inside the pages of the book. Standing guard over the body was Journey, a male saber-toothed cat, and a large mammoth. The tip of the mammoth's trunk was gently caressing Timbrook's face. It was obvious to Kurt that this creature was the leader of the herd. Several indentations in the soft earth, which extended underneath Timbrook's upper torso, indicated that the mammoth had tried to move Timbrook's body with its ivory tusks in a vain attempt at reviving him.

Dr. Sedrak scurried past Kurt and Mischa and stepped into the pit. He immediately began assessing Timbrook's vital signs. The doctor first checked for a pulse in two different areas—neck and wrist. Next, he checked Timbrook's respiratory rate by observing his chest and also by placing his right ear against Timbrook's mouth. Lastly he checked his body temperature by resting his hand against Timbrook's forehead. When he stepped out of the grave he purposely avoided Kurt and Mischa's eyes. After clearing his throat he finally looked up. He tried to speak, but his tongue was unable to form any words. He grimaced and then slowly shook his head. "I'm so sorry," he said in a voice that was barely audible. He then quickly turned away and buried his head in his hands. Dr. Sedrak was crying. Mischa went over and hugged him. She was also weeping. Kurt suddenly felt emotionally drained and sat down. Journey started howling again. The mammoths and saber-tooted cats quickly joined in. Their song was both melancholic and spiritual—a final farewell by an unusual group of friends who truly loved Timbrook. *It's beautiful,* thought Kurt, *nature honoring Timbrook.* When it ended Kurt felt an overwhelming sense of peace. Mischa and Dr. Sedrak sat down next to him. They watched in silence as the animals began to leave. After five minutes they were all gone except Journey, the male saber-toothed cat, and the large mammoth.

"The cat's name is Diego," said Mischa, "and the mammoth, Kilimanjaro, and of course everyone knows Journey."

At the mention of their names, the animals joined the humans, and together they sat in silence for another ten minutes. Sitting together, humans and creatures, was comforting to Kurt. Their companionship helped him deal with his own grief. Timbrook had obviously left behind a legacy with these animals; the manner in which they celebrated his death was a testament to that.

"Why?" asked Mischa. "Why did he have to die?"

"I don't know," said Kurt. "I knew he was sick, but I didn't realize the extent of his illness. In his Bible there's a white envelope. I'm sure it contains a message for us. It may answer your question."

"I'll get it," said Dr. Sedrak. When he returned he handed the envelope to Kurt.

Kurt held it for a moment before he carefully opened the end flap. He knew the document was precious—it contained a man's final words. Inside he found a four page hand-written letter. On the very top of page one was a yellow smiley face. It set the tone for the entire letter. Kurt read it out loud.

> *Please don't be sad!*
>
> *This is actually a blessed moment for me. I've lived a good life and now it's time to go home.*
>
> *I will obviously miss my new friends—Kurt, Mischa, Jake, Eva, and Dr. Sedrak, but I also look forward to seeing Maria again. She's been waiting almost seven years for our reunion and I know she has a lot to show me.*
>
> *I'm sorry about not giving you any advanced warning (other than a rider-less Gabriel). I knew the day was coming, but it arrived a bit sooner than I expected.*
>
> *Approximately two years ago I was diagnosed with Stage 4 Melanoma. The skin cancer was located on the back side of my head which is probably why I never noticed it. Obviously (I'm trying to add a little humor here), even a dark-skinned Indian is not immune from the harmful effects of our sun. The doctors recommended radiotherapy, chemotherapy, and surgery, which I turned down since the cancer had already spread to other parts of my body, and aggressive therapy or even surgery would've just delayed the inevitable. Anyway, that was my decision, which looking back I don't regret. I've lived longer than predicted, and I've thoroughly enjoyed my final moments here on earth, especially the last two months.*

Mischa . . . Hi . . . knowing your determined person-
ality (which I like), I'm making the assumption that you're
probably at my gravesite.

Kurt paused and looked at Mischa. She had nodded as if she
was responding to Timbrook himself. Her face was scrunched up
in sorrow, but she was also smiling. Kurt continued reading.

I wanted to let you know that I have a special gift for
you. It's in the closet in my bedroom. I've been working
on it for the last two years, and when I met you, I knew it
was for you. You'll understand when you see it. I'll also
need you to watch over Journey. She's pregnant, and her
puppies are due any day.

"She's pregnant?" Mischa interrupted.
Kurt looked at Mischa and gave her a warm smile. Puppies
would help heal his daughter's heart.

As an Indian dog Siberian huskies know how to
whelp a litter; they're also doting mothers. But, like all
mothers (humans included), Journey will occasionally
need some extra help with her brood, plus lots of meaty
treats (supplemental protein to help with her milk pro-
duction). In addition, the puppies will need to be social-
ized, which means you'll have to hold each one several
times each day. That's your job, and it's okay to let Jake
help out. P.S. I bred Journey because we'll need some
additional canine hands once the Pygmy mammoths
and saber-toothed cats leave their sanctuary and start
roaming this island.

Kurt—Thank you for what you've done, or about to
do, on behalf of the Chumash Tribe of Indians. I don't
know all the specifics, but I do know your heart, and it's

a generous heart. Note: In the last two weeks it was obvious something was up—it was written all over your face, plus you let slip a few facts. A word of caution: Don't play poker—you'll lose every time.

Dr. Sedrak laughed. "Now I know how I can win some of that new found gold."

Regarding the next Chumash Caretaker: It's a young lady. Her name is Aria Ygnacio. She's only nineteen years of age, but full of wisdom. She's an outdoorsy type person who loves the Channel Islands, animals, and the ocean. She's from the Santa Ynez Indian Reservation. I've been preparing Aria for her new assignment for the last two years (once I became aware of my illness). She'll arrive in about ten days (I texted her just before I mounted Gabriel). Her family is special to me. I'm Aria's honorary Godfather which title I accepted seven years ago—after her dad died. He was a Navy Seal serving in Afghanistan when his unit was targeted by a roadside IED. For the last seven years I've had the privilege of functioning as Aria's substitute father, which helped ease the passing of my wife. Now I entrust her ongoing training and care to your family. Once you meet her you'll understand what an amazing person she is (plus she's a hard worker).

Kurt, as a result of this decision, I do have a special request. The adobe house needs to be spruced up; it's unsuitable for a woman. It will also require modernization—Internet and Wi-Fi since she'll be taking online college classes. Please have Eva and Mischa help with this remodeling project (it's their area of expertise). Unfortunately, you have just ten days before she arrives. Sorry for the short notice! Finally, I've set up a checking account in your name to be used on behalf of Aria (whatever expenses you deem appropriate). It contains a fair amount of money so don't hesitate to use it. The documents are in a large envelope on top of my bedroom dresser.

Kurt and Dr. Sedrak: Eva is a gift from God. Her name means "Living," or "Source of Life," or "Giver of Life." Her name symbolizes who she is. There are treasures beneath the waves but sometimes the greatest treasures are right before your eyes.

Kurt hesitated for a moment. Timbrook's words were a little embarrassing, especially in front of his daughter. He stole a quick glance at Dr. Sedrak. Fortunately the doctor wasn't looking at him. *That would have been awkward,* thought Kurt who then picked up where he had left off.

That's it! I've already said enough. It's now time to say our goodbyes. To my immediate right you'll find three items: a white linen burial cloth and two shovels. I'm assuming I don't have to explain what these things are for. As God said in Genesis 3:19 concerning death: 'For out of the ground you were taken; for dust you are, and to dust you shall return.' God's not being negative—he's just speaking the truth. In heaven I now have a resurrected body, so it's okay for my corporeal body to become dust again.

As far as a memorial service—a time of silence would be nice. I've always liked Ecclesiastes 3 where God said: 'To everything there is a season, a time for every purpose under heaven: A time to be born, and a time to die; a time to weep, and a time to laugh; a time to mourn, and a time to dance.'

Please promise me you'll laugh and dance as you remember my life. I'm laughing and dancing in heaven

*right now—so keep the 'weeping' and 'mourning' to a
bare minimum.*

God Bless You, Your Friend Adam Timbrook

After Kurt finished reading Timbrook's message, he held the
pages in his hands for several minutes. No one said a word—
even the animals were quiet. Kurt glanced at the last page again.
Timbrook was pretty certain about his future life in heaven. It
probably made dying that much easier when you had that kind of
hope. *Laughing and dancing in heaven—that might be worth the trip,*
thought Kurt with a smile. "God bless you, my Indian friend,"
Kurt whispered. "You'll be dearly missed."

Mischa got up and wandered around the cemetery, picking
wild flowers. When she had a handful she placed them at the
head of Timbrook's grave.

Dr. Sedrak had a puzzled look to his face as he stared at
Timbrook's burial garments. "You never told me Timbrook was
a Chief."

"What makes you say that?" asked Kurt.

"His funeral clothes. Only a Chief is allowed to wear a full-length
bearskin cape or the feathers from an eagle. Timbrook was certainly
more than just a common Indian—he was a Chumash leader."

Kurt shrugged. "I only knew him for a few months. I guess
there's a lot about Timbrook's life that we'll never know. Perhaps
when Aria arrives she can help fill us in."

"Maybe," Dr. Sedrak said thoughtfully.

Kurt walked over and picked up the burial cloth. Dr. Sedrak
helped him unfold it. As they were about to drape it over
Timbrook's body Mischa yelled, "Wait!"

"Why?" Kurt asked.

"It's Timbrook . . . his body isn't positioned properly."

"What difference does that make?"

"You'll violate his cultural beliefs if he's buried incorrectly."

"I thought as a Christian he was no longer bound by superstitious beliefs."

"That has nothing to do with it," Mischa countered. "Timbrook was both a Christian and an Indian. His heritage was as valuable to him as his Bible. The 'Good Book,' as Timbrook described it, 'was never meant to destroy one's culture.' This graveyard," Mischa said as she pointed at each corner, "is constructed with four obelisks. Each obelisk is situated on a compass point—East, West, South, and North, but only the western facing obelisk is painted red." Mischa motioned toward the colored obelisk before continuing. "It's painted red because it serves as a guidepost—ensuring that the dead are buried in a fetal position facing west. Based upon a conversation Jake and I had with Timbrook it was our understanding that he was in full agreement with this practice. From the groove marks in the soil it appears that Kilimanjaro altered Timbrook's alignment. Before we shovel any dirt we'll need to reposition Timbrook's body so that it's arranged in accordance with his cultural beliefs."

"I didn't know that," Kurt said apologetically. "Of course we want to do what's right."

"I've heard of that custom, I just didn't know it applied to the Chumash. I'll take care of it," Dr. Sedrak said as he stepped into the grave."

"Thank you," murmured Mischa gratefully.

Kurt watched as Dr. Sedrak skillfully maneuvered Timbrook into a fetal position facing west, and then carefully covered the body with the linen cloth. Once he was done, they began filling the grave with soil, which took a little less than an hour. They then had a time of silence that was interrupted by occasional weeping. When Kurt sensed that the moment was right he reread Ecclesiastes 3 from Timbrook's letter.

After an additional minute of silence Mischa stood up and said, "We should obey Timbrook's final request."

"What? Dr. Sedrak exclaimed. "Laughing and dancing—next to a grave—won't that be sacrilegious?"

"I guess we'll soon find out," said Mischa. She walked over to the animals and teased them until they stood up. She then started mimicking the sounds that they had made earlier—howling, wailing, trumpeting, and roaring. She also added human laughter. The creatures looked at Mischa as if she was crazy, but after a few seconds they joined in. This time, however, the tone was more joyful, more upbeat, with a touch of high-spirited gaiety. Once Mischa had them 'laughing in their own language' she began dancing. Her style was inner-city hip-hop. As she pranced around the grave the animals followed her—the mammoth shuffling and stomping its feet while shaking its large booty, the saber-toothed cat leaping and pawing the air, and Journey racing back and forth as if on an adrenaline rush in spite of her pregnancy.

"This is insane," Kurt said with a smile, and then added, "what the hell . . . when in Rome, do as the Romans do." He then joined the unusual 'line dance formation,' and started wiggling his hips and raising his arms while punching the air.

"What kind of dance is that?" snickered Mischa.

"The only one I know . . . Disco . . . and I used to be good at it."

"Used to," is an appropriate choice of words," laughed Mischa.

Dr. Sedrak shook his head and said, "You guys are hopeless. This is what real dancing looks like—it's spicy and hot." The doctor began with a Caribbean salsa, and after a half dozen racy revolutions, switched to a Cuban rumba.

"That's a bit dangerous for Eva's eyes," Kurt said with a nervous laugh and then had Dr. Sedrak teach him the signature moves to each dance.

They danced and laughed until exhausted and then crashed to the ground. Kilimanjaro and Diego took off for the pond—thirsty for a drink of water. Kurt stood up and walked over to Gabriel where he removed several bottles of water from the saddle bags. He also retrieved a backpack. When he returned he hand-ed a bottle to each person.

Journey had apparently decided to stay and was curled up next to Mischa, her head upon the girl's lap.

"I think that dog likes you," observed Kurt.

"The feeling's mutual," Mischa said as she began scratching the fur behind its ears. After she had consumed about fifty per-cent of her water, she cupped her hands into a water-tight bowl, and allowed Journey to lap the other half.

Dr. Sedrak studied Mischa for a short time and then said, "You're not even a doctor, but that festive tribute was the best prescriptive medicine I've ever 'swallowed'. Thanks for taking this doctor beyond his comfort zone—it helped heal my grieving soul."

Mischa smiled at the compliment, and after a moment of re-flection said, "I think Timbrook was right to have us dance and laugh. If you've had a well-lived life, then your death shouldn't be a time of mourning, but a time of celebration. When you cel-ebrate a person's life you honor that individual, plus it leaves you with a sense of peace. I know Timbrook understood that prin-ciple and that's why he made that request. When I saw him lying in the grave he looked serene. That's how I want to go—with a tranquil smile on my face."

"Your mother was also someone who understood the meaning of life and lived each day to its fullest," said Kurt softly to Mischa as he removed a cherrywood urn from his backpack. "I think this sacred site is the appropriate place to disperse some of Tessa's remaining ashes. Earlier today, when I knew we were traveling to Montannon Ridge, I heard a small voice inside my head telling me to bring her ashes. At the time it didn't make any sense; we were on a rescue mission to find Timbrook, not distribute Tessa's ashes, plus Jake wouldn't be with us. Now, however, I understand why I was prompted. Today we're celebrating life, not death, which is the way your mother would have wanted us to remember her. This area is reserved for Chumash Chiefs. Tessa was never a Chief, but she is certainly their co-equal, and therefore deserves to have her remains sown among her Indian ancestors. And, because your brother's not here, we'll need to hold back a small percentage so that Jake can have his own special moment of remembrance." Kurt unscrewed the lid to the urn. He looked at Mischa. "Do you want to spread her ashes?"

Mischa silently nodded.

Kurt handed the urn to his daughter. Mischa first walked to the oldest section of the graveyard before she began sprinkling Tessa's ashes. Journey tagged along, but was unusually quiet, as if the dog sensed the solemnness of Mischa's actions. Kurt watched as his daughter carefully distributed the ashes throughout the entire cemetery, saving a few for Timbrook's grave before handing back the urn. Kurt quickly replaced the lid and stowed it in his backpack.

"That was harder than I thought," Mischa admitted, "but I know Mom's smiling—she's wanted us to do this for the last three years. But, I'm glad we waited since this was the perfect spot."

Kurt hugged his daughter. "I think so too," he whispered. *She's like her mother,* he thought, *strong but compassionate.* Kurt held her for another minute before releasing her, not wanting the tender moment to end.

"Thanks Dad . . . I needed that."

"Anytime," he said with a warm smile, "that's what dads are for."

"Amen to that," added Dr. Sedrak who had just returned from fetching the horses while Mischa was dispensing Tessa's ashes. "And hopefully that will be my experience in the not-too-distant future—I just have to find the right woman."

"I can't imagine that's a real problem for you," Mischa assured him. "Women love being married to a medical doctor, especially one that's handsome, intelligent, sensitive, and successful."

"Thank you," said Dr. Sedrak as he climbed onto Aiyana. "You've just made my day, which will make the long ride home that much easier."

"It's definitely time for us to head out," Kurt agreed. "It wouldn't be a good idea to descend a mountain in the dark." He helped Mischa mount Gabriel and then he climbed up.

When they reached the entrance to the valley they turned around to say goodbye to Journey, who had been trailing them.

"I promise I'll be back soon," Mischa said tenderly, "and when I return I expect to be greeted by a litter of adorable puppies."

Journey sat down and stared at them. When they passed through the arch she started howling. The melancholic wail lasted for several minutes.

When they were a quarter of the way down the mountain they received a surprise visitor. Journey had caught up with them.

"Why is she here?" asked Mischa.

"I don't know," Kurt replied. "She's supposed to be guarding the mammoths and saber-toothed cats."

"She's probably lonely without Timbrook," Mischa suggested.

"Perhaps," Kurt confirmed.

Journey never left their side and followed them down the entire mountain. When they reached the stables, they found Eva and Jake anxiously waiting for them. When Eva saw the somber look on their faces, and that Dr. Sedrak was alone, she collapsed to the ground and started crying.

Jake, not wanting to believe the obvious asked, "Where's Timbrook?"

Mischa slid off Gabriel and walked up to her brother. "He's in heaven," she whispered.

"He's . . . dead?" Jake stammered.

Mischa nodded and then held him as he sobbed.

Kurt sat down next to Eva and allowed her to cry on his shoulder.

Dr. Sedrak took care of the horses. After removing their saddles and bridles, he put them into their individual stalls and fed them. After that he sat down on the other side of Eva.

Mischa and Jake joined them, forming a small circle. Journey lay down next to Mischa and once again placed its head on her lap.

Eva wiped her eyes. "I'm okay now," she murmured, "but I need to know what happened? Why is Timbrook dead?"

Kurt reached into his pants pocket and extracted a white envelope. "Timbrook left us a four-page letter. It pretty much explains everything." He handed it to Eva who slowly reviewed each page, her voice wavering a bit when she read the kind words regarding her. When she was done she passed it to Jake. After Jake finished reading it he carefully refolded the letter and passed it back to his father.

Eva bit her lower lip. "Was he still alive when you first arrived?"

Dr. Sedrak looked directly at Eva. "No. Based upon my medical examination he died four to six hours before we showed up."

Eva sighed. "In a selfish way that's good news. I would have felt awful if I wasn't there for his final moments."

Mischa reached out and held Eva's hands. "He didn't die alone—Journey was by his side, as were the mammoths and saber-toothed cats. They were singing a lament when we first arrived. It was incredibly touching. We also had our own memorial service. We cried, we danced, and we laughed as we celebrated Timbrook's life. It's what he wanted, and we honored him by obeying his final request. And to be honest, it was wonderful; when I die that's what I want—a party at my funeral. I want my friends to walk away happy, not sad, as they remember my life."

"You still have seventy-five years," Dr. Sedrak reminded Mischa, "to plan that party, so don't spend too much time thinking about it."

"Don't worry," she said with a sly smile, "I still have to save the world, and based upon its current condition, that could take a while."

Dr. Sedrak laughed at her response. "That's what I wanted to hear."

Jake, who had been silent, turned to Mischa and said, "Are you curious about Timbrook's gift, because I certainly am. I can't imagine any project requiring two years to complete."

Shrugging, Mischa said, "I'd almost forgotten about it, but now that you've brought it up, yes—I'm as curious as you are."

Mischa and Jake both stood up and ran into Timbrook's house. They disappeared through the rear door, and then reappeared a few minutes later. In her hands Mischa was carrying a large picture frame. Whatever was in it was unknown—she had it turned around. When Mischa was a few feet away she stopped. There were tears in her eyes even though she was grinning from ear to ear.

"There are certain animals in the world," Mischa explained, "that touch your very soul because you see yourself in them. The creature portrayed on this canvas has always had a special place in my heart. In fact, it's my favorite, and what's really amazing is this: I don't ever recall mentioning it to Timbrook." Mischa rotated the frame.

Eva gasped. It wasn't a drawing or a painting but a mosaic, assembled from thousands of individual pieces, and the creature depicted was a snowy egret. "It's stunning, especially the sparkling white plumage and the bird's iridescent eyes. What materials were used in its construction?" she asked.

Dr. Sedrak got up and spent a brief moment examining the mosaic. "It appears to be made out of mica flakes, mica crystals, flecks of abalone shells, and ground-up volcanic rock."

"The realistic quality of the egret is truly extraordinary," Eva said breathlessly. "No wonder it took him two years—it's on par with an Audubon painting."

. "If you don't like it," teased Jake, "I'm willing to hang it in my bedroom."

"Or for that matter, anywhere in the house—the choice is yours," Kurt added.

"It would also look great in a doctor's office," Dr. Sedrak insisted.

Mischa smiled. "I think my bedroom will be just fine, but thanks for the offers."

Eva stood up and put her arm around Mischa. "I agree—your room is where it belongs. Unfortunately, most men are generally clueless when comes to fine art, and this piece is definitely fine art. I suggest we hang it now in order to avoid the possibility of it getting damaged."

"And while you're busy doing that the *clueless* men—who at least appreciate a well-stocked kitchen—will prepare a bite to eat," Kurt said with a hint of sarcasm. "I'm sure we're all starving, including Journey."

Everyone nodded at Kurt's suggestion. Journey just wagged her tail, and accompanied the group as they all headed up the path to the Nichols' house.

Eva followed Mischa to the tool shed. To properly hang a mosaic the job required a hammer, level, measuring tape, wire, D-ring hangers, and heavy-duty wall hooks. They also needed a pencil which they obtained from the den on their way back to Mischa's room.

The task ended up taking about ten minutes. As they were cleaning up, Journey strolled into the bedroom. The dog greeted them with a friendly bark and a round of licks, and then began exploring the room. In a corner nearest Mischa's bed she began pawing the carpet with her nails, tearing apart the nylon fibers.

"Stop," Mischa said in a scolding tone.

Journey ignored the verbal rebuke and continued to shred the carpet.

"What's wrong with her?"

Eva giggled. "If my assumption is correct, absolutely nothing; I'm pretty sure she's nesting."

"What's nesting? And why is that amusing?"

"It's humorous because it's taking place in your bedroom. Nesting is what a dog does shortly before giving birth. Journey's preparing a 'nest' for her puppies, the same as a bird does for its eggs. Your room is now her maternity ward, and the carpet is her nesting material. The only way to avoid having your carpet totally destroyed is to provide Journey with an alternative fabric."

"Like what?"

"Old towels or bed sheets."

Mischa hurried out of the room and within a minute returned with an armful of towels and several king-size bed sheets. "They're not exactly old but they'll work." She placed them on the floor next to Journey who began ripping them into long strips which she then arranged into an oval-shaped mound.

Eva laughed again. "You're about to become a surrogate mother."

"Hopefully not until morning; I need a good night's sleep."

"We'll see," said Eva with a knowing smile as they stepped out of the room and headed toward the kitchen. "Nature isn't bound by an alarm clock."

Mischa sleepily ignored the first tiny squeal. It was quickly incorporated into a dream about dolphins. The creatures were communicating with each other through the use of whistles and squeaks. The dream ended when the dolphins disappeared into the abyss. During the silence Mischa drifted with the warm currents, her conscience quiescent, floating like a motionless jellyfish. The stillness was suddenly interrupted when the dolphins reappeared, but this time they appeared agitated, and their whistles and squeaks were disorganized and loud. She tried to calm them down but they wouldn't listen. *This isn't the way dolphins are supposed to talk,* her subconscious warned. When the utterances turned into raucous yelps intermixed with whimpering, her mind told her it was time to retreat from these odd-sounding creatures, and she woke up.

As Mischa lay in bed, with her eyes wide open, the unusual sounds continued. *What's going on?* She asked herself. And then she really woke up. *Journey!* She immediately got out of bed and switched on the overhead light. She observed that the mound of tattered cloth was blood-stained, and that Journey was lying on her side. Nuzzled against her teats were four teacup-sized balls of wet fur. "You've had your puppies, she squealed, "and they're so cute!" At the sound of Mischa's voice Journey raised her head and stared at her belly. She then looked back at Mischa. *What do you think?* She seemed to be asking. Mischa laughed. Journey was obviously a proud mother. Mischa then assessed the color of the puppies. Two were silver and gray, and one ivory-white—all females. The largest of the four, which was sandwiched between the two silver and gray's, was a red and white male. Mischa picked him up. "I hope you like sisters," she whispered, "because you're totally outnumbered." As she was cuddling the puppy she glanced at the clock on the dresser. The time was 4:17 a.m. She wasn't about to go back to bed. Mischa held the male up to her eyes. "I'll teach you everything you need to know about females," she promised, "but you'll first need a manly name." When she mentioned the word *Kodiak* the puppy announced its approval with a piercing yelp. "You're named after the Alaskan brown bear," she explained, "so that should help boost your status." She gently placed Kodiak back among his littermates and picked up a silver and gray. After holding it for a moment, she said, "And your name is . . . "

42

Mischa checked her watch. The Island Packer ferry was approximately fifteen minutes behind schedule. In the distance she could see the ship approaching the Scorpion Cove pier. Twelve days ago Timbrook had passed away. On board the vessel was Aria, the new Chumash Caretaker. Jake, Eva, Mischa, and her dad were Aria's welcoming committee although her brother wasn't too thrilled about it. "It doesn't require four people," he complained. When Eva learned that the ferry was running late she talked Kurt into passing the time by taking a leisurely stroll down the beach. Mischa noticed they were holding hands. Since Timbrook's death their relationship had changed, becoming more intimate.

Once the boat was tied up they watched as each passenger disembarked.

"This is crazy," said Jake, "we don't even know what she looks like. She has to be the only person in America without a Facebook Page."

Mischa laughed. "That may actually be a sign of intelligence when you consider how much time we waste on meaningless communication."

"That's your opinion not mine—I couldn't live without it."

"She's mostly Indian," Mischa added, "so spotting a Native American among a primarily Caucasian crowd shouldn't be too difficult."

"I bet that's her," said Jake as a short, plumpish, dark-skinned woman stepped off the boat and began walking toward their location."

"Why do you say that?" asked Mischa.

"That's easy," said Jake. "The silver and turquoise jewelry she's wearing. It's typically worn by Indians."

Mischa nodded. Jake was probably right. The teenage girl was dressed in faded jeans, a cropped animal print tee shirt, and tennis shoes.

"Now that's what I call God's gift to man!" Jake declared as the next person stepped off the ship.

Mischa followed Jake's gaze. Her brother definitely had good taste. The young lady was about the same height as Mischa, had a perfectly balanced face, high cheekbones, olive skin, and thick auburn hair that fell past her shoulders. But what really got Mischa's attention were the pleated white cotton shorts, embroidered teal-colored blouse, and ankle high gladiator sandals. She had a natural beauty about her that was stunning. In addition, her choice of jewelry was also interesting: a pair of gold tassel earrings set with fossilized shark teeth, and a beaded necklace set with a two inch, hooked-shaped shark tooth.

When the heavyset teen-aged girl was about five feet away Mischa asked, "Aria?"

The girl stopped and smiled. She quickly removed her Apple In-Ear headphones. Apparently she had been listening to music.

"Yes," she said.

"Hi, I'm Mischa and this is my brother Jake. You've never met us, but you've talked to our dad on several occasions. He's down on the beach," Mischa said motioning, "with a friend, but he'll be joining us shortly."

"Who's your dad?" she asked.

"Kurt Nichols."

"Isn't he the person in charge of the Marine Lab?"

"Yes." Mischa confirmed. She noticed that the shark toothed lady had paused and was smiling as she listened to their conversation. *That's rude,* thought Mischa.

"Where's your luggage?" asked Jake. "I'll help you carry it."

The girl shook her head. "Why would I have any luggage? I'm just here for the day."

Jake appeared bewildered. "You're not staying?"

"No—this is just a sightseeing trip. I'm scheduled to leave on the five o'clock ferry."

Mischa eyes widen with understanding. "I'm sorry, what's your name?" she asked.

"Erika," she replied.

"I need to apologize," Mischa said with a nervous laugh, "we thought you were someone else." As the girl walked away Mischa turned and looked at the young lady who had been listening in on their exchange and who had so captivated Jake. "Aria?" she asked. "Aria Ygnacio?" This time Mischa included her last name in order to avoid any further misidentification. They had already suffered one embarrassment.

The girl flashed an innocent smile, her honey-brown eyes crinkling at the corners. "It's so good to meet you. Between Timbrook's descriptions and my discussions with your dad I feel like I already know you. Sorry for enjoying your moment of awkwardness, but it was so much fun to watch."

Mischa laughed. "We deserved it. It's not good to stereotype people." She greeted Aria with a warm hug and then stood back and watched as Aria hugged her brother. She thought Jake was going to melt. At that moment Kurt and Eva showed up necessitating an additional round of introductions.

"Welcome to our island," said Eva. "We're so excited you're here. And tonight, in your honor, we've planned a special dinner although it does come with a warning: if we end up talking your ear off, or asking too many questions, just yawn, and we'll know it's time to shut up."

"I don't know about that," laughed Aria, "I'll probably have as many questions as you do." She then turned and looked at Jake. "Can you help me with my luggage? They're just beginning to offload it from the boat."

"Absolutely," Jake said a tad too quickly and blushed.

Aria held out her arm. "Do you mind escorting me? These shoes weren't designed for this type of dock and I'm afraid of falling."

Jake slipped his arm inside of Aria's.

As they were heading toward the luggage Eva asked Kurt. "Is there a lock on the adobe house?"

"No," he answered.

"You might want to install one."

"Eva!" Mischa said in a high-pitched voice. "What are you implying?" She then started snickering. Her lighthearted mirth immediately spread to both Eva and her dad, resulting in a moment of unrestrained laughter. A few tourists stared at them as if they were a bit loco, but Mischa didn't care. Aria's presence had just made their island life a lot more interesting.

EPILOGUE

"What do you think?" asked a rich voice that resonated like thunder.

The man stared at the Ruler of Heaven and Earth whose robe was ablaze with shimmering light and said, "To be honest, I'm overwhelmed. This is beyond my wildest expectation."

The King of Kings chuckled, and then quoted from the Bible. "John 14:2. *In My Father's house are many mansions; if it were not so, I would have told you. I go to prepare a place for you.* This mansion," he said as he enveloped the man with his radiance, allowing his love to flow through him, "I prepared for you long before you were born, anticipating your arrival."

"I've read that scripture a hundred times," the man said as he wiped some tears from his eyes. "I just never thought it applied to me. You've recreated my adobe house, but it's now made out of precious stones; and the view—it's amazing—Inspiration Point, but a thousand times prettier than the earthly version, surrounded by colorful flowers, animals that defy description, and birds of unimaginable hues."

"You should see what's in the ocean," the Lord of Lords said as he motioned toward the azure-tinted sea. "Some of the creatures you're familiar with, but others," he paused and smiled, "stretched even my creative powers."

The man wiped some additional tears. "I thought there weren't any tears in heaven." He then quoted Revelation 21:4. *"And God will wipe away every tear from their eyes; there shall be no more death, nor sorrow, nor crying; and there shall be no more pain, for the former things have passed away."*

"No tears of sorrow, or sadness," the All-Merciful corrected. "Yours are tears of joy, which are as precious as nuggets of gold."

"I suppose that makes perfect sense," the man said and laughed. "To spend eternity emotionless, like an apathetic robot, doesn't sound too exciting."

Jehovah nodded in agreement. "Are you ready to have your emotions rocked?" The Breath of Life asked. "There are hundreds of individuals that have been patiently waiting years, decades, centuries, and even millennium, for an opportunity to meet you. But, before I allow any of them access, I'm exercising my Divine privilege," he said with a slight smirk, "and personally introducing the first two." The Comforter motioned toward a marble porch that overlooked Inspiration Point. Lounging in a cedarwood Adirondack chair was a young woman.

As the man walked toward the lady he mumbled, "Maria?" When she stood up he shouted. "Maria!"

The lady, who appeared to be in her early twenties, smiled warmly as the man, who was about the same age, approached her. "Adam Timbrook," she said and laughed. "What took you so long?"

Timbrook said nothing. He embraced his earthly wife and held her until God uttered a noise that sounded as if he was clearing his throat.

"I kept him on Earth," Yahweh explained to Maria, "a bit longer than originally planned, because of the Nichols family. They needed some extra guidance, which only Timbrook could provide. Aria has now taken his place. She's young, but full of wisdom, and with her firecracker personality, it'll also be fun to watch," the Almighty said and winked.

A serene howl suddenly filled the air.

"What's that sound?" Timbrook asked.

"You're joking," the Light of the World teased. "You don't recognize that voice?"

Timbrook looked at the Holy One and then at Maria. They were both smiling. "It can't be," he whispered. "I thought dogs didn't have souls."

"I'm the Author of all things," he reminded Timbrook, "and as the Supreme Maker, everything is possible." At the moment God finished his declaration, a Siberian husky, in the prime of its life, loped into view.

"Misty," Timbrook yelled delightedly. He ran to the dog, which leaped into his arms. "I've missed you," he murmured into the dog's ear.

"I've missed you too," the dog replied telepathically.

Perplexed, Timbrook looked at God. "Animals can speak?"

"Of course," laughed the Creator. "This is heaven—why wouldn't they communicate? But there's a rule—only humans can initiate the link. The animals, for reasons you'll soon appreciate, cannot; they're chatterboxes, especially the birds, which will talk from morning to sundown."

"Does Misty have all her earthly memories?" Timbrook wondered.

"Yes," God answered. "Just like you—so you'll have a lot to talk about."

"It will be interesting to get a dog's perspective," Timbrook acknowledged as he scratched Misty's head.

"You'll be surprised at what we know," Misty said and then started laughing—doggie style—enhanced with heavenly vocal cords.

Timbrook looked at the King of Glory and then at Maria. "Unbelievable," he said as he shook his head in amazement, "and to think this is just day one."

ABOUT THE AUTHOR

Dale Kornreich has earned two degrees—a B.A. from Fresno State University (English Major), and a J.D. from Pepperdine University School of Law. He is a member of the State Bar of California and the U.S. District Court of California. His law practice, located in Agoura Hills, California, is limited to plaintiff's personal injury and wrongful death cases. The author currently splits his office time between his law practice and creative writing.

The author's interests include SCUBA diving, skin diving, spearfishing, saltwater fishing, freshwater fishing, surfing, hiking, biking, reading, gourmet cooking, vegetable gardening, raising chickens, taking care of a small vineyard, and walking his three Siberian huskies.

Dale and his wife, Carole, are the parents of three grown children and make their home in Agoura Hills (Old Agoura), California.

The author is currently working on the sequel to *Santa Cruz.*

Contact Information:

Website: dalekornreichbooks.com
Email: contact@dalekornreichbooks.com

A Note from the Author

If you've enjoyed this novel, please consider sharing a bit about this book on your e-mail lists, websites, or blogs, with a recommendation that your friends read it as well. Your help at getting this book out is sincerely appreciated. Finally, please take a minute to post a customer review on Amazon.com. Thank you.